THE PREPPERS

By David F. Larson

This is a work of fiction, characters, places, and events either are the product of the author's imagination or are used fictitiously, and any resemblance to actual persons, living or dead, business establishments, events, or locals is entirely coincidental.

The Preppers Registered in the Library of Congress. Copyright © 4/18/2019 by David F. Larson ISBN 9781096323518

Library of Congress # TXu2-161611

Third printing

Also, by David F. Larson.

ABSORB THEM

Thanks to Father Dan S. for his spiritual insight, and to farmer Jim Rieck.

Can't forget my wife, Anne, who put up with me while writing this, and her sister, Mary Kay, who patiently listens to my endless line of BS. Last but not least, Darek, who told me, "Just start writing."

And to Nick...Semper fi

Severely wounded in Afghanistan, Jack Hansen's Marine Corps career is cut short. His buddies died and he blames himself...and it never leaves. He finds himself in a crumbling marriage, a boring civilian job, and he keeps his   PTSD to himself. He's been out of the Marine Corps for over 10 years but, once again, his life is about to change. On a typical Monday morning he arrives to work and the shit hits the fan.

At 8:13 AM, the Midwest's power grid goes down. It doesn't come back up and he's forced to resurrect skills he honed fighting insurgents in the Middle East. Only this time, Chicago and its suburbs are the battle-grounds. If things weren't bad enough, there's a group of serial killers in his town who specialize in abducting children and they think the shit hitting the fan is just great.

Jack Hansen is a loner, at least he thought he was. He meets others who are loners too. They have to band together or they will die. They're all preppers and thought they were prepared, but they weren't.   It wasn't anything like the SHTF scenarios they had imagined.

It was much, much worse.

Everybody is up the creek and there's nowhere to run.

PROLOQUE

The old black man eased himself down onto the river bank, sitting next to the young lady.

"Cottonwood trees are already losing their leaves, Grandpa Bobby. It's going to be an early winter, maybe a bad one."

Pulling a worn, but razor-sharp folding knife from his coat pocket, the old-timer slowly began peeling one of the apples he had brought with, all the while praying softly to himself. When he was done, he handed the apple to her, saying, "I always say a prayer when peeling an apple, giving thanks for what the good Lord has given me. Do you know *why*?"

"I don't know, Grandpa, to show you're *always* thankful?"

"Folks will *always* say they're thankful for what they have, but usually it's just lip service. They don't give it any thought. You have to take the time, every chance you get, to tell the good Lord you are thankful, because there is no such thing as making time later—time can't be made. Even for something as small as an apple, we must wisely use the idle moments it takes to peel it. Life is not long, girl, and moments are just as precious as years. Make every second of your life count, because the next moment isn't guaranteed." Bobby finished peeling the apple and held up the peel. "But you didn't come all the way down here to the river bank to hear my thoughts about peeling apples, or saying prayers…. So, I'll spare you any more lectures. I hear you been asking about your great grandfather, and the dark days. What did you want to know?"

"Tell me about the dark days and what you remember of before. You're the only one left Grandpa, you were there. There are still some books from before, but nothing after. Everything just stopped. I want to know why? Tell me everything you remember and I'll write it all down."

Taking a deep breath, the old man closed his eyes and for a few moments, said nothing. With his eyes tightly closed, he said, "I was there all right. I was only a child. A little boy. Now I'll be a hundred three. Imagine that, can you?" Opening his eyes, there was a far away sadness in them. "Good Lord, where has time gone? I was there all right, through the whole mess. I still remember, but I'd like to forget. Me and Wendel were the last. The others are all by the big red rock in the south pasture, and they're waiting for me—I'm long overdue." He reached into the sack, grabbing another apple out of it. With his gnarled hand he held it up, then tossed it into the river, saying, "A rotten one! You never know when you're going to get a rotten one, girl! Or the shitty end of a stick." Old Bobby took a labored breath and didn't say anything else. He sat there, all hunched over, his dark eyes watching the lazy current.

She raised her eyebrows, "You okay, Grandpa?"

"Yeah, I'm all right, sweetie, it's just hard to get my breath sometimes. I was just remembering, that's all. That's all I got nowadays. I've got lots of memories of this and that, especially the river. Old Jack and my Uncle Carl used to take us kids out on their pontoon boat. We'd float down the river shooting carp, with this great big old shotgun that Jack had. Yeah, those were the days, it wasn't all bad."

Bobby picked up a small stick and tossed it into the water, watching it as it lazily floated away. "So, you want to know about the dark days, and before? I don't recollect much of the before, but I do remember the lights and the automobiles. I remember them because everything stopped, even a small child could see the difference. It was... and suddenly it wasn't, everything ground to a halt." He pointed to the cornfield behind him with his knife, saying, "This place didn't look nothing like this. There used to be houses and buildings, as far as the eye can see. There were streets and automobiles; people were everywhere. It's almost all faded away now, like it was never here. And the people—only pockets of them survived. Yeah, I can tell you about it, and you write it all down. It will be quite a story."

Bobby slowly folded the old pocket knife, saying, "A good friend gave me this knife a lifetime ago. She taught me why we need to pray. Not how to pray, mind you, but why we must pray." A toothless smile crossed his deeply lined face.
"Don't worry, girl, I won't say anymore about praying. You want to know about this." Leaning back, he dug the heels of his worn boots into the black soil, saying, "Yeah, your Great Grandma and Grandpa Hansen started this farm, but before that, they worked in the ruins." He pointed the closed knife across the river, to the east, before tucking it into his coat pocket. Holding his gaze across the river, he said, "They went there every day, most of the people that lived out this way did. Back then it was called Chicago, and it was the grandest place. This whole province used to be called Illinois, and it's where the plan was hatched by the politicians."

"What's a politician, Grandpa?"

"**Rotten apples**, that's what they were! And you know what we do with rotten apples..."

Dinelli Hotel, Aruba

April 2020

"I love it here, Janice, you know that? I think we should buy a place on this island. It wouldn't hurt to look around while we're down here. God, why can't Chicago be like this?"

"Roger, assure me none of our friends will be hurt, we should at least warn Dean Northcutt."

"Good God almighty, Jan! Don't start on that again. Sit back and enjoy the afternoon, for God's sake. Do I have to explain it again? I've been telling all our friends for the past year to put their assets into something they can hold, walk on, or wear. That's warning enough. You surprise me, you know that? Aren't you the one that says, 'You have to break a few eggs to make a cake?' Just look at it that way. This is a *very* big cake. We're just going to sort of smash it and remake it *our* way."

Janice restlessly shifted in her beach chair. "I'm getting nervous, that's all. I was looking at something on the internet and—"

Roger angrily cut her off, spilling some of his drink in his lap. "Stop watching all that bullshit, will you?"

"Don't talk so loud, those people are looking at us."

He leaned forward towards her in his chair. Lowering his voice, he calmly said, "Janice, those clowns on the internet don't have a clue what they're talking about. They think they do, but they're not even close. It's just them fear mongering, that's all, and most of them are making money from it. Lots of money. The rest have nothing better to do. They like to scare people—that's how they get their kicks. I have been assured by the experts on this. The power will go off for two... maybe three weeks, tops. The cars will still run, nothing will fall from the sky, and the sun will still rise. All that will happen is that the power will be shut down in the Midwest. Communications are going to be disrupted for a couple weeks, just long enough to cause a financial panic. We've been molding the big cities for years and they're primed to go off like a powder keg. All we are doing is lighting the fuse. A fuse that will burn from coast to coast and then around the world. The markets will tank, the banks won't open and the natives

8

will riot. Everything will go down as planned. U.S. Treasuries will become worthless and every major city will be in chaos. The citizens will be begging for martial law— they'll actually demand it, and boy, will they get it. All the armed forces, the police, the whole enchilada, we're going to shove it down their throats. It's going to happen so fast there won't be time for any resistance. It'll be a beautiful thing. We'll clean out every rat's nest from Boston to LA. It gives me chills. Just think of it, every scumbag in prison will open their cell door to a bullet or a syringe. We'll clear out the prisons and start fresh. There will be plenty of room for those who oppose us. They'll come around or they'll get a syringe too. It'll be quick and it will be neat. We'll confiscate every single firearm too."

"Are you sure the police and military will go along with it?"

"Listen, when they see their own homes and neighborhoods going up in smoke, they'll be busting heads, believe me. That's why we want the natives to riot. We'll let them burn and loot for a while, before we turn the military loose. Our police and prison guards have been taking crap from these scumbags for years, and they're sick of it. We have people positioned throughout the military that feel the same way. We're going to clamp down hard. Those that don't want to go along with it will change their minds damn quick. They'll be scared to death when they see their careers and pensions about to evaporate."

"What about our homes, we have so many fine things? We just can't leave everything behind, to be looted."

"Oh my God, they're just houses, full of stuff. It's only *stuff*, it can be replaced. Hey, we have the best security money can buy. That's what we pay Luiz for. Our homes will be fine. Come the end of July, the whole mess will be over, and our girl will be in the White House. Hell, she's already thinking of tearing it down and building a new one and it won't be called the White House any more. Get this, she wants to re-name it the *Liberty House,* because that's what our country is about. Freedom and liberty—at least that's what we tell the sheeple. By the fall, the smoke will have cleared and the public will be out for blood. Our idiot president and his cabinet will either be swinging from a tree, or hiding in a hole someplace. General Thorndale has it figured down to a T. He and the team will provide the president with positive evidence that North Korea caused this whole electro-pulse thing, with a nuclear warhead placed in their weather satellite. That's when the idiot in chief will make his final mistake and that will be the nuking of North Korea. And what a mistake that will be for him. While North Korea is smoking like a fried wonton, our team will provide positive evidence that it was really the Israeli's that did it to us, to screw us, so they could finally have a free hand in the Middle East. This will turn the whole world against Israel and without our military support, they're dead. Imagine the furor there's going be? The President of the United States... nuking an innocent country, oh, the horrors. It'll guarantee us the presidency. With our little girl in the White House, the first thing we'll do is take out Iran, and make it look like it was Israel that did it. Those

Arabs hate us and each other, but they hate the Jews more. Without us backing Israel, when the rag-heads are done, Israel is going to look like a char-broiled bagel. But before Israel melts, we'll make damn sure they get their licks in against the Arabs. It's golden, Janice, pure golden. Israel and Korea will be out of our hair forever, and we'll own the whole stinking Middle East, lock, stock, and every barrel of oil they got. Then we'll team up with Russia and starve China to death. Hey, let's change the subject, here comes the waiter with our drinks. Look at him, he's walking towards us like he's got a load in his pants. These waiters think they deserve a buck every time they bring you something. Well, he took too long, I'm not giving him a dime."

Janice looked up at the swaying palm trees. "It's windier than it was yesterday."

Despite saying the contrary, Roger tipped the waiter a dollar saying, "A little faster service next time, boy, okay? You might as well run back and bring us a couple more." As he watched the waiter run off, he sipped his margarita, savoring the salt along the rim. "This wind is blowing in a new world order, Jan. No one will dare refer to me as that *little* rabble-rouser from Illinois again." Roger looked out to sea. A large freighter was on the horizon. "We'll have to make that next drink our last. Our boat to Venezuela leaves at four."

CHAPTER ONE

MONDAY- LIGHTS OUT

"What the heck?" Jack Hansen slid into the seat and immediately regretted taking the train. Feeling the gooey mess between his fingers, he was pissed and stared at his hand.

"It's spearmint gum. Sticky stuff, huh?" It was the fellow occupying the window seat next to him. Thinking Jack didn't hear him, the guy repeated, "It's spearmint gum. They must have had the whole pack in their mouth. I almost got my hand into it too. Really sticky shit in this hot weather we're having."

Jack spread his fingers looking at the gooey mess stuck between them. Clenching his teeth, he nodded his head and smiled at the guy. He wanted to say, *"Thanks for giving me a heads up on that before I sat down... asshole!"* Instead he said, "Yeah, thanks. Thanks for giving me the heads up on that. I wonder what brand is?" He glanced down at the morning newspaper, yet unopened on the lap of his neighbor and momentarily thought of grabbing it to clean his hand. The headline on the paper jumped out at him, **"GRIM CHICAGO RECORD— 251 GUNSHOT DEATHS THIS YEAR!"** He said to himself, "Maybe someone will shoot the bastard that stuck this gum to the seat and make it 252. Thank God I live in the suburbs."

Without returning a look back to Jack, the fellow said, "I heard that comment. You really think it's that much better for us? Personally, I'm glad these bastards are shooting each other, but you and me, we have to drag ourselves down here to work every day and still take our chances. I'll tell you something. I moved out to DuPage County to get away from these scumbag gangbangers. What do you think happened? They built so-called low-income housing right down the street from me and now we got gang problems out there. We can't win, no matter where we live. You won't believe what happened to me last week. Wednesday night I was riding in a cab that took a stray bullet, right in the center of the front passenger door. Thank God I was sitting in the back. Didn't hear any gunshot, just a wham! When I got out, there's a bullet hole in the door. God only knows where it came from. These bastards are crazy down here." Removing a section from his newspaper, he handed it to Jack. "Here, I never read the obits, too damn depressing. Use this to wipe that crap off your hand."

Jack had been making the daily commute to his job in Chicago for over 10 years. Because he sometimes needed a car during the day, he usually drove himself, but at least once a week he would take the train. It broke up his work week from the monotony of driving every day and usually he enjoyed it. While his fellow passengers would be reading a paper or looking at their phones, he would gaze out the train's windows, thinking about work or just letting his mind wander. This morning he wasn't thinking so much about the day's work ahead or his upcoming short vacation, but of what was currently going on at home between his wife and daughter. The problems at home were consuming most of his thoughts, but sometimes the past came creeping back in. *It never leaves…* After unsuccessfully trying to scrape the gum from his hand, he disgustedly shoved the crumpled newspaper under the seat. Now, in addition to the smeared spearmint gum, there was the black of newsprint added to his hand. It was hard to ignore his sticky fingers, but he sat back, trying to make sense of the morning's events. The day hadn't gone right from the start. First, there was the muffled argument between his wife and daughter. Then the ride to the Metra Station with Ellen was in icy silence. They hadn't had an argument and he couldn't think of any reason for her to be pissed at him, but then, Ellen never needed a reason.

The train started to slow, the conductor saying, "Next stop, Winfield," but Jack didn't hear him. He was self-absorbed, thinking about his failing marriage. Ellen was normally a chatterbox and usually it was hard to get a word in edgewise with her. On the drive from their house to the station, she hadn't said but a few words. After 18 years of being married to her, he had learned to keep his mouth shut when she was in one of her moods, and this morning he sensed a definite mood. The last thing he needed on a Monday morning was to get into a heated argument with her on the way to work.

The train had stopped and he watched the people on the platform, herding themselves into the waiting passenger cars. Some appeared worried; nobody was smiling, and most looked bored. He could tell the women who walked to the train station, their athletic shoes looking out of place with their skirt. Barely noticeable to anyone sitting near him, Jack shook his head, wanting to scream out loud, ***"How the hell did I ever end up doing this?"***

Ever conscious of the smeared gum stuck between his fingers, he tried to get comfortable in his seat, wishing he had the small bottle of hand sanitizer Ellen always kept with her in her purse. His wife's face flashed into his mind, that familiar aggravated look… This time he ground his teeth and shook his head. He was pissed and he didn't care if any of his fellow passengers noticed him. *I'm sick of her crap. What the hell was she on the warpath about this morning? She can be counted on to be in a silent huff about something at least once a week, but lately it seems like every other day she's in a snit about something. She can be such a bitch… I am so tired of it….* He thought about what he had heard that morning while he was in the bathroom shaving. It was muffled, but harsh. Ellen was scolding their daughter, Laura—again.

I wish she would just leave that poor girl alone, damn her... Neither Ellen, nor his daughter said a word to him about anything afterwards. *So now I get another morning of silence. This time from both of them....*

As he gazed out the train's grimy windows, he tried to pinpoint exactly when their marriage had taken the turn and become so complicated. *I can't go on like this, if it wasn't for Laura...*

The conductor yelled, "Next stop, Oak Park."

Looking out the window, Jack sat straight up in his seat. *Jeez, what happened to the other stops?* He had been so wrapped up in his thoughts, he hadn't heard the conductor call out at least six or seven of the past stops. His final stop, the Ogilvie Metra Station, would be coming up and he almost wished it wasn't. *If this morning's ride was a little longer, maybe I could figure this thing out...* Again, he shook his head. *Who am I kidding? I'll never have enough time to figure her out.* No matter how much he thought about it, it was of no use. He had gone over the same things in his mind, over and over, every day. The conclusion was always the same one. Besides her faults, he still loved her. He had become skilled at shoving aside their marital problems, hoping to magically reach a solution later.

It was almost time to flip the switch. He'd have to start thinking about work. He knew the problems at home would have to be faced, but they wouldn't be solved on this morning's commute. They'd be shoved aside, again... at least until tonight. Smelling the strong spearmint, he knew the first thing he was going do when reaching his office was to wash his hands.

Jack's destination every morning was Deegan and Son, Architecture & Renovation, on Chicago's Near North side. Old man Deegan was long dead and the son, who was in his late 80's, had retired to Florida. The business was small, with only eight employees, and should have folded years ago. They no longer built new buildings, but had found a treasure trove in saving existing ones. What kept Deegan in business was Chicago's endless stock of empty factories, warehouses, and formerly grand apartment buildings. Most of them were built between 1900 and the early 1950's, and couldn't be duplicated by construction techniques today. Many of Chicago's older buildings had outlived their usefulness, but few outlived their structural integrity. What politicians and city planners viewed as just another derelict building standing in the way of progress, he viewed as a clean slate awaiting a bright future. Built like fortresses with beautiful stonework buried under years of Chicago's grime, these buildings were like gold in the ground. It was his job to dig them out and make them shine. The most profitable of these buildings were in some of Chicago's roughest neighborhoods. Vacant and in disrepair, most of the buildings were already gutted by vandals and thieves. The city was eager to get them either torn down or back on the tax rolls. Sometimes the worse the neighborhood, the better. Chicago wasn't like Detroit. The bad neighborhoods in Chicago were being turned

13

around. They called it gentrifying the neighborhood. Thanks to fair housing laws, the minorities could be swiftly shuffled off and strewn across the western suburbs. The politician's unwritten answer to the inner-city gang problem was simple: the solution to pollution is dilution.

Jack glanced again at his neighbor's newspaper, still folded neatly on his lap, now with only part of the headline visible. The word *"DEATH"* jumped out at him. He laughed to himself, but it wasn't funny to him, it was a warning. It was only the third day of May, and already there were 251 deaths from gunshot. He thought, *What about the rest of the murders? How many ways can I kill you in Chicago?* Jack turned from the paper's sour headline and closed his eyes; he was tired of it. The newspaper headline seemed to be shouting a warning directly at him, and he suddenly had a bad feeling about today. Maybe it was just because it was a Monday, and of the way his morning had started at home. Conscious about the goo stuck between his fingers, he thought, *I sure hope this isn't going to be one of those days...*

The only big-ticket item on the work board this week was an inspection of a rat-infested industrial building they were buying. It was on the south branch of the Chicago River. When it would be, he didn't know, but he hoped it wouldn't end up being today. It was to be a final walk through before closing the deal. He didn't like the thought of it, in fact he never liked it when the building was vacant and in a rough neighborhood. Old buildings in bad neighborhoods often held surprises and seldom were they ever good. Sometimes they were inhabited with drug users, prostitutes, or the homeless. But there was that other group, the gun toting gangbangers. Most of the bangers were kids and that made them unpredictable and dangerous. All of them had guns and didn't think twice about shooting someone. Despite Chicago's strict gun laws, he was considering purchasing a small handgun to carry with him. He had his father's long-barreled 44 magnum revolver, that his dad called, "Little Red." He also had an old semi-automatic army 45 that had belonged to his grandfather, but he wanted something newer and definitely smaller. A little 32 semi-auto that could easily be concealed under his suit coat would be powerful enough. He looked around at his fellow passengers and wondered how many of them were packing a firearm.

He started thinking again about the building inspection he had to do. He was hoping that whatever day it was, it would be held in the early morning, or at least before noon, before the gangbangers woke up. If it turned out he would have to inspect it today, and he could do it this morning, then he'd be done by noon. That would give him an excuse to get home early. His partner, Don, could meet with the owners in the afternoon and cement the deal. The day was already feeling unlucky and he didn't want to end up being gunshot victim number 252 on Tuesday's newspaper headline. After getting off the train, he hailed a cab for the short hop to his office. During the ride down Canal Street, he reconsidered if he should start carrying a gun on his forays into the bad neighborhoods. It was a

14

tough decision to make. He was no stranger to firearms or dealing with tough situations, but Chicago's strict gun laws sometimes favored the criminals. Many a good citizen saved themselves with their gun, only to be crucified by the city or some gangbanger's lawyer later. As he exited his cab, a decision was made. *Yeah, I better start packing a gun.*

Entering his building, he always took the second elevator. Sometimes it caused him to wait for a bit, but he figured the short wait was worth it. There seemed to be recurring problems with the first elevator and it was frequently out of service. When it was operating, it would hesitate, and give a hard *bump* before it stopped. Usually the doors would take forever to open. He didn't like that. Also, was the ominous fact that the city inspection ticket was missing from its metal frame. Was it conveniently over-looked by a crooked inspector? After all, this is Chicago. The morning was already going south, and with the way the city worked, this would be the morning the elevator finally quit. He pictured himself stuck in it, the frayed cable hoisting it finally parting, sending the elevator crashing into the basement floor.

As he waited for the second elevator's doors to open, he could hear two women behind him talking. Just before the doors opened, he glanced back at them. One was an older lady with tightly pulled back grey hair. She didn't look friendly and was wearing a grey suit, that he thought would look much better on a guy. The other woman, who looked to be in her late 30's or early 40's, he saw regularly. She was attractive with a nice figure and long black hair, with a few strands of grey just starting. Her butt was tending to plump, but that was okay. Some mornings she wore her hair up. This morning it was down, and he had decided months ago that he preferred it down. She never wore one of those man-suits either. He also liked her smile. She always gave him that great smile, with those nice white teeth. *How the hell do they keep their teeth so white?* Since he knew she went to the tenth floor, he automatically pushed number ten for her, and had pushed six for himself. He knowingly glanced at her, almost saying out loud, "*Here it comes… here it comes… yes!*" She looked at him and with that warm smile, and said, "Thanks." He glanced at the older lady in grey, who could apparently talk without moving her lips. She quickly mumbled, "Eight for me, thank you." He didn't expect a smile from her, but he didn't care. He couldn't recall if he ever was alone with the younger lady, though he had often shared the same elevator with her many times. It bothered him that he didn't know her name. As the elevator started its ascent, he wondered as he had in the past. *What would her name be? Sally? No…hope not. No, no… she looks like a Jennifer. Maybe Jenny. Yeah, Jenny… Probably a Democrat, oh well, it's Chicago—can't be perfect. I wonder what her job is? Probably married to a lawyer…ugh!*

She was just like the other familiar faces he shared the train with. The pleasant and the sad, the fat and the skinny, the good and the ugly. Sadly, this

15

lady was pleasant and nice looking. She would always be just that, another face. Another familiar face, with no name, during the boring commute to work. *Every stinking day of my boring life. God, I wish I was back in the Corps....*

His floor would be coming up first and he would leave, giving both the women a nod and a smile. Whatever fragrance the lady with the long black hair was wearing, she wore it every time she had shared the elevator with him. It smelled really good and he always wished the ride was longer. *God, I wonder if I could find that fragrance for Ellen and get her to wear it? "Ellen, wear this, will you? You'll smell like this lady I share the elevator with... it'll improve our marriage." No, no... I better not do that....*

On more than one occasion he thought of striking up a conversation with the elevator lady, but what would he say? *"Pardon me, Miss, but you smell really great. What's that fragrance you're wearing? I'd like to get some for my wife, so she will remind me of you...Oh, by the way, I like it when you wear your hair down, and you know, your ass isn't really fat. It's nice and rounded, it's... okay."*

He wondered if she ever thought about what his name was? He hated Chicago's anonymity. *I should start wearing aftershave, and during the morning ride up, she'd say to me, "Gosh you smell fresh, what is it? By the way, my name's Jenny...."* As the door opened onto his floor, he vowed that someday he would introduce himself to her. Maybe he would start wearing aftershave too.

After exiting the elevator, he reluctantly geared his mind back to his wife and his daughter, Laura. *Here I go again, about to walk into the office, with problems at home unresolved. Why is everything so complicated? Maybe it'll be easier when Laura leaves for college in the fall. Something is always eating at Ellen, especially lately, if I could just figure it out. Yeah, things will be better after Laura leaves for college....*

As his hand reached for his office door, he forced his thoughts into work mode, forgetting Ellen's moodiness, his daughter, and the fragrant lady on the elevator. *Another day starts. Here I go.*

Entering the office, he almost bumped into Don Jenks, his longtime friend and boss. With his usual coffee in hand, Don turned towards him and snapped to attention. Raising his cup in mock salute he said, "Enter, Jack Hansen, the slum lord king!" It was Don's typical way of sarcastic humor. Jack didn't like the slum lord part and tried not to take it seriously, but Don knew it got under his skin and said it often.

Jack's job title at Deegan's was architect and structural engineer. Renovating old buildings was lucrative, but could turn negative mighty quick if something structural was missed. The miscalculation of the thickness of century old concrete could break a project in cost overruns. Jack's job was to insure things like that didn't happen. Don's job was to "put the deal together," for the least amount of dollars. Jack and Don were complete opposites, but they were good at what they did. Since the clean-up of the Chicago River, property along it was hot, and the sturdy old brick buildings flanking it were ripe for lucrative redevelopment. The city wanted these building redeveloped but, as always, a few palms had to be greased to get the project rolling and more important, to keep it rolling. Don Jenks was the one who carried the grease gun.

Lowering his raised cup of coffee, Don continued his sarcastic assault. "I hope you finally decided to start packing a gun, Jack, because you might need it today!" Jack immediately got that sinking feeling, thinking, *Oh shit, he's going to want me to go over to that building again...today. Well, at least I'll get home early.* He gave it right back to Don. "What do I need a firearm for? I got a Rottweiler with a big mouth to go with me and that's you, buddy. So, what's for me to be afraid of?"

Don was smiling and shaking his head, "No, big guy." He took a sip of coffee saying, "Not today, Jackie my boy, my services are needed elsewhere. You'll be busy down there *all* day without me, and that will be too bad for you buddy." He winked an eye and smiled back at Jack, all the while thinking, *Yeah, Jack, you'll be tied up all morning and most of the afternoon.... while you're mired with the rats downtown today, looking over that crap building, I'll be with your wife. With your precious little daughter away at school, I might even use my new key and have my fun in your bed.*

Don kept talking to him, all the while reveling in the fact he was partying with Jack's wife. He got a real thrill out of it and continued spewing his pitch. "You and Bill are going over there this morning to meet with the owners and pretend like you're giving the building another once over. They're playing games with us, so we'll give it right back to them. We're down to the wire, so let's make them think we're having second thoughts. You stress our concerns with it, that we may not make the deal. We'll let them sweat a little bit. Billy is running a little late, but don't worry, he'll be here soon. You can ride shotgun with him over there. Afterwards, the owners' attorneys are expecting a free meal out of this, so you and 'Billy the kid' take them out to wherever they like and pump a few drinks into them. You got Bernstein's number. Excuse yourself and make like you gotta go to the can or something and call him, he's expecting it. Let him know which way the wind is blowing. After your call, he'll send that cute little paralegal, or whatever they call her, over there to meet you with new contracts. Man, she is a hottie." Don once again raised his coffee cup, took a drink and rambled on.

"Those two Jews think they're screwing us, but remember, we know something about that neighborhood that they don't. They'll be all too happy to unload that building on us." Don could see a tinge of doubt creep into Jack's eyes so he continued, "Look, Jack, I put lots of work into this one. I greased that Alderman Dickhead..."

"It's Dickman," Jack corrected him.

Don started laughing, "Dickhead, Dickman, whatever. The guy's a crooked little weasel. Thing is, he's my weasel because I own him. He's got the re-zoning for this property in the bag. This job is gonna pay off big time, Jackie. Lofts and condos, that whole area is going to turn around and we're on top of it."

Jack wasn't even listening to Don. He had heard it all before and tuned him out. Often, he would tune himself out to what was going on around him, and think about the time he had spent in the Marine Corps. He wished they hadn't turned him out to pasture... *if I only hadn't gotten hit...oh God, not now Jack, let it go...don't start thinking about that shit.*

After he had left the Corps, it was Don who had gotten him the job with Mr. Deegan. Don was an old friend from grade school days, and there were some things he just had to put up with, and Don's mouth was the main one. Donnie hadn't changed one tiny bit since school days and Jack had learned to ignore his mouth.

Don was about to continue, but the office door opened up and Sarah Finnegan, the office manager/ secretary, walked in. Don's happy demeanor immediately clouded a bit when she appeared. Sarah had started out as a secretary for old man Deegan himself. When he retired to Florida, she had taken over running the office for him. Sarah had been there well over 35 years and was about to retire herself.

Jack was first to greet her. "Good morning, Sarah. Looks like you got some sun this weekend. How was Wisconsin?"

She gave Jack a warm smile. "It was really nice, Jack. Thanks for asking. Walter and I went to Lake Lawn Lodge, it's over on Lake Delavan. We had a wonderful and relaxing weekend. It was really nice to be up there before the Memorial Day rush. Nice and sunny too."

Jack liked Sarah. She had been at Deegan's more years then Jack and Don combined. She treated everyone right and did everything by the book. She was well liked and, lately, Jack was concerned about her health. She had heart trouble and recently had a defibrillator implant.

Sarah eyed Don. Turning towards him, she greeted him first, "Good morning, Don." Don had gone over by the coffee pot and was pouring himself another cup. He had his back to her and partially turned towards her, giving her a warm, "HI, Sarah," before turning back to his coffee. As Sarah went to her desk, Don shot her a short sideways glance, his eyes narrowed and his lips thinned. *You dried up old bitch.... you think you know something, but so what, six more weeks, just six more weeks and I'll be out of this hole. I'll be set forever!* Turning around with his fresh coffee in hand, he faced her and said through his teeth, "Yeah, Lake Delavan is nice, Sarah. Glad you and Walter enjoyed it."

Jack could always smell when something was wrong between people, no matter how well they tried to conceal it. At that moment he was getting a strong odor between Sarah and Don. He recalled how, on Friday, Sarah had said there

18

was something she wanted to talk to him about. With the vibes he was getting, he figured it had to concern Don. She was taking off at the end of the month. She and Walter were going to visit her family in Ireland for a few weeks.

Jack was about to ask her about the upcoming trip to Ireland, when suddenly the lights flickered and then went to a dim glow, as if they were struggling to stay on. Finally, they flickered bright for a second, and went dark.

"Shit, shit, shit! I can't see!" It was Don. "Oh crap**.** I just spilled hot coffee all over myself, damn it—shit that's hot**!"**

No one could see her, but Sarah was shaking her head and rolling her eyes as Don made his little commotion. "Don, calm down and get a towel. I'll open the street side doors and we'll have plenty of light, no need for the foul language."

Sarah opened the inner doors and immediately the bright morning light poured in from the outer office windows. Still upset from spilling coffee all over himself and even more upset for Sarah scolding him, Don continued his tirade, "Why the hell aren't the generators kicking in? This building has its own generator, and it always kicks on right away."

Jack looked at the office clock, it had stopped at 8:13.

Jack was the one who noticed it first. It was like somewhere far away, a giant motor had been shut off, and it was gradually winding down to a stop. "Listen," he said.

With an exaggerated smirk across his face, Don glanced at Jack. "What now?"

Jack held up his hand, and said, "The city noise, it's gone, everything is going quiet."

Don shot back, "Yeah, so what? I got hot coffee all over me, and Hey, my phone isn't working, what the hell..."

Jack checked his phone and it was dead too.

Don was fidgeting with his phone, getting madder by the second. He was thinking of the party time he had planned with Jack's wife. *Geez,* he thought, *Ellen's expecting me to call her in a couple minutes to plan our fun-time today.... Hell, no worry, she's got my extra key to the condo, maybe she will just hang out over there until polka time....* Don glanced at Jack and smiled to himself. *Oh Jackie, you are so stupid....*

"Oh my God!" It was Sarah. "Look, oh my God!" Jack and Don quickly moved to where Sarah was standing by the windows. She was pointing at something out over the skyline. About a mile out, they could see what appeared to be a jet airliner. It seemed to be falling from the sky.

It was hard to tell what kind it was, but it was a big one. It was no longer flying; it wasn't gliding or diving, it was settling, like a helicopter about to make a landing. From the distance they were at, it looked like it was dropping slowly, but in reality, it was coming down like a big flapjack about to hit the griddle with a splat! All of them watched in horror as it disappeared beneath Chicago's bright

19

morning skyline. Jack momentarily stayed at the window, mesmerized by the large aircraft, waiting for the inevitable explosion. He heard Sarah cough and turned towards her. She was standing there, still looking out the window, but clutching at her chest with both hands. An expression of both pain and terror was frozen across her face.

Don started shouting and pointing down to the street, six stories below. "Look, everything has stopped down there, nothing's moving. What the hell is going on?"

Jack was about to say something to Sarah when she collapsed to the floor like a bag of rags, violently striking her head on the sharp corner of her metal desk. Instantly, a large bloody gash appeared on her forehead; she was knocked out cold. Jack dropped to his knees and felt for a pulse, but there was none. During his tours of duty in Iraq and Afghanistan, he had seen many people violently die. He had seen insurgents instantly reduced to a pile of bloody pulp and he tightly held his buddy, Nolan, as his life drained into the Afghani sand. Sarah was dead and blood from the gash on her head had stained the carpet. He had never noticed it before, but the office carpet was the same color as that sand. Jack closed his eyes. *It never leaves…*

With both hands grasping the sparse hair on his balding head, Don stared down in disbelief. "Is she dead? What the hell! She's bleeding, is she dead?"

He stared at Jack and then back to Sarah, screaming, "**Jack, what the hell is going on here?** We gotta call 911 and get somebody up here!"

Jack was already slowly and gently straightening out her body, as Don quickly moved towards the door. "I'll go out into the hallway—somebody's got to have a working phone!" He rushed out into the hall and Jack stayed kneeling next to Sarah. She looked different, and for the first time he noticed she had one of those faces that people would say had the map of Ireland written across it. This had happened to him before, after buddies had died. In the milliseconds after they were gone, he noticed something about them that he had never noticed before. Her blood staining the sandy colored carpet flashed his mind back, but he didn't want to go there. He glanced down at the blood-stained carpet, quickly looking away, thinking, *Reminders, there's always got to be reminders.*

There was a blue quilt that Sarah's daughter had knitted hanging on the back of her desk chair, and he realized he had been staring at it. He reached for it and completely covered her upper body with it, leaving only the lower part of her legs exposed. Standing up, he looked out at the skyline to where the airplane had disappeared. A column of thick black smoke was slowly rising behind the tall buildings, marking the airplane's death. Far out to the west of the city, he saw another pillar of black smoke rising in a similar fashion. *Had another plane gone down?* He stood at the window for a few moments, looking at the silent streets below. Mentally he checked off everything that had just happened: *An airplane dropped from the sky, traffic is stopped dead, no power, and the phones are dead. Sarah's pacemaker fails.   And it's dead quiet....* That giant motor-like hum that Chicago, like every big city has, was no longer there. The city was silent. He felt a sinking feeling creeping into his chest. He had a habit, that when stressed, he would sometimes grind his teeth and bite his lower lip. He clenched his jaw hard, thinking, *This is going to be a really bad day....*

Suddenly, the office door burst open, slamming hard against the wall behind it. Don ran in, out of breath, his words quickly tumbling out. "Nothing works, Jack! The whole stinking city looks like it's just stopped! None of the elevators work, and that screwed up one they're always having trouble with? They're saying it crashed all the way down to the basement! Holy shit! I rode on that one this morning! Oh my God, nothing works! All the computers, even the desk tops, are down, and nobody's phone works. Eddie, across the hall, said he saw a traffic chopper drop like a fuckin rock! It crashed on top of a building a couple streets over." Don looked down at Sarah, and jerked his head back to Jack. "Holy shit! You covered her face? She's dead, isn't she? What the hell we gonna do? She can't be dead; we were just talking to her!"

"Don, I'm afraid she is. Her heart defibrillator failed. It's electric. Just like everything else, it's off."

Don stared at Jack, his eyes searching Jack's face for an answer. Jack gave him one. "Chicago, maybe the whole country for that matter, is dead."

"What the hell do you mean, dead? How could everything just go off at once?"

"An electromagnetic pulse." Don continued staring at Jack, his mouth wide open. For once he had nothing to say.

Jack asked, "Do you know what an EMP is, Don?" What Don said surprised him.

Still out of breath, Don's words tumbled out, "As a matter of fact, I do. It's a sudden burst of high energy from the sun or a nuclear explosion, detonated high above us, and it knocks out everything that uses electricity." Don noticed a hint of surprise on Jack's face that he knew of such a thing. Don shrugged his shoulders, saying, "I watched a show on TV about it one night. There was nothing else on. I thought it was all a bunch of bullshit... You think that's what this is, Jack?"

Glancing out the windows, Jack noticed that two of the elevated trains were stopped dead on their tracks. Turning back to Don, he said, "Even the elevated trains have stopped. I think we're in deep shit. We have to get out of the city, Don, pronto... This isn't just a power outage. The country could be at war, and we certainly wouldn't be safe here in Chicago." He sadly looked back down to where Sarah lay. The sandy beige carpet had a large bloody smear on it. For a split second, he again imagined the endless grains of sand in Afghanistan. Were any of them still stained red from his friends' blood? Jack tightly closed his eyes. *Damn it, can't I ever get that out of my mind? Not now, Jack... you have to think!*

Don was staring at Sarah's covered body and asked, "What about Sarah?" Don had known Jack for years and knew they were in trouble when the big guy was silent and clenching his jaw. When Jack didn't answer, Don waved his hand in front of Jack's face, "Are you with me here, Jack? You look like you're a million miles away."

Jack slowly nodded his head and opened his eyes, saying, "Yeah, I guess I was." Jack looked down at Sarah, "She's gone, Don, we have to go, right now."

Don too quickly agreed, "Okay, big guy, let's get down to the parking garage and get my car."

Jack rolled his eyes, thinking, *you've got to be kidding me*? "Don, do you see any cars moving down there? Yours won't be any different."

"Jack, it's brand new. Holy shit, I just can't leave it here!"

Jack knew that Don owned several handguns and sometimes carried one in his car's glovebox. "Don, you wouldn't happen to have your piece in your car, would you?"

"No. I was just thinking the same thing. Shit, of all days not to be packing!"

Jack firmly placed his hand to Don's shoulder, already pushing him towards the door. "We gotta go, Don. Nothing will happen to your car in the parking garage. With all these stalled cars, even if yours did run, you'd probably be blocked in. We can come back later and get it after this mess is done. I think the best thing to do would be to first get down to the street, flag down a cop, and tell him about Sarah. Then we can decide how we're going to get home."

With no elevators working, they joined the crowd of fellow office workers heading for the stairs. Passing the frozen elevators, Jack recalled how he always avoided taking the one that had fallen to the basement. Sucking in his breath, he thought, Jeez, *that was a close one, thank God I wasn't running late and took the other elevator.*

The stairways were jammed with panicked people, forcing their way down. Surprisingly, some were actually fighting their way up. *Like they're really going to be able work today,* Jack thought. Out of shape, he heard Don mumbling something about, *'quitting smoking,'* as he huffed his way down the crowded stairs. With a mass of people crowding and shoving them from behind, they spewed into the first-floor lobby. There wasn't any time to stop and think. The crushing crowd emptying all at once into the building's foyer decided their path for them. They were roughly pushed out of the building's front doors, and into the packed sidewalk. Every building was dumping its contents of workers all at once. The streets and walkways were teaming with panicked people.

Jack spotted a cop near the building's entrance and wanted to inform him about Sarah. He was only about ten feet away, but he couldn't get near him. The poor guy was overwhelmed with people asking questions he couldn't possibly know the answers to. As they were shoved past him, Jack stole another look back, thinking he might be able to get the cop's attention. His hope of getting any help from the police officer was dashed as a man dressed in a suit, with a pink tie, hauled off and belted the officer in the face.

Wild eyed, Don looked over to Jack, yelling, **"Holy shit, did you see that guy clock that cop? This town is going to go nuts!"**

"Monday," Jack said, half aloud to himself, "God I hate Mondays. I hate Chicago too." Not being able to notify anyone about Sarah would soon become the least of their problems.

Vehicles of all types were stalled on the street and most had their frustrated owners standing next to them. Some cars had people standing on top of them, and many appeared already abandoned. Everyone had a confused expression on their face that was quickly becoming one of terror. What Jack couldn't understand was why some of the cars were still running? Their drivers were frantically trying to maneuver through the mass of pedestrians and around stalled vehicles. As they pushed on with the crowd, Jack tried to figure out why a few cars worked, but the rest didn't. What was special about these vehicles? Nothing made any sense. He spotted an old work van, whose elderly driver was frantically trying to smash his way out from between two stalled cabs. He was ramming the yellow Cab in front of him, and backing into the green Cab behind him, again and again. Both cab drivers, their cabs hopelessly hemmed in between stalled cars themselves, were out of their cabs screaming at him. One was kicking the side of the van and pounding on the driver's side window. The same scene was being repeated all over Chicago, as frantic commuters fought to leave the city, kicking and clawing their way home.

The streets and sidewalks were packed with people, all pushing and running south, in the direction of the train stations. Jack doubted if many of them knew where they were going. Don barely managed to keep up with him as they blindly went with the crowd. In front of them was an older delivery style box truck that was slowly trying to make its way down the sidewalk, pushing pedestrians along with it. People were yelling and swearing at the driver, and some were hanging onto the sides and standing on the truck's bumpers. The old truck didn't get far before its high cargo body hooked the corner of a huge old neon sign. The vintage sign that read: "Johnnie's Come on Back Inn," suddenly ripped off the building, and came crashing down on top of the truck, narrowly missing the men hanging onto it. Further ahead, the CTA's elevated train was stalled on its tracks, high above the street. Frantic and confused, people stared from its dirty windows, waiting for someone to tell them what to do. Two young men were prying the doors open, trying to get out. They were both dressed in business suits and took it on their own to escape from the stopped train. After exiting the train's doors, they attempted to climb out onto the tracks and lower themselves to the street, some 15 feet below. One of them, a young man with bright red hair, suddenly slipped and fell off the tracks, landing hard on top of a

23

trash can. Clipping his forehead on the can's sharp metal edge, he rolled onto the concrete sidewalk. Covered in week old trash, he sat there dazed and bleeding, the crowd pushing past him—no one stopped to help. *That's how it's going to be,* Jack thought. *If we get hurt, we're screwed.*

Across the street from them, a line of cars was slowly exiting an underground parking garage. Unaffected from the EMP, their drivers tried to shove their way through the crowded street, as angry pedestrians kicked and pummeled their cars. The cars soon became hopelessly locked behind a line of stalled taxis. None of them were going anywhere. Jack finally figured it out. Older vehicles with no computer chips were immune to the EMP, and vehicles that were parked underground were protected from the EMP's effect.

An hour hadn't passed since the power went off, and it was already turning ugly. Criminals wasted no time in taking advantage of the chaos. On the left, not far ahead of them, was a jewelry store. Jack heard gunfire and its front window suddenly exploded outward, sending missiles of glass onto the crowded sidewalk. Immediately following the shower of glass, two young men jumped through the shattered window, shoving their way through the frightened crowd. Each of them had a semi-automatic handgun in one hand and a bulging fabric shopping bag in the other. One of them fired several rounds over the heads of the people on the crowded sidewalk in front of him. Both of them were laughing as frantic people fell over themselves, trying to get out of their way. The gunshots spooked everyone. Like the starting gun at a marathon, people instantly pushed harder towards the stations. The crowd had been steadily picking up the pace. Now all were running—full panic had set in.

Jack thought it would only be logical for everyone to head towards the Ogilvie and Union train stations, normally a good idea if the trains were still running. From what he had seen so far, he had serious doubts that they would be. Dismissing the train as a way home, he decided to go with the cattle-like crowd for the time being, then veer off and somehow get to the Eisenhower Expressway. He figured they would go with the flow of people until they intersected with an alley or another cross street. He knew that no matter what, they had to get out of the crushing mass of panicked people. Even if some of them had an objective, most would end up following the crowd, running in circles. Jack mumbled to himself, "We're running like a bunch of scared cattle. We've got to get out of this shit." Like open flood gates, the massive crowd cascaded down the street, stopping for no one. Folks that couldn't keep up stumbled and fell, disappearing from sight, trampled into the pavement. Jack glanced back at Don. His partner was woefully out of shape and falling behind fast. What would normally be a short cab ride down Canal Street had become a stampede, and they were stuck in it.

Finally, the train station was in sight, but thick smoke was everywhere, choking the street. Jack thought, *and why not? It's just what I expected. This is*

Monday morning and everything is wrong. There was no place on the crowded street for anyone to stop and figure out what to do next. No time for anyone to think, only to follow the crowd. The station's main atrium entrance looked like it was on fire inside, and Jack didn't waste any more time thinking about taking a train out of it. They would have to continue with everyone else, racing down Canal Street, past their station.

Plumes of thick black smoke poured from the station's mass of windows, and frightened people were running, shoving their way out of all the exits.

Don frantically yelled to Jack, **"Now what?"**

Swiveling his head from side to side, Jack looked for a hole through the crowd, spotting a familiar face near him. He thought the man's name was Ray, so taking a chance he loudly yelled, **"Ray!"** When the fellow looked his way, Jack waved and yelled again, pointing to the station, "What happened?"

Ray yelled back, "Inbound commuter crashed. It came in fast and it couldn't stop! The whole place is filled with smoke from the fire.It's a real mess in there, stay away!"

Jack waved and yelled, "Good luck, Ray!"

Ray mouthed, "Thanks," and disappeared into the crowd.

The burning station had further spooked everyone, and it was no longer a crowd of scared people. It had turned into a crazed mob, pushing and shoving each other down Canal Street. There was another train station about four streets down. Union Station also had commuter trains going west, but none to Jack's suburban town. If by chance there were any trains running west out of it, they'd hop one, just to get out of the crazy city.

They continued with the panicked group for about a block, when Jack noticed an older building on his left had a front entrance with a deep alcove. *We have to step out of this craziness. I have to stop and think....* Turning around, he motioned to Don to make his way over to it. He figured they might have to hoof it out of the city, so it was as good a time as any to stop, give Don a rest, and discuss their escape plan. They were near the intersection of Madison and Canal Street, north of the next station, and as Jack looked towards it, he felt sick to his stomach. *Union Station can't be on fire too, could it?* Everyone around them was staring at a pillar of smoke rising high into the air a few blocks ahead, towering above the tall skyscrapers. Someone yelled that the other station was burning too, and people started trying to turn around, pushing and shoving, going back the way they came. Others followed and within seconds everyone was frantically turning around.

Jack pushed himself towards the small alcove, shoving his way in. Already there was a young and very frightened Hispanic-looking girl. Huddled tightly into a corner, she stood there terrified, her lips trembling and her eyes wet with fear. Her long black hair was disheveled and she had a bloody scrape on her chin.

She said nothing to him, but her eyes were pleading. He felt he should say something, and wanted to help her. Reading his thoughts, as he had read hers, she said, "I'm scared and I want to go home. What should I do?"

She looked about the same age of his daughter, who he hoped was safe in school. He started to say something to her, but Don was shoving himself into the tiny space and already loudly complaining.

Squeezing himself in tight against Jack, he pushed Jack into the girl. Out of breath, Don yelled, **"Now what the hell are we gonna do, Sherlock? We should have tried my car, that's what we should have done, but no, not you. Shit, look at this mess we're in! Did you see all the smoke in the air down that way? I heard someone say an airliner smacked into the top of Union Station, and that's what's burning!"**

Holding his temper, Jack turned halfway around and said, "If Union Station is on fire, we'll head west down Adams over to Clinton. Then we'll head south to the Ike. I know there's a lot of smoke down that way, but do we know for sure it's coming from the station? Maybe it is, maybe it isn't, but I am not turning around. Tell me, where are we going to go, back to our office? And what if by some chance the trains are running? We have to go by the station anyway to get over to the expressway, so let's at least check it out. If we can't get a train west, we'll go around it, and we can walk all the way home. We'll hike right down the center of the Eisenhower Expressway, to where it empties onto west Roosevelt Road.

Rolling his eyes, Don quickly shook his head, snarling back at Jack. "Jack, everyone's turning around, getting away from here! A tall burning building... hit by a plane? Think about it! Don't be stupid—it can collapse on us, just like the Trade Towers in New York. We gotta go back the other way with everybody else, they must know something we don't. Did you ever think of that? And I ain't flat footing it down any fuckin expressway! Don't be so pig-headed, Jack. Your bullshit thinking got your team killed in Iraq, so let's turn around, like everybody else."

Don's crude remark cut deep. Jack was instantly pissed, but he held on to his temper. "Do you want to get us trapped in this madhouse overnight? I'm going south to the Ike and then west to home, and that's it. You got it? We might have to zig zag around a bunch of crap, but we **will** get home! You think this is crazy now? Wait until the sun goes down and this city is pitch black." He could see Don thinking about Chicago with no lights. Jack's face went dark. He fought a sudden urge to grab him by his scrawny neck and squeeze it—really hard. Sticking his face, nose to nose, with Don, Jack cocked his head, and in a low snarl said, "And by the way, Donnie, it was in Afghanistan, not Iraq. Thanks for reminding me about that—you can be a little asshole, you know that?"

Turning back towards the scared girl, Jack's face softened. He said, "Do you live in the city or at least have relatives nearby?"

"No, I live in Lombard. All my family lives in the suburbs, west of the city."

"Then you should go with us, we're going right past there. Believe me, we're getting out of here right now."

There was a slight tremble in her finger as she pointed it. "But everybody's turning around, going that way."

Jack shook his head, "They're fools. I don't think but a few people out there have an actual plan...but I *always* have one."

"No," she softly replied, "I 'll stay here."

Jack started to say something else to her, but Don was impatient. "I don't care what we do, but let's do it now. That fire is getting bigger by the minute, and we have to get past it. Tell the little senorita adios." Don grabbed Jack's forearm, pulling him out onto the sidewalk saying, "Come on, let's go—and don't get so pissed at me, I'm sorry. You made the decision, so let's do it!" As Don led him away, Jack gave the girl one last pleading look, but she shook her head. He again thought of his own daughter and wife. *Thank God, they're safe out in the suburbs... how I hate Chicago...*

Fighting their way against a torrent of oncoming people, they pushed themselves through the crushing mass and continued south down Canal Street. Approaching the station, Don yelled to Jack, **"Look at that, huh? What did I try to fuckin tell you? The station's burning, I was right!"** The heat from the burning building was tremendous. Like a broken furnace, billowing flames were roaring out of the old station's roof and upper windows. Something big had hit the building. Like the New York City Trade Towers, a corner of the top floors was missing, it had to have been hit by an aircraft. Jack ignored Don's comment and pushed ahead harder.

Jack thought, *"Damn, Canal Street is blocked with burning cars and shit is falling off the top of that building.* He yelled to Don, **"Let's get on Adams and go west!"** The intersection of Canal Street and Adams was a wall of stalled cabs, all jammed together like sardines. Scrambling between them, and out of breath from the thick smoke, they rounded the corner onto Adams. They were about half a block safely past the burning station when there was a deep rumbling roar that vibrated the pavement beneath their feet. The upper floors of the station were collapsing outwards and onto Adams Street, pulverizing everything below it. Jack looked back and an exploding wall of impenetrable smoke and debris blasted around the corner, racing towards them! They were running for their lives and Don surprised Jack, as he not only kept up with him, he nearly passed him!

They shoved their way down Adams, sometimes having to climb over stalled taxis and finally crawling under a bus to get through the blocked street. Emerging from under the bus, the next intersection appeared easy, as the crowd had visibly thinned out and the wall of dust and smoke was behind them. Jogging to the intersection of Adams and Clinton, they started around the corner. Both of them stopped dead in their tracks, not believing what lay ahead, blocking them.

Out of breath, Don stopped and bent over. Spitting out chunks of dirt and soot, he mumbled, "Holy shit, is the whole city on fire? How could my morning turn to shit this fast?" All they had to do was to turn the corner onto Clinton Street and head south, but now they had hit another dead end. The buildings on both sides of the street were turning into an inferno.

Oblivious to the blaze, an older black man was leaning up against a corner newsstand, casually taking everything in. The old guy turned to Jack, almost laughing. "A news chopper fell outta the sky like a sack of shit on top all them cars down there. I watched the whole works blow up from here. Better than the Fourth of July, you know what I'm saying? Looks to me like the whole city is gonna be look'n like an over broasted chicken…. You boys see the old Union Station? It looks like a torch. Hearing loud boisterous yelling, all three of them turned to see a group of black teens running out of a clothing store, carrying armloads of sports jackets. Sizing up Don, the old guy gave him a toothless smile, saying, "Don't worry boy, just some kids out doing some early shopping. Things turn to shit, real quick, huh? It reminds me of 1968." Glancing back towards the youths, he said, "I guess school will be out for a while—Ha!" He eyed Jack and again looked at Don, laughing and shaking his head. "You two honkies look like you crawled through a pile of dog shit. You should see yourselves; your faces are as black as mine.. . . You wouldn't be making fun of me, would you, boys?"

Don stammered, "No, no, not at all. We're just trying to get home."

"Well—you better get your honky asses outta here—quick. It'll be uglier than a pissed off whore tonight." The old man spit, hitting Don's left shoe. Shaking his head, his smile faded. "Sorry, boy. . .." Turning away from them, he went back to watching the fire.

"The old timer's right, Jack." Wiping his face with his shirtsleeve, Don ignored the gob of spit on his shoe. Clearing his throat, he nodded towards the old man, "Thanks for the tip, Pops!" Don grabbed Jack's arm, "Let's get the hell outta here!"

Wasting no time, they continued west down Adams Street. Jogging towards the south side of the street, the intersection of Jefferson was ahead. Jefferson was a one-way street, running north from the expressway. This was the first intersection that wasn't gridlocked solid with cars or burning buildings, and that was exactly what Jack was looking for. Finally, they could make their turn south towards the Ike, and hopefully head straight for home. Both of them immediately started sprinting down the empty side-walk, anxious to turn south onto Jefferson.

They were just about to step off the curb when a white, vintage 1960s Chevy Camaro blasted upon them from across the street. It was going against traffic on a one-way street. The old car was almost airborne as it flew through the intersection heading towards them. Halfway in their descent off the curb, the white car shot past them, heading south on Jefferson. The left side of the car brushed against Don, banging into the briefcase he was carrying and nearly yanking it from his hand. Jack felt a breeze as the speeding car whizzed by a fraction of an inch from taking him with it. They stood there in disbelief, following the sight of the old car as it flew down the open street, going the wrong way. A huge black man, wearing a 1970s blue leisure suit, was hanging on for dear life on top of the car's hood. Another smaller, skinny white guy, was being dragged while holding onto the car's passenger door handle. The white guy lost his grip right in front of them as the car vaulted past them. Catapulting off the side of the car, he somersaulted head first into a large square curb, almost at their feet. His head smacked it with a bone shattering, **splat!**

   "**HOLY SHIT!**" screamed Don. "**DID YOU SEE THAT?**" That black-haired bitch driving that thing, she's going the wrong way! She clipped me! **She could have killed me!**" Don timidly took a step towards the skinny guy, who's head had struck the curb. As if he was afraid to get too close, Don craned his neck forward, saying, "**Look at that guy's noggin!** Holy shit, what's all that bloody grey crap squeezing out of it?"

   "His brains, Don. C'mon, he's done for, let's go."

   Although Jack didn't see the driver's face that nearly hit them, with that mane of tangled black hair, it definitely was a woman, a very determined one. She had somewhere to go and nothing was going to stop her. *That makes two of us*, Jack thought.

   Already forgetting the man with the crushed skull, Don was holding up his scraped briefcase. "Look at what that bitch did to my new briefcase, now it's all scuffed up! **Can't keep nothing nice!**"

   Jack looked sideways at Don, raising his eyebrows. He impatiently jerked his head left, motioning down Jefferson.

   Don gave Jack a look of disbelief. "What, you want to follow that crazy bitch?" He paused a second, nodding his head in approval, "You know, that's good idea. I'd like to catch up to her, and wring her stinking neck."

   Jack stood in the center of the street, looking down it. He said, "Compared to the others, this street looks clear, let's go."

   They entered Jefferson Street and finally headed south towards their goal of the expressway. Jack felt his racing heart finally slow. He was relieved to be on a street that wasn't totally blocked. Other than a few stalled cabs and delivery trucks, Jefferson looked like it might be clear all the way through. There were only a few people on foot, and all of them looked scared.

   Ahead, a ragged looking fellow with a badly split and bleeding lower lip, was walking towards them, talking loudly to himself. As he approached, Jack veered to the other side of the street with Don nervously following his lead. As they passed, the guy looked at Jack saying, "Don't worry man. I won't hit you. I won't hit you." The ragged looking man eyed Don, taking two steps towards him, blocking him. Extending his right arm, he pointed his dirty forefinger directly into

Don's face, saying, "Not much time left for you, smart ass." He was dressed in old clothes and like Jack and Don, he was filthy. He stepped back and continued walking a few feet before whirling around, and once again pointing his finger at Don, "You will knock, and he's not going hear you... nope. You're done for, boy."

As the man walked away, Don shrugged his shoulders and made the crazy in the head motion with his manicured finger, saying to Jack, "This shit is bringing out all the crazies. Where are all these nut-jobs coming from? I can't wait to get home!"

Don started briskly walking away, when Jack yelled, "Hold up, we got something up ahead." Jack motioned to a body lying in the middle of the street, about 60 feet ahead of them. A man was sprawled out next to a humongous Chicago pothole. His neck was lying cocked at an impossible angle, with a large pushed in bloody patch on the right side of his head. He was wearing a blue leisure suit.

Don said, "Holy crap, that's the guy we saw hanging onto that broad's hood!" He added, "Looks like that bitch shook him off when she hit this big pothole here," Then he smirked, "That's what happens when you wear clothes like that—never liked disco... Jeez Jack, this is crazy."

Chapter 2

THE PAST

Jack and Don had been buddies since grade school. They had the same friends, and once dated the same girl. After high school, Don went to college, and Jack to the Marines. Jack signed for a four-year enlistment that went on to last nine more. Don started out as a commercial real estate salesman at a Chicago company that was owned by his wife's father. Jack never found out exactly what Don did to end the gravy train, but messing around with his wife's younger sister was at least part of it. He pulled something underhanded and the State of Illinois yanked his broker's license. Don never sold real estate again, and his wife divorced him. Two years later he started working for Deegan's.

Jack was the opposite of Don and never wanted anything to do with college or the business world. He wanted high adventure and he found it in the Marines. He became a Combat Marine and his first tour of duty was in Iraq. During his second month there he was slightly wounded and earned the Purple Heart and a Bronze Star, with a "V" for valor. He felt guilty about getting the Purple Heart and, as far as he was concerned, the small scar on his forearm didn't warrant any medals. After Iraq, he had a six-month sea assignment, training with a Marine Corps detachment out of San Diego, aboard various naval ships. There was another tour of Iraq and one tour of combat in Afghanistan. Earning his stateside shore duty, he spent two years at Camp Pendleton's School of Infantry, teaching boots how to fight. When he was offered an opportunity to instruct some Navy brass at the Great Lakes Naval Base in Illinois for a month, he jumped at it. For the first time since he had been in, he was unexpectantly given a chance to be stationed near his hometown. With the leave time he had accumulated, he figured he could stretch it out to six weeks. That was when he met Ellen. She got pregnant and they got married. Living in California was fun for Ellen, until she had the baby and Jack deployed to Iraq. Somehow, it had never occurred to her that her husband would be gone for the better part of a year, leaving her alone with a child she never wanted. There was another stint in Iraq, and then two in Afghanistan. It was on his last tour of duty in Afghanistan that he was badly wounded. He earned another purple heart, but this time it wasn't just a little shrapnel in his arm. He caught chunks of metal everywhere from an IED—and it was bad.

While Jack was in the hospital, he had too many hours, whole days, just to think. He never had so much down time, and many a night he lay awake, his last thoughts about things. The things—tucked away to deal with sometime later… The things that shouldn't have happened, but did. He had made many friends while in the Corps. Most of them put in their four-year hitch, went back home to civilian life, and he never heard from them again. While he laid on his stomach in that hospital, he thought of all of them, all the way back to bootcamp. And as bad as he felt, sometimes he found himself laughing to himself about some funny incident that happened. Most everyone was scattered across the states, and he hoped they were all doing well. He'd probably never see any of them again, but he still thought of them. Then…there were the others. Some he barely knew and some were close. A couple of them he didn't like, but none of them deserved what happened to them. Killed in action, or by accident, it didn't matter. Their life was ended, instantly… and Marines keep going, always moving. You're not afraid to die, but you are afraid that your buddy will. One moment you're with them, and the next second, they're dying, and they're gone. Just gone, and you can't do a thing about it. Gone, a four-letter word that he hated. No goodbyes, just carted away and gone. You can't dwell on it, because that's the way it is and you're a Marine with a job to do. You pray you're not next, but really, did he ever worry about himself?

The days in rehab were busy, but the nights, those long and silent nights that he laid in that hospital, one thought kept creeping into his mind. Sometimes it tried to seep in during the day, but he was busy and could shut it out. At night it was a different story. The gates to his mind were wide open and there was no shutting them. Jack wished he'd had died too.

The event he dreaded the most would be the memorial. *The memorial…* if he could somehow avoid it, he definitely would. Back at Pendleton, there was a board with photos of every man lost. Pictures and names of guys he knew, buddies he had lost. He had attended them before. There would be a row of Marines, usually in the back row, sitting in wheel chairs. He had seen them before at other memorials and now he felt ashamed of himself. Ashamed because he never gave his wounded comrades the attention they deserved. They would leave the Corps and leave his life forever. He had never contacted any of them. He didn't know why, he just didn't—he couldn't. But this time—*he was one of them* and he felt different, completely different. He would be shuffled to the side, back to the civilian world. There would be a speech and then a final playing of taps. The families of those killed, would always be there too, aimlessly walking around afterwards, sad faced and searching, wanting to hear something, anything about their dead son or husband. He had talked to families before; he knew what they would ask. "Are you Hansen? Our son told us about you. He said you were his best friend. Tell us…you were with him…. Did he say anything to you, *that day*— before he—died?" The wives, the sweethearts, the moms and dads, all searching for one last moment of their loved one's life. Tears would flow, the toughest Marine had them. Some could hide them and hold them back, but they were still there. Everyone thought he was tough, but he knew the truth. Jack Hansen cried a river inside.

Nolan's memorial would be gut wrenching. He played it out over and over in his mind, weeks before the dreaded day. Nolan had talked about his dad so much, Jack felt like he knew him. He felt like he knew the whole family. Dying was easy, but for those left behind it was hell, and what was he going to say to them? His buddies' parents would feel sorry for him because he was in a wheel chair, and the last living link to their sons. There was nothing he could say; he certainly couldn't tell them the truth. *"I'm sorry, so sorry…. I let your boys down. We shouldn't have been on that road… It's my fault they died. I got your sons killed!* When he was medevacked out, he swore he heard someone say, "*Hello civilian world.*" No, not, Jack Hansen! He regained his sense of balance and was finally able to stand without falling over. He went from a wheel chair to baby steps behind a walker and finally to jogging. The Navy shrink said he suffered from PTSD and had suppressed anger issues and possibly sustained some brain trauma from the explosion. He had already told the shrink too much, and he wished he had kept his mouth shut from the beginning. He wasn't going anywhere; they would have to kick him out of the Corps. He wasn't about to provide them anymore ammo to do it. Sure, sometimes during a conversation he would lose his place, but who didn't once in a while? The shrink said certain things would trigger him and they had to find out what they were, because that's what PTSD is about. Jack didn't need anyone to figure out for him what triggered it. It was waiting inside his mind all the time…*it never fucking leaves.* PTSD was like being in a sunny room and the shades suddenly being lowered all at once. It just came over him instantly and the sadness that encased him couldn't be stopped. He sank down, down, and further down. That hot day and the short ride with his friends would come back to haunt him, over and over again.

He decided not only to keep his mouth shut, but to lie to them. They couldn't read his mind. He was physically getting better and he wouldn't give them anymore reasons to get rid of him. He'd seen his service record and, typical of the military, the report of the *incident* was short and vague. Only he knew the whole story. It was a roadside bomb during the end of his second tour in Afghanistan that got him. He was one of four Marines riding in a Humvee that hot afternoon and only he returned to the states alive. His buddy, Nolan, was in that Humvee with him, and it was Jack that turned them around on that blocked off road. They should never have turned around. They should have sped up and gone around; forced their way through. But no, **he turned them around**, and that's what the insurgents wanted. They had driven down that road many times before, but this time was different. It was blocked. They should have plowed their way through it! Why didn't he do that? They were talking, joking around, kidding each other, and he didn't think it through—it happened too fast! Three buddies—Owens, Weaver, and Nolan, all of them dead, **because of me and my bad call!**

At first, they said he might never walk again without a walker, but sometimes he just didn't care, because this was *Hansen's* punishment, **his hell**. He was missing a kidney and there was a long period when his hearing wasn't so good in his left ear, and almost gone in his right. Most of his hearing did come back, but they told him the loud static noises that played in his head would remain forever, blaring like a thousand crazy bugs night and day. The worst was that he lost his sense of balance. Without hanging on to something, he couldn't stand up to pee, let alone walk without falling over. To go from what he once was to what he had become was an evil blow. Months went by but *he got better*! They weren't going to kick him out! When his thinking got screwed up and he lost his place in a conversation, he'd just pause, and get his shit together, *they never knew*. But those dark thoughts, they kept creeping in. He thought the shrink suspected, but he wouldn't tell him. If it wasn't for his young daughter back home, he probably would have blown his brains out. He sold all his personal weapons and made up excuses to his friends as to why he sold them. Only he knew why...

When he finally returned to Camp Pendleton, he was given a temporary assignment. All the guys he had served with had gotten out or were deployed elsewhere, mostly back to Afghanistan. He was still in the Corps, but felt alone and out of the game. He was put in charge of a bunch of short timers. Twenty-some men who were just killing time, waiting for their early discharge. They had only one goal and that was to get out of the Marine Corps. A possible disability pension for post-traumatic stress would be an added bonus. He had seen their service records. Most of them had never been anywhere even close to combat and some never left the states. He couldn't understand it and resented them, blowing the only chance they had of making something of themselves. If they wanted to know about PTSD, he could tell them all about it, but he had nothing in common with them. He didn't even consider them Marines. The military was then *cutting back* and he saw the handwriting on the wall. Jack Hansen was being shuffled around, that's all it was, but he no longer cared. He had gone from being a fighter to a babysitter. After receiving two purple hearts, it was time to call it quits and join the civilian world, where Purple Hearts and V's for valor got tucked away in the back of a drawer. But it would be on his terms, he wouldn't wait for the ax to fall. At 32 years old, he beat them to the punch and put in for a medical discharge. The now former Marine did something he thought he would never do. He was enrolled at the Veteran's Administration for health benefits, entered college, and joined the VFW. After graduating with a degree in architecture, he

34

found himself back with his old high school buddy, Don Jenks. He was in a new career that was a million miles away from the Corps and maybe it was better. He had planned on putting 20, maybe 25 years in the Corps, and never gave any thoughts past that. Being cut loose after 13 years, 4 months, and 3 days, he was for the first time in his life scared at what lay ahead, but he was also excited. In the years to come, he would often think about his last hours in the Marines.

In the minutes before being processed out, he was sitting in a long hallway on a rickety wooden bench next to an old lifer. The guy had been in for twenty-five years and with the deep scar running across his face, he looked it. They were waiting to get their walking orders, and the older Marine said, "Whole different world we're going back to, buddy. You won't be using the shit you learned here. Nope, you'll be out of place like an old police dog at a kid's birthday party. That's the long and short of it, pal. Got out once myself, but I came back. I worked in my father-in-law's hardware store, stocking shelves and dealing with his asshole customers. After a month I was ready to kill someone. As much as I sometimes hated the bullshit the Corps tossed at me, I had to admit it, it had gotten in my blood. For some of us—*it never leaves*. Good luck to you, pal."

******

As he and Don warily jogged down Jefferson Street, he recalled the conversation he had with the old lifer. In the years since he got out, he ran that conversation over in his head more times than he could remember. It was really insignificant, but it was his last minutes in the Marine Corps. Like so many other things that happened while he was in, the good and the bad, it frequently came into his days and nights over and over again. *"It never leaves."*

Unlike the streets they had just escaped from, Jefferson was quiet. It was still cluttered with abandoned vehicles, but it was at least open, with only a few people. It was too quiet and he found himself instinctively eyeballing every inch of it. He was thrust back a into the world of shit he knew only too well. He cursed himself for not having searched the two bodies for a weapon, even a knife. *I'm rusty,* he thought.

Jack mumbled to himself, "We're in deep shit…"

"What did you say, Jack?"

"Nothing, Don, just thinking about something that's all, but there's something you gotta do."

"What's that, Jack? Anything you want, name it."

35

"Don't be right next to me, okay? Good God almighty, you keep bumping into me, quit crowding me! Move over to the side and stay back from me, at least a few feet. You've got to be looking around too, eyeballing everything and look behind us every so often. There're some bad dudes on the street and I don't want to get ambushed by them or have anyone double back on us. God, I wish you had brought your gun today."

Suddenly Don looked more shaken than he was before, **"What the hell do you mean, ambushed?** Like when you were in Iraq? Hey, I'm no fighter, Jack. I 'm not like you.. . **I just want to get the hell out of here. I wanna go home!"**

"I'm just saying, Don, stop crowding me, we're making ourselves a target. These punks can smell it when you are afraid and will be on us like flies on shit. Quit gabbing and be on your toes. I can't see everything. And yeah, now you know how it feels to be in combat... Come on, let's go. You gotta keep up with me."

"God, Jack, can we at least stop and rest a couple minutes, I'm out of breath. It looks safe here."

"No."

They had just crossed Van Buren Street without incident and were cutting through a parking lot when gunfire erupted behind them. A black stretch limo had suddenly pealed out of a parking lot down the street from them and was being shot at by three youths trying to chase it down on foot. Jack motioned Don to follow him as he jumped behind a parked delivery truck, hoping the thugs hadn't noticed them. As the limo sped away, the youths gave up the chase.

Don urgently whispered to Jack, "You think they saw us? They had to see us. Oh shit, we're in for it now, we're fucked—oh God..."

Through clenched teeth, Jack growled, "Shut up or they will see us! They'd be on us by now if they did. We'll wait here a bit and see if they double back. Now be quiet and for God's sake, stay down." They stayed hidden behind the truck until they were sure that the armed youths had left.

 Jack faked a smile, saying, "Okay, Donnie, you've had your little rest. The next street will be Tilden and the expressway will be after that, let's go." Jack pushed harder towards the expressway, their jog becoming a run.

The last and final street that lay between them and the Eisenhower Expressway was finally before them, and Jack prayed they could cross it without incident. He let out a deep breath in disgust as he motioned Don to come to a halt. About 20 yards ahead, stopped in the middle of the street, was the old white Camero that had nearly hit him and Don earlier. It was sitting sideways where it had spun out. The back end of it looked like it had swiped the side of a nearby parked cab. Standing at the driver's door was a young black gangbanger with purple shorts worn down to his knees, and a red ball cap on backwards. He was repeatedly thrusting the barrel of a small handgun into the face of the black-haired lady. She was sitting behind the wheel of her car as the young gangbanger screamed at her, while trying to choke her with his other hand.

Jack heard Don mumble, "Screw that stupid bitch, serves her right, let him shoot her." Ignoring Don, he was already making his approach to attack the preoccupied gangbanger. He had quickly sized up what had to be done and did it. It was as if he never left the Corps. He could see that the assailant was a boy, maybe not even 15 years old, but he was just as dangerous as the young Iraqis he had faced in Fallujah. The gun he held looked like a short-barreled revolver and that canceled out his young age and punched the boy's forever ticket.

As he rushed up behind him, he could see that the young thug's hand wasn't clutching the lady's neck, but was in her mouth. She had his left hand clamped tightly in her jaws, with her teeth buried in the meaty area above his thumb. Blood was squirting out between her buried teeth and his hand. The kid was screaming and repeatedly thrusting the gun's barrel into her right cheek, trying to break her clenched jaws from his hand. Suddenly, he pulled the short-barreled revolver back to shoot her in the head, and would have, had he not seen Jack rushing him. As taught by the videos that he had watched, the boy whipped the small gun around, holding it sideways, gangster style. He was either really scared or high on something, as he was shaking the gun from side to side while bouncing it up and down. All the while he was yelling curses, trying to free his other hand from the women's vise-like bite.

Jack crouched down, rushing in low, lunging into him as two shots zinged past his left ear. He planted his right knee deep into the punk's bright purple shorts, burying it into his crotch. At the same time, he had both of his arms up, deflecting the small gun upwards and into his grasp. Wrenching the gun from his hand, the kid's fingers popped like twisted gristle. In one fluid motion, Jack had the young thug's gun and fired one shot into his face. Only when a geyser of blood shot out from where the boy's right eye was, did the woman open her mouth and release his bloody hand. The boy fell against the car, slowly sliding to the ground. The bullet had entered through his eye, and was somewhere in his head. It was over, but the young man wasn't dead. His head was violently convulsing back and forth, splattering the car's white door red with blood.

Jack hesitated only a second. As a river of blood poured from his missing eye, he fired another round into the boy's forehead.

Jack got his first look at the women he had just saved and backed away from her car. She didn't bother to get out. She looked a mess and sat there, trying to clear the young gang banger's blood from her mouth, spitting gobs of red mucus out her window. Interested in his new-found weapon, Jack hefted the small revolver in his palm and opened the cylinder. It was a five shot 22 caliber, hunk of junk. Deep grinding marks had removed any traces of serial numbers and who the gun's maker was. There was one 22 caliber bullet left in it. Snapping the cylinder closed, Jack cursed to himself, saying, "Shit! I've got a 22, with one round left, that's great." He bent down and frisked the kid. Finding nothing, he stood up and said to the lady, "You're lucky, you know that? For the life of me, I don't know why he just didn't shoot you and take the car. He could have been long gone. Why the hell didn't you just give it to him?"

She spat out her window and screamed, "He didn't want the car. He wanted me—he was going to rape me!"

Looking at her face, Jack sucked in his breath. The kid had thrust the small gun's barrel into her face so violently, it had torn a large bloody gash from under her left eye to her jaw. Her cheek was laid wide open and a once pretty face would never be the same. Her long black hair was a tangled mess, already matted in blood and sticking to her face. Some of the young punk's blood from his torn hand had flowed down and covered her chin. It crossed Jack's mind that she looked like a vampire. Don's right he thought, *This broad is tough!* Suddenly, the distant sound of gunfire sent that old familiar warning shooting through his body. It sounded close, too close. No bullets whizzed by him, but he ducked down, and took a step back, giving the area a quick sweep with his combat trained eyes. *It never fuckin leaves,* he thought....

He looked back at her, and as she pulled back the tangled mat of her bloody hair, he started to say, "Look lady, we have to get out of here now, let's—" Jack pulled back in astonishment. "What the hell! It's you?" Turning back towards Don, he started to say something to him, but again stopped. Something wasn't right. His buddy was sitting on the pavement, about 20 feet back. He was staring straight ahead, tightly clutching his briefcase to his chest. His frightened eyes slowly rose to meet Jack's.

Jack said, "It's all right, Don, the punk's dead, we'll be outta here quick." But Don said nothing, he just sat there, clutching his new briefcase, staring at Jack.

"Don, are you okay?" Jack didn't see the small bubbles of blood forming on Don's lips. He had seen guys fold up in combat before. Knowing Don, he figured he had suddenly reached his limit. He'd have to go back and give him a kick in his ass and get him going.

Holding a white scarf to her torn cheek, the lady got out of her car. Jack turned and looked back at her. She had a bottle of water and was washing her mouth out. Bent over and still spitting out the taste of the gangbanger's flesh, she wiped her mouth with the red stained scarf and slowly stood up. While looking at Jack, a hint of a smile showed on her bloodied face. She tossed the blood-stained scarf to the ground between them and they both stood there for a couple of long seconds, staring at each other. The open gash on her cheek was deep and about five inches long. Jack watched as a small rivulet of blood ran from it and jogged down her neck, spreading into her already blood-soaked blouse. She broke the stare first. Her eyes shot past Jack to Don, who was still sitting, tightly clutching the briefcase to his chest.

Ignoring her own wound, she quickly walked past Jack to Don. Kneeling next to him, she gently pulled the briefcase forward from his grasp. There was a small hole in his upper chest on the right side. Don went into a coughing spasm, and bubbly blood poured from the hole. She got partway up and looked at his back, checking for an exit wound. Jack was immediately behind her and she stood up facing him.

Holding up her right forearm to her bloodied cheek, she urgently said, "Your friend has been shot in the right lung. There's no exit wound, that means the bullet might have hit a rib. A small caliber bullet like a 22 might have ricocheted in his chest cavity, doing lots of damage. We have to get him to an emergency room fast, and I'll be needing some stiches myself."

Suddenly, they both heard a crash, and spun their heads to a building on their right. A man's body had been catapulted through a plate glass window, landing on his face in the parking lot with a sickening thud. Three laughing men emerged through the shattered window opening. As the helpless man lay on the pavement motionless, they began violently kicking him.

Jack looked down at Don, and then at her, motioning his head towards her car, saying, "Think that will start?"

She nodded her head, saying, "It just stalled when I spun out." Then she pointed to the dead kid. "I was trying to start it when he attacked me." She bent down and grabbed hold of Don's left arm, "Let's get your friend into my car and over to the emergency room at Boeger Hospital."

Following her lead, they gently placed Don into the car's right front bucket seat. She reached behind Don and snatched a small bag off the back seat, pulling out a grey sweatshirt top. Holding it to her bleeding face, she asked Jack, "Could you please drive?"   Jack quickly snapped back, "You bet, let's get out of here." She got in the car on the driver's side and climbed into the back. Jack tossed Don's briefcase in behind her and slid into the driver's bucket seat.

He was about to turn the ignition key when Don suddenly grabbed his right arm. Gasping for breath, with tears flowing from his eyes and blood bubbling out of his mouth, he weakly said, "I screwed you over big guy...really bad. You're going to find out soon." Don went into a coughing fit with frothy blood spewing out of his mouth, splattering the car's dashboard and windshield. He gasped, "Please forgive me, Jack."

The black-haired lady grabbed Don from behind, pulling him tightly into the bucket seat. She was about to tell him to be quiet, but instead pointed over Jack's shoulder to the three thugs in the parking lot. **"They're coming!"**

They had lost interest in the man on the ground they were kicking, and started walking towards their new interest, the 1960's white muscle-car.

Jack tried to turn the Camaro's ignition over, but it refused. The car was a four-speed manual transmission and had stalled out while still in gear. The men had broke into a run, coming straight towards them. He shoved the gearshift into neutral, turned the key, and the old V8 roared to life. Jamming the shifter into first gear, he made a hard-U turn. Both of the rear tires started to scream as he peeled away, retreating north on Jefferson, away from the expressway.

The three running men, two with guns drawn, suddenly stopped. Preparing to fire, one of them yelled, **"Where you going with our car, boy?"** Jack floored the old car, the car's rear tires smoking, tearing at the cracked concrete pavement. Laying down two huge streaks of burning rubber, the powerful old V8 bolted away from the attackers. The two men, with their weapons drawn, advanced a few feet and came to a stop in the middle of the street. They took careful aim, letting loose a volley of bullets from their small semi-automatic handguns. Two of their rounds hit the car's back glass, completely shattering it. At least three more bullets slammed into the back of the trunk lid. Jack instinctively hunched down, tensing his muscles, praying the car's thin sheet metal would stop the penetrating bullets. The gunshots, thank God, didn't sound like they came from a 45 or all three of them would be dead. More gunshots followed as the old car fishtailed wildly, roaring down the street and out of sight.

ELLEN

CHAPTER 3

Ellen Hansen felt shackled and it was time to break free. When she was young, she had what her parents called, "a wild streak." Back then, most of her friends found it made her a fun person to be around. Ellen's wildness was fun and Jack was attracted to it while they were dating. He had known others like that, girls and guys. He figured once he and Ellen were married, and she became a mom, she would change. The only thing that changed was that Ellen became bitter. As she neared 18 years of marriage and her 40th birthday, she felt she had missed something and it was time to move on. Their marriage may have had a chance if she ever really loved Jack or the baby. Her marriage to the good-looking Marine had been a convenient ticket away from her controlling parents. Now, instead of her parents, it was her marriage that felt controlling. Too many years had been lost playing house with two people she never loved. Ellen Hansen had a plan, and that plan didn't include Jack or their daughter, Laura.

Nearly 20 years earlier, a 19-year-old Ellen Kelly was out with a friend one Friday night. With their newly acquired false IDs, the two girls had managed to get themselves into a night club. They were picked up by this fast-talking guy and his friend, a tall rugged looking Marine. The fast talker was Don Jenks; the friend was Jack Hansen. Don had talked Jack into wearing his uniform to a bar. Don had said, "These girls around here have probably never seen a Marine—it'll be a real chick- magnet." It worked. Ellen had made a beeline to Jack. He was temporarily stationed at the Great Lakes Navy Base, and was visiting old high school buddies while staying at his parent's home. She and Jack hit it off that night and started dating. Three months later, Ellen was pregnant. She wanted to get an abortion, but Jack wouldn't hear of it. She had an abortion about four years earlier, which she never told Jack about. For her, getting pregnant was an annoyance, with a quick abortion the only solution. But Jack wanted the baby. He told Ellen he loved her and wanted to get married. The only problem was that she didn't love him and had been fooling around with Jack's friend, Don, when he was away on duty at Great Lakes. She called her parents and asked for help. They had helped her out of several jams before, including her first abortion. This time their answer was, "No." She ended up having a baby she wasn't sure who the father was and marrying a Marine who would be gone on long deployments for months at a time. Leaving the young and restless Ellen alone with a baby she would have rather aborted, was a stamped ticket for cheating. Jack never suspected. It wasn't until almost a year after Laura was born, that Ellen finally became convinced the baby was Jack's. By the time Laura was a toddler, it was obvious. Laura showed the unmistakable likeness of that nosey, skinny bitch that was Jack's mother. There were so many times she looked at Laura and wished she would have had that abortion. Ellen wasn't completely without heart. When Jack was wounded, as much as she wanted out, she couldn't leave him. She figured she'd wait, at least until he recovered.

If Jack had stayed in the underpaid Marines, she would have certainly left him and the baby years ago. She began to rethink her plan when he got out of the Marines and secured a well-paying job with Don at Deegan's. When she found out how much money Jack stood to inherit when his mother died, Ellen postponed her divorce plans a little longer. Actually, she had become quite fond of Jack. He was a good man, and made plenty of money... just not quite enough. Don made much more, lot's more on under the table deals, than Jack had any idea of. Soon, the little charade would be over for Ellen's marriage and Don's boring job at Deegan's. In about six weeks, Jack's marriage and his career would be over and he didn't have a clue. Whatever heart Ellen had; it was gone.

* * * * * *

It was Monday morning and Ellen had just dropped Jack off at the train station. She was driving her prized Volkswagen convertible to the dry cleaners and would make a quick stop for gas, and then run a couple more errands. Coming up to a red light, she slowed and downshifted into first gear before stopping. While waiting for the light to turn green, a thin smile appeared on her lips. She was looking forward to the fun time she so badly needed later that morning. While Jack was tied up looking at some old dusty buildings, she would be doing the "polka" with his partner, Don. The light turned green and she laughed out loud to herself as she pulled away. Don was Polish. He always referred to their little rendezvous together as having a "polka party." *Don is so much more fun than you, Jack, and he's loaded.* Her smile faded as she remembered the argument she had with her daughter, Laura, earlier at home. *That little bitch thinks she has it all figured out, but she hasn't a clue. Leaving Jack and his little princess is going to be so easy, no regrets.*

She figured Jack suspected something, but never between her and Don. By the time he did figure it out, it would be too late. Ellen wasn't just good at the

42

art of deception; she had perfected it. She had been cheating on Jack before they got married, and continued shortly thereafter. *Just have to continue the charade a little bit longer.* Her smile reappeared, only this time wider, as she licked her lips with anticipation. *With all that money Don has siphoned from Deegan's shitty old buildings and the city, the rest of my life is going to be on easy street. I'll finally get what I deserve....*

Her little car was thirsty and needed some gas, but the first stop would be at the dry cleaners. She was dropping off a suit of Jack's and picking up two dresses for Laura and one of hers. Pulling into the dry cleaner's parking lot, she thought to herself, *I won't be coming into these sad little places much longer, thank God for that*. Lately, everything she did, she viewed in those terms. She was not only going to leave Jack and Laura behind, but also the whole boring little town and everyone in it. It was a good feeling, and this morning she reveled in it.

She handed the clerk the ticket and, in a few moments, he returned with her black dress and a rose colored one of Laura's. He hung both of them on the clothes stand next to the register. While he was looking for Laura's other dress, Ellen couldn't help but compare the difference in the fronts of them. The top of her black dress looked like it had run out of material to contain her ample full figure. Laura's dress looked like a pillowcase. She smirked to herself while thinking, *With a body like a sheet of plywood, no wonder she has no boyfriends. She didn't inherit anything from me. She has a figure like Jack's mom, a crooked stick.*

The clerk came out with Laura's other dress and a couple minutes later, Ellen's little car sped out of the parking lot. She had the radio on, and turned it up full blast and was loudly singing along with a song, *"can't get enough of it babe..., no, no, no..."* as she happily drove down the street. She suddenly grimaced and her good mood darkened. She remembered the divorce papers she had left on the dining room table in Don's condo. They needed to be completed before dropping off at the lawyers' office tomorrow. She smiled to herself thinking, *I guess I can get that done this afternoon—after polka time.*

The gas station was her next stop, and it was coming up on the right. She spotted the Sheriff's Deputy, Chuck Hayes' patrol car, parked at the front of the station and made sure she pulled to the furthest pump. Getting out of her car she warily eyed the deputy's squad while walking into the station to pre-pay her gas. She would have paid with her card at the pump but she had to get a carton of cigarettes inside, and hoped the deputy hadn't seen her. She wanted to avoid him and his big oaf of a brother, Dirk, or "pig face" as Jack called him. She had an affair with the deputy back when Jack was in the service. Unfortunately, Hayes was the cop that patrolled the unincorporated subdivision where she and Jack lived. She often ran into him around town and sometimes, if Jack was gone, he'd stop in front of their house and hint about coming in for *old times*. She wanted nothing to do with *old times* and besides, the man had more than a few kinks, that even she found disturbing. His older brother, Dirk, was worse, and one of the scariest men she had ever met. He was a county sewer and water worker, who the year before was working on the sewer in front of their home. He was digging a large hole with a machine out by the street when he and Jack got into an argument. All she knew was that Jack pushed the man and then kicked him into the hole, almost getting himself arrested over it. No charges were ever filed, but it ended with Dirk Hayes threatening Jack.

Walking back to her car, she could see the deputy sitting in his squad car, talking on his radio. As she pumped her gas, she steeled a second look towards his car. She frowned and shook her head, saying to herself, "How could I have ever been so stupid to have gotten involved with him?" As the gas flowed into her car's tank, she recalled that time so many years ago. Unknown to Jack, when they were first married, she had a little run in with Sheriff Hayes.

Jack was overseas on duty in the Middle East when she was pulled over by *Officer* Chuck Hayes. She and another friend had been out at a bar and had shared a joint afterwards in the bar's parking lot. Ellen was driving and had no sooner pulled out into the street, when the blue lights of a police car was behind them. Her car reeked of weed. There were two policemen in the squad car. One was older, fat and bald headed, and the other was short and skinny. The skinny cop was Officer Hayes, and charges were never filed. Officer baldly head and Hayes were taken care of while sitting in their squad. She and Hayes shared more than a few more late nights together while Jack was away. Hayes was not a good-looking man, in fact far from it. He was abusive and she never liked him. What she and her friend did like were the bags of free weed that the officers always provided them. In the years since then, she avoided him like the plague.

Ellen sped out of the gas station, giving the squad car a last look in her mirror, and was glad Hayes had not seen her. Going through the gears, she recalled those nights in the back of his squad. *If Jack only knew….*

From time to time, she would run into Hayes when she was out together with Jack. One time they were at the county fair, another time a village picnic. Hayes had given her that thin-lipped smile, followed by a little wink. Ellen smugly smiled to herself, thinking, *After the divorce, I'll never run into Hayes, or Jack again.* She downshifted and quickly turned into Jay's Foods' parking lot, a little faster than she should have.

Instead of parking in the supermarket's lot, she parked next door in front of the Mandel's Department Store. It wasn't open yet and the lot was empty. She hated the supermarket's parking lot. People were always bumping their shopping carts into someone's car. No one cared. Her little car would be safe and sound over there by Mandel's. She intended to stop back there later on this afternoon. It was too bad it wasn't open now. This morning she had to do the grocery shopping for the princess' high school graduation party. It was to be held next Saturday afternoon, and she wasn't looking forward to it. Before getting out of the car, she checked her phone. It was 7:43. Don would be calling in a few minutes and she didn't want to miss it. Shaking her head, she smiled again, thinking of her secret get together with Don. *Jack, you are so dense.*

After she did the shopping, she figured she would drop off the groceries at home and get ready to meet Don for their fun time. It was like a big game, cheating on Jack. She felt like she was in high school again. Opening her purse, she searched through it for her shopping list, annoyance suddenly crossing her face. *Oh shit. I had that list in my hand when I was at Don's last night, I must have left it there…. Oh well, I think I can remember what's on it.* Before getting out of the car, she placed the key to Don's condo in the glove box, thinking, *Jack could spot it on my key ring and leaving it in my purse wouldn't be a wise move either.* She closed the car door, locked it, and headed towards the store, happily humming to herself.

The automatic door opened and, grabbing a shopping cart, she noticed the handle was dirty. Impatiently shoving it aside, she took a different one, saying out loud, "Don't you people ever clean these damn things?" As she started wheeling the cart into the store, a wry smile appeared on her lips, *This will be the last time I ever come in this dumpy little store anyway, so who the hell cares?*

Ellen knew the layout of the store by heart and went down the aisles, quietly talking, holding a private conversation with herself. "All right, Laura, your little party, let's see… you're lucky I am even doing this after the way you talked to me this morning, you little bitch. You really think you are going away to college this fall? You're going to be sooooo disappointed. Let's see here, ice cream, chocolate cookie dough, pecan butternut-crunch, bottled water. I'll get some soda too…. Jack loves those cheese nut logs." She thought of Don and smiled to herself, *Don loves those nut logs too. I'll pick one up for him, an extra big one….* She started laughing to herself out loud. Feeling self-conscious, she looked around the store thinking, *people will think I'm nuts.*

"An extra big one," *she* whispered to herself and chuckled some more as she continued down the aisle. Holding her little conversation with herself, she stopped just before the checkout lines, trying to visualize her forgotten shopping list, "Damnit, there's some-thing I am forgetting. What is it?"

"Are you all right there, Ellen? I can hear you talking to yourself all the way over here."

Ellen looked over to the register and saw Doris Sorensen, her neighbor who lived across the street. She was one of the cashiers at Jay's Foods. Ellen had always felt sorry for her because of her abusive husband, Glen. Doris was too far away to notice Ellen purse her lips and the slight distasteful shake of her head. *Good God Doris…as much as I piss Jack off, at least he never hit me… why does she stay with that bastard, Glen?*

Feigning a genuine smile, she entered Doris' checkout line saying, "Hi Doris. Don't mind me talking to myself. I don't have my shopping list with me and I know there's something I forgot. It's driving me nuts."

While Ellen started placing items on the conveyor belt, Doris initiated her usual checkout banter, "Beautiful day out today, going to be a warm one too, sure wish I was off. Looks like you're getting ready for a party, huh?"

Ellen kept her smile, and through her teeth said, "Yeah, a graduation party for Laura, she's such a sweetie... Why don't you stop over on Saturday for the party?" *Just leave your abusive husband at home....* At that moment Ellen noticed Doris' right eye. It had a faint black mark under it that her makeup wasn't quite covering. Ellen moved up in the checkout lane and stopped even with Doris. Making eye contact, she leaned towards her and softly said, "Doris, why do you put up with Glen? Why don't you just get a lawyer? You know, if you need someone—."

Doris held her left hand up in protest, cutting Ellen off while continuing to ring up the groceries. A tense moment passed and neither of them said anything.

Without looking at Ellen, Doris shook her head and self-consciously brushed her blond hair back, saying, "Sometimes Glen plays a little rough, but maybe I like it."

She finished adding up Ellen's total saying, "That comes to $109.35. Will that be cash or charge?" Her friendliness had suddenly chilled.

Holding up her charge card, Ellen said, "Let's make it a charge."

The big clock on the front wall over the service desk said 8:13. There was a low popping sound and the store suddenly went dark. The only light was coming through the store's front windows.

A loud groan was heard from the back of the store and Ellen heard a man in line behind her mutter, "Oh shit, not again."

Doris repeated what the man said, "Yeah, not again. This happened last week, the emergency generator should go on any second."

"I'm sorry folks." It was the store's manager, "Our generator will kick in and the lights will come back on. Please be patient, we'll only be without power a few seconds."

Doris icily eyed Ellen, then leaned over the conveyor belt saying, "If you weren't so busy with your extracurricular activities, Ellen, you'd find out there's lots of fun things happening right in our own little neighborhood. You just have to see things through a different eye...you're welcome to join us sometime."

Feeling anger rising, Ellen replied, "I'm sorry I opened my mouth, Doris. Excuse me for being concerned. And who says that I have extracurricular activities?"

"Well, you're a *church* goer aren't you, Ellen? You know what your Good Book says, 'Everything done in darkness comes to light', doesn't it?" Doris stepped back and smiled, suddenly becoming polite. "Anyway, you're all rung up,

Ellen, but without power you can't use your plastic. If you had cash, you could pay and go..."

Wanting to get her groceries, but more importantly, wanting to get away from Doris, Ellen hurriedly went through her purse. "I do have some cash, but it's so dark in here I can hardly count it. Here, this should be enough, I rounded it out to $110. Jay's Foods owes me 65 cents."

The bag boy had already placed Ellen's bagged up groceries in her cart when Doris handed her the receipt saying, "I don't understand why the generator hasn't kicked in, it always goes on by now, but I kind of like it being dark..."The coldness between them fading, Doris bent towards Ellen, saying, "Let's hope it stays out, I'll get to go home early." She added, "There are things that go on, Ellen, that you wouldn't believe, I mean it. Awesome things. Leave Jack at home some night and join us." The morning light was breaking into the darkness of the store and Doris' smiling face took on an eerie glow, sending a chill down Ellen's back. Already pushing her cart out, Ellen said, "I'll take a rain check on that, Doris." Shooting a glance back at her as she left, Ellen added, "I've got a feeling that you're going to be out of here right behind me. Bye, Doris." She wheeled her cart towards the exit and was forced to stop at the jammed automatic doors. With the chill lingering, Ellen shot a puzzled glance back to Doris. *What did she mean about things that go on, and seeing with a different eye? What things that go on? Ellen mumbled to herself,* "She's just like Al's wife—weird." She didn't have the time to think about it further as one of the store's managers appeared in front of her, trying to get the doors open.

"Sorry about that, Mrs. Hansen." It was Lenny, the produce manger. He knew Ellen and what a pain she could sometimes be. "The doors won't work without power. I'll give them a shove and they'll open up." He pushed on the door and it slid open for her. "Don't have a clue why our generator isn't working. Sorry again for the inconvenience, Mrs. Hansen."

Ellen rolled her eyes, but still thanked him, and wheeled her cart down the sidewalk, towards the parking lot. Fishing in her purse for her phone, she took it out and discovered it was dead. "Oh shit, I just charged this thing too!"

An older lady walking towards the store noticed Ellen aggravatingly looking at her phone. She stopped next to her, and said, "I have the same problem. I was just on my phone talking to my daughter and it suddenly went dead. I don't know what's going on, they're probably sticking Chinese batteries in these things."

Ellen replied, "You're probably right, they make junk and we're stupid enough to keep buying it— *Batteries!* That's what I was supposed to get! My husband had written on my list that he needed D cell batteries." Ellen started walking away, then smirked back at the lady, saying, "Oh well, I guess he'll have to buy them himself."

Stopping at the curb, she checked her phone again, "Damn, it's still dead." Hesitating a few seconds more, she frowned, figuring out what she was going to do. Her frown changed to a smile as she thought, *I guess I could go over there early. Don did give me a key; I could surprise him!*

She was about to wheel her cart out to the car when she saw a bright flash in the sky to the south. The loud sonic boom and the shock-wave that followed stopped her in her tracks. It frightened her and she said out loud, "Good lord, what the hell was that?"

She was startled again when a disheveled old man suddenly grabbed her shoulder, excitedly saying, "Did you see that, lady, did you see that?" He was pointing his boney hand towards the direction of the flash. He turned into her, putting his pinched face right in front of hers, excitedly spitting out his words, "Big jet airliner just fell from the sky. It went straight down, and then **Ka-boom!** Didn't you see it?"

Raising her eyebrows, she moved her face back from his. Whether it was his breath, or a combination of breath and B O, the old man reeked. "I am sorry, sir, I didn't see anything. I saw a flash and heard an explosion, but I didn't see an airplane." The old man hurriedly moved away and began pestering another lady. Before starting off with her cart, she took a final look at her phone and frowned again, shaking her head. "Shit." *It's dead alright…. Don is probably wondering why I'm not answering it.* Shoving her phone back into her purse, she looked around for the old man, but he was no longer in sight.

She wondered if the old fellow really did see a plane crash. Whatever it was, it was pretty far away and wouldn't affect her. She recalled a news program she had seen the week before of a house being leveled in an explosion. The owner was selling illegal fireworks he had purchased in Missouri. She laughed to herself as she thought, *It was probably just some stupid hillbillies blowing up their house with their bootleg fireworks.*

As she started to push her cart into the parking lot, she paused, looking towards her car in disgust. Someone had pushed one of the store's metal shopping carts up against her car's rear fender. *"Shit! Look at that, it better not be dented! What else is going to go wrong today?"*

* * * * *

High above Able County and about two miles north of where Ellen stood, a big passenger-jet airliner was in a holding pattern. The pilot, George Betts, had been flying civilian airliners for 30 years and was about to take his retirement. His co-pilot, Bob McKendrick, had been flying for seven years.

"Jeez, Bob, we're up here just killing time today. I wish this plane was smaller. We could slip into Midway."

"I hear you. They got us stacked like pancakes today. You know, they say at any given moment there's some 4000 aircraft over the country, all at one time. I think all of them are right here this morning, all of them over Chicago. How long is O'Hare going to be having that runway work going on?"

George shook his head saying, "I don't know. All I know is when we finally do land, Sharron wants me to stop at a store on the way home. She wants me to pick myself up two new pairs of shoes before they go off sale. Can you believe that? Sometimes I think she thinks I drive a city bus. Funny thing is, somewhere down there, about two miles south of us in Melville, is the Mandel's Department Store I'll be stopping at on the way home today. And we're wasting all this time stuck up here, flying over it. Heck, we're so close to my house right now, if I could spit out this window, I'd hit my roof."

WHOMP! Bob jumped in his seat, "What the hell was that? Everything is dead! The engines are shutting down... nothing!"

The pilots couldn't notify the control tower at O'Hare Airport. The aircraft's internal communications wouldn't work to notify their passengers. The fasten seat belt sign would not go on. The aircraft's instruments were simply, "off." In short, nothing, including the plane's massive jet engines, were functioning. They were gliding south with no power and no control. The big plane was losing altitude fast and quickly started what would be its final descent, now a rock with wings. To the observers on the ground, it looked like the big airplane was barely moving, but at 400 miles per hour, that was hardly the case. The horrified passengers screamed in panic, as the plane silently tilted, starting its plunge towards the ground. The two seasoned pilots struggled to re-start the engines, and searched in vain for an open field. There was nothing clear, only houses, shopping centers, schools, clogged roads and more houses. A mile ahead was the tall steeple of an old church and to the right, a two-story brick building that was a school. They were losing altitude fast and could only steer the plane a little to the right or a little to the left. If they were only a mile east or a mile west of their position, they would find open land, but to get there would require a 90 degree turn. George lived only a mile away from their position and knew the choices. There was no way they could execute a turn like that. They'd have to go straight in, veering left or right, that was it. George checked off his choices in his mind, saying aloud, "If we clip that church steeple, we'll veer off and dive directly into the top of the school. We go straight down the middle; we may miss the school and slide into the football field behind it. If we're lucky, we'll come to a stop in the parking lot between the grocery store and Mandel's. It's early, that parking lot is long and it should be pretty much empty. Damnit, if we go right,

49

we'll hit a strip mall and then plow into Mandel's. I think there's a children's daycare center in the strip mall!"

Bob screamed, **"What about the highway?"**

"Look at it! It's jammed with cars. There's a gas station on the corner with apartment buildings across the street from it. We have no choices but one, and it's not a good one. Let's try to angle it into the field behind the school. Pray we can fit her into that parking lot between those two stores."

Bob cried, "George— if we come in too low and clip the roof of that school, were screwed, it'll nose us down..."

"It's our only choice. God help us."

The decision was made, they'd take the aircraft straight down the middle and aim for the field. The plane's nose was up but the tail was down. It would be close. The aircraft's tail section could possibly hit the roof of the school. Both of the pilots were frozen at the aircraft's controls. A choice had been made and it was too late to change it. The tail section might not clear the school, but then again, maybe they would get lucky and only brush it. Both of them screamed in unison, **"Stay up! Stay Up! Stay Up!"**

It didn't stay up. The tail section dipped too low, slicing into the school. As easily as a farmer's plow running through a spring field, it cut a swath through the entire second floor. Bricks from the building's walls were sent flying like missiles through the air, and the sound of the aircraft's impact rattled every window for a mile away. Like a giant hand reaching up to stop it, the aircraft's tail section was momentarily hooked by the second floor of the school. The passenger's bodies strained against their seat belts as they were thrown forward by the impact, then violently yanked backwards into their seats. The solid masonry construction of the school ripped the aircraft apart behind the main wings, spraying the school with jet fuel. Screaming passengers, some still strapped in their seats, tumbled like confetti out of the ruptured fuselage. With almost a third of the massive aircraft gone, the rest of it continued on. The end of the broken fuselage was on fire. It shot like a missile, with Jay's Foods the intended target. Like a flying flamethrower, the cockpit was seconds away from hitting the back of the supermarket. Thirty yards to the right, they would have skidded in between the market and the Mandel's building, into a mostly empty parking lot. Co-pilot Bob McKendrick's eyes were riveted to the huge yellow sign directly in front of them, **JAY'S FRESH PRODUCE.** He closed his eyes, knowing in about three seconds his life would be over.

Captain Betts kept his eyes open. There was a little red Volkswagen convertible parked next to Mandel's. He had always wanted one like it....

50

Ellen was about to push her grocery cart over to her car, when suddenly from somewhere far behind her there was a shattering   **Ba- boom!** It violently rattled the store's windows and in an instant, a sonic-like shock wave echoed past her, bouncing through the store's parking lot and ricocheting back into her face. Startled, she yelled to herself, *"**What the hell was that?**"* An earthquake? Frozen in fear like a child, a monster from the unknown was behind her. She could feel it coming, but stood riveted in place, wasting precious seconds. There was another loud penetrating boom as the nose of the huge aircraft disappeared into the rear of the grocery store, followed by its massive wings. Like a hot rag cleaning a table of bread crumbs, the airplane's wings sheared through Jay's Foods. As easily as a snowplow clearing a driveway, the store and its entire contents was pushed forward, racing towards Ellen.

She stood there, her knuckles bone white, gripping the shopping cart. She couldn't move and in two seconds it was over. The front of the store erupted upon her in a hailstorm of shattered bricks, ruptured food cans, and the pulp of human remains. The debris field, pushed on by the aircraft's crumbling wings ground through Ellen, and continued through the parking lot. Like a giant tidal wave of bricks, it was followed by the burning remains of a wide-bodied jet. In an instant, Ellen Hansen was gone. Condensed into a 30-foot red-hot smear across the parking lot, there wasn't a trace of her.

A trail of blazing jet fuel followed the disintegrating aircraft. A fuse lit at the impact of the school; the plane exploded like a bomb upon hitting the store. Ellen, her neighbor, Doris, the remaining passengers and crew, all became one. All of them ground up together and incinerated on the burning asphalt parking lot.

The customers refueling their cars at the corner gasoline station had front row seats to the crash. Some stood riveted in horror as the broken aircraft cloaked down upon the supermarket. A few of the smart ones ran, wildly running away from the station as fast as they could. But others continued to stand there, mesmerized by the 60-foot wall of burning debris blasting through the parked cars. Opposite of Jay's Foods, just across the parking lot from it, was Connie's Beef. A popular spot for lunch and dinner, it hadn't opened yet. The 12-foot-high wall of burning debris slammed into it. The restaurant collapsed upon impact, but finally stopped the airplane and tidal wave of destruction that was in front of it. Parked behind the gas station, nearest to the now burning remains of Connie's Beef, was a gasoline tanker truck. It was in the process of dumping a load of fuel into the gas station's thirsty tanks. Upon witnessing the initial impact of the aircraft hitting the school, the young driver of the tanker truck didn't waste precious seconds with indecision or curiosity. He ran faster than he had ever run in his life. His truck held almost 9000 gallons of highly volatile gasoline and was still two thirds full. He was already safely across the street when it blew. The entire service station, and everyone in it that had not immediately run for their lives, was now engulfed in flames.

THE FIRE CHEIF

CHAPTER 4

Across the road and about a half mile down the street from the crash site, was the new Melville fire station. Fire Chief Tom Kirhman and his crew of firefighters watched in horror as the inferno engulfed a half mile swath of their town. They already knew they were in deep shit, as only minutes before the plane crash, everything electrical in the firehouse stopped working. Their radios went dead and none of the department's new vehicles started. With some of the personnel already out on calls, it couldn't have happened at a worse time. None of their expensive high-tech gear was working; everything was dead or malfunctioning. The station's state of the art emergency generators kicked on, but were not providing near the power they were capable of. Something was definitely wrong with them. Tom had a hunch. He jumped into the town's old antique firetruck that was used only for parades, and it started right off. An older ambulance that was scheduled for scrap also popped right off. He had all of the personal start their private vehicles, only the older models ran without problems. Somewhere inside, he had filed away a Federal Government brief from the Office of Homeland Security about what was called an electrical magnetic pulse, or EMP for short. It was the side effect of a powerful burst of energy high above. It could occur naturally from the sun or be man-made. If it happened above a country, it would disrupt anything electrical below it. This wasn't a normal power outage, that had to be it.

It was discovered as an unexpected side effect of a high-altitude nuclear detonation. It had happened back in the 1940s after the "A" bomb tests in the deserts of the far west. At that time, it wasn't a serious problem and the idea of an EMP being used by itself as a weapon wasn't considered.

There also could be a naturally occurring EMP, caused by eruptions on our own sun. Explosions on the sun, more commonly known as sun spots, happened regularly, but seldom were they large enough to give off enough energy to seriously disrupt the earth.

A major EMP from the sun had happened before, and was well documented, in the mid-1800s in the United States. There were reports at the time of telegraph lines being knocked out of service. They named it the Carrington Event. It didn't do much damage in the 1800s, or the 1940s, before computers and advanced electronics, but today electricity ran everything. Anything that had a computer chip in it that wasn't shielded and designed to be protected against an EMP was vulnerable. Tom never knew what to believe, but the fear mongers appeared right. We were in deep trouble. Everything we use is run by computers, and how many of them are shielded from an EMP? Airliners were falling from the sky; fire trucks and ambulances wouldn't start, and every computer was dead. What really pissed Tom off was the fact that our government knew about this, and did nothing. The military and congress also knew it was not *if* this EMP could happen, but *when* it was going to happen. He read about that, but at the time didn't believe it. Would our own government ignore something so catastrophic?

Electrical circuits could be *hardened* to protect them from such an event. To do this meant there would have to be a nationwide crusade that would have enormous costs. Enormous costs meant Congressional meetings and committees, and more meetings. When it came to something that had enormous costs, but could not be seen or understood, pork barrel projects like a new bridge or defense plant shoved aside the EMP thing. No one could agree on it anyway. Some of the so-called experts said it was all a bunch of nonsense, and vastly overblown. With very few in government in agreement, little was done. As far as it got was the hardening of mostly military equipment and in key areas, such as nuclear plants.

The Chief had a dim view of the State of Illinois' government, and felt the same way about the Federal. Illinois was a crooked mess and some of the most revered politicians in Washington made John Dillinger look like a choir boy. America was done for long before this terrible Monday morning. An EMP could be the blow that finished it.

Tom had watched a television program about it. It emphasized that any two-bit enemy of ours could fire a single missile equipped with a nuclear warhead to detonate high above our country. It didn't have to be a powerful country like Russia or China. This warhead would do no physical damage to anything below and would give off very little radiation. What it would do is create an electrical pulse that in a flash, would disable, or disrupt everything electrical under it. The documentary had warned that three such warheads spaced out above the United States, could effectively knock out the entire power grid in our country. The missiles need not be sophisticated and could easily be concealed and fired from a small fishing trawler in the gulf, or a container ship approaching either of our coasts. It could be launched from the deserts of

Mexico, or the forests of Canada, it didn't matter where it came from. A single missile would cripple the United States instantly.

A warhead could be cleverly concealed in any of the so-called weather satellites that orbit our planet every day. An insignificant, backwards country like North Korea, could bring the powerful United States to its knees by one explosion, high above the continent. Before Tom learned about the EMP, he wondered why countries as big as the United States could be bullied by a two-bit country like North Korea. A primitive country with a population that is accustomed to starvation and living without electricity has an advantage over an industrialized country. The United States would be the loser.

The Chief figured somebody "pulled the plug" on the Midwest and maybe the whole country. Who did it, or how it was accomplished, made little difference to him.

What he did know was this: most cars, trucks, trains, ships, and airplanes in the affected part of the country simply stopped wherever they were at the moment of the EMP. Not good, if you happened to be a passenger in an airplane. He had heard that at any given time, there are at least 4000 or more aircraft above the United States. As he looked out the station's open bay doors at the inferno taking place just down the road, he thought, *What if this EMP had affected the whole country? How many pilots would be able to safely land their aircraft with all their onboard computers malfunctioning at once?* He asked himself, "How many people have died in air crashes this morning, just around Chicago, thousands?"

Another fact Tom knew, and 95% of the American public didn't, was there were no public store houses of food for them. Everyone had heard of FEMA, the Federal Emergency Management Agency, but did they actually think it could feed a whole country? Americans had been led to believe their entire lives, that even in times of mega disasters, their benevolent government will magically come to their rescue. Tom knew that there would be no rescue.

Other than for small emergencies, only the military and the *elite* had any real amount of food set aside for them. Any warehouses of food and medical supplies that did exist would also depend on transport to the affected areas. In an EMP, transport would cease to exist. Silos filled with grain and fields of wheat would rot before they went anywhere. Fields of produce would not be harvested or replanted. Trucks loaded with produce destined for market would rot in the warehouses, or the back of a truck.

American agriculture and commerce had been developed into a very efficient machine that depended on a continuous chain to operate. The nation's products are produced, packaged, shipped, and promptly consumed. Nothing much, when compared to population density and amounts of food to adequately feed them, is stored up to be distributed for a *rainy day*. This system even had a name, the *Just in Time System*. It's very cost effective with minimal and acceptable waste of product. It works like an unending chain and works extremely well.

What the American consumer should know, but doesn't, is that when it comes to food supplies, there are only about four days of food in this chain. If the chain is disrupted for over four continuous days, store shelves will go empty.

If the general public becomes panicked, store shelves could *empty within hours*, and they will stay empty until the chain is mended. Hurricane Katrina and the power outages of Puerto Rico were excellent examples of what can happen on a *small* scale.

He knew if the power grid were to go down across the board, the use of common things that we take for granted would cease immediately, sending us back to the 1800s. Every single appliance that is in every home would be instantly useless. The list was endless and would affect everyone. Heating and air conditioning units would cease. Every hospital and nursing home would, within one week, become a building of dead people. Anyone that required dialysis, chemo, insulin, oxygen, or needed major surgery, would be dead or dying within the first week.

Nuclear power plants presented a whole nightmare of possibilities. Unless the facility had been secured, those unfortunate enough to live nearby or downwind would have about 30 days to move.

Being that his job was emergencies, he had often discussed emergency preparedness with friends and relatives. Most everyone he knew had told him, "I have some emergency food set side." Unfortunately, nearly all of them *would not have enough*. Many had nothing extra in their pantry. Within three weeks of an EMP, most Americans would be out of food. Within six weeks they would be scavenging for every scrap, facing starvation.

In his career as a fireman he had seen some sad and tragic events. Over the years, those terrible things were tempered by lives that he had saved. Saving lives and helping people gave Tom a feeling that nothing on this earth could compare to. In his own personal life, he had seen more than his share of tragedy. Diane, his wife of over 30 years, had died of cancer the previous year. Their only daughter was struck and killed by a murderous hit and run driver that, to this day, was never found. That Christmas Eve night, it didn't seem like 10 years ago, but it was the worst night of their lives. He was convinced that his wife had *just given up* after their daughter's tragic death. Then there was his older sister, also a hit and run victim. Her death was clearly murder, and like his daughter's death, it went unsolved. God, how many years had passed, was it really 50? And both of them were killed on Christmas Eve, 40 years apart. A coincidence? He didn't think so.

Co-workers always commented about how many extra hours he worked and everyone said he should retire. But what else was left to live for? Other than his job, nothing really held his interest any longer and the department was all the life he had.

Many a night at home, Tom spent the evening looking at old family photo albums containing happier times. Now it looked like America could be at war with someone. To Tom it didn't make much difference who it was or why it was done to us. He only knew he couldn't deal with any of it. He was tired, tired of it all. After reviewing all that he and the department faced and what every American now faced, he walked into his firehouse with a sense of total defeat, but also a feeling of relief.

The crews were saddled up; everyone was ready with what equipment they could get running and he was really proud of these young kids. They should have been at the scene already and no doubt the delays and lack of operable equipment was going to cost a lot of lives. Tom's heart was heavy but, beneath the heaviness, there was this strange sense of closure. *Was it really going to matter what lives they saved today?*

Knowing what he knew about an EMP, within a month, all of them would be fighting for their lives.

Jimmy Sullivan, his young lieutenant and next in command, briskly walked up to him. Sullivan snapped to attention and informed him, "Every person in the station and all operational equipment has been gathered. We're ready to go to the crash site, Chief!"

Tom smiled a genuine smile, took a deep breath, and exhaled heavily. "I know you are Jimmy, and I want you and everyone to know I am proud of each and every one of you. Please excuse me though, there is something I have to do." Quickly walking towards his office, Tom thought of the last time he had been together with his daughter. They were placing the finishing decorations on their Christmas tree. It was Christmas Eve and he had lit a fire in the fireplace and his daughter had poured him and her mother a glass of homemade eggnog. She said she was going to walk down to her friend's house for about an hour. It was snowing heavily but her friend lived close, only one block away, and she assured them she'd be right back. Christmas morning, her mangled body was found on a seldom used, snow covered road, about two miles away from their home. His daughter was murdered, just like his sister, and their deaths had never been solved. Tom knew what he quickly and without any further thought had to do. *Yeah, no further thought, Tom, just do it...do it now!* He walked fast, his heart pulsing in his chest; blood rushing into his temples. *I was going to do it years ago anyway, plenty of folks will be doing this soon.* He entered his office and quickly looked at the family photos on his desk one final time. He nervously fished a ring of keys out of his pocket and dropped them. Picking them up off the floor, he fumbled with them, attempting to unlocked his bottom desk drawer. His otherwise steady hands were trembling and he was having difficulty with the seldom opened lock, cursing under his breath, "Come on, open up, damnit!" A

57

small voice inside his head pleaded, *"Tom, don't do this!"* but he blocked it out. The other voice was louder, ***"Just do it, go ahead and do it!"*** He had heard it many times in the last few years, but this time he obeyed. The lock's cylinder was stubborn, but it started to turn. The lock clicked; the metal desk drawer slid open, and there lay his dad's WW2 Navy revolver. The old 38 was heavy and the short, blued barrel felt cold as he shoved it into his mouth and closed his eyes for the last time. A single gunshot echoed throughout the bays of the fire station.

Everyone in the station momentarily froze and looked towards the Chief's office. No one said a word.

CARL

CHAPTER 5

Carl DeFries was one of those neighborhood kids that everyone knew and everyone liked. He was ambitious, always either building something or tearing something apart to see how it worked. At 10 years old, he took apart his dad's lawn mower. At 11 years old, he was bringing home lawn mowers he found on trash night and fixing them up to re-sell. He built a tree fort in his mom's apple tree and dug a *secret* tunnel under his parent's garage. He tried making a pond in his mom's garden that ended up draining into his secret tunnel and cracking the garage floor. Some things worked out and some didn't. One of his big accomplishments was a windmill in his parent's backyard that actually generated power. But what young Carl loved most was his chemistry set. He made his own toothpaste and deodorant, and a mosquito repellant that worked really well, except for the brown stains. On the Fourth of July, he made smoke bombs, stink bombs, sparklers, and rockets. The neighbors would never forget the one 4th he made up something "extra special." Fire Chief Kirhman told Carl's dad, after the garage fire was finally put out, "If he ever makes anything like this again, I will personally lock him up."

Carl never lost his love for chemistry and at 25 years old, he was the chemistry teacher at St. Paul's Lutheran High school in Melville. His students called him the *mad scientist* and he didn't mind it one bit. He had just started his third year as a teacher and he loved it. He was single and he didn't date much. His parents had been killed in an auto accident when he was in his last year of college. He lived with his elderly aunt for a while, but had a condo for the last three years. His aunt had recently died and left him her house that he was planning to renovate and move into before fall. School was about to break for the summer and he was thinking of reviving his aunt and uncle's garden that had grown over with weeds. Other than that, his only summer plans were to teach summer school classes twice a week and work on his future home.

He began Monday morning the way he started most days, with a short jog around his neighborhood before his school day started. It was a nice way to clear his mind and plan his day. The school year was almost up and for this morning's senior class he decided, instead of the usual day, he would give the kids a break and let them start off their last week of school with an easy class. They were all good kids and had worked hard all year. He always tried to make his classes fun. He enjoyed his students and they enjoyed him. Today he decided to let each student stand up at their lab station and tell the class what their plans were for the summer and fall. He had done this with the last two senior classes and liked hearing the kid's plans. The years before, he had randomly picked out any student that raised their hand first to start out. This year was going to be different; he would ask Laura Hansen to start off. She was a friend to everyone and the type of person that, upon meeting, you would instantly like. She was muscular and lanky, with sharp chiseled features, like her Marine Corps father.

Carl wasn't much on fast foods, but he found himself going to the Burger Chief where she worked a little more than he normally would have.

If she was a little older and he wasn't her teacher, he would have asked her out.

Lately, he had seen a change in Laura that worried him. Something was different about her and he was sure there were problems at home. Carl wanted to help her, but remembered what one of the school's counselors had told him, "The less you know about these kids, the better. Get involved too much with one kid, the less time for the rest. Get involved with family problems and mom and dad, and often even the kid, may turn on you. Then you're the problem. We're here to teach, not get involved in their lives. Whatever it is, short of suspected child abuse, best to just stay clear of it." The fact that it was a Christian school and not a public school he chose to teach at, sometimes made that prospect unacceptable to him. Besides being the school's chemistry teacher, Carl was also the school's track and basketball coach. He had met with Laura's father and mother at teacher conferences and the many sporting events that Laura participated in. He immediately liked her father, Jack. After an evening basketball game, the entire team had gone out to celebrate at a local restaurant. He sat across from Laura's dad and had a good conversation with him and found the man to be extremely interesting and easy to talk to.

Ellen, Laura's mother, was the opposite. She had left him with the same feeling he had gotten with that real estate lady he dealt with recently. He couldn't wait to get away from her. He had met with both of her parents together at Laura's games. Ellen, he had met alone, three times at parent teacher conferences. Each time he felt that the older woman was coming on to him and it made it awkward to talk to her.

Looks-wise, Laura's mom was a real knock out, and it was plain to see that Laura did not inherit any of her mom's features or figure. Her mom did have a very outgoing personality, and she appeared to be cheerful and fun.

But there was something else, something subtle about her mom that made Carl feel uneasy. He had picked up on it the first time he had met with them. It was the way her mom looked at him while they were all standing together talking after one of Laura's freshman basketball games. It felt like her mom wasn't looking at him, but *in* him. He felt like she was physically sizing him up as he talked to Laura's dad.

He got that same uneasy feeling the next time he was with her. The last time they were together, his suspicions were confirmed. He had met with her mom in his classroom at a parent teacher conference and it was the first time he had been totally alone with her. About a third of the way through the conference, he suddenly felt uneasy with her and found himself stumbling over his words. Knowing she was aware of it, Carl felt she was secretly enjoying it and prolonging his agony. He felt himself blushing during their talk about Laura's school work. Stumbling over his words, he wanted to end the conference as quickly as possible. The conference finally ended, but it was the first conference that ever closed with a mom of one of his students giving him a hug. A hug where the mom pushed her more than ample breasts into him and then lightly kissed his neck.

There were problems in Laura's life and Carl knew why.

NEIGHBORS

CHAPTER 6

The suburban town of Melville is located in Able County, Illinois, about 40 miles west of Chicago. It was founded on the banks of the Fox River in the 1850s by German immigrants. Like most of the small towns in northeastern Illinois, it was extensively developed, starting in the 1960s. The sprawling farmland gave way to housing developments, shopping centers, and highways. It's now part of what is referred to as the far western suburbs of Chicago. Jack and Ellen bought their bi-level home in a small unincorporated section of town consisting of three block long streets. The streets run east and west and are bordered by the Fox River on the east and an exclusive 36-hole country club golf course on the northwest.

Directly north, the subdivision's streets run parallel to a large farm that is currently partially planted in corn. The land was recently sold to a housing developer and will add approximately 300 homes to Jack's small subdivision when completed. A small industrial park and a forest preserve border the south.

Jack and Ellen's house is located on the middle street, almost in the center of the block. From the backyard of his house, Jack could look between the homes behind him and catch glimpses of corn standing in the farmer's field. From his second-floor bedroom windows, he could see nothing but crops and vacant farmland to the north and the tree lined-banks of the Fox River to the east. From the front bedroom windows, he could see scattered forest and the tops of some industrial buildings to the south. The golf course, forest preserve, and cemetery separated him on the west from the downtown of Melville.

He dreaded the day that the farm would be developed. Their little section of town was secluded, tucked away, and as he often described it, "We're off the main drag." That suited Jack just fine. He and Laura often walked to the east end of their street, to sit in the small park that was on the river bank. He often thought of getting a small pontoon boat to take advantage of being so close to the river.

Jack got along with his neighbors and liked most of them, with the exception of Glen, who lived with his wife, Doris, across the street from them. Jack couldn't prove it, but he suspected Glen knocked Doris around. The problem was, no one had actually seen him do it, and Doris was the kind of wife who would never press charges anyway.

Behind him lived Barry. He was one of those nosy-neighbor types that wanted to start a neighborhood watch. He had a perfect yard and complained about everyone else's. He always had to know what you were doing, and Jack did his best to ignore him. Barry wasn't a bad neighbor; he was just a persistent complainer. Mostly he complained about his next-door neighbor to the east, "that biker," as Barry referred to him. Rick was the neighborhood motorcycle fan. He also lived partly behind Jack. A small corner of his lot backed up to Jack's. He was single, loved loud motorcycles, leather clad women, and kept to himself. Jack had no problems with him or any of his biker friends and had never even talked to him.

Next door to the east of Jack lived old Charlie Mills and his extremely over-weight wife, Dottie. Charlie's older brother, Ted, also lived with them. Ted was born with a learning disability and had lived with Charlie most of his adult years. He was in poor health and had been diagnosed with dementia. He seldom talked. Charlie was a retired Chicago fireman, whose passion was old guns and his two Golden Retrievers, Max and Toots. Every year he planted the largest garden on the block and would talk to anyone who would listen about his shotgun collection. Dottie was known for her canned vegetables, fried brussels sprouts, and love of food.

Get Charlie talking about his shotgun collection and you weren't going anywhere soon. Get Dottie talking about gardening and canning produce and your day was lost.

Both Charlie and Dottie suffered from diabetes, and, as of late, Dottie was constantly tethered to an oxygen hose because of end stage emphysema. Jack noticed that Ted, seemed to be going steadily downhill. He wondered how Charlie could take care of his wife and brother without a full-time nurse.

The neighbors to the west of Jack were Jake and Ronnie Wells. They had a four-year-old little boy named Bobby. Jake was a construction crane operator who worked in downtown Chicago, usually on new high rises. Ronnie had been a first-grade teacher at a Chicago public school. She was over eight months pregnant and had just taken a leave of absence to have their second child, and was contemplating becoming a stay at home mother. Jake and Ronnie were the newest residents on the block and had moved in about three months prior. The night they moved in; someone slashed their car tires. That, and other incidents, proved that the secluded rural subdivision wasn't as welcoming as it looked, at least not to African Americans.

The glue that held their entire subdivision together was Al. Al was a pudgy, amiable little guy, who lived in the corner house at the west end of Jack's street. He seemed to know everyone and was well known for his summer block parties and barbecues. Jack really liked Al, but didn't care all that much for his wife, Lois, and some of the people that regularly attended their parties. Al always referred to them as "Lois' friends." There was something about Lois and Al that just didn't figure. She was the exact opposite of him. Except for occasionally seeing her on their front porch smoking her thin cigarillos, she seldom was seen outside their house. She kept to herself and other than Glen and Doris, had no friends among the immediate neighbors. Ellen noticed that while Al was outside being the life of the party, Lois would be inside with her friends, and usually they were men. Ellen was convinced something was going on, and either Al didn't care, or was too absorbed in being the jovial host of his frequent parties. When she voiced her suspicions about Lois to Jack, he laughed it off saying, "Are you kidding me? With that long, straight black hair, she reminds me of that pasty white broad on that old creepy '60s monster show. What's her name? She could be pretty, but really, what guy would want a woman that dresses like her?" Ellen didn't agree, and Jack wondered if she knew something he didn't know about Lois. They say opposites attract and those two were definitely opposites. Al was short and pudgy and loved colorful Hawaiian shirts. He was almost bald and generally good-natured. Lois was tall, skinny, and laid back. She seemed to prefer long dark dresses and had no apparent sense of humor. If Lois laughed, she kept it hidden. On the other hand, she had a pretty face, and those beautiful deep green eyes.

SUNDAY

THE DAY BEFORE SHTF.

CHAPTER 7

It was a Sunday afternoon and the usual hustle of the weekend was winding down on Jack's street. He took a stroll across his front yard, wondering if he made a mistake by not hiring a lawn service company like Ellen wanted him to do. His grass was vastly out gunned by the weeds and it looked like the grass was going to lose the battle. Glancing both ways down the block, he seemed to be the only one out. Since it was already the start of May, he hoped it wasn't too late to spread some lawn chemicals. The week's long-range weather forecast said that heavy rain was headed into the Midwest the following week, and he figured he better get something on the lawn by tomorrow. Ellen wanted to get some flowers to plant and he wanted a few tomato plants, so they were going to the home center later. He was thinking he should plant a big garden, but he had the same thoughts every year about this time and he would never get around to it. Usually the tomato plants he put in died anyway, and he thought that maybe he should just give the garden idea up.

Jack was standing out by the street when Charlie's Golden Retrievers, Max and Toots, ran out to greet him. Their tails were wagging and both dogs pushed their noses into his legs, demanding the attention they knew Jack would provide. Old Charlie was just stepping off his front porch, slowly walking towards Jack. He noted that Charlie was limping more than usual and thought the old man's feet must really be hurting."

Charlie said, "Those old doggies limp around like me all day. They see you out here and they fly out of the house, running like a couple of pups."

Jack stood up, gave a laugh, saying, "They just know a good friend when they see one."

Charlie had can of beer in his hand and idly fingered it. He lifted it saying, "I'll drink to that." and took a long sip. Swallowing his beer, he let out a little belch and continued, "Been a long weekend, and I'm bushed." Taking another sip, he let out another belch, and said, "I gotta take a little break for a bit. It's tough taking care of Dot, and now Ted is having a tough time swallowing his food. We found out on Thursday that he'll need a feeding tube put into his stomach this coming Tuesday. They say his dementia is affecting his ability to swallow." Charlie put the beer can to his lips, this time taking a long slug. Lowering the can, he wiped his mouth with the back of his shirtsleeve and let out another belch, saying, "Never get old, Jack."

Jack smiled, saying, "Is that beer good, Charlie?"

Holding up the icy wet can towards Jack, Charlie shot back, "Sure is, Jack, you want a cold one?"

Jack refused, shaking his head saying, "I don't know how you manage it, Charlie. How's that new nurse you hired? Isn't she supposed to be here today?" Charlie gave a short laugh, "Her? Ha, no, not today. She comes every other day." He gestured his now empty beer can towards the dogs, saying, "Hey, that's why I got Max and Toots, they're always here and never let me down." Hearing their names, both dogs stopped pestering Jack and jumped up towards Charlie.

He noticed Charlie wince when one of the dogs stepped on his foot. Pointing to the old man's feet, he said, "Are your feet all right, Charlie, did you get that infection in your toes under control?"

Charlie gave him his best convincing look, saying, "Oh yeah, everything's fine. I'm just an old man with a few old man problems. Just an old complainer too. I won't bore you making you listen to them."

With that, Charlie patted his hand on his thigh a couple times, while saying to the dogs, "Come on kids, let's get some chow." When he had walked only a few feet away, he pointed down to the grass and gave Jack a sad look over his shoulder, sarcastically saying to him, "You really should do something about these damn dandelions you got growing out here, Jack. You don't want them to get out of control!" The old man started laughing to himself as he walked to his house. His lawn had more dandelions than Jack's.

Jack yelled back, "That's good advice, Charlie. We're going to the home center this afternoon to get some weed killer. Want me to get some for you?" Charlie didn't answer.

Jack silently watched as old Charlie ambled back towards his house. He really liked the old man, but Ellen didn't care much for Charlie, or his wife, Dottie. She thought people like them should live in the country, or the backwoods someplace. Maybe she was right, because that's exactly where Charlie wanted to live. Charlie had once said to him that he felt like he was not only living in the wrong place, but also in the wrong century.

Ellen couldn't understand why three old people needed to plant a humongous garden every year. It didn't take her long to figure out that Charlie and his wife were those "doomsday types," as she referred to them. When Jack had brought up the idea of setting aside some emergency food and supplies,

Ellen quickly put two and two together and knew old Charlie had put the bug in Jack's ear.

She also didn't like all the unsightly firewood Charlie kept stacked along both sides of his house. Jack tried to explain that Charlie had a modern woodstove in his basement, one that would not only heat his whole house, but also provide all their hot water.

He recalled Ellen's reply, "Who the hell heats their house with wood in this day and age? Those people live like hermits up in the woods, they're weird."

It was true that Charlie and his wife kept to themselves and didn't fit into their younger upscale suburban neighborhood. Their house was the oldest home by far in the small subdivision, and their large 1950s brick ranch didn't fit in with the newer homes surrounding it. Charlie had showed him pictures of a small house he and Dottie had bought years ago on several wooded acres in rural Tennessee. He had once referred to it as their "bug-out place," and told him how they had planned to move there when he retired. Jack figured that what stopped them from moving to the isolated area was their deteriorating health and the lack of any hospitals close by. He liked the old couple and, if anything, they probably thought Ellen was the weird one. He also knew that they had a 14-year-old daughter named Linda, who was murdered back in 1978. Although neither of them ever talked about it, Jack had heard about it from a former neighbor and later read the account in the Melville Sun archives.

It happened in late May, just before school let out for the summer. She had left school late and missed her bus. It had been a typical spring day and heavy rain was pouring down. Someone had offered her a ride home, but she never made it. Her dismembered and decapitated body was found three days later in an old falling down dairy barn about two miles from their home. The newspaper account of the girl's gruesome murder had included two photos. One was her eighth-grade graduation photo that had been taken just before her death. Jack had seen that same picture in a frame in Charlie's house. It was easy to spot that she was Charlie's daughter. She had his round face and mischievous smile, and Dottie's warm brown eyes. The other photo in the paper was one of an old dairy barn where her body was discovered. It looked like any of the hundreds of dilapidated farm buildings that dotted the Midwest. It was a large turn of the century barn that had long ago given up most of its white paint. Alongside it was the typical old farm windmill, and a decorative multicolored brick silo was a short distance behind it. Nothing sinister about it, except a young girl was brutally murdered there.

The 36-hole golf course that bordered their subdivision to the northwest was once that dairy farm. Jack had golfed there several times and had wondered where the old barn had stood. The picturesque golf course, that was once that working dairy farm, was now dotted with large million-dollar homes and mature trees. The years had erased all traces of that old farm, and all chances of finding Linda Mills' killer.

Jack was staring at Charlie's house, thinking about what he would do if someone harmed his daughter, when he was suddenly startled by the horn of a car coming up behind him. Feeling himself jump, he turned quickly around to find a smiling Al Lange behind the wheel of his black Oldsmobile convertible, slowly edging up to the curb. Shutting off the engine, he looked up at Jack and gave a short laugh. "Ha! You should have seen yourself jump when I blew Nancy's horn! You looked like you were a thousand miles away."

Jack eyed Al's beautiful old car saying, "Jeez, Al, only you would give a name to a car. First ride of the year with the top down?"

Al dreamily gazed up towards the open sky, then back at Jack, smiling and nodding his head, "You got it pal. No good having a convertible on a beautiful Sunday afternoon like this if you're not gonna put the top down. Wanna take a ride with me? I just got her back from the shop. I laid out a fortune restoring her. It's hard to get parts for a 68' Oldsmobile. She's like new, Jack, just like back in the day."

Running his fingers along the smooth black finish of the fender top, Jack replied, "Yeah, they sure did a good job. I would like to take a spin with you, but Ellen and I are going over to the home center. She wants to get some flowers to plant and I want to pick up some lawn care stuff to kill these dandelions before my whole yard turns yellow. I also want to look for some tomato plants, maybe some peppers too." Motioning towards Charlie's house he continued, "I don't think Charlie will put in his big garden this year. He always keeps us supplied with plenty of vegetables. I'll miss it."

Al looked up at Jack inquiringly, "How's the old folks doing?"

Jack frowned and slowly shook his head, "Not good, Al. Charlie's diabetes has really taken its toll on his legs. Dottie needs oxygen nearly all the time now; Ted's dementia has gotten worse, it's bad. To top that off, it looks like Ted's pretty much stopped eating."

Jack and Al had discussed the murder of Charlie's daughter before, so it was no surprise when Al said, "Gets me why they stayed in that same house all these years? After what happened to that poor girl, I would have moved as far away as I could."

He was about to agree when Al added something that surprised him. "I heard that there were some parts missing from that girl's body that they never found. There were some other similar murders of kids that happened in different parts of Illinois and Wisconsin, going back into the late 1960s with the same MO that go unsolved. Some sick shit, aye Jack? Your *own neighbor* could be a mass murderer, and you wouldn't even know it. Welcome to suburbia."

Jack ran his fingers through his thick hair, gave Al a tight-lipped smirk, then shook his head, saying, "Now that we've ruined a perfect Sunday afternoon, what else is new?"

Al let out a long breath and began drumming his fingers on the convertible's steering wheel while looking thoughtfully out the car's windshield. "Well, we got the block party coming up, down by my place on Memorial Day. I'll have the pulled pork in the smoker, like I do every year. Lois has rented a big tent in case we get rained on like last year. I'm going to put it out front near the street, right on the corner. Everybody's welcome at Al's!"

Jack mulled that over for a few seconds, then cocked his head towards the end of the block where Al lived, "You got everything else under control down there, no big news scoops?"

Al always had the latest scoop, and Jack wondered how the little guy was always so well informed. It seemed Al knew everything about everybody.

He thought about Jack's question for a couple seconds. Then he glanced from side to side, like he was looking if someone was near enough to overhear what he was about to say. Jack laughed to himself as Al lowered his voice and said, "Well, since you asked. You know that gal, Joan, who lives across the street from me on the corner? Ever notice how she always wears those army pants? I heard she was in the army; by her looks she probably drove a tank."

He caught Jack's smile, shook his head, and continued, "Seriously, Jack, I think somethings up with that lady. I've been watching her closely. She's got more testosterone then you have, Jack, and keeps that house always closed up tight. I can't see inside. She's one of those, you know..." Al dramatically rolled his eyes. "Ever see her girlfriend? It's too bad, because she's really a hot pistol, a petite little blond. She always wears those army pants too, with one of those green camouflage T shirts. And get this, big guy, never no bra. Not that I mind that, but it really browns Lois, I'll tell you. They never come to any of our parties either, *very* unsociable women. They're a couple of dikes, Jack, and they're up to no good. Them kind should stick in the city. Lois hates both of them; I don't think they fit on our block."

Al was easily excitable, so Jack egged him on. "What do you think, they're some women's lib army? Maybe one of those terrorist cells?"

Seeming not to pick up on Jack's sarcasm, Al pointed his left hand up at Jack saying, "You know, those broads have lived here at least two years and never even say '*Hi*' to me. I don't like that. It's not nice to snub people, especially your neighbors. I mean, hey, has she ever talked to you?"

Jack shrugged, "I've given her a neighborly wave, but no, we've never spoken. As far as what she does, or who she does it with, doesn't concern me."

"Well, it should concern you. Like I said, I've been keeping an eye on her lately. Just listen to this and no funny comments. Last week, at 11:00 at night, I see her and that blond unloading all this shit outta their van. Wanna know what it was?"

Jack bent down close to Al, and in his best conspiracy voice asked, "Explosives?"

Al stared at Jack a second, with Jack's sarcasm apparently not registering. "No, nothing like that, at least I hope not. It was rice, flour, and beans. Fifty-pound sacks of the shit, and lots of it."

Jack laughed, "Maybe she's opening up a Chinese restaurant, ever consider that?"

Al said, "Now you're screwing with me again. No, Jack, I'm serious here. Why the hell are they bringing big supplies of food into their place in the *middle* of the night?"

Jack asked, "I'm curious, how could you see from your house what was in those bags, especially if it was late at night?"

Al hesitated, and slowly placed his forefinger to his left eye. "I got really good vision, Jack." Then he continued, "Another thing, you know that guy that lives on the next street, in the corner house next door to Wilson's place? I think his name is Ken.

Jack shook his head, "Nope, never met him."

Al pointed back towards his house saying, "Well, him and my rainbow soldier girl neighbors are thick as flies. Wilson says he's seen this Ken guy bringing stuff in at night too. He wears the same get up, and is *very* unsocial, I mean to an extreme. And get this, he's single and has a *young guy* living there with him. What's up with that? We don't go that route, Jack, not out here." Jack started to say something, but Al added, "Look, Jack, you spent years in the military but you don't run around wearing your old uniforms, dodging in and out all hours of the night smuggling stuff in."

Jack threw up his arms saying, "So what are our plans, Al? Should we sneak into those girls' house tonight, look around, maybe fix ourselves some rice and beans, cook up some Spam?"

Al shook his head. "I'm trying to be serious here, Jack, and you're goofing around. All I'm saying is we should be aware of what people around us are doing. You have to always be aware of your neighbors, Jack, especially the weirdos. Trust no one…. You're an ex-Marine—"

"Former," Jack corrected him.

Al shrugged his shoulders, "Okay, Former. Maybe come the Memorial Day block party, you go over there and get GI Joan and blondie to open up to you. Talk to them about ways of killing people, or whatever you military types like to talk about. Check out this guy, Ken, too. Get him to come over to my party. Offer him one of Lois's barbeque pork specials, but whatever you do, get those girls to join us, so I can scope them out. I wanna know what they're up to, that's all." Al started up his old convertible, saying, "Gotta get home, maybe Lois will want to

70

take a ride with me now." As Al drove off, he shoved in an 8-track of a long-forgotten disco band, singing, *"Gotta keep on rolling now... gotta keep on rolling on... never gonna stop, never gonna stop....*

Watching as Al roared off down the street with his old stereo blaring, Jack couldn't help but smile. *Al, what a crazy guy....* Glancing down, he kicked at the head of a yellow dandelion with his toe before starting back towards his house. He slowly walked up the driveway, thinking about what Al had said about being aware of what people around us are doing. He looked at Ellen's red sports car parked next to his truck in the garage and thought, I *don't even know what my own wife is doing, let alone the neighbors.* Something just wasn't right between him and Ellen and hadn't been right for a long time now. With his marriage in trouble, he didn't have time for Al's nonsense.

He flashed back to something his dad had always said, *"Mind your own business. Who cares what the neighbors do?"*

Walking into his open garage, he glanced back to the street and saw the local deputy sheriff, slowly driving by in his squad. Spotting Jack, the sheriff smiled and nodded his head as he drove on. Staring back with disapproval, Jack ignored the deputy's greeting. *Deputy Hayes, what a prick....* Jack heard footsteps and turned around. Ellen had entered the attached garage from the house. She was facing him. He didn't know if she had seen Hayes or not, so he said nothing about it.

She smiled at Jack, saying, "You and Al been out there gabbing away like a couple of old ladies, maybe worse. Is he *watching* everybody?"

"Yeah, he keeps an eye on everyone, that little guy doesn't trust anyone."

Ellen scoffed, "Right, he should keep an eye on his weirdo wife." Changing the subject, she asked, "I just came out to tell you I'm ready to go to the home center, if you still want to go?" Suddenly, she cocked her head like she had forgotten something, adding, "Since there's a possibility of you getting home late tomorrow night, maybe I'll go see Brenda during the afternoon and have lunch with her." Jack got that uneasy feeling again and thought, *You sure spend a lot of time at Brenda's lately, don't you?*

He decided to ignore the Brenda comment, and pointed to his new pickup, saying, "Let's take the pickup to the home center, we'll have more room. I want to get some tomato plants and a few other things."

Ellen protested, "Don't tell me you're going to try and plant a garden again. Don't we get enough produce from those rednecks next door?"

Ignoring her comment, he got into the truck and backed it out of the garage. She got in the passenger side and made another snide remark about Charlie and Dot, but he pretended not to hear it. He thought of confronting her friend, Brenda, about the time she and Ellen supposedly spend together. He quickly dismissed it, knowing that Brenda would no doubt cover for her friend, and then be on the phone a minute later telling Ellen of his inquiries.

71

He had that sinking feeling that she was cheating on him again… *but with who? Maybe Al was right, he should be more aware….* Trying to figure her out was tiring and very frustrating, so he switched his thoughts to what he had to do at work the next day. He was happy that they had gotten through most of the weekend without an argument, and he actually looked forward to going to work in the morning. Monday would be an easy day.

ESCAPE FROM CHICAGO

CHAPTER 8

A score of bullets had hit the rear of their car, blowing the rear glass out. At least one round continued through and put a hole in the windshield, dead in the center, shattering the rear-view mirror. Jack yelled back to the lady, "Are you all right?"

She yelled, "I'm okay! Thank God they didn't have heavier weapons, or all three of us would be dead!"

The heavy weapon comment surprised him, and he said, "Yeah, I was just thinking the same thing, your car is a shot-up mess." Chunks of safety glass were splattered everywhere and covered Jack's shoulders. Don appeared unconscious and had slumped almost to the floor, his clothing glistening with shards of glass. She was still staying low, crammed down on the rear floor. Jack said, "You can get up now, we're out of their range." She jumped up and leaned over Don. Grabbing him by the shoulders, she pulled him up straight into the seat, pressing her hand against his wound.

Jack checked the car's side mirror and could barely see the two thugs who had been shooting at them. They looked as if they were jumping up and down in the middle of the street. *Idiots*, he thought.

He pushed the car's gas pedal to the floor as he swerved around wide-eyed pedestrians and stalled cars. He was still on Jefferson, only driving back the way he and Don had just come from, going away from his goal of the expressway. Instead of getting on the expressway, they had to go south and over it to get to Boeger Hospital. Thanks to constant gangland shootings, it had one of the best gunshot trauma centers in the nation. Chicago didn't get the nickname "Chiraq" for nothing. If anyone could save Don, it would be the doctors at the Boeger trauma center.

Jack shot a glance at the woman in the backseat and above the roar of the car's engine shouted, "Is he going to make it?"

She wasn't listening to him, her arms were around Don's chest; her fingers held tightly to his wound, trying to save what blood he still had.

Keeping his eyes on the street ahead, he loudly said, "I'm going to head up to Adams and then west to Damen Avenue. I'll take Damen south, over the Ike and the hospital will be about a mile away. I'm going to floor it. It's a bit of a drive, so hold on tight." They drove on without talking for several city blocks, the only sound being the car's loud exhaust. Jack was weaving the powerful old car in and out, around stalled cars and panicked pedestrians. Damen Avenue was just ahead and he approached it too fast. Making a hard left, he nearly lost control of the car on the turn and Don let out a painful moan. He knew Damen Avenue would lead them directly to the front of the hospital. He floored the old car down Damen and soon was in sight of the expressway. He could see the overpass and he thanked God it wasn't blocked.

Threading his way between two stalled taxis and a delivery truck, he scraped both sides of the car as he roared between them. Reaching the south side of the overpass, they had to drive up onto a sidewalk to get past several stalled cars and trucks, and ended up driving past the hospital, missing the short street to the main entrance.

Jack yelled, "Shit! That's Hastings Avenue ahead! We passed the street to the emergency entrance—Hang on!" Hitting the brakes, he hung another hard U-turn. After driving the wrong way down the short one-way street, he pulled into a long circular drive that said, **EMERGENCY ENTRANCE ONLY.**

Breathing a loud sigh of relief, Jack looked over to her saying, "By the way, I'm Jack, Jack Hansen."

She fired back, **"You almost rolled this car back there, do you know that?** You could have killed all of us! You're driving like an idiot!" Pointing to the hospital she said, "The emergency entrance doors are up ahead there, do you think you can get us through this crowd to them, in one *fucking* piece?"

"**Well *excuse* me missy**. I wouldn't complain about my driving if I were you. You nearly killed Don and I— plowing across that intersection, driving the wrong way down Jackson. And there's a black guy wearing a blue leisure suit, whose smashed in head looks like it's on backwards. We just passed him sprawled out at a pothole at Jefferson and Van Buren. I should have pointed him out to you!"

Without looking at him she snapped, "I didn't invite him to jump on top my car! Let's just get your friend up to the emergency entrance."

Jack swore under his breath as he tried driving up to the emergency room entrance. Warily eyeing the chaos around them, his stomach was tight and his heart felt like it was sinking into it. The craziness unfolding around them was unbelievable. There were injured people everywhere. Some of them looked to be in worse shape than Don, and no one was helping them. Dead bodies were lying unattended, uncovered on the sidewalk, with people stepping over them. The street and the large circular drive in front of the hospital were packed with people. Most of them were hurriedly leaving the building. For a hospital trauma

74

center, it didn't any make sense. Some of the people leaving were obviously patients, as they were only partially dressed or wearing a hospital gown. Injured people crowded the walkways leading to the hospital's main entrance and no one seemed to be helping them. They were shocked at what they saw. There were lots of people coming out and hardly anyone going in, and all of them looked scared to death. From the way some of them were dressed, they had to be doctors and nurses, abandoning the hospital like sailors jumping a sinking ship.

The entrance drive to the hospital was about 300 feet long and nearly blocked with empty vehicles. As Jack tried to weave the car up it, two irate cops started yelling and waved him off. Still applying pressure to Don's wound, she said, "Let's just stop here, get out, and get him over into that entrance. Some of those people coming out have to be doctors."

Her face was only inches from Jack's and it was hard to believe this was the same women he had rode the elevator with earlier that morning. She was a nice-looking lady, who was just nearly raped and had her face ripped wide open. He felt terrible for the way he had yelled at her minutes before and wanted to say something, but couldn't find the words.

He said, "You're right, this is as close as we're going to get. We'll have to carry him over there ourselves." He paused before getting out of the car, then turned towards her saying, "Look, I'm sorry for what I said to you. I can be a real jerk sometimes. Your cheek must really hurt, and we'll have to get you fixed up. Thanks for taking care of Don, he's an old friend."

With blood seeping out of her torn cheek, she said, "You're not a jerk, and I'm sorry too, my name is Lynne. After riding that elevator with you nearly every morning, I never thought we would end up meeting on the street... especially in a situation like this. Let's get your friend in there."

It was hard to get Don out of the car. He was going unconscious and couldn't walk. They each grabbed him under an arm and carried him towards the emergency entrance. The sidewalk leading up to the emergency room was crowded with people exiting the hospital. None of them could miss the dire straits that Don was in, but no one would make eye contact with them. Everyone hurried by. Jack tried to ask anyone who looked like a doctor for help, but was ignored. People dressed like nurses and doctors shook their heads and quickly walked by them in silence. He felt himself getting pissed.

Nearing the entrance, they had to maneuver around injured people who were lying on the sidewalk. Some were dead, covered with their own coats. Others lay with their mouths open and their un-seeing eyes staring at the blue sky.

With Don held propped up between them, they stopped for several seconds, searching impassive faces that ignored them. No one was willing to help, and he knew at that moment Don was going to die. Another friend, an old buddy, and he had let him down...just like the others. Suddenly Jack felt it hit him. It started with the smell. The unmistakable smell of fresh blood. That rusted, steely smell hit him and overwhelmed his senses. Like a terrorist attack on his body, a panic attack quickly engulfed him in its vice-like grip. He closed his eyes for a moment trying to shut it out, telling himself he was not back in Afghanistan, but it didn't matter. Suddenly his heart was racing and every muscle in his legs started screaming at his brain to make them run! Death hung in the air all around them and was feeding the panic racing through his heart. He had told himself he was long over these stupid panic attacks, but he could clearly see Weaver, Owens and Nolan. They were a bloody mess and only he was alive. **Only him! He had to get away!**

"**Jack! — Jack, Jack!**" Lynne screamed at him – "**Are you all right?** I yelled your name *three times*! Are you deaf? Who is Nolan?"

Taking a deep breath, Jack swallowed hard. It He felt like he never came home. Afghanistan and the present, it was all jumbled together. He blocked the impulse to run. —*What the fuck is wrong with me?*

Lynne whirled to the left, leading them towards some medical personnel who were hurriedly tending to people near two open ambulances.

The whole side of her face hurt, and she needed medical attention herself. She didn't want to be there with these two strangers and wondered what she was getting herself into. She had read the faraway look on Jack's face because she had seen that panicked stare before. She knew exactly what it was. She prayed this new-found friend would be able to keep his act together, as she felt like she was about to lose it herself. She prayed to herself, *Oh God, please help us, don't let this guy fall apart on me, I'll never make it out of here by myself....* Trying to hold up her side of Don, she yelled at Jack. "What's with you? I'm scared enough without you losing it on me! You're sweating like crazy. I know a panic attack when I see it! You helped me back there so I owe you one, but this is as far as we go if you're going to lose it on me!"

Jack heard her yelling at him and he shut his eyes tight, saying to himself, "*Jesus help me,*" as he fought to regain control. It was weird, the events around him didn't scare him, they really didn't, but the sudden ferocity of a panic attack and its affects did. He could deal with combat and death, he had proved it over and over, so why was this happening to him? Since the death of his friends, when it came on him, it was like he hit an impenetrable black wall. No matter how unreasonable it was, he couldn't get through it. And it was totally unreasonable—no way this should be happening to him. He told himself, *I'm not afraid of anything...* His heart was pounding and his brain was still telling him to flee, but it was thankfully fading.... He opened his eyes and looked at her. As quick as it had come on, it was gone. He said, "I'll be all right, I'm okay." His heart was still racing, but he could think again. The blackness that was blocking him was gone. As quick as it had hit him...it just disappeared, like it was never there. Letting go of his side of Don, he stopped an African-American man who looked like he could be a doctor, and urgently pleaded with the man to help them. "Help us please, my friend has been shot in the right lung."

Lynne eased Don down onto the grass, as the doctor quickly eyed him . "Give me a minute." He pointed to a lady that was lying on the ground, about ten feet away. "I have to look at her first."

Jack pleaded, "He doesn't have a minute, he's dying."

The doctor was impatient, "I said give me a minute!" He knelt down beside the older lady and placed his stethoscope to her heart, then got up. He said something to a younger black man, who was standing near her. Slowly turning away, he started walking towards Jack, asking, "How long ago was he shot?"

The young man who was standing over the old lady, quickly walked over and grabbed the doctor by his shoulder, spinning him around, saying, "What the hell man, you gonna let my mother lay there and die to go help these crackers? You're a black man, help her, not them!"

The doctor turned and stood toe to toe with the young man and said, "Your mom is gone. She has passed and I am truly sorry."

"But she's my mother, man, she's my mom." With tears welling up, he walked back to his mom and knelt down next to her, sobbing.

The doctor knelt next to Don and repeated his question about how long it had been since Don had been wounded.

Lynne, was still keeping pressure on the wound. She replied, "At least 20 minutes. I'm a nurse. The bullet is still in his lung." Suddenly she made a deep frown and sighed, shaking her head. "I can't feel his blood pressure anymore."

The doctor stood up, tight lipped, saying, "Sorry, your friend is gone, I can't help him."

Jack stepped in close to him, "You didn't even try! You didn't even look at him. You can't let him die!"

The doctor lost it, "Look around us, will you? We had people on respirators, in the middle of operations, and on dialysis. Every one of them is now dead or will be soon. We have no power, none. Even if you had gotten your friend here 20 minutes ago, he still would have died."

"He's gone, Jack—he's gone." Lynne bent over Don, gently closing his eyes.

The doctor touched Jack's shoulder saying, "I am sorry about your friend, I don't mean to sound rough. You can leave him here if you want to. If he has a driver's license, or some other form of ID, place it in his top shirt pocket, and button it...Unless of course you wish to take his body to the Cook County Morgue yourselves. Under conditions like these, that would be acceptable."

Jack knelt on the grass next to Don, feeling helpless. With tears in his eyes, he looked up at the doctor, saying, "I'm sorry too, I shouldn't have talked to you like that. I think it would be best to leave him here. His mother is alive and lives downstate. I'll write down her name and address and put it in his pocket with his driver's license."

Lynne leaned close to Jack, and placed her fingers lightly on his forearm. "Sorry about your friend…and sorry about yelling at you. Are you going to be alright?"

"Yeah, but I'm the one who's sorry. That shouldn't have happened. I lost some good buddies in Afghanistan, and I think about them all the time. I didn't expect to lose a good friend back home, not like this. It won't happen again, I promise you."

Blam! Blam! Jack instinctively crouched low. Two shots were fired near the emergency room entrance doors. People were screaming, and running away from the hospital. There was one lone gunman, a small handgun in his right hand, a gold chain swinging from his neck. He was bending over a person lying on the ground. He pointed his gun at the person's head, but didn't fire. Satisfied his victim was dead, the gunman stood straight and defiantly looked around, before calmly walking away.

The doctor was still standing near Jack and under his breath he mumbled, "Oh my God, that's the thanks we get! I have to get out of here. God help me, I have to get out of here—"

Jack was still bent down over Don. He placed Don's driver's license in his shirt pocket and buttoned it. He looked up, and the doctor was bending over him, his face almost touching his.

With pleading eyes, he quickly said to Jack, "You drove here in that old car, I saw you pull up. You wouldn't be heading west, would you?"

"You're going to leave?" It was Lynne. "You're going to run out on these injured people?"

He stood up; his eyes locked with Lynne's. "Yes, I am. For one thing, I'm a nurse, not a doctor. Most of the docs have left already. I've worked down here for eight years. Even on a good day, it can be like a war zone in some parts of this city, including around here." He turned and faced Jack. "I'm warning you, if we don't get out of here right now, we'll all die here. Even the cops are leaving." He pointed to the gunshot victim. "Look at that, the killer just walks away and nobody is stopping him."

Jack said, "What about all these injured people, who's going to help them?"

The nurse pointed to his dead colleague. "That man was a doctor and that's what's going to happen to me if I don't get out of here. You think it matters that I'm black or dressed like a doctor? Good Lord, it's not just the gangbangers we have to worry about, they're just the tip of it. Spend a week working in the emergency room down here dealing with the relatives of gangbangers who have been shot, then you will see where the problem is. Most of them are as rational as a six-year-old. Yeah, I know, you're surprised to hear a black guy talk like this, but it's the truth. There's a surplus of ghetto mentality down here and there's no reasoning with it. I don't understand it myself. They don't think like you and me. They're just angry, and anyone who doesn't immediately agree with them is against them. If you're white, then you must be a racist. If you're black, you're acting white and they hate you for it. I'm done playing this stupid game. I'll walk home if I have to, but I'm not sticking around here, *no way*. I have a wife and an infant daughter who come first."

Jack asked, "Where do you live?"

The nurse pointed west, saying, "Oak Park."

Jack got up, offering his hand to Lynne, pulling her up, while saying, "I never asked you, where are you heading?"

She hesitated for a second, as if she didn't know where she wanted to go, before saying, "I was trying to get home. I live in a condo not far from here, near McCormick Place."

The male nurse shook his head, "No, it'll be crazy over there and you know it. We should all get out of here, right now. We have to get out of Chicago."

Jack agreed, "He's right. This place, and the whole city with it, will go insane tonight and you don't want to be anywhere near it."

She protested, "But I have some things I have to get and where would I go?"

"Do you live alone?" He noticed some more blood oozing from the gash on her face.

She answered, "Yes."

He lightly touched her shoulder, saying, "You shouldn't stay in the city alone. Look, I live out west, in Able County. It'll be safe out there. Heck the lights might still be on. It's very easy to get to, it's a straight shot down the Ike. By the end of the week, they'll have the Illinois National Guard in here and have this rats' nest cleaned out."

She eyed Jack for an instant. A few minutes ago, it was obvious that the man was having a full-blown panic attack. She didn't know a thing about him. Did she want to trust her life to him? She said, "I don't know what to do. If my eye wasn't swollen shut, I'd take my car and leave."

Jack made the decision for her. Turning to the nurse, he said, "We're headed west down the Ike. Is the Harlem Avenue exit good enough for you?"

He saw the man crack a small smile of relief. "Thanks, that would be great. I really appreciate it." He eyed the jagged wound on Lynne's cheek, then held up his hand saying, "Give me one minute." He ran to an open ambulance and jumped into the back of it. He emerged from the rear of the ambulance not even a minute later with a fistful of bandages, three small yellow tubes, and a brown bottle.

Sprinting back to them, he gestured to Lynne's torn face saying, "You need stitches in that, but this will have to do, I'll patch you up on the way."

79

Jack nodded his head at the man, and knelt down next to his old friend. With a slight tremble in his right hand, he placed it on Don's shoulder and bent forward, close to his friend. He whispered, "Sorry Donnie. This is the way it has to be— gotta keep moving. I wish it wasn't like this, but it's just how it is. Goodbye little buddy." Slowly standing up, he wiped his eyes. Jerking his head towards the car, he said, "Let's go." The three of them sprinted to the car. Only Jack looked back.

As Lynne and the male nurse got into the back seat, a female voice behind them said, "Hey Jimmy, got room for one more?" It was a young black lady, wearing the same uniform as the male nurse. He shot a pleading look towards Jack. "She lives right off Harlem."

Jack nodded his head, saying, "Make it quick, get in." Jack was about to enter the car, when suddenly three tough looking youths jumped out from behind an ambulance parked next to them. One of them held a small semi-automatic handgun and the other, a long-blade knife. The youth with the gun ran up to Jack, his arm extended, pointing the gun at Jack's head. For a couple seconds, none of them said a word. The small metallic barrel pointed at his face was saying everything. The one with the knife leaned his head into the open driver's door and with a heavy Middle Eastern accent said, "Hello everybody. Our car doesn't run, so we're taking this one, and if you have any cash, we want it and anything else of interest you got." With his head still in the car, he said to Lynne, "Oh man, somebody cut you good huh? Get out of *our* car!" Gesturing to the male nurse with the knife, he said, "You too, get the hell out!" He just smiled at the young black nurse. "You stay where you are sweet face, you're going with us. Don't worry, we won't hurt you…. It'll be fun." The third member of their group was just a boy, maybe 16 years old, and was unarmed. He looked scared and stood behind the other two, saying nothing.

Jack kept his eyes locked with the young man pointing the gun at him. The man had steadily advanced towards him, where the small weapon was almost easily within his reach. Jack thought, *Yeah, get a little closer stupid. Just a little bit more and I'm going to grab that gun and shove it down your throat.*

Lynne had other ideas. Her decision had been made when the knife wielding leader told the young nurse they were taking her with them. She could feel the small revolver that Jack had taken from the boy she had bitten earlier. It was on the floor, next to her foot. She remembered Jack saying that there was one round left in it. The only thought racing through her mind was who to fire the only bullet at?

The man withdrew his head from the open car door and stood straight. Puffing out his chest, he looked at Jack and said, "How about you, quiet man— cat got your tongue. What are you staring at?" He sneered, "You look like trouble, you know that? I should let him blow a hole in your head or maybe I just slit your throat, huh?"

The youth with the pistol answered Jack's prayer and held it closer to his face. Without moving his eyes from its ugly little barrel, Jack's right hand shot up and grabbed it, twisting it away from him and out of his hands.

Lynne grasped the small revolver and, in an instant, brought it up, and leveled it at the center of the knife-wielding boy's chest. She pulled the trigger, and as the little gun fired its single 22 caliber bullet, she said, "Jesus forgive me."

The little 22 popped like a small firecracker and for a second, she didn't think she had hit him. Then he dropped the knife and took a step back clutching his chest, staring at Lynne in shock. She knew she had hit his heart, as a fountain of blood rhythmically started to shoot out between his clasped fingers. The younger boy, who had stood behind them, turned and ran. Jack had control of the other youth's gun. Within a second, he had it in his hand, and pointed at the youth who, a moment before, had pointed it at him. The man that Lynne shot sank to his knees, falling backwards, dead.

Possessing his assailant's weapon in his right hand, Jack shoved the boy away with his left, and snarled "Start running, asshole!"

The young punk quickly turned and slipped, falling to the ground. He scrambled to his feet and ran, disappearing behind the parked ambulance next to them.

Jack hefted the small semi-automatic in his hand. It was cheap and light, too light, and something about it didn't feel right. He inspected the small pistol, pulling back the slide. Then he shook his head and smiled, letting out a short incredulous laugh.

With terror stamped across their faces, their two new passengers glanced at Lynne, as if she would explain what Jack was finding funny.

Jack held the gun up in the air and pulled the trigger saying, "It's empty, no magazine, no bullets."

He picked up the dead man's knife and got in the car, saying, "Their gun was useless, but we didn't know that. It was a prop, but that knife he held wasn't." He looked down at the body of the dead youth, then back to Lynne. She still held the small gun in her hand and it was shaking. He said to her, "Thanks. That was quick thinking, and don't give it a second thought. You did what you had to do and it saved our lives. You and I are going to do two things right now. We're going to leave our personal baggage right here. I won't let my past sneak up on me again, and you're going to forget about shooting this asshole." He buckled himself in and looked down at the man's body. "You're right, Jimmy. There is a surplus of ghetto mentality down here, both black and white. Without this car, we're all dead, and nobody is going to take it from us. Now, how about we get the hell out of here?"

He turned the ignition and the engine roared. Shoving it into reverse, he floored the old car down the long drive, making people jump out of the way. Backing into the crowded street, he jammed it into first gear and laid rubber, tearing away from the hospital towards the expressway. One of the car's dual mufflers broke away from the exhaust system and shot out like a bullet from under the car. It tumbled and bounced across the street as they left Boeger Hospital. With part of the exhaust system now gone, the old V8 was unbelievably loud. He noted that at any other time it would be really fun, tearing down Chicago's side streets in a powerful car like this. Checking the gas gauge, he prayed that none of the many bullets that had been shot into the car had found their way into the gas tank. The gauge was holding steady at half full. *Thank you, Lord. Thank you.*

As he floored the old car down the hostile streets, the panic attack that had gripped him back at the hospital was gone, like it was never there. That's how they were. Without warning, one would instantly grab him. It was blinding and there was no logic to it. As unreasonable as it seemed, it would suddenly be right in his face, with no way out. As quickly as they came on, they would leave. But this time it was different, he could feel it. It was not only gone, but something positive had taken its place. As he drove off, running the gauntlet of thugs, a calm washed over him. He had something he hadn't had in a long time, and that was a mission. *It never leaves.* He thought about Don and the buddies he'd lost. If any good had emerged from the Monday morning of chaos, Jack would fully realize it in the months to come. It was the absolute futility, and downright craziness of letting the past negatively control the present. As he wildly drove Chicago's pothole-filled streets, he didn't have the time to sort it all out, but something good had just happened, he could feel it. Somehow, right then and there, he knew that wall of terror wasn't going to grab him ever again. Jack left his baggage at Boeger Hospital, and he hoped Lynne did too.

Boeger Hospital was about a mile south of the expressway, off Damen Avenue. To enter the expressway going west, they'd have to cross over it again to get on the north side, and they had to do it quick. Cook County Juvenile Center was close to the hospital and they had to steer clear of it at all costs. Staying on the south side of the expressway, even to drive a short distance was not going to be an option. He knew the whole area was bad news and had to be crawling with gangbangers, especially if they got loose from the detention center. As he turned towards North Damen Avenue, he hoped the bridge to the other side was still open. There was an entrance ramp to the Ike a short distance west of Damen. The ramp was a narrow one, and he prayed it wasn't blocked with stalled cars. With any luck they'd soon be off the crazy streets of Chicago and, hopefully, be on an uneventful drive down the Ike. He figured once they got on the expressway, he would head west to where it merged with the Illinois Toll Roads. There was an exit there that emptied out onto a main road called Roosevelt Road. From there it would be a straight shot west, almost to his front door. He couldn't wait to get home to his secluded suburban subdivision. His mind was reeling, *Soon as I clear Chicago, things have to be better.*   A thousand thoughts ran through his mind on the short drive back to the expressway, so many things could easily go wrong.

The Damen Avenue bridge was still open, but there was a group of kids on it, tossing rocks onto the vehicles below. He gunned the car through them as they tried to block him, pelting the car with stones. With chunks of broken pavement bouncing off the car's sides, he plowed across the bridge, making a hard left for the short drive on Van Buren Street. The entrance ramp to the Eisenhower was in sight, and in a few moments, they would be flying down it. As the car bounced down the pothole-filled street to the entrance ramp, Jack took a second to eye his passengers. Jimmy was already trying to clean Lynne's face while the other nurse was cutting small butterfly stitches. Maybe now, he'd finally be able to slack off and drive a little slower. Don was right about one thing, Lynne was tough. Through all the bouncing around and the male nurse cleaning up her torn face, she hadn't said a word. If she hadn't shot that thug with the knife back at the hospital, those punks would have left them stranded in the city—and that might have been a death sentence for all of them.

There were lots of people walking down Van Buren Street, and all of them were heading towards the safety of the westbound expressway. Nearly all of Chicago's westbound streets ran clear through to the suburbs. In fact, most of them kept the same names, even as far out to where Jack lived. The problem was that they all ran through tough neighborhoods. Taking any of them out of the city would be asking to get killed.

Jack was prepared to find the entrance to the expressway blocked, but it was wide open with no vehicles blocking it. What he wasn't prepared for was the sheer amount of people on foot that were making their way down the ramp and onto the expressway. All of them, upon hearing the approach of their loud car, turned around and gave Jack a hopeful eye. Some grabbed at the car's door handles, loudly demanding a ride west, while launching kicks at the car's sides.

There was a continuous line of vehicles making their way down the expressway. It reminded Jack of the caravans of refugees he had seen in the Middle East. There were pickup trucks with their open beds overflowing with passengers. Jammed in together like livestock, out of place in their disheveled office clothes, all of them looking scared. Every vehicle was bumper to bumper, packed with people with no empty seats. While trying to make his way into the line of escaping vehicles, a car passed them, its trunk wide open. There were two men dressed in suits and ties sitting in it, fear across their faces. Everyone knew what was coming and wanted to get away from Chicago as fast as possible. At the most, the traffic on the expressway seemed to be crawling at 10 to 20 miles per hour. With the traffic lanes mostly blocked, all of the vehicles were driving on the shoulders.

Jack wondered what he would do if the shoulders were to become blocked?

83

He didn't have to wait long, for everything suddenly came to a grinding halt. It looked like someone up ahead had gotten tired of walking and tried to force their way into a car at gun point. There was a man lying dead in the middle of the shoulder, blocking it. A small handgun was lying by his body, and the thought of stopping and picking it up passed through Jack's mind. He decided against it. It was either drive over the body, or get out and drag it to the side. No one wanted to vacate their cars for fear of someone car-jacking them, so no one stopped. Everyone started driving over the body. Jack and the three cars in front of him swerved over to the right as far as they could, running over the corpse's feet. He watched in disgust in his side mirror as the truck behind him didn't veer and stayed a straight course. It went up and over the body's head with its left front wheel.   When the truck's tire was directly on top of the skull, it collapsed, with a sickening "plop!" No one was stopping for anything.

Driving slowly made it easy for the nurses to work on Lynne's face. They were almost to Austin Boulevard, and out of Chicago's limits. Harlem Avenue would be coming up next, and it was the exit for the first western suburb, Oak Park.

Jack was starting to breathe a little easier, and he suddenly felt guilty. He was so wrapped up in his own predicament, he hadn't given much thought to Ellen and Laura. As he drove, he prayed they were safe.

Suddenly, there was a commotion up ahead. A crazy looking middle age white guy, dressed in a gray suit with a pink tie, was frantically waving a gun in the air. He was kicking at the sides of the passing cars, demanding they stop. He looked familiar to Jack, and he realized he was the guy who had punched the cop out in front of his office building. Giving the car directly in front of them one final kick, the man's gaze turned to theirs. He walked towards them, defiantly stepping between them and the car in front of them. He stopped and pointed a small handgun, aimed directly at Jack's face, screaming for him to stop.   Quickly gunning the car forward, Jack clipped the fellow in his left knee. Shoving him into the rear bumper of the car in front of him, he heard the bones in his leg crush. Jack stopped as the car ahead of him pulled forward. The man screamed in pain, dropped the gun and fell sideways, clutching his shattered knee. As he drove at a snail's pace past him, he spotted the man's gun lying on the pavement. It was old police special 38 revolver and was lying only a few feet from him. Stopping the car, Jack jumped out, and retrieved the gun. He was back in the driver's seat in a couple of seconds, opening the gun's cylinder. He was ecstatic to find it was fully loaded.   The man with the shattered leg was lying on the road, screaming profanities at him. He could tell he smashed the guy's leg pretty good. It was bent the opposite way at the kneecap. Jack knew that any severe injury at this point would become a death sentence by tonight. Glancing in his side mirror, he took one last look at the guy and shook his head, saying to himself, "Nice tie, asshole."

Other than hushed words to each other, the two nurses hadn't said anything since their escape from the hospital. They were almost to their stop at Harlem Avenue, and he could see they were nervous about getting out. The female nurse was sitting up front next to him. After the last incident, she had started to shake and was crying. He figured she was in her late twenties and was scared shitless about getting out of the safety of the car. He glanced over to her and then back at Jimmy.

"Your stop is coming up soon, Jimmy. I'm going to come to a rolling stop, just as we approach the Harlem exit ramp. It looks like a lot of people are getting out up ahead. You two are going to have to jump out quick, because I won't come to a complete stop. Sorry about that, but I'm afraid I'll get car-jacked if I do. Do you live close to each other?"

Shaking with fear, the female nurse answered, "No."

Jack continued, "You two stay together as far as you can, and don't stop for anyone. *Run home*, if you can. I wish both of you good luck."

Jimmy placed his hand on Jack's shoulder, "Thanks for getting us out of there. We'd probably both have ended up dead, if you hadn't given us a ride." He turned to Lynne, "I want to thank you too. You said you're a nurse, and that's good. You 'll know how to take care of that wound you got. There's plenty of antibiotic left in those tubes. Sorry we couldn't stitch it up the right way, it's going to leave a nasty scar."

Lynne tried to smile, and said, "You guys were great. I'm sorry for what I said back there. I don't blame you for leaving the hospital. Chicago's got so many crazy people armed with guns, I can't imagine trying to survive there tonight. I wish you both the best, and I pray you get home safe to your families."

Jack interrupted, "Harlem is coming up, get ready to jump out. I'll barely be moving. As soon as you clear the car, I'm going to hit the gas. There's a lot of people up ahead by the exit and they'd do anything for your vacant seats."

Jack handed Lynne their new-found weapon. "I know you can handle this; it's got six rounds in it. I'm worried about someone trying to jump in through that shattered back window. Anybody attempts it, shoot them. One shot only, we don't want to waste any ammo. We have a long way to go yet." Jack handed the female nurse the knife and gave Jimmy the unloaded pistol he had taken from the carjackers back at the hospital. He said to them, "Keep them in your hand, in plain sight. Run home as fast as you can and look like you're crazy. No one will mess with you."

When they were about even with the Harlem Avenue exit ramp, Jack slowed the car and said, "Good luck." As the young female nurse jumped clear, he realized he had never gotten her name.

Jimmy was climbing over the front bucket seat from the back when he said, "You two take care of each other and thanks again for getting us out of there. Good luck." He scrambled out the passenger door, slamming it shut behind him.

Jack was right about people making a mad rush for the two vacated seats. No sooner had Jimmy jumped out, when a grossly overweight white guy belly flopped on the car's trunk lid. Trying to jam himself in through the shattered rear window, he promptly slid back and fell off, when Lynne pointed the revolver at his pudgy face.

Another man managed to hang on to the passenger side door handle, as Jack dragged him along the pavement. He floored the car just for a second, and then hit the brakes, sending the swearing man flying off against a steel guard rail.

A second after they lost the fellow that was hanging onto the door handle, there was a loud bang! Someone hurled a large chunk of broken concrete against the passenger side door. It was immediately followed by a smaller piece that bounced off the hood and flew back, adding another star to the already badly cracked windshield. The entire expressway was a gauntlet of desperate people on foot and in every kind of vehicle, all trying to escape Chicago. The assault on the slow-moving parade of vehicles reminded Jack of the ducks in a shooting gallery. Jack liked ducks, but he didn't want to be one.

Suddenly, the expressway opened up, and the unlikely parade of vehicles spread out and increased in speed. If there were any planes in the air, the road would have looked like a checkerboard of abandoned cars and trucks when viewed from it. Jack followed the line of cars in front of him, as they threaded their way through the blocked roadway.

Turning his head back to Lynne, he motioned her up to the front seat. "You might be safer up here."

Agreeing, she started to climb into the front, pulling herself over the floor shift's council and around the front bucket seat. It was a tight squeeze for her to climb into the front, and in the closeness, he couldn't help but get a good look at her. Despite her having a line of fresh band aids laced down her torn cheek and one eye swollen almost shut, there was something about her— something Ellen could never possess. With her long black hair blowing around in a wild mess and her ample figure, she reminded him of that 1950s actress in that Howard Hughes western film. *What was her name?* Brushing her shoulder up against him, it was the first time their bodies had touched. At the same moment he caught a trace of that perfume... Jack felt something—and it was electric.

Catching his look or maybe feeling the electricity herself, Lynne instantly knew what Jack was thinking about. She shook her head, and Jack saw her lick her lips before saying, "You're really something, you know that? I look like shit! I feel like shit, and the whole side of my face hurts! We've killed people and you about lost your mind back there! You almost rolled this car...twice! The world is probably ending, and now you're sitting there giving me the look. Looking at my fat ass, checking me out. You're an asshole, you know that?" Turning her head away, she stared vacantly out the car's open side window, as she roughly belted herself into the bucket seat.

Jack drove on in disbelief, trying to figure out what just happened… *Good Lord, all I did was look at her! Oh shit, she's got the gun too….*

He felt ashamed of himself because he knew that she knew, and she was right. He had to quickly change the subject, and hoped she would let him and not shoot him with the gun he had given her. He back pedaled, "I was just thinking that your boyfriend or husband, is going to be really pissed when he sees what happened to his classic car. I've wrecked it."

Tight lipped, she turned her head facing forward, her eyes like iron, staring straight ahead. Seeing everything, but looking at nothing, she stayed silent for a few minutes. He couldn't see it, but a single tear made its way down her right cheek.

She nodded her head distantly like her mind was someplace far away, before she said, "The car's my husband's. And yes, he would be extremely upset. He bought it back when he was in high school and restored it about ten years ago. He kept it in perfect condition and we would go to car shows together in it. He was very proud of this car." There was a long uneasy pause, and she took a deep breath and exhaled, like someone about to give up. "He died from an aneurysm three years ago. I considered selling it, but we went on dates in it while we were in high school, so I decided to keep it." She paused a few seconds and swallowed hard, as if there was a lump in her throat she couldn't clear. "Once in a while—on a nice sunny day like today, I take it out. I always check the forecast first. The day has to be perfect." She kept staring straight ahead as she talked, now with a line of wetness trailing into her wounded cheek. "This morning I decided to take the car to work and park it where it wouldn't get dented, or scratched. Now look at it…."

She clenched her teeth, then parted her lips slightly, letting out a long sigh. Placing both of her hands upon her head, she tried to smooth back her tangled hair.

"His car is ruined…I'm ruined— everything is ruined." She bent forward and placed her face in her hands, sobbing.

Jack was at a loss; he didn't know what to say. *Aw Jeez– shit, now I've done it…* He had to say something to her, but couldn't think of anything, so he took a deep breath, taking his time to find the right words. "Listen, I'm sorry about everything. I wasn't giving you any kind of look, at least not in the way you interpreted it… Aw hell, maybe a little, but we've been through hell this morning." He paused, and wiped the back of his hand across his forehead. "Lynne, I was a Marine for a long time, and have seen lots of combat. I screwed up this morning, bad, and you set me straight. You're right, I was giving you the look. I hardly know you, but I already admire you and I'm glad we met. We might not have made it out of that madhouse back there if we hadn't. I also want to apologize again for how I lost it at the hospital. I spent quite a bit time in Iraq and Afghanistan. I was never scared while I was there, at least not for myself. A roadside bomb in Afghanistan ended my career in the Corps. It wasn't until I got out... that I started having some problems. You want to know what it's like over there? What we went through this morning getting out of Chicago is pretty damn close. Losing Don—it flipped a switch in my head and put me in a place, a really bad place. It won't happen again, I promise you."

Holding a bloody pink T shirt, she dabbed the clean part of it to her swollen cheek and then wiped both her eyes. Jack bit his lower lip and started to say something more, but she cut him off. "I'm sorry too. I'm sorry for swearing at you, I'm not like that, I'm just very upset. You've done a fine job keeping us safe. If anyone was checking anybody out, it was me. You've always been a perfect gentleman during our short morning elevator rides. I already knew you're Jack Hansen. You're married, with a daughter named Laura, about to go to go off to college. I sometimes took the elevator with your office manager, Sarah." I was hoping you weren't married. I would never come on to a married man... I was just... lonely, I guess. That's all, just lonely. I am a very lonely, sad person, with few friends. My husband was everything... I am so sorry for swearing at you."

Jack was seldom at a loss for words, but this time he didn't know what to say. "Let's put all this behind us, okay?" He glanced from side to side, and looked into the side mirror, "Looks like we are free and clear here, we're almost out of Cook County. We're actually doing the speed limit and nobody is trying to stop us. There is an exit up ahead where there's a big Super Center Store and a Drug Store. What do you say we take a chance and stop at one of them? We can use the rest rooms, get cleaned up, and grab something to eat and drink. We can get an ice pack for your swollen eye, and we'll start off fresh. How about it?"

"That sounds good, thank you. I do have to go to the bathroom. You think they will have electricity? There's still so many abandoned cars. I don't see any lights on anywhere.. . . it doesn't look good."

Jack wheeled the car off the expressway and onto the Mannheim Road exit, saying, "We're about to find out."

Getting off onto Mannheim, things didn't look good, all the traffic lights were out. Like the expressway, there were groups of people walking down the middle of the street. The loud car made all of them turn around and stare, immediately giving Jack an uneasy feeling. He didn't see any other vehicles that were moving and knew he had made a mistake. He had just made them a target. Abandoned cars were everywhere and it didn't take but a few seconds for a gang of tough looking youths to run towards them. One of them held up something in his hand, and Jack didn't wait to find out if it was a gun or not, as he peeled off in the direction of the Super Center Store. While approaching it, he slowed down, and their hopes sank.

The store's parking lot was covered with a surging mob of people. The huge store looked like it was being dismantled and carried away by a sea of ants. Most of the store's windows had been shattered, and people were jumping out of them with armfuls of items. They hurried away in every direction; it was a free-for-all. From the looks of it, whole families were involved. Moms, dads, and the kids; everyone was carrying something. The store was being looted to the bones, and the drugstore further down the street looked worse. It had flames erupting out of its front windows and there were no firemen or firetrucks to be seen.

Lynne stared at Jack in bewilderment, "Where are the police? How could they let things get so out of control?"

Jack shook his head gloomily, "I would expect right about now they're sitting in front of their own houses with a shotgun on their lap."

A gang of young men walking up ahead suddenly turned around towards them and bolted towards their car. One of them was carrying a long pipe, and the others quickly scooped some up rocks. Wasting no time, Jack floored the old car while making a heavy U turn, spewing road gravel at the advancing youths. As the pipe glanced off the car's roof and fistfuls of gravel showered upon them, Jack spun the car around and headed back to the expressway. The entrance to the expressway going west was about half a block away and he floored the old car towards it. The suburbs were as bad as Chicago.

The speed limit sign at the entrance ramp to the expressway said 25. Jack took the cloverleaf at 50. They would only be on it a couple miles before they would hit the Roosevelt Road exit and finally be in DuPage County and the western suburbs. As they left the Chicago skyline behind them, Jack's mind was passed overload. There was a massive cloud of black smoke off in the distance that didn't look good. It was hanging over the area where he would be getting off the expressway, and there was no way around it. The only good thing was the road remained wide open ahead. For the first time since leaving the city, there were no obstacles in front of them.

Jack relaxed a little and let his mind wander back to the events of earlier that morning. Lynne had mentioned she knew Sarah, that they had talked while on the elevator. He thought about whether he should tell her about Sarah's death. He decided against it and tried to push the morning's events from his mind. But Don's lifeless eyes kept popping up in front of him, blocking him. They were still a long way from his home and he had to stay alert. Just like his buddies who he had lost while in the Marine Corps, he had to shut Don's face out. *Sorry, Donnie, not now, I'll think about you later....* They were doing about 70 mph, and in between the roar of the car's engine and the wind blowing through its shattered windows, it was almost impossible to talk.

Lynne had to yell, "Jack, where am I going to stay when we get to your town? You think any hotels might be open?"

He yelled back, "You're welcome to stay with us. I don't think there will be any other options. Nothing's going to be open and nowhere will be safe, but I guarantee you'll be safe with me. It'll be fine with my wife, so don't give it a second thought. You and my daughter, Laura, will hit it off. You can stay with us until it's safe for me to take you back to your home."

She wanted to protest, but was in no position to refuse his offer. He was right, she had nowhere to go. She silently nodded her head in agreement, praying she made the right decision to go home with a person she didn't know.

Just ahead, the Eisenhower expressway merged towards the Illinois Toll Roads and the final leg of their journey would begin. They were finally out of Cook County and, on a normal day, in 25 minutes Jack would be home.

Getting off the expressway, they exited onto West Roosevelt Road. It would be as wide as the Eisenhower for about two miles before it would narrow down to two congested lanes. They'd be passing through several different towns before they would enter Jack's hometown of Melville. It seemed like Roosevelt Road always had road construction going on and he hoped the usually crowded roadway would not be blocked. There was smoke ahead of them and it was hanging low. It was thick, and as they entered it the smell was horrible. They hadn't gone far when they found where all the black smoke was coming from. About a city block ahead, they faced what looked like an impenetrable wall of black smoke. It was pushing quickly towards them and, like a heavy blanket, it spread across the roadway. Just ahead on the right was the new county hospital; the entire building was encased up to the upper floors in smoke. Somewhere ahead on the south side of the road, a massive fire was burning out of control. Occasional licks of flames shot into the sky from the solid cloud of black smoke.

The hospital's parking lot and main entrance were visible to them, and it was a repeat of Chicago's Boeger Hospital. They were close enough that, even with the thick smoke, they could see that the hospital was in meltdown. Like at Boeger, dazed and injured people were scattered across the huge parking lot. Any hopes they had about things getting better, now that they were out of Chicago's grasp, were fading fast.

With all their car's window glass badly cracked, or entirely missing, it was impossible to keep the choking smoke out of the car. Both of them were coughing, gasping for breath. As they entered it, the putrid smoke got thicker. Afraid he'd run into something, and more afraid to turn back, Jack slowed the car to a crawl. Their eyes burned and they felt the air temperature suddenly getting hot.

The road was six lanes wide, running east and west, with heavily wooded acreage on their left. Directly behind those woods was a somewhat secluded residential area with many high-end homes. They had finally discovered what was burning. Jack knew the area well as he had two clients who lived here. It looked like the whole neighborhood was being incinerated. Flames were shooting out of the treetops, the black smoke funneling into the sky. Deep in the inferno, he could make out the shapes of houses totally engulfed in fire and something else, something that didn't belong there. Sitting in the middle of the gated community,

90

where no aircraft should ever be, the burning remains of a large jet airliner was melting into the ground. Like the aircraft that Jack had earlier watched from his office window making its death plunge into Chicago's skyline, this one had wiped out an entire suburban neighborhood.

If Jack had felt any relief after escaping Chicago, he just lost all of it. So far, they were about a mile into sunny DuPage County, and it didn't look any better than the inner city. He plowed the old car through the thick smoke, praying they wouldn't hit a pedestrian or rear-end a stalled vehicle.

All at once, it was like someone turned on a bright light. They suddenly exited the wall of smoke into a beautiful sunny, spring day. A flock of Canadian geese, honking to each other, flew low across the road directly in front of them and landed in a nearby open field. The air temperature instantly turned cooler; the smoke was gone, and everything appeared normal as they left the massive fire behind them.

Jack tried to talk, but he couldn't. Lynne was in the middle of a coughing spell herself and he felt like someone had punched him in his chest. He sucked the fresh spring air deep into his lungs, trying to clear the smoke out. He thanked God that they had finally made it through. He knew they wouldn't have been able to breathe the thick smoke much longer.

"Oh my God, I can't seem to get my breath," Lynne was bent over, holding her left hand to her chest, coughing up chunks of phlegm and spitting it out her window.

For the first time that day, Jack actually felt like making a wise-ass comment. He was so relieved that they had made it past the raging fire, he couldn't help himself, so he nudged her on the arm saying, "You always spit out the window like that?"

Still gagging and coughing up chunks of soot, she held her left arm up towards him, flipping him the bird. As bad as the situation was, that little bit of humor was sorely needed for what they were about to face that afternoon.

Jack attempted to wipe the greasy soot from his face with his sleeve, and he smelled a hint of spearmint that lingered on his hand from the morning train ride. He started to laugh to himself, saying, "Still minty fresh."

Lynne looked at him questionably, as he held his fingers under his nose. "I put my hand into a wad of gum stuck on the seat of the train on the ride in this morning. Ha! I can still smell it. I was really pissed about it too. If that was only the worst thing that happened to me today, huh? That's why they say, 'Don't sweat the small shit.' Thank God we made it out of there alive, and good riddance to Cook County."

Coming out of Chicago to DuPage always seemed like a breath of fresh air to Jack, but now it tasted sweet. Until the early 1960s, DuPage County had been mostly a farming area. Far removed from the sprawl of Chicago, it was dotted with typical little farm towns. During the last 40 years, most of the county was eaten up by large, cookie- cutter-like subdivisions. All of them were given quaint names, recalling the area's rich farming heritage. Now, nearly every trace of the past was bulldozed and paved over. Dotted through the county were remnants of these farms. Every one of them was under constant assault from the greedy towns, abhorring any vacant land, only wishing to expand their tax base. The small subdivision where Jack lived was next to one of these soon-to-be-developed farms. The wall to wall buildings, whether in the city or the suburbs, would become a living hell for the people trapped there. As Jack attempted to make it home that morning, he didn't know that the key to him surviving the shit-hit- the-fan scenario, would be the buffers that surrounded the neighborhood where he lived. The golf course, the farm, the cemetery, and the Fox River secluded his house, removing him off the beaten path. The suburbs didn't have the inner-city congestion, but they had some of Chicago's gang problems and their own share of suburban scumbags. The scum box was wide open and all of them were out in force on that sunny Monday afternoon. Two decades of suburban gangs, hidden amongst the minorities; a large welfare class of whites, coupled with ramped-up drug use, was a powder keg that was ready to blow. The EMP was what lit the fuse.

Jack was in familiar territory. He drove this stretch of roadway every day, and regularly stopped at many of the businesses along the way. He had a couple stops in mind, not knowing what to expect when he got home. There were some things he wanted to pick up, including information. Lynne also needed some things. If she was going to be staying with them for a while, he figured they may as well get them now.

The first thing he noticed was, like Chicago, all the power was out and the streets were crammed with people on foot. Some vehicles were running, but not as many as he had seen driving out of the city, and most were older models. He wondered if Ellen's little convertible would run, but didn't give much hope to his new truck.

None of the traffic signals worked, it was like they were never there. Even the stop signs were ignored. Laws were being broken, but no one cared. He had tried the car's radio in the city with no success. He turned it on again, but it only played static. Like everyone else that day, every so often he would check his phone hoping to see the display light up, but it remained dark.

There was a large supermarket up ahead that, with much fan-fare, had opened last fall. He and Ellen had attended the grand opening, and it was like no supermarket he had ever been in. It had a party atmosphere to it, with a buffet, a salad bar, and a large sit-down eating area. Sitting in the middle of the store was a baby grand piano with a pianist dressed in a black tux playing it. There were stations scattered through-out the store where free samples of food were given out. Without a doubt, if it had been a little closer to their house, this would have become his favorite place to buy groceries. The store was ahead in the next block and Jack decided to stop there. Both he and Lynne were filthy, but they had to make a stop somewhere. Looking like they did, Jack hoped he wouldn't run into anyone he knew.

Turning into the parking lot, he quickly hung a U turn and pulled back onto the roadway. Like the stores near the city, the new supermarket was being torn apart, piece by piece. The only difference was, out here in the burbs, the looters were mostly white. Once a few people got in a store and started walking out with free stuff, the mad rush was on. No store was immune. It was easy to spot the stupid thieves; they were looting the electronics.

Just like the city, there were whole families pushing stolen shopping carts full of food down the road. Some people were fighting and once when they heard gun shots, both of them instinctively ducked low in the car's bucket seats.

Like they had seen on the expressway, a body was lying in the middle of the road. Jack slowed down and drove around it. It was a young white girl, maybe in her 20's, and he didn't have to give her more than a glance to see that she was a bloody mess. She was dead and no one was paying any attention to her, but at least people were driving around, and not over her. Jack thought of his daughter, Laura, and again prayed she was safe.

Lynne still had the handgun on her lap. The way she looked, there was no doubt in his mind that she would use it in a split second. After their hasty U turn out of the supermarket, he had about given up on finding anyplace they could safely stop. One look at Lynne and he knew he would have to find a place soon.

Sitting forward in her seat, she said, "Jack, I'm sorry, I have to go—really bad, I don't think I can't hold it much longer." He took a quick detour off Roosevelt Road and drove into the empty parking lot of a vacant car dealership. Stopping in a secluded part of the car lot, they both got out. Lynne ran to a spot by the building where there were some bushes for a little privacy. Jack kept the gun in his hand and kept a watchful eye for anyone who would approach them. As bad as their car looked, it was still a running automobile, and he knew people would kill for it. As he stood there, he wished he hadn't stopped smoking. He badly needed a drink of water, but just as badly needed a cigarette.

While Lynne did her thing, he took the time to sort the situation out. Every store they had seen was being rushed by people, and he had no doubt in his mind that within a day, the shelves would be empty. He got his wallet out and checked how much cash he had. The small amount of cash and the eight credit cards in his wallet told the whole story. America ran on credit; hardly anyone used cash. Everyone was panicking at once. Word quickly spread and people ran to the stores, gas stations, banks and ATM's all at the same time. Only this Monday morning was different—nothing worked. Every product today had a bar code on it and Jack hated them. Those crazy little lines that were on everything had to be electronically scanned to be entered into the system. Often it was done by a clerk, who was lost without the aid of the computer to do simple math.

Gone were the days of price stickers. Even an apple had a bar code on it. Few folks carried cash anymore and the use of checks was quickly disappearing. It was now debit cards, credit cards, store cards, welfare, and bank cards. In one fell swoop on a Monday morning of a perfect spring day, everything that used electricity stopped working, and all commerce stopped. The plastic cards in everyone's wallets were useless. No one could buy or sell, and the result was panic. Looting followed, and it didn't matter what kind of a neighborhood you lived in, everyone seemed to be going nuts. He softly said to himself, "Talk about the mark of the beast. God almighty, what have we done to ourselves?"

Earlier, Lynne had asked him, "Where are the police?" His answer of "Sitting shotgun on their own houses," would become true almost immediately, because the police were panicked too. If anyone knew the score, they did.

As he quietly stood there, standing guard for Lynne, he could clearly see the street. He watched a young mother with two little children struggling with a shopping cart full of groceries, trying to push it down the pothole-filled road. He thought to himself, *How many people are still at work? How many people are at home and unaware of what is happening? Holy crap... what's tomorrow going to be like?*

Fighting the urge to look at his phone and see what time it was, he wished Lynne would hurry up. He was glad he was finally out of the car to stretch his legs, but he didn't feel safe and wanted to get back on the road. The tension in his body from the harrowing ride out of the city had taken its toll. For most of the drive down the expressway, they were lucky if they did ten miles per hour. The last time he had experienced anything like this was during his final tour in Afghanistan.

With relief showing on her face, Lynne hurried back to the car. She was a nice lady and Jack felt terrible about what happened to her face. For the first time he thought of what Ellen's reaction was going to be when he introduced their new guest to her. Ellen had a jealous streak in her and things could get ugly really fast. What most people didn't know about Ellen was that her fun-loving and easy-going personality ended at their front door. He could just hear her reaction after bringing this strange woman into their home. At first, she'd be really nice to their guest, and face to face it would be, "Oh *you poor dear." Later,* when she got him alone, it would be something like, *"My God, Jack, what did you bring her in here for? Tell her to get a hotel!"* That might not be her exact words, but he knew it would be close. He figured he'd cross that bridge and deal with Ellen when he came to it.

Lynne was eyeing her battered car and she didn't look well. Jack walked around the car to her and gently placed his hand to the side of her face. "That punk really did a job on you. Are you all right?"

She nodded her head saying, "The whole side of my face is just throbbing. I think that pain medication Jimmy gave me is wearing off. It made me a little drowsy before and now I'm afraid to take it again. With things the way they are, we both have to stay alert. I do feel much better now that I went, I couldn't have held it much longer. Thanks for stopping."

Jack feigned a smile, "I know the feeling and now it's my turn for a little walk." He pointed to the corner of the building, "I'm going over there. I'll be able to keep an eye on everything, but if you see something—anything, lay on the horn." He walked over to the building's corner and relieved himself, thinking, *We're not going to even find a bathroom that works.*

While standing there, he spotted a water spigot on the side of the building and thought, *what are the chances of the water still being on?* Just for the heck of it, he tried the spigot. Water came out, but not with the usual pressure. He noticed a high municipal water tower about a block away with the town's name, Glen Ellyn, boldly painted on it. That explained why water was still coming out of the spigot. He thought about the small amount of water that was in people's hot water tanks. No electricity meant no pumps to pressurize the water. Jack stared at the stark white tower, imagining its precious contents draining away. He thought to himself, *When that big old tank is empty, this town will be bone dry.*

There was a large white plastic cup lying on its side next to the building. He decided to put it to use. Grabbing the cup, he carefully eyed the empty dealership and parking lot. They hadn't attracted any unwanted attention, and for the time being, the area looked safe. He jogged back to the car and said, "There's a spigot on the side of the building that can still give us some water." He reached into the car, grabbing a bag she had with a scarf in it, saying, "How about we drive the car over there before we go. It'll be out of sight from the street. I'll clean up this cup and we can get a drink and wash up a bit, as long as you don't mind drinking out of an old cup and using your new scarf as a wash rag?"

Lynne eyed the scarf, and said. "That was to be a gift I was going to mail to my niece. It seemed important yesterday. Things change fast, huh? It's a washrag now. It'll be nice to clean some of this soot off, plus I could use a drink."

There was hardly any pressure, but the water was cold and tasted good. As Jack tossed back his second cup of water, he thought back to those terrible months he had spent in the scorching deserts of Iraq and Afghanistan. His Marine Corps desert training had stressed water conservation. He had heard that the average civilian used between sixty to eighty gallons of water every day. That seemed a little exaggerated, but he thought about his long showers, and the many times he would let the water run when he wanted a cold drink. And how many times a day did he flush a toilet? That amount could be rationed to just a little more than drinking and meal preparation in the field, but these suburbanites? Accustomed to taking their long showers, hot baths and just letting the water run, they would soon be out of clean drinking water. He wondered how many people at that very moment were wisely filling their tubs

95

and every container they had with the last of the fresh water flowing from their taps?

After Lynne drank her fill, he soaked the scarf in the cool water and rung it out. Then he carefully washed her face around the bandages on her cheek. He didn't know much about this woman, but she was no complainer, that was for sure. She had a really clear complexion and cool blue eyes. One of her upper front teeth had a large chip missing from the corner, that he had never noticed before.

He had found out earlier that she was very perceptive and could read his thoughts. She further confirmed it when she said, "That kid broke my front tooth when he shoved the gun into my face. Thank God he didn't knock it out."

After cleaning up, they took one last drink and got back in the car. Jack stretched back in the bucket seat and realized it was the first time he had stopped to rest since he had left his office. He lingered a moment longer, vacantly staring out the cracked windshield. Nervously fidgeting with the car's gearshift, he turned towards her and said, "I want to say I'm sorry again about what happened at the hospital." Tightening his hand hard around the gearshift knob, he said, "Like I said, I was in a lot of combat over in Iraq and Afghanistan. I was damn good at what I did. There's one particular thing though—it keeps dogging me. I tried to bury it, but it never leaves. Everything flashed back to me when we were carrying Don. It used to happen every so often, but nothing like it did today—I couldn't escape from it—it's just that losing Don brought it all back. It's so damn hard to forget things. I lost some good buddies in Afghanistan because of my bad decision, and I still beat myself up over it. I let my guys down, and it cost them their lives. My decision got my friends killed and it haunts me *every single* day. I guess I'm some tough Marine, huh? Sad part is, I spent my last six months in the Marines babysitting clowns that wanted out. Almost of them claiming they suffered from some form PTSD. They all looked healthy to me, but none of them could do their Marine Corps job. I saw their service jackets. Some were deployed to Iraq and Afghanistan but had never seen any combat, yet they were getting out with a disability for PTSD. Can you imagine that? At the time it really pissed me off and I thought it was all a line bullshit. Now that I've had years to think about it, they probably did have PTSD, but it wasn't from being in the Marine Corps. Sometimes life is just a bitch, no matter where you're at, and you have to suck it up."

With his hand still tightly gripped around the car's floor shift, she gently placed her left hand on top of his saying, "With you, it's obviously not a line of bullshit. That's why it's called post-traumatic stress and I understand it. It's okay, Jack, you're *only human*. Who are you? Ask yourself that. Are you a bad person? You made a terrible mistake—and that's what it was. There would be something wrong with you if what you've seen didn't bother you. It's over. We can't change our past, and you can't beat yourself up over it. You can't bury it, either. Your friends are in a better place. They're spirits are with you—right here, now, and they know what's in your heart——they forgive you. *But you've got to forgive yourself.* Let the voices you hear be theirs, and listen to them. They'll help get you through this. Your friends died, but their spirits didn't. My dad was a Vietnam combat veteran. He was there in the spring of 68', so I know he saw some heavy fighting, but he *never—ever* talked about it, and as kids we never thought to ask him about it. But thinking back, he drank and smoked himself to an early grave, so something was eating at him. A lot of veterans commit suicide every day, without telling anyone their problems. My Dad had that John Wayne attitude, so yeah, he sucked it up. He drank and smoked himself to death—just a slower form of suicide. I think a lot of you guys ask too much of yourselves. The blood of your friends isn't on your hands. It's on the hands of the criminals that sent you there…. but they always sleep well. They wrap themselves in the flag and let the military do their dirty work. You get the medals and they get the dollars." Neither of them said anything for several seconds. Lynne said, "You know, I liked what you said about leaving our baggage in Chicago. Let's do it, Jack. I have a feeling a lot of people are going to have nightmares after today. Maybe you and I will be one of the few that don't. Like they say, 'Sometimes you need some of the hair of the dog that bit you.' I think you grabbed plenty of that this morning."

Conscious of her warm hand on top of his, he looked directly into her eyes. "I can't believe I told all this. I don't even know you. You're sitting there hurting and I'm unloading my shit on you. Other than the people at the VA, you're the only person I've ever told, and I even bullshitted them. It's not that I didn't want help, it's just—I don't know—maybe I feel I don't deserve it." He looked out the cracked windshield at the vacant auto dealership and slowly shook his head. "You know, my wife and I have been married almost 18 years and I have never talked to her about it—I could never talk to anyone about it. No one wants to admit they're weak."

She gave his hand a light squeeze and held it for a couple seconds. Returning her hand to her lap, she grabbed her seat belt and fastened it, saying, "I think it's easier to tell your problems to a total stranger, because there's no commitment. Even the people at the VA have skin in the game, because it's their job and they truly want to help you. You just have to take the barrier down and let them. I don't know you well enough to judge you. I'll tell you something though, from what I've seen this morning… you're anything but weak."

Jack tightly clenched his teeth, embarrassed that he had so quickly unloaded his deepest fears so easily. Suddenly the image of Don's lifeless body lying on the sidewalk shot through his mind like a sharp blade. He said, "I've already got regrets about this morning creeping in." He let out a nervous laugh. "Shit…Sometimes I'm my worst enemy. Ok, Lynne, let's leave it here. We'll get to my place. It'll be safe there. Are you ready to hit the road?"

"Yeah. I'm glad we stopped."

"What would really make me feel better is if we had a full tank of gas." Jack started the car and glanced at the gas gauge. The needle sat at a quarter of a tank. If the old gauge was accurate, they would make it to his house with gas to spare. If not, they'd be in big trouble. He sat there a few moments more and strapped himself in tight. He felt better after their short talk. It was like something that had been lurking unwanted inside of him since Afghanistan had left for good this time. He hoped it wouldn't be replaced with something else, but he didn't think so. He didn't know how, but he could *feel* it. *Maybe something good will come out of this rotten day.*

Carefully pulling out of the empty car lot, they headed towards the street. People were walking down the middle of it and everyone stopped and looked at them, eyeing the old car like it was the last bus for the day. The very last bus, and they were wanting to board it at any cost. Jack hit the gas and sped away from the crumbling parking lot, leaving in a cloud of dust.

It looked like that the businesses lining the street that were faring the best were the ones that closed immediately after the power went out, or never bothered to open in the first place. The stores that tried to remain open were just asking for trouble and had gotten it. It was obvious by the amount of frantic people scurrying about that everyone was waking up to the fact that this was no average power outage. It was well past lunch time, and the crowd that normally relied on carry-out and fast food restaurants had found every place closed. That had to explain it. With their pantries at home empty, they were hungry and agitated. Unable to get their fast food fix, people were already acting desperate. Folks were quickly waking up to the fact that they should have stocked up for that rainy day. For the first time in their lives, people who had money and good credit were denied the use of their credit cards. Whether rich or poor, anger flashed in everyone's eyes. No one was immune, including those on welfare. With the food pantries closed, and the sense of entitlement so ingrained, nothing could make them understand what was happening. Jimmy, was right. Ignorance, combined with entitlement, sparked outrage.

Jack had read a couple books on the shit hitting the fan. They predicted that within three days, store shelves would be looted bare. They were wrong, it looked like folks caught on quick. In the far reaches of his mind, He thought about the supplies he had salted away, some as long as three years ago. But the doubts were sneaking in too. There were items that he still needed to get. *Damn! Why didn't I get that shit while I had the time? I could just kick myself!* He didn't think the outlying suburbs would be immune from the craziness of Chicago, but he never expected the looting to spread so quickly. Continuing to drive west, they soon were out of DuPage County. Like Chicago and Cook County, they bid DuPage good riddance. With DuPage fading behind them, they entered the next western Illinois county—Able.

ABLE COUNTY

CHAPTER 9

    Able County was less developed than DuPage. It had its share of housing developments and shopping malls, but it was more laid back and spread out. The far-reaching urban sprawl of Chicago had not yet engulfed it. The county was on the fringes of rural Illinois and there was still open farmland. They were on the final leg home and Jack tried to relax a little. Chicago's Roosevelt Road had changed to simply "Route 38," almost in defiance from the big city it descended from. There was farm land on both sides of them now and not many buildings. He looked over at Lynne and her head was down, her chin resting on her chest. As loud as the car's open exhaust was, she had somehow managed to doze off. With the windows missing, her long black hair was blowing about. He caught another faint reminder of the lingering fragrance that smelled so good in the elevator that morning.

    For the first time since making their escape out of Chicago, he allowed himself to think about something other than their dire situation. Glancing sideways at her, he thought about the many times in the elevator he wanted to strike up a conversation with her. He always heard that being unfaithful to a spouse always starts with a seemingly casual and innocent conversation. He smiled to himself, *It's never casual or innocent.* It's a game that he never wanted to play, and he always steered clear of it. Taking his eyes off the road for a second, he looked at her again, thinking to himself, *She said she was lonely. There are a lot of married people who are lonely too… maybe more than are single….*

    Being married to Ellen was never easy. He had always thought that the wedding vows of for better or for *worse* referred to taking care of a spouse who had become sick or handicapped.   Other than that, he had never given those vows much thought until recently. Ellen definitely had a screw loose. Did that count as sick? Maybe it did, but what about his life and, more importantly, Laura's? His wife made their daughter's life hell and was always at her. Was that also covered by the *for worse* part? He could deal with Ellen, but he didn't think Laura should. If there was any justification for leaving Ellen, it was the torment she constantly put their daughter through. He was doing his part to stay married to her, and would never be so bold as to start an affair, but the cracks in their marriage were getting wider. He was running out of patience and had enough of her bullshit. He glanced again at Lynne and she was still sound asleep. This time he allowed himself to hold his stare. As rough as she appeared, he found it hard not to look at her. He smiled to himself, thinking, *This is the interesting black-haired woman in the elevator. She finally has a name, and it's not Jenny... and I'm sitting in her car next to her... what a crazy world....* Unlike the concealed glances he made during their morning elevator rides, this time he was drinking in a long look at her. He wondered if she had ever read his thoughts during those short rides together. Secretly he hoped she did, and as she slept, Jack felt a tinge of red creeping up his neck.

Straight ahead there was another huge cloud of black smoke coming into view, lazily drifting across the horizon. This was directly where they were headed and he felt his stomach getting that tight feeling again. There were also similar towers of black smoke to the far west and north of them. Recalling the fire and carnage they had driven through earlier, he prayed it wasn't more downed airplanes. *But what else could it be?*

The thoughts of his failing marriage were quickly dashed by the image of Laura and Ellen fighting for their lives. "God, let them be safe," he said to himself.

There was that time last year when he discussed with both of them a shit-hit-the-fan emergency plan. If something really bad happened while they were separated, the plan was to try to communicate with each other and, no matter what, immediately get home. He recalled how Ellen looked away and dramatically rolled her eyes, as Laura intently listened to his little talk. Afterwards, Ellen made the comment, "Jack, why can't you ever be more positive about things? You sound like that old couple next door more and more. I'm surprised you don't want to get a woodstove."

He thought that any time you had a plan, that *was* being positive. As much as she pissed him off, he prayed she was safe at home... *I should have told her to buzz off, and gotten that woodstove.*

There was a gas station /convenience store about a mile ahead where he regularly bought gas and snacks. The station was off by itself with no other buildings nearby. He thought that maybe they might have a generator going and be able to pump some gas. A soft drink and some junk food would be good too, so he pulled into the station's drive. The front entrance door was open and the station owner was standing in it. Since there was no one else there, he decided it would be safe for them to stop.

The owner's name was Ali, and Jack assumed he was from Pakistan. He was always a very friendly man. He ran the business with his wife and their two daughters.

Today Ali looked anything but friendly. He was standing in the doorway with both of his arms crossed in a defensive stance that said, *"Don't mess with me."* He was wearing a shoulder holster with what looked like a semi-automatic in it—that confirmed it. Jack pulled up in front and parked the car by the closest pump to the station's entrance door. Lynne was awake and he instructed her to stay in the car and be alert, holding the gun on her lap. He asked her to give a short beep on the horn if anyone looked like they were going to pull into the station. When he got out of the car, he made sure Ali could see both of his hands by holding them up, palms toward him. Before he could speak, Ali coldly said, "No gas."

Feeling that the station owner didn't recognize him, Jack said, "Ali, it's me, Jack." Smiling and gesturing to their beat-up car, Jack gave a short laugh, and continued, "Not my usual ride, I know—How are you doing?"

Ali curtly replied, "No gas or running water. I only take cash if you want groceries."

Seeing that Ali's holster was open and that he held his right hand nervously near it, Jack made no advances towards him. He pointed his index finger past Ali, towards the inside of the store, saying, "I can go without the gas, but I sure could use some bottled water. Maybe some soda, and some chips too." Seeing the look of mistrust, he continued, "Ali, don't you recognize me?"

Ali held his bearded chin up, slowly nodding his head. "Sure, I recognize you. I recognize lots of people, but today some of those very people turned on me and tried to rob me."

Jack could see the clock on the wall inside behind Ali. It said two thirty. Changing the subject, Jack pointed to the clock. "Ali, is that the right time?" Ali simply nodded his head. Sorry that he had stopped, Jack was getting an uneasy feeling and shot a glance back at Lynne. After an uncomfortable pause he said, "Ali, we don't mean you any harm." He pointed back to the old car. "This morning when we left Chicago that car was in mint condition, look at it now. There's not a straight piece of sheet metal on it, and when I get home, I'm afraid of how many bullet holes I'm going to count. We've had a terrible day, and I just want to get home. We barely got out of Chicago alive."

Ali relaxed and softened a little. "Yes, I know, I hear it is very bad. I have a cousin who has a station on the south side, on Halsted Street. We're very worried about him."

Then looking west towards the town of Melville and the black clouds, Jack asked, "Have you heard any news as to what caused this? All hell is breaking loose everywhere, and what's burning up ahead?"

Ali rubbed his fingers through his short black beard, "It's being said we are at war. Maybe the Russians, or maybe the Chinese. Something about an EMP attack. I do not understand it. All I know is everyone is acting crazy. In my country, we lose electricity sometimes for days with no big deal. Here, you

Americans are spoiled, and you go crazy." He threw up his arms in disgust. "You can come in, select what you like, but cash only—no change. I'm closing up after you leave, it's been a very bad day." Ali did an about-face and disappeared into his store.

Before going into the store, Jack eyed the empty street and gave Lynne a cautious "thumbs up." Entering the station, he noticed what looked like two bullet holes in the front door glass. They weren't there the last time he got gas, two days ago. Quickly getting what he needed, he decided not to ask about the bullet holes. He selected two large bottles of water and two bags of corn chips.

Ali and his wife were both standing by the counter closely watching him. His wife kept nervously looking out the door, her coal black eyes scanning the street. As Jack placed the items on the counter, Ali said, "That will be 20 dollars—cash."

Jack thought 20 dollars was a little steep, but he handed it to him, asking, "Where exactly are you from, Ali?"

"Pakistan. Punjab, Pakistan. And yes, sometimes we lose power, but we patiently wait."

"Well, I don't think this is an average power outage, Ali. Good luck to you." Before going out the door, Jack turned back, "About all that smoke up ahead, any clue what it is?"

Shoving the 20 into his front pants pocket, Ali flatly said, "They say an airliner crashed into a school and shopping plaza. That is all I know."

The battered old Chevy peeled out of the gas station.

LAURA

CHAPTER 10

St. Paul's Lutheran High School and Church was originally built in 1874 by German Lutheran immigrants. The original church and school were now long gone. The "new" church was built in 1926. The school was a hodgepodge of brick buildings dating from 1948 to 1994.

Laura's first class of the day was in a classroom located on the first floor of the newer two-story addition, built in 94'. This class was, by far, her favorite. It was her senior year and she was in chemistry class. It was taught by one of the school's youngest and most popular teachers, Carl DeFries. Her father thought that Christian schooling was important and had insisted that she attend parochial schools through high school. He left the choice of college up to her and was happy she had picked out a private Lutheran College in nearby Kenosha, Wisconsin. Ellen had thought it was a waste of money, but agreed to it as Jack's mother had paid all the costs of Laura's schooling through high school. If Ellen had her way, Laura would not be going to any college.

A comment that she had made to Jack, after an argument about it, summed up what she thought. "If Laura had my body, she wouldn't need any college."

It was true, Laura didn't have her mother's body or any of her sculptured looks. She was tall and lanky like her dad and very muscular. Her Norwegian heritage evident. She would be in excellent shape well into her 60's, when someone with Ellen's body would be giving up on weight clinics and on her second face lift.

Laura's Monday had started off with another nasty confrontation with her mom. Laura had become friends with Mary Kay O'Hare, a young mother who lived at the end of their block with her husband, Brian. They had an 18-month-old baby boy, named Wendel. She would sometimes babysit Wendel while Mary Kay ran errands. The week before, unknown to Ellen, Laura had returned home early from babysitting at the O'Hare's. Ellen didn't hear her daughter enter the kitchen from the back door. Laura was pouring herself a glass of milk, while her mother was talking on the phone in the dining room to her dad's friend and co-worker.

She could hear every word her mom said, and what she overheard... made her sick.

She and her mother had been having a running battle ever since. *How could she hurt Dad by cheating on him with his friend, Don?*

It was Monday morning and Laura was standing out near the street curb in front of her house. Her friend, Karen, had just got her graduation present of a new convertible and was going to give her a ride to school with the top down.

Her mom had already left, without as much as a goodbye to her. She seemed in a hurry and Laura had a good suspicion as to why. Karen was right on time, pulling her car up to the curb and giving the horn a short "Beep." Laura got in and they excitedly talked about Karen's new ride for a bit, but as excited as Karen was about her new car, she wanted to know how her friend was handling what had happened with her mom. Laura didn't want to be a downer, but on the way to school she shared with Karen the heated argument she and her mom had that morning. Surprisingly, Karen said something to her that had been lurking in the back of her own mind for some time. "Laura, your mom is beautiful. I mean like wow, she's a real knockout. I would die to have your mom's bod, but lots of people assume people as good looking as her have their shit together. They just look so perfect; you know what I mean? Did you ever consider your mom might be—kind of off?"

Laura looked at Karen and frowned. She hesitated a second and drew a deep breath before saying, "Yeah, I have thought about that... I think it's a good possibility. Maybe she has some kind of mental illness. Like she's a psychopath or something, I don't know what it is, but I'll tell you one thing, Karen, looks don't mean anything. I'm happy the way I am, but you're right, something's wrong with my mom. She's always restless and never seems happy. I love her and I don't want to make her unhappier than she is, but I can't let her hurt my dad. It's just so much to think about, I don't know what to do."

A few minutes later, they arrived at the school. Karen pulled into the lot and parked the car, but before getting out she turned to Laura, "When I was in seventh grade, I hated my mom, and one time I told her so. Of course, I was just being a little bitch and didn't hate her, I was just mad at her about something. She didn't deserve it, but I did it anyway. She had cancer, and I didn't know or consider what she was going through or how bad it was. I'll always regret saying that because I never told her I was sorry, there wasn't enough time. Lots of times we say mean things to people, especially our parents, that we don't mean, but we do it anyway and they don't deserve it." Karen hesitated for a second before continuing, "Laura, in the case of your mom, it's a two-way street. She's the one who's screwed up and somebody has to set her straight. Don't you start feeling guilty about it."

They got out of the car and the subject changed to what they planned to do that night, but Laura was still thinking about her mom. She did love her, but

105

would never understand her. Mental illness or not, Karen was right, something had to be said. She would talk to her dad tonight. For now, she had to put her mother out of her mind, enjoy the fresh spring day, and savor the last full day of her favorite class.

Walking into the main entrance, she and Karen high fived and spilt up, each going to their lockers, Karen saying, "See you in class, *skinny*."

Laura had just left her locker and was on her way to class when suddenly the lights went out. Immediately there was a loud round of cheers heard throughout the school, and some boys in front of her started wildly jumping up and down at the prospect of the day being canceled. Almost instantly there were numerous complaints of cell phones being dead. They had power outages before and Laura didn't think much about it. This would be their last full day in school anyway and she figured, power on or not, it wouldn't make that much difference. Her chemistry class was a large room with portable lab stations positioned throughout the classroom. Each station consisted of a large movable metal roller cabinet with a black slate countertop. Two high stools sat behind it, with plenty of room for two students to perform their experiments together. The outside wall of the classroom was a large, bright expanse of windows, facing the north. Power or not, the room didn't need any lights. Laura and Karen shared the first station together at the front of the classroom. Karen entered the classroom after Laura and took her seat next to her. She knew as soon as she saw Laura that she was still troubled about what to do about her mother. As Mr. DeFries walked into the classroom, she gave her friend a reassuring nudge, whispering, "It'll be okay," as Mr. DeFries started to speak.

"Good morning class! I've got some bad news today. The final exam results were lost because the power went off and goofed up all the computers. Your test results just got erased and everyone will have to take them over today." There were loud boos and jeers from the class, and one of the boys from the back loudly shouted "No way, let's go home!"

DeFries held up both his hands in mock protest, "No, you won't need to take them over, all of you passed, except maybe one." He looked at the boy who had just yelled the loudest in protest and smiled, "Just kidding, Eddie, all of you did fine."

Carl continued, "The power is off, but I'm sure it will come back on at any second. It seems like the phones are off too. More than likely the outage has affected the cell towers. At any rate, it shouldn't bother us, we have plenty of light from the windows."

Carl had been standing in front his desk, but moved to the center of the classroom, standing near Laura and Karen's lab station.

"What I planned to do, since tomorrow morning is the last time you will officially be in this school..." There were loud cheers from the entire class, and some of the boys started jumping up and down. Carl started again, "What I would like to do is give each one of you a few minutes to tell everyone what you plan to do this summer and what your plans are for the fall. We don't need any lights or computers for that. I know all of you have big plans after graduation, so let's keep it short, but let's share them. Hopefully, we will all keep in touch and see one another as time goes on."

Karen yelled out, "What are your plans?"

Carl laughed, "I'll be jogging every morning, teaching a short summer school class, and getting an old house I inherited ready to move into. And maybe I'll get a little garden started, if I have time."

One of the boys sarcastically added, "A *garden*?" He smiled and shot the boy a look over the top of his glasses saying, "Yes, Richard, a garden. The world would be in much better shape if everyone had one." Carl suddenly placed his right hand over his eyes and extended his left arm out, pointing his finger into the class, supposedly at random. When he uncovered his eyes, he was pointing at Laura. "Laura Hansen, you're going to start us off. How about sharing your plans with the class?"

Somewhat embarrassed, Laura got off her stool and faced the class. One of the boys who regularly came into the Burger Chief, where she worked on weekends, yelled, "I'll take a double with cheese!" Everyone in class, including Carl, knew Laura worked at the Burger Chief Restaurant and started laughing.

As they laughed, Laura laughed too, saying, "Don't laugh, their doubles are actually very nutritious, and a *bargain* for the price." There were some more laughs, and Laura started to tell of her plans. She had barely started speaking when she noticed some of her classmate's attention had turned away from her and were staring out of the classroom's windows.

Suddenly everyone's attention was diverted towards the windows, including her teacher's. She heard him softly say, "Oh no." An instant later he screamed, **"Everybody down—now!"**

She turned her head towards the windows to see a large airliner off in the distance, getting bigger by the second—it was aimed directly at her classroom!

The sound of the aircraft hitting the school was deafening. Laura hit the floor just as the bottom of the tail section sliced into the second-floor classrooms above hers.

The rear of the plane had been much lower than the nose section when it hit and it cut through the second story floors like a giant plow. It carved a swath directly above her, through two classrooms full of students who never knew what hit them. Had she been in Social Studies, or Spanish, she would have been ground to pieces. As if she was suddenly in some other place, nothing made sense to her. There should be another classroom above hers, but now there was only a giant hole with bright blue sky above, where a white tile ceiling should have been. The air was full of what looked like snow-flakes. It was thick, with a fine powder raining down on her. It was so thick, it was hard to breathe, and a sharp pain was shooting through her leg. Something heavy was holding it down.

A second before impact, Carl managed to dive partly under his heavy metal desk. After the crash, he crawled back out and looked up. There was a giant hole in the center of the ceiling where it had collapsed into his classroom. His whole body felt stunned, and he had to force his muscles to move. Shaken, he gazed up through the gaping hole. There were clouds where there should be another classroom. Like his students, his brain couldn't immediately comprehend that the top floor of the building was gone. The air in his classroom reminded him of a pillow fight he had been in while at college. He had been hitting another kid so hard that his pillow had burst, sending a wall of white fluff through the air. His entire classroom looked like that now, he was in a snowstorm of dust.

The smell of kerosene was strong and a river of it cascaded out of the open ceiling. His mind was foggy and as he forced himself up, he looked out where the windows had been, all the glass was broken or missing. The center of his classroom was flattened by part of the heavy floor collapsing from above, and several of his students had to be under it. Some of them he could only partly see. They were lying motionless, crushed under the broken concrete and twisted steel. Others that were fortunate to be seated near the classroom's outer walls were slowly getting up. All of them were standing there staring at him, panicked and dazed. Everyone was coughing and gagging on the thick dust.

Carl screamed at them, "Grab someone who is hurt and get out together through the missing widows! Get far away from the building as fast as you can, it's going to catch fire. Let's move!"

Laura wanted to get up, but she had been knocked flat and was covered in dusty debris. She was dazed and felt like she had sand in her right eye. Her lab station was overturned and partially on her leg. Trying to get up she turned her head, and found herself staring straight into the eyes of her friend, Karen. She was on the floor next to her, their noses almost touching. Karen said nothing and her open eyes didn't blink. Struggling to sit up, Laura grabbed Karen by her shoulder and shook it. She tried to yell, "Karen get up!" but the words couldn't come out. The choking dust was horrible and was filling her lungs. As the white dust blanketed her friend's face, she looked in horror at what was holding Karen down. There was a long length of silver pipe impaled completely through her chest, with another shorter length sticking out of her back.

She couldn't think and she couldn't breathe; she felt like she was about to pass out. As the white insulation rained down upon her, she became confused, thinking maybe the room was full of snow spinning around her like a giant snow globe. Coughing and fighting for breath, it all was so crazy. Her friend *couldn't be dead….* Someone grabbed her, pulling her up.

"Come on Laura, let's get you out of here!"   It was her teacher, Carl DeFries.

THE SHERRIFF AND HIS BROTHER

CHAPTER 11

Chuck Hayes had worked as a sheriff's deputy for the county for many years.

A good physical description of him would be a wiry little bastard with beady eyes. A better description would be a skinny crook with a badge He decided that morning when he went into work that it was going to be an easy Monday. Not that any day working for the Sherriff's department was ever hard. By easy, he meant, *easy* pickings. He'd start off the day by stopping at that corner gas station over in Melville and paying a visit to those two Arabs who owned it.

Chuck had no authority in the town of Melville, but he did in the unincorporated section where those two Arabs owned another station. He knew they were selling cigarettes and beer to underage kids and decided he wanted a cut of it. The unincorporated areas were known by the kids, to be lax on those kinds of things. It was a real money maker for the owners of that particular station. He had a little talk with the two of them one evening, and told them that for a small monthly fee, he could grant them a license to make sure things stayed lax.

He was sitting in his squad car counting the fee he had just collected, when he observed Ellen Hansen pull into the station, driving her little red VW. She parked at a far pump, got out and went into the store. Hayes eased back into his seat a bit as he eyed Ellen. *Man, she's still a hottie....* As he watched her, he allowed himself to reminisce a bit, back to the day many years ago that he busted her and some other girl for smoking weed behind a local bar. He and his partner had some fun with them, and later let them go, but he got to know Ellen *really well*. She was married to some jarhead Marine, who was serving in those oil fields that were burning up over in Iraq.

He started laughing to himself as he pictured her stupid husband. While her hubby was off fighting the hodgies over in some sandlot, he drilled an oil well of his own back here with his wife. That well didn't produce oil for long, but it was a gusher while it lasted. Hayes' smile faded as he thought about her husband, that asshole Marine.

He wasn't afraid of her husband, but he would be the first to admit that the guy was one tough bastard. The only way he would ever face him was with his gun drawn.

He would see Jack Hansen sometimes when he patrolled the unincorporated area where Jack and Ellen lived. He would always wave and give the stupid Marine a big smile as he drove by, because he knew it really pissed Hansen off.

As fate would have it, his older brother, Dirk, had a run in with Hansen last year, it was right in front of Hansen's house. Dirk didn't know Hansen, but he worked for the sewer department, and had been using a backhoe to dig an excavation on the parkway in front of Hansen's house. He had a nit-wit kid directing the dig for him when he brushed the sewer line with the bucket. He cracked the main sewer pipe and was pissed off, so he cuffed the kid and tossed him into the hole. Hansen and some other neighbors had seen the whole thing and confronted Dirk.

Dirk Hayes was just the opposite of his sheriff brother. Dirk stood about six-four and was built like an ox. Unlike his little brother, Chuck, he didn't need to carry a gun or a badge. His hands looked like a couple of baked hams and his chest like a concrete block wall. Nobody ever messed with Dirk. The only resemblance Dirk had to Chuck, were his eyes. On Chuck, they looked like they belonged to a weevil. On Dirk's fat, pug-nosed moon face, those dark beady eyes made him look like a pig. One would expect the man to say "Oink," when he spoke.

The afternoon that Hansen and the neighbors confronted him, Dirk had started to fill in the excavation to quickly conceal the damaged storm sewer pipe. Hansen came out, yelling at him about shoving the kid into the hole. Dirk didn't like being talked to like that and decided to take a swing at him. Hansen ducked the blow and smacked Dirk in the mouth. Grabbing him by the collar, he shoved him headfirst into the hole, giving him a kick in the ass to add further insult. As luck would have it for Hansen, Charlie Mills, the old bastard who lived next door, had videotaped the whole thing, including Dirk smacking the kid and shoving him into the hole. Chuck would have loved to arrest Hansen, or maybe have some more fun with Ellen, but with that video tape and the witnesses, Hansen had his brother Dirk up the creek. Had Jack Hansen chose to pursue the matter, Officer Chuck would have had to arrest his own brother for assault on his young helper and on Hansen. Both of the brothers agreed that sometime in the future, when the opportunity presented itself, they'd have their comeuppance with Jack Hansen.

Hayes watched as Ellen walked out of the station and began filling her car with gas. He kept an eye on the little car as it left the station until it was out of sight, thinking what he would like to do to her husband. Taking a sip of coffee, his mind drifted back to his brother, Dirk.

Dirk was the oldest of three brothers and Chuck was the youngest. Jerry was the middle brother who was doing life in prison down in South Carolina for kidnapping and murder. Nobody up here knew about that. After he quit high school, Dirk got a job as an apprentice butcher. Chuck was surprised his oaf of a brother actually went and took classes for it. Hayes laughed to himself as he recalled how he got ma to pay for it. He promised her she would, "Never run out of fresh meat." He laughed to himself when he remembered Dirk's meat comment to ma. Dirk had worked as a butcher for National Foods until he got fired for carving up his hunting pal's ill-gotten deer carcass while on the job. Besides butchering illegally hunted game, there were some other charges that were never substantiated, but nonetheless, the state health department got involved and Dirk not only lost his job, he almost went to jail. Chuck had pulled in some long-held IOU's to get Dirk a job in the county sewer and water department, and even more to enable his brother to keep it. Hayes stopped his laughing to himself because he again thought of Hansen, but warmly smiled as he thought of Ellen...*if that jarhead only knew the fun I've had with his pot smoking wife.*

Seeing Ellen in the gas station had set off a whole train of thoughts. Hayes put the cruiser in gear, slowly pulling out of the gas station. He had a taste for a chocolate long john and a couple cream-filled donuts. That little bakery down the street should be putting out a fresh tray of them right about now. As he drove to the bakery, his twisted mind turned back to Hansen. He had never seen her, but he heard Ellen Hansen had a teenage daughter named Laura, who worked over at the Burger Chief. He wondered if she was built like mom? *Laura...* he thought. *It must be a family name or something.* Hayes smirked and shook his head as he pulled into the parking lot of the bakery. God, he hated the name Laura, it sounded fat. *Who would ever name their kid Laura?* Maybe he would cruise through the Burger Chief's drive-up tonight....

He parked the squad and called dispatch to tell them he was stopping for a break. He was informed of some illegal trash burning being done in an unincorporated section near him. The dispatcher told him to check it out when he was done. He figured if he took his time, maybe whoever was doing the burning would be done by the time he got there. Maybe he'd let the guy slide for fifty. He sat in his car for a few minutes and made some calls. He had lots of things going on the side and liked the freedom his job gave him. Unlike the village police that were confined to a particular city, he had free roam over the whole county. He had been on the force long enough that he could have gotten off the streets and retired, but he wanted no part of that. The streets were where the fun and action were, and it kept him feeling young.

Every morning when he put that badge and gun on, Chuck Hayes was no longer the skinny little kid who was always getting big brother, Dirk, to fight his battles.

He was more than content to be a simple cop and wanted nothing to do with retirement. They'd have to drag him out to get rid of him. From time to time he would bust some kids for something, and it would turn out that one of them had rich parents or was some politician's kid. One hand washed the other. He kept his mouth shut and his hip pocket full of IOU's.

He got out of the squad, put on his mirrored glasses, and headed inside the bakery for his free coffee and rolls. He knew the young woman who worked the counter was intimidated by his cold stare and it always gave him a rise. Smiling to himself he thought, *The average citizen hasn't got a clue what goes on in this little town….*

After he got his coffee and rolls, he figured he would go check out that fire.

He started shoving the end of a big chocolate long john in his mouth as soon as he cleared the bakery door. His vest radio was in the middle of a dispatch and suddenly stopped working mid-sentence. He became puzzled when several cars that were driving by slowed down and came to a stop, blocking the street. Two vehicles were still running, but seemed to be having some mechanical problems and were unable to move.

Hayes swallowed a hunk of long john, and slowly wiped his mouth with his sleeve. There was a fellow standing next to him, looking just as puzzled as he was. Hayes turned to him saying, "What the hell is wrong with those people. I don't have time for this crap today." Walking out towards the street, he thought, *I should just ticket every one of you bastards.*

The fellow behind him said, "Hey, look at that jet out there. It looks like it's going into a dive!"

The big airplane appeared to be moving really slow, but Hayes knew it wasn't.

It was a commercial jet airliner and it was dropping fast, coming in like it was going to land. It might be able to land in some of the open fields nearby, but for where it was headed, there was nothing but buildings with lots of people. Hayes shoved the last chunk of long john in his mouth and checked his radio and phone. Both were dead.

He jumped into the squad and its radio and computer were also dead. Pushing the ignition button, the engine started, but quickly died. He tried two more times with the same results, then got out.

Everyone who had been driving their cars were getting out of them. All were watching in horror as the big jet glided in, straight for St. Paul's school. Hayes opened his coffee and took a sip, then inhaled one of his chocolate cream-filled donuts in two bites, followed by more coffee as the massive jet's tail clipped the top floor of the school. The coffee was hot, but he didn't feel it. He washed down the last bite of his donut, as the aircraft's tail section took off the whole second floor of the school.

The solid masonry of the upper floor was swept off the building like a child kicking over a stack of wooden blocks. The top of the school exploded, sending bricks and debris far into the air, trailing the airplane. The entire back

113

half of the aircraft ripped apart just aft of the main wing and crashed into the parking lot on the other side of the school, bursting into flames. The front half of the big aircraft continued on, minus its tail and midsection. There was a huge gaping hole where the fuselage had broken in two, spewing out screaming passengers still strapped in their seats. Scattered like confetti onto the open field below, their bodies bounced and tumbled like dice.

Hayes quickly took another gulp of his coffee and tossed the cup, as the front half of the plane slammed into the supermarket, clearing the big box-like building off its slab.

He had the final cream-filled donut in his fist, as Connie's Beef was obliterated by the cascading remains of the supermarket and the burning remnants of the jet. He shoved the final donut into his mouth in one squished-up wad, as the gas station was blown sky high. Hayes had so much dough in his mouth that what he yelled aloud sounded like, "Oly puk!"

He did what any police officer would do, he quickly raced across the street. He made a beeline for the open area where the bodies were scattered, some still strapped in their seats. The long field between the school and the back of the supermarket was the only area not engulfed in fire. Sure enough, Hayes was immediately rewarded for being the first to get there. Next to a seat, with what looked like the lower part of a female passenger still strapped in it, he found a little gold box with some expensive looking bracelets inside it. Taking a quick look around, he tossed the box and shoved the gold bracelets into his pocket. There were many seats scattered about. Some of them had passengers still strapped in them, and all of them were dead. With the price of gold at nearly 1200 dollars an ounce, he'd check all the bodies out. Being a first responder had its perks.

RESCUE

CHAPTER 12

Laura Hansen was in the baseball field, about 100 yards from the burning school. Carl DeFries had dragged her and at least five other students from the burning and collapsed classroom. She was sitting on the ground with about 80 other students and teachers that were, for the most part, uninjured.

The rest of the not so fortunate were over in a parking lot by the church, being attended to by the teachers and staff. Some of the kids looked the same as when they walked into school that morning. Others, like Laura, were covered in so much filth they were barely recognizable. Many were crying and coughing from the dust and smoke they had inhaled. Laura's leg was sore and had a cut on it. Her nose hurt and she wondered if it was broken.

All of them were scared and in shock, and many of the kids just started leaving to walk home on their own. Laura didn't know what to do. Her dad had made her promise during one of his "emergency talks," as he called them, that if something bad ever happened, she was to get home no matter what.

She couldn't get Karen's eyes and the sight of the pipes sticking in her out of her mind. She looked at the burning school. Her classroom was an inferno, and her friend, Karen, was still inside. Karen was being consumed by the fire and Laura would never see her best friend again. Sadness and shock gripped her. She had never been so scared and she started to shake. She remembered a comment her dad once said about being in heavy combat and losing his buddies. *"Start thinking too much about what just happened and you'll lose it. You have to keep your shit together."* She said to herself, *"God, Daddy, I wish you were here!"*

Laura and her classmates had been milling about, mostly unattended for about an hour. Her nose hurt and the side of it felt dented in and crooked. Mr. DeFries had come by once and asked her how she was doing. He looked at her nose and told her it was definitely broken. She didn't know how it happened and didn't feel any pain until after she got out of her collapsed classroom. All the kids wondered why they were all left sitting out on the field with no one telling them what to do. She hoped a nurse or someone would look at her nose, but there was no one assisting them. *Where were all the ambulances and paramedics? Every fire department from miles away should be here.* She never felt more alone in her life.

And where is Mom? No one's phone worked, and nobody knew what was going on. The other thing was that the fire in her school was spreading to other parts of the building, and they were just letting it burn. There were no big firetrucks and no ambulances. *Where was all their equipment?* Nothing made any sense to her. Some of the kids were getting impatient and more were starting to walk home. The teachers all looked panicked and a few of them were walking away too. The kids who drove cars to school said their cars wouldn't start, and no one's laptops worked.

She and some other students decided to walk over to the church to use the restrooms. The church was dark; only the emergency lights were on, and the water barely trickled out of the washroom's faucets. There was a large decorative fountain on the west side of the church that had plenty of water setting in its basin. They were all washing up in it when an older parishioner walked up and started screaming that they were being disrespectful and to get out. It wouldn't matter, because by the end of the day the Church would be burning. The students just naturally looked to the teachers and adults for help, but some of them looked panicked, like they knew something the students didn't, and that scared Laura even more. Finally, after what seemed like at least an hour after the plane crashed, two old emergency vehicles approached, followed by a line of older cars and small trucks. One old ambulance and one fire truck pulled in with their sirens blaring. The fire truck was the old one used to pull the float for the annual Fourth of July parade.

She heard one of the boy's mumble, "If that's all our fire department has got, we're fucked."

* * * * * *

About a half mile away from crash site, the Melville City Fire Department was facing an unconceivable crisis. The station was built two years before, and as the town officials liked to boast, "Our department has all the bells and whistles money can buy."

The problem on this Monday morning was that none of those bells and whistles worked.

The whole crash site could clearly be seen from the top of the firehouse, and some of the firemen had witnessed the airplane crash into the top of the school. There were several other aircraft above the city, within sight. Two helicopters were seen dropping out of the sky like dead flies. They knew at least one other plane had crashed somewhere about a mile and a half south of them.

Their radios didn't work and they couldn't call for assistance from other police or nearby fire departments. The station's switchboard should have been jammed with people calling in, but it was dead silent. Engine company number three was assisting another nearby community, putting out an out-of-control residential fire, and one of their ambulances was out on a heart attack call. They couldn't communicate with either of them. The station's crew of paramedics and firefighters looked to their chief to give them orders, but to add to the horror, he suddenly walked away from them, mumbling something about doing, "One last thing." No one thought that meant blowing his brains out. It had been almost 40 minutes since the plane crash, and only three emergency vehicles were readied to leave the firehouse. Two were outdated antiques.

Jimmy Sullivan was now in command. He locked up the chief's office before they left, his body would have to wait. He ordered every person who was in the building, except the dispatcher, to man any working vehicles, including their personal ones, and to drive to the crash site. They stripped supplies and gear from the inoperable emergency vehicles and went to the crash in a parade of mismatched cars and trucks. With no source of water nearby and most of the equipment inoperable, Sullivan doubted they would be putting out any fires. Saving lives would be the order of the day. He prayed that the new county hospital was in better shape than the new firehouse.

Sullivan decided that the area of the most possible survivors would be the school, so they headed there first.

There were nine survivors from the two second-floor classrooms that took the direct hit from the aircraft and all nine were severely injured. Five students and one teacher died in the first-floor classrooms, and twelve students were seriously injured. All the badly injured were taken to the county hospital, some of them in minivans and in the open backs of pickup trucks. Any vehicle that would run was placed into service. The rest of the students were carefully checked over by the paramedics. Those requiring medical assistance were taken into the church. Students who weren't hurt and lived within walking distance from school, were allowed to go home.

Laura was one of those taken to the church. She was examined by a paramedic who cleaned up her face, but basically did nothing but give her two white capsules and some water. Sullivan and four men started to follow the airplane's path of destruction from the school. There was a trail of debris and passenger's bodies leading from the school, across the field, and to where the supermarket once stood. He'd seen only one person alive amongst the terrible carnage in the field. A lone county sheriffs' officer was on the far side, bending over a lifeless looking body, most likely checking for a pulse.

Carl DeFries was uninjured and stayed busy, constantly checking on all the students. He brought Laura some bottled water to drink and told her he would get her home as soon as the paramedics were done using his truck. He

117

regularly took a ribbing from fellow faculty about "Old Blue," the old pickup he drove to school. But today, he was the only faculty member with a working vehicle.

* * * * *

Carl wasn't the only one with an old vehicle that was still running. Jack Hansen floored the old car as he pulled out of Ali's service station, panic ripping through his body. When Ali said a jetliner hit a school, it wasn't the word school that scared him. When the word "high school" was mentioned, most folks immediately thought of the big Melville High on the city's south side. The smaller St. Paul Lutheran, on the north side of town, was overshadowed by the big public school and most people didn't even know it existed. What hit Jack was Ali's mention of the "shopping plaza," that also got hit. There were no stores of any kind near Melville High. Though he would pass by his destination of the subdivision where his house was, Jack floored the car to go straight to Laura's school. On the way, he explained to Lynne that his daughter's school was the only high school near a shopping center and it had to be the one hit by the aircraft.

The mass of fire that was once the service station was what they saw first. It wasn't just the building that was burning, the entire corner was on fire. The building was already a charred shell, with the remains of a melted gasoline tanker truck sitting next to it. There was a huge pile of rubble, maybe 30 feet high, furiously burning where Connie's Beef should have stood. Mixed in with burning building materials was a tangle of automobiles and something massive with a row of window openings in it. Jack recognized it as part an airliner's fuselage. Where he and his daughter had enjoyed an Italian beef sandwich only two nights before, was now a huge pile of burning rubble, with the remains of a jet airliner skewered through it. Jay's Foods, the town's largest supermarket, was gone. Only the concrete slab, with a thin even pile of smoking debris strewn across it, remained. It was easy for Jack to imagine the giant airliner, with its massive wings, slamming into the rear of the market and clearing it off its foundation. It had plowed the entire building and all its contents across the parking lot and slammed into the restaurant. Everything was being incinerated in one massive heap.

With the large store leveled, it was hard to miss the path the fallen airliner had taken. Behind the store was an open field and parking lot, now strewn with bodies and debris leading from the school. The entire west section of the school's second story was gone; the rest of the building was a raging inferno. Jack stopped the car in the middle of the road, uncomfortably close to the burning gas station. They both got out and just stood there, feeling helpless. Laura's entire school was a mass of out-of-control flames, and no one was attempting to extinguish it.

118

Jack motioned Lynne back into the car, saying, "This heat is too dangerous for us to be standing here, let's get in the car and back up down the street. I have to figure out how we can get around the fire and over to the school." He backed the battered old car down the street, and when they were far enough away from the intense heat, he stopped and again they got out.

"What the hell." Jack stared at the open field. He hadn't noticed it before, but he and Lynne were the only ones there. Even at a small house fire, there were bound to be crowds of bystanders. Firefighting equipment and personnel should be everywhere; the whole area should be crawling with rescue people and police. He glanced at Lynne questionably, "The school's ball playing fields should be packed with people." Jack had his hands on his hips, as he surveyed the area. *"Where the heck is everyone?* It's got to be no later than three in the afternoon, and the only people I can see are those two guys standing next to that old firetruck over there." The next words he kept to himself. A sick feeling was taking over his whole body. *This is not good, Jack, not good at all. Where is my Laura?*

As far away as they were from the fire, it was still uncomfortably hot. He decided to try and drive over to where the old fire engine was parked. Hopefully he'd get some answers from the men who were standing there, then he'd head for home. He was praying that when he got home, he would find Ellen's car parked in the drive, and she and Laura safe inside the house.

Lynne got in the car first and closed her door. Before Jack got in the car, his attention was drawn to the Mandel's store, standing unharmed, next to the flattened supermarket. Mandel's wasn't touched, but Jack's heart fell lower to what it already was, when he saw what was parked next to it. Parked right in front of Mandel's, patiently waiting her return, was Ellen's little red convertible. Yesterday she had said she'd be doing the grocery shopping sometime the next morning. He recalled seeing her shopping list and adding batteries to it. Jay's Foods opened two hours before Mandel's…. shortly after the power went off. Where was Ellen?

HOME

CHAPTER 13

Jack jumped into the car and raced home. Flooring the car down the street, he explained to Lynne his fears of what it meant seeing his wife's car parked in front of Mandel's. He told her of his suspicions that Ellen was in the store shopping when the airplane hit the building.

Lynne tried to suggest that maybe she had been in the store, and because of what happened, couldn't start her car and walked home.

He assured her that wasn't the case. He explained to her about the store's hours and why his wife's car would be the only one in Mandel's lot. That Ellen would have purposely parked her car there because she did stuff like that all the time. She hated to have other cars parked next to hers, afraid her precious little car might get dented. Jack thought to himself, *Just another one of her stupid quirks. God help me....*

Leaving the crash site behind them, they sped off towards his subdivision. On the way there, it was hard to imagine something so catastrophic had just happened. Everything looked like any normal weekday summer afternoon. Lawnmowers must have not been affected by the EMP, as one lady was mowing her front yard.

They passed two guys out on the golf course, putting on the green. Jack gave them an incredulous stare. *They're playing a round of golf as if nothing had happened!* He turned onto his street and there was a kid shooting baskets on his front drive. *What the hell is going on?* He shot a look to Lynne as if saying, "What gives?"

Before he could even see his house, he spotted Laura's chemistry teacher's old blue pickup truck parked in his driveway. Quickly pulling into his drive, he was barely out of the car when Laura jumped into his arms. The only clean spot on her was her face. Like him, she was covered in filth from head to toe. Her nose was swollen and looked crooked. There were black and blue marks forming under her eyes. Her left pant leg was ripped wide open. His daughter looked a mess, but she was in his arms, safe and sound. Her chemistry teacher, Carl DeFries, was awkwardly standing right behind her.

It took Jack a moment before he could get his voice. Choked up, he looked back to Lynne, and then to Laura. Lynne was out of the car but, like Carl, awkwardly standing back.

"Laura, this is Lynne, she's my friend. We work in the same building. She helped me get home."

The two women looked at each other and Laura said, "Glad to meet you, Lynne. Thanks for helping my dad."

Lynne simply gave a short nod, saying, "Thank you, Laura. I'm pleased to meet you."

As if just realizing Carl was there, Jack said to him, "We were just at the crash site. It's horrible, the whole school is going up in flames."

Laura, who still had her arms around her dad said, "Did you see mom's car parked in front of Mandel's? She told me she would do her shopping first thing this morning at Jay's. She was really mad at me this morning, Dad—she was in that store. Dad, Mom—is dead."

Jack wanted to say, "*We can't be sure honey*," but he knew she was right. All he could say was, "Let's wait and see if she comes home...."

Laura stood there facing her dad, tears rolling down her swollen cheeks, shaking her head, "Karen is dead too, she's still in the school."

Jack could see Carl was starting to cry and was slowly nodding his head. Carl spoke for the first time, "Could have been worse, lots worse, Mr. Hansen. It was bad, we lost a lot of good kids and teachers." Carl shrugged his shoulders. "I am at a total loss as to what to say. We were in class and that plane just came down, sliding into the school. We barely made it out." Carl started shaking and tears were streaming down his cheeks. Everyone stonily stood there on the driveway, staring at each other and saying nothing. Each of them had gone through hell that day and their world had been ripped away from them. Yet as they stood there, a noisy old pickup truck drove by the house, and a little sparrow was on the front of the garage gutter cheeping away. Someone on the street behind them was mowing their lawn, and the smell of grilled hamburgers filled the air. In short, everything seemed so normal. As they stared at each other, all of them were thinking the same thing. "*This has to be a nightmare, please let me wake up....*"

Lynne was awkwardly standing about three feet behind Jack, never feeling so alone and out of place. As if reading her mind, Jack turned around. He looked at her, and then at her battered car, and then back to her. Both of her arms were crossed, held up tight against her chest. The adrenalin that had surged through her was clearly drained, and she looked it. He sensed defeat closing in on all of them, including himself. Like an old emergency generator suddenly coming to life, Jack's Marine Corps training kicked into gear. "All right. We *know* we're all in a world of shit, but we don't have time to be licking our wounds and feeling sorry for ourselves." He turned and faced Laura, "Sweetheart, we're going to

121

have to do something about that nose of yours." He tried to make light of it, "Your face is facing south, but your nose is pointing west." He turned to Lynne. "Lynne's a nurse, and I think she can fix it up for you."

Lynne felt hopeless, but managed a smile at Jack's south-west comment. She nodded her head and said, "Yes, of course, I'll fix you up like new."

Jack continued, "Lynne is in rough shape herself, and I owe my life to her. She's going to stay here with us."

Laura warmly smiled at her, saying, "We have a spare bedroom right next to mine. My mom would want you to stay. You've been hurt, I can help you clean up."

Jack glanced at Carl, who was still standing a few feet behind Laura. Although Carl looked like his mind was someplace a thousand miles away, Jack could see his eyes were concentrated on his daughter. Jack let go of Laura and walked over to Carl, stopping directly in front of him. They stared at each other for a moment before Jack said, "No one has to tell me that you're the one who is responsible for Laura being alive. Carl, I am indebted to you for the rest of my life." He hugged Carl and led all of them into the house. The meeting on the driveway had only lasted a few minutes, but in those few minutes, a bond was formed between them. It would make the difference between life or death in the months to come. They didn't know it yet, but the world as they knew it was changed forever.

Tiredly walking into his dark kitchen, it already looked different. He paused for a few seconds, before heading over to the refrigerator. Everything in it would already be getting warm. He was surprised as he opened it. Though the power had been off for at least eight hours, a cool gush of air met him as he pulled the door open. He grabbed a six-pack of beer that was on the shelf, saying, "I think all of us could use at least one of these.... He handed Laura a cold beer, saying, "Bottoms up, sweetie, this will help take the edge off of you. We're going to have a full day tomorrow, I guarantee it." Everyone took a beer and sat down around the kitchen table. Jack continued, "Lynne and I have seen things today that I've only seen while fighting in Afghanistan and Iraq, and we're only about eight hours into this shit. If this is how it starts, I can't imagine how it's going to be a week from now. From what I've seen today, unless this power comes on mighty quick, like by tomorrow—this country will be in a civil war." Jack's eyes bored into each of them sitting around the table. "I'm not shitting you, we're in for it."

Carl thoughtfully placed his beer down, unopened, and stared at it a moment before saying, "You really think it can get that bad, Mr. Hansen?"

"It already is." It was Lynne who spoke up. "Chicago will be totally destroyed by the end of the week, or sooner. You should see it, it's well on its way now."

Jack opened his bottle and took a long slug of the cold beer. Finishing it, he nodded his head, "Lynne's not exaggerating. Not just Chicago, but all of Cook County. By the end of the week, DuPage will get Cook County's spillover, and after some of the terrible things Lynne and I experienced today. I'm worried about DuPage County too." Jack grabbed another beer saying, "Right now, I wish we were clear out in the middle of a cornfield in Iowa, but we're not, so we'll have to make the best of it. Tomorrow morning, we have to wake up with the attitude that we are on our own, and no one, including the government, is going to come to our rescue." He looked at Carl and hesitated before saying, "I came to that conclusion about an hour ago. When I saw your school burning to the ground and no one was there trying to put it out, it made everything perfectly clear."

Lynne could see Laura's nose was going to need immediate attention and spoke up, "Laura, we're going to have to set your nose right away." She noticed Laura hadn't had any of her beer and continued speaking, while pointing at the bottle in Laura's hand. "I wouldn't have any of that. I have some powerful sedatives that I am going to give you and they don't combine with alcohol. I won't lie to you—setting your nose straight will hurt."

Laura glanced at Carl, saying, "Maybe Carl could take me to the hospital or to a clinic?"

Both Jack and Lynne looked at each other, shaking their heads, and in unison said, "No."

Lynne repeated, "No. No hospitals or clinics. After what your dad and I have witnessed today, we have to take care of ourselves. The hospitals are overwhelmed. They won't help you. I spent six years in the U.S. Navy as a Corpsman at the San Diego Navy Base, and I served onboard the aircraft carrier USS. Enterprise."

Jack was in the middle of tossing back a slug of beer and nearly choked on it. He looked at Lynne in astonishment, saying, "You were in the Navy?"

Lynne said, "Yes, and I've fixed lots of broken noses, mostly on drunken sailors," Looking at Jack she added, "And Marines." Lynne stood up. "What do you have around the house as far as medical supplies?"

Laura and Jack knowingly looked at each other. "My mom is one of those people who always worries about medical stuff. She has plenty of pills and supplies, you name it."

Jack added, "Her father was a general practitioner. She saved lots of his medical belongings, it's all packed away."

Lynne said, "Sounds like your mom is a real smart lady. Now let's get you cleaned up and I'll fix your nose. I want to look at your leg too. Let's go outside into the sunlight, so I can see you better."

They went outside together, Laura saying, "What about your eye and cheek, Lynne, it looks pretty bad. What happened to you?"

"I'm okay. I'm just tired. Long story short is I had a run-in with a car-jacker and your dad saved my life. You and I are going to be really sore for a few days. I'm going to take some of the same sedatives I'm giving to you. Both of us are going to be knocked out tonight."

Jack and Carl were sitting in silence at the kitchen table. As soon as the two women went outside, Carl started running the morning's tragic events over in his mind …. *Could I have saved more of my kids? Should I have done something different when the power went out?* Jack was doing the same thing. He was thinking about Ellen's car sitting in Mandel's parking lot, asking himself for one logical reason she could still be alive… *She had to be in that store when the plane hit. Why else would her car still be there? Unless maybe she was in the car when the plane hit…and watched the whole thing unfold and walked away unharmed. I know she wanted out of our marriage. Maybe she sees it as an opportunity to walk away… walk out of our lives forever.* Jack slowly shook his head. *No, no way would she just walk away without the money, no way.* So much had happened, it was hard to get everything straight in his mind. He had felt the same way after patrols in Iraq and Afghanistan. You'd get back to base, and thank God you're okay. Then you start thinking, over and over in your mind…. Jack pondered that last thought. It had been years since he was out of the Corps, and he still went over and over in his mind every inch of those patrols— especially that last one. *And here we go again…* He broke out of his thoughts and noticed Carl staring at him.

"Are you all right, Mr. Hansen? You looked far away just now."

Jack breathed out heavily saying, "Yeah, I suppose I was far away. Just trying to sort a few things out, that's all. So much has happened today. I guess you're probably doing the same thing." Jack took a swig of beer, swallowing it slowly. After a moment he said, "Carl, have you given any thought as to what you are going to do? With everything that has happened today, I haven't given tomorrow much thought myself. I've talked to you at school and after a couple games, but I really don't know much about you. What are you planning to do? I know you must have someplace else you should be right now. Where's your family?"

Carl shook his head, as he opened his beer. "I have no family, Mr. Hansen." Jack corrected him, "Call me Jack. Mister makes me feel old."

Carl nodded, "Okay, Jack it is. I don't have anyone, Jack. My parents died in an accident before I went off to college. I stayed with my aunt and uncle, but now they're gone too. My aunt just died last month and she never had children, so she left me her house and everything in it. I have no relatives, at least none that I'm in contact with. I don't even have a girlfriend. It's just me. I live alone in my condo."

Jack rubbed his hand thoughtfully on his chin. "I've seen some unimaginable shit happen today. I've killed people today, Carl, shot them dead."

124

Carl's eyes widened, and he just stared at Jack in disbelief. Jack continued. "My best friend died in my arms this morning, gunshot in the lung. He was killed by a little shit-head punk. I shot the kid in the face with his own weapon." Jack pointed outside to where the girls were and with a low voice said, "Lynne shot a thug too this morning. She blasted him right in the heart and he died on the spot." He added matter-of-factly, "I purposely had to drive that wreck of a car out there into some nut job wearing a business suit with a pink tie. Crushed his leg and left him lying on the Eisenhower. He's probably dead by now too."

Jack gestured with his thumb outside, towards the driveway, saying, "By the way, did you get a look at that busted up old car out there? It was in mint condition when we left Chicago this morning." Jack made a smirk, "Reminds me, I gotta count the bullet holes in it."

Carl stared at Jack speechless while Jack continued, "Lynne and I left a trail of dead bodies from here to Chicago. If someone wanted to make a movie of our day, it would be a non-stop action flick." Jack sat back in his chair and stretched out his legs. "Oh jeez, what a day. I haven't even wrapped my brain around the fact that my best friend is dead and probably my wife too.... God knows what tomorrow is going to throw at us."

Jack got up from the table and grabbed Laura's untouched beer. "Not a word of this to Laura, she's scared enough. I intend to erase this day from my mind and you will *never* hear me speak another word of it. I learned a valuable lesson today. Right now, I'm going to find a way to clean up a little and finish this beer. The girls are using bottled water I stored to wash up with. We have to conserve. I have an 80-gallon hot water tank down in the basement and about six 5-gallon jugs. That's about it for the drinkable water. Do you have any food or water at your condo?"

Carl shook his head no, saying, "Not much. I pretty much only buy what I need for the week. I eat out a lot. Never thought about something like this ever happening."

Jack was holding his bottle of beer on the table, absently looking at the label as if he was reading it. He took a short swig and sat the bottle down. "What you just said is exactly what I was thinking about. Nobody is prepared for this shit. I think most folks will expect our government to magically come to the rescue, and in two weeks this will be going down in the books as another 9-11. But I don't think so. I meant what I said earlier. I really do believe we're going to have a civil war after what I witnessed today. Everyone is going to be fighting their neighbors for every scrap of food that's left. I never thought things could fall apart this quick. I know you have your own place and all, but I would like you to consider staying with us if you want to, especially if you're all alone. It's best to band together. You think about it." Jack stood up and walked towards the back door, "Excuse me, I have to go outside and take a leak." He pointed to the refrigerator, "After I clean up, I'm going to grill us up some gourmet burgers and

125

sweet potato fries that are in the freezer. We might as well start using the frozen food up tonight, it'll be defrosting by tomorrow. We have fresh hamburger buns and tomatoes, too. I don't know about you, but I'm starved."

Carl got up from his chair, saying, "Jack, let me grill everything up. I like grilling. Just show me where everything is."

Jack made a sweeping gesture with his hand, motioning around the kitchen, saying, "Everything you need is here. I'd start with what's in the fridge and use that stuff up first. It'll all go bad if we don't use it up right away." He got up and gave Carl a "thumbs up "as he went out the back door, saying, "Glad you like to cook, because I'm bad at it. I burn everything. . . . The grill is in the shed, I'll go dig it out for you." Jack walked to the back of his lot and opened the shed door. Rolling the gas grill from the shed, he was glad he had replaced its gas cylinder the previous fall. It had a full cylinder, and there was another full one buried in the back of the shed somewhere. Lots of the folks he knew had gotten rid of their old bottle-type gas grills and had installed the newer grills that were tied directly into the city gas lines. Now with the natural gas supplies shut off, most of the big expensive grills would be worthless. As he rummaged through his shed, he remembered the small *rocket* camp-stove that he had made last year as a little Saturday project. He had seen Charlie make one and he had copied it. The total cost was under 15 bucks and it could do everything his gas grill did. Its fuel was small sticks and branches found around the yard, and he was glad he had made it. As he relieved himself in the bushes next to his shed, he thought of the two bathrooms in the house that were now pretty much useless. *The things we take for granted every day*. Not being able to use simple things like a flush toilet or microwave were going to radically change things. *Welcome to the 1860s.* After rolling the grill up to the house, he went back to the shed and pulled out two empty 5-gallon buckets and filled them each with water from one of his 55 gallon rain barrels. He recalled the many times he had chances to get more of those cheap 5-gallon plastic buckets from the home center but didn't. He now wished he had 20 more of them. As the water slowly flowed into the bucket from his rain barrel, he eyed his garden shed. *Might have to turn the shed into an old fashioned two-hole outhouse....*

Carl was digging out some frozen hamburger patties from the freezer and thought about what Jack had just said and knew he was right. He didn't have hardly any extra food at his condo, and he was on the fourth floor, with no water and no gas to cook with, even if he did have food. He seldom cooked at home because, being single, it was just easier to eat out. He had inherited his aunt and uncle's old house, and he had seen lots of canned goods in their pantry, but he didn't know how old the stuff was and if it was any good. He looked out the kitchen window and could see Jack going through his shed. He had been so wrapped up with everything that had happened at the school today, he hadn't given himself a thought. He'd have to consider what Jack said, and besides that, he really liked Laura. As he worked by himself in the kitchen, the images of his students trapped in the burning school kept flashing through his mind. If he took Jack up on his offer, he would be able to make sure nothing happened to Laura. He had seen Laura's friend, Karen, lying next to her, the electrical conduit pipe sticking through her neck, and couldn't get it out of his mind. Karen was a good girl, and he wished he could have saved her too. As Carl went through the freezer, he selected some other items to toss on the grill and his decision was made. *I won't let anything bad ever happen to Laura, never. I'll go home tonight to get some clothes, but tomorrow I'll come back here to stay until this thing blows over.* He knew it wouldn't be long for everything in the freezer to start defrosting, so he took out a full carton of hamburgers, two bags of fries, and a whole package of hot dogs. He figured the neighbors would want something to eat too and nothing would have to go to waste. He was opening the carton of hamburgers, when Laura walked into the kitchen. She was wearing a piece of white tape Lynne had placed across her now straightened nose.

As Carl eyed the tape, Laura said, "When Lynne said she'd nudge my nose back, I didn't think a little nudge meant that much pain." She shot a glance towards Lynne, who stood behind her, and said, "I sure hope those two pills you gave me work. Thanks for fixing me up, Lynne."

Lynne had tied her hair back and was wearing a red checked flannel shirt of Jack's. She placed her arm around Laura's shoulder and gave her a hug saying, "I've fixed broken noses in the same way on Marines. They usually cry, but you didn't." Both of the girls' faces looked terrible. Lynne had a full-blown shiner under one eye and Laura had one on both. Although they were hurting, they pitched in and helped with making the meal. Lynne found everything for a salad, while Laura helped Carl with the grill. Everyone sat down at the picnic table outside. Before digging in, Laura said a prayer of thanks for what they had, adding a tearful moment of silence for everyone they lost, followed by an amen. All of them sat there a few moments guiltily looking at their food. As hungry as they were, none of them wanted to be the first to eat.

Jack broke the spell, "We've all lost someone today, people we love and cared about. They're gone... to a better place. Life for us goes on and we can't change what happened or start thinking, 'We should have done this or should have done that.' Believe me, I've spent a lot of time in *that* rut. We have to move on and we need to be strong. We have lots of hard work ahead, because the horror of today will hit us hard tomorrow when it sinks in—and if we let it, it'll never leave. God bless this food, let's eat."

Lynne said, "Amen." She thanked them for helping her and for letting her stay with them. None of them talked during dinner. The silence around the table told Jack something. He would have to come up with a plan really quick to keep them all from thinking too much about what had happened, and more importantly, *what was going to happen?*

As the group ate in silence, all of them were buried in their own thoughts. Carl kept thinking about his students who had died in his classroom, and why didn't he have a scratch? Lynne was hoping there would be some possible way she could get back to her condo, to at least get some of her clothing and the two emergency bags her late husband had packed. She knew she couldn't stay with these people. Laura was concerned if she should somehow contact the Burger Chief and tell them she wouldn't be at work tomorrow night. She couldn't get Karen's eyes out of her mind…. The meal was tense, because it was heavy with dark thoughts and maybe some wishful thinking. Jack didn't break the silence. He figured all of them already knew the answers. As long as the power was out, nobody was going to be doing anything for a long time. It felt really late, but if the battery-operated clock on the kitchen wall was right, it was only five thirty. In a span of about nine hours, more than a life time of grief had happened to each of them. Jack excused himself from the table, he was worried too. He had a good hunch what tomorrow would bring and it was anything but good.

He went out to the garage and, just for the heck of it, tried to start his new truck. To his amazement, it popped right off, but died when he placed it in gear. He was encouraged that it at least started and thought, *maybe with a little tinkering around, it could be made operable.* He looked up at the garage ceiling, figuring that the second-floor bedroom above had somewhat shielded his car from the full effects of the EMP. *There should be thousands of cars buried in underground parking garages in Chicago that would be able to start.* Getting them out of the garages would be the problem, as the inner city was hopelessly gridlocked from end to end. Leaning against his new truck, he shook his head in disgust, *What a mess. How am I going to get us out of this one?*

He eyed the plants and lawn products that he and Ellen had purchased the day before and an idea struck him. Carl had mentioned before dinner that he liked to garden. Jack's mind started racing, jumping ahead like it often did, just like when he was back in the Marines. What he suddenly had in mind involved way more than six tomato plants. He walked to the front of his garage and was looking at his yard, unaware that Lynne had come up and was standing beside him.

"You're not much on yard work, are you Jack?" She was commenting about his full crop of dandelions that had taken over his front lawn.

Jack turned around and for the first time that day, managed a genuine smile, "No, I'm not. Never had much of a green thumb, but believe it or not, I was just standing here thinking about getting a garden in. Not a small plot either. Charlie next door, he has a huge garden rototiller. He usually has his whole backyard ready to plant by now. I can't do it by myself. I was talking to Carl and he told me he hasn't any family. Good looking kid like him doesn't even have a girlfriend. He lives on the fourth floor of a condo, all alone. I told him he could stay here with us if he wanted to." Jack's smile faded as he walked to the back of his garage and opened the rear door. He stood in the open doorway a few moments, his back to Lynne, staring at his empty backyard. Turning to face her, ahe said, "I know my Laura, and I think I got Carl pegged too. They'll both need a purpose to keep them going, and they'll need it right now, or they'll get to thinking how bad everything is. The same goes for you and me. All those looted stores we passed today. . . we're going to run out of food. We don't have much time. This house is on over an acre lot, and you're right, it's mostly weeds. We're going to change all that—starting tomorrow. If we bust ass this week and get the backyard turned over, we can get one heck of a garden in. I just have to come up with some seeds."

"Sounds like you think we're going to be in for a long haul. Do you really think this could go on for that long? Vegetables from a garden won't be available until late summer or fall."

"Yes, I do. You've seen how the store shelves were being stripped of food today. Come summer and way before fall is when people will be completely out of food. We'll have a nice harvest to take us through the winter, that's when we'll need it. There's something you don't know about me. I'm a prepper. Not to an extreme, but I believe in being prepared for the unexpected—and we're not prepared. Not for something like this.

Lynne nodded her head, "My husband, Bill, was one."

Jack was surprised at her answer. "Are you one too?"

"No, not really, but I went along with it. I don't know exactly how much he spent or the extent he went to. He worked for The Office of Homeland Security and knew things that the average person never thought about—or cared about for that matter. He thought it was important to be prepared and that was good enough for me."

Jack gestured next door to Charlie's house saying, "Old Charlie got me into it about three years back. Don't get me wrong, I'm not one of those extreme preppers. Ellen—well, let's just say she wasn't on board with it. My goal was at least a year's worth of food and water. I thought that was reasonable. I didn't make it with the water, but I have the food. I have a supply of ceramic water filters and some other things that most people would never think of. I don't know the extent of what Charlie went to, because he kind of keeps to himself over there, but he laid in plenty of supplies. He convinced me to install those 55-gallon rain barrels I got out back. With our water off, now I am glad I got them. Ellen and I had several arguments about it. Not just about the ugly rain barrels, but of the extra food I stockpiled. She knew Charlie put the bug in my ear about it. She went over and gave the poor guy hell."

At the mention of his wife, Lynne brought up something that was bothering her. "Jack, about me staying here. I'm not sure where I will go, but I think tomorrow I should look for another place to stay. It's not right that I stay here, especially with what you think has happened. . . to your wife."

129

Jack felt his shoulders sag. His arms suddenly feeling weak. As if he was searching for something small he had just he dropped, he gazed down at his garage floor. Her mention of Ellen being dead had unexpectedly taken all the steam out of him. Feeling deflated, he *was* searching. Searching for the right words to say to her. Words that would hide his sudden feeling of defeat.   Still looking at the floor, almost in a whisper, he said, "There *is* no place for you to go." Looking up, he took a half step towards her. Placing his hands on his hips, he was inches away from her. He felt like a school crossing guard blocking her. "There's no place for any of us to go, Lynne. We're all stuck here." He gestured towards the inside of the house. "This is it, welcome to the Hansen life boat. I think you know that already, especially if your husband worked for Homeland Security and he went to the extent to prep. That alone tells me everything. I'd love to be an optimist and say that in two weeks we'll be whistling a happy tune, but everything I see tells me it ain't gonna happen. I hope I'm wrong, but. . . I don't think so. The whole country could be looking like this."

Lynne said, "Don't you have faith in our government, not even a little?"

"Our government? Yeah, right, that's a laugh. You were in the United States Navy and I was in the Marines, so let's don't bullshit each other. Our government takes care of itself first. Your husband worked for Homeland Security, and *he* prepped. That says it all, don't you agree? So much for his faith in the government. Lynne, from the way you handled yourself today, I can see you are definitely one tough woman, but alone out there, how would you make it? I mean really? Think about it... Do you have any friends that live nearby? Anyone that could help you? Besides, you've seen the hospitals and have a nasty wound on your face. If that gets infected, it's all over and you know it. You should stay here and keep that wound clean. Let it heal." Jack paused for a few seconds, letting his last words sink in. "I'd like to think there's still a chance that my wife could come walking in. If you stay here with us, you'll find out that Ellen and I had our problems." Jack gestured to the front sidewalk. "I half expect to see her come walking down the sidewalk right now and start giving me hell about something... but she was in that store when the plane hit, I *know* she was. I'm trying not to think about her last moments and get down about it, or I'll be mentally sunk. Those people in that store. . . I don't think they ever knew what hit them. Death had to be instant. If I lose it,even for a little bit,I'll lose Laura. I can't let that happen. I like Carl, he's a tough kid, but he's alone and inexperienced. I know I'm sounding negative, but after what we've seen today, it's hard to be positive about anything." He paused for a couple seconds, "I know one thing though, you were a Navy nurse and I was a combat Marine. We have two young people with strong wills and strong backs. They just need guidance and, of more importance, *a purpose*. We all need a purpose. Let's stick together and with our skills and their youth, we'll get through this." He took a step back, pointing towards the garage ceiling. "Look, you can have that backroom upstairs all to yourself. We'll get you some clothes that fit and anything else you need. If by some miracle Ellen returns, nothing will change. We're going to all pull together." Jack bent forward a little, lowering his head to her eye level. "What do you say, Lynne, we made a good team today, don't you think?" He saw her eyes well up and a tear roll down her cheek....

Taking a deep breath, she quickly exhaled, her decision made. "Thank you, Jack. I 'll stay, but only if Laura agrees too. When things get better. . . you'll help me get back home, right?"

Jack nodded his head, " Of course I will."

" I don't want to be a burden on you, and I don't want Laura to think I am moving in on her mother. She's in shock and it'll be terrible on her when it sinks in."

He gave her arm a light squeeze, "That's another reason I'd like you to stay, she likes you, I can tell. You'll be good for each other." He gestured his thumb towards the house next door. "I have to talk to some of the neighbors before it gets dark. I want to see what's going on. Will you be all right if I leave you alone for a bit?"

Lynne nodded her head and Jack started off down the driveway. She watched him leave, and after he had gone about 20 feet, he turned his head back and saw that she was still standing there, her eyes following him. Their eyes met and Lynne softly said, "Be careful, Jack."

THE FIRST STOP

CHAPTER 14

Jack's first stop was Charlie's house. He knocked on the front door, immediately hearing Charlie's raspy voice, "Be right there." Opening the door, Charlie shook Jack's hand like he hadn't seen him in years. Grabbing Jack's elbow, he pulled him inside saying, "Man, you look terrible." Max and Toots started jumping up on Jack, wanting their usual playful pats, but Charlie shooed them down, saying, "Let me put the dogs away, Jack, so we can talk. Why don't you grab yourself a seat in the study and get yourself comfortable? I'm getting myself a cold beer, you want one? You look like you could use one."

Jack told Charlie, "No," but the old man came back with two ice cold ones anyway and handed one to Jack. The old man sat down in a comfortably worn leather recliner opposite of Jack. He opened his beer, immediately taking a quick swallow. Reaching to his side, he grabbed his pipe off an ashtray stand next to the chair and started packing it with tobacco.

Jack popped opened his beer, but unlike Charlie, he took a long, cool swig. The beer was cold and good. He could have easily downed it. Instead, he lowered the now half empty can, resting it on his lap. Neither one of them said a word for a few moments.

Charlie lit his pipe, taking a couple long puffs, firing it up. His mind was obviously far away, but he was first to speak. "Bad?" he asked.

Jack solemnly nodded his head. "Really bad, Charlie. Ellen's missing and we fear the worst. I think she was in Jay's Foods this morning when the jet crashed into it." Jack hesitated, and bit his lower lip. "What the hell... I know she was in it."

"Oh my God, Jack, I'm so sorry." Charlie shook his head and continued, "I feared that. I saw her leave this morning. I know she usually goes grocery shopping early on Mondays. Jack, I don't know what to say. What are you going to do?"

Jack took another drink, swallowing slow. Still holding the cold can to his lips, he paused and mumbled, "What a terrible day," before finishing it. Lowering the empty can to his lap, while partially crushing it, he said, "I'm not sure what I'm going to do. I'm in shock. . . I guess. So much happened, so quick. I lost my best friend, Don. He died this morning right in front me. He was shot by some punk-assed kid, and there was nothing anyone could do. Also lost Sarah. You remember me telling you about her, don't you?" Charlie remained silent, slowly nodding his head. Jack was fingering and spinning the top of the smashed beer can on his lap. "She had a heart attack and died right in front of me in my office this morning. She's still there, covered up with her quilt, lying on the floor by her desk. I couldn't even notify her husband."

Charlie interrupted, "I am so sorry, Jack, but thank God Laura's okay. I saw her in the backyard grilling with that boy. He came over and offered us some chow, but we had already eaten. Real nice kid there..."

At the mention of Carl, Jack explained to Charlie that he was Laura's chemistry teacher and how he rescued her out of the burning school. They sat in silence for a couple minutes. Jack exhaled deeply and said, "I could have lost Laura when the plane hit the school. Other than a broken nose and some scrapes, she's all right. And for that, I will be eternally grateful to Carl. You asked what am I going to do? *We're going to survive this shit, Charlie*, that's what we're going to do. Thanks to you and your advice, I have plenty of preps. Maybe not enough, but what the hell, is there ever enough? I'll tell you something, from what I've witnessed today, 90% of the public has nothing for a backup plan, and no extra food. I've already got a plan, Charlie, and have at least a year's worth of food for four people. I just wish I would have put in a garden, but that's neither here nor there, but it's still not too late."

Charlie took a couple long pulls from his pipe and let out a large puff of smoke. Thoughtfully lowering his pipe to his lap saying, "What can I do to help you, Jack?"

"I'd like to borrow your rototiller tomorrow, Charlie. I want to plant a big garden. If not, we're going to run out of food."

Charlie took another drag of his pipe. Setting it in the ashtray, while giving Jack a questioning look. "A big one, huh? Sounds good."

"Yeah, more like a small farm." Jack held up his hand saying, "Right now, though, how about you filling me in on how you and Dottie are doing. I know you probably think I'm nuts talking about a garden with what's happened and all. I'll explain it to you tomorrow. Tell me what have you heard and what's going on around here?"

Charlie took a healthy drink of beer, letting out a small out a belch. Lowering the can onto his knee, the old man didn't say anything for a few seconds. Slowly shaking his head, he said, "Lots of people say if something terrible, like nuclear war ever goes down, they'd just rather die. Well, we know that's a load of horseshit. Everyone wants to survive. I've been ready for a long time for the shit to hit the fan. Figured it would have happened years sooner. Not necessarily this EMP thing, but I thought something would come along to screw everything up. Never thought about getting old though. By the way, your garden

133

idea is clear thinking, and clear thinking will save your ass. I hear people are already looting the stores, that figures. That's short thinking by assholes. You 'd expect that kind of stuff later, not right off the bat. I'll tell you something, there are low people in high places who knew something like this was going to happen. They've been counting on it and they've planned for it. They might have even caused it. Everybody has always got their eyes glued to California and what the loony left is doing. They count on us watching the circus but missing the show. We've got some really evil people on this planet running things, and they're buried deep. They figure culling three quarters of the human population is the only solution. Of course, they'll come out of it fine, and keep enough of the little people for their serfs. They want to kill people off, any way they can. That's the bottom line. There's all kinds of ways they can do it. Cull the population and save the planet for their own private playground. If you ever talk about that kind of stuff, people shut their ears to you. They think you're some kind of conspiracy nut. Some folks do think about it, but they shove it to the back of their mind and believe if something really bad ever happens, they won't be around afterwards anyway, so why worry? I think most folks figure that, you know? Why should they worry about it, much less prepare? Fact is, most people do survive any kind of catastrophe, even a nuclear war. Unless you're right under ground zero, the majority of people will survive... until they run out of food and water. After they pull their head out of their ass and realize they survived, they'll be the first ones out looting and killing their neighbors for a meal. If I am right, Jack, and you know I usually am, three months from now half the population will be dead from starvation. A year from now, this country will have the population it did when Washington was elected president, and maybe a lot less. Only then will the rotten bastards that caused it come out of their holes. Just like rats."

Charlie finished his beer and slowly folded the can in between his hands. Their eyes locked, staring at each other for a second. Charlie slowly shook his head in disgust. "The Thompsons, next door...they were supposed to be on a plane coming back this morning from Florida. I've been getting their mail for them. They called me on Saturday and said they'd be landing at about 9:00 am. I'm sure their plane went down somewhere between here and Florida." Charlie stoked his pipe up, blowing out a cloud of blue smoke, then continued, "Bob Daniel stopped by here earlier and told me what was going on. He didn't know their names, but he heard two little kids from our subdivision are in critical condition from a car wreck this morning. Jane Pierce, who lives near the end of the block and is a good friend of Dottie's, had a heart attack. She more than likely would have survived... if an ambulance had only showed up."

Charlie took a couple more puffs from his pipe. He hesitated, looking Jack in the eyes. "We were worried sick about you kids, Jack. I didn't breathe a sigh of relief until I heard the dogs yapping when you pulled into your drive."

Jack said, "What about you guys?"

134

Charlie fingered his pipe, letting out a long sigh. "As good as can be expected, I guess. I can't do a thing about any of this, and I am too old to worry."

Jack interrupted, "Charlie, if you need anything at all..." Charlie held up his hand, stopping Jack mid-sentence, slowly shaking his head.

"I am an old man. I always knew the shit would hit the fan someday, but I thought it was going to happen years ago, when we were still young. You can prep all you want, but if you're old and got serious medical problems, you're pretty much done for, and that's where we're at. Pretty much done for." Charlie took another puff of his pipe, "Right now, it's you and Laura that I am worried about." The old man's eyes shifted to a group of framed photos that were hanging on the wall behind Jack. "Something that Dottie and I never told you and Ellen. We had a daughter who died. That's her picture behind you, on the right."

Jack turned around to see a smiling little dark-haired girl standing next to a much younger and thinner Dottie. He'd seen the photo on previous visits. He knew the tragic story about their daughter, but since neither Charlie nor Dottie ever talked about her, he never brought it up.

Now it was his turn for a loss of words. All he could manage was, "I'm so sorry, Charlie."

"That's all right, it was a long time ago. She was our little girl. God, I loved her... I loved her so much... Someday when we have some time, I'll tell you about it. It's a long story *that isn't over yet*." Charlie fell silent for a moment, crushing the can flat "That's when Dot started gaining all that weight, after Linda's death. When we got married, Dottie was such a skinny little thing." Charlie weakly smiled. "You asked how we're doing? Well, let me tell you. I'm enjoying a good smoke and talking to a good friend. That counts for a lot. Got a couple of good doggies in there that, from the sound of them, will have to be let out soon. I've got a food supply that would rival a supermarket and have an endless supply of fresh water. I got a propane freezer and fridge, so I'll have plenty of ice-cold beer, at least until the propane runs out. The only problem is that we're old, too old to give a shit anymore. I'm a little past due on getting my insulin supply, and don't have much left; that's my own stupid ass fault. My ole' foot isn't doing too good lately, but what else is new? Because of her emphysema, Dot is on that oxygen machine most of the time. And, of course, pretty soon that piece of crap will be cutting out because my solar panels aren't big enough to keep it going all night. Sometimes she can do without it, but If she gets really bad, I'll have to break out my generator. She's got two little portable oxygen tanks left and the better part of a big one, and that's all." He gestured with his thumb to the back of the house where his disabled brother lived. "Ted? He's already in bed. Dementia is a great thing, Jack. He doesn't have a care in the world, and his health is failing every day. He's pretty much stopped eating, and like I told you the other day, he was about to get a feeding tube put in. Fat chance of that now. We hired that nurse to come in and help us, but now that isn't going to happen. Ah, what the hell, I might as well tell you. I didn't like her anyway, I let her go. She was useless as tits on a boar hog. She started rooting around in my stuff. Nosy gal, and liberal as all hell, one of those *Green Deal* nuts. She didn't like my guns either."

The dogs started barking and Charlie got up. "Excuse me a second, Jack, I have to let these doggies out."

Jack got up with him, but stayed in the study. He noticed Charlie favored his left foot as he walked to the back of his house.

Old Charlie was back a few seconds later and went directly to a gun cabinet that was next to his desk in the study. He produced a key, unlocked the squeaky, oak framed glass door, and stood back, pointing to an ancient looking double barrel shotgun. "Ever show you this one, Jack?" Jack shook his head, but of course Charlie had. Charlie was repeating himself more and more. Jack let him go on, knowing the old guy loved to tell his stories, especially about his gun collection.

Charlie carefully took out the old shotgun, saying, "I've got several of these real old ones. This one's a 10-gauge. It's pre-teens and it takes them old, long brass shells. I reloaded a box of spent ones I bought at a gun show with bird shot. I was pretty loaded myself, if you know what I mean, when I reloaded them. I got them laying around here somewhere, but I've decided not to shoot with them. I saw an old double barrel about the same age as this one blow apart last fall. The guy shooting it lost two fingers. I think the shells were overloaded with modern powder and it wasn't a pretty sight. At my age, I don't want to risk it. You know, get close enough, even with birdshot, you could bring down anything with this old boy, but it might take part of the barrels with it. That's what makes guns fun though, huh?" Charlie turned around, and the smile he had a moment before was gone. He placed his right hand on Jack's shoulder, saying, "Really sorry about Ellen."

Jack got up, gave Charlie a hug and turned to leave, but Charlie stopped him. "Jack, one more thing, if the worst happens, you come over and help yourselves. I never told you kids, but you guys are in our will. Kind of wanted to surprise you when we kicked the bucket. The place is all yours, Jack. It's all legal."

Jack turned around saying, "Jeezz Charlie, don't talk like that. Commonwealth Power Company will surprise us yet, they'll probably have the power on by the end of the week. The Illinois National Guard will clean this mess up and things will be fine.

As Jack went out the door, he heard Charlie ask, "Jack, did you ever hear ducks fart under water?"

Jack shook his head, "No, not lately Charlie."

THE WALK

CHAPTER 15

There still was plenty of daylight left and it was a beautiful spring evening. Jack was tired and debated whether he should still take a quick walk around his block before heading in for the evening. He looked down his short street and saw Al Lange briskly coming towards him. As he approached, Jack could see Al was agitated and out of breath. "Jack, I was down at the crash site. Please tell me that's not *Ellen's* car down there in front of Mandel's?"

"It is, Al. Ellen was inside Jay's doing her shopping when the plane hit. We're sure of it."

Al looked up at the sky and back to Jack, "I knew it, Jack, I just knew it, but hoped it wasn't so. I don't know what to say to you, Jack. I am so sorry. Is Laura all right?"

"She's fine, Al, a little banged up is all. We have a friend staying with us, her name is Lynne. I am not going to tell you about my day, Al. I 'll fill you in sometime later. Let's just say besides Ellen, I lost some good friends today and somehow—I'll have to deal with it. To tell you the truth, Al, I don't know what to feel sad about most, so much happened today. It was crazy."

"You're in shock, Jack, that's what it is. It's really going to hit you later. I think we're all in shock, it's a damn nightmare. I just want to tell you that Lois and I are here for you buddy, anything you need... Did you guys eat yet?"

"Yeah, we ate, Al, thanks. So, tell me, how was your day? You and Lois doing all right?"

"I think my day was nothing compared to yours, Jack. I can't imagine what you're feeling, losing Ellen. Lois is fine. I've just been dealing with assholes all day. I won't burden you with my problems."

Jack shook his head. "No, Al, no burden at all. Let me know what's going on." Shaking his head, Al continued, "I was at the store when the power went off. We had a big sale in the meat department and the guys were still putting the product out, when all of a sudden, the stinking power blew. Thought it was no big deal because we've got one hell of a generator. We had the usual early birds in

138

the store, some of them with their carts fully loaded. When the power didn't go back on, we just locked the place up. We let the folks who were in the store walk out with what they had in their carts, absolutely free. I mean, the registers didn't work, no lights, no nothing. What the hell could we do? That kinda stuff builds customer loyalty anyway and is just good business, so you would think, right? Anyway, we were letting some customers out of the store and trying to stop others from coming in when things went downhill really quick. A couple of people who only had a few things in their carts saw other folks walking out with way more free shit than they had, so they got pissed off. They wanted to grab more items and walk out, like its supermarket sweep or something. Then some asshole barges his way in. I mean right off the bat people gotta be assholes. I got two baggers and the cart chaser trying to control the front door and this jerk punches the daylights out of one of them."

Al took out a pack of cigarettes and pulled one from the pack. Putting it between his lips, he lit it up and took a long drag. He looked up at Jack and then down at the ground, letting out a quick exhale, saying, "Sorry, Jack, I know my day was nothing compared to yours."

Jack motioned to Al's cigarette, "Mind if I have one of those?"

Al fingered the pack out of his shirt's top pocket and offered Jack a cigarette, but withdrew it slightly. "You sure, Jack? You been off for quite a while."

Grabbing the cigarette, Jack replied, "Yeah, I know. Let's take a walk towards your place, you can finish your story."

Jack put the cigarette between his lips and Al lit it up. He took a long, hard drag on it as they slowly walked down the sidewalk.

Jack's next-door neighbors to the north, were Jake and Ronnie. They had a little boy named Bobby. There was no sign of life as he and Al walked by their house. Jake's truck wasn't in the driveway, and none of Bobby's toys were outside. Jack hoped they were safe. They walked along in silence, smoking their cigarettes for a few moments, before Al continued were he had left off.

"Anyway, we finally get the store cleared of customers, but we still got people out front wanting in. We're praying the power goes on, because all the stuff in those open freezers in the frozen aisles will turn to mush, lickety- split. It gets to be about ten o'clock and we've got quite a crowd of people out front, and one of them smashes the front door glass." Al stopped for a moment, facing Jack. "Jack, I'll tell you, I have never seen anything like it. Remember them riots in L.A? In that town, what the hell was it called, Watts? That's what it was like. The whole store went up for grabs and most of the help left, running for their lives. Jack, it was mayhem. The store that I've spent 22 years of my life in, was stripped to the bones by lunch time. Some asshole even stole my personal lunch that I made for myself this morning, a lousy pastrami sandwich." Al Paused and disgustedly shook his head. "It was unbelievable—then, just when I think it can't get any worse, some hillbilly with a rebel flag on his piece of shit old truck plows right in through one of the front windows. What an asshole. He ruptures the gas tank on the hunk of shit, and Star Foods, that has faithfully served this town for 32 years—is now a burnt-out shell. It's probably still burning. There were no firemen or water to put it out. I'd like to know where the cops were, because I never saw any. The other thing that really fries me is, how come that jerk's rusted out piece of shit was still running, and my new car won't?"

Jack didn't feel like explaining everything he knew about an EMP attack to Al and wanted to change the subject. Al was the easily excitable type and ordinarily it made him fun to be around. He was also the type of person who, because of his outgoing personality, could get things done. It was Al's idea for the annual Fourth of July pulled pork party and the Memorial Day block party. He also held a New Year's Eve party every year for anyone on the block who wanted to attend.

They reached the corner where Al's house was and he finished telling Jack of his terrible day. Jack asked him what he planned to do.

Al flicked his cigarette into the street and thought about it for a second. He shrugged his shoulders, "My plans? I always got plans, Jack, you know that. My store is gone and I guess so is my job. I heard that two of our other stores got hit really hard too. Time to retire, I guess. Red Kelly, the general manager, stopped at my store before I started the long walk home. He gave me a ride in that old sedan delivery truck of his. Thank God too, or I would still be on the road walking. He filled me in on what he intended to do with our inventory of frozen goods.

We've got three other stores that didn't get damaged, and everything in them that's frozen is going to defrost and turn to shit. With no power, by this time tomorrow, half the food in every grocery store in the state will be garbage. With everything bar chipped and coded, we need a computer to sell the stuff, and once it's defrosted, that wouldn't happen anyway. He told me he went around to every store this afternoon. He wants any of the stores' employees who can get in to work tomorrow, to try and make it in. Somehow, without starting another riot, he wants to empty the stores of all the perishables. We can take home as much as we want. His idea is to just bring it all out to the front parking lot. We gotta get rid of everything, or we'll have a rotten mess on our hands. We don't have dumpsters big enough and won't be able get any hauler to take it to a landfill if we did. He figures if it's all free, folks will eagerly haul it away for us. This will be a first for us, we never give stuff away that's expired or defrosted. The company figures someone could get sick and sue us. God knows how many thousands of pounds of good food in this country are just wasted every day because of bullshit like that... stinking lawyers. Anyway, I'm going to our Naperville store. I worked with the manager of that store back in the day when we were just a couple of stock boys. I'll put the top down on old Nancy and load her up with all she can carry. That old girl runs great. I'm getting Jerry Billings and his kid to follow me in their old pickup trucks. Gonna get whatever charcoal, bottled gas and dry ice they got too. I ain't getting just any old chow here either, I'm grabbing steaks, shrimp, lobsters, and all the pork tenderloins and slabs of ribs we can carry. We'll make a few trips, if we can. I'd like to get a load of hamburger and buns too. With the top down on the convertible, I'll get a really big haul. I guarantee you, Jack, we'll have the biggest and best cookout this town has ever had. Everybody on the block will eat like damn kings this week."

They stopped in front of Al's house, and he said, "As bad as it looks, Jack, this shit will be just another one for the history books a month from now. If you think about it, this could be a good time to do some things you couldn't normally do."

"Like what?"

"Opportunities, Jack, they abound anytime there's an abrupt change. Think about it."

"I already have, Al, I'll catch you later."

Jack left Al and continued his walk around the block. It didn't surprise him at all that Al was already planning a party and was so optimistic about the future. He didn't share the little guy's optimism, though, and had two nagging thoughts. *What's everyone on the block going to eat next week and more importantly, the week after that?*

As he approached the corner, he got the feeling he was being watched. With a quick glance across the street to the corner house, he saw her. Al's reclusive neighbor was standing on her front porch. Just as Al had described her, she was wearing a military style camo t-shirt, and was talking to a petite blond-haired woman, also wearing a camo-t. Out of the corner of her eye, he knew she was watching him. Before he turned the corner, he stopped, took one last exaggerated drag on his cigarette, then flipped it into the street in her direction. He paused long enough to see her take a quick drag of the cigarette she was smoking and flick it towards him. Jack continued on around the corner, knowing her eyes were still on him. She wanted to talk to him, he could feel it. He wanted to get to know this reclusive woman and her blond-headed friend. The way she flicked her cigarette butt at him told him a something about her—and he liked her already.

It seemed like everyone was out in front of their houses, mostly standing in groups, talking in hushed tones. It wasn't hard to gauge how people felt. There was definitely a worried edge to every conversation. Some of the people he knew, and most of them he'd seen at least once before in the small neighborhood. Two women were embracing each other, both were crying. They had lost someone close, he could gather that, and he decided he was done telling his tale of woe. Unless someone specifically asked about Ellen, he was going to keep his problems to himself.

He had walked halfway around the block without saying much to anyone, other than a casual greeting, and was on the next street almost directly behind his own house. The street was about a block long and had houses only on one side of it. Across the street was open farmland that stretched for at least a mile. Except for the last couple years, the farm had always been planted with corn or beans. Now it was spring planting time and it sat unplanted, waiting for a developer's bulldozers to plow it under for good. He slowed his stride and paused, looking out over the open fields. The events of the day had brought his spirits down, but the sight of the old farm and knowing it had a stay of execution from the developers made him suddenly feel good. He stopped in the middle of the sidewalk and eyed the vacant farm. There was a slight breeze out of the northeast, carrying the smells of the openness to him. He thought about all the other farms across the Midwest that would go unplanted this spring. Everything was going to come to a halt and get a long overdue rest.

The word "famine" slid into his mind as he gazed across the empty farmland. It was while he was looking at the open, unplanted fields that his idea of planting a garden took on an urgent tone. *The empty field was telling him something….*His thoughts were interrupted by a certain irritating neighbor whose house unfortunately backed up to his. The guy was walking up to him and Jack cursed to himself for stopping in front of his house. Barry and Liz lived behind him, and they were trouble. They had a young son, about 12 years old, named Dwayne, who would probably grow up to be just like his dad. As Barry approached him, two words came to mind, *Oh shit*. Jack usually was able to avoid them, as their yards were separated by a six-foot stockade fence. He was glad they lived behind him and not next-door. Every time he had a conversation with Barry, the man had some kind of complaint. Liz was worse and the kid was just like his dad, a little know-it-all. The other thing that irked him about Barry was that he never let you get a word in. If you started to tell him some-thing, he would interrupt and change the subject. He would never ask, "How are you doing?"

Jack cussed again under his breath as Barry hurriedly approached him. He didn't enjoy talking to Barry on a normal day, much less today.

"Hey—Jack, good to see you. You got a book of matches or a lighter I could borrow? Starting to get dark out. Liz has a couple of candles, but we have no way to light them. They're scented, vanilla I think, at least they'll smell nice and us provide us some light tonight."

Shaking his head in disbelief, Jack sarcastically said, "You don't keep any matches or at least a lighter in the house? And you only have two scented candles?"

Catching Jack's sarcasm, Barry took on an exasperated look and placed his hands on his hips saying, "Maybe you like breathing cancer-causing nicotine into your lungs, and God knows what else from those smelly campfires you have Friday nights, but not us. We normally have no need for matches."

Jack was in no mood for Barry's bullshit. He now knew who had complained to the county about his fire-pit and weekend campfires with Charlie. He was tired and didn't feel like getting into it with him, so he let it go. "I'll put a couple books of matches in a plastic bag and toss them over the fence for you when I get home. How's that?"

Barry smiled, "Thanks, Jack. Hey, we're in real trouble here, huh? That jet come crashing down and smashing into that school and all, good Lord. Those poor kids in that school never had a chance. Sure glad Dwayne, goes to the public school." Jack wanted to get away from the man, but Barry was blocking him and talking up close to his face. He backed up a step, hoping Barry would get the hint, but he only moved closer and continued to talk. Barry was a *close* talker. Jack recalled this was another reason he disliked the man.

Smelling garlic, Jack said, "Italian night?"

Missing the sarcasm, Barry replied, "No, that was last night, I did have some leftovers for lunch though. Except for picking up Dwayne at school, we've been home all day. Everybody is complaining about their cars not running, but our old van is fine. I hear Jay's Foods really got clobbered by that plane; too bad, they really had good produce. Really feel bad for those folks who were inside it."

Jack had enough, so he tried to break away from Barry, "I have to go Barry, I had a rough day and want to get to bed."

But Barry didn't miss a beat, "I hear Mandel's is okay. That's good, because Liz and I are going over there tomorrow after we go grocery shopping. Liz wants to use up her Mandel's Cash, probably will stop at Green's too." Gesturing to his next-door neighbor to the east, Barry started again. "Hey, did you hear that jerk, Rick, last night? Sunday night for gosh sakes. Him and his atheist biker friends were revving up those choppers, or whatever they call them, at ten o'clock at night. I'm calling the sheriff's police next time."

"Barry, shut up. I've had a really bad day, and I'm not in the mood to hear any of your bullshit complaints. Try not to burn yourself with the matches."

Barry said nothing more as Jack walked past him. He just turned and stared. When Jack was out of earshot, he slowly shook his head and mumbled, "Lotta nerve."

Jack kept walking and regretted getting in a conversation with the man. He should have known better. He wondered how the guy could be so ignorant about what had happened. *Going to Mandel's and Green's in the morning. The idiot doesn't have a clue.* It had been such a terrible day. By the time he reached the next corner, the annoyance of Barry was already forgotten and he was mad at himself for not staying home with Laura. Disgusted, he asked himself, *Jeez Jack, your daughter just lost her mother and best friend. What are you doing walking around the block? Get home!* As he approached the end of the block, he recalled Al telling him about the reclusive fellow that lived in the corner house. Like Al's two reclusive neighbor girls, Al thought this guy was also acting suspicious. The guy was standing on his front porch, smoking a cigarette and wearing a camo-t shirt, same as the girls. Jack felt the man's eyes on him as he approached his house. He was almost in front of him when he realized that the guy wasn't looking at him. He was staring at something beyond him, something that was slowly moving out in the empty cornfield. Jack turned to see what the fellow was looking at. It was getting dark, but he could just make out two deer that were standing by the fence line of the field. Jack turned his head away from the deer and looked directly at the fellow on his porch, but the guy made no effort to greet him. He just eyed Jack suspiciously as he came nearer. *Almost as if this guy and that Joan are standing sentry duty*, Jack thought, *keeping a wary eye on their neighbors... I'm going to try something.*

When he was passing almost directly in front of the man, Jack paused and greeted him, giving a short, but crisp salute. Just as Jack suspected, the fellow straightened and promptly returned it. Jack said, "I'm Jack, semper fi. I live on the next block."

The guy said, "Oh yeah, sorry, I didn't recognize you at first. I know who you are, you're Jack. Thanks for your service. Glad to finally meet you. I'm Ken Martinez, I live here with my son, Ben. Your place has the Marine Corps flag out front, and your house backs up to that nosey guy.... you're lucky."

Jack had started walking again, but stopped and shook his head saying, "You mean Barry? He just asked me if I had a book of matches. He wanted to light a vanilla-scented candle for some light tonight."

Ken let out a laugh and looked down, shaking his head. He sarcastically said, "Yeah, that sounds like him. He asked me a couple weeks ago about starting a neighborhood watch. Whippy twang...."

Jack shook his head. "A neighborhood watch, huh? First time I've heard about that. Are you going to join it?

Ken replied, "Are you kidding me? No—I don't think so, they're not my type." Jack nodded his head, "Yeah, I hear you there. You'd probably get to wear a badge though."

Ken's house wasn't just the last house on the block, it was the last house in the subdivision. The vacant farm was to the north, directly across the street from him. The side of his house faced a couple acres of woods, flanked by the Fox river to the east.

Jack pointed out into the open field, "I got a feeling deer will be in short supply soon, just like candles and matches." Then he added, "Your place is like the last outpost here."

Ken replied, "Yeah, I got the back door all right."

Before Jack continued his walk, he said, "And Joan and her friend, they have the front?"

Ken replied, "Yeah, they sure do. Jo and Kathy are good people."

Jack hadn't taken two steps before Ken added, "And you and old timer got the middle. You know, I think it's going be just like Fort Apache here soon, let's hope it isn't the Alamo."

Jack replied, "Yeah, it's secluded back here, a good place for a last stand. Nice meeting you, Ken. I think we have some things in common. I was thinking of starting something like a neighborhood watch myself, but I don't have any badges to give out."

Ken pulled aside his loosely-worn flannel shirt, revealing a shoulder holster with a semi-automatic in it. "Who needs fucking badges?"

Jack Laughed, "Heh, heh. I like that. Hope we'll be getting together to talk some more."

Ken took out a cigarette, but before lighting it, he said, "Real soon, I would expect, real soon. Nice meeting you, Jack."

"Likewise."

Jack was on the last leg of his walk with one more corner to round and he would be home. He had passed several houses that had gas generators running, the hum of them echoing between the homes. He was glad he had met Ken and knew an alliance was in the making. The sun had gone down and it was pitch black. It was eerie to see the off and on glare of flashlights, as people went from room to room inside of their darkened homes. He wondered how many of them had extra working flashlights, let alone a large supply of batteries. The houses that had generators running were easy to pick out, as they were the only ones that had multiple lights on. It looked like their neighbors had run extension cords to their generators. The neighboring houses all had at least one light on. Other than the few scattered lights, the neighborhood was hauntingly dark. Jack and Charlie both had portable Honda generators and had previously discussed a situation like this. They had both decided that lights were not a necessity and would run their generators only if they absolutely had to. He wasn't sure how much gas Charlie had stored up, but expected he had plenty. Charlie still had a big old oil tank in his basement from the days when he had oil heat, and he wouldn't put it past the old guy to have filled it with gasoline. Jack had six, 5-gallon cans of gasoline stored in the back of his shed. He would leave it there and pretend he didn't have it. Neither he nor Charlie would waste their precious fuel on running their generators for the luxury of lights when a candle would do. Approaching Charlie's house, he could make out the glow of one dim light in his den. Charlie was smart and had four large solar panels on his roof. Jack had bought a small one last fall, but hadn't taken it out of the box yet.

Not wanting to get a lecture from Ellen, he had stuck it out of sight in the basement.

His house was coming up and although it was dark, he could see someone standing front of it. Whoever it was started quickly walking toward him and it was a woman. She was alone and it was so dark, he couldn't see her face, but as she got closer... her height and the way she walked...Nearly bumping into her, he said, "*Ellen?*"

She said, "Sorry, I didn't mean to startle you. It's so dark—I can hardly see."

Jack hesitated and he sensed he frightened her. "No, I'm the one who is sorry, I... I thought you were someone else. Yeah.... it's crazy with no lights on. Have a good night."   Feeling like a fool, he continued walking. *God, I really thought it was her.... She's dead. She has to be and she's never coming back.* His heart was racing and he stopped for a moment, out of breath. *Good God, I'm going to drive myself nuts, but jeez, I could have sworn it was her.* He laughed to himself, *Yeah, what if it was? I could just hear her, "You thought I was dead, didn't you? You've already replaced me. Who the hell is that broad in our house?"* Before he continued walking, he turned around, but the lady was gone, there was only darkness. He laughed to himself, *I think I scared the shit out of her. She probably ran home. Oh God, I have to shove Ellen out of my mind and think about survival. I have to plan what we are going to do to get through this shit.* He passed Charlie's and recalled earlier seeing a flat of six tomato plants near his front porch. Seeing that big empty farm field that wouldn't get planted this spring bothered Jack as much as anything he had seen today. That's what he had to think about. The empty fields and survival!

Six tomato plants were nothing. What they needed were 60 plants, plus beans, carrots, turnips, and potatoes; a harvest that could be easily kept through the winter. He would get the rototiller from Charlie tomorrow and, no matter what, turn over every square inch of Charlie's and his backyards. Somewhere he would have to come up with the seeds to plant. He thought again about mistaking the lady for Ellen. *What if it really was her?* He knew he was overtired and there would be so much to do, he just wanted to get some sleep and not think about anything else.

The dark nighttime clouds parted some and the moon shown through, dimly lighting his front yard. Before turning onto his own walkway, he saw Glen, across the street. He knew Glen's wife, Doris, worked as a cashier at Jay's Foods. He wondered if she was working when the airplane hit the store and had died with Ellen? He didn't know—he hadn't thought about it until now. It would seem natural for two neighbors who had both lost their wives in the same tragedy to come together in their grief. He thought, *I should I go over and talk to him.*

Glen was one strange dude, who neither he nor Charlie could figure out. The man seemed perpetually pissed off about something, and all the neighbors, including Jack, had learned stay clear of him. The moonlight was bright enough that Jack could see a stagger in Glen's gait as he ascended the steps of his front porch. He figured Glen was probably drunk and was glad the streetlights were out, as Glen apparently hadn't noticed him. Glen was halfway up his front steps when he suddenly stopped and turned towards Jack. In the dim moonlight, Jack could clearly see what the man was doing. He was holding out his arm pointed towards him, his middle finger extended.

For several seconds both men stood on their front porches facing one another, Glen giving Jack the finger, and Jack standing there staring at him. Not a word was exchanged between them, and Jack did not return the single finger salute.

His crazy neighbor just eerily stood there in the moonlight, his arm and finger extended defiantly at him. Jack decided he had had enough confrontations for the day, so he entered his front door and locked it behind him. Parting the window curtains slightly back, he peered out his front window. He had a feeling Glen would still be there, and he was right. The man knew Jack was watching him. He was still standing on his front steps, his arm and middle finger boldly extended towards Jack's house. He felt a sudden chill and the heat of anger rising up his neck. Not many things did that to him, but some people could always be counted on to do the unexpected. He didn't know what his neighbor's problem was and after what he went through today, he didn't give two shits. *Screw him*, he was dead tired and just wanted to get some shut eye before facing a whole new set of problems tomorrow. He'd sleep with his dad's old Army 45 tonight. He was out of patience with assholes. Glen Sorensen had better stay out of his way.

TUESDAY

CHAPTER 16

The bedroom window curtains swayed as the early morning breeze blew through the open windows, carrying the sound of a male cardinal's springtime call. The sun was just starting to come up and last night's darkness still lingered in the bedroom. Jack slowly his opened his eyes, but he didn't move. Lying there motionless, he kept the right side of his face buried in his warm pillow. He could only see out of his left eye, and when it came into focus, it was fixed on Ellen's dresser. Everything was on top, exactly like she left it. Like thousands of other people this morning, he would wake from the fog of sleep in the comfort of his own bed to a new and frightening world. He reached over with his left arm and pulled Ellen's pillow close to him, her familiar smell filling his head. Her fragrance was strong, but her side of the bed was cold. Something else was cold. He felt the hard grip of the old Army 45 that was next to him under the covers. He suddenly remembered Glen and pushed Ellen's pillow away, mad at himself for not confronting his belligerent neighbor the night before. *What an asshole. Now I have to deal with him. I hope I don't have to start carrying a gun all the time.*

He quickly sat up, his bare feet hitting the cool oak floor. Normally he would immediately get up and head for his morning shower, but this morning he sat on the edge of the bed, slowly looking around the room. The clock radio on the nightstand next to him was dark, as was the cable box below the TV. He felt that morning urge to use the bathroom, but remembered he had used the last flush before he turned in last night. There was also a taste of something foul in his mouth. The last time he had brushed his teeth was the morning before. He got up, walked into the bathroom, and peed into the already dirty toilet bowl, making a mental note to bring up a plastic bucket and use it from now on. He stood in front of the vanity and eyed the two faucets that might never carry water again. Seeing the shadowed reflection of himself in the vanity mirror, he ran his hand over the stubble on his face, longingly eyeing the image of the shower behind him. Heading back into the bedroom, he stopped at his dresser and opened a drawer. While pulling out a fresh set of underwear, he counted the clean pairs he had left, all neatly folded and stacked by Ellen.

He hadn't been out of bed five minutes, and the realities of living without electricity was already having its effect. Sitting down on the edge of their bed, he lingered in the dim light, slowly taking in all of Ellen's belongings. Everything was neatly arranged on her dresser, nothing touching. *That's Ellen,* he thought. Whether something was tucked away out of sight in a drawer, or in plain view, everything had to be organized just right, with nothing touching. As he sat there, it was like he was viewing her things for the first time. How many times had he walked past her dresser without even noticing this stuff? How different from his cluttered workbench in the basement. Did she ever stop and look at his tools, the same way he was looking at her stuff now?

He felt like slipping under the bed covers and going back to sleep, as if things would be better when the sun was fully up. There were times while serving in Iraq and Afghanistan, he had the same feelings he had now. After their crazy escape from the city yesterday, what he needed now was some down-time and some space. He wanted to wake up knowing it was over, or soon would be. He laughed to himself, *God, here I go again, only this time instead of being stuck in a world of shit with my buddies, I'm at home, with some of my own neighbors being the bad guys.*

As he sat there, he thought back to those times when he was in still in the service. When he came home on leave, some of his civilian friends would ask him if he was ever scared. There were times when he was over there that he felt overwhelmed and sure he missed home, but scared? No, not really. Frustrated maybe, but not scared. Afraid? Yeah, he was afraid one of his buddies would get it. Afraid he would get it and not see his baby daughter again. Afraid she would grow up and never know him.

The thing that kept him and all of his buddies going was knowing that they were a plane trip away to a familiar place. A place where there was order and normalcy. That in a few months, the madness of the Middle East would be over for them and they would get on a plane and go back home. *Home.* What a word, it meant so much. Home, a place where there was love, safety and a future.

As he sat on his bed staring at Ellen's blouse neatly folded on a chair, he had but one thought that early Tuesday morning. *How the hell did we let this all slip away?*

He looked through the open bathroom door and again longingly eyed the empty shower. To himself, but out loud, he said, "Shit!"

"Jack, is that you? What are you swearing about? Are you okay?" Lynne was in the hallway outside his closed bedroom door.

"Yeah, I'm fine, Lynne. Sorry, I'm just getting up and trying to get myself going. I always swear to myself when I get up, it gets me moving. I'll be out in a minute."

He quickly changed into fresh underwear and slipped on a pair of blue jeans. Opening his bedroom door, he saw Lynne was standing there. The area around her eye was fully black and blue, but at least the swelling had gone down some. She was wearing a grey flannel work shirt of his—he noticed she had nice looking legs.

"Good morning, Jack. Really, what were you swearing about?"

Standing in his bedroom door opening, he scratched his unruly hair, saying, "I wanted to take a shower. This is really going to suck. I guess the days of bathing every day are gone. We'll have to figure something out so we can shower or take a bath at least once a week. I just counted my clean underwear too. I only have five pairs left."

He suddenly felt uncomfortable standing in front of Lynne. He realized that his old flannel shirt was all she had on.

Sensing Jack's uneasiness, she said, "Carl said I could go with him to his aunt's house today and look through her clothing. He said she looked to be about my size, maybe a little bigger in the butt." Lynne let out a little laugh. "She was 80 years old; it'll be interesting what we come up with."

Jack smiled and let out a little laugh himself, some of the uneasiness leaving him. "We have lots to do today. We're going to have to decide our priorities pretty quick. I know it's early, but I' am going to wake Laura up and get ourselves in gear. We'll cook up those eggs and that package of bacon that's in the fridge for breakfast."

"Sorry, Jack, Laura's already gone. She left a half hour ago. She went with Carl in his truck. They went with your friend, Al, to pick up a load of food from the grocery store chain where he works. She said a whole bunch of other people were going with them so it would be safe. Al assured me that, because it was so early, they'd be all right."

"You met Al?"

"Yes, I did. He came down about an hour ago. He seems like a nice man and feels really bad about your wife. He wants to help you any way he can. Sorry we didn't wake you. Laura looked in on you and said you were out like a light."

Jack ran his fingers through his tangled hair. "I can't believe I didn't wake up, especially if Laura opened the bedroom door. Jeez, I must be losing my edge."

"After what we went through together yesterday? I don't think you lost anything, or ever will. You were dead tired and needed the sleep."

Jack looked closely at Lynne's face. He was going to ask her if she was in pain, but she interrupted before he could speak.

"I know, my face looks horrible. I just got done redoing the bandages and cleaned myself up. Everything looks like it will heal together, but I can see I am going to have a nasty scar. It doesn't hurt like it did yesterday, it just feels stiff. I'm just thankful that you happened by when you did, Jack—I wouldn't be standing here now." She hesitated a few seconds then continued, "Jack, I am so sorry about Don. If you hadn't stopped for me…"

He cut her off. "Don't think like that. I've been doing too much thinking myself already, and I just woke up. We have to put everything bad aside that's happened. We have to bury it, or it'll sink us. I know it's hard, but from this point forward, the past is just that. I told that to myself last night, but what did I do right after I woke up? I started feeling sorry for myself. We just can't afford to do it." Jack slightly raised his hand, saying, "Hold on a second." He went back into his bedroom and brought out a pair of grey sweat pants. Handing them to her, he said, "You can cut these down and wear them just for this morning. I'll get you some clothesline for the waist."

While Lynne fixed up the sweat pants to fit her, Jack went down to the kitchen. It wasn't but a month ago that Ellen had insisted they buy all new kitchen appliances, and they all had to be black. New appliances or not, all of them had been off for almost 24 hours and everything was starting to defrost. The age or color of them meant nothing. In a few days or less, every freezer in the state would be permanently warm and worthless. He thought to himself, *Damn, why didn't I get one of those little propane freezers like Charlie has?* Beneath Ellen's new refrigerator, there already was a puddle of goo on the floor. It was dripping from the bottom of the freezer door and looked to be chocolate ice cream.

Jack opened up the freezer and saw he was right. The meat was still frozen solid, but the ice cream was right next to the door and it was wet and soft. He was bending over, wiping up the mess on the floor with a paper towel, when Lynne entered the kitchen wearing his cut-down sweatpants.

"What can I do, Jack? Would you like me to fix you up some breakfast?"

He stood up and pointing to the refrigerator, he said, "Going to have to use up some more food this morning. Other than the ice cream, the stuff in the freezer is still frozen, but the refrigerator is getting warm. I'll go down to the basement and drain some water out of the hot water heater. While I am down there, I'll bring up—Ellen's iron frying pan."

He was conscious that he hesitated before he said Ellen's name and suddenly felt awkward in front of Lynne. He walked over to the kitchen sink and placed both of his hands on the countertop. Looking out the kitchen window, he started to laugh and slowly shake his head. Then he laughed some more before saying, "I checked the dishwasher, it's full of dirty dishes. Can't get any slack here, huh?" He started laughing again and shook his head some more. He was leaning against the counter, intently watching something in his backyard. He turned around and noticed Lynne standing behind him, a concerned look on her face.

He said, "I can see by the look on your face you think I've lost it, because there couldn't possibly be anything that's funny, right? I was looking out the window, wondering if we could use unfiltered rain water to wash our dishes, and

I see this." He turned back towards the window and pointed to the house behind his. "Want to have a good laugh? Come here, look at my idiot neighbor back there. That's Barry, look at him. He's up on a ladder washing his windows. Can you believe that? The world as we know it has just ended, and that idiot, instead of figuring out a plan to survive this shit, is wasting precious water. He's washing his stinking windows!" Lynne looked out the window. There was a man in the yard behind them, climbing a step ladder and holding a bucket.

Jack reached for the kitchen sink's faucet handle and flipped it up. "Yep, it's still off, no miracles. I've got maybe 50 or so gallons of drinking water stored up and some full 55-gallon rain barrels. We have 80 gallons of fresh water downstairs in the hot water heater, and we have to conserve every drop of it—if we want to survive." Jack frowned as he watched Barry wipe down a window. He turned back to Lynne and pointed to the crumpled paper towel he used to wipe up the melted ice cream.

"See that paper towel I just used? It'll be a rare sight within six weeks. The same goes for toilet paper... especially toilet paper. People will be running out of that by the end of the week. I feel sorry for any parent who has a kid in diapers."

Jack watched his neighbor for a few seconds more before saying, "You know, I never particularly liked him or his wife, or their kid for that matter. He's irritating as hell. But my personal feelings aside, they're not bad people. They're actually very good people. They're hard workers and church goers. Their boy, Dwayne, is probably the smartest kid in his class, and I wish no harm to them. But I'm afraid a good part of the population is like them. Short of a miracle, come fall they'll be starving. Come winter, they'll all be dead and there is nothing I can do about it. All I can say is, 'Oh well, too bad."

Jack sadly shook his head and turned away from the window. "I'll go get that frying pan and some fresh water. We're going to eat good the next few days before everything goes bad. Maybe I'll send a couple steaks over to Barry."

He was down in his basement, looking for the old cast iron frying pan, when he was startled by his sump pump kicking on. He had a battery back-up pump that would activate if the power to the main pump was off. It hadn't rained for over a week, but being so close to the river, there was enough ground water to activate it. Apparently, the auxiliary pump hadn't been affected by the EMP. *Interesting*, he thought. *Why is it some stuff was not affected*? He stared at his sump pump, still trying to figure this EMP thing out. The maximum time that pump would run before draining the battery dead, would be about 12 hours. Jack had heard the five-day weather forecast yesterday, before going into work. A period of heavy rains was forecast for most of next week.

If he was going to get a garden in, he had to act fast. They had to beat the coming rain. Looking around his dark basement, he realized how many things he had that would be ruined if the basement were to get flooded. He would have to move everything that was valuable upstairs before the weekend. His basement had never flooded, but without a sump pump, he didn't want to chance it. He decided he would also drain the water heater of the last of the precious city water.

With no electricity to run his two sump pumps, it wouldn't be just the little seepage he normally got. There could be three or four feet of muddy, contaminated water filling his entire basement. He wished his house was like Charlie's, a raised ranch with a walkout basement. Charlie wouldn't get a drop.

Lynne removed a carton of eggs, milk, and a package of bacon from the refrigerator. Everything was already starting to get warm. With a box of pancake mix from the pantry cabinet, she started to make a big breakfast for them. There were leftovers from last night's cook-out that they could eat for lunch, and there was plenty in the freezer for dinner. She opened the pantry cabinet and scanned Ellen's canned goods; it was just the basics. Other than the usual cans of tomato products, green beans, and some cans of soup, the rest was mostly condiments and gravy mixes. She hoped there was another pantry shelf downstairs.

Glancing out the kitchen window, she could see the neighbor was still washing his windows. Jack had scared her when he started laughing. After what they had seen yesterday, what could possibly be funny? As she watched Barry so thoroughly washing his windows, she wondered if the man knew something they didn't, or as Jack had said, "He's just an idiot."

Working in Ellen's kitchen, she felt like an intruder and wanted to leave as soon as possible, but the same question kept popping up... *Where will I go?* She barely knew these people, and Laura's mother had just died... *Maybe she died, but maybe not? What if she walked in right now... and here I am in her kitchen, what would I say? They owe me nothing. What are his friends and neighbors going to think? I'll have to find a place to go... it's not right that I stay here.*

She couldn't get Jack's wife out of her head. She saw a full-length picture of her in the bedroom. The woman was beautiful and had a perfect figure. Lynne gently placed her hand to the wound on her face. *They don't even have her body, and here I am in her kitchen— using her things. Oh my God, please help me, this is crazy. What do I do?* She wished her husband, Bill was alive. *Bill...why did you have to die and leave me alone? I'm so scared.* She continued to watch the neighbor, and now his wife was helping him. As if it was a normal day, a husband and wife were working around their house. *Everything is going crazy. Jesus, please help me...*

Hearing the back door open, she quickly wiped away the wetness from her face. Grabbing an egg, she broke it into a bowl.

Jack walked into the kitchen saying, "I have the grill ready to go. I found the griddle and I have the big frying pan too."

Grabbing another egg, she turned to Jack, "I've been watching your neighbors over there. Do you think they know something that we don't?"

"No, they don't. I was out front just now. There's a guy down the street edging his lawn, and his wife had a watering can and was planting flowers. I just talked to Mike Pierce, who lives down there next to them. He's bugging out later this afternoon to his place in Wisconsin. His old van is almost loaded and he has enough firepower with him to start a war. He told me his neighbor said, 'People are overreacting, the power will soon be back on and everything will be hunky dory.' Those were his exact words."

Lynne seemed a little too quiet, and he sensed he had interrupted something. He was sure she had been crying before he came in.

"Lynne, are you all right?"

"No, I'm not." She wiped her face and sniffed. "I don't belong here. You don't even know me and you already treat me like family. I'm an intruder... I'm going to leave this afternoon."

"You're not an intruder. I thought we discussed this yesterday and you decided to stay. I can't stop you if you insist on leaving, and yes, we hardly know each other, but think about it. How are you going to survive out there alone? People are going to have to stick together to survive."

"I know that, but what are your friends going to think? It just looks bad. You just lost your wife—we think... What if she came walking in here right now, what would you say to her?"

"She's never coming home. She was in that store when the plane hit, I know she was. But let's say she did come home and was injured. Who would have the medical knowledge to care for her? Not me. I have survival and combat skills, but you were a Navy Corpsman. We need you, Lynne. Laura can be put to work doing anything and can learn to do anything. Carl, that kid's a wizard. He's not just a chemist. He can figure out things, build stuff, weird shit that I'll never even think of. We need to pull together and use our collective skills to stay alive. Loners only make it in the movies. Let me tell you something, I feel sorry for all these banker, lawyer, and salesmen types out there. Unless they also happen to be an Eagle Scout, their skills are now worthless. The same goes for all the computer geeks. The days of the computers are finished. Unless the power magically goes back on, most of these office types are going to be dead within six months, I guarantee it."

Jack glanced out the kitchen window and scoffed in disgust. While shaking his head, he pointed at Barry. Barry was struggling, together with his wife, trying to place an extension ladder up to their house's second floor windows.

While Lynne looked out the kitchen window, Jack said, "Look at those two, will you? Even with his wife's help, he can't set a ladder up. We'll survive this, but people like them, I don't think so. Our little lifeboat over here can't help them either because they'll sink us. I think better than half the population is like them. Good people with good intentions aren't going to make it. It's not that they're stupid, but they sure are ignorant. People like old Charlie, your husband and me, we see things differently. I think most people don't want to think of anything bad happening. They go with the flow like everyone else."

There were tears running down her cheeks, and he had to convince her. "Listen to me. If people saw the shit I've seen during my deployments in the Middle East, they'd sing a different tune. They think it can't happen here? Well, everything has to have a starting moment, and this is how the shit starts for us. Old Charlie gave me a talk on prepping a few years ago. With the crap I've seen in my life, it made perfect sense to me. Only an idiot would think it didn't.

I'll tell you something else. Ellen threw a fit when I told her I wanted to plant a big garden like Charlie's. I had to give up on that idea. I have better than a year's worth of survival food stocked up downstairs for four people. She about had a cow when she saw me buying it. She said it was a waste of money. I told her so are our insurance policies, but we still get them." Jack cocked his head towards Barry and his wife, they finally had their ladder up to a second story window. "Try to talk to people like those two about storing up some emergency supplies. Not a whole year's worth, let's just say in addition to what they normally have, one month's worth of food. You know what their response would be? I'll tell you. They'll look at you like you're nuts, that's what. And they're no dummies, both of them are college educated and have good jobs, but they're ignorant as to what could go wrong. Did I tell you last night he asked me for a book of matches, so they could light a candle? A vanilla-scented candle, what idiots. Who the hell doesn't keep a book of matches in their house?"

"You and my husband, would have been good friends. You sound just like him. He said the same things. People will laugh at you and call you Chicken Little."

"He was right. I would think it would be common sense to want to protect your family. Nope, most people will laugh at you, and some even get mad. They'll think you're some kind of far-right militant extremist who belongs on a government watch list. I gave up saying anything to people. The other comment I get is, 'Well, if we run out of food, we'll just come over to your place. Yeah—right....'" Jack stopped to take a breath and exhaled tiredly. "Lynne, please stay with us. You won't be a burden, and believe me, you'll earn your keep, if that's what you're concerned with. Who cares what anyone else thinks? I sure don't."

The back door opened and Laura walked in. She was carrying a large watermelon, followed by Carl who had two large paper shopping bags in his arms.

Jack breathed a sigh of relief. "Man, am I glad to see you two home safe and sound. Please, next time let me know when you go out. I've been worried about you."

Laura set the melon on the counter and gave her dad a big hug, kissing him on his cheek. "I'm sorry, Dad. Carl and I helped Uncle Al, along with a bunch of his friends. We got several truck-loads of food."

Carl added, "They have some freezers with a big generator like yours hooked up to them at Al's house. They also got a truck load of bags of charcoal and extra propane cylinders. Al said we could eat at his place every day for helping him. I got these for us to eat this afternoon." Carl placed the two large shopping bags he was holding on the counter. One was full of fresh vegetables and three loaves of Italian bread. The other held four huge slabs of spare-ribs. "We have three more big bags of fresh produce in the truck, plus a big box of assorted frozen meats."

Jack was impressed, "Wow, I won't argue with that. You guys did pretty darn good. Lynne has started to make us some breakfast—pancakes, bacon, eggs, and cold orange juice to wash it all down." Jack's face turned serious, "Did you run into any trouble getting the food?"

Laura shot a look at Carl, letting him do the talking.

"Al's friend had all this food set aside for us. It wasn't even light out—we didn't expect many people to be out. As soon as the store's workers wheeled stuff out, people started showing up and were grabbing it. About a dozen store employees were there and all of them had old trucks or vans. One guy even had a 1950s hearse. After the employees filled their vehicles with mostly vegetables and frozen meat, they wheeled loads of stuff out into the parking lot, where anyone could take it for free. People kept walking in from the street and within minutes there was a big crowd. They were grabbing the free food, but started insisting to be let into the store. The manager was there and he just locked the place up. I don't think their plan to empty the store of perishables and give the stuff away in an orderly manner went too well. There was a lot of yelling and shoving. People thought we were looting the store and started demanding they get their share. They started kicking the store's doors in.

Lynne was beating up some eggs. She stopped for a second, asking Laura, "Did anyone get hurt?"

Carl started to say something, but Laura cut him off, "When we were about to leave, when two women started screaming at us, saying we were looters! A guy who was with them opened Carl's door and tried to pull him out of the truck." Laura looked at Carl with a look of admiration, then added, "Carl hit him in the nose!"

Carl quickly cut in, "It was no big thing, Mr. Hansen. The guy was little, and as early as it was, I think he was drunk."

"You were justified in smacking him, Carl. I would have done the same thing if I was there. No one has a right to open up your door. It might actually have saved the guy's life, anyone else might have shot him. Thing is, all of us are going to have to look at things differently from now on and avoid any conflict. I think that most people within the next few days, if they haven't already, will all be carrying weapons. You'll run into people who instead of arguing or even asking a question, will pull out a gun or knife and not hesitate to use it. The important thing is you're both home safe and sound." Jack gently touched his fingers to Laura's cheek, "Speaking of getting hit in the nose, how's yours feeling?"

"It still hurts some, but Lynne did a great job putting it back in place last night." She turned and embraced Lynne, giving her a warm hug.

Laura said, "I'm glad you're staying with us, Lynne. Carl will take you to his aunt's house to get you some better clothes than my dad's sweats, unless we can find a clothing store open."

A half an hour later, they were all sitting outside at the picnic table about to enjoy the breakfast Lynne had prepared. Before they dug in, Jack led them in a prayer of thanks, ending with a few words about Ellen. In turn, Laura and Carl mentioned prayers for friends they lost at school and for the grieving families they left behind. Lynne gave thanks for being taken in by such nice people.

They made some small talk while eating and were almost done, when Jack spoke up in a serious tone. "I think from now on we have to consider the possible consequences of every move we make, every place we go." He glanced at Carl, "Have you thought about what I said last night?"

Laura answered for him, a little too quick, surprising Jack. "He wants to stay with us, Dad."

Carl spoke up, "I stayed at my condo last night. I live on the fourth floor. I always use the elevators, except when I use the stairs for a work-out. It's a real haul getting up there. The battery emergency lights were already dead and it was pitch black. My place was so dark I couldn't see a thing. There's no water or any sources for it nearby. I really don't think I can live there."

Laura said, "Carl, tell my dad what happened last night."

"Somebody woke me up, pounding on my door in the middle of the night. I didn't answer it. I figured they would just go away, but then they tried to kick it in. They must have thought no one was home and wanted to rob the place. I started yelling and they left. This morning I go down to my truck, and the driver's side window is smashed in. I had it in the condo's parking garage, but people saw me pulling it in earlier. I think they tried to steal it. I don't know what stopped them. I guess I'm lucky it was still there this morning, I don't think I'll be that lucky again. I was thinking about moving into to my aunt's house. I plan to eventually live there anyway, but it needs some work before I can stay there."

Laura suddenly interrupted, "You can't stay there, Carl, you'll be all alone at night in that old house. Besides, there's no water and you don't know anyone nearby.... He'll stay with us, Dad."

Though her face had to be hurting, Jack swore he saw the trace of a smile on Lynne's face and wondered if he had missed something that was funny.

Carl said, "I'd like to take you up on your offer to stay here, if it's still open?"

Jack was relieved that Carl wanted to join their group and smiled at him, saying, "You bet it is, Carl, but you won't be sitting around. I want to put you and Laura to work immediately on a little project I have in mind. I understand you like to garden?"

Jack explained his plans for a massive garden and was relieved by Carl's instant enthusiasm. He and Laura were anxious to jump right in on it.

After they finished eating, Jack said, "Before we get up, I think all of us should get to know more about each other. How about if each of us briefly tells every-one about their life, where they were born and what they do." He shifted his eyes to Lynne, and said, "Lynne, although I already feel like I've known you for many years, I don't even know your last name. How about you start us off."

"Okay, sure. My married name is Lynne Townsend. I was born in Topeka, Kansas. I won't say what year. My maiden name was Discipio. I'm 75 percent Italian, and the rest Irish and German. I have two big brothers. One lives in Canada, the other California. My mom died of an aneurysm when I was in eighth grade. My dad tried the best he could, but he just folded up after mom died. He was a bricklayer and worked really hard, but he drank and smoked excessively and it killed him. He died years before he should have, during my senior year of high school. I had nowhere to go and there was no money for college, so I enlisted in the U.S. Navy for six years as a Corpsman. Basically, that's between a paramedic and a nurse. I was stationed in Pearl Harbor and at the Navy base at San Diego. I spent one year aboard ship where I met my Bill. He was the senior Weapons Officer aboard ship. He left the Navy to work for the Department of Homeland Security, and I became a nurse at a hospital for three years, until we moved to Chicago. I was offered a job at Labspect and have worked there almost four years." She glanced at Jack, and then to Laura. "Your dad and I have shared the same elevator for the last year. We see each other just about every morning, he works on the fourth floor and I'm on the tenth." With her face bandaged, Lynne couldn't smile, but her eyes showed it. "He saved my life yesterday."

Jack laughed, "I don't know about that...let's just say we saved each other."

Laura asked, "What's your job, Lynne?"

"We mostly inspect hospitals, nursing homes, and clinics. There are two nursing homes here in Melville that my company inspects. It's not an official state inspection, but we help them to know and follow state and federal regulations, of which you know there are a ton of them." Lynne took a sip of water, then added, "I live alone. Just like my mom, Bill died from an aneurysm three years ago. Some coincidence, huh?" She paused and took a deep breath, "We had a baby boy named Mathew, who passed away just before his second birthday. That was eight years ago. I'm all right though, that's how life is, none of us are promised anything. I am grateful for today and this moment with all of you."

Laura got up from the bench and gave Lynne a hug and gently kissed her bandaged cheek. "Lynne, we're your family from now to eternity." Laura turned to her dad as he nodded his head.

Jack said, "Yes, Lynne is part of our family and so is Carl. We're going to stick together and make it through this."

Carl said a few things about himself and how his life growing up compared to Lynne's. Jack was the last to speak. He gave a short history of his life for Lynne and Carl. When he was done, he stood up and widely gestured to the large expanse of weeds that was invading his backyard. Everyone looked at him expectantly, not understanding.

"By Friday, I'd like to have our yard looking like Charlie's yard used to look like. We're going to plant the biggest garden this neighborhood has ever seen." He pointed at Charlie's turned over, yet unplanted yard. "I've already talked to Charlie about it. He thinks it's a great idea. He agrees with me, that no matter if this crisis gets resolved or not, enough damage has been done to the food supply already. Anything we plant, we'll harvest and it won't be wasted. Charlie and I have no doubt in our minds that we may be facing something that this country has never seen before, and that's a possible famine. There's lots of rain in the forecast for next week, so we'll have to get everything planted before then. The goal is to plant both of these yards with vegetables, every square foot. Sometimes I tend to go overboard on things." He shot a smile to Laura, "I think my daughter will agree on that, but we have to think big. Anything we can grow to supplement our canned and dry stores will stretch our existing food supply, especially come winter and next spring. And next spring, before the growing season starts, even a lot of preppers may be starving."

Carl said, "I have a friend who's the manager of Madsen's Home Center. They have an excellent garden center. I'll get over there this morning and see what I can get."

"Great idea, Carl, get all the plants you can. I'd like to plant stuff like potatoes, sweet potatoes, beets, turnips, and carrots. We need things that will stay fresh through the winter. Also, tomato, bean, and pepper plants, and get all the seeds you can carry. It'll be cash only, so I'll give you 1000 in 20's and some 100-dollar bills. You pay when you're done and quickly come straight home; don't slow down for anyone. Try to make out a deal for two or three truckloads of stuff, if you can get it. I'm going to check out some other places. If I'm here when you return, I can go back with you. Another thing we'll need is fertilizer, get as much as you can haul. I know you're an expert on chemicals, so pick up anything you can easily make explosives out of too."

Laura gave her dad a surprised look. "What would we need explosives for?"

Jack raised his eyebrows, "Clearing stuff, you know, stumps and trees."

Satisfied with her dad's answer, she asked, "Can I go with Carl, Dad? No one will be fighting over fertilizer and seeds."

Jack hesitated, "Yeah, sure... but please don't take any chances," He nodded to Carl, "Remember, the first sign of trouble, come home. Meanwhile, I'll be checking out a couple smaller places. John's Hardware, and Andy's Home Center. I know the manager of Andy's, he's a former Army drill sergeant. A good friend of Charlie's runs the garden department over at John's. I'll see what I can get there." Jack stepped in front of Carl and placed his hand on his shoulder, "We more than likely will only have one shot at this, Carl. You go for the best stuff, but don't come home empty handed. If those stores aren't stripped clean already, they more than likely will be by tomorrow, so we might not get a second chance at this."

Lynne, who was sitting there listening, cleared her throat. "I know something about potatoes." Everyone looked at her and she continued. "I see you have a big bag of red russets in the garage. If you cut them into cubes, each one with an eye, we can grow them into a new plant."

Jack smiled and said, "Lynne, you can be in charge of planting the taters. Believe it or not, those are top on my list of what we have to grow."

Lynne got up and started cleaning up the table. Jack stopped her, saying, "I'll clean up the dishes later. Right now, I would appreciate it if you could come with me and check on things over at Charlie's place. Give me your opinion on the condition of Dottie and Ted, and see if they need anything. I will check with you over there before I leave. Also, could you stay here and hold down the fort this morning while we're gone, if that's all right with you?" He took the keys to her car out of his pocket and held them up to her. "I was going to ask you if I could use your car to go over to the hardware store and Andy's Home Center. The tank is almost empty, but I have some gas in the shed to fill it up."

"The car is yours, Jack, but please, no more bullet holes."

Laura and Carl drove off in Carl's truck, going to the Mega Home and Garden Center. Jack took Lynne over to Charlie's and introduced her to them. She wasn't in Charlie's house two minutes before she asked him why he was limping. As Jack left to go back to his house, Lynne was already examining Charlie's legs.

GARDEN SUPPLIES

CHAPTER 17

Mega Home and Garden Center was about a one and a half miles from Jack's house. It was much larger than the one Jack was going to and had an excellent garden department. The building supply department was at the far end of it and was separate from the garden center. As Carl expected, it was in chaos. There were three men standing outside of the main entrance doors. One of them Carl recognized as his friend, Ed, the store manager, and all three of them were armed. They were open, but it wasn't business as usual. Before entering, customers would tell the manager what they wanted. He told them they'd have to pay in cash. The place was in shambles, and it looked like some of the people were trying to walk out with merchandise they hadn't paid for. The three men standing outside would have none of it and were doing a good job keeping a lid on things. He talked to his friend, Ed, who told him, "Carl, the garden department got really trashed yesterday. The whole place went up for grabs. Everything got knocked over and now it's mostly junk. You're welcome to anything in there for a 100 bucks per truckload. If we get one more night of looting, I'll be surprised if the store is still standing tomorrow, so you better get what you want today. You can pack your truck with all it can hold and pay me in cash when you leave. Don't get your hopes up. It's a mess in there, but you're welcome to salvage what you can. If you think you can use it, take it."

And salvage they did. Like Ed had said, most of the racks containing the plants were knocked over. Broken pots and trampled plants were scattered everywhere. Carl and Laura lifted an empty rack five feet high by eight feet long, and slid it into the pickup's bed. They packed each of the metal shelves with flats of assorted vegetable plants. Laura found hundreds of flower and vegetable seed packets, mixed together and scattered about, trampled on the floor. She gathered all of them and quickly dumped them into the back of the truck. There was potatoes, onions and garlic sets, all mixed together, it didn't matter. Everything was tossed into the pickup's bed until every square inch of the truck was jammed. They made four quick trips home, each time the truck filled to overflowing. His friend, Ed, had said, "Take all you can carry," so they took full advantage. They piled large plastic bags of fertilizer high on the roof and hood of the old truck, covering it. The first four loads went smoothly. There were other people picking through things, but everyone kept to themselves. They were going to call it quits after the fourth load, but Carl spotted something he knew they had to come back for. He had found a large pallet of fertilizer, hidden from view in a secluded corner, so they decided to make one final trip. After dumping off the forth load, they went back for the fertilizer. Carl filled the entire truck, stacking the large plastic bags over the top of the cargo bed. While Carl was busy tying down the load, Laura decided to take one last look inside the building to see if she could find anything else, they could use. She was disappointed to find the garden tools mostly gone. Every rack and all the shelves were pretty much empty of any hand tools. She was about to turn back when she spotted one of those old-time hay-forks with its five needle-like tines. It reminded her of a famous painting of an old man and woman she had seen in Chicago's Art Institute. They were standing beside each other, the man holding an upright pitchfork and somber looks on both their faces. She never understood what that painting was about, but liked it. Since they didn't have a hay-fork, she decided to take it.

Carl was still tying down the load, out of her sight, three aisles over. To get back to the truck, she had to cut through two aisles that were stacked several feet high with bags of top soil. She started back to the truck, her only find being the pitchfork. She couldn't see Carl, but was within sight of the roof of the truck when she heard a man's voice growl, "Give me the keys, *asshole* or you're dead."

Keeping low, Laura silently rounded the stacked bags of topsoil. It wasn't a man; he looked like a boy, maybe only 16 years old, and his white shirtless back was to her. He held a long blade, threatening Carl. She could see Carl's scared face. He was just standing there, riveted in place. Silently raising the pitchfork with both arms above her head, she threw it at him, thrusting it into him, skewering the boy through his bare back. He was young and he screamed, and he screamed and he screamed! The long rusty knife he was holding clanged to the floor. Grabbing the end of the pitchfork's handle, she had total control of him, like a puppet on a stick. The sharp tines of the fork had plunged easily through the soft white flesh of his back, piercing his heart and both his lungs. The thin young man grew silent and jerked, trying to pull himself off the pitchfork. Unable to pull free, he looked down in horror at the five glistening points protruding out the front of his hairless chest and started to cry. She had him. As five rivulets of blood drained his life away, the boy was shaking, as she slowly lowered him to the floor.   "Oh my God! Oh my God—Carl, don't tell my Dad what I've done! God help me."

* * * * *

Andy's Home Center was closest, so Jack made it the first stop. After what he and Lynne had experienced during the ride home from Chicago, he didn't know what to expect. He was pleased to see that the home center was open, but he wasn't pleased with the mob of people that was assembled out in front of it. There were four employees by the main entrance and one of them had a tag pinned to his shirt that said, "Manager." There were two tough looking guys standing alongside him and another man sitting in a lawn chair with a shotgun across his lap. All of them were armed with handguns.

He started thinking about Laura and Carl. *Why did I let those two kids go out without me? God, please let them be safe.* He debated with himself if he should go into the store or go home and find Laura and Carl.... *As long as I'm here, I might as well go in. From the looks of things, there won't be a second chance later.*

Jack sat in the car for a few minutes, watching people going in and out of the store. They were letting only a dozen or so people inside at a time. When someone came out, they would let another person in. Some of the people were mad and were being turned away. There was a big sign that boldly read, **"Cash Only."** It looked like hardly anyone had any cash, and people were pissed. Jack slowly got out of the car and edged close to the entrance. He wanted to see exactly what the deal was, before he rushed into anything. It was well organized and anyone who wanted to enter the store had to wait in a straight line. Surprisingly, it wasn't as long of a wait as he would have expected. Before they were allowed to get in the line, one of the three men would demand to see their money and ask them what they wanted. Jack showed the man his cash and told him what he needed. He and about a dozen other people were told the rules by the man wearing the manager's tag.

He said, "It's cash and carry, folks. All items will be scanned with a hand-held scanner at the checkout line inside. The price you pay will be double the total. That's to cover tax and our *special* operating costs. If you don't like it, go somewhere else."

Jack assumed the special operating costs were the three burly armed guards standing next to the door. He figured there were probably at least two more guards, somewhere out of sight. The manager said, "Only one shopping cart per person and all sales will be rounded off to the nearest dollar. And listen, we're not going to take any crap from anyone. Troublemakers will be immediately shown the door; we won't stand for any bullshit."

Jack was standing in line next to a troublemaker. The man was angry, and said, "I have cash, but I really don't feel like using it up at this store! It's bad enough you won't honor this 100-dollar Andy's gift card I have, but doubling the price? You're crazy. It's price gouging and it's illegal! Where the hell do you get off charging double?"

The manager said nothing. He shot a look at the security guards and cocked his head towards the guy who was complaining.

The guards tried to grab him, but the fellow decided to put up a fight. The burlier of the two guards placed him in a headlock and led the complainer, who was screaming profanities at them, out of sight and into the parking lot.

The store manager climbed on top of a picnic table near the store's entrance and defiantly placed his right hand on his holstered weapon.

He yelled, "We're open today strictly for your convenience! We don't want to be here! Like I've explained, the surcharge is a reasonable charge, to cover sale tax that will eventually have to be paid and putting up with the bullshit like you just witnessed. Nobody is price gouging. We don't have to be open, so be nice or we'll just close up!"

Jack was nice. He grabbed a cart and, as always was his luck, one wheel was wobbly and started making a thumping sound as he pushed it. He shoved the cart to the side and grabbed another one. The burly security guard holding the shotgun actually smiled, saying, "Don't you just hate that?"

Jack returned the smile, and agreed.

Jack had a big wad of cash and wanted to spend every cent of it. The first things he placed into the cart were several large packs of batteries. He took the last package of D's and two packs of double A's. The battery-operated drill he had at home still worked but was on its last legs, so he grabbed one of those too. He also bought a solar panel. It was bigger than the cart, but he figured he'd place it on top of it when it was full.

The shelves in the store were already being depleted of any items that would normally be considered used for a disaster. Not a candle was in sight, except for some big peppermint scented ones. He wondered if Barry and his wife had bought their candles here. They were out of propane, kerosene, matches, lighters and flashlights.

One item that Jack was surprised they did have was a large manual water filter for campers. He got the last one of those and two gallons of bleach. They also had a nice selection of first aid kits, so he grabbed three of them and some boxes of assorted band-aids. He found hydrogen peroxide, alcohol, and white vinegar, along with antiseptic wipes. It all went into his cart. He would have liked to go into the building supply section, but the big shopping cart was nearly full.

The last section was the garden section, and his heart sank. It was picked clean.

The only seeds that were left were two full racks of assorted flower seeds. On a hunch, he started going through each rack of seeds and his hunch paid off. He found at least thirty packets of vegetable seeds that had been misplaced. He was about to leave when he spotted three large boxes on the floor, hidden behind a display that was labeled, **NON-GMO VEG. SEEDS**. He took all three. His heart was beating so fast with excitement, he felt like yelling out a cheer. It was exactly what he was looking for.

He paid for all his items and hurriedly left the store, thrilled with the cache of seeds he had gotten. He was finishing loading the car when the shooting started, instinctively making him crouch down low beside the car. Mr. Complainer had come back. Only this time it looked like he was carrying a semi-automatic rifle. Jack couldn't see what kind it was and it didn't matter. The man with the manager tag on his shirt and the two guards were the first to fall. The guy with the shotgun shouldn't have been casually sitting down. He went over backwards, dead in his chair. Mr. Complainer was far from done. He was crazy with anger and was randomly firing into the running crowd. Jack wasn't about to become a victim or a hero. He was in the car in a split second, jamming the key into the ignition. The old Chevy Camaro's V8 engine roared to life, Flooring it, he fishtailed it out of the parking lot, blasting the old car down the street.

As he floored the car away from the home center's parking lot, he said to himself out loud, "That's the thanks they get for being nice guys and opening their store today. What a screwed-up world."

His next stop was going to be the hardware store. After what he just witnessed at Andy's, he was considering going straight home. Because the hardware store wasn't really out of his way, he headed towards it. He figured he'd at least drive by it before heading back. It was late morning, maybe about 10:30, and lots of people were out walking the streets. There were a few older cars and trucks out and, like Jack, they were out running around, getting last minute supplies. Every vehicle was overloaded with goods. Like his escape from Chicago, some people tried to get him to stop. One kid threw a rock at him, hitting the car's front fender. He remembered Lynne's comment about not getting any more bullet holes in her car and felt like turning around to run the little bastard down. Who would stop him?

The hardware store was coming into view and it didn't look good. The store's parking lot was mobbed, and people looked out of control. He decided to drive right on by and check Tammi's Foods next-door. The same scene was being repeated at every store. Some windows in the store's front were broken and missing. People were grabbing shopping carts and going through a shattered glass door. There was a steady procession of carts being pushed down the street. Every one of them was loaded to overflowing with boxes and canned goods. Just like yesterday, there wasn't a cop in sight. It was a free for all and the looters were white. He was about two blocks away from the store when a young woman, struggling with a grocery cart, caught his eye. Her cart had lost a front wheel, and she was trying to keep it from tipping over. It was overloaded with canned goods and what looked like potatoes. Jack drove slowly alongside her and took a good look. They weren't just any old potatoes; they were sweet potatoes. They were easy to grow, easy to store through the winter, and were top on his garden list.

One cut up sweet potato might be able to produce at least three plants or more. They were an ideal long-lasting and fresh survival food. He slowed the car and a young, rough looking lady eyed him suspiciously. He pulled up beside her and decided to take a chance.

"I don't think your shopping cart is going to make it. Sweet potatoes, huh?"

She wasn't friendly looking, and in a raspy street voice, she answered him. "Yeah, I grabbed what I could. Most of the canned goods were already gone. All I got was some creamed corn, Lima beans, and this crummy cart full of potatoes. A lousy selection and now this stinking cart is shot."

"Would you like to lighten your load and sell those sweet potatoes to me? She mulled the question over for a few seconds. While she was thinking, Jack noticed she was probably a lot younger than what she looked. Some of her teeth were missing and what was left looked to be a dentist's nightmare. She had a bad complexion, but at one time must have been an attractive girl. Jack thought to himself, *She must be a crystal meth addict...*

She said, "How much you give me?"

Jack replied, "How about a hundred bucks for all of them?"

She laughed. "Do I look stupid? You're going to plant these, aren't you? That makes them valuable. I'll take 200, cash."

There was no denying it, she had Jack pegged. Then she said, "I'll tell you what, sweetie, give me a ride back to my place and you can have some fun, then you can go plant your potatoes. I'll make it well worth the two."

Jack smiled, shook his head. "How about two and we'll....eh, call it a day?"

"Okay, suit yourself, two it is. Let's see the cash."

Jack got out and gave her the money. The two of them emptied the cart of potatoes, tossing them into the back of the car.

When they were done, she asked him, "How about that ride? I live about a mile away and this cart is a real pain with only three wheels." Jack suddenly noticed that his car had attracted the attention of three not so pleasant looking men who were quickly moving their way.

She noticed them too, saying, "I know who those guys are and they're big trouble. Please take me with you, would you? Just get me a couple blocks away from them."

"Okay, let's throw your stuff in the back and jump in." It was against Jack's better judgement, but he could see that she was afraid of them and he didn't want to leave her there. Flooring the old car down the street, Jack shook his head in disgust. This was becoming routine, fleeing from thugs at every stop. He looked in the cracked side mirror. The men had lost interest and were walking in the opposite direction. His new passenger sat back and breathed a sigh of relief, "My name is Sheila. What's yours?

"Jack Hansen."

"Well thank you, Jack Hansen. Those guys back there would have either beat the shit out of you or maybe killed you for this car. Then they would have been all over me." She leaned over a little too close to Jack and gave him a tight lipped smiled, "So… thanks for the ride, *Mr. Jack*."

"Where do you live, Sheila?"

"Just keep going straight for about three blocks, then turn right on Lincoln. The address is 1431. I'm staying at a friend's house. I just got in from California last week. Haven't seen my parents in over 10 years… figured I'd surprise them… I ran away when I was 17." She started laughing, "My parents and I didn't get along, let's hope they've changed. I know I have." Sheila was very talkative. Jack figured the girl was just nervous, so he kept silent and listened to her. "Yeah, things are really going nuts huh, Mr. Jack? There's a lot of real weirdos out roaming around looking for trouble, like those guys we left back there. They just love what's happened. They think they died and went to scumbag heaven." She turned in her seat and nervously looked out the car's missing back window. "Looks like someone's been using your car for target practice." After letting out a nervous laugh, she got serious. "It's getting really bad. I saw a guy this morning shooting people, just for the fun of it. No one stopped him either, he just walked around laughing."

Jack pulled up to a small 1930s style brick bungalow at 1431 Lincoln.

The chain-link fenced yard was tidy, and a woman in a long dress was sitting hunched over with her back to them on the front porch.

As he paid Sheila her money, she glanced at the lady on the porch, then turned to Jack and in a low voice said, "Oh shit! That's my mom. How did she know I was here? Oh crap, she still looks the same. I guess I better go face the music, huh? Thanks for the ride, Mr. Jack—I can see you're a real nice guy, and you probably think I'm a scumbag for, you know…. Sorry, I just really need the cash. My debit card is no good. I used to be on meth, but I 'm clean now, been good for almost a year. Planned to start my life over from scratch. Fine time I picked, huh?" She got out of the car and closed the door, pieces of the door's shattered glass falling to the street. Sticking her head back inside the car, she said, "World's really screwed up, Mr. Jack. Thanks for the ride. You be careful, big guy, okay?" She turned towards the house carrying her bag of canned goods and had walked about ten feet when Jack beeped the horn and motioned her back to the car. He leaned towards the passenger door window, handed her something, then sped off without saying a word. Sheila stood there and watched the battered old car until it faded away. In her hand were five, 100-dollar bills. That was the first time in her life that a guy had given her money, for *nothing* in return. *Thank you, Jack Hansen, God bless you….*

Jack didn't know why he handed Sheila the extra money, he just knew he felt good about it. Glancing back at her in his shattered mirror, he could see her fragmented reflection standing on the curb. Every few seconds he checked his mirror until she was out of his sight. *I pray you make it, Sheila*….

He decided there would be no more stops, no matter what. He was worried about Laura and Carl. Picturing in his mind all the things that could go wrong, he called himself an idiot for letting them go off to the garden center by themselves.

From the position of the sun, he figured it had to be getting close to noon and he was suddenly very thirsty. He reminded himself he should have carried some drinking water. He decided that, in the future, an extra weapon and some water would be carried in their vehicles at all times.

His mind was working overtime, calculating all the changes in their everyday lives that would have to be made. From now on, no one would dare travel alone and everyone would have to be armed. He wondered if he would ever see a policeman, let alone the Illinois National Guard. He was on the last leg home as he turned onto the stretch of road that led into his subdivision. The north side of the road was taken up by a large Catholic cemetery, followed by a 36-hole golf course surrounded by luxury homes. The south side was bordered by a county forest preserve, and a small industrial park. After witnessing the mayhem that was going on in town, he was glad he lived in his isolated subdivision off the beaten path. The river that bordered his subdivision to the east would serve as an important barrier that would help keep intruders out.

It was a perfect spring day and, like yesterday, apparently not everyone shared Jack's view of impending doom.

PARTY TIME

CHAPTER 18

Jack couldn't believe his eyes. All hell was breaking loose and people were out on the golf course, carrying their clubs, enjoying the sunny day. It was just like yesterday. *While Rome burned....* he thought. It was so incredulous to him that people would actually be golfing, it was hard to keep his eyes on the road. It looked like a normal Saturday. *Do these people know something I don't? Did the power go back on?*

How could there be such a contrast between what was happening all around them and the tranquility he was seeing on the golf course?

If what he was witnessing on the golf course shocked him, nothing would have prepared him for what awaited him when he turned onto his own street. Al's house looked like one big Fourth of July picnic. There must have been half the subdivision's residents standing on the front lawn of Al's corner home. A volleyball net was strung across the side yard and horseshoes were being played in the back. He counted at least eight gas grills lined up, with several picnic tables nearby, all with bright red checked tablecloths.

As he drove by Al's house, the Camaro's loud exhaust caught everyone's attention. Every person there had drink cups in their hands, and all of them eyed the noisy car as it drove by. A short fat man, wearing a green Hawaiian shirt, turned towards Jack and raised his glass high in a toast. It was Al. Al motioned Jack to stop, running to the curb to greet him. Jack could see that whatever Al was drinking was splashing out of his cup and all over his shirt. He wanted to get right home, so he kept the loud car running as he pulled up next to the curb. Jack quickly scanned the people in Al's yard and two men stood out. Both of them had him in their cross-hairs. Standing next to a smoking grill was Deputy Chuck Hayes and his pig faced brother, Dirk. Both of them held a beer bottle in their hand and were giving Jack the eye. It wasn't a friendly one.

Excited and out of breath, Al leaned into the car's driver's side window. "Ain't this great? This is what I call a community coming together. Wait til you see all the food we got. I got stuff stashed in freezers all over the place. I got generators, ten grills and plenty of fuel." Jack could hear late 60's rock music blaring out of some big black speakers near Al's garage. Al caught Jack's look and said, "Yeah, this is going to be like Woodstock. I got food, music, games and a shit load of beer." Al pointed to a beer truck that was parked in front of the house next door. "I scored a whole friggin truck load of suds, great huh?"

Jack nodded his head towards the sheriff. "I see the sheriff and his pig-headed brother couldn't pass up a free meal."

"Jeez, Jack, don't start nothing with those two. You know, they aren't so bad once you get to know them. I'll give them a couple prime ribs and they'll be on their way." Al stepped back and eyed the old car saying, "Why don't you shut this turd off and have a beer? I got a shit load of shrimp, lobster, steaks, you name it.... Hey what's wrong, buddy?"

Al was excited and more than a little drunk. Before Jack could reply, Al continued, "Don't tell me you're going to give me all that doom and gloom, Armageddon stuff?"

"No, Al, no doom and gloom. I've been out all morning and I just want to get home. I'm worried about Laura and her friend. They've been out getting some stuff."

"Stuff? Are you kidding me? What are you doing at your place, Jack, starting a garden center? Holy crap, those two kids have been driving by here all morning, with every kind of plant under the sun."

Jack looked towards his house, but didn't see any sign of Carl's truck. Seeing Jack's concern, Al leaned into the car and placed his hand on Jack's arm, "Hey, they're fine, buddy, and they're home. The kid's truck is in the backyard and they're unloading all their shit. They just stopped by about 15 minutes ago; said it was their last load. I asked them to come on down and join the party when they're done. Those two have worked hard." Al finished his beer and pointed to Jack's car, "So, hey, shut this hunk of junk.... Hey! Are those bullet holes?"

"Yeah, I used it for target practice."

"Holy shit, you better be careful. It's bad out there. Glad we're tucked away safe and sound back here. Anyway, you get home and check things out. Bring everybody back here for some fun and food tonight. Lois is making her specialty, pulled pork.... Soon as we get some shit grilled, I'll bring some down for old Charlie and his wife, and I'll bring you and him a case of cold beer."

Lynne was already out on the drive when Jack pulled in. She said, "I could hear you coming with that loud exhaust from a mile away. How was it out there, as bad as yesterday?"

"Yes and no. The stores are getting looted, with not a cop in sight. I think I was right in my guess that they're too busy getting their own places fortified. I don't fault them though. If anyone knows the score, they do." Jack looked back down the street to Al's. "All except our idiot sheriff down there. Instead of doing his job, he's mooching free food and beer, the worthless piece of shit. I get back here and it looks like one big party. There were even people out golfing, I can't understand it. Al said the kids got back all right. I could just kick myself in the ass for letting them go off without me this morning. Did everything go okay?"

"Yes, they're fine, and you should see all the plants they've got. They made five trips, come out back and see." Lynne looked into the back seat of her car. "How about you... sweet potatoes?"

"Yeah, sorry about the way I tossed them in there. I was kind of in a hurry. Your beautiful car is really beat, but I'll make it up to you, I promise."

"That's okay, it's only a car and it saved our lives. Looks like I'll be making plenty of sweet potato pies, huh?" She pointed at the large box on the back seat. "What's that big thing?"

"That's a small solar panel. I think we'll find it very useful. I have another one that I haven't used yet. Charlie has some big ones on his roof."

"Yes, he showed them to me."

"Thanks for going over there to check on them."

"That's no problem. I've been over there all morning. I checked over Dottie and Ted. Jack, we're going to have to discuss them. They all have serious health issues, and I think all of them, as bad as they are, would normally be admitted to a hospital. Dottie is in end-stage emphysema and needs almost constant oxygen. Charlie's solar panels don't produce enough power to continually run Dottie's oxygen machine. He told me he has a gas generator. We'll have to get it running and plug her machine into it at night, otherwise her bottled oxygen might run out. I didn't tell Charlie, but he has gangrene in his left foot; it's out of control, creeping up to his ankle. It has to painful. I don't know how he can walk. The toes on his right foot have it too. I think he knows how bad it is, but he plays it down. His toes look horrible. I think he's taking some kind of pain medicine, but he denies it."

He stopped her, asking, "Why wouldn't he want to tell you about what he's taking?"

"Probably because it's pretty powerful and he shouldn't be using it. He has other issues too. God knows what medication it is, or who prescribed it, but he has to be taking something, believe me. Plus, haven't you noticed he drinks all the time? It's not a good combination. I also checked over Ted. He has severe dementia and refuses to eat. He should be on a feeding tube. Charlie said they have a nurse. From the looks of things over there, she wasn't a very good one. Do you know he's almost out of insulin?" Lynne took a deep breath and continued the run-down of their health issues. "I changed Ted's diaper twice this morning and gave him a bath. It was obvious that he's been sitting in his feces since yesterday. He should be in a nursing home, or worse yet, in hospice. To top that off, there are only nine diapers left." She ran her fingers through her hair and gave Jack a pleading look, "Honest to God, if they don't get the medical help, they need...."

"I don't know what to say. I'm sorry about you having to change Ted's diaper."

"Jack, unless a miracle happens, without hospitalization I think we'll be burying Dottie and Ted within the next week, or sooner. And Charlie, soon after. It's that bad."

Jack was trying to wrap his mind around everything Lynne was telling him, when Laura and Carl came walking around the corner of the garage. Laura ran up to him and gave him a long hug, kissed his neck and hugged him some more.

"Dad, I was so worried about you."

He gently pushed her away to arm's length, "Are you all right? I should never have let you two go to that place by yourselves." Carl was quietly standing behind her. Jack asked him, "How'd everything go? I heard you scored really big. Did you run into any trouble?"

Carl lied, "No, no trouble at all."

"That's good. I was really worried about you kids. Let's see what you brought back."

All of them walked into the backyard. Jack was amazed at all the plants and seeds they had. He stepped over to a tall stack of bags of fertilizer and placed his hand on the top bag. "Nice job, Carl. This stuff is like gold."

Pointing in the direction Al's house he said, "I know you've seen what's going on down there. This looks like just an excuse for one big party. Everyone's trying to stay optimistic and all, and that's good, to an extent, but we're not going to be like them. We're going to prepare for the worst."

Lynne said, "And pray for the best."

Jack laughed, "Yeah, so we can party later."

Laura said, "Dad, we're going to Carl's aunt's house this afternoon before it starts getting dark. It's only a few minutes away, across from the big Catholic cemetery. Lynne is going to look through his aunt's clothing to see if she can find something to wear. Carl wants to go there to feed Harry and the girls, his aunt's chickens.

You know, Dad, I would like to stop at the crash site on the way there. It's close by. Carl and I were going to stop there after our last trip this morning, but we were afraid to."

They stood in the backyard, staring at each other. The mention of the crash site silenced them. The happiness they'd just shared about the garden supplies faded, as the memory of yesterday crept back in. For a few seconds no one said anything. All of them were thinking along the same lines, about loved ones and good friends that were gone. Ellen was gone without a trace. Laura's friend, Karen, was gone. Sara had to still be lying by her desk in the office, and Jack pictured Don's body still on the sidewalk.

172

There were no funerals or planned memorials, no caskets to grieve over and no cemeteries to visit. It was hard enough for Jack to wrap his mind around it, let alone what Laura must be going through. He didn't know what to say to her and there was nothing anyone could say to him.

Jack said, "Boy, we're a sad group, aren't we?" He nudged Lynne's shoulder, "Come on, let's go get you some clothes." He shot a glance to Carl, shrugging his shoulders as if looking for an explanation. "Harry and the girls?"

Carl replied, "My aunt and uncle always kept a few chickens. They liked the fresh eggs. I've been taking care of them since she died. I bring eggs to the other teachers at school. Harry is the rooster." Chickens! Jack's mind was racing again. He was thinking about the chickens. He had never given livestock a thought. Sheep, goats, pigs, big tom turkeys, who would stop them? Ellen tried to creep back in, but he quickly shut her out. She would never allow chickens running around their yard. He decided it was as good a time as ever to go to the crash site, and if Ellen's car would start, he would bring it home.

Jack said, "All right, let's go to the crash site and then to your aunt's. These chickens sound interesting. We'll take both cars and we'll go armed."

Lynne started walking towards Charlie's house, "I'll let them know where we're going. I'll be right back." Laura went with her.

Jack stepped up alongside Carl, giving him a questioning, sideways glance. "You spent the morning with Laura. Do you think she's ready to go to the crash site, because I'm not so sure?"

"Yes, I think she is. I think we should all go there. There's no funerals or cemetery—no planned memorials we can go to. I don't know what else we can do, except say goodbye. It's really sad. That's why you're getting us so gung-ho about this garden. I mean, we need it and all, but keeping us busy keeps our minds off how bad it really is...right?"

"Yeah, that's about it. Make no bones about it, it's about to get bad. Don't let the party atmosphere down at the street fool you. Those people are wasting valuable time, they really are. That's something I have no intention to do. Let's saddle up and get over to the crash site while there's still daylight." Carl drove and Jack rode shotgun next to him, with a 12-gauge over-under shotgun on his lap. Reaching the corner, they slowed down approaching Al's. The afternoon air was alive with the smell of grilled steaks and beer. Rock music was blaring from Al's stereo speakers.

Joan and her girlfriend were standing on their front porch, silently watching the excitement at Al's. They were dressed alike, wearing faded camouflage T shirts, keeping to themselves. As they drove by, Joan eyed Jack and gave him a short salute. Her blond-haired girlfriend cheerfully raised her glass. Jack returned them a salute as they drove on past. He would have liked to stop and maybe have a drink with them, but he had too many ideas racing through his head. They were running out of daylight. He'd make a point of stopping at Al's party tonight, and then walking over to talk to the two women.

Lynne drove her car for the first time since leaving Chicago. Laura went with her, setting her grandfather's heavy old 45 on the floor, between the bucket seats.

As Carl drove, his mind was drawing a blank. He was searching for something meaningful to say when he got to the crash site. He was methodically turning the tuning dial on the truck's radio, trying to get any station that was broadcasting, but all he was getting was static.

The day had been so hectic, Jack hadn't thought much about Ellen's death, or what life was going to be like without her. To avoid putting himself in a bigger rut than he was already in, he purposely blocked out the lingering thoughts of her and everyone else who had died. They would be at the crash site within 10 or 15 minutes and it wasn't enough time for him to think deeply about Ellen, or how he felt. He didn't know what to say to the others. He knew how he *should* feel and what other people *thought* he was feeling, but he couldn't help the creeping feeling of guilt. Was he actually feeling some relief? He had to say something at the crash site, for Laura's sake, but the words weren't there. He still loved Ellen, maybe that was enough. He briefly re-entertained the thought that maybe she was alive and had concocted a way out of their marriage by using the plane crash as a means to escape. That was more believable than her being dead. He was sure their marriage would never have been one of those to celebrate a golden wedding anniversary, but to end like this?

Her little red VW convertible was still parked right where she left it, only now it was more of a dark gray, the color of ashes to be more specific. Ashes? *Was it some of Ellen's own ashes that now covered her car?* They parked close to Mandel's, only a few feet from the front entrance. Everyone slowly got out of their vehicles and hesitantly walked as close as they could to the still smoking tangle of wreckage. It was weird. Jack looked back at the closed Mandel's store. It was amazing no one had looted it yet. It was like the whole crash site was hallowed ground.

Smoke drifted towards them from the hot debris. The smell of burnt plastic permeated the air. They could feel the heat on their face, radiating from the cooked pile of wreckage. There was nothing, absolutely nothing, to indicate to an untrained eye that an aircraft had caused all this destruction. He carefully searched the wreckage with his eyes. Nothing was recognizable. The destruction was complete. Everything that could melt or burn was mixed into a charred, twisted heap. There was another smell, though. It was faint, overwhelmed by the burnt plastic smell, but he smelled it, and wondered if the others did too. Jack tried to shut it out, because he had smelled it years before when a Humvee burned up. When you smell something burnt, it's because you're breathing in charred particles of what burned. He was smelling charred human flesh.

174

Wrapping his arm around Laura, he pulled her close.

Lynne and Carl stood silently behind them, Carl giving a mournful look towards the burned-out shell that was his school. Nothing escaped the fire. It had spread from the school to the roof of the church. Old St. Paul's was gone. The entire roof of the church had collapsed. Only the brick steeple and cross remained. Jack and his daughter didn't share it with each other, but they were both searching for something. They would know it when they found it, but it wasn't there.

There was no sign of Ellen's remains, no small object that she may had carried. He thought of all the old movies he had watched. Wasn't he supposed to find something, an article of clothing or a piece of jewelry? There was nothing but her dusty car.

Laura was the first to speak. "Mom was so hard to understand. It was like she was always searching for something, never content." She slowly scanned the smoldering debris. "Wherever you are Mom, I pray you're at peace. We love you." Turning around, she motioned Carl and Lynne to step forward and join them. They all took hold of each other's hands and Laura led off. They prayed together, as each of them had been taught. "Our father, who art in heaven hallowed be thy name. Thy kingdom come, thy will be done on earth as it is in heaven. Give us this day our daily bread and forgive us our trespasses, as we forgive those who trespass against us and lead us not into temptation but deliver us from evil. Amen."

"We love you Mom." Laura kept the rest to herself... *and I forgive you. I won't ever tell Dad...* She and Carl sadly eyed their charred school. Only the blackened outside masonry walls remained.

As Jack carefully scanned the entire the crash site, he was surprised they were the only people there—or was he? As he stood there, he thought, *The people who are in mourning today are maybe the only ones who know how serious this is, and what deep shit we're in.*

The remains of the victims in the store would never be found. The answer was there, all around them. The fact that they were all alone gave him the answer. There were no police guarding the wreckage. No NTSB or FAA officials telling them to stay away, or telling them they'd be informed when remains were found. There was no one, just four people on a beautiful spring afternoon saying the Lord's Prayer at the site of a terrible plane crash. For all they knew, it was one of hundreds, maybe thousands of crash sites scattered across the country. Jack knew this site, and the others, would be left untouched—for a very long time.

Life is for the living, he thought... *we could soon be joining them, we have to leave now.*

He said to Laura, "Let's see if Mom's car will start." He was holding up a set of spare keys that he had brought with and pointing them toward the filthy car.

Like leaving a cemetery after a funeral, Carl's truck, followed by the other two cars, slowly left the crash site. As Laura drove her mother's little car away, she sadly gazed into the rear-view mirror. With the crash site disappearing behind her, she wondered if a memorial plaque would ever be placed there.

The sun was no longer overhead, and Jack figured it must be pushing at least 3:30. They were all hungry, but their stomachs would have to wait. The smell that would be coming off the line of grills when they passed Al's would make it really tempting for them to stop and eat, but they would have to pass. Lynne had the spare ribs, that Carl had brought home that morning, ready to go when they got back. Jack didn't want to stop at Al's. The party atmosphere reminded him of the band that continued to play as the Titanic sunk. As they passed the golf course, Jack pointed out to Carl someone riding in a golf cart. It was weaving across the fairway, its occupants plainly drunk. People were wasting precious time and resources; behaving like idiots.

About ten minutes after they left the crash site, Carl's aunt's house was within sight.

His aunt lived on a dead-end street, across from the entrance to a large Catholic cemetery. There were only three houses on the street. The house next door was vacant, and the other one had people living in it, but was for sale. His aunt's house was the first one on the end. It was an old white sided Dutch-Colonial that looked like it dated from the 1920s. The house next door was a typical 1960s brick ranch, somewhat like Charlie's. It was a beautiful late afternoon, nice and quiet, but Jack didn't want to take any chances. He'd been through too much already and didn't want to walk into trouble.

Carl pulled into his aunt's driveway, as Jack motioned out his door window for Lynne and Laura to hold back. He wanted to take a good look around before the girls got out.

"Okay, Carl, let's check the place out. I want to make sure we're alone." Getting out of the truck, each of them quietly closed their doors. They walked around the house, keeping an eye on the vacant ranch house next door and the woods behind. With only three houses on the short street, there were no signs of life.

Only when Jack was sure they were alone, did he wave Lynne and Laura to come. The two women stopped at the front door, while Jack and Carl made a quick walk-through. The house had that musty smell that houses lived in by older people always seem to have.

Jack said, "Pretty secluded place your aunt and uncle had here. I've never been down this little street, but I've noticed it before. It lines up with the entrance to the cemetery."

Carl pointed towards the ranch house at the end of the short street. "John Nesbit and his wife, Mary, lived in the ranch that's for sale over there. They both worked at the cemetery. Their son and his family live there now with John. Mary

176

died last year. The vacant house next door is a rental and it's been empty for a while." Carl motioned to Lynne to follow him. "My aunt's bedroom is over here. All her clothes are in the back closet. My uncle's stuff is in the other one. He's been gone for about ten years, but she kept everything. They were married for 51 years." Carl placed his hand to Lynne's shoulder, "You take anything you want, Lynne." Lynne stepped in front of a dresser and hesitated, picking up a gold framed photo. It was an old wedding photograph of a young couple. There was a date neatly printed on the back of the frame, May 5, 1957.

"Your aunt was very pretty; they were a nice-looking couple."

She gently set the frame back down on the dresser. "I don't feel right about going through your aunt's drawers."

Carl was standing in the door frame behind her and shook his head. "Don't be. She'd love for you to take anything you want." Carl turned and left Lynne and Laura standing in the bedroom together. A second later he reappeared at the door and said, "Lynne, she was a nurse, just like you." He smiled, "You both look too serious. Really, if you see something you want or think we might need, please take it, don't be shy. Make sure you take her jewelry box too." He turned around and went into the kitchen, where he found Jack. He was examining a rather well stocked pantry. Jack reached in and pulled out a can of chicken soup.

"Your aunt has a good selection of canned goods here."

Carl nodded his head in agreement, "There's lots more downstairs. They grew up in the nuclear fallout shelter days and always kept lots of canned goods."

Jack put the can back on the shelf and turned to Carl. "I'm glad you're moving in with us."

"Thanks for letting me. There's no way I can live in my condo without power and I have to admit, I don't think I'd want to live alone here." Laura walked into the kitchen and heard Carl mention about living alone.

"No, you certainly can't, Carl. It's a nice house and all, but you just can't be here alone, directly across from a cemetery. I'd be scared to death something would happen to you."

Jack let out a short laugh. "Ha, that cemetery makes the best neighbors around. Dead people aren't hungry." He turned to Carl, "Since you're moving in with us and this house is vacant, I suggest we load all this food into some boxes and get it out of here right now. All I've seen the past two days are stores being broken into and looted. After the stores get cleaned out, vacant houses, especially isolated places like this, will be next. Let's load up your truck with everything we can take with us. If we have to, we can come back again before it gets too dark. If we don't, by the end of the week this house could be stripped clean. We should hang a "trespassers" *will be shot* sign on the front porch."

Carl agreed. "Sounds like a good idea. We'll do it before we leave. All right, let's go room to room. Set aside anything we can use. There are flashlights, batteries, candles, and matches in these cabinets. Some camping gear and old

177

hand tools are in the basement." Carl pointed out the kitchen window to the garage. "I think there are a couple 5-gallon cans of kerosene out in the garage and, hey, I bet my aunt's old van will start! If it does, we can pack it full of stuff too. I know she has some gardening supplies we can use and also some vegetable seeds."

Jack cocked his head to one side, raising his eyebrows in a hopeful expression, "By any chance…. any guns, maybe some ammo?"

Carl made a wide smile, "Oh yeah."

"That's great, now introduce me to Harry and his girls."

Jack knew only two things about chickens: omelets and drumsticks were good to eat. He'd also heard that they were easy to raise. Out behind the garage was an attached shed with a small fenced in area. Inside were six adult chickens and Harry, the rooster.

"Carl, this is amazing. I don't know a thing about chickens, other than they taste good. Right now, I don't have the time to learn a thing about them either. I've got just one question; how long would it take to set this whole operation up at my place?"

Carl laughed, "Gosh, Jack, when you move, you sure go fast. First a big garden and now chickens. Are we getting a cow tomorrow?"

"No, but I've thought of goats or pigs, and maybe a couple turkeys."

"Are you serious?"

"Carl, my mind is going so fast it's spinning. Over in the industrial park, there's a fence company that puts up those portable construction fences around building sites. We could score some fencing from them. We'd probably will need some of that chicken wire too. I bet we can move this whole set-up to my place, and maybe use the garden shed for a coop… if that's all right with you? I know I'm being pushy, but after what we've seen the last two days—we have to get our shit together really quick. Let the others party and put their faith in the government to come to their rescue. We're going to have to really bust our balls this week, because next week, opportunities like these will be gone."

"I'm with you, Jack, but what about the garden? I've got to get all that stuff we brought home planted."

"Tell you what, I think we should take these chickens today. We can let them loose in my garage for a couple days, until I get a coop ready. If any looters stumble upon this place, Harry and the girls will end up in a pot. You take care of turning over the garden this week, and I'll take care of the rest. Wait til you see that big rototiller Charlie has in action; it'll will make short work of my weeds."

Laura and Lynne packed Lynne's car with Carl's aunt's clothing. Everything from short-sleeved blouses to winter coats were stuffed into the back seat and trunk. The contents of the medicine cabinet and bathroom hall closet were emptied of toiletries and anything else that could be used for medical emergencies.

Next, they carried out the contents of the kitchen and basement pantries. Nothing   edible was left behind. After rummaging through the basement, they went out to the garage. His aunt's old van started right up and promptly received its new tenants: Harry and the girls, along with nine baby chicks and several fresh eggs. The back seat of Ellen's car was packed tight with weapons and ammo, and looked like a rolling armory. It turned out Carl's uncle *really* liked guns, and Jack wondered if he knew Charlie. Rifles, pistols, shotguns, and ammunition filled the entire car.

There were many other things that they'd come back for at a later time. As they would learn in the months to come, common everyday things that everyone took for granted would soon become very hard to come by.

They left in their parade of vehicles, with Laura leading in Carl's pickup truck, followed by Lynne in her car. Carl pulled out with his aunt's old van and Jack drove Ellen's car. As her little sparkling crystal ballerina dangled back and forth from the rearview mirror, he softly said to himself, "*Sorry, Ellen, I can't think of you now, there is too much I have to do.*"

Ten minutes later they were pulling into their subdivision and approaching Al's. It looked like everyone in the neighborhood, and then some, were there. There were more grills lined up, and Al's stereo was still blaring. What really floored him as he drove past, was that someone had managed to get one of those big inflatable bouncy houses set up. The electric blower that kept it inflated was plugged into a generator setting next to it. It was filled with the neighborhood kids, having a ball, oblivious to what was awaiting them. The sight of the children sent a shiver up Jack's spine. He thought, *What's going to happen to all those kids when the shit really gets rough? God help us…*

Laura, Lynne and Carl drove by the party, barely slowing down, but Jack, who was coming up last in Ellen's car, stopped. Al was already by the curb.

"Holy crap, you got Ellen's car back! I'm sorry, Jack, for the party atmosphere over here. I know it doesn't look like it, but everyone is pretty depressed about all this shit, including me and Lois. We figure this is kind of a morale booster." Al pointed to the children having fun in the bounce house. "Especially for the kids, they don't understand any of this. Hey, me and Jerry just paid a visit to old Charlie, and Dotty. We brought them some of Lois's pulled pork and a case of cold beer. You know, Dotty doesn't look too good, and Charlie's brother, he's in bed and looks like shit. He smells like it too. Charlie says that lady you took in is a nurse and has been tending to him today. The other thing is the old guy ain't walking too good, his toes look horrible."

Jack agreed, "Yeah, Lynne's a nurse, thank God. They're supposed to have a live-in nurse with them, but with what's happened, that's history. We'll just have to take care of them. All the hospitals are in meltdown with no emergency services, and from what I've seen, I doubt there are any drugstores that haven't been broken into. Just like your store, Al, everything is going to hell."

Al raised his eyebrows optimistically, "Well, I've talked to a lot of people today. Some are saying that the Illinois National Guard is slow getting ready because of no transportation, but in a couple days they're going to kick ass and this shit will be over. They'll knock the crap outta them gangs in Chicago once and for all, and good riddance to them bastards. I also heard they'll be getting the power on by Sunday. Apparently, the only place that is without it is us here in the Midwest. Tim Johnson, who works for Commonwealth Power and Light, says they'll send in crews from other states to get us back on line." Something caught Al's eye. He made a face, stuck his head into Jack's door window, and looked in. "Holy shit, Jack, you gonna start a war? What the hell is with all these guns?"

"Just want to be prepared, that's all."

"Gosh, Jack, don't you think you're going a little overboard here? Charlie told us about your garden plans and all. I've seen your backyard, and it looks like MacDonald's farm back there. I mean, we got this so-called FEMA group and the Homeland Security people. Those government agencies have whole warehouses full of food for just this type of disaster, and don't forget the Red Cross. Then we have the National Guard and all that to clear this riff-raff out. I admit it's bad, but we have to look on the bright side of things. That's what we pay taxes for."

Jack didn't think this was the time to discuss his dim views about any so-called help from the government. He just said, "Yeah, maybe, let's hope. Anyway, I've got to get home. Thanks for all those spare ribs. The kids should be getting them ready for the grill, right about now."

"Don't mention it and hey, you wait right here a second."

Al came running back a minute later with a case of cold beer. "Here, take this home and chill out. Better yet, after you eat, bring your whole clan back down here and join us."

Jack took the case of beer and put it on the passenger seat. "How you keeping all this beer so cold?"

"That's a secret, Jackster. Now you get home and eat. And hey, stop worrying about shit. Everything will turn out all right. Remember, we got a president who's a Republican."

"Yeah, whatever you say, Al. That makes me feel so much better. See you later."

BOBBY

CHAPTER 19

Jack pulled into his drive and decided he would park the gun-laden car in the backyard, just to be safe. There was no use tempting someone by parking it out front. As he got to the corner of the house, he saw Carl standing in front of the grill, slathering barbecue sauce on the ribs.

Carl asked, "Parking back here now?"

Jack got out of the car and tiredly said, "Yep, too many strangers down at Al's. We're going to have to change the way we do things. I hope there's no more excitement tonight. Did Lynne check over at Charlie's place?"

"Yes, I did." It was Lynne and she was still wearing his sweatpants, but now had a women's yellow blouse on. "Ted is going to have to be cleaned up again, and he's totally unresponsive. Even if he was in a hospital receiving the best of care, he'd pass in a day or two. What are we going to do if he dies? With what's going on, we won't be able to get an ambulance, let alone a funeral home to take him."

"I don't know, Lynne, I really don't know. Let's clean up and eat. Then we can go over and talk to Charlie about it. They all sat down and Laura led them in giving thanks. They prayed for all the friends they had lost and asked for courage to face tomorrow. As Jack prayed, he thought about that morning and how he had given Sheila the money, and how she had just stood on the curb, watching him until he was out of sight. He silently wished her and her mother well in patching up their past. The spare ribs were excellent. Carl had slathered them with their last bottle of barbecue sauce. Lynne made a salad, and they feasted on a thawed-out Chocolate Cheesecake for desert. They were sitting outside at the picnic table finishing up and Jack had just started his second beer. Lynne and Laura were about to clean up and go over to Charlie's, when Lynne suddenly cupped her hand to her ear. "There it is again, Laura. Did you hear it this time?" Laura sat still in her chair. Jack and Carl looked at each other without saying a word.

Laura said, "Yes, this time I clearly heard it. The first time it sounded like a cat, or maybe a kitten."

They heard it again. This time, all of them. Sitting still, they listened, all of them hearing the sound again.

"That's a child's cry." said Lynne. She and Laura both stood up, staring at the house next door.

"Dad, it sounds like it's coming from Jake and Ronnie's house."

It was 35 hours after the shit had hit the fan. Jack had just finished a good dinner and was about to kick back and finish beer number two. It had been a long day, and he was afraid of what tomorrow would bring. He was glad today was finally drawing to a close. He had taken to wearing his dad's old 44, Little Red, in a holster, but had removed it before dinner. Getting up from his seat, he reluctantly strapped it back on. He was beginning to think he should just stay armed from the moment he woke up.

With Laura and Lynne in the lead, he and Carl followed them to the house next door, where Jake and Ronnie lived with their little boy, Bobby. The house was a three-bedroom ranch with an attached garage. Jack had checked it out earlier that morning. The house had appeared to be locked up tight, with no one home. He looked through the garage windows and saw it was empty. He had concluded that the young couple and their little boy were more than likely stuck somewhere, still trying to get home.

The back door that had been locked up tight that morning, was now wide open. The door jamb was broken, splintered at the lock, like someone had kicked it in. The cries of a child were clearly coming from inside the house.

Laura and Lynne were in the house and out of sight before Jack could protest. Carl was about to follow, when Jack grabbed him by his shoulder and pulled him back saying, "Don't! Go back and get a gun and stay by this door until you hear me say it's clear."

Carl ran back to Ellen's car and retrieved a 12-gauge shotgun, while Jack cautiously went inside. He could clearly hear the crying coming from a front bedroom. With his gun drawn, he checked out the first floor of the house. Lynne was kneeling on the bedroom floor next to Ronnie and her little boy. Ronnie had been brutally beaten and possibly raped. He left the room and met Carl at the back door, "You wait out here where you can cover the front and sides. I'm going to check out the basement and garage. Any guy comes running out that isn't me, don't say a thing, just shoot him!"

Jack checked out the attached garage and then the basement. He really didn't expect anyone to still be hiding in the house, but he was already mad at himself for letting the girls run in before the place was cleared. He didn't want to make any more mistakes and miss a hiding intruder. When he was sure the house was clear, he waved Carl in and joined the girls in the bedroom.

Ronnie was a mess; someone had beaten her mercilessly; the left side of her face was caked with dried clots of blood. Bobby was sitting next to her crying, holding onto her arm, with Laura trying to pull him away.

Lynne took the little boy and gently pushed him towards Laura, saying, "Laura, he's unharmed. Take him to another room. He needs to be changed and given something to drink. See if there's any food in the kitchen. Some fruit would be best." Laura scooped up Bobby and quickly left the room.

Jack knelt down next to them. Ronnie was barely alive, but able to talk and was trying to tell Lynne what happened. Lynne was bending over her, holding her ear close to Ronnie's blood-caked mouth, listening.

Jack made out one word. "Glen!"

Lynne stood up, followed by Jack. She turned around and grabbed the end of a bedspread. Sliding it off the bed, she spread it over the young mother's body.

Jack said, "I only heard one word and that was *Glen*. What happened?"

Lynne didn't say anything for a few seconds, sadly looking down at the covered body. "She was pregnant and lost the baby, it's so sad. She said the name Glen Sorensen—said he raped her and beat her. He probably thought she was dead. Do you know who this animal named Glen is?"

He was about to answer her, when Al's reclusive army veteran neighbor, Joan, came into the room.

Joan looked at Jack and down to the covered body of Ronnie. "What happened? I was just on my way down here to see you."

Jack motioned for everyone to leave the room and go outside. Laura was with the boy on the back patio, changing his fecal and blood-stained clothes.

Joan said, "We just saw her this morning, maybe around nine. She was walking home, pulling the little boy in a wagon. She was expecting another child. My girlfriend, Kathy, asked her to stop. We offered her something to eat, but she refused. She said she had to get right home. What the hell happened?" Jack looked expectantly at Lynne.

"All she said to me was she heard someone kick in the back door, and it was this Glen Sorenson. She said, 'He raped and beat me,' and then she died. I think she was bleeding pretty badly internally. She lost the baby. I hope the little boy was hiding and didn't see it. Her blood is all over him."

Joan said. "Glen was in front of Al's when she walked by this morning. He was drunk and acting really nasty. Everyone felt sorry for him. I heard his wife was working at Jay's when the plane crashed into it. He walked down the sidewalk in front of our house before he crossed over to Al's. He saw us in our yard. I'm not going to repeat what he said to us, but we kept an eye on him until he went across the street. God, I wish I would have shot that bastard. He'd be dead, and this wouldn't have happened."

Jack turned to Lynne and Carl and filled them in on who Glen was. Then he brought up the barrel of the 44 and said to Carl and Joan, "Let's go across the street to his house and see if he's there. I don't expect him to be, but if he's drunk enough, who knows? We could find him in bed, passed out cold." Jack said to Carl, "How about fixing Joan up with one of your uncle's rifles. Joan, you were in the Army, right? See any combat?"

I've seen it, but never engaged. I was in for 20 years. I've been trained and can handle myself and any weapons you have."

"I bet you can. You come with me; we're going in his front door. He lives in that brick two story across the street. Carl, you go around the rear of the ranch house next door to him and cover his back door. I've been back there before and there's a big brick barbeque grill in the yard, right by the deck. You get behind it, and if he comes out, you don't hesitate, got it?" Carl nodded his head and Jack repeated himself. "You just shoot him. You don't say a word, just don't shoot unless you know it's him. He's not easy to miss. He's blond-haired, skinny, and about 6'2", with a short beard. He's covered with tattoos and looks like an asshole."

A petite blonde headed girl joined them, "I'm Kathy, Joan's friend. I'll go back there with him. I know what he looks like, and I'm good with this." Kathy was holding up a Shotmaster 9 mm. pistol. "I have a carry permit. I won't hesitate, and I won't miss."

The four of them ran across the street like a commando team: Jack with Joan, and Carl with Kathy. Jack figured they would to have to kick in the front door to Glen's house.

What they weren't expecting was that the door would be wide open, with a greeting painted in large black letters on the far living room wall,

HAVE A GREAT DAY ASSHOL

Joan spoke first, "He spelled asshole wrong."

Jack motioned Jo to be silent and pointed to a gruesome sight dangling above them. Hanging by its leash, from the second-floor stair banister, was Glen and Doris's black Doberman, Satan. The fur around the dog's neck looked wet, matted with its blood. Together, they carefully made their way through the house, checking every room. The entire house was trashed. It was like a madman had torn through it, destroying everything in his path. Special attention had been given to framed family photos. The frames were smashed and every picture was torn into tiny shreds. In the master bedroom, high on the wall at the head of the bed, was painted the word Satan, in dripping black letters. A large upside-down cross was painted under it.

Only when Jack was sure the house was clear, did he speak.

"This guy's a killer and he's whacked in the head. We're going to have to put the word out about him. Looks like he slit the dog's throat before he hung him up." Like the front door, the rear entry to the house was wide open. Knowing Carl and Kathy were standing guard in the backyard, Jack shouted out, "We're clear, Carl, but take a good look around you before you come in."

A chill ran down Jack's spine and he was again moving, cursing to himself out loud. He ran from the kitchen, back to the front door, with Jo close behind him. Carl and Kathy followed. Kathy shot a confused, "What gives?" look to Jo.

Jack stepped out and stopped on the front porch of Glen's house. He looked across the street surveying his own house, and breathed easy. Everything looked all right.

He saw Laura inside his garage, getting something off a shelf. Charlie was sitting in a lawn chair on his front porch, his old M1 carbine across his lap.

Charlie gave him an "All clear" wave and Jack waved back, carefully eyeing the other houses near them. The four of them all stood together on the porch, spooked by Jack's actions.

Everything looked quiet, and Carl asked, "What is it, Jack, what's wrong?"

Jack was silent for a moment, then slowly shook his head. "Notice the message painted on the wall reads, 'Have a nice day asshole,' and not assholes. I've got a feeling that I'm the asshole. Bad speller or not, I think that note was directed towards me. Sorry to alarm everyone, but I suddenly got the idea that maybe this was a set-up and he wanted us over here, so he could do something over at my place." Jack paused, wishing he had a cigarette. "You know, all of us brush elbows with perverts and killers like this Glen every day, and we don't even know it. What keeps these bastards in check and acting normal is prescription medicine and the plain old fear of getting caught. Now that the law is done for, these killers and perverts are going to have a field day, and we have to be prepared...prepared for anything." He turned around and looked at Joan and Kathy. "This is the kind of shit I'm really afraid of. While we're out of our houses checking his place out, he's at our place doing his thing and waiting for us to come home. He might be in any one of these vacant houses on the block, watching us right now, laughing at us...and you know what?" Jack looked around at the neighboring houses. "I think he is. He's hiding nearby, enjoying this."

Kathy's eyes went wide with alarm, "Oh my God. He could be back at our house hiding, waiting for us..." Jack nodded his head. "I don't want to scare you, but from now on, each of us has to be armed, 24/7. There's a lot of Glens out there and we have to expect the unexpected. I don't mean looking under your bed every night before you get in it, but every time you leave your house unattended, it has to be locked up tight. Unless you have a dog, you should set little markers around the hallways and doors before you leave. I'll explain about that later. You come home and something is slightly out of place, you've got yourself an intruder. We're going to have to band together and I don't mean a neighborhood watch." Jack motioned down the street to Al's barbeque. "That party bullshit will be coming to a halt really quick once these people figure out how deep the shit they're in is."

Joan gave Kathy a nudge with her elbow, "Let's you and I walk down to Ken's and let him know what's going on. We'll stop back later."

185

Kathy said to Jack, "When we come back, could one of you walk down to our house with us...to check it over? I'm scared."

Jack nodded his head, "That goes without question, ladies. That's the way we're going to operate— from now on." As Joan and Kathy started walking down the street to Ken's, Jack and Carl walked across towards Charlie's.

"Carl, why don't you check on the girls and Bobby. Take a good look around the place too. We're going to have to be on our guard tonight and every night from now on. I'm going to fill Charlie in on what's happened." He added, "We have to be thinking about Ronnie's body too. With no funeral parlors, she's going to have to be buried tomorrow morning, at the latest. I wish we knew where her husband was."

Before they parted, Carl stopped at the curb. Facing Jack, he seemed afraid to speak. "How are we going to survive what's coming, Jack? I mean, this is just the start, and I already feel overwhelmed...."

Jack placed his hand on Carl's shoulder, "We're going to survive this shit, Carl, make no mistake about it. We're going to take each bump in the road as it comes and not become discouraged. Lots of people are going to simply fold up, **but not us**. Tomorrow morning, before dawn, you're going to be plowing us a big ass garden. Better get plenty of sleep." Jack turned away from Carl and started walking over to Charlie's. Max and Toots ran out to greet him.

CHARLIE

CHAPTER 20

Charlie was still sitting in his lawn chair holding the carbine. It was a vintage Korean War M1 Garand. Three full clips of 30-06 ammunition sat on the small table next to him. Jack was walking up to him as he said, "Did you carry that in Korea?'"

"No, but I carried one just like it, and I was hoping I'd get to use it again tonight. Didn't think the bastard would still be in there, but I was hoping. I knew that guy was no good the day they moved in here. It's funny, you can just tell with some people, don't even have to talk to them. The way they dressed. That Doris went out on weekends looking like she was attending a funeral, always dressed in black. Didn't you ever notice that? And him, you ever see that eyeball tattoo on his face? Weird people, I tell you. Who the hell gets a tattoo of an eyeball on their forehead? You get a tattoo; you get something like this." Charlie held up his left forearm, displaying a faded eagle, globe and anchor.

Jack grabbed the lawn chair next to him and sat down, saying, "Someday I'll show you mine... Did you hear the whole story of what happened?"

"Yeah, Laura came over and told me. Asked me if I'd seen Glen, the son of a bitch."

"Have you?"

"No, not today, but I saw him out here flipping you the bird last night. I knew he was an asshole, but I didn't think he'd rape and kill that poor woman. Any news of her husband?"

"No, he works in Chicago. Heavy crane operator on the far south side. He could be trapped in the city or anywhere in between. So, you saw Glen give me the finger last night, huh? I wish I would have confronted him then and there. Maybe this wouldn't have happened. He beat Ronnie to death, Charlie. Just beat the hell out of her and she lost the baby she was carrying. Right in front of the little boy too. I could have confronted that animal and ended it last night."

"Can't go that route, Jack, don't blame yourself for not confronting someone. Crazy people like that, you never know what they're thinking, and it's usually a safe bet to just avoid them. Everyone around here is really going to have to sleep on pins and needles from now on. Not just because of this murdering bastard either, it's going to get really nuts. I'm afraid we ain't seen nothing yet."

As Charlie was talking, Jack was intently watching Glen's house. "I was just telling Carl and Joan the same thing a few minutes ago. I wish he'd come back. I'd shoot him on the spot."

Jack bent down and gave Max the attention the dog was asking for. Charlie was scratching Toots on her head.

Jack said, "He killed his dog too. Slit its throat, then hung him from the second-floor stair banister. That dog always seemed friendly to everyone." They both sat there a few moments, not saying anything.

Finally, Charlie said, "That tells me he won't be back to that house ever again. A man gives away his belongings or kills his dog, he's gone for good."

Jack shook his head. "I don't know. He may like us to think that, but he'll be back. I can feel it."

Changing the subject, Charlie said, "That's quite a lady you got staying with you. She spent most of the morning over here. She changed Ted, must have been three times, and gave him a bath. He can't hold his bowels anymore, what a way to end up. She cleaned up Dot too and helped me get my generator going. Got Dot's oxygen machine plugged into it for the night. Can't run it 24 hours a day though, or we'll be out of gas pretty quick." Charlie scoffed, "Ha! Make sure that Lynne never gets in a poker game."

Jack didn't say anything, not understanding the poker comment.

"I had her take a look at my legs, damn feet have been killing me. She said. 'It looks worse than it is.' I could tell she was shoveling me a load of horseshit by the look on her face when I took my socks off. The smell is the corker. I got gangrene, Jack. She knows it, and I know it. I can tell by the way she is when she's with Ted that he's on his way out too. And Dot, it's not so much her emphysema, but her heart. She's so worked up over what's going on, well— it's just bad news all around."

Jack started to say something, but Charlie cut him off.

"Would you do me a favor and get me my pipe and tobacco from the study? On your way back, how about grabbing us both a cold beer from the propane fridge?"

Jack went into the house and peeked in Dottie's room. She was sound asleep, as the oxygen machine was pumping its lifesaving gas into her lungs. When he returned to the porch, Lynne was standing there, talking to Charlie. He handed Charlie his beer and pipe and held out the other beer to Lynne. She waved him off.

"No thanks. I was just telling Charlie that Bobby is fine, but he hasn't said a word. He's about four years old, and Laura said he normally doesn't speak much. Seeing his mother like that, it had to be horrible on him. We fed him, and Laura put him to bed. He went right to sleep. What are we going to do with his mother?"

"We'll have to bury her in the backyard tomorrow."

188

Charlie opened his beer with a **pop**! "Better dig two, Teddy's on his last legs. I wish I was in better shape; I'd do it myself. What the hell, better dig four." The old man let off a weak laugh and took a swig of beer.

Jack scolded him, "Don't talk like that, Charlie, we have to..." He cut Jack off mid-sentence. "Listen up, because time grows short. You know, like I was telling you, I wish I was in better shape, but what the hell, that's life, huh?" Charlie looked over to Lynne and motioned her to sit in Jack's chair. Then he shot a glance to Jack, nodding his head over to the porch step. "Grab yourself some concrete, big guy, and sit down. There's something I gotta say and I want you both to hear it, and *don't* interrupt me. I'm going to spare you my tale of woe and make it short. As I was telling you yesterday, I thought the shit would have hit the fan years ago. It really surprised me it didn't. Me and Dottie been prepping a long time and we thought we had all the bases covered. We just never figured we'd be too old and too sick to play the whole thing out. Thought of everything we could possibly need and stocked up. Aw what the hell, never get old." Lynne started to say something but Charlie waved her off. He took another swallow of beer, letting out a small belch, saying, "Anyway, where was I? Oh yeah—now Jack, we've been neighbors for a long time and we've talked in the past about prepping and all, but you don't know a quarter of what I have got stashed away here." He paused while he packed his pipe with tobacco. Lynne shot Jack a look as if she was going to say something, but Jack shook his head, and mouthed, "No."

Charlie continued, "You know those guns and book cases in my study that you've always admired? I built those myself, all of knotty pine." The old man smiled and looked over at Lynne. "When Dot and I were married, the place we honeymooned at in northern Michigan had all these cute little log cabins. We just fell in love with the place. The insides of them were all finished in these natural knotty pine boards. I've always liked knotty pine since then. Thing is, the north wall of the study is false, and so are all the book cases and shelves. There's a couple feet of dead space behind them pine boards." He looked over to Jack and winked. "You start poking around, you'll figure it all out. There are more than a few surprises hidden behind them walls."

The old man lit his pipe that he'd been packing; took a big puff, then started laughing to himself. "Yes sir, a few surprises. I got some special stuff I brought home after Korea. Boy that was one cold ass place, if they only let MacArthur— Aw shit, where was I? Oh yeah, scout around in our bedroom too, you'll find some loose paneling. That will really make your day." Charlie raised his beer and took long drink, then belched. "Also, down in my basement, over in the north corner is a big wooden box standing all by itself. You lift it up and you'll see a pipe coming up out of the floor going to a pump. Me and Ted sunk a well down there years ago, when the village wanted to cap our main well, the bastards. Sunk a sand point down 23 feet and got good clear water. Try driving pipe by hand in a basement. Boy, that was a job I'll tell you, but it was fun. It's a shallow well, but I send a water sample to be tested every other year, and it's as good as the city water. Andy's Home Center does it for me. Hard as hell and got an iron taste to it, but it's good. Probably better then all that cancer-causing fluoride and God knows what other crap the city water has got added to it." Charlie started scratching his head like there was something he forgot. "Oh yeah, one last thing. There are several spiral bound notebooks in my side desk drawer. I keep detailed lists of everything I got, where it is and what it's for. I did that in case something ever happened to me." Charlie pointed towards Joan and Kathy's house. "I see you've made pals with Joan, and her sidekick, Kathy. I've talked to them several times. I saw them out in their backyard one day when I was driving by. I noticed the way they dressed and figured they'd been in the military, so I stopped to shoot the shit. Joan was in the army and is one tough woman. She put in the 20 and got out an E 8. Kathy, she's younger and a nice kid. She wasn't in the military, but she works at the big Veteran's Hospital over in Berwyn. I had a long conversation with them and guess what? They're survivalists." Charlie seemed out of breath and paused a moment. Jack was going to ask something, but Charlie held his hand up, stopping him.   "Listen to me, Jack. You're going to have to align yourself with fighters—people that have what it takes to survive. Those two girls down there are politically as far left as I am right—but this is life or death. Political bullshit has to be buried. They're friends with a guy over on the next block. He's a strange one and a real loner. His name is Ken Martinez, and I've talked to him. I don't think he has any politics one way or the other, but he's a prepper and a gun nut. Met him at a gun show and you should have seen the shit he was buying, holy crap. I hope he never has a fire in his house. His son lives with him, but I think the mother died. This Martinez is a former Army Ranger—I'm surprised you haven't crossed paths with him. I'm telling you this because I think you need to team up with these people. I don't think you'll make it if you don't. I don't think they'll make it either. Maybe if you were out in the Rockies or Smokies you could make it by yourselves, but here in the burbs, close to this over-flowing shit-tank called Chicago? No way. This place will be like General Custer's Last Stand." Charlie paused for a moment, out of breath, then said, "Years ago, I had a buddy plan myself, unfortunately he died three years ago... and he was six years younger than me... damn cigarettes." Charlie took a long pull off his pipe. After he blew out a cloud of blue smoke he said, "I ain't going to make it, kids, I'm just too damn old, but you're going to and my place is yours. That crowd of idiots down the street think this is just an excuse for a party. Don't fall in with them, because they'll suck the life right out of you when it gets bad." Charlie laughed, "You know, it's a funny thing when you think about it. All of us are preppers and we're all loners. Even you, Lynne, you're a loner, I can see it. I'll tell you something; loners got a fatal flaw. We all think that we know best and that means doing everything ourselves. Preppers who are loners aren't going to make it, Jack, not here. The have-nots will overwhelm them and they'll drop like flies. You'll have to band together to make it. Don't be afraid to take in others... but *only* if they have skills you need."

Jack noticed Lynne quickly wipe her face with a tissue. It looked like she started crying and didn't want to be noticed. Charlie saw it too, and turned around in his chair, and opened the screen door saying, "Go on dogs, get inside now. Go check on Mother." Charlie turned to Lynne, "Let's don't start that stuff, honey. No crying, preppers don't cry. They also don't look back and they don't ever complain, unless they're out of beer, so no crying. In a way, I've always thought about preppers as pioneers, they don't give a brown turd about what everyone else thinks. So, don't get misty on me. I ain't going anywhere just yet, but the handwriting is on the wall. One other thing, could you gas up my generator before you turn in tonight, Jack? I'd really appreciate it. And hey, that neighbor behind you, what's his name, Barry? What the hell is his problem? He got all pissed off at me this afternoon. He came over here demanding I let him plug in a bunch of extension cords he had put together. He had them laid out from his house over to my generator. Damn cords must have totaled over 400 feet. I told him it wouldn't do him any good because it was too damn long, so he wanted me to move my generator to the back of my lot, closer to his place. He got all pissed off when I said I wouldn't do it." Charlie started laughing, "By the way, did you happen to see him and his wife trying to stand that big ladder up against the side of their house? *What a couple of morons!* They were wasting precious water to wash their windows. God help us." Charlie pushed himself up out of his chair. "See you two tomorrow morning." Before he disappeared behind the door, he added, "The rototiller is ready to go. I'll be up at five, maybe earlier. Goodnight, kids."

Charlie went inside and closed the door. After Jack heard the click of the deadbolt, he got up from his spot on the step and leaned against the porch railing. "Jeez, what do you make of all that? He's got everything already planned out for us."

Lynne got up from her chair and tiredly ran her fingers through her hair. "He certainly thinks of everything. It's too much for me to think about tonight, but he's right, at least about the loner part. It's funny how old people can see right through you. Right now, I'm just too tired to think about it. It could be a long night. I hope Bobby sleeps through it."

Jack gently touched the bandage on her face, "Your cheek doesn't seem as swollen as it was last night. Even with having this nasty injury, you worked hard today, Lynne. Thanks for helping my neighbors."

Because Charlie's front porch faced the west, the setting sun's last rays were shining upon them. As they faced each other, Jack saw the remnants of a single tear, sparkling in the dimming light on her cheek.

Lynne drew a deep breath, "We're going to be okay... right?"

191

"Yeah, we're going to be all right."

"I guess I better go check on Laura and Bobby."

Jack laughed, "I'll go down to Al's and get Charlie a couple steaks for breakfast, while I can." His smile slowly faded, and it was his turn to take a slow deep breath. He could smell a slight trace of fragrance, the fragrance that she worn in the elevator only two days before. He didn't know if he imagined it, he only knew it already seemed like a lifetime ago. As the sun was taking its final plunge, the cool night air started rolling in and the music coming from Al's seemed to be playing louder. Jack cocked his head towards Al's. Both of them listened... ***Gotta keep rolling now... gotta keep rolling on... never gonna stop, always gonna rock....***

Lynne raised her eyebrows... "Disco?"

Jack let out a laugh, "Yeah, Al loves that old stuff, especially disco."

For a few moments, they both stood awkwardly close, only inches away from each other. In the cool evening air, Lynne was close enough to feel the warmth radiating from Jack's body. They were standing a heartbeat apart, when a cold breeze came up and blew between them. Jack backed away and let out a breath he was holding. "I'd better go see what the news is at Al's.... Maybe I'll take a walk around the block and check things out. I'll be back in about an hour. You going to be all right?"

Lynne looked down for a second, then up at Jack. "Yeah, go ahead, I'll be okay. Carl gave me his uncle's 12-gauge pump shotgun to keep in my room." She hesitated, "Jack—please be careful." He gave her arm a light squeeze and stepped off the porch into the darkness. The only place on the whole block that was completely lit up was Al's.

THE COOKOUT

CHAPTER 21

The cookout at Al's was going full out. Most of the grills were manned by familiar faces that Jack recognized from the neighborhood. As he searched for Al, he noticed there were lots of faces he didn't recognize, most of them eating and all of them drinking. Word about the cookout had spread, and the offer of free food was acting like a magnet. Some people gave him a wary eye when they noticed the long-barreled 44 he was wearing holstered on his hip. Surprised to see Joan and Kathy there, he started making his way over to them. Before he could approach them, he was stopped by a neighbor who lived on the next street to the south of him. They had both seen each other before, but they had never stopped to talk. The fellow approached Jack from the side, firmly putting his hand on his shoulder. He immediately didn't like the guy, and the conversation that followed went downhill quick.

"Hey, I'm Bob Dorfman. I live over on the next block." Placing both of his hands on his hips, he continued, "Couldn't help but see you and your group today pull in with all those vehicles. Three cars and that truck. There isn't a running vehicle on my whole block. Where did you get them?"

Jack backed up a step and faced him. "I don't think it's any of your business, Bob."

Bob placed his right hand to his mouth, thoughtfully rubbing the two-day old stubble on his chin. "Look, buddy...I really need to borrow that pickup truck tomorrow morning."

Jack instantly didn't like the man and could smell he'd been drinking more than beer. "Sorry, Bob, not mine to lend out. The only one that's mine is the little red convertible. That belonged to my late wife and I don't want to loan it out."

"I'm not interested in that. I need that truck. Look, I got cash. I'll rent it from you or buy it outright."

"Like I said, the fellow that owns it won't loan it or sell it, and that's final." Jack was closely watching Bob's body language and didn't like what he was seeing.

Bob looked down, eyeing Jack's sidearm, then moved in closer. He was at least four inches shorter than Jack and held his chin up defiantly. "You're the guy who has that Marine flag always hanging in front of your house. A real patriot, huh?" He glanced back down at Jack's gun. "You got a permit to open carry that thing?"

Jack made a thin smile. "Who cares?"

"What do you mean, 'Who cares?' I'm an officer with the State Police, and I just asked you if you got a permit to openly carry that weapon. If you're in law enforcement, show me your badge, but don't talk to me like I'm some kind of dick."

"I don't know what kind of dick you are, Bob, but I think it's safe to say you're a pretty big one." At that moment, Joan and Kathy appeared alongside the man. Joan was on the left, Kathy on his right.   Bob thinly smiled, briefly eyed Joan, then stared at Kathy. Wearing a wide smile, he sneered. "Well, if it isn't the rainbow twins." Bob slowly pulled a leather packet from his chest jacket pocket and quickly flipped it open, revealing a State Police badge.

Unimpressed, Kathy said, "Tell me, Bob, do you ever brush your teeth? I'm a dental assistant and I'll bet you got a mouthful of carries…"

Jack let out a laugh, and so did Joan. He couldn't help it. He remembered his grandmother using that term.

Bob turned and faced Joan, then looked back at Jack. Locking his eyes with Jack's, he forced a smile and sarcastically snarled, "These two little girls your body guards?"

Joan didn't hesitate, "He doesn't need body guards and you're no cop, are you Bob? You're a clerk…" Joan paused, scrunched up her nose and moved her head back, away from his. "Man, Kathy's right. Your teeth *could* use a good cleaning, ugh——." Kathy burst out laughing, and Jack could see rage rising in the man's eyes.

Joan continued, "I'll tell you something else, Bob. If you don't walk away from here, like right now, you'll be needing full dentures. Maybe implants and someone to figure out how to get that badge out of your colon."

Bob was doing his best to look cool, but his left eye started twitching. "Okay, I got it, I'll go. You just threatened me and you think it's really funny. You may think because of all that's happened, it's okay, but it's not. You have no respect for my authority because I'm alone. What can I say? But let me tell you something. I know what goes on around here and you people don't have a fucking clue. You think you're so brave, we'll see. You better watch your backs, ladies, especially in this neighborhood." He shot an aggravated sneer to Jack, and said, "You too, pal."

Kathy and Joan moved sideways, giving him space as he turned to leave.

Joan said, "Watch our backs… is that a threat from you?"

Dorfman stopped mid stride and slowly turned around facing Joan, a tight-lipped smile on his face. "No, it's not a threat, but like I said, you don't have a clue what's going on around here, you really don't. You'll find out that I'm not the enemy. Have a nice night, ladies."

194

Al's wife, Lois, was standing behind Jack and lightly clapped her hands, "Thank you, he's finally gone."

Jack said to Joan, "Who the hell is he? And what was he talking about, watching our back?"

Joan didn't answer. Lois did. "He's an asshole and he's had way too much to drink. He's just a little man with a badge. He came over here and started snooping around. He wanted to know where we got all the food and was asking all kinds of questions, as if we had stolen it. Of course, before he left, he had a steak. Of all the nerve. Can you believe that?"

"It might get worse, Lois."

"I expect it will, *especially for him*." Lois said nothing to Joan or Kathy, but coldly eyed Bob Dorfman as he walked away. She turned and walked back towards her house. Jack extended his hand to Kathy and then Joan, saying, "Kathy, Joan, once again, thanks for the back-up. That Dorfman guy looks like a real asshole, but he did get my curiosity up. I wonder what he knows, that we don't?"

Joan high fived Jack. He's just a drunk with a badge. It was no problem, Jack. Call me *Jo*, that's what my friends call me."

"Then Jo it is." Jack looked from Jo to Kathy, "You girls come over here to get some chow?"

Kathy said, "No, the welcome mat isn't exactly out for us. That Lois is a real piece of work. We've been over here asking everyone if they've seen that murdering bastard, Glen, or anyone who answers his description. We figured someone here might have seen him, but no one has seen him since this morning. We got the word out though, and if he shows up, there's more than just us who'll shoot him on sight. We're going to head back home. We have plenty of our own food."

Jack bid the women goodbye, then headed to find Lois. He found her in her kitchen.

Lois gave him a hug, saying, "Thanks again for running that man out. I don't like nosey people." Lingering in front of him, Lois stood close to Jack. "Jack, you've been through so much. Losing Ellen like that. Al and I feel terrible for you. I don't know how you're managing to keep yourself together. I was good friends with Doris. She was like Ellen, a good person. Glen's not strong like you, Jack. He must have gone crazy after losing her. Killing that young mother like that and leaving that little boy all alone. It's too bad, those people probably should have never moved here."

Jack quickly exhaled, disgusted at Lois' comment. He eased back from her, saying, "I don't understand you and Al. It's great what you're doing here, feeding everyone, helping your neighbors. But why did you just snub your neighbors, Joan and Kathy? And why did you say *those people* probably should have never moved here? My God, Lois, this world is a mess, and that kind attitude has made it that way, for God's sake!"

Raising her eyebrows, Lois lowered her chin. "For God's sake, really, Jack? That's a good one. The God you believe in doesn't run this planet. He *abandoned* it. Take a look around, he skipped out 2000 years ago. I'll be back... yeah right." Lois turned her back to Jack, staring out her darkened kitchen window, shaking her head. "You know, Jack, your weak thinking will be your end. I'll help who I please and I'll like who I please, and God has nothing to do with it." She turned around and faced him, slowly moving up to him. Stopping with her face uncomfortably close to his, her green eyes were wickedly alive, boring into his. "I don't like those two women, and as far as the black family, I have nothing against them, but they made a bad decision moving here and now their little boy is an orphan. Who's going to raise him—you? I like you, Jack, but I don't have to like everyone you like and certainly not your version of God. He's a phony and so are his so-called commandments. Where is he now when everyone *really* needs him, huh? Do you believe in those commandments, Jack, *all* of them? Or are you like most good Christians, you pick out the easy and convenient ones? Today Al and I are helping people, Jack. No lofty words or sermons, *we are feeding our neighbors.* Now come on, Jack—it's late, let's not talk about all this. I suppose you came here looking for Al?" She moved closer, almost against him, her green eyes looking upwards into his, a hint of a smile in them. Barely discernable, Jack edged back a fraction of an inch.

Lois coyly smiled, rolling her eyes towards the ceiling. "Al's upstairs—he decided to take a little nap about two hours ago, and now he's out... dead to the world." She backed away from Jack, leaning seductively against her kitchen counter. "Too much of that free beer, I suppose. The beer truck is gone and good riddance." She tossed her head and ran her fingers through her long black hair. "Did you know that Jerry stole that truck and all that beer from where he works? He drove it back home with him an hour ago, beer and all, I hope. He's loading up that truck as we speak. He and Dawn are leaving tomorrow morning for his parent's summer home up in Wisconsin. Jerry told me they're *bugging out*, while the getting is good. After today, I'd like to close up shop and get the hell out of here myself."

Lois made a disgusting face and pointed to her side yard. "I got people using my yard as a damn toilet, *peeing* against the side of *my* house and in *my* bushes. Jerry and his stinking beer truck."

Lois slowly moved away from the counter and again stepped uncomfortably close to Jack. With not a trace of alcohol on her breath, she moved closer, her green eyes darkened and fixed on Jack's. Slightly cocking her head to the side, the tip of her tongue lightly licked her lips. "Want to break a couple of those commandments, Jack? It'll be good for you... it'll help you forget."

"I don't think so, Lois." Jack backed away from her, her lips making a thin smile.

She huffed, "Jack, don't look so serious. Don't be afraid of an older woman. I won't bite you…" She changed the subject, "How do you like our disco tunes? That was Al's idea, but I think the music will end tonight. What I really would like is for people to take whatever food they want and then leave. You know, *take out*. Speaking of taking food home, Al put some frozen steaks in a cooler by the garage door for you. Unless someone else has grabbed them, take them home. They were frozen solid, but will probably be soft by the morning. There's a tub of my pulled pork in there too. It's good—enjoy." She placed both of her hands on her hips and cocked her head. "Jack, now you quit looking at me like that. I just offered you a little warm diversion. I wanted to comfort you, that's all…" Lois turned around and walked over to a chair by the kitchen table. Sitting down, she started removing her shoes. "Sorry, my feet are killing me. This is getting to be too much. Would you believe it, one guy was yelling at Al, saying he was burning his steak. Can you imagine that?   Al worked his ass off to salvage all this food and people are walking all over him." She stood up, rubbed her hands across her face and straightened the front of her black blouse. She stood there a moment and stared at Jack, puzzled by his silence. Taking a deep breath, she tiredly exhaled. "Thanks again for running that asshole out of here. Looks like I may have a yard full of people most of the night. I don't care, I'm going upstairs to bed. I think I'll sleep in the guest bedroom…Al snores all night when he's had too much to drink. Good night, Jack."

"Good night, Lois." Jack went out the front door, his head spinning, *what more could happen today*? He grabbed the cooler and thought about Al, peacefully sleeping upstairs in his bed. He felt sorry for him when he woke up.

Al's front yard must have had over 60 people in it, some were eating and all were talking about the power outage. He started walking towards home when someone yelled his name. He turned to see Jo across the street on her front porch. She was waving at him to come over. As he made his way over to Jo, he couldn't help but hear people's conversations. It was FEMA this, Homeland Security should be doing that, and where are the police?   Why hasn't the authorities done anything to stop the looting? Jack thought to himself, *Help will not be coming folks.*

Reaching Jo's porch, he said, "What's up, Jo? Tell me something good."

"Nothing good, I'm afraid. The man in the house behind us was just found hanging in his garage by the people next door to him. His wife and teenage handicapped daughter were found in an upstairs bedroom. Mother and daughter were in bed together. Suicide, I guess. Their name was Reynolds. Did you know them?"

Jack slowly shook his head. "No, I didn't. Suicide, my God, what next?"

"I don't know, Jack. It's too much for anyone to deal with—I just wanted to let you know. I better get in, Kathy is really upset. She was good friends with the wife and daughter." Jo started walking inside, then turned around as if she forgot something, "Jack, how well do you know Al and Lois?"

Jack shot a glance toward Al's. "I thought I knew them really good. What do you want to know about them?"

"Lois can't stand Kathy and me, and I always have the feeling they're watching us." Jo took a drag on her cigarette and exhaled, her tongue touching her upper lip before continuing. "Jack, I know Kathy and I are still the new kids on the block and some people don't care for our lifestyle, but that aside, something is—I don't know how to say it, phony about those two people. I don't think they know half the people in their yard, yet they give Kathy and I the cold shoulder. Do they have any kids?"

"One. Al mentioned to me once, while we were out golfing, that they had a daughter. Sounded like she and Lois didn't get along. Small wonder there, huh? I guess the daughter got into drugs and left after high school. I don't think they have a clue where she lives, or even if she's alive. They haven't seen or heard from her since she left, about 10-15 years ago. I had the feeling that Al regretted telling me about it. Sad subject, I guess." Jack paused, "Jo, can I have one of your smokes?" Jo took out a pack of cigarettes and handed Jack one, then lit it for him. Jack took a long drag, then said, "We all have our cross to carry, Jo. Some folks keep it pretty well hidden. They're a strange couple though." Jack again looked back over to Al's, as he took another puff off the cigarette. "I wouldn't worry about Al and Lois, they're harmless. Lois is just really judgmental. They both have some screwed-up views of life." Jack bid Joan goodbye and was going to call it a day. He had intended to walk around the block, but the events of the day had finally caught up to him. He felt like he hit a wall and was suddenly stopped cold. He glanced over at the house of the family that had committed suicide, *God help us...* He stood at the curb for a few seconds, before crossing the street. Two people were walking across towards him. *Oh no, please... I don't want to talk to them...*

"Hey, Jack." It was Jerry, and his wife, Dawn. Jack's mind and every muscle in his body was screaming at him to say, *Sorry, Jerry, I don't feel like dealing with any more problems today, I'm fresh out of patience, and sympathy...*

"Glad I caught you, Jack. I came over to see Al, but hear he's wasted for the night. We're trying to find Lois. I feel bad about not being able to say goodbye to the little guy. Me and Dawn are heading up to Wisconsin in the beer truck I borrowed. We're leaving before dawn. Got every inch of that truck packed with our shit. Even got my new aluminum fishing boat tied down up on top. We're going to stay up there until things blow over. From what I've heard, Chicago and Cook County are going nuts. You should clear out too, Jack, while you still can. I hear you got four running vehicles. Load them up with whatever shit you can and

198

get the hell out of here. All them gang-bangers in Chicago will be coming our way after they burn everything down in the city. We just ran into Mike Pierce. His son just made it home from the college in DeKalb. The kid walked the whole way home. They're packed up and are pulling out for northern Wisconsin tonight. Things will be lots better up in cheese land. Hell, I might even come back as a Packers' fan."

Reaching out to Jack, Dawn gave him a hug, then stepped back her eyes suddenly filling with tears. "Jack, we are so sorry about Ellen. We don't know what to say. Thank God that Laura is all right. Jerry told me about your neighbor, Ronnie—that poor little boy. I'm afraid things are going to get terrible here." Dawn moved in close to Jack, looked around and lowered her voice. "Seriously, Jack, why don't you pack up your cars and come up north with us. There's a murderer loose here. It's not safe for any of us. Jerry's folks have a secluded place on the Rock River, on the west end of Lake Koshkonong. They have a couple cabins and an empty trailer. We can stay up there this summer and live like hippies. You and Jerry can fish every day. We heard the Illinois National Guard will be out soon to clean this mess up. When everything blows over, we'll all come back."

"Thanks for the offer, Dawn, and I know you are sincere, but I have to stay here. My neighbor, Charlie, and his wife are old and in bad shape. They have Charlie's older brother living there with them, and he's in bad shape too. We're also taking care of the little boy next door to us. His dad never came home from work. We don't know if he's still somewhere in the city, or if he's even alive. With his mother murdered, we have to take care of him, and Charlie's family too. We can't leave them alone."

Jerry placed his sweaty right arm on Jack's shoulder, his left around his wife's. Pulling them all together, he announced, "Group hug here." Jerry's breath reeked of beer. After they parted, Dawn bid Jack goodbye and left to find Lois.

Jerry looked around Al's, and smiled, "Man this has to be the biggest party Al has ever had and he's missing it. Too bad what Lois is going to do to him come morning, huh?" Jerry let out a laugh, but Jack remained silent. Suddenly Jerry got serious, "Jack, I know you'll have your hands full taking care of that little boy and Charlie, but if you are going to stay, would you do me a favor and kind of keep an eye on my place? There's a cement block on the ground, near the garage door. I keep a spare key to the back door under it. Anything you need, feel free to grab it. My house is your house, big guy." Jerry wet his lips and smiled, "And if you run out of suds, there's 15 cases of beer stashed in the basement. They sort of fell off the back of a truck a couple weeks ago. It's yours if you want it." Jack managed to distance himself from Jerry's drunk embrace, but Jerry continued, "Also, on the shelf above my downstairs workbench, there's a whole cigar box of Cubans that sort of fell off another truck, enjoy them buddy." Jerry pointed to where Dawn was standing by the front door of Al's house, talking to Lois, and said, "Lois and Al

199

should head up there too. Dawn is trying to convince Lois to get Al to load up their old convertible and join us later this week." Jerry handed Jack a folded slip of paper, "I wrote down the directions for you, Jack, in case you change your mind. It's easy to find, first exit off 90, soon as you cross over the Rock River. Jack thanked him.   As Jerry walked away, he turned around saying, "This time tomorrow night big guy, I'll be out on the in-law's pontoon boat, fishing for cats on the Rock River. I'll see you in a couple months or so. Be safe, Jack."

While Jerry was talking about fishing on the Rock River, Jack was already edging his body towards home. He didn't want to stay a second longer, and after what happened with Lois, he wished he hadn't gone down to Al's in the first place. The last two days had enough action to last him a lifetime. As he walked home in the darkness, only one thought was in his mind... *getting a good night's sleep.*

Walking up his drive, he saw a single candle burning on his front porch. Laura, Carl, and Lynne were sitting next to it.

"I hope you guys weren't waiting up for me?"

"We were worried about you, Dad." Laura stood up and gave him a hug. "People are acting crazy."

"They sure are. You think you know someone, but let something like this happen, and they show their true colors, I'll tell you."   He hesitated for a moment. He wasn't sure if he should bring up what Jo had just told him, but he said, "Laura, do you know the couple who have a disabled teen-age daughter, who live behind Jo and Kathy?"

"No, I don't know them, Dad, but I've seen the mother outside with the daughter. She's in a wheelchair. They moved in last fall, why?"

"The mother and daughter were found dead in bed, and the father hung himself in the garage. Probably a murder–suicide, Jo just told me."

Lynne covered her mouth with her hand, "Oh my God..."

Laura said, "Good Lord, I don't understand it. Why are some people giving up? Yeah, everything looks bad now, but lots of people think this whole thing could end in a few days, and it could, don't you think?"

Jack tiredly said, "I don't think so, but no matter what happens, lots of people will pull through whatever comes. Some people just get scared and panic; they become very short sighted. They take what they see as the easiest way out, and in their mind, they'll justify it. Anyway, I just wanted to know if you knew them. Now I wish I would have kept it to myself. You guys have enough to be sad about, no use me heaping more on tonight. Changing the subject, did anything happen while I was away?"

Carl spoke up, "I saw this guy squeezing between the opening in the fence out back. He went over and opened up your shed, so I confronted him."

"What?" Jack planted his hands on his hips. "Who was it?"

Laura answered, *"Barry."*

"Barry? What on earth did he want?"

Carl said, "Your generator. He said he knew we had one, and we should have it out and not be hiding it from everyone. We should be willing to *share* it. He asked me, '*Who the hell are you, and why are you pointing a gun at me?*' The guy's a real idiot."

"You didn't… shoot at him?"

"No. I told him that who I am is none of his business. I told him to get back over to his side of the fence, that he's lucky he didn't get shot. He went back through without saying a word, but as soon as he was out of sight on the other side of the fence, he started yelling. He said he would get the police over here."

"Ha!" Jack scoffed, "That's a good one. Police… that'll be the day. You did really good, Carl, and you exercised restraint."

Jack asked Lynne, "How's our little Bobby?"

"We fed him, gave him the last of the milk and he's sound asleep. He didn't say a word. Hopefully he sleeps through the night. We brought his bed over here. He's sleeping with me, I'll be near him if he wakes up. I'm hoping he'll start talking to us, but the poor little guy has been badly traumatized.

"Lynne, you're a godsend. I don't know what we'd do without you. Let's pray that tonight is quiet. We all need a good night's sleep. This day's been another tough one." Jack eyed Carl, "You ready to plow up the backyard tomorrow?"

Carl said, "I'll be out there before the crack of dawn. After what happened at my place last night, I'd like to crash on your family room couch tonight, if that's still all right with you?"

"Sleep wherever you want, Carl. There's extra blankets and a pillow in the upstairs hall closet. I don't know about you guys, but I'm beat. Lock all the doors and keep your weapons handy. Grab one of the big plastic buckets. If you have to go during the night, use the bucket. Don't anyone go outside alone, *for any reason*. If you hear something, wake me immediately. I'll see you all bright and early… good night." Jack held up the cooler he got from Al's. "Oh, by the way, I'll set this cooler on the kitchen counter. Steaks and pulled pork, courtesy of Al and Lois."

WEDNESDAY

CHAPTER   22

A young child crying…. somewhere there's a child crying, you're a hoarder, that's what you are… Jack slowly opened his eyes. The first thing he saw was the window curtain. It was dark and swaying slightly. Daylight was showing around it's edges. There, he heard it again, a child *was* crying. He remembered Ronnie, and sat bolt upright in bed. He was wide awake.

Talking to himself, he muttered, "God, what time is it?"

He heard some type of motor running. It was coming from the backyard and it was too loud to be his generator. Getting up from bed, he pulled aside the window curtain. Carl was already working at the back of his lot behind Charlie's rototiller, making short work of the soft spring ground.

Still mumbling to himself, he slipped on his pants and a fresh T shirt and started for downstairs. He had barely made it through the bedroom door when he heard Laura's voice, "You finish your juice and we'll be eating a big breakfast in a little while. You don't have to cry, there'll be plenty to eat."

Entering the kitchen, he found Bobby in a chair, with Laura sitting next to him.

"Good morning Dad! Boy, you were sleeping like a log."

Bobby turned around in his chair and stared at Jack, but didn't say a word.

Jack moved over towards him, bent forward and grabbed his bare toes. "How you doing little buddy?" The boy ignored Jack and finished his drink.

Laura said, "He eats by himself, don't you Bobby? She raised her eyebrows at her dad, "But he's a man of few words. He hasn't said anything yet. How are you doing this morning, Dad?"

"I'm doing good, sweetie. How come you let me sleep in so late? I have things to do."

"You needed it. You're overworking yourself, so we decided to let you sleep. Besides, we have everything under control. Carl's turning over the garden, Lynne's next door with Charlie, and I'm holding down the fort here."

"I woke up and heard Bobby; I thought I was dreaming." Jack looked at Bobby, then back to Laura. "Is everything all right, no problems last night or this morning, other than him not talking?"

"No, Dad, no problems. Those steaks you brought back from Al's last night are all defrosted, so we're going to grill a couple of them up with some eggs for breakfast and have the rest for lunch. We'll bring some over for Charlie too. We'll eat the pulled pork tonight. We'll eat good today."

He left Laura and walked outside. Carl shot him a quick "Thumbs-up," as he continued plowing up the yard with the big machine.

He started walking to Charlie's, but was met halfway by Lynne. Something was wrong. They both stopped short. This time it was Jack who read her mind.

"Ted died, didn't he"?

Lynne clenched her teeth and slowly shook her head. "No, it's Dottie—this morning."

Jack felt his body sag. "Oh my God, no."

"She must have passed shortly before I got there."

"Does Charlie know?"

"Yes, I told him. He's in their bedroom with her now. Ted doesn't look good at all. Here we thought he would be first to go. Their situation is really bad. The generator somehow quit running last night and Charlie had to put her on the bottled oxygen. I don't think that had anything to do with it though, her heart probably just gave out."

Jack could sense there was more she had to say. He asked, "Something else I need to know?"

"You won't want to hear this, but did you know Charlie uses oxygen too? One of those bottles isn't an extra. It's for him. He's not supposed to smoke; he's got emphysema too. I just found that out. He didn't want to tell me, he thought I'd take his *smokes* away... That's the reason the nurse stopped coming here. She insisted he give up smoking, so he fired her. Can you believe that? The man has always got a cigar or a pipe in his mouth. What the heck happens when we run out of gas for that generator? It might have to run constantly if he needs oxygen too."

"I don't know, Lynne. We only have enough gas to run one generator for a few days." Jack scratched his head, "After that, we're out, other than what's left in our cars. Charlie has some more gas stashed, but I don't know how much. Maybe we can get some more bottled oxygen from the hospital so we don't have to run the generator. How's Charlie doing?"

"The man's calm, strangely calm. Something doesn't add up. He's in pain because of his toes, there's the situation with Ted, and now Dottie's death. I would think he'd be at his wits end. I don't want to say he's giving up—but gosh, Jack, you know him better than me. Is he always this calm about things?"

"No, maybe he just can read the handwriting on the wall and knows there is nothing anyone can do about it. I'll talk to him. He looked down at his grass. Kicking the head off a dandelion, he started to laugh.

Lynne cocked her head, asking, "What could be funny?"

Jack kicked another dandelion, "Sorry, Lynne, nothing's funny. It's just that last week, Ellen was on me to do something about our lawn. My big project for this week was to get rid of all these damn dandelions. Now look at us, people are about to be fighting for their lives." He looked over at Carl, who was starting another row with the rototiller. "Did you tell Carl?"

"No, just you."

He watched Carl walking behind the huge machine, and neither of them said anything for several seconds. Jack broke the silence first. "Good thing it's still early springtime. If it was later, this ground would be a lot harder to plow up. We've got to get our garden in by Friday to beat the rain that's coming." Jack noticed Lynne had fresh bandages on her face.

She caught his stare and knew what he was about to ask. Raising her left hand to the side of her face, she said, "It's better, my cheek just feels stiff. I cleaned it and changed the dressing this morning. I guess my beauty pageant days are over."

They locked eyes in silence for a couple seconds and Jack said, "You'll look fine. Before this shit is over, I think lots of folks are going to be left with a few scars, and they're going to be the lucky ones."

Jack gestured towards Charlie's house. "We didn't need this today. Everyday it's something. I better go in and talk to him. We'll have to decide what to do with her body. Jeez, what's next?"

Lynne excused herself, "I have to change Ted."

Jack started to walk back with her to Charlie's, but only got a few feet when he heard the rototiller stop. Carl came running over to him.

"Morning, boss! That tiller works really well. Charlie must have spent a fortune on it. It's bulky, but works a lot easier than I thought it would."

"Yeah, it's a good one. Charlie always buys the biggest and best when it comes to his garden. He has a big brush shredder too. How are you doing this morning?"

"Good, but I noticed that guy behind us, Barry or whatever his name is, has been staring at me. I guess he's pissed I pointed the shotgun at him last night."

"Don't worry about that asshole. Later today, I intend to take a walk around the block, there's few things I want to check out. If I see him, I'll straighten his ass out. He's just a big dick, who likes to stick his head in everyone's business."

Carl started laughing, saying, "I hope someday I can talk like you and Charlie, you both have a way with words."

204

"It comes with age and being pissed off all the time, Carl. Don't worry, you'll get there." Jack jerked his head towards his house, "Hope you're hungry. Laura's got steaks ready to go on the grill and a shitload of eggs." Jack hesitated and wet his lips. Carl knew something was wrong.

"What's the matter, Jack?"

"Dottie passed away this morning."

"Oh no. I thought she was doing all right. I was expecting it would be Ted."

"Yeah, me too. We only had one unpleasant thing to do today and that was to bury Ronnie. Now we have to bury Dottie, and soon Ted." Thinking to himself, Jack rubbed the stubble on his chin as he his gazed at Ronnie's back yard. "After breakfast, I'd like you to take the rototiller and break the ground up as deep as you can along Ronnie's back fence line. Make it about eight feet wide, maybe twenty feet long. It'll make it easier to dig graves. I've got a gut feeling we're going to be digging a couple more soon, and one may be Charlie's. Don't say anything to the girls about that."

Jack started walking away, then suddenly stopped and turned around. "Nothing, Carl, and I mean nothing, will slow us down this week from meeting our goal. Our lives depend on it. I don't want you or the girls to think I'm callous and unreasonable. I'm not. We'll get through this, no matter who dies. If something happens to me, it's up to you. There's one other thing. Those chickens of yours have taken over my garage. They think my new truck is their place to crap. I'm going to work on solving that problem today. I have an idea, so we're going to be doing some shopping. I just have to figure out the list of materials."

He left Carl for his first unpleasant task of his new day. Visiting Charlie was always something he looked forward to, but with the death of Dottie, he hoped it wouldn't be the start of another day of tragic events. The smell of fresh coffee greeted him as he neared the back porch. Lightly knocking on the door, he let himself in. The two dogs were first to greet him. Charlie was sitting at his kitchen table, having his morning coffee.

"Thank God for coffee. How you doing this morning?"

"Morning, Charlie. Lynne told me what happened. Charlie—I'm really sorry about Dot... I don't know what to say."

"That's all right, Jack, I'm actually glad it happened quick. That's the way it used to be back in the day. Nowadays folks get rushed to the hospital and pumped full of God knows what. With feeding tubes and IVs and all them painkillers, they keep people going like they're some kind of machine. That's no kind of life."

"I know, Charlie, but still, she was your wife and I know how much you loved each other..."

"Grab a chair, I'll pour you a cup. You look like you could use one."

"I sure could, thanks." Jack paused, searching for the right words to say. "You know... Charlie... I wish there was another solution for us, about Dot and all... but I don't see it. I heard yesterday that the unidentified bodies from the plane crash might be placed in a mass grave in the cemetery, but there won't be any attempt to identify anyone. They don't even have the proper vehicles to transport the bodies there with any dignity. Would you like us to bring Dot to the Catholic cemetery? Carl and I will dig the grave."

"No, Jack, next to Ronnie will be fine. I've been anticipating this. I just figured Ted would go first..." Charlie wiped his eyes with the back of his hand. "God, I never thought it would end like this. Always knew the shit would hit the fan and figured I was prepared to put up a good fight—but to go out this quick, the fun has barely started." Jack was going to ask him something, but Charlie cut him off. "Listen, before I forget, I gotta tell you something. Mike Pierce stopped by here last night before he bugged out to Wisconsin. He had his brother in-law with him, who's a Cook County Sherriff. He works, or I should say *worked*, at the Cook County Jail. He said everything is in complete disarray and all the criminals were being turned loose for humanitarian reasons. He said that the big prisons in Joliet and Marion are letting them go too. I always heard they'd put a bullet in their heads before they opened their cell doors. God help us, stinking do-gooders. Can you imagine what it's going to be like if they're turning the criminals loose? Holy shit, what the hell are they thinking? Anyway, he said the bottom line was not to expect any help. No matter what your problems are, you're on your own. Everything in the state that's run by the government has pretty much stopped working. Now this isn't some rumor, this is fact. You're going to have to make your house into a fort, because nobody is going to come to your rescue."

Charlie set a dirty-looking red, white and blue patriotic mug in front of Jack and poured him a cup of coffee. Jack watched the steam coming off the top of his cup, and neither one of them said anything for a few seconds, as a somber air settled between them.

Charlie broke the silence. "I couldn't help but hear that loud music coming from your buddy's house last night. It appears that lots of people think this is just an excuse for one big party. They're in for a rude awakening. They're wasting valuable time bullshitting. They're bullshitting each other and themselves about how things will get better. Don't fall for it. People are trying to reassure themselves that everything will be all right. You know the line. 'Don't worry about it, the government will come through.' Well I'll tell you right now. If there's a little voice in the back of your head telling you to do something, then you better do it now while you still can." Charlie took a sip of his coffee and pointed to Jack's, "Drink up, boy, it'll cheer you up. Lynne told me you plan to build a chicken coop on the back of your garage. That's a great idea. She says you're going over to that place in the industrial park that puts up temporary chain link fencing. The fellow who owns it is a friend of mine, name's Walt. His son and grandson have the

206

same name. Tell them I sent you, and make sure you're waving some cash in front of them. They'll give you whatever you want. Make them chickens a nice big outdoor enclosure and they'll be happy as pigs in shit."

Jack got up, hoisting his mug of coffee. "Thanks Charlie. I'll bring this cup back later...clean. Breakfast will be done soon. Would you care to eat with us?"

"I know I gotta eat, but I'm not really hungry right now. I just want to be alone for now."

"I understand, Charlie. I want you to know something though, no matter what, we're here for you. You're not alone."

Jack went back to his house wishing there was something he could do for the old guy, but there wasn't. The breakfast set before them was a real feast. They had fresh eggs, grilled prime rib, buttermilk biscuits, bacon, and fresh fruit. There was a generous amount of hot coffee and assorted juices to wash it all down. At any other time, especially about to eat a feast like that, everyone would be talkative, but the air was somber, and Jack wasn't hungry.

As they sat outside at the picnic table, Jack led them in prayer. "Lord please bless this meal and we thank you for it. We know all good things come from you and the bad we get comes from the other guy. Let us never forget that, and continue to fight the good fight of faith."

Lynne added, "Lord, give us the strength we need today to bury Ronnie and Dottie. Please help Charlie deal with the pain he's going through and give us the strength to help him and Ted. Amen."

Bobby looked up from his chair and said his first word since his mother had been found. "Amen."

THE BURIAL

CHAPTER 23

After breakfast, Carl went back to his rototiller, and Jack to figuring out what he needed to build the chicken coop. Chain-link panels were generally available in two different sizes. The size Jack wanted was 10 feet long by 8 feet in height. He figured the fenced-in area would be up against the entire back of the garage, projecting about 10 feet out. That would make the ground area approximately 10 feet by 30 feet. Including the panels for the roof, he would need eight of them and maybe a few extra, including some metal posts for support. He was still figuring out what he needed when three teenage boys walked into his backyard. They were all carrying shovels....

A tall blond-haired boy did the talking. "We hear you may need our services. Forty dollars per hole, three feet deep, six long, and about thirty inches wide. We call ourselves GDH. 'Grave diggers for hire.' We just finished digging three in the backyard of the corner house on the next street over."

Jack was a little taken aback, but wasn't surprised, as he recognized the tall blond-haired boy. He had a summer business mowing grass and last winter he was shoveling snow. The kid was a real entrepreneur and now he was digging graves. They didn't have the time to stop and dig graves, so he started walking to the rear fence, saying, "You boys have yourself a deal. Follow me."

The blond-haired boy didn't move, "We only take cash or silver."

Jack turned around, "Cash it is." Eyeing up the boys, it was obvious that blondie was the oldest, so Jack asked him his name.

"I'm Tony."

"Well, Tony, I think you may have hit on something here, probably going to have lots of holes to dig."

"We sure hope so.... I mean, someone has to do it."

He left the boys to dig and started walking towards Al's. The 44-magnum revolver he carried on his hip no longer felt foreign to him. He never thought he'd have to be openly carrying a weapon in his own suburban backyard. Walking past Ronnie's house, the image of her battered body flashed through his mind. She was still in her house, lying on her bed, awaiting her burial. He wondered if they would ever see Glen again. He unsnapped the strap on his holster and he'd leave it unsnapped. He'd be ready for him, if they did.

The sun's position told him it was about ten o'clock, and there were already more than a dozen people in Al's front yard, some of them cooking on the grills. Al was hunched over a generator, trying to start it. He was swearing to himself and though Jack was about 50 feet away, he could clearly hear what he was saying.

"Son of a bitch! Start, damn it...." Jack waited until he was right behind Al before he spoke.

"Morning, Al. Problems?"

"Oh hey, Jack, yeah lots of them. Can't get this stinking generator to start, for one. I went to bed early, and no one gassed them up for the night. This one ran itself dry and now it won't start. The other generator, which belonged to me, is gone.... Some asshole stole it late last night. And without power, the frozen food I got stashed here will defrost in no time. Luckily, I have stuff at some of the other guy's homes. Hopefully, their generators are still working."

"You're going to have to keep them off at night and put them away, unless you plan to stand guard all night on them. That idiot who lives behind me was poking around in my shed last night. Carl ran him off with a shotgun."

Al stood up. "What did he want?"

"To *borrow* my generator."

"Maybe he's the asshole who took mine... I'll tell you, if I find who glommed it, they'll be missing a few parts themselves...."

Jack assured him, "If I hear a generator running at his place, we can check it out. Otherwise, I would say it's long gone. I guess you won't be playing any more disco tunes, huh?"

Al jerked his head towards his house. "No more tunes, no more beer truck, or party. Lois is really pissed at me, Jack. The whole south side of our house smells like a damn urinal. Oh, and get this. Some drunken asshole decided to use our downstairs powder room last night to take a dump. No one was supposed to go into our house. I was already tucked in for the night. Lois don't have a clue who the guy was, and it **had** to be a guy. No woman could physically leave a mess like that. We got no water, and some moron uses our shitter and plugs it—but good, then pukes all over the floor and bathroom door....and then—they just walk out! Can you believe that?" Al wiped his brow with the back of his hand and moved closer to Jack. "Lois told me that you tangled with that asshole, Dorfman last night. Sorry I missed it. I heard my two rainbow neighbor girls made an ass out of him in front of everyone. That's great! Lois doesn't like those two gals across the street, but she hates Dorfman more, and personally, so do I. She said that Joan broad really put that asshole in his place."

"Al, is that guy really a state cop, or what?"

209

"No, not really. He's more dangerous than a cop. He's some sort of evidence technician who likes to flash his badge, you know the type. I really don't know him, but his wife comes into the store a lot. Real piece of work she is too, just a bitch. She thinks everyone working there is her personal servant. I'd like to chop her up, and toss her on that grill there." Al's eyes suddenly got glassy, "Whatta you think about that Jack, wouldn't that be fun?"

The sound of a helicopter in the distance suddenly caught both the men's attention. Coming in straight and low was a military National Guard helicopter. The sound of it had everyone staring into the sky as it flew over their street. The people in Al's front yard began to jump up and down and wave. The sound of the rotors got louder, and Jack realized there was another chopper following the first one. Behind it were two more.

Al was ecstatic, "See there, Jackie my boy, the cavalry has arrived! It won't be long now, they'll get this shit cleaned up, and just in time!"

Jack excused himself and left Al to his sudden merriment and fixing his generator. It was burial time. Charlie had wanted to keep Dottie's burial private, so Jack decided it might be best to keep Ronnie's private too. In the back of his mind was the nagging thought that before long, many people might not have the final dignity of a formal burial. He watched the horizon as the helicopters disappeared from sight. He had little faith that they were here to save anyone, especially in the insignificant town of Melville.

He left Al's without running into Lois and breathed a sigh of relief, especially after what happened the night before. He felt sorry for Al, who had no idea that his wife was ready to cheat on him with a good friend. He slowly walked home, not looking forward to the funeral procession that would end in his own backyard.

The burial was like one that had taken place during wartime. Like soldiers hastily gathered on a far corner of a battlefield, with the battle still raging over the horizon, they buried Ronnie and Dottie. It was good that Bobby didn't have a clue what had happened. This would be one memory the child didn't need. He thought about that for a few moments. He had great memories of his childhood. *What kind of memories would Bobby have?*

They were all gathered at the first grave, where his mother was about to be laid to rest forever. He was busy playing with clods of dirt that soon would be covering her. There was a lawn chair for Charlie and a small tank of oxygen in case he got short of breath. Jack and Carl had carried the bodies out on a makeshift stretcher. There were no fancy caskets or wooden coffins. They had placed them into the graves before the others had gathered.

Ronnie was wrapped in a powder blue sheet, and Dottie was in a beige linen. Everyone had tears in their eyes and stood there silent. Lynne was first to speak and led them in the Lord's Prayer. Charlie told a story about how Dottie had a pet turkey when she was a kid. When it came to Ronnie, Jack recalled her

210

saying she intended to plant lots of flowers around their house. He made a vow to always have flowers planted on her grave and never let Bobby forget he had a mom and dad who loved him.

The service was simple. They filled the graves in and marked each with a two-foot-high wooden cross, vowing that they would somehow get a permanent stone marker in the future.

Laura and Carl helped Charlie back to his house; Lynne took Bobby for a walk, and Jack stayed there a few minutes alone. He watched Bobby as he walked away with Lynne and wondered about his future, if there was to be a future. Alone in his thoughts, he was interrupted, and it was Barry. This time his wife, Liz, was with him and neither of them looked happy.

Barry blurted out, "Did we just witness what we think we did? Are these graves? Did you just bury two people here, adjacent to my backyard?"

"Yes, we did, Barry. Dorothy Mills and Ronetta Johnson, both laid to their eternal rest."

"Are you out of your minds? You can't bury people in their backyard! My God, did you folks ever hear of a cemetery? Do you know how many laws you just broke? What happened to these people? How did they die and what gives you the right to just bury them wherever you please? God, Hansen, are you going nuts?"

Jack was fed up with Barry, and his mood slid from grief to anger. Without saying a word, Barry's wife abruptly turned and walked back towards their house in an indignant huff. If the situation were different, Jack would have been amused, watching her big ass trying to squeeze through the gap in the fence. She left the two men alone at a stand-off, facing each other.

"Look at yourself, Jack, will you." Barry pointed to Jack's side arm. "You parade around here like you're the law, wearing that big gun. Seriously, do you even have a permit to carry that thing?" Barry extended his arm towards Carl, who was back to rototilling, "That boy over there, running that machine, are you aware he pointed a shotgun at me last night? I just came over to see if you had a generator going and if I could plug into it... and what the hell is that kid doing now, tearing up the whole yard with that thing? Oh my God, Hansen, what does your wife think about all this?"

"My wife? You mean Ellen?" Jack sadly shook his head. "Barry, your wife's name is Elizabeth and your boy's name is Dwayne. You work at North Western Bank and your dog's name is Kippy. I know all that, as I should, because I've lived behind you here for 10 years. But you don't even know my wife's name, do you Barry? How about my daughter, do you know her name?"

Barry pointed his finger at Jack's face. "Don't start trying to side track this whole thing with your nonsense, Hansen. I won't stand for it."

Jack shrugged his shoulders, "Listen, butthead, I'm not trying to side-track anything. I've had a terrible week. When that plane came down, I lost—" Barry

211

cut Jack off. "We've all had a terrible week Hansen, so don't start calling me names because you're not mature enough deal with it. I demand to know why you just buried these two people next to my property line and how did they die?"

Jack pointed to Ronnie's grave. "She was your neighbor, Ronnie. Did you ever take the time to meet her?" He pointed to Dotty's grave. This is Dotty Mills. Ronnie was raped and murdered in her own bedroom by Glen Sorensen, who lives across the street from me. He's crazy as a bat and is still out there. That's why I'm wearing this gun."

"Murdered? Well for God's sake, who is this Glen guy and have they caught him?"

"I just told you who he is, and no, *they* haven't caught him. There is no *they*, Barry. Have you seen a cop lately? Why do you think I'm wearing this gun?"

 "So, you make yourself the law and the county coroner too, is that it? I'm not going to stand for this. I have a friend who's a state policeman. He lives on the next street over. I'm going to go over there and talk to him, and I'll get some answers, you better believe it!"

"His name wouldn't happen to be Dorfman, would it? Because I met him last night. He was drunk and belligerent. What an asshole!"

"Yeah, go ahead, Jack. You keep talking like that. You're just getting yourself in deeper. A couple days from now, the power will be back on and you'll be going to jail."

Jack felt every muscle in his body screaming at him to jump on the man and beat the living shit out of him. Instead he said, "I don't have the time for this, butt head. I'm building a chicken coop on the back of my place today, almost as big as your wife's ass, and I have to get started." With that, Jack did an about-face and quickly walked back to his house, leaving Barry standing there with his mouth open.

"Chicken coop? What do you mean a chicken coop? This is a residential area, Hansen. You can't raise chickens here! Don't walk away on me! And where do you get off calling me butt head? You're a jerk, Hansen! Do you know that?"

WALT

CHAPTER 24

Jack didn't have time to argue with neighbors, nor let it bother him. He left Barry standing at the fence and approached Carl, as he stopped the machine.

"Carl, I'd like to borrow your truck. Charlie has a friend over in the industrial park who rents those temporary chain-link construction fences. They have 10 x 8-foot panels that would be perfect to build an outside coop up against the garage. I was thinking we could wall off the inside of the garage, about three or four feet in, for their roosts."

"My truck is yours, Jack, it has about half a tank of gas left."

"Thanks. I'm going to head over there now. I'll see if Lynne can go with me." Lynne was waiting for Jack when he returned to the house. "Is everything all right? As loud as that rototiller is, I could hear that guy yelling at you."

Jack glanced towards Barry's house, saying, "He's just pissed about the graves. He and I have never seen eye to eye and I'm done talking to him. I'm going over to the industrial park in Carl's truck, it's close by. I want to pick up some fencing. Would you ride shotgun for me?"

"Sure, if Laura can keep an eye on Bobby. I'm hoping he might take a nap. I think he's still exhausted from what he's been through. I'll check over at Charlie's and then we can go."

"I appreciate that, Lynne. There're so many little odds and ends we need. I've been thinking that maybe tomorrow, you and I could make a run over to the big home center, where Laura and Carl went. We're going to need some chicken wire, and they sell those big sacks of wild bird feed. You go check on Charlie, I'm going to bring up some more things from the basement. With the sump pump not working, I'm afraid we'll flood out when the rain comes." A half hour later, Jack backed the pickup out of the driveway. Lynne was in the passenger seat with her 12-gauge shotgun across her lap.

"Thanks for riding with me, Lynne. This place isn't far, it's just about a mile away. It's in the back of the industrial park and it's kind of isolated, so we'll have to be careful." He looked thoughtful for a couple seconds, "I mentioned to Carl about going back to the home center tomorrow, and he wasn't so hot about it."

He furrowed his brow, "I wonder if something happened there, and now they don't want us to go back. Did you get that feeling?"

Lynne sat quiet for a couple seconds, then said, "I did. I got that feeling when they first returned. I asked them how it went and both of them seemed kind of vague. They didn't want to talk about it. Maybe something did happen, but I'd just let it go."

"Yeah, you're right. Carl probably got in a tussle with someone. It more than likely upset Laura. Sometimes I forget that she's only 18 years old. You know, she's still a kid."

Approaching the corner, they could see Al's front yard was again looking like a picnic ground. Al was in a better mood and he waved for Jack to stop.

"Hey, Jackster, you guys hungry? We're grilling lobster, shrimp and salmon. I got a shitload of sweet potatoes and red russets in the coals too. We've got 15 big bags of charcoal spread out on the ground out back. It's like a blast furnace back there." At the mention of potatoes, Jack felt his pulse quicken.

"Do you have any potatoes left?"

"Sorry, Jack, we're out. I got all of them in the coals. Too bad I had to toss out a bunch of them because they were sprouted, or we'd have more. Come back in a half hour and they'll be done."

"Can I have the ones you tossed out in the trash?"

"Sure, Jack, they're in trash bags out back. You're not supposed to eat them when they get like that. I don't know why, but at the store, we always toss them out if they're sprouted."

Jack parked the truck and he and Lynne got out. Lynne smiled and winked at Jack, saying, "We want all the potatoes we can get, especially ones that have sprouted. This afternoon we'll cut them up in pieces, each with a sprout on it. After they dry out a bit, we'll plant them next week. We'll be growing taters!" Ten minutes later, they loaded the truck with at least two bushels of sprouted potatoes.

While Jack closed the truck's tailgate, Al said, "Jack, you're taking this farming thing way too seriously. Did you forget all those choppers we saw this morning? Faye Biddle was here earlier and said she saw four more of those big double-bladed jobs. She says the government's got warehouses full of emergency food and shit. We're in the clear here, Jack, why don't you relax a bit? You don't need all these rotten potatoes."

"That's good, Al. I hope Mrs. Piddle is right."

"That's Biddle, with a *B*, and she's right, she works for the federal government."

"What's does she do?"

"She's a big shot, works up near O'Hare airport, head honcho with the FAA. She used to work at the DuPage Airport. She's a friend of Bill McArnold.

Believe me, Jack, those FEDS know what the government has got stashed, as far as food and shit."

Jack thanked Al for the potatoes, as he and Lynne got back in the truck. Al placed his hands on the door and leaned in close.

"Let me give you a word of warning, big guy. I don't know where you're headed, but your buddies, Deputy Hayes and big brother Dirk, were here a while ago. They're driving a jacked-up 4x4 pickup truck with those big monster wheels on it. They told me the county was going to be requisitioning vehicles that are still running, especially pick-up trucks and vans. Just thought I'd give you a heads up."

"Thanks for the info, Al. Anyone who tries to take my vehicles, state, federal or county, will be wishing they didn't mess with me.... I suppose you fed those two assholes?"

"Come on, Jack, they're not bad guys, really. You just got off on the wrong foot with them. I've known them awhile, they're just a little rough around the edges."

Jack started the truck and put it in gear, "See you later, Al, and thanks for the taters!" He drove off and as he turned the corner, he was flagged down by Jo and Kathy. They were standing together on their back deck. Upon seeing Jack, they walked out to greet him.

Jo said, "Did Al tell you what Hayes said?"

"Yeah, big deal, he's just a big windbag. I'm not afraid of him or his lummox of a brother. County cop or not, nobody's taking any of our vehicles."

Jack changed the subject, "Hey, we got some chickens and they had a mess of chicks. They're in my garage and we got more on the way. Would you ladies like some?"

Kathy gave an excited little jump, "Oh my gosh. Yes, you bet!"

"Good, we're on our way to get some fencing for a coop. If we can get it, I'll double my order so you can build one too. We'll help you with it."

Jo reached in and roughly pulled Jack to her, giving him a kiss. She said, "Jack, we're so happy we hooked up with you guys. Do you need any help?"

"No, not yet. Let me see if I can get the stuff first. It's not far, only about a mile away. We'll be back soon." Jack pulled away from the curb heading towards the industrial park. Lynne looked in the truck's side mirror and watched the two women as they walked back towards their house.

"They're quite a pair, you know that? That Jo is tough..."

Jack interrupted her, "No shit, did you see her grab me and plant that kiss? She about ripped my shoulder off."

"Yeah, she looks a bit rough, but I like her. Kathy is such a little thing. I wonder how they met?"

"I don't know, but I'm glad they're on our team. They both got their share of guts, I'll say that. They proved that to me already."

215

They left the subdivision and turned down a tree-lined side road that led towards the industrial park. Lynne scoffed, "People are so naïve, Jack. I don't know who that Faye Biddle is, but she's woefully mistaken. Remember me telling you about Bill? He worked for Homeland Security and he knew a lot of the FEMA people. There are no warehouses of MRE's or any appreciable amount of food stored up for the people of this country. Sure, they have stores for small, state-wide emergencies, but not for something as big as this. They can't feed the whole country, every day. Unless you're in the military or a political elite, when it comes to something this massive, the average citizen is out of luck. Most of the folks in this country don't have a clue what is awaiting them. I feel sorry for people like Al. He just doesn't get it."

"Al is my buddy, and I've tried to talk to him, but it's of no use. His idea of emergency food is a supply of snacks and three cases of cold beer. Lois's idea probably isn't much better. She's probably got six cans of soup, a gallon of water and a flashlight set aside by itself somewhere. I think most of the country is like that. Try to tell them any different and they look at you like you're nuts, so I gave up trying. The really sad part about it is, when the Titanic takes the big plunge, and I think it's about to, we're not going to be able to save those who didn't prepare. If we do, they'll take us down with them. If the U.S. Calvary comes to the rescue, it'll be towards the end, and by then—the unprepared will be dead."

As they entered the industrial area, Jack slowed the truck. Up ahead of them was the first building of the industrial park. There were four men loading a flatbed semi-truck, and a forklift was hoisting a large wooden crate onto the trailer. They all stopped what they were doing and eyed them suspiciously as they drove by. Jack could see two of the men were armed with rifles. As they passed, Lynne gave them a wave. They waved back and resumed loading their crate.

The next building was a rental center for portable toilets. Jack had seen them before, scattered around town, mostly at building sites. On the door was the company's logo, *"GOT TO GO."* There was a large fenced in area that must have had over a hundred of the grey and white portable toilets, all lined up in neat rows. Jack motioned to them as they drove by.

"That's another thing we're going to get. We can't keep wasting our fresh water by dumping it into the toilet every time we use it. Besides that, our bathrooms are becoming a mess from spilling water on the floor. I figure we could get a new, or at least a clean, portable shitter and cut the bottom of the holding tank out of it. That way we could dig a hole and place the shitter over it."

Lynne laughed, "Jack, you have such a fine command of the English language. That's a good idea though. God, it's like we are reverting back to the 1800s."

"Yeah, not a nice thought, huh? Look, there's our place." The sign on the side of the building read, **Commercial Construction Fencing,** rental and sales.

Driving along the side of the building, they came to a gate that was partially open. Behind it was a young bearded man, pouring fuel from a can into the side tank of a large flatbed stake truck. He looked up in alarm when he saw Jack. Jack stuck his arm out, flashing a fistful of cash, yelling, "We need to buy some fencing. I have cash."

He had quickly learned that in the new order of things. Cash was everybody's friend and would open any door. In this case it was a chain link gate. The man opened the gate and waved Jack in.

Jack pulled through the open gate, parking the truck next to the old flatbed. Getting out of the truck, he noticed the guy flinch when he saw his holstered 44. "Sorry about the gun, no worry. It's just that we've had some run-ins with some real jerks and we have to be armed." He noticed that other than a large knife in a sheath on his belt, the man appeared unarmed.

The bearded young man walked over to Jack saying, "No kidding, I just walked three miles here to pick up this old truck. It's like all the idiots in the world have hit the streets. All have is one small 22 target rifle and I wished I had carried it with me."

Jack extended his hand and the other man shook it. "I'm Jack, and this is my friend, Lynne." Jack handed him the list of what he needed. "Here's my list of what I can use. Everything that's on it. . . I'd like it doubled, if you can do it. I'd really appreciate it."

"I'm Walt, glad to meet you." Walt eyed the list, nodding his head. He looked up at Lynne, his eyes settling on her face. "Man, something really clocked you one, sister, that looks like it hurts."

Lynne said, "Only when I laugh."

"Well, I won't tell you any jokes." He looked again at the list of materials and then back to Jack. "I have everything you've got listed, except the 30-foot lengths of pipe. We have 20's and double female slip connectors. You could make them into 30's. He looked at their pickup truck and shook his head. "No way you're getting all this on that little truck. How far away you live?"

Jack said, "Just outside the park, over in the River's Edge subdivision."

Walt said, "Really? My grandfather's buddy lives over there, Charlie Mills."

Jack smiled, "Charlie sent me here, he's my next-door neighbor."

"Charlie's your neighbor? That's great, he's a good guy. He and my grandfather served in Korea together. They've been friends for a long time. How's Mr. Mills doing?" Jack's jaw tightened. "I'm afraid not so good, Walt. His wife, Dottie, passed away this morning."

"Sorry to hear about that, it's been a while since I've seen them. Lots of bad things happening this week." Walt looked down at the list saying, "If you're a friend of old Charlie's, no need to itemize everything on your list. Looks to me like a grand cash would cover it and I think that's a deal for you. It's a deal for

217

both of us, because I can sure use some cash, damn plastic won't buy shit. We can load it up in the big flatbed here, and I can deliver it right now. That would give me a chance to stop in and see Mr. Mills."

Jack stuck his hand out, "We got a deal, Walt."

"Lucky you caught me here. I had to walk all the way from my apartment, what a hike that was. I live on the top floor and it really sucks without any power. My girlfriend lives with me too and we hardly have any food. We mostly eat out and now everything is closed. Wouldn't matter though, all we have is those damn plastic debit cards and nobody will take them." Walt pointed to the old truck, "My dad has a trailer out in Marseilles, on the Illinois River. I'm sure glad he kept this old truck, we're going to drive it out there this afternoon. It's great, you showing up with this cash, it'll really help us out."

Lynne asked, "Are your parents out at the trailer?"

"No, they're down at their place in Florida with my grandparents, and hopefully safe. Let's get you loaded so I can get going, my girlfriend will be worried about me."

Jack eyed the huge old truck and got an idea. "Walt, do you know the owner of the portable toilet place?"

Walt smiled, "You're looking at him—well sort of, my dad owns it. It goes hand in hand with renting construction fencing."

Jack said, "I know those things are pretty light and can be lifted easily. I'd like buy three of them? Is 600 bucks enough? We could tilt them up onto the truck...."

"You got it, Jack. I need all the cash I can get, but we'll have to do it quick."

They loaded up the truck and Walt hastily tied the load down. Without saying a word, he jumped into the flatbed's cab and drove the big truck next door. Ten minutes later, they were pushing three brand new portable toilets onto the flatbed.

"One more little thing." Jack was pointing to some blue 55-gallon barrels that were lined up outside the building. "Those blue barrels over there, what's in them?"

Walt laughed, "What, now you want barrels too? They're empty, the disinfectant that we wash the shitters out comes in them. They're clean, we hose them out and resell for twenty bucks each for rain barrels. In fact, Charlie, bought a bunch of them from us a couple years back. I delivered them to him."

Jack said, "How much for all of them?"

Walt started laughing and looked at Lynne, "Is he always this demanding? All right, you can have some, but you can't have them all. There's about 20 there. I want to take at least six of them out to my trailer. You can have the rest, if you have some cash left?"

218

"I'll pay you when we get home. And about the route we're going to take to get into the subdivision, I'd like to come in the back way, through River Road. There's a lot of people gathered on the corner of my street and I don't want to draw any attention to us. Also, pull your truck into the side yard, on the south side of Charlie's house; don't worry about the lawn. There's a nosey neighbor who lives behind me, he's nothing but a pain in the ass. I don't want him to see what we're bringing in, especially the portable shitters. He won't like it."

"Okay, Jack, I get it. Nobody likes these things. Let's finish getting loaded and get out of here. Why don't you go load your pickup with some of the barrels? I have to hurry to get back to my girlfriend, she'll be worried sick."

The east side of the subdivision was bordered by the Fox River and River Road was nothing much more than a small side street that ran alongside it. It ended at a small park and boat ramp, near the entrance to Jack's street. No one from Al's noticed the big truck as it entered the subdivision from the back road. Walt expertly backed the truck alongside of Charlie's house without raising any attention from Barry. Carl was there to greet them, followed by Laura, who was holding Bobby's hand.

"Dad! Where did you get all this?"

"We scored pretty big, thanks to our new friend, Walt. We have to get this stuff unloaded really fast. Walt has to get going."

Walt said, "You guys can slide this stuff off. I'll go run in and see Charlie."

Carl and Jack were just about done unloading when Walt came out. "Man, the old guy's foot looks terrible. He was resting it up on a footstool with his sock off... his toes are turning black. His brother, Ted, doesn't look like he's going to last long either."

Jack said, "They're both in bad shape and there isn't much that can be done. Lynne is a nurse, and she's trying to keep them as comfortable as possible. I know you want to get out of here, so I'll go get the rest of your cash." Jack came out a few minutes later and handed Walt the cash, a shoe box and a 20-gauge shotgun.

"Here's the money I owe you, plus an extra twenty. Walt, I want you to have this too, I know you're going to need it."

Walt took the shotgun and the box. In the box was the small revolver that Lynne had been pistol whipped with. Next to it were two full boxes of 22 caliber cartridges and four boxes of 20-gauge shotgun shells."

"Gosh, I don't know what to say, I was happy just to have the cash. Because of you, my girlfriend and I will have some cash and now a way to protect ourselves." Walt pointed to the 55-gallon drums. "I wouldn't have thought about taking some of those barrels out there with me to store some water, if you hadn't shown up."

Jack placed his arm on Walt's shoulder, "Listen to me, Walt. If I were you, I would go back to your place and carefully look everything over. I don't have a

219

clue what you have in your businesses over there, but there are some things you're going to need and you may not get another chance to get them. This is why we're scrambling around this week getting everything we can. I'm talking about fuel, bottled gas, hand tools, batteries, flashlights, medical supplies, even toilet paper. Throw some of this fencing and posts on your truck, and maybe take one of those portable toilets."

Walt thought for a couple seconds, "Yeah, there's some stuff I could definitely use, now that I think about it. I have some full 5-gallon gas cans and a big Honda generator. The portable toilet idea sounds crazy, but you're right, we aren't going to have any place to even take a dump. There's no power to pump the sewage out of the trailer's tank. And I never even thought about bringing toilet paper with me. We got a ton of the stuff in our warehouse. Trouble is, I can't lift it all into the truck by myself." Walt was quiet for a few more seconds, thinking of more things he should take. "Man, you're thinking of things I've never given any thought to. Do you really think it's going to get that bad?"

"Let me tell you something I learned in the Marine Corps, Walt. Everything goes good until all of a sudden, it's not, and things slide to the *not* side really quick. Something insignificant now may make your life a lot easier later. It might even save it." Jack laughed, "Imagine a world without shit paper." He gave Walt a fatherly pat on the back, "Look, Carl and I will follow you back to your place. We'll stand guard and help you load up. Let's get going."

Walt looked like he was about to cry, "Thanks, Jack. I don't know what to...." Jack cut him off. "Don't even think about it. You helped us, it's the least we can do for you." About an hour and a half later, Jack and Carl returned home from helping Walt. Carl's truck had the tailgate down and was piled at least eight feet high with cases of toilet paper, all stacked on top of various hand tools Walt had given them.

The girls had dinner ready, and Jack's mood was the best since Monday morning. Carl wasn't talkative during dinner and Jack could see why. Nearly both backyards were turned over, ready for planting.

"Carl, like my grandfather used to say, '*You look like your hay is in, buddy.*' You really kicked ass plowing up these yards today, you've got to be beat."

"I am, Jack. I'm going to *hit the hay* early tonight; I want to finish up by mid-morning. If we all chip in tomorrow, we might get everything planted before it rains." Carl thanked Lynne for another excellent meal, then got up and excused himself.

Bobby was sitting on Laura's lap, taking small pieces of apple from Lynne, when he suddenly said, "Mama.... Daddy."

Laura glanced at Jack and then at Lynne, "That breaks my heart, that just breaks my heart. That makes three words he's spoken. What are we going to do?"

Lynne stopped handing him the apple slices, saying, "This is what we're going to do." She reached over, taking the little boy into her arms. Holding him close, she gently kissed his neck saying, "Bobby, you will never be alone. We love you with all our heart. You'll have a good life, a long life, we promise you."

They sat like that for a few minutes, Lynne slowly rocking him every so often giving him a slice of apple, until Laura said, "How about I get him cleaned him up and put his PJs on. I'll read a story to him."

She led him away from Lynne saying, "Bobby, let's get you cleaned up and we can read some bedtime stories. Would you like that?"

As Jack watched Laura leading Bobby back into the house, he picked up his bottle of beer from the table and took a long swig, finishing it. Idly looking at the empty bottle's label, he said, "Thank heaven Charlie has room for some beer in his fridge. You know, sooner or later these generators that folks are using so freely will start failing, or gas will become too hard to get to run them, then watch out. It'll be the big thaw. I have gas in the shed and have yet to use our generator. I don't want to use it unless I absolutely have to. It's got to be a life or death thing, you know what I mean?"

Lynne was gently rubbing around the bandaged area of her cheek, when she asked, "Do you have any doubts, Jack?"

"About what?"

"You know, about what we're doing, the chickens, the garden, getting all these supplies. Do you ever think we're wasting our time? Most of Al's friends do."

"No, I don't. No doubts at all. What we're doing is giving ourselves some hope that we need right now, but more importantly time. The longer we can stretch out our food, the longer we'll live. Things will eventually get better, we just want to be around to see it." He set the empty bottle on the picnic table, "What about you, Lynne, do you think we're spinning our wheels here?"

"No. If we hadn't experienced what we did trying to get out of Chicago, we might be like most of the people out here. But after what I've seen…. I think it's like you said the other day, something tells me that we're about to be in a world of shit."

They locked eyes for a few moments. Jack said, "Your cheek is looking better. I don't see any more swelling and the redness is gone. Is the wound still hurting?"

"No, it's starting to itch. Like my mother used to say, 'That means it's healing.' I can't wait to get it uncovered. I'll probably scare everyone though."

Jack smiled, "I doubt that, you'll look fine."

He pointed towards the basement door. "I'll drain some fresh water out of the water heater so you can wash up. I think I'll drain it completely tonight, before it gets dark. If the basement floods out, the valve will be under water and we'll never be able to drain it without contaminating it."

They locked eyes again in silence for a few more moments. Jack was the first to talk. "What are you thinking about, Lynne? I can see your wheels spinning."

"I'm thinking that you should have known my husband, Bill. You're a lot like him. Always thinking, always wanting all the bases covered. Working in Homeland Security made him that way. Talk about doubts…. One thing though, Bill always made me feel safe and secure. I don't know if a lot of married women feel that way, even in normal times. I feel safe here, Jack. As screwed up as things are, you make me feel safe. Thanks for taking me into your family."

They were interrupted by the distant sound of loud music. They both heard it, and Jack smiled, "Now that's *hope*. Unless my ears deceive me, that sounds like disco. Al must be out of the dog house. Lois let him start his stereo up again."

After listening to the music a few moments, Lynne said. "They're an odd couple, aren't they?"

"Yeah, they sure are, but that's what makes life interesting." Jack slid his chair back a little from the table. "After I help you clean up here, I'll get you that clean water. Then I think I'll go down there to see him. I would like to steer clear of his place, but all those people stopping there makes him a wealth of information. It's like he's running a news anchor desk. How about coming with me?"

"No, I'll help Laura with Bobby, check over at Charlies, then *hit the hay*. You just be careful over there."

"Careful is my middle name. I'll also let Jo and Kathy know what we got today. They're going to be really happy with all that fencing. Can't wait to see their reaction when we give them a portable shitter and some water barrels. Maybe I'll be able to finish the walk I wanted to take around the block."

"Jack, there is one thing I want to mention. I told you about my husband being a prepper. We kept emergency bug-out bags that are still at my condo in Chicago. We had a cottage near Jasper, Indiana that I sold. We also had a couple snowmobiles and an old 1970's Dakota camper motor-van. I haven't seen any of it since before he passed. It's all in a self-storage place over in Downers Grove, maybe a half hour drive from here. He didn't want to store it in Chicago. He thought it was safer out here in the western suburbs. I never got around to checking it out or getting rid of any of it. I've been paying the rent on it all this time. Jack, he spent a lot of time there alone and I don't have a clue what's all in there. I know he stored up a bunch of emergency supplies, and God knows what else. If I have any regrets, it's not taking more of an interest in his prepping. I went along with it because I knew it was for our best interests but, truthfully, I never thought something like this would happen, at least not to this extent. So now he's gone, and I'm left with all these supplies and things I don't even know how to use, and it's all going to go to waste. He insisted I take a firearms training class. Thank God I did that. The key to the storage unit is on my car's key ring."

Jack got up from his chair saying, "Looks like sometime this coming week or so, we're going to make a little road trip to Downers Grove."

IN THE NICK OF TIME

CHAPTER 25

A melody of 50's rock tunes was blasting from Al's stereo speakers. The smell of charcoal was strong in the air as the sun was setting. Al was sitting in a lawn chair, drinking from a bottle of water, as Jack walked up to him.

"What Al, no more beer?"

"No, I had enough of that yesterday. I'm taking it easy tonight. Unless Lois and I want something ourselves, no more grilling either. It's self-serve, everyone grills their own. We got some dynamite hamburgers tonight with all the fixings. No buns though, but we got a load of week-old rye bread. There should be a few baked potatoes left, if you want one."

"Thanks, Al, but I'm good. Did you ever find your missing generator?"

"Nope. It's gone, big guy, but I wasn't the only one who got hit.

Guy on the next street lost his generator, his cords, plus two cans of gas. Larry Milner said someone made off with his can of gas and all his extension cords. I guess we have to expect it. This bullshit is sure bringing out the assholes."

Jack looked around at the people in Al's front yard. There were about 50 people there, many were unfamiliar faces. Some were taking plastic bags of food and walking away. One person with a tank of propane gas was getting out of a car.

"You want anything, Jack, please take it. I'm encouraging everyone to take stuff home with them if they want and fix it themselves."

Al gestured to the fellow carrying the propane tank, "Thanks, Bill, we can really use that."

Al looked up at Jack, "We're running low on propane for the grills. I can't believe how much gas we've used. I'm sure happy about FEDUP showing up, in the nick of time too."

"FEDUP?" Jack eyed Al suspiciously. "Is that what we're calling them now?"

"Yeah, FEMA sounds like some kind of fucking sickness. Anyway, where you been, Jack, haven't you heard? Those big National Guard choppers landed at the county building, and I heard some big shit from FEDUP was with them. They said there would be first-aid centers set up, most likely at Melville High for one. Also, all the hospitals are going to start opening back up. The best is, the power will be going back on!"

"Where did you hear all this news from, Al?"

"Everybody is talking about it, Jack. Where the hell you been? Some guy and his wife that were here earlier claimed they were there when the choppers landed. Happy days are here again, Jacko, that's why I got the tunes back on."

Al hollered out to a man and a woman who were standing by a cooler, "You just help yourselves there, take whatever you want over to a grill and cook it up. Try some of my wife's pulled pork, it's special and it's great! There's bread and condiments over on that far table. Hope you brought your own drinks though." Al took a long drink from his bottle of water. "Almost out of bottled water, glad this mess will be over. Hey, Jack, try some of Lois' pulled pork, she mixed a couple other types of meat in with it. It really tastes good, you'll love it."

Jack thanked Al for his offer and excused himself. He walked over to Al's garage and opened up his big freezer; it was nearly empty. There were several large coolers that were mostly full of various packages of meat and poultry, all wrapped in white butcher's paper. Jack stood on Al's driveway and looked from person to person. There was an air of optimism about the place. As he stood there, some forgotten group was singing about dancing through the night. He couldn't help but visualize the band that played on as the Titanic slowly went down. He decided to go over and check on Kathy and Jo, ask them what they've heard and tell them what he got for them.

Before he could walk across the street, he heard Al call his name. Turning around, the little guy was now at his side.

"Jack, I got a big favor to ask of you. I hate to ask, but I have a big problem."

"Sure Al, whatever you need."

"I hate to ask this, but could you ask Carl if I could borrow his truck for about a half hour tomorrow morning? It's the garbage. I got a truckload of plastic bags packed with crap from all this cooking and shit. I don't want any animals pawing through it, opening it up. Got lots of spoiled meat in them too. Lois wants it out of her sight, you know how she is. I really don't want to put it in the trunk of the convertible. I want to dump it over in the industrial park somewhere. It might require two trips. I'll have a rotting mess before any of the city garbage trucks ever get here."

"No problem, Al. We have a pile too, plus Charlie has some. I was thinking of burning it. There's an old gravel pit by the golf course. Nobody ever goes over there, so we can dump it in there and set it on fire."

"Great idea about the gravel pit, Jack, but I don't know about sticking around to burn it. I just want to dump it someplace far out of the way. What the heck did they do in the old days?"

"Everybody took it to the town dump or burned it in their back yards. That's why there was such a problem with rats and disease. The good old days weren't so good, huh?"

"They sure weren't, big guy. I'm glad this crap is coming to an end. Another week of this and we'll *all* be going nuts."

Jack walked across the street and knocked on Jo and Kathy's front door. The house was dark and no one answered his knocking, so he walked around to the back. He found the two women sitting together near a small campfire in a fire pit. Kathy was roasting some hot dogs on a long fork over the dancing flames. She looked up at Jack and held the hot dogs up high, inspecting them. "You want one, Jack? They're almost done."

"No thanks, Kathy, I'm good."

Jo lifted a water bottle high in a toast, "Here's to the last of our hot dogs. We have six dogs and only two buns."

"How are you ladies doing?"

"We're good. We decided to keep to ourselves. Too much conflict across the street, and that Lois, she hates us. Jack, I know she's your friend, but something is really weird about her."

"Don't let Lois get to you. Al more than makes up for her. Anyway, I see Al's got his music going again. He was just telling me the power is coming back on. I'm surprised he doesn't have a live band."

Jo rolled her eyes, "Yeah, *right*. That's a lot of crap. Reminds me of when I was back in the army, you know how that went. There'd always be word of something going down. We're going to go here, we'll be deploying over there, better get ready for this…. I'll believe it when I see it. Take a good look at those people over in Al's front yard, Jack. I bet not one of them ever spent a day in the military. If they did, they'd be home either digging in or bugging out. Instead, they're standing around like a bunch of sheep waiting for the slaughter."

Jack clapped his hands together and laughed, "Okay… that makes me feel good about what I've accomplished today. Hey, I have a little surprise at my place for you two."

Like a little girl all excited, Kathy jumped up from her lawn chair. "You have the fencing for the coop?"

"Oh, much better than that. I don't know about you girls, but our bathrooms are becoming a mess. Slopping 5-gallon buckets of water through the house to dump into the shitters is a pain in the ass, let alone the water we're wasting. Not only that, when you dump anything into a sewer, it doesn't magically disappear. No power means no wastewater treatment. Sooner or later the crap will start backing up into people's houses, and when it does, you don't

226

want to be living on the low end of the block. I got you girls a brand spanking new portable toilet! I'm going to cut the bottom of the holding tank open, so it'll drain directly into a pit. You're going to have your own private outhouse. You can even cut a moon in the door, if you want." Jo sat back silently eyeing Jack. Her questionable stare caught Jack's attention.

"What's wrong, Jo? I thought you'd be excited to hear that."

"We are excited, Jack. But you know, it's because of all this crap going down that we fell in together this week. I mean, we've lived down the street from you for almost two years and have barely said hello. You've just lost your wife, and Lynne told us what happened to you in Chicago. Most people would be back at their house feeling sorry for themselves, licking their wounds. Some would be blowing their brains out. I'm sitting here wondering just what kind of glue holds you together, because I'd like a tub of it. Jack, I don't want to look a gift horse in the mouth, but I'm also wondering why you're helping us?"

He was about to answer Jo's question, when Kathy got up, almost knocking over a small pan that was over the fire.

"Whoa, those pork and beans are really hot! I almost dumped the pan. Jack, you sure you don't want anything? I've got some potato chips, and we actually baked some chocolate chip cookies on the grill. I'll go inside and get them."

"I won't refuse a chocolate chip cookie, Kathy."

She disappeared into the house with the hot dogs and beans, Jo eyeing her as she left.

After she was out of sight, Jo said, "Kathy always looks on the bright side. She tries to see the best in people. Always cheerful, too."

Jack sat down in a chair next to Jo, "Aren't you?"

Jo let out a laugh. "What, me cheerful, or looking for the best in people? I seldom see the glass as half full, and I'm not necessarily the easiest to get along with. Some people are just naturally happy, I guess. I wish I could be like her. Kathy has always been like that, but you would think she wouldn't be. Her father, may he rot in hell, abused her from the time she could walk. He didn't stop until she was in eighth grade." Jo leaned in close to Jack, "She stuck a ball point pen in his eye and blinded the bastard. She's really upset about this Glen guy being on the loose. It brings back memories of a time she's done the best to blot out."

"Here we go, beans and franks!" Kathy came out carrying two plates and a paper bag. She handed a bag that contained six huge chocolate chip cookies to Jack. "This is for our big Marine, enjoy."

Kathy sat down, "We want to know how are you doing, Jack? We're so sorry about your wife, you've had a terrible week. And your neighbor, Ronnie. It's hard to imagine the terror she went through."

Jack thought for a moment, and for the first time spoke with some uncertainty. "Maybe I'm in shock, I don't know. If that's what it is, I'm glad I have it. To tell you the truth, I don't know what I'm feeling. I just know I have to keep moving, and I don't feel that I can spare the time to think about it. Too much is happening for any person to comprehend. Your neighbors committed suicide, so have others, right in this subdivision and we're barely into the first week of this mess. Across the street it's been looking like a big party, but look closely at those people, they're scared. So how am I doing? The answer to that is, *I am doing*. I'm doing something that's not short term. I refuse to kill myself in grief and worry, and I won't sit back and think someone else is going to do something for me to solve my problems. I sometimes feel like kicking myself in the ass for not being more prepped, but I can't change the past. I've got my ass in gear and there are things that I have to do this week. Come hell or high water, I *will* get them done."

Kathy fingered the hot dog on her plate, suddenly uninterested in it. She said, "I believe you will get them done, Jack, and we're glad you've included us in your plans. Thank you." Changing the subject, she asked, "How's Bobby? I pray he didn't see what that bastard did to his mother."

"Lynne and Laura are watching him closely. Considering what he must have seen, I think he's doing good. He's started asking for mama and daddy. I don't know what to say, it's just sad what human beings do to each other." Jo got up and placed another piece of wood on the fire. She sat back down, and Kathy suddenly got silent.

Jo took up where she left off earlier, "That lady that's living with you, Lynne. I like her. You didn't even know her, yet you took her in. And that boy, Carl, who's staying with you, and now us. We hardly know you, and now you're helping us too, why?"

Jack leaned forward in his chair, "Carl asked me the same thing. If I was alone right now, living in some secluded place in Idaho, I wouldn't be worried. But we're stuck here, in this suburban sewer we live in. As far away from Chicago as we are, unless we pull close to people who are on the same page we are and come up with a plan to protect each other, we're screwed. I don't care if you're an experienced cop or an armed to the teeth prepper, you'll be overwhelmed. I think there're will be a wall of people exiting every city that has had gang and major crime problems. When the cities have been destroyed, the gangs will leave too. We have to take the time to hunt for food and supplies and leave our homes sometimes. We also have to sleep, and it's then we'll be vulnerable. I don't plan to build an army, but unless we pull together, and I don't mean what Al over there is doing, we won't make it to winter. If you go on any military base, there are multiple men on sentry and a roving guard duty, 24-7, and that's what we'll have to do. A typical family of a husband and wife with a couple of kids, aren't going to be able to do that day in and day out. Anyone who even looks like they're well fed is going to be under constant assault. We have to get serious and join forces, and we have to do it now. If it turns out I'm wrong about how bad I think it's going to get, no harm done. I can take people making fun of me."

Kathy spoke up. "We're with you, Jack, you can count on us."

Jo added, "Count us in."

"Good. How are you fixed for supplies? As good as I think you are?" Jo was taking a bite out of her hot dog and started to cough. Kathy looked over to Jo and back to Jack. "What do *you* think?"

"I think Jo already answered me...."

Jack sat back in his chair, thoughtfully rubbing his chin. "What I'm thinking is, that tomorrow morning Lynne and I will be making a road trip over to the home center. We need anything they have that chickens will eat. I know zero-point shit about chickens, but I've always heard they're not fussy eaters. Whatever they got, if it looks like a chicken might like it, we'll take it. I'll bring some cash with me to grease the skids. I'd like you to ride shotgun for us, follow us in your van, just in case.... We can also fill your van with supplies."

Kathy said, "Thanks for helping us, Jack."

Speaking of your van, just out of my curiosity, how come you girls have such an old 1970s van?"

Jo shrugged her shoulders, "Old is good, new is bad."

Jack got up from his chair. "This week has sure proved that right. Thanks for the cookies, see you ladies tomorrow. Is 0900 all right?"

Jo said, "We'll be waiting." Kathy gave Jack a "thumbs up," and they both said, "Good night."

Jack stopped and turned around, "One other thing. Early tomorrow before we go, Al and I will be making a garbage run. I'll be hauling Charlie's and our stuff, plus picking up Al's. He's got a big load, it'll be mostly spoiled meat, I guess. You guys get your trash bagged up and I'll dump it for you. This will be a one-time thing, I hope. I don't plan to ever do this again. We have to find a spot nearby that we can carry our stuff to before it piles up in our yards, or we'll get rats and God knows what else. I'm thinking we should burn it."

Jo laughed, "Garbage pick-up too?"

"Only this one-time. I'm not going to be wasting gas on garbage runs."

Kathy said, "Jack, on the way back tomorrow, could you stop and pick me up an ice-cream sandwich?"

Jo added, "And bring me back a popsicle?"

Jack laughed and waved goodbye.

He decided to call it quits for the evening. He had planned to take a walk around the block to further cement a friendship with Jo and Kathy's friend, Ken, but now he figured they would do it for him. He was talked out for the day and did not cross back over to Al's. Instead, he walked home on the opposite side of the street, avoiding the large amount of flashlight-carrying people in Al's front yard.

Ever since the sighting of the helicopters and the rumors of the power coming back on, the mood on the block had turned to optimism. Al's stereo was

229

back to blasting disco music, and someone on the next street decided to celebrate the 4th of July early. Bottle rockets and packs of firecrackers were going off and kids were yelling. If it wasn't for the dark houses and running generators, it would be like any other suburban spring night. Reaching Glen and Doris's house, his heart got heavy. He thought about Doris and Ellen; the store's walls crashing in on them. He wondered if they were talking to each other when the aircraft plowed through the store.

He was about to cross the street over to his own house, when he stopped in front of Glen's. Dark and vacant, the two-story house towered over his bi-level. He carefully eyed each of the home's second floor windows, looking for any signs of movement. Any tell tail flash of light that would indicate Glen was back, hiding somewhere inside. *Where are you holed up, you bastard?* He turned and looked across the street at his house. The only sign of life was the dim light of a candle that flickered from Lynne's room. He focused his eyes on the candle light, his mind always planning, constantly thinking of everything that could possibly go wrong. He made a note to keep some 5-gallon buckets filled with water for fire safety. He didn't like having to rely on candles and dangerous kerosene lamps inside his house. He recalled how Ellen would always say, "Jack, you worry too much." Maybe he did. Sometimes he wished he could just flip a switch and turn his mind off. He cursed himself again for not having prepared enough, *there's so much more I have to get done this week....* Next door at Charlie's, the entire house was dark. Like his own house, Charlie's generator was not on, precious gas had to be conserved. The sound of generators echoed through the neighborhood, still foolishly being run for the convenience of lights. He stood on the sidewalk for a few moments listening and observing... thinking.

There was no need to look for an oncoming car as he stepped onto the vacant street. Crossing to the middle, he stopped, pausing to look up. With the lights of Chicago-land switched off, the stars in the nighttime sky over Illinois had been turned back on. He thought about what Lois had said in her kitchen about God. *"Where is he now?"* He wondered how many believers would soon be turning their backs on God, because he didn't keep his part of the deal. With no one around to hear him, Jack said, "No deals from me J.C. I know you're not my cosmic servant, and I do believe. Tomorrow, like Noah, I'll continue gathering what my family needs. Thank you, Lord."

THE DUMP

CHAPTER 26

The sound of the rototiller woke Jack up. The sun hadn't yet come up and Carl was already at it. He had said he had a little more he wanted to turn over and had gotten an early start. Laura had already planted the tomato plants and most of the other plants she and Carl had brought from the home center. All the rain water barrels were nearly empty. Carl and Laura had watered plants with watering cans, until well after sundown. Hopefully, Friday afternoon would be spent planting seeds.

From here on, it would depend on the rain. Jack got up and grabbed a clean T shirt. It had been over a week since the laundry had been done and he was running out of clean clothes. He wondered if they would be forced to use the generator just to run the washing machine. He hadn't thought yet about washing their clothes without power. That would be a bridge he'd have to cross quick, because he only wanted to use the generator if he absolutely had to. He could smell himself and he smelled ripe. The last shower and shave he had was on Monday morning. The girls were using the last of the city water that he drained from the basement water heater to keep themselves clean, and he'd have to talk to Charlie about getting water out of his basement pump.

He hadn't noticed the rototiller shutting off, but he clearly heard yelling coming from the back yard. It was Barry. This time he was standing on the lower boards of his fence, yelling over the top of it at Carl. Jack smirked; it probably was about waking him up so early with the noise of the rototiller. He was about to quickly dress and hurry out there and give it to him, but he decided not to. Instead he stayed behind the curtain of his open bedroom window and listened. He wanted to hear how a young chemistry teacher would handle his idiot of a neighbor. Barry was bigger than Carl, and Jack watched with concern as his complaining neighbor entered his yard, confronting Carl face to face. He couldn't hear what they were saying to each other, they just stood there talking in low tones. A few minutes later, he watched as Laura brought them each a cup of coffee. Jack smiled to himself. Laura and Carl obviously possessed a trait that he didn't have... *patience.*

He had a small pail of water in the bathroom and washed himself up before putting on the clean shirt. He briefly thought about jumping in the river, but decided against it. He laughed to himself, thinking, *Welcome to the new world.* When he entered the kitchen a few minutes later, Laura was mixing pancake batter. She turned around and cheerfully greeted him as he entered the kitchen.

"Good morning, Dad! Sure wish we had some milk for these pancakes, but I think they'll be just fine without it. We're having blueberry pancakes, eggs and the last of the pork sausage for breakfast. I think after today, the freezer and fridge will be pretty much empty. Everything is defrosted and won't keep much longer. It's weird, we're eating better than we ever did."

"Morning, sweetie. Just enjoy it while you can, it'll all be ending soon. So, what's going on outside with our pesky neighbor today?"

"I guess Barry was upset that Carl woke him up again. I made a fresh pot of coffee at Charlie's and brought them both out a cup. At least Barry isn't yelling at him anymore."

"Geez, I'll never figure that guy out. Well, I'm going to stay out of it. Whatever his problem was, it looks like Carl handled it." Jack poured himself a cup of coffee. "Where's Lynne?"

"She's next door helping Charlie and Ted. I'm making breakfast for them."

"Gosh, am I the last one up again?"

"Afraid so, Dad."

"What's your plans for the day?"

"Play with Bobby for awaile and plant vegetables. Carl wants to get everything planted by sundown; he says there's rain coming in tomorrow. That's good because most of Charlie's rain barrels and all of ours are empty."

"Thanks for reminding me about the rain barrels. I'm going to the home center today. I want to pick up some PVC fittings and some pipe. I want to connect some water barrels up together." At the mention of the home center, Laura tensed. He sensed something was wrong and waited a few seconds to see if she would share anything. Not wanting to push the issue, he said, "Anyway, me, Lynne, Jo and Kathy are going there this morning. I'm bringing a wad of cash. Right now, I'm going to load up all our trash and dump it in that old gravel pit by the golf course. Al's going with me. I hate to start burning it here, it'll be a big mess. In the long run it'll only create more problems, but I don't want to waste the gas by carting it out of here every week either. The weekly garbage pick-up, that's another thing we took for granted. Going to miss it."

"Just be careful, Dad, there are so many terrible people—"

Jack got up, hugging his daughter from behind, "Don't worry, old dad will be careful. Lynne and I have a couple more trips planned in the next day or so, but after that, I plan to stay near home and conserve fuel. Once we run out, we're not going anywhere."

Laura turned around and faced him. "Carl and I have been doing all this work on the garden and all, and its hard work, but it's been fun. I know you're doing this to keep us busy and that's good. It's keeping my mind off what has happened…. Dad, is it *really* going to continue to get bad? I mean, some of the neighbors think we're crazy, tearing up the whole yard and pack-ratting stuff."

"Some of the neighbors, huh? Is some of the neighbors Al and the people partying down there with him?"

Turning away from the counter, she faced her dad. "Well. . . Al said the National Guard will be here soon, and that Commonwealth Power is going to get the electric back on by next week. He also heard they're setting up shelters and mobile kitchens."

"If this was just a city-wide thing or even a county-wide black-out, I would agree with Al. But we can't get any radio stations. We're near two major airports and haven't seen any airplanes. Not one. As far as I know, the whole country is like this. I don't know these people Al is getting his information from. I'll believe it when I see it."

"All right, Dad, we don't doubt you. I know you'd rather be safe than sorry. We should be done with the main part of our little farm today. You and Lynne get your potatoes in, and we're finished."

"That's my girl. I'm going next door to talk to Lynne and Charlie. Later, Al and I are going on a garbage run. Maybe he can convince me to be a little more optimistic. Make me a plate of food and save it for me, would you? I'll have it when I get back."

"Dad, I love you…"

"Love you too, sweetie…"

Before heading out, he glanced out the kitchen window. Carl was back to turning over the sod. Thankfully, Barry was nowhere in sight. He left for Charlie's without stopping to talk with Carl. Carl knew more about gardening than he would ever know, and didn't need an old Marine telling him what to do. He went over and talked to Charlie and had a second cup of coffee with him. Lynne was attending to Ted. When Jack left, Lynne walked out with him.

"How is Ted?"

"Not good, Jack, his legs are huge. They're filling up with water and he has this cough… his heart is just plain giving out. I'm afraid he's going into renal failure. He's just lying in bed moaning and he's in pain. His body is shutting down. We'll just have to make him as comfortable as we can. If we could get an IV and some morphine, I could at least help him some. Also, Charlie needs insulin. I know the hospital would be a long-shot, it's probably in shambles. I remember we passed a sign for a nursing home just before the golf course. It's close by and they should have it. We could also try the fire department, but I think that nursing home would be the best bet."

"Do you think they would give something like that to us?"

"That nursing home is part of a group of private homes that was bought out by Brandon Health-Care, and I deal with them regularly. In this situation, I would expect all of their residents have been evacuated. They would have insulin, and I think they'd give it to me."

"The first thing I was going to do this morning was to go down and get Al, and then do a trash run. The three of us can go right after breakfast, and then we can check out that nursing home."

An hour later they were loaded up and pulling into Al's driveway. There was a huge mound of black garbage bags on Al's drive, each one bulging with spoiled meat and produce. Jack got out and started tossing bags into the back of the pickup, while Lynne went in to get Al. A couple minutes later Al and Lois came walking out with Lynne.

Al said, "Be careful with those bags, big guy, you don't want them stinking things breaking open in your truck. Hey, you should have come back last night, lots of news from the front."

Jack avoided eye contact with Lois, as he said, "Morning Lois... morning Al, what's the news?"

"First of all, Chicago and a good part of Cook County are in shambles, but they landed the National Guard in there to kick ass. They also got more choppers coming in and dropping off supplies to set up relief camps, that's what they're calling them. They say power will definitely be on within a week or so. In the meantime, they're dropping generators off at every hospital. It's like that lady from the FAA said it would be, Jack, it's not a bunch of hearsay bullshit."

"Where did you hear all this from, Al?"

"Wally Olsen. I don't know him really that well, but he's on the county board. He told Jimmy Chen about it yesterday. Jimmy was over here last night with his wife and two kids. Cute little girls, huh, Lois?" Lois smiled at Jack while nodding her head. "They're Chinese or something.... filthy rich too. They got a big place over at the country club. Lois and I have been there."

Lois said, "Yes, they're very cute, a sweet family..." Lois kept smiling at Jack. He could feel her green eyes boring into him.

Al said, "Anyway, they walked over here from their place. You and I have walked by it when we golf. It's overlooking the 13th hole. You should see the insides of their place, it's huge. They got like six fireplaces and the biggest kitchen you've ever seen. They had dinner over here last night. They heard about my Lois' good cooking, I guess."

Jack continued to throw the black bags into the truck, avoiding Lois' stare. When the bed was heaped high, he motioned to Al and Lynne, "Let's saddle up, Lynne's got shotgun."

As the three of them got in the truck, Al said, "How come you're coming with us, Lynne? Don't you think old Al can take care of Jack?"

Jack answered for her, "We're making a stop after this first run. We need some medicine and an IV drip to make Ted comfortable. Lynne doesn't think he has much time left. We're going to the Valley View Nursing Home. It's over by the golf course and shouldn't take much time. You're going to stand guard on the truck for us while we go in."

"Oh boy... I don't know, Jack, that may be a bad idea. I hear the cops are confiscating vans and trucks for emergency services. We should just dump this shit and get right back."

"Nobody is going to take anything from me, Al, I guarantee it."

Al was sitting in the middle and gave a look to Lynne. He raised his bushy eyebrows and shrugged, saying, "He's the boss." She smiled back, raised her eyebrows and shrugged her shoulders. Al glanced at her bandaged cheek. "That looks a lot better than it did a few days ago. Is it still hurting?"

"No, I may take the bandages off tonight or tomorrow morning." Lynne couldn't put her finger on it, but there was something phony about Al and she suddenly didn't care for him. Jack started the truck up and the three of them headed towards the gravel pit.

Just before they got to the golf course, there was a small overgrown drive with a faded sign. Half buried in the brush, the words: Sand & Gravel, were barely readable. Jack turned the truck into it.

"Gosh, Jackster, I've never even noticed this little road. Have you been back here before?"

"Nope, but once we get back there, you'll recognize it. There's a shallow gravel pit, you can see it from the ninth hole. I figured we might be able to back up to the pit and toss everything right in it."

Overgrown bushes and trees were scraping the sides of the truck as they drove down the narrow road. Jack pulled the truck in as far as they could go, stopping at a fallen tree. He clenched his teeth; something didn't feel right. "I don't want to do this, but we might have to dump this crap right here. I hoped we could get right up to the edge of the pit. The only other alternative is to burn the stuff back home."

Al was shaking his head. "Nah... I don't think that's a good idea, burning this shit. These bags got a lot of spoiled meat and stuff in them. That kinda stuff needs a really hot fire, and I sure don't want to bring this crap back home...let's just dump it and get the heck outta here."

"Listen," It was Lynne. She had her head partly out the door's window. "Shut the truck off, Jack, I hear talking up ahead."

Jack raised his eyebrows, "Probably someone out golfing. Let's get out quietly... don't slam the doors. We'll see who's out there."

The three of them got out of the truck and silently made their way up the rest of the overgrown road. They had gone about 50 yards, when the road

235

narrowed down to a path. The voices were louder, and they heard a vehicle running.

Al shot Jack a worried look, "That don't sound like no golf cart, Jack. Why don't we just dump the shit and get the hell out of here?"

Jack placed his forefinger to his lips, motioning Al to be silent, as they slowly made their way to the edge of the gravel pit. The pit was about 400 feet long and about 200 feet wide. A narrow gravel road was on the western edge of it. The depth was about 20 feet deep and most of it was filled with murky water. Jack was bent forward, spreading some bushes, when he motioned for Lynne and Al to hold up. Getting down on his hands and knees, he crept ahead on his own. Pushing his way through the heavy brush to the edge of the pit, he slowly moved some spiny brambles aside... *Holy shit!*

He recognized it immediately for what it was, he had seen one before in Northern Iraq. An entire Kurdish town had been massacred and their bodies had been hastily thrown into a shallow pit. Some of the bodies had been bulldozed over and covered with sand, but most were only partially covered.

Jack sunk himself further down into the brush and signaled the other two to stay back and be quiet. He didn't know what he had stumbled upon and didn't want to be seen. Silently creeping forward a little more, he again peered through the bushes, cursing himself for not having his field glasses in the truck. There was a large flatbed truck slowly driving on the edge of the pit, with three men were standing in the back of it. One of them was a huge man, but he was too far away to clearly see his face. He was tossing human bodies over the side of the truck like rag dolls, splashing them into the swampy water! There was another truck, this one a beat up old semi-dump, backing up to the pit and stopping. Something was familiar about the old flatbed truck. He could barely read the letters painted on the cab's door, but he had recently seen them.

WALTER CASS & SONS
Construction rentals

It was Walt's father's truck! The same truck that Walt had delivered the fencing materials on, only Walt wasn't driving it. The dump on the other truck started to raise. He couldn't believe his eyes. When the dump was all the way up, one of the men walked over and released the catch on the truck's gate. The back of the huge dump truck was full, almost to the top with human bodies. With the its huge box raised up, the driver bucked the truck backwards, sending lifeless bodies sliding out. Like a fluid load of sodden garbage, the bodies splashed into the dark water. There were heaps of bodies already in the pit. Some wrapped like mummies in blankets and sheets, and others fully clothed. Many were floating, partially submerged, drifting away to the far corners of their watery grave. Only God knew how many were submerged under them. He could make out men, women and children. There were hundreds, maybe over a thousand.

Jack silently backed himself out of the heavy brush, shaken at what he'd seen.

"Big guy, whatta you see, whatta you see?"

"Be quiet, Al, shhh, let's get out of here…. Now! Keep quiet…both of you, back up and stay down!" Jack followed behind them, whispering, "Get back in the truck and don't slam the door." He got in the driver's seat and prayed no one heard the pickup truck's old engine as it started. Slowly, being as quiet as he could, Jack backed the truck out, leaving the way they came in.

"Jack, are you going tell us what the hell you saw that's got you so shook?"

"What I saw, were two trucks. One of them was a big flatbed truck that stopped at my house yesterday, the other one a large semi-dump. They were dumping dead bodies, men, women, and children, into the pit. I'd say there were over a thousand."

Once out of the overgrown drive, Jack paused on the main road. There was no one in sight either way. Parking on the shoulder, he quickly got out and lowered the truck's tailgate. Jumping back into the driver's seat, he said, "Hang on to something," as he floored the truck in reverse for about 50 feet.

Al yelled, **"What the hell are you doing?"**

Jack didn't have to answer Al's question. He suddenly slammed on the brakes and all the black garbage bags slid out and shot off the back of the truck's tailgate, spewing into the roadside weeds.

Al looked alarmed when two of the tumbling bags broke open, spilling their bloody contents into the middle of the road.. "Jeez Jack, a couple of those bags busted open… they're in the road."

Shoving the gearshift into first, Jack floored the old truck towards home, saying, "You want to go back and clean up that mess and be seen by those people dumping those bodies?"

Al glanced into the rear view mirror. Half open bags were strewn across the road."No, I guess not. The rats and coons will eat it up tonight."

Jack bent forward, looking past Al to Lynne. "What do you think? I'm thinking they're the victims from the plane crash and bodies from the hospitals. We saw what Stroger Hospital looked like, and that was within a couple hours."

Lynne bent forward, talking over AL, "Has to be, they've got to be overwhelmed with bodies."

Jack slowly nodded his head, licking his dry lips, badly wanting a cigarette. He said, "All those bodies at the crash site, with no morgue and no refrigeration… what a mess. I can understand. . .but what spooked me is they were using Walt's truck. I wonder if he got nailed in a road block or something and the county took it from him? I bet that's what happened.. . . The poor kid stops and helps us and gets his truck confiscated."

Jack suddenly made a hard right, turning the truck towards the industrial park.

Al worriedly said, "Where the hell are we going now? We should be going straight. Whatta we driving this way for?"

"Hang on, Al, I just want to check a place out. Someone who helped us yesterday may need a ride and one of your free meals."

Jack intended to drive to either the portable toilet rental or the fence place to see if Walt was still there. He was a nice kid, and he figured he at least owed him some help. He hadn't driven 50 feet into the industrial park when he saw a body lying on the side of the road. Before he even got of the truck, he already knew who it was. It was Walt and he had a bullet hole in the back of his head. It looked like he had been kneeling, shot execution style. Jack picked up a single flattened brass shell casing laying on the road's gravel shoulder. "Look at this shell casing, Al. It had to be run over by whomever killed him." Examining the the mangled casing, Jack said, "It was fired from a Shotmaster 45."

Al rolled his eyes. "That shell is smashed all to hell. How can you tell what kind of gun it was fired from?"

Jack handed Al the flattened shell casing. "You don't have to take my word for it, Al. Look how long that shell is. Then look at the end of it. See the number 45? You can barely make out the letter S next to it. It's not that common of a gun. The ammo for it has been hard to get. I don't know why, but the government has been buying it up. Your neighbor, Jo carries a Shotmaster 45. I'm pretty sure your sheriff friend carries one too. I don't care for them myself, but it's a popular gun with law enforcement, and it's the only 45 that uses this shorter shell."

"Jeez, Jack. Neither one of them would shoot this poor kid."

"I didn't say they did."

Jack and Al placed Walt's body in the back of the pickup, and the three of them drove home in silence. There would be another grave to dig in the backyard.

A few minutes later, they loaded the rest of Al's trash into the truck, Al was pleading with Jack, "You have got to be kidding me. We just dropped a kid's body off in your garage, and you're still going to some nursing home, after you dump this shit? Jack, you're nuts!"

"What do you want me to do, Al, sit home all scared? I just saw over 1,000 bodies being slid into a sand and gravel pit. If we don't keep our shit together and stay the course we need to be on, we'll be joining them. Now, let's load up the rest of your crap. Then I'll go get the girl's garbage. I wanted you to stop with us at the nursing home to be a look-out for us, but you can stay here, if you want to. We can handle it by ourselves. It might be better if you stay home. Locate those boys doing the grave digging and ask them to dig another one in my backyard, near the big red rock." Jack fished in his front pocket and handed Al two 20's. "Give them this ahead of time, in case I don't make it back until late. I'll be stopping at Jo and Kathy's when I get back. They're going with me and Lynne to the home center. We have to get food for our chickens."

"Oh my God, chickens? Chickens? Jack, you're really starting to worry me. Barry, was down here last night bitching to everybody about you starting a cemetery behind his place. Now I got nothing against a backyard cemetery, strikes me as convenient, but he also saw those portable shitters you stashed over at Charlie's place, and now chickens? He was talking about getting all the neighbors to sue you when this shit is over. It wouldn't be bad if it was just him, but a couple other people think you're hoarders. That asshole Dorfman has been talking to Barry too. They're college buddies, did you know that? He's a forensic investigator, and believe me, he's trouble. I know you don't think so, but this shit will be over soon. How are you going to explain to a judge what you've done? You've got a cemetery in your yard, holy cripes."

"I don't give a shit what anyone thinks. I'm digging in, Al. The neighbors who don't like it can go take a flying leap. By the way, write down the names of all these people for me. I want to remember them when they come to my door next month looking for a handout, crying for help. See you later."

Al stood by his curb and watched Jack speed away, "Be careful with those bags, big guy, don't let them break open..."

Jack dumped the last load of garbage, just like the first load. He pulled off the road into a vacant lot near the industrial park. After dropping the truck's tailgate, he accelerated in reverse and hit the brakes hard. Boxes of garbage and overstuffed black plastic bags, shot out from the back of the truck, tumbling into the weeds. Ten minutes later, he was back home, picking up Lynne.

Lynne was holding her shotgun, standing near the closed garage door waiting for him. He stopped the truck by the curb as she walked out to the street. Getting into the truck, she said, "I told Carl and Laura what happened. Laura is a little freaked out about Walt's body being in our garage."

"Did you tell them the rest, about what we saw at the sand pit?"

"I told them just what we figured, that it was probably the bodies from the plane crash, plus the county hospital and nursing homes. With no one able to claim those bodies and nowhere to store them under refrigeration, it's the only logical thing to do. She understood. . . I only hope they're keeping good records of everyone they bury."

As Jack drove down his street towards Jo and Kathy's, one thing bothered him. *Why was Walt's truck being used to transport the bodies, and who killed him for it?*

Jack parked the truck in front of Jo's house. Both her and Kathy were already sitting in the van waiting for them. Jo was in the driver's seat. Jack and Lynne got out together. As they walked up to the driver's side of Jo's old Chevy van. Kathy sang out, "Good morning!"

239

Jack pulled off the sunglasses he was wearing, sticking them on top of his head. Jo had both hands on the steering wheel, a tired expression already on her face. Kathy was holding a large coffee mug. Jo smiled at Jack, saying, "She's a morning person, I'm not, but we're ready to go."

Jack said, "Whatever she's putting in her coffee, give me a full cup of it. In fact, get us each a cup."

Jo said, "That's not a bad idea. I've got a six-pack of cold beer at the bottom of our freezer. Let's sit out on the back deck and have a couple brews before we go. We can make a game plan for our supply run."

Jack agreed and the four of them sat on Jo's rear deck. Jack explained to them what he had seen earlier at the gravel pit. He told them what happened to Walt and the questions he had in his mind about his death. The four of them came to the agreement that the county was most likely overwhelmed with decomposing, unclaimed bodies, and had no other option. No one would want to face a decision like that lightly. Jack thought to himself. *What would I do?* The troubling part was that none of them could come up with a reason for a nice young man ending up dead, and his truck being used by the county to transport the dead bodies.

Governments were known to sequester property during times of war and disaster. If it was needed for the common good of the people, private property could be used or outright confiscated by the authorities. Jack had no problems with that, as long as it wasn't his property that was being confiscated. The whole concept was ripe for abuse and the average citizen seldom benefited from it. But a county official killing a young man for his truck, and then leaving his body on the road? It shouldn't have happened.

Someone, possibly a rogue county official, killed Walt for his truck. They decided it wasn't going to happen to them. They would surrender their property only if faced with an overwhelming force. And in Jack's mind, an overwhelming force meant a whole army.

While they were having their impromptu meeting, Ken and his son, Ben, joined them. It turned out that Ken had met Kathy at the VA Hospital while having dental work done. When they realized they lived in the same subdivision, they became friends. When they realized they were both preppers, they became allies. Now, Jack joined their team, and he explained to Ken how he intended to make a run to the home center. He also informed Ken about his portable toilet idea and that he had one for him. A bond between them was formed and it was over something as simple as an outhouse. *Simple, yet necessary.* They talked about what was going on in the subdivision and about how Al's house had become a mecca, not only for the free chow, but for rumors. Jack also brought up the problem of nosey neighbors. He mentioned the issues he'd been having with Barry, and Ken confirmed he had the same problems with his neighbors, the Wilsons. He said that he'd been friends with the Wilsons at first, but they started treating him differently when he had a campaign sign in front of his house, with a certain candidate on it. When they found out he was in the NRA, they stopped talking to him.

Jo and Kathy expressed their concerns too. They said the only neighbors that they liked, and were friends with, were Sue and Ron and their handicapped daughter, Dawn. They explained to them that they family who lived behind them and who had committed suicide earlier in the week. Ron had left Jo and Kathy a note saying Sue and he had agreed to do it together. They were afraid there would be no one to care for Dawn if something happened to them...their only solution was to kill themselves.

Kathy made eyes towards Al's house, saying, "I think all of you know, up until this week, good old Al has shunned us. The same goes for his wife, Lois— she's a real piece of work. We've tried to be friendly with her, but she ignores us. I guess Jo and I don't fit into their perfect little world. There's other people around here too. . . they've made it known that they don't like us. We don't have a rainbow flag hanging up. We mind our own business and keep our house looking nice. I don't know why anyone wouldn't like us."

Jo scoffed, "I notice that Al always stares at Kathy. There must be something he sees that he likes."

Ken said, "To hell with all of them. Let them play their suburban games of bullshit, I don't have time for it. I've known what's coming for a long time and I only have a high school education. Four years in the army was my college. If it wasn't this EMP shit, it would have been something else to tip the can over. Let them party and play their mind games. We have work to do." He faced Jack, "Do you mind if we go with you to the home center? If you could give us a lift back home, I'll go in and get some cash and follow you guys there in our van."

Jack said, "We'll wait for you." Ken and Ben jumped into Jo's van and she gave them a lift home. Ten minutes later, one pick-up truck and two vans drove out of the subdivision.

Al and Lois watched from their second-floor bedroom window, as the three vehicles drove off together.

Before they left for the home center, Jack made it clear that he would stop for no one and would drive around or through any road blocks. "Our friend, Walt, lost his life for his truck. I'm not giving anyone a chance to take ours. I'll take the lead. If any vehicle is in front of me and going too slow and I can't get around them, I'll give them a nudge. He looked at Jo and Ken. All three of us have been in Iraq and I know, Jo, that you drove a truck. We've all done this before, so let's hit it!" They got in their vehicles and headed towards the home center, driving fast, with Jack in the lead. They had mapped out their route and agreed to take the side streets and stay clear of all major intersections. It wasn't far, but they wanted to avoid any possibilities of hitting a roadblock.

It was almost ten o'clock and lots of people were out. They saw mostly older vehicles on the street, but a couple newer ones too. There were many people thumbing for rides, but no one was picking up any hitchhikers, especially armed ones. It also seemed like everyone was carrying something. It was like the whole town knew there was a bad storm coming and everyone was last minute preparing. Jack checked his mirror and could see Jo and Kathy following him, keeping back, as agreed. There was one major intersection just before they got to the store and it couldn't be avoided. Jack resisted the urge to slow as he approached it, looking for any signs of trouble. As they crossed the intersection, he could see thick black smoke drifting across the street ahead. He hoped it wasn't from the home center.

"Aw shit!" Jack cursed out loud. Up ahead, the lumber yard and home center were engulfed in smoke. Across the street from it was the Hobby Room, the $ Buck $ store, and Tool City. A solid mass of fire was shooting through his favorite stores' roofs. The Hobby Room was Laura's favorite store. The $ Buck $ Store and Tool City were excellent sources of prepping supplies. The whole block of stores was going up in flames, without a firetruck in sight.

Mega Home Center consisted of a huge two-story block type building in the center, with two lower additions on each side of it. On the right was a full-service lumber yard, to the left was the garden center where Laura and Carl had gotten the garden supplies. Although the building was blanketed by a cloud of heavy smoke, it was unscathed from the blaze roaring across the street. There were about a dozen vehicles in the parking lot, with people loading them up with items taken from the store. Jack wanted to go to the building materials section first and was happy see the main gate wide open. He spotted a fellow from the VFW he knew, a former Navy Seabee, with his pickup truck parked just inside the gate. He was taking plywood from a huge stack and loading it into the back of his truck. The guy was also a sergeant on the Melville Police Department, but he wasn't wearing his uniform. As Jack pulled near, he saw him stiffen and place his right hand by his side. He was wearing a long flannel with the shirt tails out, and Jack knew a handgun was somewhere under that hanging fabric.

Jack didn't waste any time identifying himself. "Hey Val! It's me, Jack, how you doing?"

"Hey Jack, semper fi, sorry— I'm a little jumpy. I'm doing good though, how you holding up?"

Jack had decided the less said about his problems, the better. He said, "We're doing okay." Jack motioned to the open gate, saying. "My daughter was here yesterday and bought some stuff. I don't see any employees, are they still open?"

"Not any more, Jack, come in and take what you want. I'm surprised the place is still here." Val pointed across the street to the Hobby Room Store. "Look what those SOBs did to those stores over there. We got crazy, punk kids running around torching places for the hell of it. The only way to stop them is to shoot them, it's gotten that bad. With no fire department to put out the fires, it places everything else at risk. Look at this place, it's a tinder box with all these building supplies. It won't be here much longer." Val slid a 4x8 sheet of 5/8ths plywood into his truck, then walked over to Jack. He tipped his ballcap to Lynne and continued, "I know the owner of this place, he was here earlier. He'll be lucky if his buildings are still standing tomorrow morning. It's bad, Jack. If you get a chance, providing you like climbing stairs, get up high on some tall building and look east. Do it at night if you can. Chicago looks like it's burning, like one big torch. It really got going late last night, with all this wind that's started blowing in. Thank God the wind is blowing away from us, towards the lake. I'll tell you who's doing it, it's the street gangs. They're going nuts. The Black and Hispanic gangs are fighting each other and torching everything. And now the local crazies are starting it out here."

Jack asked, "What about the Melville Police Department, Val. Aren't you guys trying to do anything about what's going on?"

"Honest to God, Jack, the first couple days were rough, but we tried. Some of the guys have personal vehicles that still run. My old pickup runs great. We tried running patrols. We ran folks to the hospital and stuff, but now.... No way—we all got families, you know how it is.... My wife is freaked, she wants me home. Some of the guys got places or relatives up in Wisconsin and have already bugged out. Yesterday we had two officers seriously injured in a car wreck. At any other time, an ambulance would have gotten them over to the hospital and they would have survived. They both died, there was no one there to help them. Our whole department has disappeared. Some of the guys never showed up for work after the second day. They're scared, and can you blame them? And now— I'm sorry, it's every man for himself. Me, I'm hunkering down in my home, that's what I'm getting this plywood for. I live in a two-story house and I'm boarding up all the first-floor windows, and I suggest you do the same. Look, I gotta get going, best of luck to you."

Jack held up his hand, "Hang on for one minute, Val, I just want to ask you a couple quick things. Is the county hospital open at all and do you know what they're doing with the people who die? The other thing I want to know about is if the county confiscating private vehicles?"

Val moved close to Jack's door. "The county hospital is in really bad shape; they all are. Most of the staff is nowhere to be seen and you can't blame them. They have no way to get to work, plus they have families too. To top it off, the hospital's emergency generators failed. They have no power at all. As far as the deceased go... they don't want this spread around, but what the hell, everyone's going to find out soon enough. They're overwhelmed with bodies over there. People are constantly being dropped off at the hospital and if it's for something serious, they just die. And who's going to go back home with grandpa's body in their trunk? Not to mention everyone who was already in the place on respirators and shit. Plus, there was a shitload of people having surgery that didn't make it when the power went off. It's really sad. They're putting them in the old gravel pit, over by the golf course. We also have all these nursing homes around here full of old and sick people. They're dropping like flies. They got those who died when the two jets came down, too. You drive around enough; you'll see dead bodies just laying out on the street. People are killing each other left and right. The county coroner and sheriff's department are in charge of picking the bodies up. They identify the deceased, if they can, and into the old pit they go. They said they have to do it to stop the spread of disease. Things are really screwed, what can I say? I'll tell you what though, they aren't going to shove me or my loved ones into that pit, no sir... What was your other question? Oh, yeah, confiscating private vehicles. There was talk about that and also going after the looters, but what the hell, with the whole force off protecting their own shit, that isn't going to happen. Good luck to you, big guy." Val walked back to his truck, and as he got in, he turned back towards Jack, saying, "And hey, watch your ass around here. Lots of crazies running around. There's a dead kid lying face down in a bunch of busted up tomato plants in the garden center. He's got a pitchfork sticking out of his back, jammed to the hilt. The manager said it happened yesterday afternoon, that's why they're closed today. Good luck to you guys."

Jack thanked Val and wished him luck. He turned to Lynne and they silently stared at each other for a couple seconds.

Lynne raised her eyebrows and broke the silence, "You think?"

He said, "The kids were here yesterday afternoon. Maybe someone threatened Laura—I've noticed that Carl is very protective of her...."   Lynne nodded her head in agreement, "They were acting strange when we said we were coming here. They didn't want us to come here, that was clear."

"Well, let's get what we need and then get home." Jack waved back at Jo and Ken, signaling them to drive up.

Once everyone was together, Jack got out and quickly gave the others the low down.

"That guy loading the plywood is a Melville cop and a buddy of mine. He gave us the scoop on what's going on. I'll let you know what's happening later. He told us there may be a crazy person roaming around in there, so be on your toes. Someone ran a pitchfork through some kid...he's laying somewhere in the garden center. I'm going to grab a load of this plywood and some nails for boarding up any vulnerable windows in our houses. Let's load up my pickup and then go into the yard together. At least two of us have got to keep watch at all times. Warn off anyone that tries to approach us, but if they keep coming and you don't know them—use your best judgement, but don't hesitate. Unless they moved it, the animal feed and that kind of stuff is on the far right of the main building. That's where I'll be heading first."

The store was like a free for all. There was an assortment of older cars and trucks in the parking lot, all being loaded down with everything imaginable. Jack spotted a beautiful 1950's yellow Packard convertible. The top was down and a guy was carelessly stacking sheets of plywood across the back of it. He even saw a Model A Ford truck pulling out with a load of fencing. He thought to himself, *anything that is running is out on the road.... what's going to happen when we run out of gas?*

The thick, acrid smoke from the burning stores across the street started blowing directly on them, making it difficult to breathe. Working in a cloud of smoke, Jack and Lynne madly finished sliding over 20 sheets of plywood into the truck. Pulling the truck next to the building, Jack jumped out and was surprised to find an empty shopping cart. Quickly wheeling it into the building, he cursed to out loud, *"Shit! It's got a lousy wheel ...every time!"* Fighting the wobbly cart, he knew exactly where the hardware aisle was and wasted no time filling it with boxes of nails and screws. The others had found the mother-lode of wild bird feed. Boxes and bags, large or small, they took it all. There were several large bags of dog food which they also grabbed. Jack figured the chickens would provide them with plenty of eggs if they were healthy and happy, and he intended to make sure they were.

They only had one confrontation in the store, but when Jo leveled her 45 at the man, he quickly backed off.

There were more items they needed, but they'd loaded the vans to the point where the doors wouldn't close. The back of Carl's pickup was piled to overflowing, and the tops of the vans as well. There wasn't an inch of space to fit anything else.

Their luck held out as they pulled out of the smoke-filled parking lot and headed for home. There were so many other things in the store that Jack wanted to get. As he drove out onto the street, the heat from the burning buildings across from them was almost unbearable. *Did they dare try another run?* The warm spring winds were steadily blowing harder from the southwest and high clouds were blowing in. The flames were whipping out of the burning buildings, sending flaming debris sailing through the air towards the lumberyard. Jack figured Val, would be right. If the winds got any higher, the home center would be burning to the ground before evening. *Maybe one more run...*

Their first stop was Jo and Kathy's. They quickly unloaded some supplies into Jo's house, before continuing to Jack's. The final stop was Ken's. While they were unloading the last of their load, Ken nudged Jack's arm and gestured next door to Wilson's house.

Defiantly standing in Wilson's front yard, was Wilson and two other men, whom Jack hadn't seen before. The three men were in a straight line, warily watching them. He had met Wilson before, and with the sullen look on his face, he knew that something was about to go down. Wilson was staring at Jack, his eyes blinking like he had a nervous tic. The two unknown men, one short and squat, the other one tall with a big handlebar mustache, were the only ones armed—both of them wore badges. The two of them cockily advanced, stopping a few feet away from Jack. The short, stocky one wore a shoulder holster with what looked like a standard short barreled 38 revolver in it. Another handgun was holstered low on his right hip. It looked like a nickel-plated 44, similar to Jack's 44, Little Red. The short guy snarled, " **Look at all the goods you've stolen. Proud of yourself? You're nothing but a bunch of looters, scum of the earth, and now you're all under arrest!**" The tall one with the mustache had a holstered semi-automatic, high up on his left hip with the flap open. He was carelessly holding a sawed-off pump shotgun in his right hand, pointed towards the ground. His mustache badly needed a trim

The mustached man smiled and said, "Martial law has been declared. Do you know what that means?"

Jack already had his gun drawn and leveled at the man's chest before he had the "s" in means out. An open mouth immediately appeared from under the unruly hair- covered lip, and Jack figured he would let loose in his pants next. Jo was a split second behind Jack, her Shotmaster 45 aimed at the head of the shorter man.

 Mustache was the smarter of the two men. He was immeadiantly scared and looked it. Jack thought the shorter man's close-shaved big head was lacking a neck. He was too stupid to be scared. Instead he eyed Jo with a cocky smile, saying, "You're not going to fire at me... *sweetheart*. We're the law here."

Jo must have had the same thought as Jack about the man's big head, because she snapped, "Shut up, *bullet head*!" She stood there for a couple seconds with her arm extended, and without warning, coolly fired her pistol, blowing the top part of the smiling man's right ear clean off.

Jack shot an exasperated look at her, "Jeez, Jo!" The mustached man dropped his shotgun and raised his arms. All three of them started pleading for their lives at once. Wilson fell to his knees, his eyes screaming at Jack, *"I'm not part of this!"*

Jo snarled, "Shut up!   We're not looters and you're no cops. You're just bunch of pricks." Jo kept her pistol pointed at the bleeding man's head. He held his hand tightly cupped to his bloody ear and was starting to cry.

Jack could see a slight quiver in Jo's hand and her finger was touching the trigger. He calmly said, "Jo—ease off, lower your weapon. He's not worth it."

But Jo didn't move. She kept the black pistol pointed at the man's head. Jack kept his 44 aimed at Mustache, who had proved him right, because after he dropped his shotgun, a wet spot appeared in the crotch of his blue jeans

Jo's voice raised high. "Don't think I don't know who you and your friend are. You're the two assholes who spray painted all that vulgar shit on the front of our house!" The wounded man, still holding his ear, backed up a couple steps. Jo yelled, "Aha— yeah, surprised huh? You didn't think I knew that, did you? You and your bush-lipped buddy here, who's busy wetting his pants. That was the first week, when my girlfriend and I moved in here. You're the ones who were picked for the welcome wagon, weren't you? I'll bet you two were the ones who flattened Jake and Ronnie's car tires when they moved in." Jo moved her finger off the trigger, but shifted her aim towards the mustached man saying, "Listen up, Leroy. I know where you live. I bet you didn't know that.. . . You mess with us again and I guarantee we'll come into your house in the middle of the night and kill you where you stand, sleep, or whatever." She looked down at Wilson, "You want to see some martial law?" Wilson quickly shook his head, too scared to say anything.

Jack glanced at Wilson and looked away, almost embarrassed for him. He wondered if anyone else had noticed that Wilson had joined Mustache. The front of his pants was soaked.

Jack ended it. He said, "We're relieving you two boys of your weapons." With Jack still holding Little Red leveled at the tall man, Ken and Ben removed the men's firearms. "They're ours now, thanks. We'll take good care of them. And take those phony badges off your shirts. Throw them on the ground, and get out of here." Jack said to the mustached man, "Consider yourselves lucky, Leroy, we could have killed both of you. Don't get any ideas about coming back, it's not worth it. And one other thing, the next time you decide to go into battle, stop and take a piss-break first."

Jo said, "Thanks for the 44, asshole. I've always wanted one."

The three men split up. Wilson hastily retreated home to change his pants. The other two got into an old pickup parked next to Wilson's garage and roared off. Jo holstered her pistol. Jack noticed she was shaking.

Jack was the first to speak, "God, Jo, I thought you were going to kill him."

Jo said, "I know where Leroy and his friend live. Bullet-head lives over on the next street *with his mom*. He's a security guard at the York Field Mall. His name is Len. I was planning on spray painting something vulgar on the front of his house, I just couldn't figure out what."

Jack replied, "A security guard at a shopping mall, that figures."

Ken handed the big nickel-plated 44 to Jo, saying, "This is a nice one. If you don't want it, I'll take it."

She said, "No, you can have the other gun he was wearing. I might start carrying this one. I'll be just like Jack..."

Jack said, "Oh great."

Ken was the one to get business back on track. "Now that we're done having fun with the neighbors, how about we go back for another load."

Jack said, "My thoughts exactly!"

247

Lynne had an astonished look on her face. She gasped at Ken and then back to Jack. **"Are you guys crazy?** After what just happened, you want to leave and go get another load?"

Jack said, "Yeah, I've been thinking about it too. I think we should. Those guys won't give us any more trouble, at least not today, probably never. They were about to shit in their pants. Didn't you notice, all of them were starting to cry? Yeah, let's do it. Let's get anything else we can before that place burns down." Jack looked pleadingly at Lynne, "You okay with that, Lynne?"

"I suppose. If everyone thinks it's all right... I'll go along with you. It just seems like it's never ending, people wanting to kill us. All right, let's do it and get it over with."

Ken said, "Pretty soon we're not to going to be able to go anywhere. We'll be stuck here; everything will be either burned or looted out." He turned to Lynne, "You got more guts than those three guys put together, Lynne."

Lynne sighed and said, "I'm glad you think so."

Ken faced Jack, saying, "Jack, you mentioned you wanted to get some plastic pipe and rolls of chicken wire and to see if they had any tarps and ropes. That's a good idea. I think we should get some metal garbage cans to dump this feed into. It'll keep it dry and also keep the mice out of it. I wouldn't mind looking around the hardware section some more. I'll think of more stuff we can use, as I see it."

Jack agreed. "I think it's a good idea, but you shouldn't leave your places totally alone. I'm not worried about Wilson, he's like my neighbor Barry, a big gas bag. But those other two assholes, they're cowards, we know that, but they're also pissed off and they're sneaks. There are lots of others just like them around here. They won't have the guts to face us, but they'll hurt us any way they can, especially if they think we're not at home."

Lynne said, "That's what I'm talking about. They could come back..."

Ken turned to his son, "Ben, you all right with staying back and guarding our place?"

"You bet, Dad!"

Jo glanced at Kathy but didn't speak. Kathy said, "No problem, I'll stay back."

Jack said, "Good. If we're all agreed, then let's go. Lynne and I will have one more stop on the way home. We can split up from you after we leave the home center. We can handle it alone. There's a nursing home called Valley View, maybe you've seen it, it's on Golf Lane. It's set way back from the street, it shouldn't be a problem. We need some medical supplies for Charlie and Ted, and Lynne knows just what to get." He shot a questioning look at Lynne, "You still okay with that?"

She hesitated, "Yeah, I'm good—let's do it."

Ken motioned to his van, "Okay, let's saddle up and move out!"

248

They started walking to their vehicles when Jack suddenly stopped. Jo eyed Jack, and she instinctively looked around.

Jack said," You know, something's bothering me and I meant to mention it earlier. Do you guys smell that? It's kind of like a sewer smell."

Ken snorted, "Yeah, it smells like shit. I figured it was coming from the river. With the power off, the treatment plants may have dumped all the raw sewage directly into the river without treating it. Not only that, but people are still flushing their toilets. Where the hell is it all going?"

Lynne noticed Jack had that faraway look he sometimes got, while he looked towards the river.

Jack said, "That's a good point, Ken, and one I never thought of. We better be careful and stay clear of the river until we sort this thing out. I figured it might have been something that Dirk Hayes screwed up when he was working on the sewer in front of my house last year. Something really stinks bad though. I hope our sewers don't start backing up into our basements. All right, let's go, let's get some more supplies."

Jack hesitated mid-sentence. A thought suddenly shot through his mind…. *Earlier, at the gravel pit, the huge man throwing bodies off the side of Walt's truck looked familiar, if he had only brought field glasses….Could it have been Dirk Hayes? And his brother, the sheriff, he carries a Shotmaster 45 for a side arm….*

Jack forgot what he was talking about and struggled to finish what he was saying.

Jo said, "Something wrong, Jack?"

"No, just thinking about too many other things, it's been a crazy week."

Jack continued, "Where were we? Oh yeah, I wanted to mention the weather. We haven't had rain for a while. It's been a dry spring, and we're really overdue and could use it. The last forecast I heard was on Monday morning. They were calling for lots of rain next week. That's tomorrow… This wind has been blowing like mad all day." Jack looked to the skies. "It's too early in the year for the temperature to be warm like this. Something is blowing in for sure. I don't know about you guys, but my sump pump runs even when it's not raining. My battery back-up just went dead yesterday. If we get a downpour, my basement is done for. I moved all my stuff out of it and drained the water heater."

Ken said, "We did the same thing, everything is out. Living this close to the river, who knows? I've never seen it go over its banks down here, but my basement is a different matter. I'm up pretty high and it's never flooded, but with no power, I don't want to chance it."

Everyone looked at Jo and Kathy. Jo shook her head, "We're high and dry. We only have a half basement and our sump pit is always dry. Our corner of the street is up high." Looking at Jack, she raised her eyebrows. "Your buddy, Al—his

249

place is down pretty low. We should warn him when we get back. Everybody in the neighborhood will be there and he can spread the word."

All of them stood there staring at each other for a few seconds, waiting to see if anyone had anything else to add, maybe some common sense. Ken broke the silence. Cocking his head, he winked at Jack, "I guess we're ready, huh? Into harm's way we go."

Jack smiled back, "Yeah, let's hit the home center before we change our minds."

Ben and Kathy stayed behind to guard their houses. Jack and Lynne led the way in Carl's pickup truck, with Jo and Ken following in their vans. When they arrived back at the home center, they knew it would be their last trip.

The winds had picked up, and flaming pieces of molten roofing were blowing off the inferno that had been the shopping center. Like flaming kites, sizzling pieces of asphalt roofing were landing on the home center across the street. Some of it had landed on the north side of the building where the garden department was. There were rows of balled up evergreens inside the open-air garden department. Like a line of dried out Christmas trees, all of them were ablaze. Jack figured it wouldn't take long for the inferno to spread to the main building and into the lumber section. They would have to get what they wanted fast, before the whole place went up with them in it.

The group didn't waste any time. Squealing into the lumber yard, Jack jerked the truck to a halt next to a pile of ½ inch plywood. Jumping out, he shoved about 20 sheets into the truck bed as fast as he could. Next, he drove over to where the roll roofing was and grabbed several rolls of it, hastily tossing it onto the plywood. Next stop was the fencing, it was all the way in the back. He topped off the back of the truck with six big rolls of chicken wire, then left Lynne to guard the truck while he ran into the main building. Luck held out and he found a shopping cart, but as usual, it was a wobbly piece of shit. As he struggled with the lousy cart, he thought of Sheila, pushing her broken grocery cart loaded with sweet potatoes. *What a crazy world...* The store was packed with people running around, pushing carts, and quickly tossing stuff in. Everyone was trying to take what they could, before the building went up in smoke.

Ken was struggling with a cart with a bad wheel too. He flew by Jack with it, loudly swearing to himself in Spanish. Jo whizzed by him with a big flat cart loaded with 50 lb. bags of ammonium nitrate fertilizer. He could only imagine what she planned for that. Smoke was rolling through the open store like a thick black wall. Shoving his way through it, Jack wildly pushed his cartload out to the truck. Lynne was in the pickup's bed, half sitting on the roof, wielding her 12-gauge. Despite the smoke and the heat from the burning buildings across the street, the lumber yard was still full of people. No one paid attention to anyone else. Everyone was in too much of a hurry to cause any trouble.

Jack needed a wheelbarrow and knew exactly where they were. He blindly ran back in, forcing himself through the wall of thick smoke. It would mean a trip all the way into the back of the garden center. The whole front of it, that had been filled with bushes and small trees, was up in flames. If the wheelbarrows weren't within sight, he would have turned back because of the intense heat. Spotting several against the back wall, he grabbed a sturdy looking metal one and ran, madly pushing it away from the fiery hell that was closing in on him. The back of his shirt felt like it was on fire, and the intense heat was sucking the breath out of him. He was hacking up crap from the acrid smoke and was about to call it quits, when he spotted him. It was just as his friend, Val, had described. A young, shirtless man was lying on his side. his head was half buried in a tangle of trampled plants. An old-fashioned hay fork was stuck in the center of his back. The sharp tines were sticking through the front of his stark white chest. Tt looked brutal. His body was crawling with maggots, and a long rusty knife was on the floor next to him. There wasn't any time to think about it, but a brutal scene flashed through Jack's mind, *of the shirtless man attacking Laura, and Carl running him through with the tines of the pitchfork... again saving his daughter's life.*

Something massive suddenly crashed to the floor in the front of the building, instantly sending a tidal wave of flames roaring towards him. Swearing to himself, Jack quickly glanced to the entrance of the garden center. He could see the fire was already racing through the roof above it. There was no time to linger, soon the entire building would be collapsing on top of him. Running towards an open exit like a mad man, he crazily pushed the wheelbarrow. Randomly slapping items off the shelves into it. By the time he returned to the truck, his hair was singed, but it was worth it. The wheelbarrow was overflowing with cleaning supplies and disinfectants.

His shirt was soaked with sweat and caked black with soot. There were other people in the parking lot, and all of them were as filthy as he was and most were coughing from the thick smoke. The winds had gotten stronger and every corner of the garden center was ablaze. The flames had spread to the roof of the main building, and the lumber yard would be going up next. He would have liked to return for another trip, but it'd be only a matter of minutes before the high winds whipped the flames into the dry stacks of lumber. It was time for them to go. Jack and Lynne met up with the two vans in the parking lot and drove out into the street together. They were met with a blast of intense heat from the burning shopping center across the street. There was a closed-up clothing store next to the $ Buck $ Store. The faux stone front of the building was melting away like hot butter, sliding off its walls. There was no doubt that the restaurant next to it would soon go up as well. As they left the burning stores behind them, Lynne handed Jack a bottle of warm water; he downed it in several big gulps.

"Gosh, Jack, you're a mess. Your face is black as coal."

He laughed, "How do you think you look? That shirt you're wearing was a light pink when we left home, it's almost black now." Jack grabbed some tissue that was in the truck's console and wiped it across his face. The tissue was instantly black with soot. "God, my face feels like it's burning up, man that fire was hot. Let's pull over up ahead and see if everyone is all right. If everyone's okay, we'll then split up. You and I can stop at that nursing home."

The group pulled over by a deserted section of road. Jack got out and ran back to Jo and Ken's vans. "Everything okay, nobody got burned?"

Jo looked like she had been dipped in tar. She was coughing and spitting out her window, gagging on the soot she had inhaled. "Yeah, I'm all right. Holy shit, that place was hot. We got some good stuff, though."

Ken pulled his van alongside of Jo's, "I'm fine and I did really good. My van is packed with stuff we'll need."

"All right then, Lynne and I are heading over to that nursing home. We'll see you later."

Ken said, "Sure you don't want us to back you up? They'll think you're looters and crazy, you're faces are black as shit."

"Thanks, but I think we'll be all right. You better get back to your place in case those two assholes we ran off decide to come back with some friends. Don't clean up. You'll scare them to death."

Jack got back into the pickup and they drove off toward the Valley View nursing home.

Lynne said, "Gosh, we do look like a couple of pigs. We walk into that nursing home looking like this, they won't give us anything. They'll run us out."

"To tell you the truth, I'm not expecting to run into anybody. It's probably empty, so it won't matter how we look. Let's wipe our faces off the best we can and see what happens. I would think the nursing homes went the same way as the hospitals. We'll scope the building out before we go in. It's been five full days since this crap started. The residents have to be gone. Val told me they were putting the dead from nursing homes into that pit. If the county was removing the bodies of people who died, I would think they evacuated all the surviving residents too. They just wouldn't leave those poor people there to fend for themselves. And speaking of bodies, we're going to have to bury Walt, tomorrow morning at the latest. Maybe we can do it later this afternoon. What a sad day. I wonder if Laura told Charlie about it, they were good friends." Jack wiped his filthy hand across his face. "You know another thing, I haven't even talked to Carl today, we've been so busy. Good God Almighty, give us strength. There's just not enough time to do everything we have to do."

"Could you believe Jo shot that man's ear off? If I hadn't seen it, I wouldn't have believed it. What if she had missed?"

"Maybe she did miss. I think she wanted to kill him." Jack looked over at Lynne, "She's almost as tough as you...."

252

"Yeah, right. I'm anything but tough." They drove in silence for several minutes and Lynne said, "You know, something's bothering me. Did you notice how Al got nervous when you dumped the load of garbage off the back of the truck? A couple of those bags broke open, and I saw a bunch of bloody meat spill out of them. He was acting strange...."

Jack was silent for a few seconds. "Well, we'd just left that mass burial site...it had me shook, and I've seen something like it before, back in Iraq. I'd imagine it shook him too."

"I don't know.... It was like he didn't want anyone to see what came out of those bags."

"It was probably something Lois forgot to cook up. . . .Hey, the nursing home is up ahead. I don't see anyone around, but there's cars out front. It doesn't mean anyone is there, they've probably been sitting there all week. Let's drive around to the side and park by that other exit door. We'll see if it's open and maybe take a peek. I'd like to avoid just walking in through the front door, until I know the place is safe."

After parking the truck, he grabbed a couple flashlights from the center glove-box. "It's probably going to be really dark in there. We'll need these, but don't use them unless I say so. I don't want to become a target. Let's just sit out here a couple of minutes. You watch those upper windows in the taller building, and I'll keep an eye on the lowers. Watch for any signs of movement, let's see if we draw any attention."

They sat in the for truck several minutes, before, quietly getting out. Jack unsnapping the flap on his holster,as they approached the building. Lynne was alongside him, carrying her shotgun.

Jack said,"I'm not so sure about us approaching this building openly carrying weapons. If anyone is watching us, they'll assume the worst. They may take a shot at us."

Suddenly they heard a **"POP"** and followed silence.

Jack instinctively flattened himself and Lynne against the brick wall of the building. Whispering, he said, "Sounded like someone fired off a small 22 or a firecracker out back." He had his 44 out and motioned Lynne towards a small alcove near the corner of the building. It was next to a wheelchair ramp and surrounded by thick bushes. "I don't think anyone is shooting off fireworks. You squeeze yourself tight in there, behind those bushes. I'm going around back and see what's up. That definitely sounded like a gunshot. No matter what, you do not come out. If you hear gun fire, but don't see me right after, that means anybody who comes past you is a bad guy. You keep that shotgun pointed up and ready. Stay hidden and shoot them only if you have to, but don't hesitate. If they don't spot you, let them go. Just don't shoot me. I'll say your name before I walk out." Jack turned to her, feigning a smile, "It's Lynne, right?"

"God, Jack, this isn't funny. Please, let's just go. I'm scared. Let's turn around and go home."

"I'm sorry. . . but we should do this. We have to at least make the effort for Ted and Charlie, we owe it to them. Don't worry, I'll be back. Remember, I'll say your name as I come out."

Lynne crawled backwards into the thick bushes and laid down. Hoping there were no spiders, she settled herself into a pile of dried leaves and debris.

Jack carefully made his way around back, in the direction of the gunshot.

He didn't have to walk far. A nurse, or maybe it was an aide, wearing a filthy uniform, lay dead on the walkway. He was right about the popping sound. A small 22 caliber handgun was lying next to her, a fresh pencil-sized hole was in her right temple. There was no doubt about what she did. She was older and Hispanic-looking. There were fresh and dried blood splatters down the front of her uniform and on her arms. The dry ones were numerous and couldn't have been hers.

Slightly moving the gun with the toe of his shoe, he fought the urge to pick it up. If anyone came out of the building and saw him standing over her body holding the murder weapon, it wouldn't look good. Stepping around her, he tried a nearby door. It was unlocked and opened into what had to be a rehab or physical therapy room. There were several different types of exercise machines facing a wall of huge picture windows.

The vacant room was sunny, but the air was dank a stale. Winding his way around the silent machines, he spotted a pair of wooden doors on the far end. Praying the doors wouldn't squeak, he slowly opened one. It led into a long dark corridor. He had barely opened the door when the stench hit him. Like an open septic tank, the smell was overwhelming. The corridor led to another long hallway that had rooms on both sides. The stench of urine and feces permeated the entire hallway and got stronger the further he walked into it. Switching on his flashlight, something on the floor gave off a familiar glint, something that should not be on the floor of a nursing home. There were several spent 22 caliber shells on the gray tiles, the bright brass casings reflecting from the beam of his flashlight.

The nurse who committed suicide must have stopped in the hallway and unloaded her handgun, carelessly dropping the shells to the floor. As he moved from room to room, he found out why. Her victims were everywhere. Some were in wheelchairs, others in their beds. An old man was slumped over on the toilet. All of them were dead. A little further down the hallway, there were more 22 caliber shells scattered about on the floor. Jack counted six of them. Another re-load and more dead bodies. Ahead was what looked like a day room, with more shells on the floor and more bodies. Six women were sitting in their wheelchairs in front of a long counter, and each one had the same pencil-sized hole in the back of their heads.

254

Jack reached the vacant nurses station and stood for a moment, listening for any sounds of life, but there were none. He started down another corridor and was met by more empty brass shells, and more death. Most were in wheelchairs, some had been using walkers. All were dead, and not all were old. At least a quarter of the rooms had a body in it, and in each, the stench of death and feces was overpowering. By Jack's count, at least half the residents were left abandoned without care for the last five days. It appeared the lady that he found dead had taken it upon herself to end their suffering. He decided he would get Lynne, so she could find what they needed and get the hell out of there. He hoped he was near the front entrance and he was right. Ahead of him was the main entrance and reception desk. Before pushing through the two heavy entry doors, he carefully looked through the door's windows, surveying the parking lot. As much as he wanted to get some fresh air, he wasn't about to rush out. Not seeing any movement, he slowly exited the building, filling his lungs with the fresh springtime air before calling Lynne's name. A few moments later, with dead leaves sticking to the front of her filthy blouse, she appeared.

"I was getting scared, what did you find? Are there residents still in there?"

"Yeah, they're in there all right, and they're all dead. All of them were residents except one. The gunshot we heard was the suicide of the lady who killed them. It looks like mercy killings. She must have been a nurse, or maybe an aide. She shot all the residents in the head with a small 22 handgun. She killed herself outside behind the building. That was the shot we heard."

"Mercy killings...my God. No one's alive?"

"Not a one. I guess we can take whatever we want, but I'm warning you, it's bad in there. Looks like at least half the residents were left on their own after the power went out. The smell is unbelievable."

Lynne braced herself, taking a deep breath, and said, "I'm no stranger to smelly nursing homes. I can imagine, let's go in." Approaching the door, she added, "At full capacity, I think this home has about two hundred beds. If half were left to fend for themselves, that would mean approximately 100 bodies are lying in a week's worth of their own filth. Yeah, it's got to be bad." They both took deep breaths before opening the front door. Jack taking the lead. As soon as they entered the main corridor, Lynne's hands went to her face. The stench hit her like a wall, a wall of pure fetid shit. "Oh my God, Jack, this is horrible! I've never been anywhere that smelled this bad. What are we going to do?"

"Let's get what you need and get out of here, before someone shows up to get grandma. We don't want to get pulled into this mess. I'll admit, you were right. We shouldn't have come in here. Every hospital, every nursing home, they're probably all going to look like this." Switching on their flashlights, they shot two beams of brightness down the dark corridor. "I passed a nurses station at the far end of this hallway when I came in. Let's see if it has what you need. If

255

it doesn't, we'll get out of here." They had barely entered the long hall, when jack stopped. Shutting off his flashlight, he motioned Lynne to do the same.

Lynne whispered, "Jack, what's wrong?"

"I thought I heard something. . .voices. Didn't you hear it?"

"No."

Not two seconds later, the dead silence of the nursing home was pierced by the sound of shattering glass, echoing down the dark hallway. Jack pushed Lynne back with his forearm, flattening both of them against the cool tile wall. The windowless hallways were pitch black, and only where there was an open door of a resident's room, did faint rays of outside daylight shine in. Feeling a doorknob behind him, he was relieved to find it unlocked. Instinctively as he opened the door, he pulled up on the knob, taking the door's weight off possibly squeaky hinges. Entering a small windowless room, he pulled Lynne in with him, bumping his leg against what could have only been a toilet. Both of them knew they were in a small restroom, *with no other way out*. Before he could close the door behind them, beams of two flashlights pierced the hallway's darkness. Like laser beams, they shot past their open doorway, particles of dust sparkling in their light.

The male voices they heard confirmed Jack's suspicions. There were two of them and they were looking for drugs.

"Man, this place stinks like fucking shit. Where do you think they stash the stuff? It's gotta be locked up somewhere. Holy shit, look in there, all them old geezers are dead. Looks like somebody put them out of their misery. Let's hope they didn't beat us to the shit."

"Be quiet, man, ssh! I thought I heard something...."

At least one of the men carried a shotgun. The distinct sound of a shell being racked into it echoed down the hall.

Jack hadn't closed the bathroom door, nor did he want to. He stood just inside the doorway; his back pushed hard against the heavy wooden door. Lynne stood rigid, squeezed in next to him, His taunt muscles feeling hot against her. There was dead silence for a few moments. One of them yelled, **"Hey! If anybody's in here, you better come out. We won't hurt you—we promise."**

Slowly, but not soundlessly, the thieves crept forward. The beams of their flashlights nervously crisscrossing in the dark hallway.

Jack felt a rivulet of sweat roll down his forehead and into his left eye. He didn't blink. Lynne's right shoulder was up tight against his left. He could feel her muscles tense against his. Up against the open door, they both stood silent, not moving. . .waiting. Jack knew these were druggies and not experienced felons, because they were breaking every rule. What criminal in his right mind would make himself a target, walking down a narrow hallway, talking to a perceived opponent? Racking a round into a shotgun didn't scare Jack. It just proved their intent to him. A bad guy saying, "Come out, I'm not going to hurt you," while racking a shotgun shell, is really saying, "Show yourself, so I can get a good shot at you." Lastly, two men walking down a narrow hallway with flashlights on when they suspect hostiles ahead— well, that wasn't breaking a rule, that was just plain stupid, especially when Jack could swear, for a moment, he saw three...

Jack had a couple rules of his own. Silence, patience, and be very, very quiet...

Blam! Blam! Blam! Blam!   Blam! Blam!

Handing Little Red to Lynne, he whispered, "Two down." He didn't have to tell her to reload, as she had already taken a speed loader off his belt. Grabbing the shotgun from her, while she reloaded, they waited, Jack listening for any sound. He knelt down low and took a quick "look see" down the hall. One of the flashlights was lying on the floor, a couple feet from two bodies. It was still on and cast the bodies in an eerie shadow. It revealed both of the men lying on the floor, splayed out in death poses. But something bothered him. Was his mind playing tricks on him? He was sure he had seen three beams of light. It was only on momentarily, like a light being turned on and almost immediately switched off... He shot two men, both holding flashlights, and they heard only two men talking, but could there be a third? Someone smarter than his two buddies who shut his flashlight off, and kept his mouth shut? He could be further back in the dark hallway— with a gun pointed at them…. *Nice try asshole….*

Lynne's face was inches from his. He put his lips to her ear and whispered, "We wait, there's another one." He was sure there was a third person; he could feel it. Whoever he was, having just lost his buddies, he had to be scared. He and Lynne stood frozen for five minutes, maybe more.

They both heard it. It was a slight scrape. Someone bumped something, very lightly. Jack strained his ears for any sound. . . *Someone was getting ready to do something stupid. They're scared, they have to take a piss really bad and they want to run….they're going to run!*

Sweat was running into his eyes, and he was so close to Lynne he could feel her pulse. Jack knew it was coming, but they would have to wait, it would be any second now. *This guy is scared and he's going to run….now!*

He bolted! Beyond the dead men's flashlight, that was still shining on the bloody floor, someone wildly started running away. Jack couldn't let him escape to ambush them later, outside. He fired Little Red four times at a shadow fleeing down the hallway, dropping the third person in a death curdling scream. Once again, they waited, but Jack could feel it—they were alone. Their third assailant had bled out. It was time to go. Advancing towards the two dead men splayed on the floor, he picked up their still-lit flashlight, quickly shutting it off.

In the brief moment of illumination, he saw that both of their mouths were wide open, each revealing a mass of rotten stubs for teeth. *Meth, or maybe heroin*, he thought. One was shot above the left eye, a large portion of his skull missing. Typical damage from a 44-hollow point. The other man had two holes in his chest. Jack decided he wasn't going to go down the hallway to check out the third.

Pocketing their flashlight, he picked up their shotgun, moving his back against the wall, listening. His heart was beating fast and his ears were ringing from firing the 44 in the small confined bathroom. *Was there somebody else in the building with them… or maybe waiting outside?* He listened…. Silently, he edged backwards. His eyes darting from side to side down the dark hallway. He whispered, "It's okay, Lynne. I got them."

Lynne whispered back, "Jack, let's just get home. Oh my God…. I can't take all this death, let's get out of here—now! God, my ears are ringing. I'm so scared!" They left the nursing home the way Jack had entered. Stepping around the dead nurse on the sidewalk, he picked up and pocketed the small 22 caliber revolver. Cautiously, they made their way to the front corner of the building. Lynne wanted to run to the truck, but Jack stopped her. He offered her Little Red. "Have you ever fired one of these big boys?"

"Yes."

"Good, I'll take your shotgun. You stay here and cover me. If there is anyone else out here, they'll be behind those parked cars. I counted the cars in the parking lot when we pulled in here. Everything looks the same, but someone may be hiding behind them. I'll run to the truck with the shotgun. You shoot at anyone who sticks his head up, just don't hit me. I'll pull the truck over here to pick you up. Use both hands to fire it. Don't let it kick back in your face."

A few minutes later, they were safely driving away from the nursing home. A building of death. Lynne thought about all the dead people they left behind. Good people. Grandmas and grandpas. She knew were loved. *Would they ever be buried? Would their loved ones come looking for them?* Her hands were shaking.

They drove in silence at first, letting the carnage they had just seen sink in. After a short time, Lynne said, "We're being desensitized to death and violence. It's become an everyday thing for us, and I don't like who I'm becoming. That was really terrible back there. All those people had families; now they're just going to lay there and rot. Their families may never know what happened to them."

"It is terrible, but you've got to look at it in a differently. Their families might be already dead themselves, and how in the world would they take care of them if they brought them home? It's a new world. To survive in it we have to adjust, it's just the way it is."

Neither of them said anything else for a couple minutes. Jack's eyes were busy, searching the road ahead, scanning for anything that looked like trouble. Lynne stared out her door's window. They were passing the golf course. Everything looked so normal. Her heartbeat was finally starting to slow. She turned to Jack. "How did you know? How did you know there was another one of them hiding in that dark hallway? You couldn't have seen him."

"It was only for a second, but I could have sworn I saw three beams of light. One thing I learned in the Marines, and that's to trust what I see, not what my mind thinks it's seen. I didn't want to second guess myself. There was a third person. He had to be further back, behind the other two."

"You thought about all that, and made your decision with one quick look?"

"Yeah."

Neither of them said anything else for the rest of the drive. It was late afternoon when Jack pulled the truck into the subdivision. Approaching Jo and Kathy's house, they saw the girls still unloading their van. As expected, Al's front yard was full of people and activity. Two men were carrying propane tanks over to a line of grills, and there was a large white catering truck parked in front of Al's driveway, with **SNAPPY'S BARBEQUE,** painted on its sides. Jack pulled the pickup into the girl's driveway and parked next to their van. Jo had already gotten herself all cleaned up and was first to greet them.

She said, "How'd everything go? Did you get what you needed?"

"It didn't go, and we left empty handed, except for a nice 12-gauge pump and a heavy metal flashlight. There were maybe 100 or more dead bodies in the place, three of them I contributed to."

"Oh my God, I knew we should have gone with you! Are you guys alright?"

Lynne said, "Physically fine, mentally, I'm not so sure."

They quickly filled the girls in on what happened. Jack just wanted to get home before running into Al or anyone else. Before leaving, he looked across the street, jerking his head towards Al's, "What's going on over there now, and what's with the big catering truck?"

Jo smirked, "I think your little friend bought it. Now he's selling spare ribs, whole slabs. He must be in a really good mood because he ran one over to us for free. It's huge. We haven't tried any of it yet. Would you guys like some?"

"Sounds great, but no thanks. Lynne and I have some thawed out stuff at home that we have to eat up tonight. I wouldn't trust it for tomorrow."

Jo said, "You two better get out of here fast before he sees you. He told us that when this is all over, he's opening a restaurant. Says he's going to call it, *Al's Place.* Let's hope he doesn't have his wife as the hostess."

Jack placed the truck's gearshift in reverse and started to pull away, but stopped, saying, "By the way, did you tell Al about getting all his stuff out of his basement? That rain could hit us tonight."

"We both told him, but he said he would just plug his sump pump into a generator. I told him about what you said about the smell and the sewers backing up, but he said, and I'm quoting here, 'Jack thinks he's an expert on everything. I'm not worrying about no sewer.' He just blew us off."

"Well, you warned him, what more can we do?" Come on, Lynne, let's go home and get cleaned up." Before driving away, he took one last look at Al's, "Man, those ribs smell good."

They had barely pulled the truck into the driveway when Laura ran out to greet them, "Oh my Lord, look at you two, you're filthy. Carl and I have been so worried."

Jack said, "Sorry, it's been a tough day. Lots has happened and it's not over."

Carl joined them a few seconds later. He excitedly said, "The garden is almost planted. We'll be done by dinner time!" With less excitement, he said, "Gosh, I thought I was filthy, but you both look terrible, holy crap. Are you all right?"

Lynne said, "Were fine. We just need a bath. How's Bobby doing?"

Laura said, "He's fine, if we could just get him to talk. Hopefully he's still young enough to completely forget what happened."

Carl was inspecting all the things Jack had on the truck. "Wow, I thought you brought home a lot on the first load. This truck is packed! Are you home for good now, or will you make another load?"

"No, not from the home center or any of the other stores. When we left, both sides of the street were going up in smoke. These high winds are spreading the fire from one building to the next."

Jack tiredly got out of the truck and went into his garage. Stopping at Walt's wrapped-up body, he asked, "Did those boys come over and dig the grave today?"

Carl said, "Yes, they did, it's ready."

"That's good." Jack looked up to the heavy clouds that were rolling in. "This wind is blowing in a lot of high clouds and it's been awfully hot today, something big is heading our way. This is typical spring tornado weather. With no weather service to give us an early warning, we better be ready for it. We're going to have to pay attention to the sky from now on. Lynne and I are going to clean up and eat something." Jack stopped mid-sentence. He sadly eyed Walt's body lying on the garage floor, "We'll bury Walt this afternoon. It'll probably be pouring rain all day tomorrow, not a good time to bury someone."

Speaking quickly, Laura said, "Carl, tell my dad what Barry and that man said to you today." Jack turned to Carl with a most aggravated look was on his face.

"Barry and what man? And while I'm thinking about it, what was that idiot complaining about this morning?"

"This morning he was mad about me working out there so early. He was also demanding to know what we intended to do with the three portable toilets. I

260

told him farmers always start early. Then I told him we weren't going to use all three johns, only one of them, for an outhouse. When I asked him if we could put it by his fence, he totally lost it, but Laura gave him a cup of coffee. I think our generosity caught him off guard."

For the first time that day, Jack smiled, "Good job, Carl, but I wouldn't have offered him a coffee. Now you're learning how to talk to assholes."

Carl continued, "He came back later with another guy. They both came into Ronnie's yard. They had seen the two kids digging the grave.

The guy demanded that it be filled in and said the county was burying people in graves near the golf course. He also said to tell you a warrant would be issued for our arrest— all of us, including Jo and Kathy. The guy's name was Dorfman and he had a Illinois State Police badge."

"Did you say anything back to him?"

"I tried to think of what you would say."

"And what would I have said?"

"You would have told him to blow it out his ass and get the hell off your property."

Jack laughed, "*Please*, tell me you said that to him?"

"No, I guess I was afraid. I've seen that other man before and I know he works for the state police." Carl took a deep breath. "The guy was really pissed, Jack. He said the power will be back on sometime next week and when it is, a bunch of people are going to be arrested, including us."

Jack turned to Lynne, shaking his head, "Not even one week has gone by and idiots are starting their bullshit."

Lynne said, "They want to arrest someone? Tell them to find the owners of that nursing home we just left. I'm so tired. Every day this week has been an ordeal. I'm going to clean up before we eat and before Bobby wakes up. I don't want him to know how cruel this world is. Even if things are going bad, let's pretend they're not, just for him." Lynne turned, and tiredly walked into the house, leaving Carl and Jack alone.

Jack said, "I don't need to make enemies of my neighbors, because basically they're right. You can't use your backyard as a cemetery, or keep portable shitters in it, or raise chickens. But these people just don't get it. Give them another week or two. They'll be coming around with their tails tucked between their legs. Once they figure out that we're right and they've been dead wrong, they'll change their tune and be nice as pie to us. In the meantime, we're not going to take any crap from them."

Carl asked, "Charlie told me that he heard Jo shot at a guy this morning and blew off his ear. Is that true?"

Jack mused, "How the heck did Charlie find out about that so quick? He's like Al, nothing gets by him. Yeah, it's true, but it wasn't his whole ear, just a chunk off the top." Jack shrugged his shoulders and laughed to himself, thinking

261

of the man running to his truck crying, holding his hand against his bleeding ear. "The guy was a prick. He's just the type we're talking about and he's lucky it was only the top of his ear. Jo and Kathy have never bothered anyone and neither did Bobby's parents. But certain people have always got to mess with their neighbors, especially if they're different from them. Some of them do it because they're jealous or on a power trip, that's how that guy was. Some aren't bad people, they're just plain idiots." He glanced towards Barry's house. "I don't think Barry has ever done anything malicious against anyone in his life, but he's being an idiot, and he can hurt us if he keeps his bullshit up." Jack started walking through the garage, but stopped, staring back at Walt's body. "What a rotten shame. He gets murdered, and we can't even call his parents or girlfriend. Then some asshole with a badge wants to arrest *us* for not tossing his body over the side of a gravel pit." He tiredly looked back at Carl, who was still standing on the driveway. "Nobody is going to arrest us, Carl, so don't worry about it. Enough of this bullshit. I'm tired. I just want to clean up and eat. While I go wash up, I'd appreciate if you could fire up the grill for us. I'm going to stick the last of our thawed-out meat on it."

He and Lynne used water from the rain barrels to clean up. Their water supply was starting to get low. Since Monday, between cooking, drinking and washing, they'd used nearly sixty gallons of fresh water for four adults and one child. All of Jack's rainwater and a good part of Charlie's was gone. Most of it was used up to keep the plants taken from the home center alive. Jack washed his face and hands thinking, *I'd give anything to jump in a shower right now....*

At the bottom of his basement freezer were three large packages of thick-cut pork chops that he and Ellen had bought at Super's. He pulled them out of the freezer and thought back to when they had purchased them. *Super's, God, I'm going to miss that place. Aisles of never-ending food, with little stations set up throughout the store serving free samples...Will I ever see that again?* The pork chops were totally defrosted, yet still cold to the touch. There was also a frozen pizza. It sagged in the center when he picked it up. *Pizza... God, what I'd give for a Chicago pan pizza ...* Everything else was warm and a sodden mess that had to be thrown out. He placed all of it on the kitchen counter, saying out loud to himself, "This the last of it, we'll all eat good tonight."

After dinner, he and Carl unloaded the truck. He filled Carl in on the horrors they discovered at the nursing home, and the run-in with the three addicts.

They also buried Walt. Jo and Kathy, as well as Ken and Ben, were there for Walt's burial. They had metal folding chairs set up at the side of the grave. Charlie sat in one; Lynne was next to him, with Bobby on her lap. Carl stood with Laura, holding her hand. Jack stood at the head of Walt's grave and began to speak, "Up until a few days ago, most of us were strangers to each other. Walt didn't know me and owed me nothing, but he helped me. He helped all of us and it cost him

262

his life." He paused, struggling with the words he wanted to say. "This morning, I witnessed hundreds, maybe a thousand bodies being dumped into the old gravel pit. People who a week ago were alive, good people, being dumped like trash. Today, Lynne and I discovered residents of a nursing home who were murdered for being a burden and unable to care for themselves. No one is burying them. They're still there, rotting where they fell.   Someone loved all these people, I would hope..." He looked over to Bobby, who was playing with the small silver cross Lynne wore on her neck.   "All those people once had parents who loved them and wanted the best for them, and look how they're ending up."   Jack looked down into the open grave, his eyes sadly resting on Walt's body. He hesitated, searching for the words he wanted to say. "This week, they died horrible deaths, and many of them, like Walt... died alone. I left my best friend's body at one of the biggest hospitals in the city, next to the front entrance.   There is no doubt in my mind that his body is probably still there on that sidewalk." He stared up at the sky, "I'm trying to keep my faith, yes I am, but it's hard.. . .Before Walt left here yesterday, a voice inside my head told me to go with him, get his girlfriend and let them stay in safety with us. Somehow, I knew. I don't know how, but I knew he wouldn't make it out to his trailer with that big old truck, but I let him go—I let him go to his death and I blame myself for it. I didn't even offer him the option of staying with us. I'm ashamed of myself."

Jack vacantly stared into the open grave. Loud disco music was drifting through the yards, echoing from Al's. It was disturbing the service. He tried to block it out. Lifting his head, he slowly shifted his gaze from face to face. "I've killed several people this week. I killed three drug addicts in that nursing home this today. They would have murdered Lynne and me, if I gave them the chance. For that, I don't feel any remorse—not even a tiny bit. I am *happy* they're dead. They don't deserve to walk on God's green earth, because they destroy everything that's good. They're cockroaches and I'd like to step on every one of the bastards. I feel sorry, sorry Walt, so very sorry."

He was finished. Charlie said a few words. He recalled that he knew Walt as a child, and what a good boy he was. He turned to Jack . "The cards were dealt a long time ago for all of us, Jack, before we were born. Don't be so hard on yourself. This is the way it's going down and a line has been drawn. All of us here are on the right side of that line. God has given us the means to fight the good fight. Scripture tells us to turn the other cheek and tells us to forgive, but it doesn't tell us to *surrender*, to roll over and die. A line has been drawn. God gives us free will and lets us make the choice of which side we want to stand on. This is a spiritual war, that's what it is. Satan is going all out."

Charlie was finished. Lynne and Laura each read a passage of scripture aloud. There was nothing else left to say. They covered Walt with black Illinois topsoil, and the group went back to their work. Jack cleaned Little Red and the 12-gauge pump shotgun taken from the nursing home. Carl and Laura finished their planting. Lynne fed Bobby and gave him a bath. Ted continued to lay in his bed, and Charlie pulled out a dozen old 12-gauge shotguns. He loaded each one with heavy buckshot and placed one in every room in his house, including the bathrooms. He knew what side of the line they were standing on, and he wasn't going to get caught with his pants down.

THE STORM

CHAPTER 27

Jack was sitting alone on his front porch, listening to the oldies' music coming from Al's. The sun was getting low in the sky and the wind had suddenly gone still. It was still unseasonably hot, but he felt a subtle change. He had experienced a tornado as a kid and recalled the eerie feeling he had just before it hit. It had been an unusually hot summer day and suddenly the air had become dead still and charged with electricity. He remembered how the wind had been blowing steady all day, then suddenly not a leaf was moving. He was 12 years old, at a summer cottage with his parents, and he would never forget that feeling, and he felt it now. There was a slight, barely noticeable cool breeze. Jack knew exactly what was coming. He got up from his chair and ran into his front yard. He saw what he was looking for. There it was, a tall black cloud far to the north, all by itself. In the Midwest, storm clouds typically moved in from the southwest, but this would not be the usual spring thunder-storm. The approaching black cloud was getting bigger by the second, quickly rolling in from the *north!*

He ran to the back yard, **"Carl, get down to Ken's, a bad storm is rolling in! We could get a tornado. Tell him to close up his place and get low!"** He muttered under his breath, "Perfect day to produce a tornado...." He yelled to Laura, **"Laura, go next door and tell Charlie what's coming. We might have to carry Ted into the basement! Then get with Lynne and Bobby in our basement! Get close to an outside wall, in a corner!"**

Jack ran in and warned Lynne. Sprinting back out, he jumped into the truck to warn Jo and Kathy. They were in their garage, stacking supplies. He told them to close up the garage and immediately get into their basement, up against the foundation. On the way back, he warned the people in front of Al's. A cold wind was starting to blow and a few large cold raindrops splattered on the truck's dirty windshield.

He heard a guy say to a woman standing next to him, "It's that idiot from down the street." He shot Jack a nasty look. Saying, "It's just a spring thunderstorm, you *moron*. Why don't you enjoy the cold shower, like everybody else? You could use one."

Less than five minutes had passed and Jack was back in his driveway. All hell was starting to break loose. The hot humid air, that had laid in the Midwest all week, clashed with the ice-cold air out of northern Wisconsin.

There were no warning sirens, or phones to spread the alarm. Almost instantly, the sky turned dark green. Then instantly to night. Ominous black clouds rolled over them, bringing with them strong winds and ice-cold rain that quickly changed to large pellets of hail. With sharp hailstones pelting his back, Jack ran to Charlie's. Bolting into the kitchen, the inside of the house was pitch dark, daylight going to midnight almost instantly. Stumbling through the house, he shouted Charlie's name. A light suddenly flashed from Ted's bedroom. Charlie was sitting next to his brother, holding his hand, with both dogs huddled at his feet.

"Charlie, you have to get downstairs, now!"

"Jack, get yourself home! Ted can't be moved, we'll be all right. My place is built like a brick shithouse. It ain't going anywhere—**get home!"**

Jack learned soon after he moved next door to Charlie, that once the old man's mind was made up, there would be no forcing him to do anything.

He raced out the back door and made a mad dash for the safety of his own basement. As soon as he cleared the back corner of Charlie's house, he was knocked flat. He wasn't prepared for the heavy gusts that hit him, blowing like a wind tunnel between the two houses.

In a split second, he found himself rolling on the ground, being pelted with large, marble size hail. Clawing his way through the torrents of rain and hail, he stumbled, blindly charging between the two houses, hardly able to keep his eyes open. Finally making it to the corner of his house, he felt strong hands grab him. It had to be Carl, pulling him into the safety of the back wall of his house. Out of the driving wind and in pitch darkness, he tumbled head first on top of him. The cold rain was drenching his back, and the ground around him was alive with white bouncing chunks of ice. Through his soaking wet shirt, he felt welcoming warmth under him, but it was Lynne he was on top of, not Carl.

"Jack, you're really heavy and—I'm lying in cold mud, let's get inside."

"Yeah, let's do that—thanks for grabbing me, I could hardly see."

Protected from the high winds by the back wall of Jack's house, they both got up and scrambled towards the back door. As Jack unlatched the storm door, it was suddenly wrenched from its hinges. Like a freight train roaring down the track, they both knew what was almost upon them and had only moments to get inside. The wind suddenly became unbearable, both pushing and pulling them at the same time. Holding on to each other for dear life, they shoved their weight

266

into the back door, pushing it open. Jack pulled Lynne inside behind him, tumbling together down the basement stairs, the beam of Laura's flashlight immediately upon them. For the next few minutes, all of them huddled as one in a corner of the pitch-black basement.

The house shuddered and shook, creaked and moaned. Stories of a tornado sounding like a freight train roaring in were not exaggerated. After a couple minutes, the roaring locomotive passed, but the driving, pounding rain got worse.

Jack had his back against the exposed concrete basement wall and suddenly felt cold water pouring onto him. Shining his flashlight onto the wall, it looked like a waterfall cascading down from the sill plates above. He knew what had happened. *The high winds must be blowing siding off the front of the house, allowing the driving rain to flow in under the outside walls. God, help us!*

The basement had four windows in sunken metal wells, about two feet below the outside grade. Unknown to Jack, a lake of water was forming in his front yard, submerging two of them. More like aquariums than windows, they were unable to contain the growing water pressure. Suddenly, the window above them shattered. Like a ship getting a breach in its hull, an ocean of ice-cold water gushed in, cascading down upon all of them.

Jack yelled, **"Get to the center of the basement, next to that steel column! All the window wells are filled up with water, they're going to burst!"**

It seemed that one minute the basement was dry, and seconds later, they were in swirling cold water, getting deeper by the second. Jack shined his flashlight to the sump pump pit. Water was bubbling up out of it, like a spring.

"Dad, look!" Right next to Laura, in the laundry room, was the basement floor drain. Smelly tar like goo was shooting up from the drain and onto her.

Loudly cussing, Jack jumped up. **"Shit!** I have to close off that floor drain! There's a valve in it. I've got a special wrench for it!" Grabbing it, he shut the drain's heavy brass valve tight. Water was continuing to gush in from the broken window, but at least he had secured the floor drain. Outside, the high winds were shaking the house and the driving rain continued to pour down in sheets. He was afraid what he would find if they went upstairs....*Would there be an upstairs?* Shining his light at the sump pit, it still looked like a fountain. The water was rising faster; no pump would have been able to keep up with it. **There was a huge jolt underneath him!** They all felt it and Laura screamed! Jack had felt something like it when he was stationed at Camp Pendleton, California. Like being in an earthquake, the ground beneath them had shaken, and he swore he felt the concrete floor rise. He felt it again and this time it definitely came up. The floor violently jolted beneath them and the center of the basement floor suddenly buckled up, with a loud **crack!** It rose at least four inches, maybe more, and everyone panicked, switching all their flashlights on at once. Smelly, black water was gushing up from huge open cracks in the broken floor. Jack knew immediately what was happening. The valve on the floor drain had held, but the clay tile pipes below the floor didn't. The hydrostatic pressure of the water from the main sewers backing up had suddenly burst the pipes beneath the floor. With nowhere to go, the water pressure burst through the concrete like a geyser, lifting up the center of the basement floor, and nothing could stop it.

Like sailors abandoning a sinking ship, the five of them, with Carl carrying Bobby, rushed up the basement stairs. The filthy water was already washing over the third step, and it continued to rise the rest of the night.

SATURDAY

CHAPTER 28

With the run of bad luck they had during the week, Jack figured the storm would top it all by taking his entire roof off. For the magnitude of the storm, the damage done to his home was minimal. There was a large patch of shingles blown off the roof, and there were windows that had been broken from flying debris. The high wind gusts had peeled all of the aluminum siding off the south side of the house and garage. It was shoved in a twisted heap up against the backyard fence. His metal shed was in shambles, strewn across the yard, and would be a total loss.

The rain had continued coming down heavily until dawn. As first light seeped through the clouds, people started venturing out of their battered houses. As the sky grew lighter, the full extent of the damage was becoming apparent. The rain had diminished to a drizzle, but the morning sky was still scattered with dark, rolling clouds.

The basement was disheartening. It had at least seven feet of polluted sewer water in it, leaving only the top two treads of the stairs exposed.

Charlie's house was almost unscathed. His home was the first home built in the subdivision, and it still had the original well and septic system. Charlie was one of the last holdouts, refusing to be hooked up to city water and sewer. It proved to be a smart move on his part. He had fresh water and usable toilets. There were no village sewers to back-up into his basement. The only major damage to Charlie's house was that his roof-top solar panels were gone.

Other parts of the neighborhood did not fare as well. The houses across the street from them were fine. Glen and Doris' house was unscathed. Jack eyed that in sad irony. It was the houses behind Glen's, on the first block of the subdivision, that took the direct hit. Almost the entire block of 14 homes was in shambles. Two were completely gone, leaving only a concrete slab on one and the basement foundation walls on the other.

The tornado had torn a jagged swath, splintering everything in its path to shreds. Every front yard on Jack's street was covered in shattered building materials that had once been part someone's house. It would take heavy machinery to clean the mess up and semi-trucks to haul it away, but they would never come.

He went next door to check on Charlie. The old man was standing on his driveway, looking up at his roof. "Good morning, Jack. The higher the sun gets, the worse it's going to look. Folks thought they were screwed yesterday.... God what a mess, what a mess. Looks like all my solar panels went adios." The two men stood together, surveying the neighboring homes. "Jack, I want to thank you for everything you've done for me. Thanks for having Laura and Lynne over here. You guys have been waiting on me and Ted hand and foot. Lynne's in there now, changing Ted. He's in bad shape. I don't think he'll hold on much longer."

"I'm sorry, Charlie, I wish we could do more." Jack looked up at his roof and back to Charlie's. "I can't believe we still have a roof on our houses. That wind, it was unbelievable. I see your solar panels are gone and you're missing some shingles. Did you get any water inside?"

"A few small roof leaks from where the solar panels tore loose, that's about it."

Jack said, "Other than missing shingles, the only major problem I got is my basement is full to the top with sewer water. I got everything out of there before the storm, so I didn't lose anything of importance, but it's a mess."

Charlie was slowly shaking his head, "Thank God you had enough foresight to get your supplies out of there. Don't worry about the water. I got an old surplus U.S. Navy submersible pump, the type they carry aboard ships in their repair lockers. We'll hook it up to the generator and pump you out quicker than shit, but not for a few days. The ground is too saturated from all this rain. If we pump it out now, your foundation walls might collapse in. I wouldn't use it right off the bat anyway. I don't want to advertise I have a pump or anything that's special— including a good running generator. People who wouldn't give you the time of day are going to be coming on like your best friend after today, you watch and see.... Then they'll stick it in your ass later."

"Thanks, Charlie, and I agree with you, especially about the ass part. This storm is going to be a real game changer. Well, if you're okay, I'm going down to check on Jo and Kathy, then Ken and his son. After that, Carl and I are going over to the next street to lend a hand over there. They got the worst of it. Lynne is coming too, they'll need a nurse, I'm sure. It's too bad about your solar panels, maybe we can find them."

Charlie laughed, "The way that wind was howling, they're probably in Lake Michigan. One good thing is all our rain barrels are full, and it looks like Carl's garden made it. The hail did a number on some of his plants and he had some soil washed out, but with the amount of stuff he planted, hell, if even 50 % survives, you guys will be doing good." Charlie went back into his house, and Jack walked down to Jo and Kathy's. He got a terrible feeling as he approached their house, the entire roof was gone.

Jo and Kathy were sitting together on a white wicker glider, on the front porch. The two girls silently watched Jack as he approached. Jo spoke first. "Hey, we were just about to come down to your place. How'd you make out? Is everyone all right?"

"Yeah, we're all fine, so is Charlie. I haven't gone over to Ken's place yet. Are you girls all right? You didn't get hurt, did you?"

"No, we're fine. The house isn't so good though. The entire roof is gone. It's in a field someplace. Jack, we owe you our lives. If you hadn't warned us...." Kathy was silent and looked like she'd been crying.

Jack asked, "Kathy, how about you, are you all right?"

She wiped her eyes with her shirt sleeve. "Yes, I'm fine, just praying my rosary... a little upset maybe. We're not hurt and that's what counts. When I'm done, we'll figure out what we're going to do. Everything upstairs is soaked and covered with broken drywall and insulation. The ceilings are collapsing on the first floor too. The drywall just fell apart when it got soaked. Somehow—we'll get it cleaned up and we'll be all right."

Jo got up, "Did you see the house that was behind us? It's a pile of rubble and most of it's sitting in our backyard, up against our house. There's nothing left. They committed suicide in their house and now it's gone. It's a weird thing, if they hadn't, they would probably have died last night anyway."

Jack left the two women and went into their house to check out the damage. Kathy was right, most of the first-floor ceiling was soaked and collapsing. It had long since stopped raining, but filthy water was still dripping in everywhere. The oak hardwood floor was saturated too, and was sure to buckle. The master bedroom's cathedral ceiling, along with the entire roof, was gone. Without the roof to tie in the outside walls, the bed-room's west wall was leaning out about a foot. Every upstairs window pane was broken or missing. As a final insult, sopping-wet insulation and wet-crumbling drywall covered everything.

A three to four-man crew of carpenters could have a new roof framed and ready to shingle in a few days. With no available materials, no power, and no carpenter crews, the house was doomed. There would be no rebuilding.

Jack went back downstairs; the girls were still sitting on the porch.

"What are your plans, ladies? Tell me what you're thinking."

Jo shrugged her shoulders, "Maybe we'll call our insurance company...."

Jo gestured to Al's house, "Look at Al and Lois' place, it's untouched, I can't figure it out. The place behind us gets leveled, the whole roof blows off our place, and these other houses right next to us suffer no damage."

Kathy put her arm around Jo. "The important thing is, Joanie, we're unharmed and we will make it. God will provide."

"I hope so, Kathy." Jo looked up questionably at Jack. "Jack, you're the structural engineer. What do you think?"

"If the shit hadn't hit the fan and we had a good carpenter crew, in three weeks you'd be back in here. It would only take a few days to get the roof back on. I'm sorry, it's not going to happen, not now. What about your supplies? I know you're big time preppers; did they get wet?"

"No." Jo quickly answered, "We have about 100 plastic, 5-gallon buckets of dry chow. They're all sealed tight with oxygen absorbers in them. We have two years' worth of other stuff. All our guns and ammo are dry. We're in good shape, except all our clothing is soaked, but it'll dry out."

"Well, you're welcome to move in with us, we'll make room."

"We can't just move in with you, you've got enough problems down there. You hardly even know us. Kathy and I will figure something out."

Kathy spoke up, "Jo, tell him what happened just before he walked up here." Kathy sadly eyed Jack, "That's what I was crying about."

"Kathy, please, let it go. They're just assholes. I can handle them. Let's leave Jack out of it."

Jack's curiosity was immediately aroused, "Assholes? *Who*?" He looked from Jo to Kathy, then back to Jo. "Come on, tell me. I promise I'll be good. Please let me know what's going on and who's giving you shit."

Jo lightly cleared her throat and hesitated, reluctant to pull Jack into their problems. "I admit I have a problem with anger..."At that, Kathy said, "Oh yeah...."

Jo continued, "I know I overreacted to those guys yesterday. I should never have shot that man's ear." Joan shrugged her shoulders and let out a sigh. "I am so tired of their shit, it just never ends. I'm not going to get into all of it now, but there's been other things done to our house. Yesterday, I admit, I just kind of lost it, but it's not just him... Did you see that large group of people earlier, walking around in the dark, checking from house to house, seeing if anyone needed help?"

Jack answered, "No, Jo, I didn't."

"They're on the street behind us right now. They walked right by us. I mean, our house lost its entire roof and is a complete wreck, and they just walked right on by." Jo pulled out a pack of cigarettes and lit one. Taking a drag, she quickly blew the smoke out, visibly pissed. "They didn't say anything, not a word. No, how are you doing or do you need help? They just walked by, like we're a couple lepers. Every one of them have been partying at Al's this week and they're our neighbors. One of the women was *Lois*. She was with them and didn't say anything to us. She wouldn't even look our way. I know Lois doesn't care for us, but for God's sake, we're neighbors, we're human beings."

Kathy pointed towards Al's, "We donated a tank of propane, plus a whole load of paper plates and cups to Al for his cook-out. Now they just walk by here, ignoring us, like we somehow deserved this."

Jack was silent for a moment, searching for the right words to say. "I'm sorry. I'm sure Lois just got caught in their group, walking with them this morning. I know she can be a pretty hard egg. I'll go talk to Al. I'm sorry that I never paid much attention to what went on in this neighborhood... I've always kind of kept to myself. That's the problem of being a loner, I guess. That's why we have to band together."

Jo took a drag off her cigarette and quickly exhaled, "We'd be helping people if we could, but these people, they're really something else. Instead of offering us help, I think they're probably happy at our misfortune. Well, we'll see how they are a couple weeks from now, when we got chow and they don't."

Jack knew Jo was right. He said, "After I came to see how you girls were, I was going to walk around myself, see if anyone needed help. I've been getting snide comments myself all week and I've been trying to ignore them. People are upset and aren't thinking straight, but you're right, they'll probably be knocking on our doors."

Jo said, "Tell me something. A couple weeks from now, if Barry and his family need food, will you give them some—after the way he's been treating you?"

"Yeah, I would, of course. I'm sure he'd help us too. I'd give them a meal or two and maybe some canned goods. But people can't expect us to be the neighborhood's resource center, and that's what it would turn into if we let them—they'd sink us. If they asked for more...I might give them some. But what happens when the lifeboat is overloaded? It never ends well. It'd be nice if they could trade with me, with something that I need. Things can be worked out. I guess I'll cross that bridge when I come to it."

Pointing to the pack of cigarettes in Jo's shirt pocket, Jack said, "Speaking of sharing, can I get a smoke off you, Jo?" Removing a single cigarette from the pack, Jo placed it between her lips, lighting it with a small gold lighter. Handing it off to Jack, he immediately inhaled deeply on it. "After exhaling, he said, "You know ladies, these things will kill us.. ." Not getting a response from the women, he struggled to find the right words to say. Their house was wreck and things were sliding from bad to worse by the minute. He struggled to say something positive, even if he didn't feel positive himself. After taking another long drag from the cigarette, he said, " Ladies, We know what we've lost, but let's look at what we still have. Computers run the whole country and everybody in it. How many people have any real skills anymore? Half the country spends their life behind a keyboard. We have skills that most people don't have. Lynne can put her nursing skills to work if someone's injured." He pointed to Kathy, saying, "I bet you're the only dental assistant around here. Sooner or later, one of that group is going to need a tooth yanked. There's a comeuppance for you. I'll bet there aren't any preppers among that group. In fact, I know there isn't. Think about it, they're like sheep, all huddled together for comfort, waiting for the

273

shepherd to come to their rescue." He paused a few seconds, kicking a small piece of building debris off the porch with his toe. "If folks would only learn to get over their prejudices and help one another." Jack sadly shook his head. "Everyone who's over at Al's is really friendly with the little guy now, but watch what happens when the gravy train ends."

The two women just sat there, sullen. For Jack, it was suddenly awkward. He wished he hadn't mentioned Al. He paused for a moment, searching for the right words, but it was hard to think of anything positive when their whole world was turning to shit.. "Ladies, you're a lot better off than you think you are. Certainly, much better than those jerks who've been hassling you. All your supplies are intact. You just need dry shelter because this rain isn't done. I still see some black clouds out west. You girls start getting your stuff together.   I'll find you a place right away, but if not, *you come join us*. We'll be one big happy family." He could see his suggestion wasn't having the affect he wanted. He pointed at them, cigarette in hand, "You mark my words, ladies. The day is coming quick, when these assholes will be knocking on our doors looking for a handout. Unless they change their tune, all they're going to get from us is an 'adios and have a nice day.' We're going to stick together. You're going to make it through this shit, I guarantee it."

He started to walk away, but turned and stopped, "I know you love your house, Jo, but it's a sinking ship. It's time to salvage what you can and move on, and thank God you're not hurt. I'll be back with help."

He wanted to check on Ken and his son, but decided to go to Al's first. He found Al alone in his garage, and the little guy wasn't in a very good mood.

"Don't say it, Jack, don't say a word. You were right. I should have gotten anything of value out of my basement. It's full to the brim, full of *raw* shit and God knows what else.... so please, do me a favor and don't say..."

Jack cut him off mid-sentence, "I told you so?"

Al rolled his eyes. "That really hurts, but I knew it was coming and I deserve it."

"What did you lose?"

"Well— thankfully all the food is up here, but all my beverages are down there. I was keeping that stuff for myself. About a dozen cases of beer, a shitload of soda, bottled water, my wine cellar. Oh God, my wine collection! **Oh shit**, I forgot about that. Aw crap...all my booze...oh shit. And my hot water heater, it still had some fresh water in it. Everything is under eight feet of stinking shit. Aw man... I'm screwed. Screwed but good. How's your house, Jack?"

"Like yours,. my basement is flooded out. The water is filthy and it smells really bad. I lost some shingles off the roof and all the siding got blown off the south side. I have a couple broken windows, but we're all okay, and no one got hurt. Your place looks really good, Al, not a scratch." Jack pointed across the street to Jo and Kathy's house. "I just went through the girl's place. The entire roof is gone and the upstairs outside walls are ready to go over. Their downstairs is completely wrecked from all the water pouring through from the second floor. The whole ceiling is collapsed, or about to be. We have to find a place for them to stay."

He at least expected a response to what he had just said. Instead, Al turned around and busied himself moving some large white plastic boxes. He could see he had stacks of them in the garage.

Jack nudged one of the boxes with his boot toe, "What's in all these big white boxes?"

"Spare ribs, pork tenderloins and beef brisket, all packed in dry ice. Party time is over, buddy. Al's soup kitchen is closed, no more freebies. I'm selling this stuff for 300 smackers per box, and people are happy to get it…. Of course, one's free to you." Al excitedly continued, "Did you see that barbecue truck parked here yesterday? I'm good friends with the guy who owns it, Dino Pasqualli. We worked out a deal. He has a warehouse freezer full of frozen spare ribs and cuts of pork. But even packed like it is, it won't last forever, so I got it dirt cheap. He's been making a killing driving around with that truck of his. I let him stay here the last couple nights, he left this morning. This is the last of the frozen meat, Jackie my boy, at $300 a box, that's a $290 profit for me. There's no fresh meat left anywhere. This is pretty much it, and one of these boxes will feed a family for a couple days."

Al laughed, "Something good has to happen once in a while, huh? And speaking of something good, listen to this. Dino, he's been driving all over and he heard some good news. He said that next week, that FEDUP outfit will be coming into every town. Probably will be a big town meeting, and this bullshit will be finally coming to an end. I can't wait, Jack, I got it all figured out. I'm going to open a restaurant, going to sell barbeque. Going to call it Al's Place, no more working in a grocery store for me, no sir."

He could see that Al was excited, and no doubt serious, about starting a restaurant, but he also felt he was trying to steer the conversation away from Jo and Kathy's problem. "Hey, Al, I was thinking. It's just you and Lois here. I know your basement is flooded, but your house hasn't been damaged. You have four huge bedrooms upstairs. You know—Jo and Kathy are in a bad situation. Could you put them up for a few days?"

"Oh boy, I was waiting for that one. Look, Jack, that little Kathy, with the rack she's got on her, she's got my welcome mat anytime, especially the way she dresses, or should I say, the lack of it. But hey, Lois would *kill* me, she can't stand her or GI Jo."

Jack took a step back and crossed his arms. Al caught the roll of Jack's eyes, and said, "Listen, Jack, you've got to understand something. Those two have been kind of frowned upon around here from the get go. You never pay attention. If it wasn't for me, you wouldn't know what the hell goes on around

275

here. Some folks don't like having to explain to their kids why two grown women are keeping house together. I may not be a church goer like you are, but I still don't go for that kind of stuff. And now, after what that crazy broad did to Len Pauli's ear. Are you kidding me? She almost blew his head off! And the worst thing is, I hear you and this Lynne gal you took in were with them, and *you* backed GI Jo up. She's a complete nut job, Jack, and you want me to take her and her ditzy blond girlfriend into my house?"

Jack protested, "It would just be for a couple nights, Al. Their house is uninhabitable, they need a place to sleep tonight."

"While we're on the subject of taking people in, I know you think this Lynne seems like a nice person and all—but, you don't even know her. It's not like she's family or anything…. Remember our little garbage run? I was getting bad vibes from her. She kept looking at me funny. I was feeling really uneasy sitting next to her, and it went right over your head, Jack. You don't even pick up on stuff like that. You don't know anything about her. I don't know what she's told you, but it could be all lies. She's in a tough spot. People will tell you anything when their back is to the wall. I'd watch out for her; she could knife you when you're sleeping."

"Give me a break, Al."

"No, no—I'm serious here. Look what's been going on around here, even before this shit started—murders and all. Oh my God, you're too trusting. And another thing, you got that young teacher guy staying with you. Jack, you got a teenage daughter. What the hell are you thinking? And for the love of Mike, Ellen ain't even gone a week and your tooling around with this Lynne? Plus, you took in that little black kid—holy shit. Jack, are you nuts?"

"Lynne and I aren't *tooling* around, and she's not going to stab me while I sleep." He had heard enough. "Good bye, Al, I have to go."

"Jack, please, don't leave pissed off at me. I think you're doing the right thing, taking care of Charlie and even the little black kid. I like your farm idea too. I agree with you and got no problems with any of it. I mean, look at me, I've been feeding the whole stinking neighborhood, running a soup kitchen. But that Lynne gal, she's trouble, Jack, I can feel it. *Lois doesn't like her either*. The same goes for them two broads across the street and that guy Ken and his son, if he *really is his son*. Nobody likes them, Jack, and the word is that lots of folks around here think you're too damn arrogant. Look at yourself, walking around with that big cannon on your hip. You know, buddy—*you know*, how things are around here."

"And just what am I supposed to know, Al—huh? Exactly *how are things* around here?"

Jack turned on his heels and walked out of Al's garage, slightly shaking his head . Al followed him out and kept talking….

"Jack, you're my pal, you have to listen…. You want to run your little farm and start a neighborhood cemetery up there, that's great, but this other shit, there's going to be trouble for you. You can't save everyone."

Jack stormed off. He was pissed and blotted out what Al was saying.

Al stood at the corner of his garage, silently watching Jack as he walked back home.

STORM DAMAGE

CHAPTER 2 9

Jack walked past his house and went directly to Ken's. Ken had one of the smaller homes in the neighborhood and it received only minimal damage. His basement had some water seepage, but like Jack, he had prepared for it and lost nothing important. Jack filled him in on the plight of Jo and Kathy. Without hesitating, he immediately left to go help the girls.

Disheartened by Al's comments, Jack stopped at Charlie's. He was met at the front door by Lynne. The look on her face told him everything. Ted had fallen unconscious and death could knock in minutes or take hours. Charlie was sitting at his bedside, both Max and Toots were at his feet. Lynne said there was nothing she could do.

Upon seeing Jack, Charlie got up. Jack told him not to, but he got up anyway, grabbing a cane and limping out of the room, beckoning Jack to follow him.

"Didn't expect this today, Jack. I guess last night's storm signaled the end for Ted. God almighty, I never thought our lives would end like this. You know, you can plan and prepare, get every last detail figured out and things still don't work out. Then you sit back and do what I'm doing right now. 'I should have done this or that.' Like they say, hindsight is 20-20."

He followed Charlie to his study. Sitting down, Charlie swiveled in his squeaky desk chair and faced Jack, motioning him to sit in the other chair. "Sit down, Jack, and tell me what's going on in our neighborhood."

Jack filled him in on everything that had happened, from the confrontation at Ken's to the destruction of Jo and Kathy's house, and Al's sour comments. He spent about 15 minutes and Charlie listened without interruption.

When he finished, Charlie said, "I wouldn't feel too bad about your pal, Al. He just did you a favor by showing you his true colors and you're better off for it. Too bad about Jo and Kathy. I have three empty bedrooms and a finished basement. They're welcome to move in here." Charlie started laughing. "I'll probably have to take down my photos of Trump and Reagan though, they'd use them for dart boards."

Jack said, "Thanks, Charlie. I'll tell them that you offered to let them stay here."

"You kids should have seen this place when I built it back in '54. My house was the first place here. When it got all subdivided up back in the 1970s, all these folks started building these so-called country homes, and the first thing they did was to make it city-like. I'm sitting on an acre and a half here, and that seemed like a good size lot, before it got all built up around me—but now, hell, this is almost as bad as the city. They started putting up these big custom homes, and all of a sudden, they're telling me you can't do this, and you can't do that. No, you can't burn those leaves, that's pollution. My Johnnie's got asthma. They tried to make me take the sewer and water lines when they brought them in, told me my private well would have to be capped.

My argument was, 'It's my well. I'll use the city water to drink and keep the well for the lawn and garden.' Not with these bastards, they couldn't have that, *no* sir. I had to fight them in court on the water and sewer thing. I won and didn't have to get it. Thank God, otherwise today I'd be out of water. I got a pump in the basement—that I've kept a secret all these years, plus my private well. I've got water and a septic system. Everyone else ain't got a drop of drinking water and has a basement full of the neighbor's turds. That's progress, huh? The faces change over the years, but the attitude stays the same. We're surrounded by dickheads."

Charlie pulled up a foot stool and set his left leg on it. "Damn, my foot's getting bad. Never get old, Jack, never get old. Anyway, I know you kids got lots to do today, but there are a couple things I have to talk to you about, things I want you to be aware of. People are blind, Jack. They only read the headlines, if they read at all. They don't have to be radical preppers like me, but they do owe it to themselves to be informed. But no, it's football, baseball, hockey, basketball, or what some idiot Hollywood actor is doing. It's no accident. This is well planned out. We're under a spiritual attack to distract us. Keep the masses occupied and sedated with sex, drugs, and whatever... Then these bastards can do whatever they want, with little interference. Some states are passing these so-called women's health bills. Women's health, my ass. Abortion up to the last day, just before birth. Ask a baby how healthy they think that is? The sad thing is lots of so-called good Christians voted these bastards in. So obviously they must agree with it or they're too busy watching football. And if you're like me and side with the unborn, which is really just a word that means, 'They have no voice,' now you're the criminal. You're the deviate...because *it's the law.* The same people want to ban private ownership of guns, because guns *kill the innocent.* Figure that one out? What's purer and more innocent than the unborn? Well it's all down the crapper now. I guess their plan wasn't going fast enough, so they created this mess we're in. Depopulation, that's what it's about. These bastards just need enough of us, *the little people,* to be their serfs. If these new world order pukes ever get our guns. . . we're toast. This crap that's going on was planned and may be the perfect storm to confiscate the guns and do whatever else they got in line for us. When the government has all the cards and you don't have a pot to piss in, or a window to throw it out, folks will give up their rights for a meal. They'll sell themselves into slavery, blinded by a bullshitting politician telling them that *he'll save you.* I'll say this though, this shit-hit-the-fan thing might be a good time to go skunk hunting, and get rid of some of these bastards."

Charlie lit his pipe and started stoking it up, "Shit, I get myself all riled up and I forget what else I wanted to tell you.... God, I get so mad...." He took a heavy pull on his pipe, exhaled a cloud of blue smoke, and didn't say anything more. Jack noticed the old man seemed out of breath, so he didn't interrupt him. After a few moments, Charlie continued. "Oh yeah, remember what we were talking about the other day, me giving you this place? Well it's all set. I want you and whoever else you take in to live here. Come winter, you'll thank me. Me and Dot agreed the day before she passed, and now it's all right here, all in black and white. When I croak, the place and everything I own is yours."

Jack started to interrupt, but Charlie cut him off, "Jack, not now. You can talk all you want later. I've got one more important thing to talk to you about, and it's going to take a while to say, so don't be interrupting me. I hope I got enough wind left in me to tell it to you." He could tell Charlie was having trouble, so he said nothing while the old man caught his breath.

"I told you about our daughter and about what happened, how they never found her killer. Now I want you to listen to this because it's *very important*. Over the years, I've kept track of unsolved murders of children and young adults. Not only in Able County, but in DuPage and Will County too. I also kept track of missing children, and some clear patterns have emerged to me. I know we don't have time today to get into all the particulars, so I'm going to keep it short. There's a 60 % more chance of a child that comes up missing around here of never being found, or found murdered, compared to the lower half of our state. That means that locally, something terrible is going on around here that isn't happening elsewhere. I had to follow cases for many years to come to this conclusion. There's something police departments out here don't have, and that's time, but I had plenty of it. I've carefully researched this, Jack. I know what I'm talking about. Kids go missing in southern Illinois and there's a good chance that they show up five years later out in Nevada or California, or living with a distant relative. Kids go missing here, most never come home......or they're found murdered. A good percent of missing teenagers, nationwide, are troubled kids and end up as runaways. But the percentages don't match here. I looked up personal information about these children that went missing or were found murdered here. Compared to the rest of the state, more *good* kids are getting murdered or come up missing here. The key word here is *good kids*. They have no reason to run away. The murdered ones that are found are usually mutilated in some way; body parts are missing. Fire Chief Kirhman was a good friend of mine, and his daughter, Kathy, is a good example. She was killed ten years ago, on Christmas Eve, by a hit-and-run driver while she was supposedly walking home. What the newspapers accounts didn't print was that she was run over *multiple* times by the same vehicle. Someone ran her down, backed up, and ran over her again and again. She was found dead on a back road, *three* miles away from her house. She would have never been walking on that road on Christmas Eve. Now get this, Kirhman's older sister was murdered the exact same way, back in 1968, and it was never solved. A random act or a coincidence? No way."

Charlie started coughing and had to take a couple deep breaths before continuing. He said, "The same with my Linda, God rest her soul. She was a *good* girl. She was raped, murdered, and *mutilated*, and the police determined it was random. Some sicko, supposedly passing through, gives her a ride home from school and she's found murdered in an old abandoned barn. Trail grows cold and the case gets shelved. It's not just my daughter and Kirhman's, I've got a whole file folder of them. I've been tracking a *serial killer*. The police department has had two complete turnovers of personnel since 1968. My daughter's case is ice cold. They think I'm just a sad old persistent parent who misses their child, and all I get from them is sympathy." Charlie took another puff from his pipe. "Listen, Jack, this is what I think. It's not just one person who's doing this, it's a group. One of them is on the road a lot, at all different hours, and that makes it look like a random act of someone just passing through. I also think it's someone a kid would expect to be trustworthy. The actual abduction may be done by only one person, but I believe others participate in the killing part, like some kind of sick cult. They pick an average kid who one minute is walking or riding their bike somewhere, and the next day is listed as missing or found miles away from home—dead.

I think whoever is doing these killings lives close by, maybe right here in our little subdivision.... That murdering bastard across the street, he fits the puzzle, and I'd feel much better if he was dead. I'll tell you something else. I think something satanical is behind every murder. We've got a group of people who are very sick, and when the opportunity presents itself, they do their thing, and they've never been caught. They've been getting away with this, from what I can figure, from as far back as 1968, with the murder of Chief Kirhman's sister. I think they're some kind of satanic cult that recruits new and younger members, because that Glen bastard wasn't even born yet in '68." Charlie pulled a small flask out of his jacket pocket and unscrewed the top. "My own special brew, it's good... care for a swig?"

Jack refused. Charlie took a drink, then continued, "You and I know this is just the start of this shit-hit-the-fan bullshit; nobody is coming to the rescue. By this time next week, most people won't even have a can of tomato paste. These nosy neighbors and the people giving you trouble today will be trying to kill you in a couple of weeks for a can of spam. You're going to have to deal with them, but they'll be the lesser of your problems. Notice I said lesser, but not least. These sickos, the ones who killed my daughter and all the others, they're out there too. What separates them from the hordes of hungry neighbors that you're going to face, is the fact that they're ruthless killers and they *enjoy* it. The very fact that they are ruthless is going to make them survivors. These sick bastards will make it, you can count on it. It's going to be a field day for them because, at first, pickings are going to be good. They're going to make minced meat pie out of dorks like that Barry. They'll have people like him on a barbecue spit, you wait and see. Jack, you're going to survive this shit because it's just the way you are. You're ruthless and that makes you a survivor, but so are these people. I've got a feeling. I think within the next year, because you're such a *ruthless* person yourself, you're going to have a run-in with these sick pricks, I just know it. People like you will stand out, simply because you'll be the only ones still eating regularly. These killers will be survivors too, and they're not going to waste their time bothering with starving people who ain't got a can of beans. They'll be hunting for the preppers; you better believe it. You're going have a target on your back, Jack.

I'm giving you everything I own, Jack, lock, stock, and barrel. It'll more than triple your chances of survival. You're going to find these bastards that killed my daughter. You'll know them when you run into them. But don't worry, you won't have to search for them. They'll need food and they'll *find you*.... I want you to kill them, Jack. Make them pay hard for what they've done."

Charlie took a couple puffs on his pipe, sat back, and closed his eyes. Jack heard him quietly repeat, "Make them pay hard." He started to say something, but the old man cut him off, saying, "Don't forget, you tell those two girls they can stay here if they want to. They can have the whole lower level or the pick of the bedrooms. Now leave me be for now. I'm tired and I want to be alone with my brother. Let Max and Toots out for me, will you?" There were tears running down the old man's cheeks, and there was nothing more to say.

The rest of the day was spent moving Jo and Kathy's belongings to Charlie's house. Carl's truck, the two vans and Charlie's pick-up made multiple trips, up and down the block, emptying Jo and Kathy's storm ravaged house. Their survival stores and weapons were among the first loads taken out. All the vehicles were loaded in secrecy inside the girls' attached garage, to avoid the prying eyes of the neighbors gathered at Al's. They worked the entire day, salvaging and moving the contents of the girls' home. Jo was reluctant to move, but with nowhere to go, it took little convincing. She assured Jack that it would only be temporary.

By sundown, everything was moved, and they cleaned themselves up the best they could. All of them were filthy, longing for a long hot shower. They grilled up a smorgasbord of defrosted food and sat on Jack's back patio, enjoying the odd assortment. Jo and Kathy provided shrimp and crab, and Ken had brought wild salmon and catfish. Charlie wasn't there, but he provided ice cold beer. Everyone was thinking the same thing as they ate, *Will I ever eat, or even see food like this again?*

As the sun set, black rain clouds started rolling in. The wind turned sharp and the group broke up, as the sound of thunder echoed above the houses.

"Going to be coming down soon." Jack stood on his rear concrete patio, looking up at the rolling clouds, the air suddenly turning cold. It's going to be just an old-fashioned thunderstorm, not like last night. We should all get a bar of soap and take advantage of this free shower."

SPARKLING RAINDROPS

CHAPTER 3 0

That night it poured. Everyone brought their dirty clothes outside, where an old, antique galvanized metal tub was filled with rainwater. It became their *new* washing machine. Jack's new Maytag machines were in his flooded basement, still under seven feet of filthy water. After washing their clothing in the old tub, the soapy clothes were hung out on a makeshift clothes line to get a thorough rinsing from the pouring rain. Before turning into bed, everyone decided to take advantage of the rain to wash a week's worth of grime off their body. As Jack entered the dark house, he was met at the back door by Carl, who handed him a bar of soap and a fresh towel.

Carl said, "The girls are just about finished giving Bobby his bath. We might as well take our showers first. I don't mind telling you, Jack, your deodorant ain't making it."

Jack was already soaking wet from washing out a week's worth of his dirty clothes. He didn't laugh at Carl's comment, but replied, "You're pretty ripe yourself, Carl. You know, our whole generation is spoiled. It wasn't until the 1960's that taking a daily shower became common. Before that, folks just washed themselves up at night. They took baths, usually on Saturday night. Deodorants were pretty basic too and a lot of people didn't use them. Nobody had air conditioning either. I remember my grand-mother used a wringer washing machine. In the summer she hung her clothes on a line outside. She'd hang them in her basement in the winter. It's tempting to use the generator to power Charlie's washing machine, but that would be foolish with our limited supply of gasoline. There's going be constant temptations to use the generator for every inconvenience. We're just going to have to get used to this."

Jack found himself a private spot on the side of the house. He removed his clothing and stood in the light rain, letting the icy rain drops wash away the past week of grime. He closed his eyes and pretended it was washing away all the craziness that had happened, letting all his problems run off him, onto the wet grass. There was a bolt of lightning and the wind picked up; the rain drops hit harder and felt good against his skin. It'd been a long time since he stood barefoot on wet grass. His mind flashed back some 40 years before, when, during those hot summer afternoons his mom would turn on the lawn sprinkler and him and let the neighbor kids run through it. He hadn't thought about that in year. . ., *Oh God, we never knew how good we had it.* He wondered if times would ever be that carefree again. When he was finished, he went back in the house and dried off in the kitchen, his only light being the dim glow of a small kerosene lantern. For the first time in days, he felt cool and refreshed. Wrapping his towel around him, he started up the stairs to his bedroom, passing Lynne on her way down. The bandages were off her face, and for the first time, he could see the full extent of her wound. A jagged and angry-looking red scar ran down the entire left side of her face.

Catching his stare, she raised her hand, shielding her face from the glare of Jack's lamp. "I know, I look horrible—don't look at it."

He didn't know what to say. He would be lying and she would know it if he said, "*It doesn't look bad,*" because even in the weak glow of his lamp, it did.

There were no words to say, so without hesitation, he ever so gently placed his hand behind her head and pulled her to him. Bending down, he lightly kissed her cheek and then her forehead. Holding her close for a moment he said, "We all have scars, some can't be seen. You're safe here Lynne—that's what matters."

He felt her pull away, slightly, saying, "I feel safe here, Jack... I—better get outside... while it's still storming. You smell so fresh and clean. I can only imagine what I must smell like."

He lingered on the steps a moment while Lynne continued down the stairs. As she went outside, he slowly went upstairs and into his dark bathroom, tiredness seeping into every muscle. Setting the lamp on the vanity top, he found his comb and ran it through his tangled hair. He needed a shave, and his reflection looked old in the bathroom mirror. Without electricity, the whole house felt different, almost foreign to him. Running his hand across the heavy stubble on his face, he could hear the rain coming down, much harder now. The wind suddenly picked up, whipping ice cold raindrops through the open bathroom window into the dimly lit room. After shutting the window, he left the bathroom and went into his bedroom to close the windows from the driving rain. Entering his room, he paused at the door. The white curtains looked like ghosts dancing in the cool breeze that was blowing in. The fresh crisp air felt good, and if the rain wasn't soaking the floor, he would have left the windows open. The first window closed easily. He reached up and tried to slide down the second window, but it bound for a couple seconds, making him lay his weight into the stubborn sash. Just as the sash started its slide down, there was a massive crack of lightning that lit up the entire backyard.

As the lightning struck, the window suddenly closed down hard, slamming into the sill with a loud bang! At the same instant, the entire yard lit up, suddenly like daylight. Below him, visible for only a couple seconds... stood Lynne.

Her face was turned up to the sky, her arms hung loose by her sides. Her body was stretched out, welcoming the sparkling drops of coldness that streamed down her.

285

Jack blinked his eyes and her image was gone, replaced by his own reflection in the darkened glass. Pulling back from the window, he suddenly felt ashamed. Though unintentional, he had violated her private moment; but it was too late, her image was burned into him.

Feeling exhausted, he tiredly sat down on the end of the bed. Staring at the kerosene lamp that sat on Ellen's dresser, his eyes rose to the wedding photo on the wall above it. In the weak light, he stared up at it. Like the window curtains, Ellen's white wedding dress starkly stood out, but her face was obscured in darkness.

How ironic, he thought, *our whole marriage was shrouded in darkness...how can life get so screwed up?* Trying not to look at the photo, he got up and turned down the lamp. As the flame flickered out, he stared into the pitch blackness and at the wedding portrait hidden behind it. Hidden, but still there. The eyes in the photo seeing...knowing what was in his mind. *Should I feel guilty, or do I feel a sense of relief that you're gone? If you're dead, then you're reading my mind.*

With a thousand things running through his brain, he laid back on the bed. Pulling the bed sheet over himself, he let the badly-needed sleep overtake him. He dreamt about the wedding portrait and he dreamt about her eyes. Ellen's eyes, dark with anger—staring at Lynne, watching the rain drops trailing down her body.... *You're with me now, aren't you Ellen? You know my every thought. This strange woman in your house... you know I want her. God, please help me, let me sleep. Sparkling raindrops, let me sleep...let me sleep...*

GOODBYE OLD FRIENDS

CHAPTER 3 1

"Dad! Dad, wake up!" Jack's eyes opened, his hand already reaching for his revolver. Laura was standing over him shaking his shoulder, and she was crying.

"What, what is it?"

"You better go over to Charlie's, something terrible has happened." Jack slipped on some clean jeans and bolted out his door.

Joan, Kathy, and Carl were standing outside of Charlie's back screened-in porch. Lynne was inside the porch, an empty medicine bottle in her hand. Charlie was sitting peacefully in his rocker. Max and Toots were at his feet, and all three were dead.

Jack looked at his old friend, an all too familiar feeling of grief rising in his chest. "What happened?"

Lynne held up the clear plastic medicine bottle, letting Jack read the label.

"Oh my God, where did he get that?"

She shook her head, "I don't know, but this bottle held 45 pills and now it's empty. Ted is gone too. I think he passed naturally during the night. Charlie must have given some of these to the dogs and taken the rest himself sometime early this morning. Jo and Kathy found him when they got up."

So many friends were dying, Jack was at a loss for words. "Oh my God, Charlie, why, why did you do this?" As he looked down at Charlie, he noticed a piece of white notebook paper folded up, sticking out of his shirt pocket. He gently removed it from Charlie's pocket, and slowly unfolded it, dreading what was written on it.

Sorry Jack, it's better
this way, we both know
it's no use in me sticking
around any longer. Ted
died last night. Please put
us next to each other,
Max & Toots at our feet.
The place is yours. All
the paperwork is on my
desk. Anybody questions
why you are living in my
place, show them this
letter.   If

they give you any trouble, shoot them. They'll be gunning for all of you, Jack—You know how it will go down. Remember about the gun cases in the den. Don't forget, there's a fake wall on the west end of the basement, another one in Ted's room. You're going to be surprised. Have fun with the B.A.R. Take care of my shotguns— They're my favorite. Love all of you....... Semper fi— Charlie~

Jack handed Charlie's note to the others. They each read it in stunned silence.

Kathy handed it back to Jack, saying, "What did he mean by 'fake wall,' and what's a B A R?"

"Charlie collected old guns. He probably has a fortune in antique firearms in this house. To a gun guy, the letters B.A.R stand for Browning Automatic Rifle. They're deadly, but they're old school and they date back to World War 1. I think the last time they saw any real use was Korea, maybe early Vietnam. One of them would be nice to have, but the way things are, getting enough ammo to make it worthwhile might be tough to find. Any ammunition Charlie has might be from as far back as World War Two, and I'm not sure if I would bet my life on its reliability. Charlie has lots of old guns, but I'm afraid most of them are wall hangers. We get some time, we'll open up those walls in the bedrooms." Jack looked down at Charlie. The old man looked as though he was just taking a nap. "God, Charlie, why did you have to do this?" He knew the old man was right, but he asked himself, *Is this how it's going to be in the new world we've been plunged into?*

The morning was spent digging the graves for Charlie, Ted, and their two beloved dogs. It must have been about 11:00, when Jack saw Barry squeezing through the gap in the back fence. Jack's first thought was, *Not now, please. Anybody but this asshole.* He figured Barry was going to start bitching about the graves again and was in no mood for any of his crap.

"Hey Jack. Oh my God, who died now?"

Not wanting to get in an argument with him, Jack simply explained the deaths of Charlie and Ted. Figuring Barry was going to once again unload on him, he resigned himself to take it with no argument. He was surprised when Barry said, "Sorry for being such an asshole, Jack. I found out a couple things last night. They're just dumping people's bodies into the old gravel pit by the golf course. *Just dumping them* like trash. I heard there's over 3000 bodies in there and lots more to come. They don't even know who half of them are. No one is getting a decent burial, it's just one big mass grave. It's terrible, just terrible. There are children being dumped, just like garbage. It makes me sick. I went over there earlier and saw it firsthand and complained. Do you know what they did to me? This big guy grabs me and held me next to the edge of the pit. He threatened to throw me into it if I didn't leave. Jack, my God, where is the rule of law here? I told Bob Dorfman about it and he said there was nothing he could do. Anyway, I'm sorry about giving you the tough time here..." Barry stood in front of the two open graves, mournfully looking into them. Then he shook his head, saying, "Oh crap, I've been such an asshole, Jack, I'm so sorry about Ellen. I didn't know she was killed by that plane. I didn't know the whole story about Ronnie being raped
291

and murdered, by one of our own neighbors yet. That Carl, he's a good kid. I was rough on him yesterday morning. He tried to explain about your garden and all, even offered me a cup of coffee, and I was a jerk to him. I was just tired and too pig-headed to listen to him or you. I'm sorry, but I know it rings hollow. I don't know what to say."

Jack extended his hand, "I'm sorry too. Sorry about what I said about Liz and for calling you a butthead."

"You can call me whatever you want, Jack. I thought you might take a swing at me. I'd almost feel better if you did."

"No hard feelings, Barry, life's too short. There's too much fighting going on, and too many people good people dying. I'm sick of it. Let's just start off new."

"Thanks Jack. I feel the same way. —Look, I know you're dealing with a lot right now, but there's something important I have to talk to you about. You're the only one I trust. Those guys who came after you the other day, the one that woman shot in the ear. You've got to believe me, I never had a clue about all the things they've done around here, the things they did to those two women...." Barry paused and gestured to Ronnie's home. "Or to this young family. You did a good thing taking in their little boy."

Barry seemed hesitant, like there was more to the story than what he had already said.

Jack said, "That's all right. I've been ignorant of what's been going on around here myself, and apparently it's been plenty."

"I'm glad you mentioned that, because there has been something terrible going on around here, and it's been going on for a long time. I should know more by tonight. I think this Glen Sorensen guy is the tip of the iceberg. I know you don't like Dorfman. Believe me, everybody knows how he can be, especially when he's been drinking.

He and his wife can be really snooty too and, between you and me, she even gets on my nerves. But listen, I just want to tell you that besides how he acted the other night, he really is a good guy and knows his job. He just gets nutty after a few too many beers. I've known him a long time and we're good friends. Because of his job, he has privy to all kinds of information. He's a forensic investigator for the state. Apparently, they reopened an old investigation about some murders around here and he's been on top of it. They managed to get some DNA off some old evidence, linking the same person to at least six unsolved murders, right here in Able County—right in *our* neighborhood, Jack. Did you know Charlie had a daughter who was murdered?"

"Yeah,   I did. Charlie told me about it."

"Dorfman told me he knows who the suspected killers are. He said killers, Jack, not killer. God help us, there's more than one. They had enough evidence for an inditement and were about to get an arrest warrant when the power went out. Everything was lost when the computers went down. The suspects' names are locked in the computers and only three people know the names. Two of them were killed yesterday, one in an accident and the other in a car-jacking. Dorfman thinks they were murdered because somehow the killers found out. Now he's the only one left who knows. I asked him who they were, but he didn't want to tell me. He's scared, Jack, and I don't blame him, because I'm scared too. He told me they thought Fire Chief Kirhman's sister was possibly the first victim, way back in 1968. His daughter was murdered in the same way ten years ago, and that's where they got the killer's DNA from. It's too much of a coincidence and they think they're linked. Did you know that Chief Kirhman died on Monday, right after the power went out? I heard he shot himself. Maybe he figured out who the killers were—maybe they killed him and made it look like a suicide. Who knows? I'm telling you all this because you're the toughest person I know, Jack. You and I have always been on the other side of the fence, pretty much about everything, but you were right the other day. I don't think we have a police department anymore. There is no they, it's only us. Oh my God, Jack, never in a million years would I think this kind of stuff was going on around here. I'll be seeing Dorfman this evening—I'll get him to tell me what he knows. I'll let you know tomorrow what he tells me. They weren't going after just one or two killers, Jack. They thought it was a whole group, like a cult or something."

Jack was saddened by what Barry told him. He looked back at Charlie's grave and said, "If Charlie and Dotty could have just hung on a couple more days, maybe they would have had some closure. Barry, tell me something. Before all this came to light, did you know their daughter was murdered back in the late '70s?"

"No, I didn't. Not until Dorfman told me. It happened so long ago. Who would ever think something so terrible could be going on in our little town, for all these years? One other thing. I know that you're good friends with that guy, Al, in the corner house where all the partying has been going on. Did he mention to you that the young couple who live next door to him are gone, without a trace? Their last name is Connors. Liz and I are good friends with them, they go to our church. They're good people and they're gone. They're not the type who would just run off without telling a neighbor. Someone ransacked their house too. They were last seen several nights ago at your friend's cookout. It's like they just disappeared..."

"Thanks for telling me all this, Barry. I haven't seen them, and no one has mentioned anything to me about them. I know who they are, I've talked to them a couple times. They seemed like a nice young couple. Please, let me know tomorrow what you find out, and I'll help you anyway I can." Jack paused for a second, and changed the subject, "Tell me something, what are your plans?"

Barry kicked at a hunk of dirt, looked around, scratching his head. "That's a good one. I don't know, Jack. We're scared. As much as we love our house, Liz thinks we should leave as soon as possible, at least until some law and order are restored. My basement is flooded with sewage, and we're almost out of food and water. If it's true about this big relief camp thing, or whatever they call it, I guess we'll head over there until the power goes back on. It's funny, by some miracle, my van runs fine. If I had a full tank of gas, we'd drive out to my brother's house. He's got a place just north of Galena. It's on the Mississippi. He's pretty isolated."

Jack extended his hand again to Barry and as he shook it, he said, "Carl will be over with some food and water for you, in about a half hour. Will five gallons of gas be enough?"

"Yes, of course. God, Jack—you'd do that for us—after the way I've treated you?"

"Forget about it. Getting to your brother's place is the only way you'll be safe. Do you own any guns?"

"No."

"You pack your van up today and tomorrow morning we'll bring you the gas. I've got some extra guns. I'll give you a shotgun and some shells. I can't guarantee the security of your house once you leave. You can box up and store your valuables at my place. It's up to you."

"Jack, I don't know what to say?"

"Don't worry about it. There is one thing you can do for me. When you see your buddy, Dorfman, tell him to lay off us. You be careful tonight. Don't open your door to anyone. See you in the morning."

Charles and Theodore Mills were laid to rest, with Max and Toots at their feet. Jack was the last one to leave their gravesites. Looking down at Charlie's grave, he said aloud, "Tomorrow morning, we'll find out who murdered your daughter. I'll take care of them for your Charlie, I promise you—they'll pay hard. Semper fi old friend."

DAY 9

CHAPTER 3 2

After Charlie's burial, Jack explained to the others what Charlie had told him about the murder of his daughter. He told them the whole story and the new information that Barry had given him. When he went to bed that night, everything Charlie had told him and the new revelations by Barry were jumbled together in his mind. Nothing made sense, but murder never does.

Jack was wide awake. It was before dawn and too early to get up. There was too much going through his head to sleep, and every bit of it was important. It was the start of day nine, and so much work had yet to be accomplished. He felt like getting up and starting his day, but he would have to wait until daylight. Every task on his plate that morning was as important as the next, but all of them depended on one thing—and that was daylight. It had to be close to 4:00 AM and he couldn't go back to sleep, so he laid there, thinking—just thinking. *All of these murders dating back from 1968...they all have to be connected.... but how, and why.... and by who?* He got up and sat on the edge of the bed. He felt like going right over to Barry's, but he would have to wait. He would have the answers today—and he'd keep his promise to old Charlie. He picked up the 44 and held it. No lawyers, no trials, only justice.

The day was starting out hot and muggy and, with no air conditioning working, all the upstairs windows were wide open. He had fallen back asleep and was woken up by the sound of a generator starting up, signaling the start of a new day. He got up and looked out his bedroom window. The sun hadn't fully come up, but already there were at least two generators running somewhere on the next street. As people exhausted their gasoline, the sound of generators was heard less. During the night and early morning, the neighborhood had become quieter than it had ever been. There were no more annoying sirens, beeping horns or car alarms to disrupt his sleep. Soon there wouldn't even be the sound of a generator. The sounds of suburban life had ended.

All Jack's frozen food was gone. Charlie had kept his generator going on and off for pretty much three days straight, and had ran it intermittent after that.

Keeping Dottie's oxygen machine running was a priority that used up at least forty gallons of precious gas, but it also kept his big freezer cold.

There was still a full load of rock-hard, frozen food in Charlie's propane freezer, plus whatever was left in his two refrigerators. The item of the day was to tune up Charlie's generator and use it to keep his big freezer running. The generator would have to run for at least 8 hours each day. Once the frozen food was gone their generator would be silent. Jack gazed out his window, thinking of all he had to accomplish and the hurdles that were in front of him. Running his fingers through the start of a beard, he said to himself, "It's another day, let's hit it."

Over a breakfast of fresh eggs, bacon, pancakes, and frozen orange juice, the 'family', as they now referred to themselves, discussed their plans for the coming week.

Lynne reminded Jack about her late husband's storage garage. It was agreed that later in the week, she, Jack, and Jo would make a trip to the nearby town of Downers Grove to retrieve her Dakota RV and snowmobiles.

Jack explained to the group, that after years of bickering back and forth, he and Barry had finally buried the hatchet. There were mixed feelings around the picnic table that morning. Everyone was trying to stay positive and agreed that besides all the hurdles thrown in front of them the past week, progress was still being made. But there was still an underlying current that was written on everyone's faces. Jack didn't have to see it, he could feel it. All of them had the same question in the back of their minds, 'What's going to be thrown at us next?' For the first time since he had lived there, he was looking forward to talking to Barry and, hopefully, finding out who the killer or killers were. He felt anxious and hurriedly gulped the last of his coffee.

He didn't have to wait long and he hadn't even gotten up from the table. They were suddenly interrupted by screaming coming from Barry's yard. Jack and Carl both got up and ran to the back fence. A lady was screaming, while running out of Barry's house. Within moments, other neighbors rushed over. It didn't take long to find out why she was screaming. Barry's entire family, including Kippy their dog, was dead, all of them brutally butchered.

The murder weapon was a cheap, but razor-sharp machete, and Barry's head was cut clean off. Their son, Dwayne, was a bloody mess, hacked to death while still in his bed. Liz was found partially clothed and horribly beaten in the living room. Her assailant, also only partially clothed, was on top of her. A bloody pair of scissors was sticking out the side of his neck and the bloody machete was at his side. The man with the scissors imbedded in his neck was Glen Sorensen. Within minutes, everyone on the block was there. Unknown to any of them, a similar situation was taking place two streets over. Bob Dorfman, the state forensic technician that Barry was supposed to visit, was found by a neighbor, hacked to death in his basement. His wife was found strangled, beaten and raped in their living room.

There had to be 25 people standing in front of Barry's house. One lady incredulously said, "Someone has got to call the police."

Jack heard a familiar voice behind him say, "She's a real rocket scientist. Someone should inform her that we're back in the stone age."

He turned around and it was Al. Almost jovially, Al added, "Hey, big guy, looks like old Glen Sorensen came back for seconds, huh? Barry's wife really pounded them scissors into his neck, right in the old jugular too. I guess we can all breathe a sigh of relief with that murdering bastard dead."

"Yeah...kind of looks like it." Jack wasn't so sure. Everyone in the crowd shared Al's optimism. Glen Sorensen was dead, but something smelled wrong to Jack, it seemed all too easy. He kept his mouth shut until he got back home. He wasn't home long before he heard about the murder of Bob Dorfman and his wife.

An hour later, the 'family' was again seated at their picnic table, discussing what had happened.

Lynne said, He must have attacked the Dorfman's first. The man was a maniac. He had to know he was the one whose DNA they found, and he killed them to shut them up. If he would have just killed Barry's wife, instead of trying to rape her, he would have gotten away with it. That poor woman must have exhausted her dying breath, stabbing him with those scissors. Thank God she stopped him before he killed again."

Jo spoke up, "That seems to be what everyone thinks. That bastard got what he deserved, that's for sure." Everyone looked at Jack, expecting him to say something in agreement, but Jack stayed silent. Jo started chewing on the ear piece of her sun glasses, eyeing Jack suspiciously, "Okay, Jack, tell us why we're wrong?"

Jack leaned forward in his chair and was silent for a few seconds. "First of all, what proof do we have that Glen was ever in Dorfman's house, let alone the person who killed them. Another thing, now we'll never know if the DNA was Glen's, or how far back the evidence dates from. Glen couldn't have had anything to do with Kirhman's sister's death. He wasn't even born yet. Lastly, what proof is there that Liz stuck those scissors in him? It sure looks like she did, but anyone could have done it, to make it *look* like she did it. Charlie believed these murders were done by some kind of sick cult, probably satanic. He thought that they might be inducting new members to keep it going. Heck, the original killers might have already died from old age, who knows? Think of it, they have to be really old. You know, another thing is, I could believe that Glen could have killed Barry and his son. Barry was no fighter, especially if Glen broke in the house undetected. I can also believe he raped Liz, but right after he did the same thing at Dorfman's house?   No way. No, not two women, at different places, in one night."

Laura interrupted, "I'm totally confused, Dad. Are you saying Glen didn't kill these people?"

"I think he probably did kill them, maybe all of them, but not alone. I believe someone would like us to *think* he acted alone. I think there were at least two other people with Glen and one of them jammed those scissors into his neck."

Carl started to say something, but Jack held up his hand, momentarily placing his forefinger to his lips. "Before we buried Ronnie, did anyone notice that something was missing from her body?"

Lynne said, "Yes, her ear. Her left ear was gone. I looked for it before we buried her, but couldn't find it. I didn't think anyone else noticed it. I kept it to myself, I didn't want to upset anyone."

Jack was nodding his head. "A young black woman's left ear was taken. That's telling me something, I don't know what, but I think it's symbolic. Only a cult or someone really sick would do something like that. Charlie told me that on Monday afternoon, he was concerned about Ronnie and Bobby. He went over there and knocked on the front door. I'll bet that Glen was inside raping Ronnie while Charlie was at the front door. Who knows if Glen acted alone, or even if Ronnie was the intended target? These people enjoy killing children. Why would they switch to an adult? I think they wanted Bobby or the unborn baby. Ronnie was in her final month of pregnancy...."

Lynne gasped, "*Why?*"

After remaining silent a few moments. . . Jack said, "I can't fathom why anyone would hurt a child, but who can understand the mind of a serial killer? We may not like discussing this, or even thinking about it, but this kind of sick shit goes on. I think Charlie interrupted Glen and he ran out the back. I'll bet he was supposed to take Bobby or Ronnie's baby with him. Bobby is smart and might have been hiding, who knows? I think Glen settled for killing Ronnie and taking her ear. And why her *left* ear? Is it somehow symbolic in Satanism? I don't know enough about it and with no internet, we can't even research it, but I bet it is." Jack gave them a moment to digest what he just said, then recapped what he thought. "From what Charlie told me about these unsolved murders and abductions, most of them have always been young children, the oldest being kids in their early teens. Other than Ronnie being pregnant, her murder doesn't compute. Unless she somehow stumbled onto something about the killers, and they wanted to shut her up." Jack slowly shook his head. "But how could she have? They recently moved in here, but somehow, they're connected. I think little Bobby is the key.

Carl said, "How could anyone get away with something like this, all these years?"

Jack said, "I don't know, but that's it in a nutshell and it's all we have to go on. It's a sick puzzle, we just have to find the missing pieces. Either Glen had nothing to do with any of the past murders, or he's a newer member of a long-established cult. I'll bet Glen was killed over at Barry's by another cult member. He became a sort of *sacrificial lamb*, to throw everyone off. I think someone wants us to believe that Glen did all these killings by himself. I don't think he could have, no way. We would have heard screaming, for one thing. This was done by multiple people, experienced at what they do and it went down fast. Barry and his family didn't have a chance. The only thing I do know is that these people are animals, and now they've been let loose with no law enforcement to stop them."

Kathy spoke up, "I think we've entered the end-times, where evil is everywhere. I feel like we're surrounded by it. I can feel it."

Jack said, "I think you hit the nail right on the head. We're dealing with evil, pure evil. It's been here all the while, but now it's unleased and it's going wild."

Lynne said, "I've got chills running down my spine. I've been scared all this past week. We've all been through hell, but this scares me, this really scares me. Our world has gone crazy."

Kathy said, "Satan has always been made to look like a big joke in this world and that's just fine to his way of thinking. He'd like us to think he's a joke, but he's real, I know he is. I was abused from the time I was little, and he robbed me of my childhood. *He,* or *it,* is here and it doesn't matter what we call it. If there is light, there is darkness. If there's up, there's down, and where there's good, evil is always nearby trying to destroy it. We have to pray to Jesus always and remember, we're the good guys here, *we have to be.*"

Jo gave Kathy a hug, while silently nodded her head in agreement.

Lynne suddenly got up, "Bobby is still sleeping. I'm going upstairs to check on him. We must never let him out of our sight again."

Lynne went upstairs with Laura to check on Bobby. Kathy wanted to go back to Charlie's and took Carl with her. They searched the entire house, making sure it was safe from intruders.

Jo stayed back to talk to Jack and slid over close beside him. "Jack, let me sound this out on you. Remember when you were at the sand pit? I think we both know that it was Dirk Hayes who you saw tossing those bodies into that pit. You and I know that the sheriff and his brother must have killed Walt for his truck. The sheriff carries a Shotmaster 45, just like mine. Other than me, I haven't seen anyone else around here carrying one of those, and I would notice it. That shell casing you found has to be from his gun. I think we both know it. Both those guys have given Kathy and me the creeps ever since we first moved in here. We complained to the sheriff's department about all the vandalism that was done to our house, and I swear, somehow, that Sherriff Hayes and his brother were in on it. Not only that, but those guys are both old enough to have been at least in their teens back in the late 60's. I know they aren't married and they supposedly live together. Who knows, maybe they're not even brothers? They sure don't look alike. One other thing, all these children who were murdered—they were supposedly picked up while walking home by someone *trustworthy*. Who's more *trustworthy* than the local town sheriff?"

"I've been thinking the same thing, Jo. The problem is, we can't prove a thing. I suppose we could just go and kill both of them, but what if we're totally wrong? We can't prove for sure that they killed Walt. They're both assholes, we know that, but we can't kill them just because they're assholes. Besides, as bad as things are, someday things will be better and we'll be held accountable. I don't want to go to prison after this whole mess clears up. No, we have to have absolute proof. I don't think those two are smart enough to be doing all this killing for all these years without getting caught. What really bothers me is how come we didn't hear anything last night, no screams, no nothing? To kill two families and rape two women, there's got to be several killers involved, not just one or two. Barry got hit so quick, it was over in seconds, but Liz was raped... but then again, maybe she wasn't. It could have been staged. Without an autopsy, we'll never know. I was awake half the night, and my windows were wide open. How come I didn't hear anything? Since the power went out, you can hear a pin drop in this neighborhood at night. If we don't get *all* of them, we'll *never* be safe. We'll keep this all under our hats. We have to make sure we don't say a word of our suspicions to anyone, and I mean no one— let these evil bastards *think* they've fooled us. Meanwhile, we'll keep doing our thing. Maybe someone else might be sick of the Hayes brothers too, sick enough to kill them for us."

DAY 10

CHAPTER 3 3

The mood in the subdivision had changed after the brutal murders of the two families. People who had firearms now openly carried them, and Jack was no longer ridiculed for wearing the big 44 on his hip. The word on the block was that FEMA would be coming in with food and medical supplies. Folks said troops were seen in Cook County and the power would be back on any day.

Jack didn't believe a word of it. All he knew was that he sadly added three more graves to their cemetery. Barry, his wife Elizabeth, and their twelve-year-old son, Dwayne. Their dog, Kippy, was buried at Dwayne's feet.

The massive burial site at the sand pit was now common knowledge. An official from the county slowly drove through the neighborhood in a decrepit old ambulance, spreading the word that bodies of the deceased should be brought to the pit to be interred in the mass burial site to prevent disease. No, they would not be picked up. The families would have to find a way to bring the deceased there themselves, and no questions would be asked. No one liked it, but there were no other options. Without ambulances and hospitals, simple injuries were quickly leading to death. Inside of one week, the dead were already piling up. Burial by a relative or neighbor in the deceased's own backyard was the only other option. In the coming months, even those would stop. There wouldn't be enough living to bury all the dead.

The day had been a hard one, and Jack had lost track of what day of the week it was. Usually at sunrise, he would mark off each day without power on his inside garage wall with a black marker. As the sun was setting, he remembered he had forgotten to mark it off that morning. He walked into the garage and marked another slash. Tomorrow he would start another row. It would be day 11.

The chicken coop was almost done and all the chain-link fencing was up behind his garage. Metal posts were set into the ground and panels of fencing were laid across the top of them for a roof. The inside of the garage was partitioned off across the entire back, leaving a five-foot area for roosts and shelter.

Charlie's old Honda generator ran almost constantly throughout the day. Besides keeping the remainder of their food frozen, it was essential for the power tools they were using. Jack had attempted to pump out Ronnie's and his basements. Ronnie's stayed dry, but the putrid water still bubbled up from Jack's sump pit and broken floor. Without constant power to run the pump, his basement would never be dry again. He decided to nail up his basement door forever.

Jack knew that the day was rapidly approaching when running a generator every time they needed it would be a thing of the past. After only eleven days, supplies of gasoline were already low, and eventually the generators would permanently shut down. With no way to get parts for upkeep of the generators, let alone fuel, things would get a lot worse.

Carl measured the lower and most vulnerable windows of the three houses and cut sheets of plywood to cover each of them. Each sheet was numbered and stored in Charlie's garage for future installation. They knew that soon, they'd have to fortify the houses from the expected intruders. Jack got a sinking feeling, as he thought of what life would be like without his power tools. Using a handsaw to rip a sheet of plywood would be a nightmare.

Everything was planted, including the sweet potatoes Jack had gotten from Sheila, the girl with the broken-down shopping cart. He had thought about her several times. He hoped the money he had given her would save her from the starvation he knew was coming. He also thought about the girl he and Don had left stranded in the Chicago doorway. Did she ever make it home to the suburbs? The days of the open cook-outs and generous hand-outs at Al's had ended too. After only eleven days, things were changing quickly.

The family sat outside together that night, joined by Ken and Ben. Carl lit a campfire in the fire pit, and after a few minutes of sitting around the warm fire, everyone seemed to relax. It was a beautiful early summer night. Kathy produced a bag of marshmallows and Laura had some graham crackers and chocolate bars. Campfire s'mores were made for everyone.

Lynne was holding Bobby on her lap. The girls all started singing campfire songs, but Bobby's face was forlorn, and his voice still silent. Carl was sitting next to Jack. He leaned over to him and said, "Jack, I've been so busy with the garden, I haven't had any time to think about much of anything else. I was in my truck today and tried the radio. I went through the whole dial. There should be some type of emergency broadcasting, no matter what happened. Something just isn't right. I picked up mostly static, but I also got music and some sporadic talking... but it suddenly just stopped."

Jack looked at Carl in astonishment, "What?"

"That's right, I heard music, but I don't know where it was coming from. The talking I heard was Spanish, but who knows where it's being broadcasted. It could be from anywhere. With all the stations in the states off the air, it could be

Mexico or even South America. I couldn't hear enough of it to tell. But that's not the point. We should be hearing more than static and jumbled talking. I think that maybe parts of the country are not affected by the power outage. EMP or not, there are emergency broadcasting stations that should be operating. My feeling is that the radio signals are intentionally being jammed by our government, or maybe someone else, for God knows what reason. There are three separate power grids in this country. I've always heard that if one goes down, they all go down. I don't know whether that's true or not, but it might be that the Midwest is the only grid affected. There may be other things going on that the government wants kept secret. What I am worried about are the nuclear plants. The closest to us is to the south. We've got one northwest of us, and a deactivated one to the North. They're all pretty far from us. I guess everything depends on the winds. Who knows, the whole world could be at war, but I'm hoping to find out for sure, maybe this week."

Jack rolled his eyes, "Nuclear plants? That's just great. What are we going to do?"

"My uncle was an amateur radio operator up until the late 70's, and he kept everything. I could put that old obsolete radio equipment back in use. I saw three of those old Zenith Transoceanic radios in his basement. The wiring and some of the tubes might be shot, but maybe I can salvage parts from all three and get one of them working. They can pick up stations in South America and overseas. I think there are some old police walkie-talkies down in his basement too. We could use those to communicate between ourselves. I want to check on the place anyway, maybe I'll take a ride over there tomorrow. If we do get something on a radio, it could be all government propaganda. We might wish we didn't hear it, but we could sure use those old walkie-talkies."

"That's a great idea. You shouldn't go alone, though, I'll go with you. We can go in the morning. Speaking of going places, Lynne wants us to go get her late husband's RV and some other things this week. I plan to do that with her, maybe on Friday." Jack hesitated for a few seconds, "I'll tell you one thing, this nuclear thing scares the crap out of me. I hadn't thought about that...."

On day 11, the sun was barely up and they were on their way to Carl's aunt's house. Carl was driving and Jack rode shotgun, leaving early to avoid as many people as possible. There were still lots of small items they could use from the old house. Jack was especially interested in his uncle's collection of antique tools. With limited electricity to run them, modern power tools were becoming useless. Without modern air and power tools, it was back to using tools and practices of 1900. The contents of an antique store were now more valuable than a modern hardware store.

Driving any place had to be done speedily, ignoring speed limits and stop signs. Routes had to be carefully planned out in advance, avoiding the main roads as much as possible. Driving slowly, even on a seemingly empty street, was

303

inviting trouble.   During the day, all the main arteries leading out of Chicago were saturated with desperate people on foot. Having been displaced from the windy city, they advanced through the suburbs like a hoard of hungry locusts, devouring everything in their path.

Jack was prepared for squatters or possible looters to be at Carl's vacant home. Surrounded by forest preserve and across from a cemetery, the house was secluded and inviting to thieves. Since it was within sight of the main road, he decided it would be best to drive right past it, doing at least twice the posted limit of 35. If there were any unwanted guests at the house, he wanted to make it look like they were just another vehicle driving by in a big hurry, not someone doing a recon on the home.

Carl was glad that Jack made him do the speedy drive by. They spotted the back end of a black 57 Chevy station wagon alongside the house and an overweight man was loading it up. He didn't give Carl's old pickup truck a second look as it sped by.

"Carl, slow down and pull off the road up there. Nose the truck behind those bushes. Somebody's cleaning out your aunt's place, despite us nailing the doors shut and our 'Looters will be shot' sign. We're going to double-time it back there and see how many are there. If it's only the one guy, maybe we can shag him out, but if there's more than him and they're armed, they're going to wish they heeded our sign."

"Do we have to kill them?"

"You want to ask them to leave? You won't get two words out of your mouth and they'll be shooting at you."

Jack caught Carl's frown and the slight shake of his head in disagreement.

"Welcome to the new world order. You can stay behind if you want, but they've been warned of the consequences by the sign we left nailed to the door. They're trespassing. They made the decision. It's your property, it doesn't belong to them. This is a life or death situation because we need what's in *your* house." Jack could tell Carl was still unconvinced. "Look, if they're unarmed or look like they're kids, I'll cut them some slack and maybe try to scare them off, but if they're heavily armed, we either turn around and go home, or we deal with them. We can't confront them and give them an edge on us. If there are too many of them, we'll let it go, but if I think we got a shot to take them out, I'll go for it. That's the way it has to be."

Carl reluctantly nodded his head and pulled the truck behind the bushes. "Okay, you're right. I just wish there was another way."

With the truck out of sight, buried in the thicket, Jack jumped out, saying, "Let's go. We have to move quickly, or they'll be gone with what belongs to you."

They ran back to the house, approaching it from the driveway side, hiding in the woods about 150 feet away.

Unlike the morning at the sand pit, this time Jack was prepared. He had a set of field glasses and Charlie's M1 Carbine. Silently sneaking towards the house, they crouched down and watched from the dense woods. While looking through the field glasses, Jack whispered silently to himself, "Okay, what do we have here? There's a skinny guy walking out, he's carrying a big box—he's wearing a shoulder holster with something big…okay…. What's this, what's this? Look at that. There's a rifle conveniently laying on the hood of their car. What the hell is it? It's got a big magazine sticking out of it … could be an AR-15. But why is it on the car hood? Okay, okay… here comes another guy. He's carrying out a laundry basket full of tools…. *your* tools, Carl. He's a porker. Oh jeez, look what he's wearing, a 2016 campaign shirt. *Oh boy*, bad day to wear that… anybody but her. He's carrying a big ass revolver on his hip too. Okay… now they're heading back inside the house. Jeez… they're leaving that rifle just sitting on the hood… what idiots. And they're both looking up at that side second-floor window… and all the upstairs windows are open…interesting." He handed Carl the glasses, saying, "All right, you stay hunkered down here. *Do not* move a muscle. We got ourselves some well-armed morons who apparently can't read our no trespassing sign, so they have to go bye-bye. I'm going to get closer. See that thatch of thick brush up there, to the right? I'll be in it. You don't do a thing, do you understand? You just stay here and keep down. I'll be coming back from behind you when it's over, so *don't* shoot me."

Jack made his way back towards the road, then circled through the woods to the dense thicket of Buckthorn. Covered by weeds and heavy brush, he silently waited, watching the two men carrying out the contents of Carl's house. He was in the thicket only a couple minutes when he raised the carbine. The station wagon was jammed packed, and it looked like they were getting ready to leave.

From a kneeling position, Jack took aim with Charlie's M1 and dropped the guy who was nearest to the car and the rifle that was on the hood. Swiveling the muzzle of the old carbine up, he put a round into the torso of the person who was keeping watch from an upstairs bedroom window. He shot the third man as he attempted to run to the car, obviously to pick up the rifle.

He glanced back to where Carl was hiding. Thinking it was over, Carl started to stand up, but Jack impatiently motioned for him to keep down, saying to himself, "God, that kid worries me."

15 minutes later, Carl heard Jack whisper behind him, "Easy, Carl, it's me."

A few seconds passed and Jack was alongside Carl, and he was pissed. "Hey— you have to listen to me, Carl. Don't be in a such damn hurry to get up. I told you to stay down. You have to do what I tell you!" Jack jerked his head towards the house, "All right, let's give that guy upstairs some more time to bleed a bit, before we go in. I don't want to get shot by someone making their dying stand."

"Jack, how the heck did...."

"Carl— I want to listen and just watch for a bit, then we can talk."

They both sat in silence a few minutes. Carl quietly asked again, "How did you know there was another guy upstairs?"

"Those two guys were walking out of there way too casual. There had to be someone on watch. Both of them clowns looked up at that second story bedroom window when they walked back to the house. Didn't you notice all the upstairs windows are open? That's because their buddy was up there. I kept an eye on the upstairs windows. Sure enough, I spotted some movement. The guy was pretty much staying back and it would have been a long shot for me to hit him. I hit the guy closest to the car first, because he was only an arm's length away from that rifle sitting on the hood. Then I sighted to the upstairs window they kept looking at. These guys had the firepower, but no brains. I was hoping that my first shot would draw the guy upstairs out for a look. He fell for it. I saw the muzzle of a rifle barrel, so I aimed where someone should be on the other end of it and nailed him. I'm not worried about the two outside. I hit them dead center in their chest and they're finished. But the guy upstairs, we can't be sure of. I know I hit him, but we don't know how hard. He still may have a kick left and we're not going to be stupid enough to find out. Let's wait him out. We'll give him a couple more minutes. We don't hear him screaming, so he's probably dead. They waited five minutes before Jack went towards the house. The first thing he did was to remove an AR-15 rifle off the old Chey's hood. At the top of the stairs, under an open window, was a man dressed in green camouflaged pants. He was sitting slumped over in the upstairs hallway, with an AR-15 rifle on his lap. He had spent his dying moments waiting for the person who shot him to come up the stairs. He sat in a puddle of blood, shot through his stomach. Jack shot him once more in the head before he ascended the stairs, then gave the house a quick once through. Satisfied the house was clear, he signaled Carl to come in.

Carl slowly started coming up the stairs, but stopped. Staring in disbelief at the dead man, he said, "Holy shit! When I heard the gun shot, I thought they shot you!"

Jack pointed to the dead man. He was their lookout. My first shot got him, but he was still kind of sitting up with his weapon next to him, so I shot him again when I came in... just to make sure."

"I don't get how you spotted him. I was looking at all the upstairs windows and I didn't see a thing. How do you do it?"

Jack was looking out the open window, towards the street. He mumbled, "It's all common sense and these assholes didn't have any of it. All right, let's hurry up. You can come up here, but keep an eye out, in case they got friends in the neighborhood. Go through the house but make it quick. And don't be an idiot like this guy up here. Whenever you look out a window, keep well to the side of it."

Jack bent down and picked up the rifle from the dead man. Talking low, to himself, he said, "Look at this will you? This thing has been kicked up a notch, he's got a bump stock on it…. Nice. There's several extra magazines up here too. I bet there's some more magazines in the car. We just scored two AR-15's. This is good…*very* good." Jack unbuckled a web belt with a 9mm semi-automatic in its holster. Holding it up he said, "Nice."

Carl said, "Looks like this guy was in the Army or maybe Marines, huh?"

"I don't think so; I got a hunch he was just a wannabe. My, my, *what do we have here*? Look at this, he's got two hand grenades on him, holy shit! Thank God we got him before he had a chance to use one of these on us. I'd like to find out where he got his hands on these, Jeez." Jack pocketed the grenades, saying, "All right, go find your radio stuff and whatever else you need. Don't even look at what they stashed in that wagon because it's all going home with us, including the car. And, Carl, don't be careless like these assholes and start carrying stuff outside. Just leave it in a pile in the front hallway until we leave. I'm going back into the woods where I can watch everything. Give me a yell when you're done. I'll go get your truck and we'll load her up." 15 minutes later, Jack pulled the truck up to the front of the house. Carl was standing on the front porch, looking down at the two dead bodies.

"What are we going do with their bodies?"

"We'll prop all three of them up against these porch stairs next to our no trespassing sign. The next looters might get the message." Carl looked like he was about to be sick.

A half hour later they arrived back home. Jack pulled the old sedan delivery into the driveway and Carl parked his truck behind him.

Jack got out and was admiring the old car. "This old Chevy wagon is really something, look at it. I think it's got a 327 in it. With that four on the floor, it's a fun car to drive, just like Lynne's car. It's got a full tank of gas too. There's a mess of extra ammo for our new rifles and four more grenades in the car." Jack noticed Carl was starting to shake, "What's wrong, Carl?"

"We just killed three men, Jack, and you're talking about an old car. I'm a chemistry teacher, not a killer. God almighty, what's happening to us?"

"It wasn't us, Carl, it was me. I killed them. That guy upstairs would have wasted us with his new toys as soon as he saw us. That's why he was up there."

"There has to be another way, other than ambushing them like we did. When will it stop?"

"Carl, our sign was clear! Rob this house and you get shot. They came armed to the teeth to confront and kill anyone who got in their way. They were amateurs but had plenty of firepower, so they felt like bad asses. The guy upstairs had an AR-15 with a bump stock on it. We get some time, I'll show you what a

307

bump stock does to a semi-auto. He would have cut you in two with it. Plus, he had that 9mm pistol and two grenades. Hand grenades, for God's sake! The first guy that I took out had an AR-15 within his reach on the car hood. They weren't out for some target practice. We're at war here. You think I want to do this? Believe me, I want to avoid any confrontation. I didn't want this. I don't enjoy killing people. Listen, I've got one more hump planned, and that's to go over to Downers Grove to retrieve Lynne's RV and whatever else her prepper husband stashed. After we get that, I plan for us to hunker down and stay put as much as we can to defend this place. I think within two weeks, most everyone in the state will be out of food. We have to get whatever we need right now, before the rest of the population wakes up and discovers they're permanently up shit creek. We don't want to be out roaming around, competing with them for the table scraps." He placed his hand on Carl's shoulder. "Are you going to be okay? Please don't be pissed at me. I'm depending on you."

"Yeah, I'll be all right. I'm not mad at you. I know it's the way it is."

"I hope so, because the first time you give someone like those pricks a break, they'll kill you." Jack didn't think Carl was convinced. Placing his hands on his hips, he shook his head and said, "Carl, let me tell you how I deal with it. Someplace, I don't know where, there's this great big box. I call it the scum-box. It's full of scumbags and assholes. There's this black force that doesn't like me and it lets these bastards loose. They want to harm me and my friends—so I've got the green light to kill 'em. I squash them like a big ass bug and I sleep fine. You can work it out any way you want in your head, but that works the best for me. We're the good guys and they're the bad guys, so keep it simple. Now, let's get the girls to help us unload this shit and then we'll stash this old car at Charlie's. I plan to have Jo go with me and Lynne tomorrow to get Lynne's RV." Jack held up the AR-15 with the bump stock, saying, "Watch Jo's face light up when I hand her this baby and those grenades."

Carl remained silent, and Jack said, "Come on, Carl, buck up. When we get the RV here, we'll park it out of sight behind Charlie's place. Lynne and I already discussed that maybe, if you're tired of sleeping on my couch, you might want to bunk in her RV for the summer. From what she's told me, it's old, but still nice inside. What do you think of that, huh?"

"That sounds good."

"All right, now remember, let's spare the girls the gory details and show them what we've got. I was thinking that sometime tomorrow you can work on your radios. Maybe we can find out what's going on in the rest of the country."

Jack was concerned not only with Carl, but with everyone's mental health. He'd have to continue to find ways to keep everyone enthused and busy. After everything was taken out of the old wagon, he and Carl spent the rest of the day boarding up some of the houses' lower windows. In both houses, there were low windows that were vulnerable and would make logical targets for intruders to access the house. The women complained about losing the daylight, but the thought of someone breaking into the house through an easily accessible window changed their minds.

When evening came, they were exhausted. Without power and electronic distractions to keep them up, everyone in the subdivision had started to go to bed early. With no television shows to watch, phone calls to make and no games to be played on the computer, some aspects of life were better. Once the sun set each night, the evening entertainment consisted of a camp fire.

Everything that was once taken for granted was now a major problem. In their suburban setting, most of their neighbors didn't even have enough wood lying around to build a decent campfire, let alone feed their fireplaces come winter. That night, as the family sat around the campfire, Carl discussed his plans for a shower and placement of the outhouses. They were joined by Ken and Ben. They discussed their fears of being away from their house, as they sat around the evening fire.

Before their bodies were even in the ground, neighbors were stripping Barry's house of food and supplies. Three times Jack had to run scavengers out of Jo and Kathy's vacated house. It was decided if Ken and his son had to leave their house during the day, someone from Jack's group would *house sit* for them. The luxury of being able to go somewhere, leaving your house and belongings unattended, had come to an abrupt end. Carl had found his uncle's old walkie talkies in his aunt's basement. Getting them working to communicate with Ken would have to be a priority. Jack decided that early the next morning, he, Lynne, and Jo would take Ellen's little VW to pick up Lynne's RV. He figured because of the car's small size; it would be the least likely vehicle to be confiscated. The campfire ended early for Jack and Lynne. Tomorrow at 3 AM would be the start of another rough day.

Jack had given up wearing a watch years ago. Without cellphones, keeping track of time had gone back to the days of noting the position of the sun. He set his battery-operated alarm clock to the sunset and roughly figured when 3 AM would be.

One of the last things Ellen had ever done was to gas up her little convertible. Having a running vehicle was one thing, having one with a full tank of gas was quite another. He put the top down and loaded up the gear they needed. The heavy-duty battery from Carl's truck, some jumper cables, a bolt cutter and a two-gallon can of gas filled the tiny trunk. With the little car's top down, the plan was to have Jo sit in the back, wielding her new toy, the AR-15. Jack would drive and Lynne would ride shotgun with her 12-gauge pump and Jack's Army 45 on the floor between them. They would drive fast, with lights out. To avoid being seen, Jack had disabled the car's brake and interior lights.

Lynne and Jo each had their hair tied back tight. Jo wore her army cover and a Kevlar vest. Jack wasn't surprised when she asked him for three of the hand grenades they had gotten out of the 57-station wagon.

He had to laugh when he saw Jo in the back of the Volkswagen. She looked like a tail gunner in an old WW 2 bomber and he was glad she was on their side. He almost felt sorry for anyone who tried to mess with her.

Other than the danger of their mission, it was a perfect night for a ride in a convertible with the top down. It was a cool, pitch black and moonless night. Every star in the sky stuck out like diamonds. As they rounded the corner by Al's, they were surprised to see Lois. She was standing alone in the dark, smoking a cigarillo on her front porch. Lois suspiciously eyed them as they drove past, not returning Lynne's wave.

Jo yelled, "What an old bitch, she can't even return your wave!"

Jack laughed, "She probably didn't know who we were."

They had just cleared the golf course and were approaching the street where Carl's aunt's house was, when they spotted headlights from at least three vehicles blocking the road, about a quarter mile ahead. Jack stopped the car, not wanting to take Ellen's noisy little convertible any closer. He sat up in his seat and looked over the top of the windshield. "It looks like two vehicles have got another car stopped in a road block. I expected to hit this kind of crap. All right, they haven't spotted us—this is why I disconnected the lights. What we're going to do is pull into the cemetery and cut through to the other side. There's a small service entrance that empties out onto a side street that will get us to Roosevelt Road. I've been in this cemetery during the day and I've seen it, but it was always locked."

Lynne asked, "How are we going to get through the gate if it's locked?"

"No problem. I brought a bolt cutter from Charlie's garage, just in case we had to cut a lock at the storage place. This is going to take us out of the way, but we don't need to get snagged in a road block. If this works, we'll take the cemetery route on the way back too." The cemetery was huge. It dated from the 1890s and was packed with huge tombstones and small mausoleums, with towering trees overhead. All the roads were laid out on angles. With no lights, it was easy to get lost driving down the tangle of narrow roads.

Lynne gave Jack a nervous glance, saying, "Being in a cemetery never bothered me, but with no lights, it's really creepy.: Jo said, "I think we're safer here than anywhere. Dead people don't shoot at you."

Jack pointed ahead, "There's the gate and it looks like it's got a padlock on it. Going to have to cut it to get out of here." Jack stopped the car, jumped out and snapped the padlock with the bolt cutters. A few moments later, they were out of the cemetery and driving down a side street.

They had figured out a route to the storage lot, avoiding the main roads, taking as many side streets as possible. Being as it was dark, there were only a few people walking the streets, most of them carrying a mound of possessions on their backs. Two young men tried to flag them down as Jack drove quickly by. One of them started swearing and attempted to throw whatever was handy at them. A shower of gravel hit their open car and rained down on them. Driving down the dark side streets without any headlights was treacherous, as abandoned cars were scattered about, some left in the middle of the street. After about 45 minutes, they pulled out onto Ogden Avenue, the last main street they would have to drive on. Ogden was a main road that started in the heart of Chicago and wound its way west through many suburbs. As early in the morning as it was, there was already a steady stream of tired-looking people walking down the center of it, escaping the riots raging in Chicago. They drove on Ogden less than a block, when they arrived at the storage yard.

The yard was a large one, consisting of two long rows of single garage size units, four rows of smaller units, and one row of double units. To the south, behind the double units, was a large open area containing everything from boats to construction equipment. Lynne's unit was number nine, a double size garage in the back row. She had already explained the layout of the place to Jack, so he zipped into the yard and immediately drove up to unit number nine.

Across from them was an open storage unit with a big moving truck parked next to it. Carrying the AR-15, Jo jumped out of the back of the car and checked it out. Finding the truck empty, she climbed up onto the top of it. From the truck's roof, she climbed onto the higher roof of the storage building and disappeared in the darkness. Jack got out and removed Carl's truck battery from the trunk, while Lynne opened the lock on her unit's door. Removing the padlock, she pushed the big metal door up, revealing a classic Dakota RV. It was the older, boxlike model, with the big elongated red —D— painted on its side. She stood guard with the shotgun in the doorway of the open unit, while Jack changed the old battery out.

She didn't have a clue what year her camper was, but Jack was glad it was old enough to still be equipped with a carburetor. He undid the wingnut on the air filter and poured about half a cup of gas down the carburetor, then jumped into the front seat.

She handed him a ring of keys containing a key with a big *D* stamped on it. Sliding it into the ignition, he prayed the old RV would start. Pumping the gas pedal several times, he gave it a turn. After several revolutions, the motor caught, but quickly died. His heart was beating fast. They'd be shit out of luck if it didn't start, and Jack definitely wanted this old RV. He didn't want to leave without it and all the emergency food Lynne's husband had stashed in it.

There was so much stuff, there was barely enough room for two people in the front seats. The entire vehicle was jammed to the ceiling with white plastic buckets labeled, *Freeze dried emergency food.* The buckets of emergency food made the trip well worth it and Jack was ecstatic... if only the old RV would start.

He quickly got out and poured another half cup of gas down the carburetor. Jumping back into the driver's seat, he again turned the ignition key, while rapidly pumping the gas pedal. "Please start, please start— come on baby, start for Lynne...." The engine popped off, coughed and started to stall. He feathered the crap out of the accelerator until it sputtered, but continued to run. Oily black smoke was pouring out of the exhaust. Checking the gas gauge, it read full. Jack felt his heart skip a beat and yelled, "We're on the home stretch, Lynne. In a few minutes, we're outta here."

Jumping out of the RV, he wanted to check out what else was stored in the garage. Returning to Lynne a few moments later, his words quickly tumbled out, "She's running like a top and has a full tank! There's a couple dozen plastic buckets in the back of the garage that are loaded with freeze dried food. I'm going to jam them inside the cab. There's also some boxes. You take a look around and see if there is anything else you want. We'll have to pull her out to hook up the snowmobile trailer."

He barely had the word *trailer* out of his mouth, when Jo yelled down from above, "Company coming—fast. Looks like three guys in a truck, south side; two in a car on the north. I'll take care of the truck." Jack did a quick look-see, as a car pulled between the two corner units, purposely blocking their exit.

 He muttered to Lynne, "We got company! Shit, I was afraid of something like this." He looked to the south end where an old 50's Ford pickup truck had stopped, effectively boxing them in.

"Jack, what are we going to do?"

"I'll try and talk to them to buy us some time. There's some ammo boxes stacked back there. Put'em in the RV, then look around for anything else you want. I'll keep an eye on the scumbags here. We haven't heard any gunfire, so they haven't found Jo. She's up on the roof over the pickup truck at the other end, and I'm betting the three guys sitting inside it don't know it. You load up, we'll wait these guys out."

They didn't have to wait long before they heard, "This is my storage yard and you're trespassing!"

Jack yelled back, "Good, so *you* own the place. We rented this garage from you and it's paid in full. We'll get our belongings and leave. Thanks for keeping an eye on our stuff. Bye, good talking to you buddy!"

"You're not going anywhere, smart guy! There's five of us, and just you and the lady. We're well armed and we got you boxed in. You ain't getting past us."

"What exactly do you want?"

"What we want is for you to come out and gently lay any weapons you got on the pavement, and then you can walk out of here. You can join the homeless folks hiking down Ogden Avenue. We'll take your guns, that cute little red convertible, and whatever that's so important in that garage. You can be safely on your way; *I give you my word*."

Taking a quick peek, he could see the man who was speaking. He was fat, and overconfident, leaning on the front fender of the driver's side of the old Buick. Another skinny fellow, wearing a white T shirt and smoking a cigarette, was doing the same on the passenger side. If they had any weapons, it was too dark to see them. Stepping back, Jack eyed the roof of the building across from them. Yep, Jo was up there. There was a dark figure hunched down on the roof's overhang, directly over the pickup truck. He had Jo's attention and flashed her the "wait one" sign.

Lynne whispered, "Oh my God, Jack, how are we going to get out of this one?"

"Those two cocky idiots are just leaning against their car. The guys in the pickup truck aren't out yet. They're just sitting there; they figure they got us. If they get out and spread out, we're screwed. So, we're going to have to make this quick. It's a long shot, they're pretty far away, but I should at least hit the fat guy who's doing the talking. Even if I just wound him, it'll be enough. Jo is about to take care of the truck, so you get back and get down on the floor. Knowing her, she'll use a grenade, so once I start shooting, I got about five seconds to duck back in."

Jack figured that, since they were idiots, he'd ask them a stupid question. While fatso was contemplating a smart-ass answer, he'd pop out and unload at them with the 45. He gave it a try. He yelled, "Hey, what day is it?" He got off six shots towards the two men leaning against the hood of the old car, then ducked back for cover. About a second later, the pickup truck exploded. One of Jack's slugs hit home, smacking the skinny man dead center in his chest. Jo had dropped two grenades onto the truck when he started shooting. The first one bounced off the pickup's roof, then slid down the windshield onto the hood. Having never seen a hand grenade, the three men sat there staring at it in disbelief. When it exploded, it nearly decapitated them with shrapnel and shattered windshield glass. The second grenade landed in the bed of the truck, sending shrapnel through the back of the cab and into their spines. Jack shot a glance at the truck, and it was wrecked. The hood was hanging halfway off, blown to shreds, and it's three occupants didn't look healthy. A strong gasoline odor instantly filled the air. Amazingly, the truck wasn't burning.

The other two men who, a moment before, had been so confident, were laying on the ground. At least two of his bullets hit their car's windshield. Jack reloaded with a fresh magazine and sprinted towards them.

The heavy man who did the tough talking was bleeding from his arm, slightly grazed by one of Jack's bullets. As Jack ran up to him, he came to his knees and started pleading for his life. His James Dean look-alike partner, who not even a minute ago was so confidently leaning against the Buick's hood, was barely alive. A bright red patch of blood covered the front of his white shirt. Jack stood in front of the kneeling man, the 45 in his hand.

"Stand up and quit sniveling like a little baby, you're not even hit. Come on! I don't have much time, let's go." He herded the man towards their storage locker, telling Lynne, "If he moves, shoot him. I'll finish loading up the RV."

The man was crying and pleaded with Lynne, "I'm hurt, please don't let him kill me. Oh God, please! I was going to let you go."

Jack finished loading the RV and confronted the man, eyeing him with contempt. "I should have killed you! How on earth did I miss your fat ass and manage to hit skinny over there? What's your name?"

"Larry...Larry Berkmann."

Jack motioned to Lynne, "If Mr. Berkmann says one more word, shoot an ear off and don't miss and hit his head. I need him to help me hitch the snowmobile trailer to the RV." Jack pulled the RV out and left it running. Confronting Larry, who was still crying, Jack said, "Quit crying or she'll shoot you. You're going to help me move this snowmobile trailer out and hitch it up to the RV. Then you're going to stand there very peacefully while I finish up. Got it?"

Like a fat bobble-head doll, Larry quickly nodded his big head.

Jack looked around and was not surprised to see cases of various types of ammunition stacked everywhere. There were no weapons, but the extra ammo was like winning the lottery.

When they were loaded, Jack and Larry wheeled the snow- mobile trailer out of the garage and hitched it to the back of the RV.

"Well, porky, we're done having fun, so we're ready to go." He pointed to his car, "Hey, what year is your car?"

"It's a '62. If you want it, please take it, it's a good car and it's a classic. Are you going to let me go?"

"Tell me something, did you close and lock the yard gate?"

"Yes... Yes, I did."

"Why? Why would you do that?

"I don't know...I just did...."

Jack pointed the 45 at the man's forehead." You bastard. You wanted us to die, trapped in here, didn't you? You planned to kill us!"

Rapid fire, Larry pleaded with Jack. "**No**, I swear to God, no! We only wanted the car and whatever guns you had. We have two 20-gauge shotguns, that's it! They're pieces of shit. We only had a few shells. With you boxed in, we figured you'd give up. We'd have let you walk out. For the love of God, you gotta believe me! Please don't kill me, mister, please. I'm begging you. Look, I've got some food stashed away. It's out back, you can have it all!"

" Anyone else with you?"

"No, just me. I swear!"

"I hope you're telling the truth, because if you have a friend hiding somewhere, I won't like it."

"No, it's just me and you guys, I swear to God."

"All right. Listen up, Larry, cause here's the plan. When we leave, you're going to move your fat little legs towards that gate, *real fast*—we'll be right behind you. You're going to unlock it and let us out. If you lied to me and have any friends lurking around here, tell them not to shoot, because *no matter what. . . no matter what, Larry. . .*you'll be dead, I promise. Unlock the gate, and open it wide. We leave, and you live. That's the deal."

Larry bobbed his head quickly up and down, sputtering, "You leave, I live—got it!"

"How we looking up there, Jo?"

"Everything is clear, but it's getting light fast. Lots of people walking the street. I'm coming down."

Larry's classic car's engine started knocking. Black smoke poured from the exhaust. It misfired, gave out one last gasp and quit, with a loud backfire.

"Looks like one of my bullets hit your engine, Larry. Too bad, I wanted to add an old Buick to my collection. All right, start for the gate and no funny business or like they say in the old westerns, 'You'll join your pals.'"

Jack got into the RV and Lynne drove the VW, with Jo playing tail gunner in the back.

Larry opened the gate and the RV and trailer went through first, followed by the little VW convertible.

Jo gave Larry a big smile and the middle finger.

The ride home was surprisingly peaceful. Jack followed the same route, again cutting through the cemetery. Entering his street, he backed the RV into Ronnie's drive. Opening her garage door, he backed the snowmobile trailer into her empty garage and unhitched it.

With the snowmobiles stowed away in the garage, he pulled the R.V. into Charlie's yard and parked it alongside the back of the house, announcing, "Carl has a new home!" As Jack exited the RV, Laura rushed up to him.

"Dad! We were so worried, is everyone all right?"

The whole family was outside and everyone was hugging one another. Carl and Laura entered the RV together. Laura said to Carl, "Carl, we're going to fix this up so cute!"

Lynne glanced at Jack and smiled, raising her eyebrows.

Jack totally missed it, saying, "Hope you folks don't mind, but I had a lousy night's sleep. I'm going to grab something to eat, then catch a little shut eye. Don't let me sleep any more than an hour."

Jack slept longer than he had in the last two weeks. He dreamt of the river and an old black man peeling an apple *"Don't waste time boy!"* The three dead men they left on Carl's front porch was in it, and so was Don... *"I'm sorry, Jack,"*

315

What was there to be sorry about? The old black man...I know him... He smelled bacon and fresh coffee ... *That wasn't a dream.*

He woke up, instinctively glancing at his clock radio, it's display was dark. A week and a half ago he would have gotten up, took a pee and flushed the toilet. He would turn the shower on and let the water get just right, before stepping in. He'd soap up, wash his hair, shave and stand under the hot water as long as he pleased. He'd would get out, dry off with a fresh, clean towel, brush his teeth and get into clean clothes. He said to himself, "Them days are over." He laid there a minute longer, dreading the day ahead. Finally getting up, he sat on the edge of the bed, staring at himself in the dresser mirror. Already he had a great start of a beard and needed a haircut. Part of his dream was still in his head, the old black guy sitting on the river bank... ***"Don't waste a minute boy!"***

Rubbing his eyes, Jack ran his fingers through the greasy stubble on his chin. *I feel like taking a swim in the river. Maybe I should go over to Barry's house and jump in his swimming pool. Yes! The swimming pool, what a great idea...*

After taking a leak, he grabbed the piss bucket and emptied it out his window, while looking over into Barry's backyard.

There were several people gathered around Barry's pool, all holding various buckets and containers. Barry had gotten an above-ground swimming pool a couple of summers back. Now people Jack didn't even recognize were dipping their buckets into it. He watched a guy filling one of those big 5-gallon clear plastic water bottles with the pool water. *I wonder if that idiot is going to drink that water?* Others were filling 5-gallon pails and carrying them away. Jack sadly shook his head thinking, *so much for taking a cool dip in the old swimming hole...* There were people walking out of Barry's house with clothing and boxes of stuff. One guy was carrying out the big screen TV. Jack said aloud, "What an idiot." There were also two women. He hadn't noticed them at first, but they were standing near the rear fence, well apart from the others, spying into his backyard. Normally something like that would only raise his curiosity, but today it worried him.... *What are those women looking at?* Smelling the bacon and fresh coffee wafting up from downstairs, he knew exactly what they were looking at, and what they were thinking.

Everything that folks took for granted was already running out. Houses left unattended were stripped clean. He took another look at Barry's pool and thought, *What the heck, before it gets dark, we'll have a little pool party this evening, while that pool still has some water in it.*

The smell of the bacon lured Jack down to the kitchen. Through the sink window, he could see Lynne was outside using the grill...*God, what are we going to do when we run out of propane?*

Sticking his head out the back door, his eyes searched for the two curious women behind the fence, but they were gone.

Lynne smiled at him, "Good afternoon, sleepy head. Coming down for lunch?"

"I smelled the coffee and bacon. I didn't want to sleep that long, I figured it was still morning."

"Nope, it's well after noon. You were out like a light, so we let you sleep. I'm using up the bacon, this is the last of it. Actually, we're having hamburgers with cheese and bacon on top. No buns though. Found a loaf frozen of rye bread in Charlie's freezer, we'll use that in place of hamburger buns. I'm also using up the last of the frozen French fries. I figure Charlie's big freezer will be just about empty in three days. Just as well, running the generator for a few hours a day to keep the freezer cold is eating up a lot gas. It's a trade-off, I guess, we can't waste the food. How'd you sleep?"

"I slept good, crazy dreams though. How is everything going today? **Please** tell me there are no problems..."

"Knock on wood, none so far. Carl got two of those old walkie-talkies working, and he gave one to Ken. He says those three old radios are junk. The wax capacitors are shot, whatever that means? But at least if there's any trouble, we can call each other for help." She removed a pan of sizzling bacon from the grill and set it on the picnic table. "That was terrible at the storage place this morning. What we did to those men.... It should really be bothering me, but it's not—at least not in the way it should be. It's just like those three drugs addicts in the nursing home. I don't like the way we're becoming, all this constant violence. Carl told me about what you said; about there being a big box somewhere, filled with bad people. You're right, it's like they're purposely being sent to us. Instead of helping one another, people are turning into animals. That man, Larry. Do you think he really owned that place? And if he did, why couldn't he just let us get our belongings and leave?"

Jack was slowly shaking his head. "Three men died because of their greed. They blocked us in and we had no alternative. What more can I say? I don't understand it myself, but I can explain why you're not feeling terribly bad about it. It's because for the first time in your life, you can fight back using lethal force. For our entire lives, most of us have been at the mercy of bullies, thieves, scumbags, you name it, but now, anyone can fight back. Someone messes with you, you don't have to wait to become a victim and fill out a useless police report. Just shoot them dead, right on the spot. One less scumbag. This shit-hit-the-fan thing has been great for victims. At least now the victims can shoot back and just walk away. No cops, no lawyers, no trials—only justice."

Lynne poured him a cup of coffee, saying, "Well, you're a ray of sunshine. That really cheers me up." Pouring herself a cup, Lynne shook her head, "I don't care about justice. I just wish people would leave us alone. Why does it have to be this way?"

317

"I don't know, but it is. We have to watch and be careful with everything we do. Speaking of watching things, Barry's yard is sure busy. People are taking water from his pool. I noticed a couple women looking over our fence. I think they were watching you grill. I don't like that. It won't be long and we're going to be the only ones around here with food and water." Jack took the cup and deeply inhaled the fresh coffee smell, saying, "Thank God we got plenty of this stuff." Hesitating for a moment, he said, "You know, I don't take any of this lightly, but then again, I don't feel guilty about what we did to Larry and his buddies. When you get right down to it, Larry didn't look like a bad guy. But him and his buddies made a bad decision. They chose to rob us, and even if they did let us go, it might have been a death sentence for us trying to walk back here. We did nothing to them. If anyone should be feeling remorse this morning, it's Larry. It was a scary situation and it's over. You and I shouldn't give it a second thought, other than we played it right. There were only three of us and we put one person out of sight, up on the roof. We won. They lost. You certainly shouldn't feel guilty for not having a great amount of remorse for them. We could have taken the food he said they had. At least we left him with that." Jack picked up his cup of coffee, taking a sip. "So, come on, cheer up. Tell me, what is everyone up to today?"

"I guess you're right, now that you put it that way. It's just so crazy everyday.. .. I'm glad you're in a good mood. Carl and Laura have cleaned out the Dakota. He went over to his condo with Kathy and Laura to get the rest of his things."

"They went over there without Jo? Oh, God, they shouldn't have done that by themselves. Where's Jo?"

"She's over at Ken's with Bobby. Bobby just loves her. Carl said they'd be back in time for lunch. Ken and Ben will be eating over here too. Jack, don't underestimate Carl. Believe it or not, he's a lot like you, a little smarter maybe."

Jack laughed, "That's a funny one, but you're right, Carl is smarter than me. I like the kid, I really do."

"I'm happy you feel that way about him, and I'm glad you're in such a good mood today because there's something else, something we need to talk about."

Jack immediately got the *"what now?" feeling,* and sat down in a lawn chair with his coffee. "Oh boy, I knew there'd be something, I might as well be comfortable. Now what's up?"

Lynne pulled up a chair and sat facing him, leaning in close. "These last couple weeks have been crazy and we've grown close. I'm 42 years old and I feel like I've known you for all of them."

"No kidding, I feel the same way. Good Lord, look what we've been through. That's just the way it's going to be, I guess, we're bound to grow close."

"Exactly, Jack, I'm glad you understand that. I want to tell you something and I don't want you to get angry."

"Oh boy, I was expecting something like this. Thank God I'm sitting down. You're thinking about moving out, aren't you? You have your Dakota and all that survival food now...."

"Jack, no— it's not about me. It's about Laura. She's not a little girl anymore, but you treat her like one..."

"She just turned 18 years old."

"That's what I'm talking about. These last two weeks have been like dog years. Look how close we've all become in such a short time. Laura asked me to talk to you, because she's afraid to."

"Afraid of me? Why would my little girl be afraid to talk to me?" Jack started laughing.

"She wants to move into the RV with Carl, they're in love."

"***What?***"

"They love each other, Jack. I've talked to both of them. Jo and Kathy have too. I think they've been in love since day one."

"**Aw Jeezz.**"

She wanted to tell you something else, something that happened."

"Oh my God... did Carl—oh jeez. **Is she pregnant**?"

"Will you just listen? Do you remember the man at the home center with the pitchfork sticking out of his back?"

"How could I ever forget the sight of that, he looked like a stuck pig... *why*?"

"That man was about to kill Carl. Laura ran up behind him and stabbed him with that pitchfork. She killed him to save Carl."

"Oh my God! My Laura did that?"

"Jack, no matter what, there will be no separating those two, ever. They want to get married."

"Aw no...one day, all I ask for is just *one day. One day* without any problems...."

"Shh! They're back now, so you be nice to them... *I mean it*...

They're going to be moving in the RV together tonight, so please, Jack, be nice."

"Aw jeezz."

GOODBYE NEIGHBORS

CHAPTER 3 4

Four more days had gone by, and Jack had accepted the fact that he was powerless over any of the events around him and that included the emotions of two young people falling in love. Thirteen days after the shit hit the fan, Laura married Carl, the only documentation of their marriage being a notation in the family Bible. Every aspect of life had changed since the day of the EMP, and that included marriage. Lynne's RV became Carl and Laura's first home.

Jack never got to have his "pool party." There was a steady procession of neighbors trekking into Barry's backyard, taking water from his swimming pool. If there were any indicators of how desperate the situation was about to become, the depletion of water from the neighborhood's swimming pools was it. People were walking down to the river with their 5-gallon buckets. It was their only source of water. Within one week of his death, Barry's pool was collapsed, and his house was stripped clean of any consumables. Jack figured they had taken enough chances with their forays gathering supplies and that their luck was bound to run out. They unanimously decided they would not venture further than a mile from their houses. Everyone who came back from town told hair-raising stories of being harassed and sometimes robbed by the refugees escaping from Chicago and Cook County. As far as Chicago and its close neighboring suburbs, they'd become killing fields.

Jack and his new family started "digging in." There was much work to be done and it would have to be built from materials at hand. The days of running out to a store were gone forever. Daylight was precious, and without electric lights, not a minute of it was wasted. Carl built more rain barrels and the outside shower. Charlie's septic tank was a life saver. They were able to use his bathtub and even his toilets. All they had to do was bring buckets of water in and let gravity do the rest. Jack figured old Charlie's place was the only one on the block that had any type of plumbing system still working.

The people whose homes were connected to the municipal sewer system had continued to use their toilets. After about the third week, even the houses that hadn't flooded had raw sewage backing up their basement drains. Everyone was out of clean drinking water. All the frozen food was long gone and folks were well into the canned goods they had left. The only people doing outdoor grilling were the ones who had extra propane tanks. The sound of generators was heard less, the sounds of gunshots were heard more. Two more families had committed suicide at the end of week three. Al's two missing neighbors, the Connors, were never heard from again. Like Barry's house, their home was stripped clean.

On the late afternoon of day 18, Jack took a walk down to Al's. There was an entirely different air about the block. Most of the houses were vacant. The scattered mess from the big storm had never been cleaned up. Other than a few blue plastic tarps on top of some roofs, the houses on the next block that were damaged from the storm went unrepaired. The whole neighborhood looked like a junkyard. There were no kids playing basketball, no one cutting their grass and the music had permanently stopped at Al's. As off the beaten path that their subdivision was, strangers were often seen walking down their street. The smell of outdoor grilling was an open invitation to ask for a handout, so it had to be done secretly, hidden from sight. As he neared Al's house, he saw him grilling by the far side of his garage, his friendly good nature apparently gone. Al was having words with two greasy looking fellows, who could not keep their eyes off the two slabs of sizzling meat he was grilling.

The men were too busy eyeballing the steaks to notice Jack walking up behind them. Jack didn't hear what they were talking about, but Al's body language said it all. The men were filthy, and from five feet away, Jack could smell them.

The taller one said to Al, "You're not very neighborly, are you, friend?"

Both men turned around startled, when Jack said, "I'm less neighborly and we're not friends, so start running." Jack was out of arms reach and had his Dad's 45 leveled at them.

Both of them took off in the direction of the golf course. Just before they disappeared into the brush, the tall one yelled, "Up yours, asshole!"

Jack said to Al, "You better start cooking indoors, or at least completely out of sight in the back. In a couple days, they won't be *asking* for a meal."

Jack still had the 45 semi-automatic out, and Al pointed to it with his spatula, "You scared the shit outta them two with that. How come you're not carrying Little Red? I thought you were a revolver guy."

"I own two handguns and I like them both. Guns are tools, Al. You have to pick out the right one for the job. This week it's the 45. What I should be carrying is an M16. That's how bad it's getting."

"You got that right, big guy. It is getting bad, those two were scary looking. Thanks for running them assholes out. Why don't you have a seat, Jack. You want one of these steaks?"

"Thanks, but no, we still have some left ourselves, but I will sit down. We'll be out of our frozen stuff soon. We're at the bottom of Charlie's freezer." Jack holstered the 45 and sat down across from Al.

"Yeah, big guy, fresh meat is going to become scarce. Just think, somewhere out west there are cattle dying of starvation because no one can ship them feed, and they got no way to ship the cattle here. Go figure, huh? What a screwed-up mess." Al flipped his steaks and seasoned them. "Hey Jack, sorry about our little disagreement last week. You know me, always got my big mouth going. I guess I'm just old school. Look at them steaks, huh, they're going to be scarce."

Al closed the lid to his grill and sat in a lawn chair next to Jack. He pointed to the next street over. "Speaking of barbecuing, have you done your walk around the block yet?" Jack shook his head.

"Well, after you leave here, you take your little walk. When you get over on the next block where those two Korean guys live, Long and Dong, or whatever their names are, take a look at what they've got on the old spit. Jack, I've been a butcher and in the grocery business all my life. I've worked in meat, deli, frozen, you name it. I'll tell you something, that ain't a lamb or a calf, and sure as hell ain't a pig they got on the old rotisserie."

"What do you think they're roasting?"

"Let me put it to you this way, big guy, *Lassie* ain't coming home tonight." Al started laughing so hard he dropped his spatula.

"Coming to that already? Jeezz."

"Tell you what, Jack, right now I wish I owned a kennel full of big dogs. Dogs will eat anything, as long as it's flesh. They're going to be worth their weight in gold a month from now. Who needs a freezer? It's like your chickens, as long as you can keep them alive, it's fresh meat. You get a bunch of dogs, feed them any kind of meat, even stuff that's going bad. They're happy as a pig in shit."

Jack heard barking coming from Al's garage. He looked at Al, raising his eyebrows, "No?"

Al smiled, "Yeah, I got six mutts and one is about to have puppies! I'm going to be a grandfather, Jack!"

Jack leaned forward in his lawn chair; his hands folded on his lap. "What the heck are you feeding them, Al? People are already eating dog food, and you can't even get ahold of that."

Al was still smiling. Like I said, dogs will eat anything, even each other's shit. There's plenty of food around that you won't eat. You know, spoiled meat and such…. Anyway, hey, you're a farmer, and I'm in the meat business, kind of like a rancher… You think I would look good in a cowboy hat?"

"Raising dogs for food? My God, Al. We get through this and you open your restaurant—I don't know if I'll want to eat there."

"Jack, someday this shit will be over, in the meantime, if you can find a product to sell, whether it's bullets, booze, cigarettes, or *any* kind of meat, as bad as this shit is, you will become *rich* my friend. People still have plenty of cash, silver and gold, but they're hungry. You can't eat silver and gold. Believe me, whether it's ground up Fido, or Mickey Rat, they'll be eating it and will gladly pay for it. Mark my words, Jacko, there are people who are going to make lots of money off this shit-hit-the-fan bullshit. When the smoke clears, they'll be on top and, big guy, I intend to be one of them." Al saw Jack suddenly eying the grill. Laughing, Al said, "No, Jack, that ain't Rover, it's grade 'A' corn fed beef."

Jack changed the subject, "Okay… enough talk about your new pets. What about these FEDUP centers that you said were going to be set up? Have you heard anymore, or was it all just bullshit?"

Al wiped the metal spatula on his pants leg and removed the steaks from the grill, placing them on a plate, saying, "No it wasn't *all* bullshit, just most of it. They're going to be set up, but they're running behind. They'll be nothing but a great big camp. It'll be fun for all. It doesn't sound like some-thing old Al and Lois would enjoy. Word is all these riots everywhere are holding things up. The other thing is, I hear the Midwest is the only place that's messed up. The east and west coasts are fine, but the Feds are worried shitless about all the nuclear plants in the Midwest blowing to kingdom come. For the time being, all their resources are going towards securing those plants. The government has a broadcasting ban, or block, on the radio stations. They don't want people getting freaked out worse than they are."

"Al, where do you hear all this?"

"You know me, Jacko, I talk to lots of people. By the way, me and Lois are blowing this place in a couple days. Those nuke plants cook off, I don't want my Lois looking like a fucken glow stick, she's skinny enough. I got people a little west of here who have a finished basement that's not full of the neighborhood's BMs. Going to stay with them for a while, they're going to help us move. Hey, it's time for me and Lois to eat—talk to you later, Farmer Jack."

Two days later, Al left. He had the Old's convertible loaded to overfilling and two box trucks, with two guys Jack had never seen before helping them move. Jack tried to stop him.

"Al, you haven't been out there like I have. It was crazy a couple weeks ago. It's got to be really nuts now. People will kill for a can of beans, and I'm not kidding."

"Jack, don't you worry about little old Al and Lois. We ain't going too far and we'll be with old friends. If we get hungry or something goes wrong, I'll head old Nancy over to one of those big government camps they're building and we'll be fine. The only thing that bothers me is having to use my old convertible here as a truck like this. Damn, I just got Nancy painted. Probably will have to get her repainted again when this bullshit is over. I bought her back when I was a senior in high school, back in 1968. Hell, Lois and I went on our first date in her." Al started laughing, "Had the old top down that night, heh, heh, heh…"

"You be careful, Al. You get in trouble, we'll be here."

"I know you will be, Jack. You're a good friend. I wish everyone was like you. You keep working on your little farm, planting them tators. Carl was showing me yesterday how everything is sprouting up. I'll be back, Jack, maybe next spring. You can cook us up a turnip or something… and remember what I told you, be careful who you take into your house. Don't trust nobody."

"Come on, Al, don't start on that again. I'm not sore about you not taking Jo and Kathy in. You and I have our differences and that's the crux of the thing. People have to get along, like the book says, 'Take the plank out of your eye before pointing out the splinter in your neighbors.'"

"The book—you and your book. Tell you what, Jack, look at your book's cover upside down, particularly at the cross on it. What do you see?"

"What do you mean, what do I see?"

"You see an anchor, Jack, that's what you see, and it's no coincidence." Al moved close and faced Jack. "Nothing is hidden, Jack, you just have to be able to see it, cause it's all there. Don't let that book be an anchor because anchors, my friend, will hold you back. That's what Christianity about, it keeps the peasants in place. Lois and I used to be Catholic. We got the message a *long* time ago. You keep working that farm you got going and hey, take this, it's my front door key. Tell those two girls they can party here while we're gone, if they don't mind the smell. No hard feelings. How's that for being neighborly? I would appreciate it, though, if you kept an eye on my place and keep them looters out of it, if you can. I'm taking anything of value with me. See you later, big guy, and remember, don't be so trusting. It'll be your downfall."

He bid goodbye to Al and continued his walk around his neighborhood. He hadn't walked three houses past Al's when he saw three couples standing on the sidewalk ahead of him. They had the look of desperation on their faces and, as Jack walked towards them, all of them uneasily looked at him and then back to each other. One of the women gestured in the direction of Jack and mumbled something to the others.

As he walked past them, he felt more than a hint of belligerence, especially as he had to leave the sidewalk and walk on the grass to get around them. When he was about ten feet past, one of the men spoke up. "Hey, you're the one on the next block who's got all those big barrels in your yard, aren't you?" Jack paused and turned his head toward them, but didn't answer. "We see you people watering stuff, just wasting it. You know, everybody around here is out of water. Where the hell are you getting it from and what gives you the right to waste it watering plants?"

Jack was all out of nice, but tried his best to keep his cool. Stopping in his tracks, he slowly turned around. The fellow doing the talking had set the tone, but Jack did his best to hold his tongue. He was already mad that they made him step off the public sidewalk to get around them. He said, "Just in case you missed it, we recently had the mother of all rain storms. I like rain barrels; they save the free water that runs off my roof. Did you ever think of trying something like that?"

"Who do you think you are? Don't get cocky with me. You think because you walk around here with that gun on your hip, you're fucking Wyatt Earp and we're supposed to be afraid of you. Here's a news flash asshole, we're not afraid of you. How about instead of strutting around here like you own the place, you learn to share with your neighbors?"

Jack didn't get a chance to answer the guy. One of the women, a short, plump lady, snottily said, "It's not fair that you have drinking water and we don't. We have little children. You're just wasting that water, pouring it on your *fucking* plants! We know you people are hoarders too." She pointed towards Jo and Kathy's house. "We saw all those buckets of food and supplies you took out of their house. You've got it all squirreled away, while we go without. I've seen you and your family in church. You have the nerve to call yourselves Christians? You disgust me. All of you will go to hell!"

Jack was pissed. He said, "So, because I have the foresight to stockpile some emergency supplies, have some water and food, and you don't, that makes me the bad guy?"

The other woman shouted, "Foresight? That's bullshit—you're a hoarder who only cares about himself!"

She was pushing it, but Jack kept his calm. "That makes you feel like you're a victim, right? That makes you feel entitled to the food and supplies we bought with our own money, years ago—mind you." She tried to interrupt, but Jack talked over her. "Tell me something, fellow Christians, did you offer any help to those two women, when the roof got blown off their house? Or were you part of that group that just walked by and ignored them? You still had plenty of food and water back then, didn't you? I'll bet you had a roof on your house too. I'd tell you where to shove it...it's really deep, but that wouldn't be Christian. Have a nice day, folks."

Jack had barely started taking his walk and was regretting it. He continued on, leaving them standing on the sidewalk, yelling and swearing at him. There were too many desperate people out, and it was clear that most of them were completely out of everything. He just kept walking until he was across the street from the vacant farmland. Undeveloped and open, for at least a mile, the fertile ground had not yet been covered with concrete and houses. By now, it should have been planted with beans and corn. He stopped and faced the open land, thinking about how many farms across the country would go unplanted that summer, guaranteeing famine next year. The land was open and so peaceful, he couldn't help but stare at it. It was like it was trying to tell him something. *Yeah,* he thought, *Everyone in this subdivision should be planting their own garden on it... or at least in their yard.* He turned away from the empty farmland and continued walking. The houses across from the open land were quiet and most them were vacant, their owners having fled to the less populated areas of Iowa and Wisconsin. All of the vacant homes were now fair game and being broken into. Water heaters were being drained of every precious drop. Paper towels and toilet paper were top on the list of the *must have* items. Everything that people had taken for granted was running out, and every vacant home was being searched by its desperate neighbors.

As Jack walked past Barry's house, he interrupted two women who had hurriedly exited out the front door, each awkwardly carrying large boxes. He wondered, *The house was already looted, what could possibly be left in there to take?* The front door had been wide open since Barry's death, and hungry neighbors had long since carried away anything of value. If it was edible, drinkable or consumable, it was gone hours after his death. The women nervously passed Jack on the sidewalk, never raising their eyes to meet his. Everyone was quickly becoming scavengers of their neighbor's misfortunes.

He was almost past Barry's house when he met the infamous Jim, "*the biker.*" The decked-out motorcycle of Barry's neighbor sat in the driveway of the next house, along with four more custom bikes behind it. "Jim the Biker," as he was known, lived directly behind Charlie's house and, unfortunately, next door to Barry. He had caused Barry untold hours of grief, with their loud bikes and wild parties. Jack was thankful they lived on the next street and not right next door to him. Jim's attached garage was open and several leather clad bikers were standing inside. One of them, dressed in black leather head to toe, sauntered out towards Jack. Jack had never talked to him, but recognized him as the one who tormented Barry, and he was not anxious to meet the infamous Jim. Dressed in an open black leather vest, Jack could see the man's shirtless chest was covered in tattoos. Jack slowed his pace, thinking, *Oh shit, not another asshole....*

Jim said, "Hey, you're the guy who lives behind us—right?"   Before Jim even opened his mouth, Jack had made the decision that he didn't like him. He didn't like the way he looked and didn't like the man's opening line. He didn't appear armed, but who knew what was under that black leather vest? Jack's eyes made a quick sweep of the bikers standing in the garage. One aggressive move... and his 45 would be out of its holster, pointed at the center of Jim's chest. He glanced between the houses, looking into his own backyard. Spotting Jo, he jerked his head back and hoped she had seen him. Jack didn't reply to the man, because he didn't have to. His body language was clear and it said, "Stay away from me." He was fed up with neighbor's demands and wasn't going to take anymore crap from people, especially leather-clad, tattooed bikers.

Picking up on Jack's unfriendliness, Jim said, "Sorry, I didn't mean to bother you. I know everything is going crazy. Let me start over. My name's Jim."

Jim pointed to his house. "I live there with my girlfriend, Lorretta. I guess I should have introduced myself long before this. I wanted to ask you if you could spare some propane, or maybe let us use your grill. We have two boxes, each with a dozen sirloin steaks. They're still cold, but completely defrosted. I'll be tossing them out if we don't grill them up tonight. I'll give you a dozen steaks, plus a case of beer, for your trouble—the beer isn't cold, but it's cool. It's in the freezer with the steaks. We've got some dynamite cherry and apple pies that are also defrosted, plus a bunch of fresh onions and potatoes to cook with the steaks. One of the girl bikers sauntered out from the garage. Like Jim, she was clad head to toe in black leather, but there was something about her that looked familiar.

"Hey Jack, I didn't know you lived around here."

Jack had to do a double take. It was Anne O'Sullivan.

"You're going to need a haircut and a shave, big guy."

Anne owned O'Sullivan's barbershop in town and regularly cut Jack's hair. Jack relaxed, saying, "That's right, you told me your boyfriend rode a motorcycle and hung out with a gang of bikers."

Jim said, "Aw—we're no gang, we're friendly. We just love to ride our bikes and have fun." Jim nodded towards Barry's house "I guess we were a little rough on Barry. I wouldn't wish what happened to him on anyone. I'm a computer systems manager who also loves old motorcycles. Let me introduce everybody, looks like you already know Anne." A huge man grabbed Jack's hand and shook it vigorously, saying, "I'm Fats, glad to meet you."

Jim said, "Fats is the cook over at Jimmy's Barbecue. This is Loretta, my girlfriend, she works in a daycare…. So, you thought we were some kind of outlaw group, huh? That's funny, I've heard the same thing about you and your group."

At that moment they were joined by Jo and Carl. Jo had seen Jack talking to the bikers from the backyard and gotten his message. Jo was carrying a 12-gauge shotgun. She stopped a few feet away from Jim with Carl next to her. Kathy and Ben appeared from the far corner of Jim's house. All of them were armed and not looking friendly.

Jack held his hand up and waved to Jo, saying, "No problems, Jo, we're just talking. Let me introduce Jim."

Jim nervously said, "Good Lord, you thought we were going to start trouble with you? No way, we don't bother anyone, but lots of people bug us. You must have been talking to Barry and Liz, right? We never got along with them, but— like I said, it's terrible what happened to them and I hope they get who did it. I wasn't even home when it happened. Barry and Liz could be a real pain in the ass, but I would never do them any harm. People are going crazy, just plain crazy, and nobody is safe. We're just ordinary people. We're bikers on weekends, but we're no gang."

Jack said, "Sorry, Jim, that's what I get for judging people, bad habit I got. I just expected you were going to give me trouble and signaled Jo to come over."

Jack nodded his head towards his group, saying, "This is part of our clan. No gang either, just one big, happy family." Everyone approached and introduced themselves.

Jim introduced two more people who walked out of the garage. "This is Lainie, she's a nurse at the Berwyn Veteran's Hospital. And this is Pat, she works at Jimmy's with Fats, and that's her brother, Leo, he's Anne's husband"

"The Berwyn VA?" It was Kathy. "What department?"

The tall leather-clad woman named Lainie turned around, "I work in the metabolic lab, on the tenth floor of the main hospital. I've been there 15 years."

Ben said, "Jimmy's Barbecue, that place is dynamite!"

Fats patted his belly saying, "Yeah, no kidding!"

Jack said, "Jim, if you want, bring your chow over to our place in about a half hour. We'll have the grills ready to go and you can cook up your steaks. We'll eat with you, and we appreciate you offering them to us. Sorry again that I was unfriendly. We've had one too many run-ins with some real assholes, and they weren't dressed in black leather. What are your plans? Are you going to try and stick it out here?"

"No, we're leaving. Haven't you heard about the nuke plants?"

Jack said, "Only rumors."

"Them things could blow. We don't want to be anywhere near the northern part of the state if they cook off. Tomorrow morning, we're riding up 90, to Loretta's sister's place in Wisconsin, just outside of Janesville. Then we're all heading north to a place Lainie has up near the Wisconsin Dells. It used to be her parents' vacation home. Lots of good hunting and fishing up there. We'll go up there and sit this thing out."

Jack looked at Jim thoughtfully. "You guys been riding your bikes around with no problems?"

"Yeah, they're lots better than a car. Can't carry much on them, but you don't get stuck on some road blocked by abandoned vehicles. We spot trouble, we can cut through somebody's backyard if we have to. Also, they're easy on gas. Most of our bikes were parked in garages when that EMP thing hit, plus they're all older and have been modified. We haven't had any trouble with any of them. I'll tell you what, if you can spare say—a couple shotguns or a pistol and some ammo, I could turn you on to a nice bike. It's a good one, it's a '47 Harley. It's over in the industrial park, in storage. We'd take it with us, but we've got no one to ride it. If we leave it behind, it'll probably get stolen. Lainie is the only biker. The other girls have never driven a bike and are afraid to take it all the way up north. It belonged to one of our group. He never made it out of Chicago."

Jack stuck his hand out and Jim shook it. "You bring me that bike tonight before you leave and it's a deal, Jim. What news, if any, have you heard besides the usual bullshit rumors?"

"Lainie lives in Cicero, or what used to be Cicero. Chicago's gone nuts and it's spreading out to the whole county. She left there yesterday and has the latest news. She barely got out of Cook County alive. Idiots were trying to knock her off her bike, it's crazy. There are thousands of people on foot, trying to get out of the city and they're all headed west. The street gangs are burning everything. God help us if they come out here. That's another reason we're leaving. The power plants going boom might be rumors, but we're about to be overrun with something just as bad, gang bangers and desperate people. That's no rumor, it's a fact. Anyone who has any brains is getting out of Cook County as fast as they can." Jim scratched his chest and shook his head in disbelief. "It's bad, I mean *really bad*. The people who should be holding the fort together are bugging out. Lainie saw helicopters land and pick up people over by the big VA Hospital. Nobody could get anywhere near them." Lainie was talking to Kathy and Jim waved her over. "Lainie, tell Jack about the helicopters you saw."

Wearing motorcycle boots and a black leather vest, Jack couldn't picture Lainie as a nurse. Her arms were covered in tattoos and she had that thirsty, evening look.

"Yeah, I saw lots of them land, they had U.S. Army painted on the sides of them. They were mostly those big double rotor jobs. They came in right behind the old part of the VA Hospital. There's an Illinois National Guard base back there. You can clearly see it from the upper floors of the main hospital. There's got to be hundreds of troops back there. They're not letting anyone near it; they have guards all along the fence. I saw big trucks and armored vehicles going in and out of the place. I was in the main hospital building when the EMP hit. Most everyone stayed that morning, but by the afternoon people started panicking when they heard what was going on outside. Most everyone has families and they were scared, so people started leaving. I don't blame anyone for wanting to get home to their kids. I'm single and live by myself, so I stayed. A bunch of us did. We did what we could for the Vets because lots of them couldn't be moved, but it was hopeless. The night shift never came in and almost all of the day shift had left. By the next morning the emergency lighting started failing and patients were dropping like flies. We were overwhelmed."

Jack asked, "How many of you stayed?"

"It's a big hospital, I don't know. There were about six nurses and two doctors where I was. There were also patients' families, mostly wives. They were pleading with us not to leave."

Jim said. "It took guts to stay, Lainie."

It was barely perceptible but Lainie shook her head. "I don't know about that—I didn't stay. It got really bad late Tuesday night. I went down to the first floor to see if I could find something to eat. The vending machines were all broken open and empty, so I went to the cafeteria. It's in the older section, down the hall and just around the corner. I knew it would be closed, but I was really hungry. I figured I would find something. I felt safe, because I go down there every day. I didn't know that the first floor would be crawling with addicts and crazies roaming the halls. They were coming in from the surrounding area looking for drugs… just walking in like they owned the place. I guess most of the guards had left. All of the emergency lights were out, but I had a flashlight. I didn't see anyone and I didn't know that these creeps were roaming around. I was just about to go around the corner to the cafeteria when this crazy guy jumps out of nowhere and grabs me. I shattered the flashlight in his face. I must have got him really good, because he screamed like hell. I took off running and he starts chasing me in the dark, down this long hallway. It's the longest hallway you've ever seen, and I was scared shitless. I'm not much of a runner, but he was hurting and I got ahead of him. God, it was crazy. I was trying to get away from him, but I had to keep stopping, trying every other door, and they were all locked. He started gaining on me, so I started running again. I lost one of my shoes and I couldn't see him, but I could hear him, and he was screaming what he was going to do to me. I kept grabbing door knobs and praying one would turn and finally, one was open. I got in and locked it behind me. I could hear him coming down the hall. He was out of breath and getting closer. He knew I must have gotten into an office. He started swearing and shaking every door. He got to mine and started twisting the knob, yanking on it. I was only inches away from the door and I could hear him breathing. God, I was so scared, I couldn't move— it was like I was frozen. I couldn't see a thing, but I heard him walk away and it was silent for a while. Several minutes later, I heard the knob click a couple times. It wasn't my imagination, he was back."

Lainie paused and closed her eyes—Jack noticed she was shaking "Oh crap—look at me, I'm shaking just thinking about it. I hid the whole night, curled up under a desk in that little office. I'll tell you, that old building is creepy enough in the daytime, but totally dark—holy shit, I felt like I was locked in a tomb. It was like something out of a horror movie. There was yelling and screaming all night. It started getting light out, but I couldn't open that door. I was afraid he'd still be in the hallway, so I climbed out a window and ran to my bike. I got the hell out of there, and went home. I'll tell you something else. If this shit ends, I'll never go back there."

Jim said, "Thank God you had the Harley."

"You aren't kidding. If I didn't have that bike, I would have never gotten here. Nobody could get a car through the main gate. Stalled cars had blocked it solid. I was so scared. I kept riding around, trying to find a way out, but everything was blocked. I spotted a couple maintenance guys cutting a hole in the fence. They drove their car through it and I was right behind them." Lainie paused and smoothed back her jet-black hair. "I feel terrible about leaving, but that guy would have killed me. The patients who couldn't walk out of there were trapped. It's not a hospital anymore."

Jack knew the big VA hospital well. He had been to the cafeteria many times and could imagine the terror Lainie felt as she was chased down the "forever" hallway, as he always thought of it. Like many area veterans, he went there for all his health care. It was a good place and he was always treated well. It was sad to hear what happened to it. Just like every other hospital, it was in shambles.

Jim said," Don't blame yourself, Lainie, every one of us has had to make tough decisions this week. We know what kind of person you are."

Jack said, "Jim's right. Don't start blaming yourself. I've been a patient at the VA myself and you folks treat us really well. Believe me, every hospital went through the same thing, but it tells me how bad it's going to get when I hear one of the biggest veteran's hospitals in the country was left to go down the tubes. A country that abandons its veterans is screwed. What was the National Guard doing? Were you close enough to see anything?"

"We sure were. One of the doctors had a good pair of binoculars and we could clearly see what they were doing. On Tuesday afternoon, they started bringing in whole families in army trucks and buses, escorted by armed Humvees. We were upstairs in building number one, on the south end, so I was pretty close. They all had families with them. It was clear that the place was nothing but an evacuation site. Not for us though, just the politicians and their families. Like rats leaving a sinking ship."

Jack nodded his head, "Seems like I've heard that before. Thank God you got out, Lainie, and thanks for staying as long as you did. I know you care about the Vets."

Everyone had gathered around them, listening to Lainie's terrifying ordeal. Jack said to them, "I think every one of us has got a hair-raising story to tell. Let's try to relax tonight and have a nice steak dinner. We have lots of frozen stuff, so we might as well enjoy all of it tonight. How about everyone come over to our place. We can talk some more and then eat."

As they ate dinner together, Jack thought about how he had misjudged Barry, and now Jim and his friends. He thought about what Al had said about not knowing your neighbors, *the little guy was right.* After dinner, Jim delivered the motorcycle, and Jack gave him more guns and ammunition than he'd bargained for.

Jack and Jo went over the next morning to see them off. As the bikers roared away down the street, Jack said to Jo, "Al was right. I guess we really don't know our neighbors. I shouldn't judge people."

331

DAY 3 2

CHAPTER 3 5

Two weeks had passed since Jim and his friends had left for Wisconsin. Like most of the unoccupied houses, Jim's place was broken into and ransacked by hungry neighbors searching for food and anything of value. Jack thought about running them out of Jim's house, but the scavengers were people he recognized. The neighborhood had taken on a forlorn look that could only be described as depleted. People were out of canned goods and many stayed inside their houses, secretly eating what food they had left. Anyone who dared to grill outside was immediately accosted by their hungry neighbors, most of them sick from drinking contaminated water or eating spoiled food. There were at least three more suicides that Jack heard of, and another couple was missing, thought to have drowned themselves by jumping into the river.

On the night of Memorial Day, just before dawn, there was a violent explosion. It was so intense that it jolted Jack out of bed. He was half asleep, as his feet the floor, thinking he was back in Iraq. In only his underwear, he bolted from his room, expecting to find the house coming down around him. He was relieved to see Lynne come out of her room, carrying Bobby, unharmed. Exiting the house, they figured they'd see one or more of the neighbor's homes leveled. Everyone was gathered outside, as puzzled as he was as to what had just blown up. Nothing could be seen in the pitch-dark nighttime sky. There was no smoke or burning debris, only people standing in their backyards wondering what the hell just blew up. About five minutes had passed and there was a second explosion, this one further away and to the north, directly in line with the river.

Jack could pinpoint exactly where this explosion was by the flash reflecting off the bottoms of the clouds. It was massive, and as far away as it was, they were met with a sizable shock wave. The explosion rumbled its way down along the river, echoing off its dark banks. The rest of the night was quiet, and no one had a clue as to what had blown up...until morning. Someone had blown up the two main bridges that spanned the Fox River. The first explosion had taken out the Roosevelt Road bridge, which was a little more than a mile from Jack's house. The second one destroyed the North Avenue bridge, a few miles to the

333

north. The next night, two more bridges were destroyed, the massive I-90 Illinois Tollway bridge and the Route 20 Lake Street bridge.

Jack knew of only two possibilities of who possessed the explosives and know-how to drop those massive bridges into the Fox River. It was either the US. Army Corps of Engineers or the Able Limestone Quarry Corporation. Able Lime was the largest limestone mining and quarry operation in the state, and they definitely had a motive for dropping those bridges. The family-owned business headquarters was located in Able County, and the owner's massive home and estate was about a mile west of Melville. With those bridges down, the hordes of hungry refugees and the Chicago gangs behind them would be stopped at the east side of the Fox River, and have to detour miles away from Melville. Someone was desperate to detour them and it was easy to see why, Chicago was in ruins. The surrounding communities were being trampled by the throngs of people escaping the city, and everything in their path was being destroyed.

Residents in the western edges of Cook County who barricaded themselves in their homes were under unrelenting siege, day and night. They were ultimately overwhelmed by the looters and thugs. The most fervent of preppers weren't prepared for a 24-hour a day attack against their home.

FEMA had given up on trying to send any help to Cook and DuPage counties and simply abandoned them like an out of control forest fire. Three massive relief camps were being set up to the north, west and south of Melville. As massive as they were, there would be no way they could help the thousands of people fleeing from the violence that was raging in Chicago's Cook County. It was a well-known fact that Chicago, despite at one time having the strictest gun laws in the country, was armed to the teeth. No army commander in his right mind would take his troops anywhere near the jungles of Chicago.

The stories being told by the fleeing people were riddled with the rumor that aide was being flown in from the east and west coasts, and that the nuclear plants hadn't been secured. Jack only knew one thing for sure, and that was no rumor. Anyone who still had faith in the government was an idiot.

After the collapse of the bridges, Jack and Ken decided to do some demolition of their own. No one was around to stop them when they *borrowed* a large back-hoe from a nearby industrial yard. Their idea was to further isolate themselves from being overwhelmed by the invading army of desperate people. Ken's job had been an operating engineer with an excavating company. He assured Jack he would have no problems digging a huge trench across River Road, the only other entrance into their subdivision. Although no larger than a secondary side street, it ran parallel to the river, and was an open invitation for anyone escaping west from Chicago by way of Roosevelt Road. It took Ken a full week, but he dug a ten-foot-wide, 150-foot-long trench, cutting through the road. It started at the bank of the river and ran west into the industrial park. Along with felling 100-year-old cottonwood trees across it, the road that was the backdoor to the neighborhood was permanently blocked. There was no dissent in the remaining neighborhood residents about tearing up River Road. Blocking the east entrance to their subdivision had worked. The trench quickly filled with water from the river. Only people on a boat could enter from the east. Water from the river ran through the large trench and into the vacant land between the industrial park and the subdivision. A large shallow lake was formed in the low swampland to the south, further isolating the neighborhood from intruders.

A week had past and Jack was in his garage, attempting to siphon the remaining gasoline from his pickup when Laura ran in. She was crying and out of breath.

"Dad, you have to come with me to Mary Kay O'Hare's house, right now! Carl is still out hunting with Ben, and this can't wait."

Setting down the plastic tubing he was holding, Jack turned around and faced her. "Calm down, sweetie, what's wrong?" Laura brushed back her tangled hair and tried to catch her breath.

"I've been so busy with my own problems; I haven't thought of any of my friends these last weeks. Dad, please come with me. I'll explain on the way." Hearing Laura, Lynne and Kathy stepped into the garage. Laura turned and faced the other two women, "Lynne, we have to go to my friend's house, down by the river. She needs help, right now, please come with us…"

Jack jerked his head towards Lynne's car, "Let's drive down there, it'll be quicker."

Mary Kay O'Hare's home was at the far eastern end of the subdivision, near the west bank of the river, almost across from Ken's. She lived there with her husband, Brian, who was the head pharmacist at Wald's Drugstore in town. They had one child, a 13-month-old boy named Wendel, whom Laura would sometimes babysit.

On the way to Kay's house, Laura explained that Brian had gone back to the drugstore the previous week to try and salvage what drugs he could from the looted store. He was shot and killed by robbers in the store's apothecary and apparently his body was still there. Screeching to a halt on Kay's drive, Laura bolted from the car, pulling Lynne with her. The O'Hare's house was a split-level, located about three houses off the park, adjacent to the river. It was a beautiful home, situated on the center of a tree-filled, one-acre lot, with an idyllic scenic river view, that gave no clue as to what waited inside.

Entering the front door behind Laura and Lynne, Jack barely recognized the disheveled lady who was sitting cross legged on the living room floor. Her baby boy, Wendel, was sitting next to her. Clean and neatly dressed, he was playing with multi- colored plastic eggs, placing them in a small decorated yellow Easter basket.

From the dead look in Mary Kay's eyes and the condition of the insides of the house, something was terribly wrong. Noticing that Mary Kay was clutching a

335

small pill bottle, Lynne gently pried it from her grasp. Kay offered no resistance and didn't say a word. She wasn't surprised when she read the label. With the baby boy clean and freshly dressed and the mother looking hopeless, it was obvious. She had been holding a bottle of pills in one hand and an open bottle of fruit juice in the other. Lynne handed the pill bottle to Jack He couldn't pronounce the name on the label, but it said —90 tablets count. Jack didn't have a clue what it was, but from the looks of things he had the right idea. If Laura hadn't decided to check on her friend, the young mother and son would have been dead.

Lynne sat down on the floor next to Kay, and Wendel immediately crawled up onto her lap. Like Bobby had, the little boy began playing with the small silver cross that Lynne wore hanging from her neck. Gently placing her arm around Kay, Lynne asked, "Am I right in what I'm thinking these pills are for, Kay?" Jack and Laura crouched down in front of Kay. The stench of a sewage-filled basement permeated the house, making it difficult to breath.

Barely audible, Kay said, "Did you go next door to the Graff's house?" Jack looked at Lynne and Laura, not comprehending.

Kay continued, "They're upstairs in bed together. It was very peaceful for them; they just went to sleep. They asked me if I could help them, so I did." Kay's eyes were dry, no tears, no hope, only a solution. "My Brian was murdered. Mom and Dad are dead too, they'd be here if they weren't. My dad was always prepared. He bought us emergency food, enough for six months or more, for all of us. He was like that, always prepared for an emergency. The food was stored in the basement and was ruined by the flood. There's no more drinking water or food in the house. Everything is hopeless." She locked eyes with Lynne, her eyes vacant. "You know I'm right. All of us are going to die. You're going to be doing this too—so please leave us alone. I have to do this."

Laura had both of her hands to her face, holding back tears. Jack, usually never at a loss for words, couldn't think of anything to say. The air in the house was dank and hot, ripe with the smell of mold hanging everywhere.

Lynne edged closer to Kay. Wendel was still on her lap between them. She pointed to the silver cross on her neck, that Wendel was playing with. "Look at what he's holding, Kay… do you need a sign, are you looking for a way? Your Wendel is holding the key." Lynne lightly touched Kay's cheek, "Kay, we've all seen terrible things and some of us have done terrible things, but Wendel is your hope, and he's holding the key for the way. You're not alone, Kay, and no one is going to die. We're going to take you home with us. Your mom and dad and your husband would want that. You and Wendel will have a hot bath, a good meal and a safe night's rest. Kay, you and Wendel can be a part of our family. We take care of each other, and Jesus Christ leads the way."

Kay's eyes showed the first hint of emotion. A streak of anger crossed her face. She pushed Lynne away. "That's bullshit and you know it. There's no Christ and never was. Leave us alone!"

Lynne firmly said, "Yes, there is. You closed your ears to him, so he called for us. We're taking you and your son out of here."

Standing up, Jack and Laura gently got Kay to her feet. Lynne got up, holding Wendel high in front of her, saying, "Wendel, let's go home."

After they got Kay and her little boy back to the house, Jack and Carl returned to Kay's to salvage what they could before the looters tore the vacant house apart. Trying not to breathe deeply, Jack went down into Kay's basement. The stench of mold was overpowering. The water had receded, leaving about three inches of black river muck across the entire floor. He found what was once white plastic buckets of survival food that had been stored on the basement floor. The buckets looked like they were painted black, caked with river mud.

Carl said, "She was right. It looks like her dad had stored up at least six months' worth of food for a family of five. These containers may have been under water and are caked with mud, but you know what? They're sealed air tight."

Jack grinned at Carl, "Thank God for 5-gallon plastic buckets! Let's get some gloves and bring these pails home to wash off. Whatever is in them will be fine. It's going to be a crap shoot as to what's in them though, the paper labels on them havw washed off."

After they brought the buckets of food back to their house, Carl and Jack returned to salvage anything else that could be of use.

Carl opened up an upstairs bedroom closet and exclaimed, "Look at this!" The closet was at least five feet wide, and the two black doors of a gun safe took up almost the entire back wall. "If we don't open this safe and get whatever is in it out of here today, someone will rip this whole wall out for it. Whatever is in here will be gone by tomorrow."

With his hands on his hips, Jack surveyed the huge safe, shaking his head. "I've met her before and her husband has filled prescriptions for us. They certainly don't look like the type to be into guns. I'm trying to think what else could be stored in there?"

Carl tried the door handle, giving it a heavy yank. "The condition she's in, I would hate to press her for the combo, she probably wouldn't give it to us. But you're right, they don't look like gun people. Let's look around in these filing cabinets, maybe we'll get lucky and find the combination written down somewhere. If not, we'll see if Lynne can get it from her."

Jack said, "If there are guns in here, we have to get them. If we don't, someone else will and they might end up using them against us."

Both of them were busy leafing through filing cabinets, when Carl said, "We'll have to get her husband's body. It's going to be unpleasant, but he has to

337

have a decent burial. She has to have some closure, let's hope he hasn't been brought to the pit."

Jack agreed, "I think we should go into town today, maybe this afternoon. It's odd though, I've talked to her husband and he knew I was a Marine. If he was into guns, I'm sure he would have said something."

"That's because he wasn't." Carl handed Jack a folder of photos and awards. On the top was a marksman's award, with a photo of a young blond-haired girl who looked to be about 12 or 13 years old, standing next to an older man. The name on the award was Mary Kay Elliot. In the photo, she was holding an AR-15.

Jack took the photo and smiled. He recognized an older man standing next to Kay. "The older fellow in this picture is her dad, Bob Elliot. I've met him. He's a master gunsmith who owned a store and gun range over in Oakhill. I stopped in there about five years ago. Originally his place was out in the middle of nowhere. When it got built up around him, I heard the anti-gun nuts put him out of business. She had to have grown up in that store, and from these awards and photos, she knows a lot about firearms. We're going to have to get her to come around. We need someone like her."

"I hate to say it, Jack, but she looks like a complete nut-case. She helped her neighbors kill themselves."

Jack nodded his head. "Yeah, she'll fit in with us really good."

And so, the family added two more members to it. Later that day, they would add one more.

338

THE INTRUDERS

CHAPTER 3 6

Ken Martinez was alone in his backyard. He had just finished cleaning a Canadian Goose he'd shot and had fired up his smoker. Ben was about to join his dad outside when he heard a light knock on their front door. Carefully moving the living room window curtain aside, he peeked outside. A young couple who lived down the street was on the front porch. With them was their neighbor, a nice looking young black-haired lady, who often walked her dog by his house. They were unarmed and he had seen all of them before, so he opened the door. The attractive black-haired girl spoke first. "Hi Ben, you remember me, I'm Candi. I always walk my dog by here. These are my neighbors, Bill and Darlene. I don't know what you're grilling back there, but it's sure smelling good. We were wondering... if you had any food and some water you could possibly spare? Whatever you could give us would be greatly appreciated... I'll pay you back, Ben—somehow, I promise you."

Candi was beautiful, and Ben had secretly watched her many times as she walked her dog past his house. He quickly replied, "Hi Candi! Hold on a minute, I'll go get my dad." He turned around and ran towards the back of the house, leaving the three standing on the front porch. He made it as far as the kitchen, when he saw a man in the backyard holding a small handgun, pointed at his dad. At the same moment, he heard a loud crack of the cheap storm door lock breaking, followed by the squeak of the door's hinges. The three friendly neighbors were in the house and coming at him, a menacing glare replaced their smiles. Unarmed and with only a second to spare, Ben jumped into the entryway of the basement stairs, slamming and bolting the fortified door behind him. The neighbors, turned intruders, started wildly kicking at the door. Grabbing the two-way radio that Carl had given him, he yanked it off his belt, praying Carl would answer.

"Carl, we've got armed intruders, they have my dad outside! I'm locked in the basement!" Ben could barely get his breath. He was already feeling like a fool and mad at himself for answering the door.

Carl answered him immediately, "We're on our way! How many are there?"

"There's a guy with a gun in the backyard, he's got my dad. Another guy and two women are upstairs. They're trying to kick the basement door in!"

"Be there in a second, Ben, hold on!"

Ben grabbed a shotgun that lay propped up at the foot of the stairs and debated if he should shoot through the door. The door had been reinforced by his dad, and the intruders quickly gave up trying to kick it in. He could hear the hurried footsteps of the two women running from room to room above him. The guy upstairs yelled to them, "Those square white buckets are survival food. Jam all you can into that van, and find them keys!"

Just outside the basement door, the man screamed, **"You better come out of that basement right now, kid! We got your dad and we'll blow his fucking brains out! We want the keys to that van!"**

Hearing the commotion inside his house, Ken screamed, **"You stay put, Benny. They break through, shoot the bastards!"**

Ben heard the man outside growl, **"Shut up, pops, or I'll put a bullet in your head. Give me the keys to that van...NOW!"**

Afraid Ben would shoot through the basement door, the man at the top of the stairs stood well out of the way, yelling, **"We're loading up that van of yours, kid! We're taking your food, guns, and whatever else we find up here. We've been watching you and we know you're preppers! We know you got stashed in that basement. Open the door or we'll burn this place down!"**

Ben heard the man at the door say to one of the women, "Go look in the garage. If there's a can of gas in there, bring it to me!" Unexpectedly, in a friendly tone, he said, "Listen kid, if you don't open this door right now, Terry will shoot your dad... and I'll dump a can of gas down these stairs. It doesn't have to be this way. Open the door and nothing will happen to you, or your dad. I give you my word." There was a long pause, before he screamed, **"All right— screw you! As we drive away, you'll be cooking like that goose back there!"**

* * * * *

Carl was outside talking to Jo when he received the short, but to the point, call for help from Ben. He and Jo tore off running through the backyards, approaching Ken's house from the rear. He wished Jack was with them, but Jack had gone back to Kay's house with Lynne to try and open the safe. Kathy and

Laura were busy keeping an eye on Kay and watching the children. He and Jo would have to go it alone, until Jack heard the gunfire. Carl had his twelve-gauge pump. Jo had an AR-15, plus her nickel-plated 44. From their position behind the back fence, they could see a man pointing a small revolver at Ken and yelling at Ben to come up from the basement or he would shoot his dad. There were three other intruders, two of them women carrying boxes into the garage. Carl figured they had to be loading Ken's van. No one was on watch, and it looked like only the man with the small handgun was armed. One of the women ran out of the garage and into the house, carrying a red, 5-gallon gas can.

Is   The other woman, a tall blond-haired girl, appeared at the side garage door. She was laughing and shaking what looked to be a ring of keys in her hand. Before Jo could get into position to take a shot, Ken whirled on the man who was holding the gun on him. While Ken tried to wrestle the handgun away from his assailant, two shots were fired from the man holding the small pistol. Jo raised her AR-15 and let off two more.

Ben was at the bottom of the basement stairs when gasoline started gushing under the door, cascading down the steps. Instantly the basement was filled with dangerous fumes. He heard one of the women upstairs run through the house, screaming, **"I found them, I found the keys. They were under the van's front seat!"** Almost Immediately, he heard two loud pops, followed by two loud cracks, hopefully from Carl's weapon.

* * * * *

Their plan was to just walk up nice and friendly, then shoot the boy and his father. The only reason Terry didn't was they needed the keys for the van. Once the keys were found, the father and boy would be killed and the four of them would be off to safety in northern Wisconsin.

Things were not going well for them. The keys to the van could not be found, and the father couldn't be persuaded to tell them where they were. Terry had his gun pointed at the father when he heard Darlene shaking the keys, yelling**, "I found them!"** He was momentarily distracted as she excitedly appeared, laughing and dangling the key chain. Seizing the moment, the boy's father suddenly lunged at him. They fought for a few seconds. Terry fired two shots into him. A second later, the boy's father was falling to the ground, clutching his chest.

341

At the same time, Terry felt himself being violently shoved back—all the air being brutally knocked out of his lungs. Something very powerful had hit him and sent him whirling, flinging him to the ground. He thought someone had hit in his chest. The man he had just shot with his small handgun was sitting on the ground across from him, his blood-filled hands clasped tight against his chest. Terry looked down at his own shirt. A fountain of bright red blood was pumping out of it, pouring from **his** chest... *Oh my God*, I've been shot, *that's* **my blood**... *nothing was supposed to go wrong—we planned this out so carefully....*

ONE WEEK PRIOR

The two couples lived next door to each other and were good friends. They, along with other neighbors, had been watching with growing resentment those who had plenty of food and were not willing to share it with them. Some 32 days had passed since the power had gone out, and everyone was almost out of food and water. Some had run out within the first week, but managed to scrounge meals from neighbors, like that crazy little guy that lived in the corner house. Some folks started fishing in the river. The neighborhood rabbits were easy to catch but, just like the squirrels, they quickly disappeared. Others went over to the nearby golf course to hunt the plentiful duck and goose population. By day 25, people who had never hunted, let alone butchered anything in their lives, were eating their pets. The pesky geese, that always seemed to be everywhere, were now seldom seen, and even the chipmunks were gone. On day 26, Candi and Terry butchered their dog.

Bill and Darlene lived next door to Candi and Terry. Bill was a real estate salesman, Darlene a hair dresser, and they had no children. Their busy lifestyle could never be burdened by kids. Candi and Terry weren't married, but had been together for 15 years.

Terry was a used car salesman, and Candi a waitress. The two couples shared the same interests and the same lifestyles and frequently went out together. Totally out of food and water and with no survival skills, they were facing starvation. As the end of the second week approached, they started stealing from their neighbors. Working as a team, they would break into vacant houses. Homes that were abandoned after the storm were now open and fair game. They had gone through the house on the corner, the one where the two strange women lived, but had been run off by the man who always wore that big handgun, the one with the Marine Corps flag in front of his house. He was also the one who was still grilling food, while they were going to bed hungry. After that couple and their son were so brutally murdered, Darlene and Candi had gotten water from their backyard swimming pool and had seen a lady cooking on a grill in the yard behind them. That was the house where that crazy Marine lived. Some said he had to be the one who killed those people, probably for their food. It was said that they never got along, and it made perfect sense to Candi.

Candi and Darlene went back the next day and joined the others who were going through those murdered peoples' home, looking for anything that could be eaten. Once again, they saw that big Marine in his backyard, talking to a lady who had placed several plates of cooked food on a picnic table. Whatever those people had on that grill smelled good. Everyone on the block could smell it and everyone wanted some, especially Candi and Darlene.

Within a week, Terry and Bill had become masters at breaking into the unoccupied houses. At first, they were surprised at how much canned food they found. As days passed, others were doing it too and pickings were becoming slim. It became obvious who had food and when they were cooking it. The warm summer breeze announced it to the whole neighborhood. There were only two families who still had plenty of food and openly cooked every day. Some people had already approached them for handouts and were cruelly turned away. It was rumored that these two families were hoarders and had tons of food and water stored up in their homes. The word was that they were what was known as *preppers,* and they had looted some supermarkets during the first days after the EMP. The one who was known as, "The Marine," was the leader of one group. Many in the neighborhood were talking about him and the others who were living with him. It was believed they were probably some kind of cult, armed to the teeth, and no one in their right mind would mess with them.

But then there were those other two…. They were friends with the Marine. They must have been looters too. How else would they have so much food? They were seen grilling outside, cooking and eating well, every day. A man and a teen-aged boy, all *alone…living by themselves*—at the end of the block by the river.

Candi got an idea! These people were hoarders and looters anyway, so who would care? It would have to be quick. Surprise them, kill them, and take that big van of theirs. They'd load it up with their survival gear and food and drive up to Candi's parent's summer home in Lake Geneva, Wisconsin. They would strike fast and be in Wisconsin within two hours, before anyone knew what had happened. Once up there, they could fish and hunt…and they would survive, screw everyone else.

The only weapon they had, was a small 22 caliber handgun and a dozen bullets. Bill had found it while rummaging through one of the storm-damaged homes.

The initial plan was to walk up to them all friendly and shoot them, just empty the gun into them. Candi had befriended the teenaged son months before while walking her dog. She had seen the way he always looked at her…. She knew he had a crush on her…*it so would be easy*. She was good looking and had a nice figure, and he was teenager….

It was decided that she would approach the boy, and the men would take care of the father. The problem was that, when outside their house, the father and son always openly carried powerful guns. They would have to watch them and be ready on a moment's notice. Just because they were well armed didn't mean they weren't vulnerable, and Candi planned every detail. Sitting around their campfire one evening, while holding the small handgun, she told the others, "If an ice cube could sink the Titanic, we can take over that house. It doesn't matter how many guns they have. If we catch them at the right moment, this little pistol is all we need."

* * * * * *

The laughing blond-haired lady, suddenly popping out of the door with the van's keys, distracted the gunman for an instant. Ken made his move. He underestimated the young man's strength, and before he could wrestle the small handgun away from him, his assailant fired twice. He felt the bullets hit him in his chest. As he fell back, his assailant went down, his chest exploding into bright red. Blood splattering out of it. Despite being mortally wounded, Ken pulled out his holstered 45, wanting to run into his house to save Ben, but he felt his knees buckle. He dropped down on the grass. All his energy instantly being exhausted. Dropping his gun, he held his hands tight to his chest, trying to stop the flow of blood, giving himself a few seconds more. With every beat of his heart, blood poured out from between his tightly clasped fingers. There was no pain, only resignation...*I'm done for...oh God, I'm shot in the heart...I'm done for.* The entire first floor of his house was on fire. He could hear Ben screaming from the basement. He felt himself shutting down...down... down... he was blacking out. *Oh Benny, I love you so mu....*

* * * * *

Jack had gone back to Kay's house with Lynne. They were in the upstairs back bedroom when they heard the sound of gunfire coming from the direction of Ken's place. In an instant, he was out the door running, with Lynne close behind. They jumped into battered Camaro and headed towards the next street. Approaching Ken's, Jack hit the brakes hard rounding the corner, not wanting to run headlong into an ambush. He saw Jo and Carl running alongside Ken's house, and black smoke pouring from its open back door. Ken's big old silver-gray van madly shot out of his garage, careering towards the street in reverse. Rounding the corner of the house on foot, Jo and Carl both opened fire on it. Carl fired his shotgun three times. The van's side and front window shattering as it recklessly

345

backed down the driveway. Once out on the street, Jo took aim at the driver, and let off three rapid shots. The van sped forward, but instantly veered hard to the right, careening off River Road and down the steep embankment towards the river's edge. It rolled over twice, ending upside-down on its roof.

Jack floored the car and several seconds later was next to the embankment, overlooking the wrecked van. Jo and Carl were running towards him, as he jumped out of the car.

"Jo, what the hell happened?"

Out of breath, Jo ran by him, saying, **"Intruders! They killed Ken. Where's Ben?"**

* * * * *

There was only one way out of the basement and it was engulfed in flames. Mindful that an intruder could easily enter through a basement window, every window, including the basement's escape window, had been covered over with two layers of three-quarters inch plywood. Ben grabbed a 12-gauge shotgun and pumped round after round into the covered escape window. Emptying the gun, he reloaded it and fired again and again. Becoming overwhelmed by the smoke, he knew he only had seconds to get the splintered plywood free. Grabbing a jagged section, he pulled back with all his strength. The splintered wood cut deeply into his hands. Sharp, needle-like splinters pieced his fingers. Ignoring the pain, he put all he had into one last yank, wrenching a section of the plywood back and breaking it off. The fire was quickly spreading and the upper two thirds of the basement was filled with choking, hot smoke. He knew it might only be seconds before their massive stores of ammunition above started to cook off from the intense heat. He had to get out. He and his dad had distributed extra ammo for each weapon they had in every room of the house. The basement was no exception. His dad called the upstairs back bedroom, *the main magazine*. It held almost ten years worth of buying ammunition on every payday. The attic contained what his dad referred to as the *4thof July stuff*.   Ben was out of time. The ammunition upstairs would be cooking off any second, plus his dad had all those military explosives hidden between the basement floor joists. The choking fumes and intense heat sent him scraping through the jagged opening. Sharp splinters, like claws, dug into his back as he pulled himself through and into the steel well of the escape window. Pushing up on the heavy steel grate covering it, he was finally able to crawl up and out to safety. Thank God they had not yet bolted the outside grate down. Once out, he spotted a dead man lying on the ground, a small handgun lying next to him. To his left sat his dad, sitting up, but slumped over… dead.

Crawling to his dad, he held him in his arms, "Dad! Oh no, not you, oh no, not my Dad!" Picking him up, he carried his father away from the burning house. He didn't want his dad's body to be blown to bits by his own ordinance. He carried, half dragged his dad, finally collapsing in the ditch out front.

* * * * *

Jack had jumped out of the car, his 45 drawn, ready to face whoever was in the overturned van. Jo and Carl ran past him, scrambling down the embankment towards it. Rounds of ammo started to cook off in Ken's house. Jack turned back to the car where Lynne was still sitting. "**Lynne!** Get out! Get down the embankment! The house is going to explode!" He turned back, running up the sharp incline, roughly grabbing Lynne, yanking her down the steep embankment behind him. They had barely reached the bottom, when Ken's house blew. It wasn't individual rounds cooking off, or cases of ammunition exploding one after another. It was one massive earth-shaking explosion, leaving a smoking hole where ken's house was, and leveling the house next door.

"**Holy shit!**" It was Jo, followed by, Lynne's "**Oh my God!**"

Jo quickly recovered, **"She's getting away!"**

Jack turned around to see a young black-haired woman sprinting away towards the river. The woman obviously wasn't hurt or wounded in the rollover. She must have jumped out of the van before it rolled onto its roof.

Jo yelled, **"Get her, we can't let her make the river!"** Jo was up, followed by Carl, giving chase to the black-haired woman as she disappeared from sight.

Jack carefully checked out the van. One person, the driver, was partially still inside. She been thrown halfway out the driver's door. The top half of her blond head looked like a broken pumpkin. Some of it was missing.

There were white plastic buckets of survival food and various weapons strewn across the high weeds and brush. The van was a complete wreck. Part of its roof was ripped open, and its contents scattered everywhere.

About 20 feet from the van, Jack spotted what he was looking for, pulling himself through the weeds.

The young man saw Jack, and cried out, "**Please, help me**! My hips are crushed, please help me…"

Checking the man for weapons, Jack knelt down beside him. "Where you off to, partner? I don't think you're going far, pulling yourself through the weeds like that…" The guy didn't answer. He continued grabbing onto the high grass, trying to pull himself away. The scumbag, who minutes before had tried to burn Ben alive, was now asking for help.

Jack heard the staccato of Jo's AR-15 firing by the river. He got up and looked around, as Lynne walked up next to him. He sadly shook his head and Lynne turned away, knowing what Jack was going to do.

Jack looked down at him, "Do you have any children?"

"What?"

"Are you a father. Do you any little children at home?"

"Hell no! Help me… please!"

Jack pointed the 45 at the man's head. His finger was touching the trigger, about to begin the squeeze that would send the young man to hell.

"Go ahead, do it, you fucking bastard!"

Jack eased his finger away from the trigger and walked away, saying, " I was going to make it easy on you. Have a nice crawl…. . I don't think you'll make it back to the scum box."

Ten minutes later, Ben stood alone at the top of the embankment. He was black with soot, and the back of his shirt was in bloody shreds. Both of his hands were bleeding, but he seemed oblivious to the pain. He turned and looked back to where his house once stood. The home was leveled, as was Wilson's house next door.

Burning debris was scattered everywhere, and the sound of bullets cooking off could still be heard.

Ben looked towards Jack and Lynne, his eyes vacantly staring past them. "My dad's dead… They only had one weapon, a little piss ant 22 pistol, can you believe that? They probably never fired a gun in their life, and somebody like that took us out." Tears, black with soot, tracked down his face. "We had everything. You wouldn't believe what Pops had. He started prepping years ago and in ten minutes, it's all fucking gone! We were done in by a yuppie neighbor bitch and a little shitty 22 caliber pistol!" Ben wiped his face with his bloody hand, "I let the bastards in, it's all my fault."

Jack spotted Jo and Carl coming back from the river and started walking towards them. **"Tell me you got her!"**

Carl disgustedly shook his head, "We're not sure, she jumped into the river. It's still really high from all that rain. It's moving fast, with lots of trees and brush floating in it. She went under before Jo could get a good shot at her."

Jo said, "I don't think I hit her, she ducked under just before I fired. I hit the water where I thought she was, but the current is moving so fast. She was alongside a big submerged tree limb. I don't think even a good swimmer could survive in that current. If I wounded her, she's as good as dead. We went down the bank for a couple hundred yards, hoping she'd pop up, but nothing. She must have drowned."

Ben said, "Were there any survivors in the van?"

Lynne shook her head, softly saying, "No, Ben, there weren't."

Ben started to quickly walk away, but Jack lashed onto his arm, "Ben where are you going so fast?"

"I'm going to take the path that runs alongside the river bank, it ends at the dam. If that bitch doesn't drown, she could hang onto something and make it to the falls. If she's alive, she'll be half dead, and I'll find her. I'm going to break her fucking neck ...I'll rip that bitch's face off."

Lynne hesitantly placed her hand to Ben's shoulder, "Ben, your back is bleeding, you've got some burns...look at your hands, you've got some nasty cuts. Come back to our house with us, let's get these wounds taken care of."

"No! Get the fuck away from me!"

Ben roughly pushed Lynne away. Armed with his dad's M16, he ran towards the river.

Lynne pleaded with Jack, "Jack, stop him, he's only a boy!"

"No—let him go. He's going to have enough regrets to live with. I doubt that he'll find her, we need to just let him go. No one's going to mess with him. The way he looks, nobody will come near him."

Jack looked down at the wrecked van. Let's salvage what we can of Ken's supplies." He pointed to neighbors, who were drifting through the open yards towards the two demolished homes. "If we don't take this stuff now, it'll be picked clean by sundown. Carl, why don't you go get your truck. We'll load up what we can. Then all of you go back home, I'll stay here in the car and keep watch on what's left of Ken's place. His shed has been knocked down, but at least it didn't burn. You come back after you unload and we'll salvage what we can out of the shed. Maybe by then we can get close enough to the house—to find Ken's body."

Lynne pointed down to the wrecked van, "What about him?"

Jack spit, like there was something suddenly distasteful in his mouth. "Who cares?" He cocked his head to the armed on-lookers who were gathering, "I've got a hunch that these people gathering about were their friends, they sure as hell aren't ours. Let them deal with him." Jack leaned against the car door, looked up to the sky and closed his eyes.

Lynne stood in front of him, concerned, "Jack, are you okay? We couldn't save that man, but I'm glad you didn't kill him. These people chose their fate..."

Jack opened his eyes but continued looking skyward. "Just trying to make some sense of it all. I was asking God for strength to continue.... You know, it's funny, this morning when I woke up, I said to myself that this was going to be an easy day. Just finish draining the gas from my truck and do a few light things instead of busting my ass, risking my life and having to shoot scumbags." He

349

gestured towards the smoldering remains of Ken's house, shaking his head in disgust. "Look at this, our life is going from one disaster to the next. It's like we aren't solving anything, we're just trying to survive the next bullshit thrown at us. We still have to go into town and get Brian O'Hare's body. My God, now we have to bury Ken—and look at these people, already here to pick through the bones—like stinking vultures." He pointed to several people advancing on the still-burning remains of Ken's house, saying, "No. This isn't going to happen." Suddenly he jumped into the car, gesturing Jo to come with him. Lynne watched in astonishment as he floored it in reverse down the street, screeching to a stop in front the scattered wreckage of what was Ken's house.

He and Jo jumped out of the car. Jack faced several people who were walking into Ken's yard, all of them were armed.

Holding his 45 pointed at them, Jack faced them, "Hi assholes!

Jo moved about ten feet to the right of Jack, mumbling, "Jack, are you nuts? There's seven of them." Her AR-15 was up at the ready, following Jack's lead.

A man dressed in camouflage and carrying the goofiest looking rifle Jack had ever seen, said, "What the hell is your problem, dude?"

"Ken Martinez was just robbed and murdered. Then they set fire to his house and it blew up. I recognize a couple of you guys. You're Ken's neighbors for God's sake. The smoke hasn't even cleared and you're coming down here with your cracker-jack weapons to grab what's left. That's my problem!"

Lynne and Carl both watched in horror as Jack and Jo faced the armed scavengers. Lynne turned to Carl, "My God, he's gone crazy! We have to stop this!"

Jack held his 45 pointed at the man carrying the custom rifle. "What do you plan on doing with that piece of shit you're carrying? I'm dropping you first, asshole."

"Look man, we don't want any trouble. We're just looking for stuff, you know how it is..."

At that moment something big cooked off in the hole that was Ken's basement, making everyone, except Jack, flinch.

"Yeah, I know exactly how it is—so all of you carefully lay your weapons down... or use them. I don't care if you're neighbors or not, I'm getting really pissed."

The man carrying the custom rifle said, "Do as he says, this guy's that crazy Marine who lives on the next street. He's fucking nuts."

The group of men placed an assortment of weapons on the ground, and Jack said, "You can come back at sundown and pick them up, they'll all be here." Jack jerked his head towards the direction of his house, "Yeah, we got some food, enough for me and my family. And just so you know, my place is rigged to blow—just like Ken's place did. You tell your friends, anyone comes for our shit, they'll die trying."

Defeated, the group of men walked away.

Jo breathed a sigh of relief saying, "Jack... you are one crazy bastard, you know that? Does anything scare you?"

"Yeah. It's what Lynne's going to do to me when we get back to the car."

* * * * *

Jack's armed-stand against the locals worked. Everyone stayed well clear of the crazy family with the large garden and yard full of chickens. However, there was a new problem and it was becoming worse every day. There were hordes of displaced people, most out of eastern Cook County and Chicago. Finding no food, they continued their way west, and groups of them had somehow gotten over the river. Some were breaking away from the hoard that crowded every main road heading west. These people would drift down the side streets, searching for vacant houses to sleep in. Most would only stay overnight, but some would set up permanent residence. The destroyed bridges had diverted most of the refugees to the north and south of Melville. The numbers of homeless people coming out of Cook County were staggering. As off the beaten path as Jack's subdivision was, an almost constant flow of homeless people drifted in and most of them were armed. Hungry and desperate, they were no longer *asking* for handouts. He had a radical idea that would make his subdivision less appealing to these people. It would take another tragedy months later for him to implement it.

Ben got better physically, but the wounds of losing his father and their fortified home had left him bitter. Everyone was convinced that the young black-haired woman had drowned in the river that day, but Ben wasn't. Every day for two weeks after his father's death, he would search the debris near the dam, looking for her body. He had seen at least 100 bodies of men and women, bloated and half submerged, tangled in the snags. None of them was her. The river had become a dumping ground for bodies, and an avenue for suicide in the towns it passed through. Consumed with hate, Ben examined every putrid body he found. His logic that she survived was simple: "If she would have drowned, after a couple of hot summer days her body would have bloated and surfaced like the others." Jack didn't openly agree with him, but, in the back of his mind, he knew Ben had a valid point.

Jack was pleased that Jo and Kathy had taken Kay under their wings. They were astounded of Kay's knowledge and proficiency with firearms. Although Kay's passion wasn't any longer in guns, she had learned from her father a skill few gun enthusiasts had, and that was how to properly maintain and repair their firearms. Kathy's unbridled good cheer rubbed off on everyone and was especially helpful on both Kay and Ben. With Ben paired up with Carl, and Kay with Kathy and Jo, Jack hoped the two new members would do well. Lastly there was Wendel. He and Bobby immediately became pals and would become inseparable as time passed. And the safe...it was full of guns!

THE KEY

CHAPTER 3 7

Several things were learned from the destruction of Ken's house. Easily broken into first floor and basement windows had to be boarded up, but there had to be exits. Jack took it one step further. Taking a cue from the insurgents he had fought in Iraq, every room in the house had to have another exit added to it. Several scuttle holes were cut into the floor of Charlie's house, connecting the basement to the first floor. No one would ever get trapped by fire or an intruder. Every room was connected to the room next to it. Small square openings, just big enough to crawl through, were cut at knee height in the walls in every room. The openings were hidden and cleverly concealed. Each room had a 5-gallon bucket of water to be used as a fire extinguisher. Every room had two loaded guns, one handy and one hidden. Everyone was supposed to stay armed with a side arm at all times, and at least one person never went outside of Charlie's house during the daytime. If someone was casing the house, counting how many opponents they had to overcome, they would never know that there was always one more person hidden in the house. Carl and Laura's RV was walled off with leftover fence sections from the chicken coop. The side of the RV was backed tight to the brick outside wall of the house, allowing emergency access to the home through a window. Even bathrooms and closets had access holes cut into them. That was when they found Charlie's arsenal.

* * * * *

"The camps are open!" Laura ran into the kitchen all excited. "Dad, the relief camps are open, for real this time. We met people who have actually seen them—but they said they didn't go in." Laura and Carl had gone into town with Jo and Kathy to spend all their paper money. It had been over three months since the SHTF and a flea market had sprung up in town, where everything from toilet paper to guns was for sale or trade. The market was getting bigger by the day and was the only place anything could be purchased. No goods whatsoever were being produced or delivered to the Midwest, and box stores selling merchandise had ceased to exist. Jack could foresee when the paper dollars would soon be worthless, and was anxious to go to the new outdoor market and spend every paper dollar he had. Already, gold and silver were the preferred currency, and he figured it wouldn't be long before the once almighty dollar would no longer be accepted by anyone.

Jack skeptically asked, "For real? You talked to someone who has seen them, or is it more second-hand rumors?"

Laura said, "It's for real this time, Dad. A helicopter flew over town and dropped thousands of these." She handed Jack a paper leaflet. Each page had a different map drawn on it, with a white star marking a "Relief Camp." The small booklet was several pages long. There were two maps for their area, one showing Camp Able and the other, Camp DuPage. Camp Able was closest, about two miles from their home. The heading stated: Ample food--Clean Water--Medical treatment--Shelter. **No firearms or weapons** of any kind allowed in or near the encampment.

Tossing the small flier on the kitchen counter, Jack said, "Kind of vague, but to the point, I guess. But we don't know anyone who has actually been there. I'll believe it when I see it."

Carl said, "Bill Owens, he was a maintenance man at the school and he's a real gun nut. We saw him this morning in town. He said you can't get near the place without waiting, maybe a day, just to get to the main gate. He said he went to the one near the DuPage Airport and there were check points in the lines to get in. They're searching everyone and disarming people. If you don't give up your weapons, and that includes large pocket knives, you get turned away. They take everything and you don't get it back. He said he saw what was happening and turned around and left."

Jack said, "I don't blame him. I'd eat dirt before I let some government paper pusher disarm me. Did he have any reliable news?"

Carl nodded his head, "Have to take it with 'a grain of salt,' those were Bill's own words. He said the rest of the country isn't much better off than us. That's why help has been so slow. He said after the Midwest got hit with the EMP, all hell let loose. It took our whole economy and the international banking system down the tubes.

He also said that nuke plant, northwest of Rockford, has problems. So does the one south of us."

Jack rolled his eyes and looked up at the kitchen ceiling saying, "Great, that's just great. I guess Al was right."

Laura spoke up, "Carl, tell Dad about the east coast."

Jack sat leaning forward in the kitchen chair, "You mean it gets worse?"

"Yeah it does, somebody nuked Washington, DC."

Jack sat back, "That means we're at war—and we don't even know who with?"

"That he didn't know, it happened three weeks ago."

Jack asked Carl, "You still monitoring the radio waves?"

"No, I gave up a week ago. Those old radios need some new tubes and capacitors. I've tried to fix them, but they're junk. There's no place I can get that old stuff. I get nothing but static on the truck radio. I still think radio transmissions are being blocked. I'll try again tonight. Jack, what's this mean for us?" Lynne, Jo, and Ben had entered the kitchen and were silently listening. Everyone looked expectantly at Jack.

"As far as Washington, it's too bad about the Smithsonian. I always enjoyed that place. I liked the Washington Monument too. Other than that, it's no great loss. I can think of a few politicians who I hope witnessed it."

Lynne snapped, "**Jack!** I can't believe you said that. We're talking about thousands, maybe a million innocent lives."

"You're right, I'm sorry, at least about the general population. As far as the politicians go, those bastards sold us out years ago. I wouldn't worry though, I bet none of them were anywhere near the Capitol, and why would they be? That would mean they were actually doing some work. No, I'm sure they're safe and sound on some island in the Caribbean, or some mountain retreat, waiting for the 'all clear' to come back, so they can start their bullshit again." Jack stood up, leaning back against the kitchen counter. "What does it mean for us? Well, for a starter, I'm surprised we're getting any aide at all. *We know* there are no warehouses full of unlimited emergency supplies, and mark my words, a zillion people are going to be flocking to these so-called camps, expecting just that. Those camps will be overwhelmed in days, if they're not already. They'll turn into massive disease pits, that's a given. And this policy of disarming everyone, I know why they're doing it. They've been just itching for a reason to disarm the civilian population for years. It wouldn't surprise me if this whole thing was one big false flag to cull the whole damn country of people and guns. I'll tell you one thing, there might be less weapons, but when these camps run out of food, when the gravy train stops, people will be out for blood. *God help us.* As far as the nuke plants go, that's another whole ballgame."

Laura said, "Nuclear plants... that's scary. What are we going to do?"

Jack said, "I don't think they'll be an immediate concern for us, but anyone that fled to the northeastern part of Illinois, or southeastern part of Wisconsin, may be glowing soon. We have one south of us, but it's also a little east. Any windblown contamination would miss us. The lower part of Lake Michigan and northern Indiana might be in trouble. The wind has been consistent, mostly out of the west. Who knows where the airborne radiation from those nuke plants will end up? Probably in Lake Michigan, which will finally

355

put the Zebra mussels to work doing something good. Hopefully all the fallout lands on Detroit."

Lynne said, "Jack!"

Jack tiredly rubbed his eyes. "Sorry, I don't mean to make light of this, but it's too much for anyone, especially a simple Marine like me, to figure out. I think we should sit tight and stay here. If there is nuclear fallout to the north and south of us, we're trapped here anyway. We can't go east, and there's nothing west of us but vacant farm land and small towns that won't be welcoming us, that's for sure. I think most of all, we should resist any temptation to go to these so-called *camps*. If everyone heads there, we'll be living in a ghost town and that's good for us. Unless squatters move into the nearby abandoned homes, we may finally be left alone." Jack looked at Lynne. "What do you think, Lynne? Didn't you mention your husband worked with these FEMA people?"

"Yes, he did. You'r right about them not being able to handle the amount of people that are going to need help. They know they'll be overwhelmed come fall, especially here in the colder northern cities. Besides lack of food and water, no heat. That was the reason my husband bought the RV and the supplies of emergency food. He wanted us to get away from Chicago and head south as quick as possible." Lynne had everyone's attention. The gravity of the situation written across her face. "These government shelters will look tempting, but they have to be avoided. They'll be overcrowded and, free food or not, we shouldn't go anywhere near them. Come winter, there's going to be a resurgence of diseases that this country hasn't seen, even in our great grandparent's lifetimes. These packed camps will be breeding grounds for them. One other thing, we have to stay clear of any authorities. They see that we look well fed, or someone points us out and accuses us of looting, they can legally take our food, and believe me—they will. They'll confiscate everything we have. That goes for going to this new market place that has opened up in town. We have to be very careful. Certainly, don't eat anything from there. People are going to be dying from food poisoning and drinking contaminated water. Add bad hygiene and no toilets, it's going to be a nightmare. Speaking of that, we should limit contact with people, even people we know. If we have to go to this market for something, we have to make it short and limit contact with people. Forget about shaking hands. And that reminds me, please don't forget to carry those small bottles of hand sanitizer I gave each one of you. It's not just people we will have to worry about. It's disease."

Carl said, "You think now that they're setting up these so-called camps, you think we'll finally see some National Guard troops?"

Jack leaned forward saying, "No. We may see a helicopter fly over once in a while, but if the whole state is screwed up, I don't think anything is going to change as far as the National Guard. They're spread too thin and, really, how many of the Guard do you think even showed up for duty? We won't see the

356

military. But I'll say one thing. If any of us do run into any military or official-looking types, Lynne is right, you have to steer clear of them. Let the busybodies and Democrats talk to them, not us."

Again, Lynne said, "Jack!"

Kathy frowned and said, "I'm a Democrat."

Lynne sighed, "He's kidding, Kathy. Don't pay any attention to him. He's being an idiot. He's right on one thing; we'll have to remain out of sight as much as possible. We've got to keep to ourselves."

Jack grabbed a pencil and pad of paper from the counter, saying, "As for me, I'm going to make a list of things we need, and look around at what we have that we can trade at this flea market. Maybe I'll make a short trip into town tomorrow and do some bartering. I'm really looking forward to it because there are a few things we could really use that we can't scavenge around here. Did any of you see any problems in town? Did that flea market really get bigger, or is it just turning into a big refugee camp?"

Laura said, "No problems, Dad, but everybody seems to be armed. We didn't see anyone messing with anyone else. We actually felt pretty safe at the market. I felt it was safer there than out on the road. We saw that cop and his brother that you don't like, Chuck Hayes, or whatever his name is. They said, "Hi" to us... they're really creepy, but they left us alone."

Jack's face darkened, "Good thing I didn't go with you. I *do not* want to run into either of those two."

Carl said, "The market takes up the whole park. Everything from sweetcorn to pot is being sold. There was a guy selling beat up old cars and trucks, cans of gas, and kerosene. Guns, bullets, booze, and cigarettes seem to be the biggest sellers, next to food and bottled water... lots of illegal drugs too."

Laura said, "There's people roasting what looks like dogs, maybe cats too. They're selling large chunks of barbecued meat on a stick for five dollars, in silver change, each. I asked one of the men selling it if it was beef and he started laughing. He said it was, 'Fresh Fido.' That's pretty sick, don't you think, Dad?"

Jack shook his head, "Maybe sick to our western way of thinking, but not to some parts of the world." Jack thought of Al and the dogs in his garage. "You didn't happen to see Uncle Al there, did you?"

"No Dad, no Uncle Al."

Carl said, "We're just over two months into this mess and already the wild animal population is almost gone."

Jack said, "Tell me, while you two were in town, did you see any of those pesky pigeons that are always all over the place?" Laura shook her head. "How about at the park or, better yet, at the golf course? Did you see that flock of geese that is always there?" Again, Laura shook her head. "I bet every animal at the Yorkfield Zoo has been slaughtered and eaten. I'm talking elephants, chimps, snakes, bears, every last one.

357

Come this fall, maybe sooner, I'll bet you dollars to donuts people are going to start disappearing. It won't be Fido on a stick, it'll be Aunt Bea and Uncle Andy. And it won't be selling for no five bucks either."

Laura said, "My God, Dad, do you really think it could come to that?"

Jack sadly nodded his head, "Yeah, unfortunately, I do. We may be at that point already. People will know damn well what they're eating and will pay anything to get it... I'm afraid we haven't seen anything yet." Jack sighed, grabbed his cup of tea off the table and downed it. Looking at no one in particular, and almost as if he was talking to himself, he softly said, "We're going to have to be very, very careful...and never venture far away from here alone...."

For the rest of the day, Jack decided to walk around their houses and inventory what they had. He knew they had items that could be traded at the market. His first stop was Charlie's basement. He grabbed a couple of cool beers out of the bottom of Charlie's root cellar. It was a great little place to, at least somewhat, chill a brew. The first beer he practically downed. After the hard week and long dry spell, he figured he owed it to himself. It was cool and tasted good. He let out a belch and walked over to Bobby's parents' house. After two months, he had given up all hope that Bobby's father, Jake, would ever return home. He figured, like thousands of other good people who worked in or near the city of Chicago, something bad had happened to him. Jack knew Bobby's father would never return home, but he decided to give it at least another month. Then they would more than likely start using Ronnie and Jake's house for storage. Unlocking and entering the front door, he felt like an intruder going into their home. The last time he'd been there was to clean up after Ronnie's fatal beating by Glen. It had been a while since he thought of Glen...*Some people don't deserve to walk God's green earth.*

As he stood in Ronnie's living room, he was struck by the fact that everything was so neat and orderly. It was as if nothing so brutal had happened in the bedroom only a few feet away. Feeling awkward and like an intruder, he turned around and walked out. Maybe he would go through the house with Lynne in a few weeks, but it was still too soon. He locked the door and went over to his place. He knew he would find something there he could use for barter. Entering his own house, he slowly walked into the dark dining room and sat down at the long oak table. The house was hot and stuffy, but as long as it was summer, it was at least livable. For now, he, Lynne, Kay and the children lived upstairs, but with winter approaching, they'd all have to move into Charlie's. He had a fireplace in his living room, but in no way would it be able to provide warmth for the entire home. He tried to remember the last time he had sat in his dining room; it seemed like ages ago. Opening the second beer, he took a long slug of it. Kicking back in his chair, he had a full view of the kitchen. He sat there thinking about that Monday morning. The last morning with electricity. It had been a typical morning. He had a bowl of cereal for breakfast, with a banana sliced into it. He thought about past breakfasts and all the meals that had been prepared in kitchens, just like his, all across the Midwest. *God, I wonder if I'll ever see a pineapple again, let alone a banana?* How many people ever thought about where their food was grown and how it got to their table? *What I'd give for an ice-cold glass of orange juice... Simple things I took for granted, and may never have again—I took a train ride into Chicago, and life as I knew it ended.* He gulped another swallow of beer, wiping his mouth with the back of his hand.

God, I wish I had listened to old Charlie and seriously prepped. I was always battling with Ellen, letting her have her own way.

He took another hard swallow of beer, thinking...*What I'd give for a cigarette and some pretzels...* "Cigarettes!" Jack said aloud to himself. He remembered there was a full carton of butts in Ellen's car. Carl said they were worth their weight in gold!

Plus, Ellen always kept a spare pack or two in the glove box. He'd have one from the pack and trade the carton! With his spirits buoyed, he went outside to Ellen's car. The carton of cigarettes was still on the floor, next to the shifter. He opened the glove box, and sure enough, there was another two full packs. There were also a couple pieces of paper, so Jack took a look at them. Nothing of importance, but lying flat on the bottom of the glove box was a shiny brass Caldwal door key. He looked at it for a few seconds, finding it odd that Ellen would have a new looking Caldwal key. All the locks in their house were keyed alike and were Wesson-lock brand. Only one person that he knew for sure had Caldwal locks. Don had recently mentioned that he'd changed all the locks in his condo to Caldwal. Jack sat in the driver's bucket seat of the little car, fingering the large square key, wondering why Ellen had it and who's door lock did it fit? *It couldn't be Don's?*

So much had happened since the day that he and Lynne had left Don's body in Chicago. He sat there a few minutes, thinking about his boyhood pal. *When was the last time I even thought of poor Don? It's like he never existed...* He recalled how Lynne went through Don's pockets and had taken out his wallet and key ring. They had put them in Don's briefcase, which was sitting next to the couch in the living room. Jack palmed the key and got out of the car. He didn't know why but, just for the heck of it, he wanted to compare Ellen's key to Don's house key.

Don's scuffed briefcase was still there, sitting where Jack left it months before. Grabbing it, he sat down on his couch, placed it on his lap and opened it. Don's sunglasses where there, along with his wallet and a ring of several keys.

One of them was a Wesson-lock. Jack looked at the key for a second, thinking, *Damn.... this key is new and looks like mine...* He quickly got up and opened his front door, inserting the key into the lock. It was a perfect fit!

He removed Don's Caldwal key from the ring and placed it together with the key from Ellen's glovebox. An exact match! He stood next to his front door with bewilderment across his face, and said to himself. "What the hell is going on here?"

"Problems, Jack?" It was Carl and Laura. They had seen the front door open and had walked over to check it out.

Startled and embarrassed, Jack said, "Oh, hey Carl, hi sweetie. No... no problems, just trying to figure something out... Hey, I was thinking, maybe tomorrow when go into town to that big flea market, we'll take Ben with us. It'll do him some good to get out. Maybe on the way back, we could stop at Don Jenks' condo, it's not that far out of the way. I have the keys to his place; I'd like to check it out. I know he had some guns. Maybe there's some other things we could use."

Laura said with a smile, "That's a good idea, Dad. Maybe there will be some diapers... infant ones..."

Carl added, "I might look for some cigars too... **Grandpa Jack!**"

CHAPTER 3 8

That night, Jack had more crazy dreams. In the past he was accustomed to waking up in the early pre-dawn hours with imagines of his last day in Afghanistan, stabbing him awake, but those nightmares had finally gone away months ago. He had one of those restless night where he just couldn't fall asleep. It was like his mind was on overload. The more he tried to force himself to sleep, the more he thought, so he tossed and turned all night, with crazy thoughts running through his head. There were little children calling him Grandpa, laughing and yelling, running along the river bank next to him, but their voices faded and the children disappeared. He saw the old man again, his skin wrinkled and black, sitting alone on the river bank talking to himself. Suddenly the old man turned his head and he was almost nose to nose with him, the old man's eyes boring into his. He wanted to run, to wake from his dream, but he couldn't. He noticed he held something in his gnarled hand, and it was a key, a bright brass key. The old man said, **"The next moment isn't guaranteed boy! Make every moment count!"** The black man's face changed and it was old Charlie, **"Make them pay hard boy, make them pay hard, make them pay hard!"**

Jack physically felt himself jump as he jolted awake. His T- shirt was wet with sweat. Placing his fingers against his heart, he could feel it bouncing in his chest, like an old worn-out engine. It felt like it was misfiring. *Holy shit...I'm going crazy...I'm going to give myself a heart attack...* Everything he dreamt about was emptying, like dark turning into light. It was gone, except for the last thoughts before he opened his eyes. *The old black man by the river, dangling the brass key. It felt so real. Who was the old man? He felt like he knew him, like he'd seen him before....*

He laid there for an hour trying to make sense of his dream, but it was too far away. He tried, but he couldn't get it back. He closed his eyes and started drifting back to sleep. He wasn't asleep, but not yet awake, when he started dreaming of Iraq. It had been a long time since he dreamed about Iraq. It seemed so far away, but was so real. Him and his buddies were close, but it was like they became bonded forever while in Iraq. He thought of how he, Weaver, and Nolan had pissed on the dead insurgents' bodies. He could see the dusty sand as it washed off their dead faces and Weaver laughing, saying, "No virgins for these fucking bastards!" They would have been in big trouble if they got caught doing what they did. Jack was the leading PO and joined in with his two buddies. Afghanistan started drifting in and Jack sat up in bed. He was out of breath and it was still dark, but he wasn't in Iraq or Afghanistan, It was just a dream... another dream... *Oh God...it never fuckin leaves....*There was an early morning chill in the room, and as his feet hit the floor, he realized he had to take a piss really bad. *Maybe that's why I was dreaming about Iraq and what we did... oh shit, how is Laura going to bring a baby into this crazy world.*

He got up and grabbed his bucket, the smell of three-day old urine sloshing up at him. *Shit, I better empty this thing.* He thought of Ellen and what her reaction would be to them becoming grandparents. He laughed to himself... *She'd be pissed...*That was one thing they had never discussed. Jack smiled to himself.... *Grandpa Jack, that changes everything. It makes this all worthwhile, all that we're doing...* The thought of Ellen clouded his mind and he shoved her to the side. He finished going and raised the window sash, slowly dumping the bucket of stale piss out the window, trying not to let it splash back on the house. The morning light was just seeping into the backyard, and he could see Jo standing by the shed, the smoke from her cigarette mixing with the morning haze.

Jo looked up at him, giving him a thumbs up, as the last drops of urine left the bucket, saying, "**Nice**—real nice."

He waved back at Jo, figuring the "Nice" comment was in reference to what he had just dumped. He smiled to himself, thinking, Good *old Jo, she always says her mind.* Sitting down on the edge of the bed, he started thinking again about those damned keys. *Could there be a logical reason for them to have each other's keys?* Was he jumping to conclusions? If they were cheating on him together, *wouldn't he have known it? Am I that fucking stupid?*

He thought of an incident that he'd heard about, where a guy had come home early from work and caught his best friend alone in his house with his wife. He accused them of cheating on him, only to find out there were guests hiding in the back... it was a surprise birthday party for him.

Glancing at the wall, he knew Ellen's wedding picture was staring at him from behind a shadow. He felt like jumping up and smashing it. Lynne was asleep in the room next to him, and he wondered if she was awake and if she'd heard him muttering to himself during the night. He recalled Don's dying words, "I'm sorry Jack..." *Sorry for what? God, what a fool I've been....*

Quickly getting dressed, he felt the stiffness of his three-day old socks as he pulled them on. He wanted to get down and talk to Jo while she was alone. Maybe he could unload his problems and how he felt about Lynne on her. He felt like his head was going to burst, and he wanted to wake Carl. More than ever, he wanted to get right over to Don's. He knew there would be hard evidence there, if he and Ellen were sleeping together. *Would they do that to me?* He sat on the edge of the bed and ran his hands through his unruly hair... *I have to put this to rest soon or it will drive me crazy.*

As he slipped his pants on, anger was building and he muttered under his breath, "Don't kid yourself, Jack, damn straight they were screwing around together."

After he was dressed, he hurried outside and unloaded everything he suspected about his wife on Jo. She listened patiently and when he was done, she put her arm around his shoulders and with a grimace, said, "Hate to break this to you, big guy, but this is all very old news. I think everyone, and that includes Kay and Ben, know everything. Laura caught your wife red handed with your pal and was about to tell you that Monday night that the shit hit. After she found out that her mom and your best friend were dead, she figured, 'Why should I make Dad feel any worse?' She decided not to tell you." Jo gave Jack a moment to digest what she had just sprung on him. Jack looked stunned and said nothing. She took a long pull from her cigarette. "Laura is very upset about this and confided in us. Lynne found out about it when she accidentally found an address book of your wife's stuffed in the back of a dresser drawer in her bedroom. She burned the book."

Jack bit down hard on his lip, it was like a stick of dynamite had gone off in his head. "Holy shit, that bitch! Oh my God. That's what her and Laura were fighting about that Monday morning!"

Jo nodded her head, inhaling the last dregs of her smoke. Flipping the spent butt into the dirt, she said, "I might as well add that everyone, including Laura, knows how you feel about Lynne."

"What?"

Jo rolled her eyes, "What do you mean, 'What'? Every time you two are around each other, a blind person could feel it."

"Give me a break, Jo. We're in a bad situation here, it's only natural for us to be close."

"Yeah, maybe...but I see the way you look at her, so don't bullshit me. In case you want to know, she feels the same way about you. And don't try to tell me you didn't know that, the way she fusses over you. I'm glad this is all out in the open now, it'll make it easier on both of you. And one other thing, big guy. When things go back to normal, see a kidney doctor and get your bladder checked out. Jeez, that was about a gallon of piss you dumped out your window."

"It was about three days' worth."

"Gee, Jack, that's great. I bet your room smells nice."

He was about to say something wise-ass back to her when they both heard a loud **Snap!** Both of them stiffened. The sound of someone stepping on a branch and breaking it from beyond the wood fence put both of them on alert. Jo

363

put her finger to her lips as she went over to the fence, her AR-15 up and ready. Jack circled to the left, his 45 drawn. A tall and lanky black man, wearing a faded blue jean jacket was about five feet from the fence.

"Don't shoot me, please... I was just passing through and heard voices. I thought maybe I could ask you for a drink of water. I'm very thirsty."

Jack was alongside the man and warily looked down the fence line for any accomplices.

"I'm alone, please don't shoot. I have only my pocketknife and it's not a weapon."

Jack had his 45 menacingly pointed at him. "You always sneak up on people when it's still dark? It's a good way to get shot." He carefully looked the stranger over. He was African American, lean, and stood about 6' 2." He had a blue baseball cap on and was carrying an old wooden baseball bat.

Jack pointed to the bat, "What's the bat for? You intend to play some ball?"

"Sorry if I startled you. My name is Steve, Reverend Steve Posely. I got this bat a a long time ago... when I was a kid, from my grandfather. He played on the Negro Baseball Leagues in 1918—I really treasure it. I had to leave the rectory where I lived in a hurry. It was on fire and burned to the ground, along with the school and church. I grabbed the bat and took it with me. It's the only possession I have, other than my pocket knife, Bible, and rosary. Everything I own was destroyed in the fire. —Like I said, I didn't mean to startle you. I like to travel early, before the crazies are out. From three in the morning to about noon is the best time. I hole up during the day and evening, mostly in vacant houses, usually with people like myself. All these druggies who can't get their meds will kill you for a cigarette. It's getting much worse. There are crazies who are doing unspeakable things, and there's no food or drinkable water anywhere." Steve pointed east, towards Chicago. "The black street gangs own Cook County and have declared war on everyone they come across. It doesn't matter who you are, or what race you are. They take whatever they want and will kill anyone who is in their way. I lived in Oak Park and the whole city is lost, it's been overrun. I'm trying to make it to the Able County relief camp. I heard the DuPage one is already overflowing with refugees and they're turning people away."

There was an uneasy silence. Jo roughly said, "We don't like people poking around. How do we know you're not a scout, checking us out for your group?"

"I guess you don't, a man's word doesn't mean anything anymore.

Before all this happened, I was a Catholic priest at Divine Infant Catholic Church in Oak Park. The church and school were burned three weeks ago. I started making my way west last week. It's been terrible."

Jack felt the man was telling the truth, but he sensed skepticism in Jo. She asked, "I've seen black ministers who are Baptist, but none that I can recall who

364

are Catholic. I'm Catholic, so start reciting the rosary for me." The man started praying the rosary, and Jo stopped him. "Okay, so you at least went to a Catholic high school. What about your parishioners, couldn't they help you?" Father Steve smiled, "Of course they did. Every church has a core group of dedicated people that no church can survive without. I wouldn't be standing here if it wasn't for them. Unfortunately, most were elderly and by their very nature, quite frankly..." Father Steve sadly shook his head, "They're not fighters, at least not in the physical sense. We ran out of food. We shared what we had left with people who probably never entered a church in their life. One would like to think that when you feed a fellow human being, they wouldn't try to kill you after-wards. I'm okay though. I've spent lots of time in the inner city and was a Chaplain at Cook County Jail. I've been, as they say, around a bit. Also, I grew up on the family farm and I know things that most city folks don't. Living off the land, that sort of thing. Most of it I learned as a kid, that I'm now thankful to know. I'll be all right if I can just avoid the crazies—Can I go now?"

Jack said, "Wait a couple minutes." He ran to the house and came back a couple minutes later with a large bag filled with produce and a large bottle of water. "Here, Father Steve, good luck to you. That's Jo, and I'm Jack, and a man's word still means something here."

"Thanks, Jack." Father Steve nodded his head to Jo. "God bless you both, you'll be in my prayers."

As they watched the priest leave, Jo said, "We average at least four to six parties a day coming by and we're secluded back here, especially being cut off with the river. I can't imagine what it would be like if we lived on a main road, in the middle of a town like Oak Park. There would be hundreds of hungry people going by every hour of the day, nonstop."

As Father Steve faded from sight, Jack said, "I wish we had more people in our group just to stand watch."

Jo pointed in the direction of Steve. "You mean people like him?"

Jack watched the man fade from sight and said, "Exactly people like him. We don't need more mouths to feed, but we do need people with survival skills and for defense. After what happened at Ken's" —Jack trailed off, "I still can't believe those neighbor kids got the drop on Ken and caused so much destruction." He recalled what Charlie had said about the local gang of satanic killers. Turning to face Jo, he said, "What are we going to do when we get attacked by a trained group of killers, who *enjoy* what they're doing? That's what I worry about every day. We already had a group of sociopaths living amongst us, right here, torturing and killing people for fun, *before* the shit hit the fan. It's like Charlie said to me, 'Their very ruthlessness makes them survivors.' God, I hate to see what it's going to be like come winter. It'll be survivors against survivors and only the most ruthless will live. That Father Steve guy solidifies something I've always thought: that when the shit hits the fan, the turn-the-other-cheek crowd isn't going to make it."

Jack wondered if he really was a Catholic priest, or a fallen Catholic who had just made it all up and scammed him out of some food... *the man said he grew up on a farm...* He gazed over his fence, past Barry's vacant house, towards the empty farmland to the north. An idea had been tossing about in his head for some time... *If we could only get that farmland back in use....* As the new day approached, the eastern sky was turning light. Jack stood silent for a moment, staring east, deep in thought. *A farm...* "You know, Jo, we do need at least two more people who have special skills. Their skills would cancel out with whatever supplies of ours they consume. The day is already here when we'll need someone on guard 24 hours nonstop, not just at night. Making a broad sweep of his arm, he pointed towards the area behind his property, saying, "I don't particularly like being surrounded by all these empty houses where squatters can set up camp. I always feel like we're being watched. It makes me feel like we're sitting ducks here. I've been thinking we will have to do something about it." His thoughts were interrupted by Carl sticking his head out of the RV door, giving them a wave.

Jo said, "Looks like everybody is getting up." She raised her eyebrows , cocking her head, "You still going into town and stopping at your old friend's place afterwards?"

"Yeah, I'm going into town, maybe get some things we're looking for and, yes, I'm still going to my partner's house."

Jo exhaled, disappointment showing on her face. She shrugged her shoulders, saying, "Why, Jack... what good will it do for you to go there? They're both dead, your wife and your friend. Our world has changed and it's not good, so find some happiness. It's that simple, don't make it so friggin complicated."

Both of them heard the creak of Charlie's back door open and looked towards it.

"Joanie, I got a cup of coffee for you." It was Kathy, sticking her tussled blond head out the door. When she saw Jack, she waved. "Oh, hi Jack, didn't see you. Good morning. Would you like a cup too?"

"Sure, Kathy, thanks." Kathy disappeared inside and Jack smiled, maybe his only smile of the day, and pointed towards Kathy, "I'd give anything for some of her good cheer."

Jo laughed, "Me too."

Jack continued their conversation, "Thanks for your concern, Jo, but I have to go to Don's. Let's just call it a... *final closing* to the last chapter of my marriage."

Kathy came out with two large mugs of steaming coffee. "Here you go, Joanie, here's yours. And Jack, black with one sugar, just the way you like it."

About an hour later, Carl pulled his pickup out of Charlie's garage and headed towards town. Ben was in the back, proudly brandishing his dad's M16, and Jack rode shotgun. It would take about 20 minutes to reach the large park that was in the middle of downtown Melville.

Carl had been around Jack long enough that he could tell something was eating at him and hoped it wasn't anything he had done. As he drove out of the subdivision, he shot Jack a sideways glance, thinking, *Boy, he is acting strange this morning, he's too quiet. Something's going on here...and what's with him wanting to go to this Don guy's house?*

Jack said, "Carl, remember, after we go to town, I'd like to stop at my partner's condo and check something out. It's close to your aunt's house, so it's not that far out of our way. I'll only be there a little while. It's okay with you, right?"

"Sure, Jack, anything you want."

Jack spotted a group of people walking towards them up ahead and shouted back to Ben, "Heads up, Benny, company on your left."

They drove past the people without incident, two of the women waved. Jack warily eyed them in the truck's side mirror. He felt like he was back in Afghanistan, constantly scanning for anything that looked out of place.

Wanting to get his mind off what he might find at Don's place, he asked Carl, "So, what's those two squawky chickens back there with Benny for?"

Relieved the topic of conversation wouldn't be one of those father-in-law/son-in-law talks, Carl said, "Just call me 'Chicken Man,' Jack. Those are two layers that are getting past their prime. Plus, Laura packed up two dozen eggs. Folks will do anything for some eggs, especially fresh ones. And what's better than a couple of live chickens? Going to make for some good bartering."

"What exactly are you looking to trade for?"

"Charlie's pontoon boat is in that little storage yard down by the river, next to the boat ramp. I want to bring it up to the house where it will be safe. I figure we can go out on the river, go fishing, maybe relax a little on it with the kids. Trouble is, somebody stole the gas tanks out of every boat down there. I need a couple marine tanks and I bet there will be some at the market. Heck, Charlie's own tanks will probably be there. The girls need some feminine stuff, you know...I got a list here. I'll look around. I'm sure we'll find something interesting we can use."

Upon arriving at the park, everyone was amazed at how big the flea market had become. There were lots of vendors and plenty of customers. It looked like many people were permanently camped there and, as Laura had said, nearly everyone was openly carrying a firearm. The parking lot was full and had numerous old cars and trucks, some of them dating to the 1920's. Carl got a good parking spot up front, but the truck couldn't be left unguarded, even for a few minutes. Jack got out, but stayed nearby, and he wasn't alone. Anyone who had driven a vehicle there dared not leave it out of their sight. Every vehicle in the lot had someone in it, or standing nearby, keeping a watchful eye.

Besides the chickens and eggs, Carl and Ben had a bushel of overripe tomatoes, some onions, green peppers, and Jack's carton of cigarettes. Ben had gathered up two laundry baskets full of small apples that were mostly taken off the ground from under Charlie's apple trees. Jack didn't say anything to Ben, but he doubted anyone would want his wormy apples.

As Carl and Ben started to walk towards the market, Carl said to Jack, "I can't say this is the safest place around, but everybody is armed. If somebody causes trouble, it's a no-win situation for them. If someone gets kicked out of here, they're screwed. I heard this is the only place like this in the county. Come on, Ben, let's see what we can find, I don't want us to go home empty handed."

Jack had been in many open-air markets when he was in the service, but nothing he had seen compared to this one. It was a cross between markets he had seen in Tijuana, Mexico and Afghanistan. Things that could normally never be openly sold anywhere in the states was available here. Gasoline was being sold in every kind of container, from the big red five-gallon cans to clear plastic one-gallon water jugs. Guns and ammo were being sold in nearly every space. Unlike most of the flea markets Jack had been to, absent from this one was the electronics, video games and stacks of old vinyl records. Liquor, drugs, cigarette's, ammo, and cans of food looked to be the biggest sellers. There were no tables. Everything was either being sold out of the back of a vehicle or was laid out on the ground. There was a big tent and a large white box truck that had the words, **FUN TIME,** crudely painted on its side. They didn't need the sign; everyone knew what they were selling. The five young women leaning seductively against the truck made it perfectly clear.

He watched with interest as a well-dressed, but disheveled man and his wife were trying to buy a rusted-out, old extended work Chevy van parked near him. The van must have been originally painted white, and had seen hard use. It was a rusty streaked cream color and looked like it was salvaged from a junk yard. The for sale sign on it read: RUNS GREAT! COMES W/ FULL TANK + 3 XTRA 5 GALLON CANS OF GAS! IT'LL GET YOU THERE!

The fellow trying to buy the truck was grey haired and middle-aged, with a thick foreign accent. Jack guessed he was Greek, and he was near enough to catch the whole conversation.

"Look, I have cash, do you understand? Just tell me how much you want for this piece of shit, will you?"

The greasy looking man selling the van, said, "Hey, don't piss me off, Zorba, or you won't get it for any price."

"What do you mean calling me Zorba? My name is not Zorba and how could I possibly piss *you* off? I will pay you $50,000 for your crummy van. I have it in cash in this brief case." He held up an expensive looking brown alligator briefcase for the seller to see.

"Look pal, I told you. I want six, one-ounce gold coins or the equivalent in silver. I might even work something out for a load of booze or cigarettes, but **NO CASH!** Can you understand that? I admit this van looks like shit, you're right about that, but it runs like a top, has great tires and comes with extra gas. Everybody wants these big vans. I won't have it long. You want to get up to Wisconsin to your bug out place, this is your ticket. Six gold coins, pal, and we have a deal." In a final desperate attempt, the man with the briefcase opened it up and displayed the most cash Jack had ever seen.

He swallowed hard and said, "I have two cases like this. They contain a total of $750,000, in one hundred-dollar bills. I will give you all of it, right now, for your beat-up old van. Tell me we have a deal."

The man selling the van smirked and shook his head. "I don't care if it was an even million, pal. If you offered me a thousand rolls of shit paper, you might have a better a chance. Those Ben Franklins you got in that case aren't even big enough to wipe my ass with." He started laughing, saying, "The dollar has dropped like a rock, go paper your walls with it. By winter, people will be using paper money to keep themselves warm. Nobody in their right mind is taking paper anymore, everyone's trying to get *rid* of the shit."

The man with the briefcase turned and faced an attractive, black-haired woman who had been standing behind him. He sighed, looking defeated, and slowly nodded his head. Her face expressionless, she reached under her coat and produced a small change purse. Opening it, she counted out six gold South African Krugerrands.

The man selling the van started laughing, and quickly turned to a guy next to him, saying, "Didn't I tell you, Mike? I knew he had some gold, all these foreigners got it."

The buyer handed him the gold coins and the seller gave him a key, saying, "It's all yours, Zorba, drive safely." Jack watched as the new owner started it up and promptly drove off. The good-looking black-haired lady was with him.

Jack continued to look around and was happy he had gotten rid of all his cash, thinking, *a single copper penny is now worth more than a thousand dollars in cash, holy shit.*

A little farther down, there was a sign next to a large covered charcoal grill that read, _Stick Dogs_. Cut up chunks of _Mutton_ on a skewer. There was another next to it that said,_ German Shepherd Pie_. Jack shook his head in disgust, *anything to make a buck.* He smiled to himself, half expecting to see Al and Lois standing behind the barbecue grill. His smile about the clever signs faded as he thought, W*hat will they be roasting come winter?*

"Jack!" He turned around, and it was Carl and Ben. Both of them were excited.

369

Carl said, "You should see the stuff we got for those chickens and eggs. Nobody here has any eggs, let alone live chickens. We did really good."

Jack asked Ben, "Anyone take your apples?"

Ben excitedly smiled, "I traded them for two bags of brown sugar!"

He was surprised someone wanted the apples and let out a laugh, but frowned when he saw Ben eyeing up the grilled stick dogs.

Ben hungerly said, "Hey guys, those look pretty tasty."

Carl started laughing, "Ben, it's time to go. You don't want any of them, believe me. You'd probably be puking your guts out in ten minutes."

Jack said to Carl, "Anyone interested in my carton of cigarettes?"

"Yeah, plenty of people. But I think you should keep them. From what I can see, a year from now there won't be any left. Cigarettes may be worth twice their weight in gold someday, but they're yours to trade if you can find something you want. We could babysit the truck if you want to take a walk around?"

"Maybe I will take a look around, but you're probably right about the cigarettes. People will go hungry before they will give up their smokes. I'll leave them here."

Jack had an uneasy feeling since the moment they pulled into the market and the feeling grew as he walked around. There were too many desperate looking people milling around the fringes. All of them were wearing dirty clothes that looked too big on them. It was apparent that for the first time in U.S. history, Americans were losing weight. Most everyone had a hollow, empty look on them, and that included the people who were selling food. He took notice of the food that was available. It was mostly canned goods and the type that would definitely not be at the top of anyone's shopping list. Many of the cans were missing the labels and were dented. It could have been cans of dog food, for all he knew. Items such as lima beans, creamed corn, pumpkin, and the like were plentiful. Hearty soups, baked beans, chili and meats were not to be found in any quantity. It also seemed like every person there was carrying something and was eager to trade it.

As he walked about, Jack listened to the conversations. There was an air of cautious optimism amongst most and that was about the relief camps. Everyone had heard that the camps were finally open. All anyone had to do was to somehow get to them and walk in. There was supposedly plenty of food and shelter for all. They were into the first week of September, and although the weather was still pleasant, October would be colder and wet, with winter following close behind. Everyone was talking about finding food, warm shelter, and the camps.

The promise of plentiful food, water and a safe place to sleep was a powerful draw. Knowing how our government worked, Jack knew folks were going to be wishing they'd stayed home.

He had seen enough and was about to walk back to the truck when a big fellow who had his back to him, suddenly turned and blindsided him with a fist the size of a canned ham, square to his face! His nose splattered and he flew backwards, slamming onto the ground! He struggled, unable to get up, and felt powerless as strong hands ripped the 45 out of its holster. Another blow followed, this one a savage kick to his ribs, sending a searing pain up the left side of his chest.

"Did you think I'd forget how you kicked me into that hole in front of your house...right in front of the whole neighborhood? How do you feel now, asshole?"

Standing above him was none other than pig face himself, Dirk Hayes.

"I see you're all alone here, jarhead, and guess what? Nobody gives a shit, so I'm going to stomp your fuc..."

Suddenly, Dirk collapsed almost on top of Jack, his knees buckling under him.

Though both of his eyes were teared up, Jack could make out a tall black man wearing a blue ballcap. He was holding up an old Louisville Slugger baseball bat, standing over Dirk.

"I don't know what you did to make this big lummox mad at you, Jack, but I don't think we should be around when he wakes up."

Father Steve helped him to his feet and picked up his gun off the ground. The priest looked down at the man he had just hit, thinking, *if he wakes up...* A crowd of people had gathered, but no one offered to help Dirk, who was knocked out cold on the grass. As quick as it started, it was over, with folks stepping over and around Dirk. As soon as Jack stood up, blood started streaming from his nose and his head was spinning.

Father Steve struggled to keep Jack standing, saying, "Jack, can you talk? Are you here alone, or with someone?"

Jack was dazed and in pain. His chest felt like someone had stabbed him.

"Jack, do you remember me? I'm Father Steve. We have to get you out of here."

"Yeah, I remember you..." Jack looked down at Dirk, "I thought... I thought you said you were a priest?"

Father Steve cocked his head, giving Jack a weak smile. "I'm doing my best... Are you here with someone?"

Jack weakly pointed towards the parking lot. Father Steve grabbed his right arm, got it up over his shoulder and helped him towards the lot. They were almost there, when Jack heard a familiar voice.

"Well— looky, looky here. If it isn't the big tough Jack Hansen, the nation's gift to the United States Marine Corps.... Looks like someone finally kicked your ass—but good. I hope that someone was my brother, Dirk. I know he's around here somewhere."

Jack was face to face with a smiling Sheriff Chuck Hayes, dressed in his civilian clothes. Hayes eyed Father Steve suspiciously, eyeing the bat he was carrying. He continued walking past them, laughing and yelling, **"What comes around goes around, dickhead!"** Hayes kept on walking, laughing, muttering to himself.

Father Steve said, "I think it's 'What goes around comes around."

About a hundred feet ahead, he could see Carl casually talking to Ben by his truck. Feeling like he could pass out at any moment, Jack said, "Yeah, whatever you say Steve. Get me over there by that pickup truck. Those two guys standing next to it are my friends. That guy we just saw is the baby brother of the gorilla you just cold-cocked. We have to get out of here fast or there will be trouble, big trouble."

Carl was first to spot Jack. He sprinted to him, followed by Ben.

Carl started to say something, but Jack cut him off, "Get me in the back of the pickup. I have to lay flat. My head is spinning and I think I gotta couple busted ribs." Carl started to ask what happened, but he cut him off again. "We have to get out of here fast, right now. I'll tell you later. This is Father Steve. He just saved my ass and he's coming with. Get me home boys, I'm really hurting."

As Carl and Ben laid Jack into the bed of the truck, Steve started to protest, "I'll be okay. I'll just continue on towards the camp..."

"**No**!" It was Jack, he spoke quickly, out of breath. "You have to come with us. You'll never make it there. They will hunt you down. You'll be dead within an hour. Carl, get us out of here—fast!"

Father Steve climbed into the back of the pickup bed with Ben, and together the four of them left the market. It would be a long time before Jack ever returned.

* * * * *

"**Oh my God! What happened?**" Lynne opened the front door, as Carl and Ben led Jack in.

Carl said, "He had a run-in with Dirk Hayes. Dirk caught him by surprise."

Jack's nose was crooked and both eyes were nearly swollen shut.

Lynne asked, "What did he get hit with? Let's get him over on the couch."

Father Steve said, "This big gorilla of a man turned around and hit him in the face with his huge fist for absolutely no reason. Then he took Jack's gun and kicked him in the chest while he was on the ground. He was raising his boot to stomp him in the face when I, ah... intervened." Father Steve held his bat up. "I don't like violence, but some people are hard to sway. I didn't expect that a person so big and mean looking would have dropped so fast from one little bop to the head."

Lynne looked up Father Steve, "I don't know who you are, but we're thankful you happened to be there and stopped it. Thank you."

While Lynne examined Jack's nose, he pointed to a spot on the left side of his ribcage. "I'm pretty sure I have some busted ribs where he kicked me. I've had broken ribs before, they hurt, but these *really* hurt. That bastard surprised me and kicked the shit out of me." Jack looked up at Father Steve, a pained look on his face. "Thanks, Steve, if you didn't happen to be there, that big lummox would have killed me."

Father Steve said, "I was about to come over and say hello to you when that man suddenly turned around and slugged you. He kicked you when you were on the ground. I couldn't let him do it again."

"All right, Jack, you can talk about it later. Let's look at your ribs." Lynne quickly cut Jack's bloody T shirt off and examined a red swollen area on the side of his rib cage. She carefully felt the area, slightly feeling the outlines of each rib.

Jack winced, "Yep, them's the ones."

"They're not pushed in or out of place. Thank God for that. I think at least four of them are cracked. Slowly, take as deep a breath as you can. Any stabbing pains?"

"No. It hurts, but not like a rib is sticking into something."

Father Steve said, "Yes, thank God for that, it could have been much worse. That man's boots were huge."

Laura, Jo, and Kathy entered the house, Laura saying, **"Oh my God, Dad! What happened, who hit you?"**

Lynne looked up at her, "He'll be fine, Laura. He has a broken nose. That makes three of us now... and he's going to be sitting around for a while, taking it easy." Sternly looking back to Jack, she said, "*Aren't you?*" Carefully wiping dried blood off his face, she said, "He has at least four cracked ribs. There's not much that can be done for cracked ribs, other than to let them heal." Still looking at Jack, she gently said, "Your nose has been knocked out of place. I'll have to straighten it. It's going to hurt a bit. You're going to have stay put on this couch for a while. Laura, go out to the garage and look in Charlie's little freezer, there's two ice packs in there." Laura hurried to the garage, while Lynne continued to carefully look Jack over for other injuries. Lynne shot a worried look to Jo, indicating that Jack's injuries may be more serious than she told Laura. Placing her hand on his forehead, she said, "How are you feeling, Jack? Do you feel sleepy or nauseated? You sure you don't have any pain anywhere else?"

"Yeah, my ego, it's crushed. I was walking around looking at everything and I forgot how dangerous life has become. And no, I'm not sleepy and I don't

373

feel nauseated. I don't have a concussion, if that's what you're getting at. I'm pissed off and what I feel like doing is going after that big sonofabitch."

Ben said, "We should have stayed there and finished it. We could have gotten rid of both those guys, once and for all!"

Jo said, "As much as people hate the Hayes boys, they do have friends and it could have turned out worse. We'll run into them again, believe me. Maybe we can go out looking for them sometime and take them out on our terms, but not now."

Lynne handed Jack two pills, and said, "I want you to take these, it'll help with the pain. If you feel sleepy, I want you to try and stay awake. Jack, what year did you go into the Marine Corps?"

He gave her an exasperated look, "1911—Good Lord. I got a busted nose and a couple cracked ribs, no concussion. The pain is better. I'm going to be sore, but I'll be all right. Wait until I get my hands on that asshole."

"All right, Jack, calm down. You just lay here on Charlie's couch." She handed him two icepacks and covered him with a blanket saying, "You try to keep the ice against your ribs, and keep the other one over your nose. We'll all be in the kitchen. I'll be back to check on you in a couple minutes. We'll have to do something about your nose right away." Once in the kitchen, she turned to Laura, "I think your dad is hurting worse than he's letting on. What do you think?"

"I agree. He's bullheaded and doesn't want to admit how the sheriff's oaf-of-a- brother caught him off guard and hurt him. I can tell he's in real pain. Are you sure he'll be all right? Aren't you supposed to tape up broken ribs?"

"They used to do that, but it makes the pain worse and doesn't make them heal any faster. Your dad is going to have to rest and take it easy, and that's going to be hard for him."

Laura said, "He'll never get any rest with that yelling going on. It sounds like Carl and Ben are having an argument."

They both went out into the front yard where Carl was unsuccessfully trying to talk Ben out of going back to the flea market. Ben wanted to exact revenge on the Hayes brothers.

Lynne stepped close to Ben and faced him, "You're not going back to town and that's final, just get it out of your head. We don't need you hurt too."

Ben's upper lip curled, "You know, Lynne, you like to boss people around. That goes for Carl and Jo too. I could leave here any time I want and you people can't stop me. I'm not afraid of anybody!"

Lynne softly said, "We know you're not afraid, Ben, but would you agree that Jack is the toughest person here?"

"Of course. Jack and my Dad could kick anyone's ass." Ben thought about what he just said and shuffled his feet. "I guess you're right. My Dad's gone and Jack almost got stomped to death. But someday I'll have the chance, and I'll know when it's right to take it. I'm sorry, it's just that sometimes I feel like my opinion doesn't count here and I'm sick and tired of it."

Jo stepped up next to Ben and said, "Your opinion does count. We have to stick together, or we won't make it." She nodded to Father Steve, who was standing apart from the group, listening. "I don't think Father Steve has been properly introduced. Tell everyone who you are, Steve, and where you came from. You've been on the road for a couple weeks, tell everyone how bad it's gotten out there."

Steve introduced himself and recounted how he had been struggling to make his way out of the city. Jo told the group how he had stopped by the back fence earlier asking for some water, and how Jack had given him not only the water, but also some food.

After to listening to Steve talk about how much more brutal it was becoming on the streets, Ben apologized. "I'm sorry. I just get so pissed off. We try so hard, we don't bother anyone, and people just walk all over us. They attack us and we let them go— when we should just kill them. I'm not a kid, I'm almost seventeen. I'm tired of people trying to take what we have."

Kathy said, "We all feel the same way. Nobody likes what is happening to us. But we have something here, Ben, something most people today don't have, certainly not those homeless who are heading towards those government camps. We have each other, and all of us have skills that will keep us healthy and safe. I don't think any of us realized we were treating you like a kid. They treat me like a dumb blond though..." Everyone except Ben laughed. Kathy continued, "It's just sometimes all of us are guilty of wanting to do something foolish. It might be out of anger or just plain bullheadedness. It's up to the group, or someone in it, to set that person straight." Kathy looked over to Lynne and smiled, "Even if it's Jack."

Ben shuffled his feet, hesitantly saying, "I know you're right.... I usually don't think when I'm pissed. I just react...it's just the way I am." Carl and Jo both gave Ben a hug. Lynne sternly placed her hands upon her hips, saying, "That reminds me, Benjamin—have you brushed your teeth this week?"

Ben pushed Lynne away, "That's it, now I'm really pissed!" He started laughing, and so did everyone else.

Kathy turned to Father Steve, "Welcome Father. I'm Kathy. Jo and I are the only Catholics here, but everyone is Christian."

Ben interrupted, "Sorry, not me. My family has never gone to church and I ain't about to start."

Kathy rolled her eyes and whispered to Father Steve, "We're working on him."

Exasperated, Ben snapped, "There you go, doing it to me again. Do you want to know what I believe? I believe we are here—period. This is it, for good or bad, and your prayers are *nothing* but wishful thinking. They might make you feel good, but nobody is there to hear them. We're totally on our own and this is

375

as good as it gets." Kathy shrugged her shoulders and faced Father Steve. "Anyway, you can see we have a well-rounded group here, but all of us are thankful that you saved our Jack. We're a tight group, but before the power went out, most of us didn't know one another. We probably might never have been friends, either. Our life styles and politics vary, but the crap hitting the fan brought us together, and now we're a family. Father, I know I speak for everyone; our home is your home, and you're welcome to stay with us. We have a shower, *with hot water*. After you clean up, we'll be just about ready for dinner. That the person you hit with your bat, as Jack would say, 'Doesn't deserve to walk God's green earth'. We suspect he and his brother are behind some brutal, unsolved murders." Kathy pointed towards the back of house. "Behind us, in the backyard, we've buried a number of good Christian people. One of them was a young man named Walt. We really didn't know him but, like you, he helped us out, and we think the two men that you dealt with today killed him. There's been other senseless murders here and we think those two might be connected to them, but we can't prove it. But we do know one thing, we're surrounded by evil. That big guy you hit hates Jack, and *you* hurt him. His brother is a County Sherriff and he'll be out hunting for you *and he will find you*— and he'll *kill* you. For your own safety, you have to stay here with us, at least for a while."

Jo spoke up. "Maybe the big ape didn't regain consciousness. Sounded like Father whacked him really good—he could be dead." Jo smiled. "We can only hope... and pray."

Father Steve removed his ball cap, revealing a sparse head of curly grey hair. Running his hand through it, he said, "No, I wouldn't ask that for anyone. I just hope I knocked some sense into him. Maybe he'll learn not to mess with people. I just wanted to stop him, that's all. I've been dealing with those types every day. I don't think all of them are necessarily bad people, but even those who are, are still redeemable. It's just that people aren't thinking clearly, they're scared, and there's many more takers than givers. So many are angry. It's hard to be reasonable when you're hungry and have lost everything. They're acting only on their emotions. So many have lost loved ones, and that changes people. Sometimes it makes them bitter and hateful, they shut God out." Father Steve placed his hat back on, pulling it firmly down, looking like he was about to leave. He said, "I was passing through that market today, hoping to hitch a ride to the refugee camp west of here. God granted me something special and I can't waste a minute of it. Folks need spiritual help, and that's my mission." He looked at Kathy, "You're very kind, but I'm not afraid and I should be going. Besides, I don't want to stay here and impose on you folks." Lynne started to interrupt, but Father cut her off, saying, "Do you really need another mouth to feed? I think not. If you want to help me, you could give me a lift towards the camp, far enough ahead to avoid those two men and their friends. I'd greatly appreciate that. Besides being a priest, I'm an old farm boy, and I'll do better out here than I can in the city. — I'll be all right."

"Did you really grow up on a farm?" It was Jack, everyone looked at him in surprise. He was standing on the front porch, leaning against the doorjamb, and holding an ice-pack to his face.

"Yes, I did, and I'm still part owner of it with my two brothers. One of only about 50 black-owned farms in Indiana."

"Jack, what are you doing up?" Lynne rushed to him. "I'm going to take you back to your house and get you into your own bed and you're going to stay there!"

"Sorry, Lynne, but I hate feeling left out... I don't know what you gave me, but I'm getting kind of groggy." Jack pulled away from Lynne's grasp and faced Father Steve. "Father, please stay with us for a few days. We'll get you safely to the camp, I promise you. There's an abandoned farm behind us, one street over. If you could give us some of your time, I have a plan, but—"

Lynne cut him off, grabbing his arm and leading him away. "Jack, you're going to drive me nuts! Come on, let's go. Carl knows your plan and will explain to him what you've been thinking about doing." As the two walked back towards Jack's house, the group stood in silence. They couldn't help but overhear Lynne, as she scolded Jack. "What am I going to do with you? You've been hurt. You're going to lie down and stay put, no more getting up. Look at you, your nose is bleeding again! And don't think you're going out tomorrow either."

Ben turned to Father Steve. "See what I mean, Steve? She's bossy, even to Jack."

The group laughed and Ben said, "Do I have to call you Father?"

Father Steve said, "Only if you want to. I won't be offended if you don't. If it'll make everyone more comfortable, just call me Steve, or Reverend. Just don't call me Leonard."

Ben looked at Steve questionably, "How come? Does Leonard mean something bad to Catholics?"

Steve laughed, "That was a joke, Ben. Really, you can call me anything you want. Just don't call me Jerry." Now everyone laughed, including Ben.

Jo said to Father Steve, "Why don't you use our shower and clean up? Afterwards we'll be ready for dinner. It'll be getting late; you should stay the night. You and Carl can talk tonight. If you don't want to stay past tomorrow, we'll understand and give you a ride to the camp in the morning. How's that?"

"Well... I have to admit that a hot shower and meal sounds good. I'm beat. All right, I'll stay overnight, and I'll listen to what Carl has to say in the morning."

Father Steve took his first hot shower since the power went out. Laura raided her dad's closet for some fresh clothing for him, and he ate the best dinner he'd had in over a month. After they were finished eating, they asked him about himself. He explained how he grew up on his parents' farm in Indiana with his two older brothers. Carl listened intently, noticeably interested. When Steve mentioned that after high school, he went to diesel mechanics school and became a certified mechanic at a truck dealership, Carl interrupted Steve. He asked, "Can you fix farm equipment?"

"Sure, living on a farm you learn to fix things yourself, if you can. My dad put my mechanic skills to use. I lived on the farm and maintained everything until I entered the priesthood. I still help out when I can."

Laura asked, "What made you decide to become a priest?"

"My family are all practicing Catholics and I attended Catholic schools growing up. I wasn't satisfied with my life and felt God was calling me to do something more important. Long story short, I entered seminary at the age of 32." They all laughed when he told them he was the only one there who could milk a cow, drive a tractor, and tear down a diesel engine. "I found true happiness."

After dinner, Carl showed Steve the garden. Before it got dark, they went to Jack's house and quietly went upstairs. From a second-floor bedroom window, the vacant farmland to the north was in full view.

Carl pointed out the window to the open land. "There it is, Steve. It's a pretty big spread, huh? Steve nodded his head and Carl continued to tell him Jack's plan. "We think it's over 400 acres. The whole thing had been farmed until about five or six years ago. The last couple years, they only planted some corn in that side section, but last year they didn't bother to harvest it. If we hadn't lost power, they'd be putting roads in right now. The whole thing was supposed to be developed into a housing project this past summer, but that's not going to happen now. Way off, in that far corner behind those trees, there's two big old steel pole barns. We've been in them and they're full of old equipment. Other than two tractors, we don't know how to use the stuff or what it's for, we're city folks. Nobody is going to do anything with this land. I may not know much about farming, but I know gardening. This topsoil here used to be river bottom and the black dirt goes down at least three feet. Steve, we want to make this a farm again. Our garden is fine, just for us, but it won't feed a neighborhood. Nobody is doing a thing. We're the only ones in this subdivision who are actually doing something. Everybody else is either giving up, running around acting like idiots, or waiting for the government to come to their rescue. We need your help, Steve. If we can get this planted, it's going to save a lot of lives come next winter."

Father Steve's eyes lit up. "Save lives, huh? You just said the magic words, Carl. I can stay for a while. Tomorrow morning, as soon as the sun is up, we'll walk those fields, then take a look at the machinery. We'll figure something out." Steve smiled and laughed to himself.

Carl said, "What are you laughing about?"

"The big man upstairs. He did it again. He sent me somewhere where I was needed. Tell me something, Carl, did you pray about this farmland?"

"Yes, I did. I'm Lutheran, and so is Jack. I know he prayed about it, because we talked about it."

"Well, I guess the man upstairs was out of Lutheran farmers who also know how to repair farm equipment, so he sent you a Catholic."

The two of them left the bedroom, Lynne was leaving Jack's room. In a low voice she said, "Don't talk so loud... he's finally asleep. As much as he's hurting, he's all excited about having a real live farmer staying here. It's a good thing too, it'll keep his mind off about what he wants to do to the sheriff and his brother." Descending the stairs, Lynne asked Steve, "You were up there in the back bedroom looking over that farmland, what do you think?"

"Fishes and loaves."

"What?"

"I think you're about to feed a lot of hungry people."

As the three of them left Jack's house, their conversation was interrupted by Jo, who yelled from across the yard. "Hey guys, we're going to have a campfire going pretty good in a few minutes, how about joining us?" She and Kathy had started a campfire over in Charlie's backyard and were setting up chairs around it.

Carl said, "We'll be right over, thanks." Turning to Steve, he said, "*You* are the answer to our prayers. Thanks for offering your help." Carl cocked his head towards the fire, "I think the girls have a couple bags of rock-hard marshmallows they're going to roast. Let's go join them." Carl and Father Steve joined the women around the campfire. Lynne and Laura sat there only a few minutes, then left to stay inside near Jack and the boys. As everyone sat down, Carl announced that Steve had decided to stay with them for a few days.

Steve said, "I'll walk the fields with Carl tomorrow and tell him what I think. We'll see if the equipment in those barns is any good. Farming is always hard work, but with what's happened, it'll be a lot harder. It's going to be tough to get supplies."

Carl said, "There are still farms here in Able County. There has to be feed and grain stores nearby."

Steve was looking around, admiring their garden, "You folks look like you did pretty good with what you have right here." Steve noticed one member of the group was missing. "Where's young Ben?" Jo spoke up, "Whenever we're gathered as a group like this, one person always stays separate, on guard. It's one of our rules. It's Ben's turn, so he's around here somewhere, watching. Also, you can see we're always armed. We're never without our firearms, or far from one. We take turns standing watch all night. We've been taught some tough lessons and we're still learning. It's not easy living here. We never go far from here alone and there is always someone in the house. You see what happened to Jack, just going to the flea market.

Steve agreed, "Yes, it's a dangerous new world. It's terrible that we have to live like this. It amazed me how quick people turned on each other, especially when the food and water started running out. It would be expected for the gangs to act as they did, but some of my own parishioners—I still find it hard to believe. It truly was a let-down. We have to pray it gets better."

Kay said, "You preachers always speak about praying. But what good does it do? Prayers or no prayers, this should have never happened to any of us, I don't understand it. We're good people. I'm not Catholic, but my husband and I regularly attended church, and so did my parents and now they're all dead. My husband was a good man and I prayed for his safety. He was brutally murdered in the back of his store." Kay turned, pointing over her shoulder. He's buried back there by the fence, with other good people who have senselessly died this summer. They died horrible deaths and what happens? God *rewards* their killers by letting them steal what they want and walk free. I hate them, and I find it hard not to hate God. If there is a God, there is no way that he listens or hears our prayers when he sends bad things to good people and cruelly takes any blessings, he supposedly gave them—away. You know what I think? It's very simple. There is no God."

There was an uneasy silence, and both Kathy and Jo wanted to spare the priest Kay's anger. Before either of them could interrupt, Kay started in on him again. "I want you to explain something to me, Father. Why is this being allowed to happen? If this God, who we've spent our whole lives following, is so almighty powerful and supposedly loves his followers, why doesn't he stop it? I'm not asking for the world to be perfect. But if he does exist, couldn't he have made it a little better, especially for those who believe in him?"

Kathy shot a "Oh no...here we go," look to Jo, and rolled her eyes. The fuse was lit, but Jo tried to cut it, saying to her, "I think we all have questions about these things, Kay. I know I do." Making a grimace, she turned to Father Steve, "You must be exhausted. I think we can ask you these questions later, maybe tomorrow, after you've rested."

"That's all right. You're not putting me on the spot. That's what the evil one wants. He's stacked the deck with logic, so I have no time to rest. Satan's logic makes fools of the intelligent and misleads the ignorant. If you have the time and an open mind, I'll give you your answers. People get pissed at God about something and forever close their ears. Even in good times most people don't want to hear anything I have to say. The folks that want to hear are the ones going to church. The folks that really need it, stay home. If this were a book, no matter how interesting, they'll skip the next few pages. —The bad guy wins."

Jo said, "Then go ahead, Father. I've spent my lifetime skipping pages. I'll listen."

Carl added, "Please tell us, Steve. We need to hear some good news for a change... as long as you're up to it."

"I'm always up to it and it is good news. The question is, are you folks up to it? I tend to be a bit long winded...."

Kay said, "Go ahead. I'll listen, but I may not agree with what you say."

"Fair enough. First off, *God does not send bad things.* He may correct us, but he does not hurt us. Some think that God sends the good and *also* the bad to us. Punishment for the sinner, no matter how harsh, can be justified, because they must have brought it down upon themselves. They probably did things that only God knows about, so they must have d*eserved it*, thus it's good, right? The answer is no. God doesn't crash a jet airliner into a school because he doesn't like the pilot or the music the kids are listening to. Anything that's causing pain, despair and confusion in your life *is **not** from God*. Our God is not vengeful. That's what separates us from Islam. Jesus taught love towards all, including non-believers. We're taught that our God is a *loving* father, who would *never* hurt us, and all *good things* are from God. Bad things may come our way, but he will use them for an ultimate good—always."

Kay interrupted, "A loving father doesn't kill his children or take away a good husband." The Bible says, 'He giveth and taketh away.' That's not loving."

"Kay, God loves us and will *not* kill his children. There is *nowhere*, I repeat *nowhere,* in scripture where the *Lord* says, 'I giveth and now I taketh away.' Read your Bible, it's *not* in there! You won't find it no matter how hard you look. Hollywood preachers say it—and who runs Hollywood? *Job is the one who said it, but God didn't*. The entertainment industry is full of people with an ax to grind against Christians. They purposely twist and misquote scripture, and it's done a lot of harm. People learn scripture from some atheist in Hollywood, isn't that just great? Someone who produces pornographic movies decides to make a movie on the life of Christ and his teachings. They film it in the Holy Land with beautiful music and a sprinkling of slanted scripture, and the ignorant public sucks it in as gospel. Listen, God's people are destroyed because they don't read his word *for themselves!* We have to pick up our Bibles and read them. Don't let some idiot in Hollywood dictate it to you. Our lives are not only affected by *our* sins, *but by the sins of others*. The hurtful things in our lives come from Satan, not God. The death of your husband was caused by the results of the sins of *another*. It's amazing the number of Christians who take the mention of Satan lightly. Believe me, he has no problem with that, and loves it when people think he's a joke or a myth—but he's not. So many people have told me these past months that they're angry with God for allowing this to happen. I ask all of you, who puts this anger in their head, who plants those seeds of doubt in a good Christian's mind? Doubt, that's Satan's favorite word, do you know that? He invented it. We have to know our enemy, and it's not God. *Never* be angry with God. As Christians, we are supposed to believe this life we have is just a blip, compared to the eternity in heaven we are promised, without pain, without suffering and with Jesus Christ. The atheist believes this is all there is. How sad is that?"

Jo cut in, "I'm not saying I don't believe in God, Father. But you have to admit, there's a lot of rich and successful atheists.

"And you want to know why, right? Why does God send blessings to people who deny and hate him? Why does he seemly reward terrible, evil people? The answer is, *God sends his blessings to all*, but *eternity* in heaven *only to those who follow his way*. Listen to me, God does not reward sinners. Their superficial lives are tragic and short. We only see the material things they have. The glamour and riches we see are like a coat of cheap paint. These people are hiding under it, and believe me, they're scared. They lead a mixed up, screwed up life, with the constant fear of being caught, humiliated, put in jail and the worst fear of all: losing the love of their family. *They worship things and fear people*. It would be much better to *worship God and fear losing their soul*. Then they wouldn't have to fear anything else. But no, they just keep stumbling down their dark paths. Look at the people in Hollywood, they're the obvious ones. They pass their sick lives off to our youth as normal and call it culture. Satan is tricky. Instead of watching the man that's wearing the suit, he's got us busy watching the stage show. Remember, it's not about what we see in the left hand, it's what's hidden in the right. Christ is not fooled by a pretty face or a well pressed suit, and we shouldn't be either. Hollywood and the media are smoke and mirrors. These people are sick, and yes, most look wealthy. But it's all going to come to light. Satan spreads sickness and God's written word is the pill. It's a prescription for happiness. We have to read it if we want to be *awake.* When you're awake you'll know the truth, because you'll *see* things that have been purposely hidden."

Kathy said, "Jo is right, they do look happy, but their lives are usually a mess. It would be interesting to see what they're doing right now."

"I think it's a safe bet to say they're scared. Satan's followers like everyone to think they're happy, but they're not. They're being punished and their mixed-up lives are the proof of it. The ones who say they hate God and deny him, they're lying to themselves. There's a shadow of fear, a drop of clarity, and it's constantly whispering to them, 'What if I'm wrong?' We don't see it, but it's there. They claim there is no heaven, but pray there is no hell. People jokingly say that all the time—but are they really joking? They deny Christ by their words and by their actions. They will lie to your face and say they could care less about God—but believe me, *they do*. God is there, and deep down, *they know* it. That's why so many of them ask for forgiveness and try to cut a deal with God when they're on their death bed. He's been in their mind and has never stopped trying to redeem them, because even though they spit on him and say they hate him— *he loves them!* Listen, he never stops until you're dead... and once you're dead— well, you've had your chance. When people deny Christ, it's like a noose around their neck that gets tighter as they get older. The superficial things we see in their lives, the power that they think they have, is the *only* reward they'll get. They lead an empty, screwed-up life that could be followed by an eternity of hell, and you know what? Moments before their end comes, as the final darkness descends, they clearly see it!

Kay, as far as someone giving you an explanation that will make you understand and fully accept your husband's death, I ask you, is there *anything* that I can say that will make you say, *'Oh, now I understand!'* Is there?"

Kay stared into the fire, slowly shaking her head. "No. I don't think so." Father Steve was closely watching her, and said, "I knew you would say that. But let's say there was… Let's say I gave you *positive proof*, right now. You know what? Satan wouldn't give up. He'd still be working on you. Neither him nor God, *ever* stops working on us… until we're dead—then it's time to pay the fiddler."

Kathy said, "If we can figure all this out about Satan, then God knows it too. Why does he allow Satan to exist? Why doesn't he just destroy him? It's not logical. There's no reason for God to allow Satan to exist. This whole thing confuses me."

"This might be a tough question to answer to your satisfaction, but remember, he will destroy Satan. He'll be tossed into the lake of fire. Until then, he's just like you and I. Satan and all the fallen angels, like man, have free will. God the Father is the Creator of them. I would like to think that like man, the fallen angles are somehow redeemable, but they aren't. It may be because of who they are, and the fact that they knew God the Father from the beginning and *know the truth*. They know it—but still rejected him."

Kathy handed Father Steve a bottle of water, saying, "I was hoping for an easy answer."

Thanking her, he took a long drink, and continued, "I'm sorry, there's no easy answers, but this is what Satan loves. This is one of those traps he sets, so let's not get sidetracked and fall into it. Let's concentrate on what we do know. God loves us and grants us forgiveness, but first we must forgive others. It's really pretty simple. We have free will, everyone does. Kay's husband and the person who murdered him had it. We can do anything we want, choose one way or the other. It's totally up to us. Following God's commandments looks like a test to some. It's not a test, never…ever. God gave us the tools and that's his *written word*. We can listen or we can walk away. *We* are the ones who decide our fate, *for eternity.* And that's a great gift. Think about that. I mean, *really* think about it. That God, the Almighty Creator, in all his glory… *stands aside* and lets *us* decide our fate! That's no test." Father Steve's eyes glistened in the firelight. He made eye contact with each of them, then turned to Kay. "Kay, God could have granted us a perfect world with no consequences of our actions, whatsoever. But imagine a world with free will and no consequences. Would people ever feel sorry for doing wrong? Why bother? How many sinners would ask for forgiveness, if they knew in the end they would still be rewarded with eternal life? Would they ever be thankful for anything? How many decent people in our world would strive to be better? Would there ever be a Mother Teresa? Our reward *is eternal life with Christ*. Think of that, **Eternal life with Christ!**" Father Steve leaned close to the fire, bending over to pick up a small piece of firewood. Tossing it into the flames he said, "Some people's reward will be like this stick." He sadly shook his head, as the group watched the stick being consumed. "I know I come on strong here, but it's important. Satan only knows the words doubt and hate, and he loves them because it keeps people in a dark hole. He knows the light of forgiveness can free them, and believe me, the word forgiveness is not in Satan's vocabulary, so it must be utmost in ours. It's hard to get out of that hole once you're in it. So, we must learn to forgive, go for the light and let God sort it out... it *will* free you! This planet of ours just didn't plop here and evolve, like the atheists would have you believe. It was lovingly made, and evil wants to destroy it." For several seconds all of them sat there, no one saying a word.

Breaking the silence, Kathy said, "It's hard to have faith when you've been badly hurt. I know that first hand. It's much easier to be angry."

"Sure, it's easy to be angry and it's hard to forgive. We've all been badly hurt at some time in our lives, and we feel justified in our anger. Some of our friends and loved ones have been murdered. For all we know, the perpetuators of our loved ones' deaths may be dead themselves, but we still carry all this hate. We feel that it's our right. Believe me, Satan loves that, it keeps it going. Many have told me they don't believe in God anymore, or they think that God has totally abandoned this world. I've had people from my own church screaming at me, calling me every profanity, as if I lied to them. One of our former altar boys intentionally set fire to our church, gutting it."

The sun had fully gone down, and the flames of the campfire were reflected off everyone's faces. Fall was in the air and a cold breeze came up, scattering bright sparks and ashes, sending a sudden shiver through all of them. Father Steve shook it off, saying, "You all felt that, didn't you? Don't be afraid. God will *never* abandon any of you, or this world. Satan wants you to think that. He's here, he's here right now, but so is the Holy Spirit. Your free will, and which way you decide to go with it, determines your spiritual fate. Satan's ultimate goal is to *steal your soul*. Remember, the battle for your soul starts in your mind, as a seed of doubt planted by Satan, *the enemy of faith*. As Christians we must pray, *constantly*. Prayer is our most valuable weapon against him and his evil spirits... that want to destroy us. God hears our prayers and answers them on his dimension that, at this time, is *impossible* for us to understand."

Kay made an audible sigh. "That's where it always ends. You're going to tell us it's a mystery and it's up to us to have faith. Then it's goodnight, see you in church, and don't forget your contribution. I'm sorry, but religion is a racket and it's bullshit."

"Kay, that's what evil wants you to think! It's not a cop-out by me to get out of answering your questions, that's *exactly* how it is. Yes, *faith*. When I was a child, my mother told me to think of God's mind as a magnificent giant oak tree, and Einstein's mind as a tiny acorn. She told me to keep it simple, because the smartest person on this planet is that acorn. That sufficed me as a child, but you and I can agree that answer isn't even close. In the beginning, God the Father created time, space and matter, all at once. Before creation there were *no* ingredients. Think about that for a second.... Not only did nothing exist, but *nothing*, however we can humanly define it, did not exist. God created— *everything*, including *nothing*. That's why we call him God. Anything less and he would not be the supreme being, because something greater than him would have had to create him. That's why our God is an awesome God."

Jo very softly mumbled to herself, "Way too much to think about."

Father said, "I heard that and you're right, it's beyond our comprehension... that's what I'm trying to say. We human beings are **so arrogant!** Who says that man has to understand everything for it to be true, Satan? If we can't taste it, feel it, or see it, it has to fully explained to our satisfaction. Someone has to always *prove* it to us. If we still don't get it, we dismiss it or say, as in the case of scripture, it's a just bunch of fairytales."

Father Steve threw up his arms. "Satan wins... So, what are we to do with something we can't understand? It's easy... man evolved from pond scum, or some alien race created all this in some cosmic lab. Folks would rather believe that, than believe in God. Holy crap—God? Give me a break! People would rather close their ears entirely or believe some bullshit Hollywood story. Remember, Satan wants you angry. It pleases him. Notice I said pleases, because nothing ever makes him happy. God doesn't want us miserable. He shows us how to be happy. He gives us his written word and it's called scripture. Scripture tells us what to do! Why people don't read it, is beyond me! We are to *walk by faith, not by sight*. We let our *faith* become the *evidence that cannot be seen*. We are the apostles in that wave-rocked boat. The roaring waves and the angry sky are what is happening around us now, right here, and Jesus is not asleep, I assure you. He's *always* with you, even when you think he's not, *but so is the evil one*. He distracts, plants doubt, and sets traps." Father Steve uncapped his water bottle and took a drink. While screwing the cap on, he said, "People have been arguing when life begins but Satan knows when it does. A demon is there from your first heartbeat. It will wait a lifetime to destroy you and along the way will help you destroy others. It knows your every weakness and desire and will reward you with whatever it thinks you want—if it will keep you away from God. Satan knows God is real, and he spends *your* lifetime trying to prove to you he isn't. But—and this is a strong but...*God was with you first! Before* your first heart-beat—he was with you, because *he made* you and he *loves you*. Think of your heart as God's home and Satan as an unwanted visitor. An intruder that has entered to destroy you!"

Everyone was hunched forward in their chairs listening to Father Steve, as the fire was starting to go down. "Kay, I know God answered your husband's last prayer and listened to *his dying thoughts*. I ask you, are you and your son safe here? Carl told me you have special skills. You have training as a gunsmith and a marksman. They're skills that this group needs to fight the evil that has surrounded them. Could you have been the answer to *their* prayers? Carl told me that he and Jack prayed for an answer on how to re-start that old farm. Was it a coincidence that I was thirsty and happened to stop by your fence, asking for a drink of water? Jack could have sent me away. Did anyone here pray for Jack's safety when he went to the flea market in town, where I happened to be, baseball bat in hand? Lastly, you prayed that someone could give you an answer. *I pray that I have.* Every day I pray that I can help people get through this madness that has engulfed us. All you have to do is say, 'Here I am Lord' and he's there for you."

Father Steve looked around the campfire and into each of their faces, "We are in a battle here, but it's not for our lives, it's for **our souls.**" He pointed to the white plastic bag on Kathy's lap. "Now, how about those stale marshmallows? Here, give me the bag. You guys really got me going here— remember, I am a priest…. Enny beeny chilli beeny..**kazamm**!..... Nope, they're still stale! Boy, these are hard as rocks."

Kay said, I'm sorry for what I said about God and for putting you on the spot. I have thought about what my husband's last thoughts and prayers were. I know he would have prayed for our safety. You're right about the anger. I've got a lot of it, and it's not doing me or my little boy any good. I'm sorry… thank you for staying with us, Father."

"Did somebody say marshmallows?" Ben appeared and stood by Kathy, eyeing the bag of marshmallows on Father Steve's lap. Ben helped himself to a few, then left to continue his guard duty.

As he walked away, Jo leaned over towards Kay, "I wish Ben would have been here to listen to Father Steve's talk. He needed to hear it."

Kay said, "Yes, he does, but after everything he's been through, I think he's doing better. I certainly know how he feels. He complains like any teenager, but he seems to have put the past behind him, more than me."

Jo shook her head. "I thought so too, until I heard what he's going to do. He's planning on tracking down that girl who killed his dad. He's convinced she's alive and in one of the camps. He says he's going to find her and kill her."

"He told you that?"

"No, he told Kathy and she told me. I started to tell Jack yesterday morning, but Ben interrupted us. Don't let his joking around fool you. He's got so much anger buried in him; he's going to explode."

Father Steve and Carl sat quietly and listened to the women talking about Ben. Carl turned to Steve and briefly explained to him what happened to Ben's father.

Steve said, "So, he's biding his time for a come-uppance. There's a lot of that going on. I don't know how much you've seen in your little neighborhood here, but in the city it's an epidemic, old grudges, neighbors who never got along and family feuds. People who were abused as children, are using this as an opportunity to exact revenge. We had a rash of suicides start after the first two weeks, as well as murders. All of a sudden, people in our parish, including one of our schoolteachers, were being murdered for no apparent reasons, leaving us asking, 'Why?' Believe me, most everyone is carrying something. People don't carry it on their sleeve, but it's there. Everything is coming to light and nothing is hidden. Something might have happened to someone 40 years ago, and they decide this is the perfect time to get even. That's why we have to quickly forgive and not let anger take root. As a priest, I've heard things and I know things—I've put them out of my mind, but it's not hard to put two and two together. Churches in the city are being burned, and innocent clergy of every faith are being attacked. The coals of unbridled anger are being stoked by Satan himself. It doesn't have to be that way; we can end it—by forgiveness.

It's so simple, just turn all the nasty baggage we carry—over to God. We can't possibly bear it, so let him carry it. Remember that anger and hate are heavy chains padlocked around our neck. *Forgiveness* is the key to that lock. If people would only use the time they spend on anger, gossip and revenge on prayers, our world would be a different place. Let our prayers become our swords. I'll talk to Ben and he'll change. I promise you he will. Christianity is not an exclusive club. It exists for the non-believers, the atheists and the agnostics. Ben will fit in fine."

Kay asked, "Are you always so confident in yourself, Father?"

"Yes."

Jo said, "Us sitting around this fire, it's been good—but you don't know us, Father. We're from the left to the right, both politically and spiritually. I guess that much is obvious, but there's other things about us that you know nothing about. Our lifestyles and things we've done—and failed to do, don't fit in with the teachings of the church. I've done some terrible things, Father. If I didn't, we might not be sitting here tonight. The anger I once had and the hate is gone. That's ironic, huh? It took the shit hitting the fan to do it."

"I'm not going to judge you, Jo. I see Christ in you. I see Christ in all of you. That's the key. See Christ in every person."

"We just want to survive this, Father—without losing our dignity or our souls."

Father Steve said one word, "Courage."

Early the next morning, Father Steve and Carl walked towards the vacant farmland. The sun had just come up, and there was a fine mist rising from the ground. A damp and early fall chill was in the air.

Carl said to Steve, "Thanks again for the talk last night, Steve. You're right about the hate. People have gone nuts. I've never even been in a school yard fight, let alone owned a gun. And now..." Carl raised his jacket revealing a holstered 38 revolver. "This belonged to my uncle. I have to wear it all the time."

Steve said, "I've noticed you folks have shotguns in every room, including the bathroom."

"Pretty sad way to live, huh?" Carl stopped and gestured with his arm to the open field before them. "This is it, Steve. This is what we want to farm. Let's take a walk out to the center of it and you can tell me what you think. It's hard to believe October is almost here. There's so much we have to do before winter. We have to preserve what we've grown. I know something about gardening, but canning, preserving and keeping stuff fresh, not so much. I had to go to the Melville Public Library to find books on it. Laura and I filled the back of our pickup truck with books. Most of them were reference books on everything imaginable, except computers." Carl laughed, "It used to be so easy to look up things on the internet, I seldom went to a library for a reference book."

"Yes, reference books—a whole generation has already grown up not knowing what an encyclopedia is. It appears computers, as we know them, are done for, doesn't it? Good riddance, I say. Someday they'll come back. Hopefully, we will have learned not to depend on them and know the damage they are capable of. I honestly don't think they'll come back in our lifetime, there's going be too many basic things that have to be rebuilt first. You and Jack are right about the farms. One year without planting, that's all it will take to kill over half the population of this country, maybe more. People in the cities are starving now, imagine what it will be like with no food a year from now? It's so sad, how could we have let this happen? I can't fathom how many people will perish and the knowledge that will be lost by their deaths. The machines will still be here, but there won't be enough people with the skills to get them going, or keep them going."

"It's a scary time, Father. Laura is over two months pregnant, and I have to tell you, I'm scared."

"I understand that you're scared, this is a tough time. But you're in good hands here. Lynne is a capable nurse. You have food, clean water and warm shelter...and a loving family with Christ at the center of it. Everything will turn out fine. Pray about it and share your fears with the others, as you did me. I will pray for you. Now let's walk these fields and see what you have."

Carl said, "You gave me another idea for my list of things to do, I'll need a bigger truck though."

Steve looked perplexed, "Why, is your list that long?"

"Oh, it's long all right. I was just thinking that I'd better get another couple of truckloads of books, or move into a library!"

Steve laughed, "It's funny, but true. We're only one generation away from losing crucial skills. It's sad. I bet there isn't a library in Chicago that is still standing."

They reached the center of the field and Carl kicked his boot heel into the dirt, loosening up a black clod. "Look at this soil. The topsoil in this part of Illinois goes down three feet. You get further up in northern Wisconsin, they got maybe four inches, and it's nothing like this black soil."

"You're right. We're standing on some of the best farmland in the country, and we haven't been good stewards of it. That should be a sin, huh?"

"It sure should." Carl pointed to several acres of standing corn. "That corn over there was planted last year, but they never harvested it. But it's still been good for us, it's attracted lots of geese and deer. I can't figure out why they never came back to harvest it. The builders just started digging that trench right into it."

Carl followed Steve as he walked over to the dried out, tattered field of corn.

Steve said, "Doesn't look like much effort was put into planting this corn. As beat down as it is, it still should have been taller and thicker. You say that this land has been owned by a developer for a long time?"

Carl said, "Yep, this field should be full of houses being built by now. There's a huge billboard on the far end of it, the developer's name is on it. They're out of Chicago." Carl pointed to the far northwestern edge of the field. "You can't see it from here, but they were digging at that corner too. It wouldn't have been farmland much longer."

Steve pulled at an ear of crumbling corn. "Developers get taxed as if it's still farmland, as long as they keep crops on a certain percentage of the land. They probably had someone plant this corn for tax reasons. That's how the game is played. They will rent land out to a farmer, who will plant hay, or corn, maybe beans on it. As long as it's being used as farmland, they're taxed at the lower rate. They make some money off the farmer when he harvests the crops, to pay the property taxes. It's all about working the system. That's why this corn looks stunted and is full of weeds. They're not going to waste money on fertilizer or weed control if the property has the possibility of being bulldozed before harvest time. A developer isn't going to let a field of corn get in his way. The farmer never harvested his corn, but he still got paid. Imagine someone doing that in some country where people are starving? That's the American way, the accountants run the show." Steve picked up a couple empty, rotting cobs. "Too bad Jack didn't think of his plan earlier. You could have harvested this corn for seed, it's too late now."

They continued to walk the fields. Every so often Steve would bend over and pull at a weed. He yanked at a small tree; its roots unyielding.

389

Carl said, "What is that stuff? It seems to be coming up everywhere."

Steve laughed, "That my friend, is a farmer's nightmare." He yanked unsuccessfully at the small bush-like plant. "That's Buckthorn, and it's bad news."

He pointed to the fence line of the property. Those tall trees you see over there on the side of the field, it's the same thing. Other than that corn, these fields haven't been planted in years, maybe four or five. Buckthorn is an invasive shrub. It'll grow 15 feet high and gets dense, super dense. It gets loose in a forest and it will crowd out and kill all the native trees, even oaks. All these invasive plants are like that." Steve kicked over a tall thistle plant that was about three feet high and then stopped. "Carl, I don't want to throw a wet rag on your plans to plant this acreage next year, but you've got some nasty stuff growing here. Most of this is the average weeds, like ragweed and golden rod. That'll be the easiest to deal with. But this woody stuff is different. You've got small trees and bushes coming up everywhere. A few more years and you won't be able to walk through here...but don't get me wrong, we'll get the job done."

As Steve surveyed the waist high weeds, he shook his head, "We've never let our farmland get this far out of hand because it's always in use. What would normally be done to a field like this is to blade it down to get these woody plants out. Blade it off, pile it up and burn it."

Carl said, "Where do we get this blade?"

"Maybe there's one in those machinery sheds you were talking about, but we'll need a running tractor to use it. Don't get discouraged if we don't find it. There's another way. September has been a dry month. Towards the end of October, the leaves on this stuff will be really dry. What we can do is set this entire acreage on fire. There's plenty of fuel, so it'll burn hot and even take out the green stuff. It'll knock this woody brush down and kill some of it. We'll burn up the seeds and a lot of pests too. We won't be able to control it, so it'll probably burn everything out, clear to the river bank."

Carl said, "There's maybe 400 or more acres here. You think we can burn off this whole thing?"

"We'll pick a dry, windy day with a steady breeze blowing out of the west. Yeah, I think we'll be able to burn most of it." Steve nodded to a line of tangled trees and bushes bordering the western edge of the farm. "That tree line looks like it hasn't been cleaned out in 30 years. It's choked with dead brush. We get a fire started along the entire length it on a windy day and it'll easily spread into the fields." He slowly spun himself around, surveying the vacant land, and almost to himself he softly said, "*This is going to be fun*. Come on, Carl, let's go over to those pole barns and check the machinery out. We've got about three weeks to get it running." Steve pointed towards the standing corn. "That area where the corn is standing will be ready to plant come spring. I don't know what you intend to plant, but that's a big chunk of land by itself. It'll be more than a good start if you just plant a couple acres of it. The rest of this place is going to take some more work. We'll plow up what we can this fall before it muddies up. The clods will break down some over the winter and make it easier to plant, come spring."

As the two of them walked towards the pole barns, Steve asked, "So, what do you have for seed?"

Carl said, "We don't have any."

* * * * * *

Jack had to get up to take a leak. It was early and the sun was just edging up. His head was throbbing, and his nose felt like an over inflated balloon. He sat on the edge of the bed for a couple minutes and lightly touched his sore ribs, cursing himself for letting Dirk Hayes get the better of him. Getting up, he stood over the piss bucket, looking out his second-floor bedroom window. Two people were far out, walking through the open farm field. It had to be Carl and Steve. Jo was in Charlie's backyard, and he remembered what she had said to him about Ben the day before. He thought, *Might as well go down and find out what she wanted to tell me about the kid.... God, my ribs hurt...* Jack cautiously descended the stairs, feeling a sharp pinch in his side with every step. With his nose throbbing, he slowly walked out into the damp September morning, regretting leaving his warm bed. Everything was wet with dew and fall was definitely in the air. Jo was sitting at Charlie's picnic table, honing an old Marine K-Bar knife.

Jack said, "Jo, do you ever take a break?"

"Only when I sleep, and I sleep lightly." She frowned at Jack and slowly shook her head. "Jack, what the hell are you doing up? You look like shit. If Lynne sees you out here, you're dead."

He eased himself down on the wet bench across from her. "I am hurting, I'll admit that. My ribs really took a whack and I'm pissed at myself for letting that big prick get the drop on me, he caught me good." He winced in pain, "I'm going to get that bastard, I promise you that. You think his face looks ugly now? Wait 'til I get done with him. I'm going to beat it to a pulp."

"Ah, revenge. That sounds so sweet." Jo lightly licked her lips and cut a long sliver of wood from the edge of the bench top. "There, that's how I want it. Someday I'll stick it right up that pig face's ass."

"You're something else, Jo, you know that? You're not the average woman. Sometimes you're downright scary."

Jo showed a thin smile, "I suppose I am; I've been told that before. Is it becoming on me?" Jack smiled back, but didn't answer.

391

She stuck the knife upright into the wooden tabletop, burying the tip at least an inch. "You missed a great fireside chat last night. Kay cornered Father Steve with the, 'I'm pissed off at God question.' I felt bad for the poor guy at first and tried to steer her away from it. But as tired as he was, he went for it and did a good job answering it."

"Did his talk change you?"

"It clarified a couple things, but no, it didn't change me. The last four months has changed my attitude and opinion about a lot of things. It's made me aware of what's truly important. I'm not so angry anymore. You know, before the shit hit, Kathy and I would go to mass every Sunday morning. I'd watch Kathy and others in church, so earnest in their prayers and their intentions. I wanted to be like them, but *I couldn't*. Instead of praying about things, I'd think about them and find myself getting pissed. No solution, no prayer, just anger. With prayer you find peace. It forces you to take a step back, even if it's only a moment. Prayer keeps me from doing something rash.

Jack interrupted her, "Like ripping my *'Make America great again hat'* off my head?"

"Yeah, right…. You're just kidding, I know you don't have one of those hats. Tell me you don't?"

"No, no hat. Although I do have an autographed photo of Ronald Reagan."

"Is it framed?"

"No."

"That's all right, I guess. Anyway, that's how I've changed. I've mellowed out and I know who the enemy really is. That's what Satan does to us. He distracts us, even in church. I was told, one time, that I have an attention deficit disorder. Imagine that? I'll tell you, in places like church it can go into full gear. Now, after what's happened to us, I'll think back and ask myself, why I ever let things bother me, because now we really got something to be pissed off about. They divided us, Jack. Divide and conquer, that's what they did. We were too busy bashing each other to see it for what it was. This was what they wanted all along. Keep both sides pissed off at each other. Let them do whatever they want, as long as their ultimate goal was reached. Now we're all screwed."

"And you think this mess was the intended outcome?"

"Yeah, I do. They let us destroy ourselves, so they can put it back together the way they want it. It's always been the men behind the curtain running the show and they're evil, just plain evil. They own the politicians. Money, sex, drugs. The politicians are paid actors and we're just the audience. Think about every president in our lifetime. We've been at war with somebody our entire lives. Our young men and women are constantly being killed. Do you know anyone who has voted for that? But that's what we always get, don't we?"

Jack shook his head. "Jeez, Jo, you think too much. As far as this attention defecate thing, I think I may have it too.

"It's deficit, not defecate. I'm being serious, Jack."

"I'm sorry, I know you are. I just don't feel much like talking. My nose feels as big as a politician's ego. As far as here and now, maybe it's a good thing we both have this attention deficit thing. I think people who have it see things differently and are unpredictable. That makes you and I formidable opponents. We think out of the box and will do the unexpected. Maybe that's why God made us that way and put us together, to defend our little flock here. I hate to see what's in store for us once this mess finally ends, I pray we can handle it. There is one thing that puzzles me—puzzles me in a good way. If we were at war with China or Russia, Chicago and northern Illinois would be a burned-out cinder by now. Why only nuke D.C. and not New York City, and Chicago? It makes me think that someone in our own military had enough of Washington's' bullshit and decided to do something about it. Put your mind to work on that for a while. But as for now, I'm going back to bed. My side is killing me."

"Hang on a second, before you go in. Let me tell you about our boy, Ben. Do you know he's planning on going to the camps to look for that girl who killed his dad? He's dead set that she's there. He figures she thinks she's safe from us because preppers like us wouldn't be caught dead in a government camp."

"Ben told you this?"

"No, he told Kathy. He's kept his mouth shut about it to the rest of us, knowing what we would say."

"What did he think, that Kathy would agree with him, or maybe help him?"

"He's got a crush on her and he tells her everything. All I know is that he's taken a sudden interest in our old Harley. I'm keeping the key on me, just in case our boy decides to take a midnight motorcycle ride."

She caught Jack eyeing her pack of cigarettes, so she pulled one out of the pack and handed it to him, sarcastically saying, "Here, this will help your sore chest." He started to stick it between his lips, but stopped, saying, "If he's made up his mind to leave, then there's nothing we can say to him that will make a difference. But in no way can we let him take any of our vehicles."

Jo pulled back, "You won't try to stop him?"

"What are we going to do, lock him up? He's free to walk away anytime he wants to. He's not my son and he's not a little kid."

Jo pulled out her lighter and lit Jack's cigarette, saying, "He may not look like a little kid, but he thinks like one."

"I'll talk to him if I get the chance. Right now, I gotta get back inside and lay down. I shouldn't have come out here—I'm hurting."

THE CAMP

CHAPTER 3 9

Two weeks had passed since Father Steve and Carl had burned the fields. They had gotten both of the old tractors running and had turned over almost half of the charred farmland. As Father Steve had predicted, the winds had whipped the fire they set into a storm that quickly engulfed the dry fields. When it finally burned itself out, the last flames were extinguished on the muddy banks of the Fox River. Jack wasn't much help with any of the work needed to clear the farmland. Although it was his brain-storming to place the unused land back into a productive farm, his cracked ribs still hurt him. He never complained, but everyone knew they still did. It wasn't only his ribs that were bothering him. He had two shiny brass keys that demanded an explanation. He sat out most of October, tending to his chickens and doing small jobs around the house. They were into the first week of November and the mornings were turning cold. Father Steve made an announcement after breakfast.

"Well folks, I think my job here is done. As cold as it is this morning, winter can't be far behind, and it's time for me to skedaddle. If you have time tomorrow, I'll take you up on the offer to drive me to Camp Able. I don't want to wait until the weather gets bad."

Jack said, "I knew this day was coming. I just wish I could convince you to stay. You won't eat as good there as you do here, and I doubt if they'll have any fresh eggs."

Father Steve gave a short laugh, "There's going to be lots of hungry people at that camp, Jack, and I intend to feed them all."

Jack cocked his head, not understanding. "Where are you planning to get the food?"

Father Steve pointed upwards with his forefinger. "I'm talking spiritual food, Jack. Long before this disaster happened, people were starving to death spiritually, they always have been. It's the reason why everything is so out of control now, it's been building since day one. This is an exciting time for me to be alive and a unique opportunity to bring people back to what is really important—to let them know they are never alone. It's a battle, Jack, and I'm heading into it."

Jack slowly nodded his head in agreement. "Maybe so, but you're always welcome back here...in case you get hungry for the real deal. If it gets too rough, you come back, even if it's for just a short rest to recharge yourself and have some good home cooking."

Jack moved in front of Steve and held up his hand in protest, "*Nothing* I can say to make you stay, huh?"

Father Steve shook his head saying, "I have to go. But don't worry, I'll be back next year to help with the harvest. My time here has been restful and I'm grateful to you folks for it. It was God's way of slowing me down. It gave me time to think and as you said, *recharge*." He sidestepped Jack, but stopped, as if suddenly remembering something. "God didn't order that kick in the ribs you got, Jack. Nonetheless, like every stumbling block that's thrown before us—he uses it to create good. Our meeting was good for both of us, and like I said that first day, it wasn't by accident. I'm re-charged now, Jack, and so are you."

Before sun-up the next morning, Carl pulled Ellen's car into the driveway of Charlie's house. Father Steve said his final goodbyes to Jack and Lynne, then climbed into the back of the small car.

Jo was about to get in the front seat to ride shotgun, when Ben quickly shoved himself past her, squeezing himself in next to Father Steve.

Jack loudly said, "Ben, where do you think you're going? Get out of there!"

Ben smiled, his lips set tight, shaking his head, "I'm tired of sitting around here. I'm going with, for the ride."

Jo stuck her head in the car, her face almost touching Ben's. She growled, "Ben, stop your bullshit and do what Jack says. Get the hell out of there! It doesn't take three of us to drive Father Steve to the camp!" Jo backed herself out and stood up, her hands on her hips, looking down at Ben. "You refuse to believe she drowned and you're going looking for her in the camps, aren't you?"

Ben snapped back, **"You're damn right I am! She's alive! She *thinks* she's safe!** She knows we wouldn't have any use for a government-run camp and wouldn't be caught dead in it! She's there I tell you; I know she is—I can feel it!"

Lynne said, "Ben, no one could have survived those swift river currents that day. Just because you never found her body—she went under, got caught on a snag and never surfaced. That girl drowned, Ben." Lynne turned to Jack. "Jack, stop him."

Jack was standing next to Lynne, shaking his head in resignation. He turned towards her, "I don't need this today, none of us do. I'm trying to keep *all* of us alive, and I can't stop him or anyone else from leaving if they have a mind to. This is a different world we're living in. We can suggest that he stay, but we can't stop him." He let out a tired breath, making a small cloud of fog in the cold morning air. "Let him go." He stepped up to the car, leaning his head inside, "You're leaving your dad's M16 here and taking your 45?" Ben patted a bulge under his coat. "Extra ammo and your knife?" Ben nodded. Jack hesitated, thinking of what else to say to him. "Ben, we think you're making a mistake, but don't be too proud to come back if you change your mind. Good luck to you. You hide your weapons someplace safe before you're anywhere near that camp, don't wait until the last minute." Jack glanced at Steve and motioned his head towards Ben, "He'll be hungry, Father... make sure he gets fed."

Father Steve replied, "I will. Goodbye, Jack, and thank you. You've helped me more than you know."

The little car sped off down the dark street with all its lights off.

Jack said to Lynne, "Steve knows the whole story about what happened to Ben and his dad. He'll keep an eye on him—he'll work on him too."

Tightly jammed in Ellen's little VW, they headed west down Roosevelt Road, towards Camp Able. Carl drove, Jo rode shot gun, and Father Steve and Ben sat in the back.

Carl said, "Sorry for making you ride in the back of this cramped thing, Steve. We couldn't risk driving the truck or the old station wagon. We've heard that vehicles, especially the larger ones, are being confiscated at the camps. We doubt that anyone would want a little puddle jumper. In case they do, we could better afford to lose this."

Steve said, "That's all right, Carl, this is fine. I want to thank you again for this nice winter coat, the boots and the other things you've given me. You know, before I found you folks, I had lost a lot of weight. Thanks to your generosity, I've gained the weight back and then some. I know it's going to be a rough winter, at least I'll be in good shape. I owe a lot to you folks."

They drove in silence for a few minutes and Steve said, "Ever since I became a priest, I've gone where the Archdiocese has sent me. This is the second time in my life I'm going someplace on orders given to me directly from the man upstairs, with no middleman." Father Steve looked sideways at Ben's flint-like face. "So... Benny, looks like you and me are going to be pals..."

They'd driven in darkness about three miles, frequently having to leave the main road and cut down residential side streets. Trying to avoid the large groups of people walking in the center of the road, Carl drove across lawns, down sidewalks and stopped for nothing. They had grown accustomed to desperate people jumping in front of them, thinking they could stop the small car. Like Lynne's Camaro, Ellen's treasured little car was collecting dents from the many rocks being thrown at it. Jo had to repeatedly point her weapon in the face of desperate men grabbing onto the car's door handles, trying to force their way in.

Jo said, "Carl, I smell trouble up ahead, cut down the next side street. Let's see if we can go around it."

Carl made a hard turn and floored the little car down a one-way street, going the wrong way.

Jo looked behind them, to see if anyone was following. She said, "It looked to me like some kind of check point. I thought I saw a man in a dark uniform. I don't like it. Let's stay off of Route 38 for a while, if we can." As the

397

cold darkness gave way to light, they drove an alternate route for about a mile, trying to get as close as they could to the camp. Suddenly, they were faced with a line of vehicles coming directly towards them. Carl had to slow down to a crawl, as a rusty old pickup pulled up across from them. Jo had the nickel-plated 44 on her lap, ready to shoot the driver of the pickup if she had to. The driver of the old truck turned out to be an old, grey-haired woman, who looked older than she probably was. She had a passenger next to her, a young girl, maybe about 12. The old woman held up a weathered hand and signaled Carl to stop.

Pulling up directly across from Carl, she said, "I had a little VW like that once. The heater worked like crap, but I loved it. I drove it until the floors rusted through. She cautiously eyed them over. "You folks aren't heading to the camp, are you?"

Carl replied, "As a matter of fact we are." Carl jerked his head back, towards Steve, saying, "That's Father Steve Posely sitting behind me. He wants to help out at the camp."

The woman eyed Father Steve, letting out her breath in a huff, giving him a skeptical look. "A sky pilot, huh? Well, let me tell you something before you even go near there, Padre. We're coming back from there. You won't get near the place in your little puddle jumper. Route 38 is backed up with desperate people who will yank you out of that car for a half bottle of water. It's clogged solid for a mile, and I mean packed. They got check points all along it. They will make you get out of your car and walk in. You won't see your little car ever again. They search everyone for weapons and take everything away, even knives. We turned back before we got too close. If you get too close and they see you, you're screwed. They'll take your guns, even if you're turning back. They have overwhelming force, so there's no use resisting." The old lady spit out her window, onto the street. "Ain't nobody forcing me to do anything, especially taking my truck and guns. Fuck the bastards" She bent her head down and peered at Father Steve. "Sorry, Reverend, but that's how I feel about it." She looked at Carl and for the first time smiled, showing yellow teeth. "You look like a smart kid. You turn around and go back home. I suggest you let your preacher friend walk from here, don't risk it getting any closer.

Carl said, "Who's they?"

She shook her head. "We don't know. They're dressed in all black uniforms, like Nazi storm troopers. Didn't want to get anywhere near them, but we talked to people who got close enough to see weapons being confiscated. Get this, they destroy them on the spot. They take your guns, unload them and they got flunkies in civilian clothes laying the guns flat on the street. They give them a couple whacks with a sledge hammer and toss them into the weeds along the roadway. The bastards. Relief camps…. yeah, sure—welcome to camp run-a muck!" The old lady spit out another gob of goo and shook her head in disgust. "People are starving, so they give up their guns without a fight. They just hand their weapons over for a cup of watered-down government piss soup. Well not me, no way! Look, we gotta get going, it's not safe for us here. Good luck to you and to you too, Reverend. You're going to need them prayers if you go in them camps."

Carl stayed stopped, thanking the lady as she drove off.

Father Steve said, "How about I just get out here, Carl. I'll walk the rest of the way. No use you getting caught in a road block."

Carl ran his fingers through his long hair, looking into the VW's rearview mirror at Father Steve's reflection. With his eyes pleading, he said, "Won't you please reconsider, Steve? I think it's too dangerous there for you. We won't be there to protect you." He gave a pleading look at Ben. "Let's go back, Benny."

Jo turned in her seat, looking back to Steve, "Please Father, Carl's right. You'll be all alone, come back with us." Jo turned to Ben. "And what you plan to do is just plain foolish. You heard the old lady. There're thousands of people in there. You're not going to find that girl. You're wasting your time and risking your life—and for what, revenge?"

Ben's face remained set. Without emotion he said, "Get out of the car, Jo. Let me out."

Steve smiled, motioning for Jo to get out of the small car. He said, "You two worry too much, you know that? Please let us out here. I have work to do and I think Ben can help me." Looking sideways at Ben he said, "You'll be my side-kick, won't you, Ben?" While Ben sat there silent, Steve smiled at Jo, "He'll be fine."

Jo hesitantly opened her door and got out, pulling the front bucket seat forward. Ben got out, followed by Steve, taking his backpack with him.

Jo said, "Father, you said that there were two times you took orders directly from God, without a middleman. When was the first?"

"The day I decided to become a priest. Look, it's never been about me. That's the whole reason I became a priest... and I am never alone. Remember this, neither are either of you." Father Steve started laughing, "Hey, that rhymes, 'neither are either!' Pretty good huh?"

Jo said, "Father, this isn't a joke... there are people killing each other for a can of beans."

Steve reached out, placing his right hand on Jo's shoulder, "I'll be careful, Jo, but I'm not alone. You know that—I'm in good hands." He pointed upwards. "Besides, I got Ben with me and he's strong as an ox. Steve bent down and stuck his head into the passenger side door opening, "I'll see you next summer, Carl. You go find some seed to plant and don't get discouraged. Even if you only get a half acre planted, it'll be a good start. Remember what I said, find an old yellow-page phone book. There's bound to be one laying around in one of these older homes. It'll have feed and grain stores listed in it. With no computers, those old phone books will be like gold, so when you find one, keep it. It'll be the only way you're going to find business addresses. You take care of Laura and the new baby. I want to baptize her in the spring."

Carl furrowed his brow, "How do you know it's going to be a her?"

Steve laughed, "Trust me, I know those kinds of things. Maybe you'll have twins."

Jo reached into the back seat of the car, "Father, you left your bat..."

Steve stopped her," I won't need that anymore, I still got my cap. You give the bat to Jack. He'll need it, especially if he runs into that big lummox. My old Buck knife is back there too. It's an antique, and it belonged to my father. You take it, will you, Jo? Carry it with you and pray for me... ah—whenever you peel an apple! Never waist a minute! When he gets old enough, give it to little Bobby for me, will you? He'll treasure it, I know he will. You teach him what I've taught you, Jo. Teach him about God's love and forgiveness. He'll have a long life and grow to be a wise man."

Carl asked, "Do you have everything, Steve?"

Steve patted his backpack. "I got everything I need in my backpack. I have warm clothes, my Bible, six tins of sardines and a small loaf of Kathy's Irish soda bread. What more could I want?"

Jo grabbed Ben by his shoulder, saying, "Come here kid." She gave him a tight hug, saying, "You be careful. When you get back, you can have the motorcycle. How's that?"

Ben, his face emotionless, cracked a hint of a smile at the mention of the motorcycle. Nodding his head, he said, "Yeah, I'd like that. You be careful too, Jo. Take care and watch Kathy for me, I worry about her."

Jo smiled, showing her perfect white teeth, "I will, goodbye Ben."

Ben bent down, locking eyes with Carl. "Bye Carl. I'll be back. Don't worry, I can take care of myself. I learned from the best, my Pops and Jack. Tell Lynne I'm sorry about the way I talked to her. Carl...you drive fast going home, don't slow down for nobody."

Carl said, "Don't worry, Ben, I won't. You take care."

Father Steve and Ben turned and walked away towards the camp together, Steve talking to Ben as he walked alongside him.

Carl said, "I hope Father Steve works on Ben."

Jo said, "He will, because God's working on them both."

Carl and Jo rode home, avoiding the main roads as much as possible. Carl figured it added at least an hour onto their drive, but it was worth it being able to avoid the mass of people heading west towards the camps. The last two days had seen a sudden explosion of people abandoning their homes. With little or no food and no fresh water, the first week of November was the last straw for people holding out in their unheated houses. An early cold snap coming down from Canada had sent temperatures plunging to below zero. Unseasonably cold weather instantly made ice boxes out of every house. Totally defeated, people left their freezing homes for the promise of the heated trailers and buildings in the government camps. Jack's subdivision was nearly abandoned. Some of the families who had fireplaces tried to stay, but they found out their fireplace was more for decoration than heat. Supplies of dry firewood were already gone, burned up by the nightly campfires of summer and fall. Shade trees that grew in yards and on parkways were suddenly being cut down for firewood. The cold homeowners found out what split and seasoned firewood meant. Their freshly-cut green wood was useless, it wouldn't burn. Unless they had a woodstove and at least two full cords of dry firewood, people quickly figured out their house would be uninhabitable until May. No one in the city or suburbs, except a prepared few, had a woodstove and a large supply of dry firewood. Families left their homes and their treasured belongings behind, walking towards the warm shelters promised in the camps. The last mile of the road to Camp Able was piled with smashed rifles, shotguns and hand guns five feet high on both sides. There was everything from full-automatics to rare antiques, all of them with their barrels flattened. Many of the refugees stopped along the way, hiding their weapons in abandoned houses with the intentions to retrieve them later. For most of them, there would be no later.

November 9th was a sobering wake-up for the new residents of Camp Able. The high school and trailers were already at nearly twice its capacity and thousands more refugees were pouring in. The camp was a sea of people and overflowing portable toilets. The promised shelter was full. The newcomers were shuttled off to trailers and heated tents.

On November 12th, it was announced that food would be rationed to one meal per day. The tents and trailers that surrounded the large high school that had been named, "Camp Able," weren't much better than the ice-cold homes that people had abandoned. What kept them there was the promise of food, fresh water and the stark realization that Camp Able was the end of the line. With everyone now disarmed, a grim realization took hold. If they wanted to leave, how would anyone ever make it safely back home without a firearm for protection?

Unknown to the refugees, the officials at the camp had seen the handwriting on the wall and were already making their own plans for escape. They realized that they were about to be abandoned by their government. They had done the math and the figures didn't lie. Even with the severe rationing, the supplies of food would not last the winter. Yet the refugees kept pouring in by the thousands. Regular shipments of government meat and poultry to the camps had nearly stopped. New sources for protein had to be found. . ..

As Carl and Jo drove home, he remembered all the old things his uncle had hoarded in his aunt's house. He wondered if his uncle had saved any old phone books. "If we had the time and my truck, I'd stop by my aunt's house and pick up some more hand tools. I think that may be the place to find an old phone book too. Gosh it's cold today!"

Jo rubbed her hands together. "Man, it's too early to get this cold. That old lady was right, the heater in this little car sucks."

Carl agreed, "You got that right. I don't think it helps much, this being a convertible. Jack said his wife took really good care of this car. It looks like Lynne's car now."

Jo said, "You know, I think Jack is a little like Ben. I know I am. We hoped that Ben had gotten over and dealt with what happened to his dad, and here all the while he's been planning how he was going to go after that girl. Jack never talks about his wife either. From what Laura has told me, her parents had a stormy marriage, and Ellen probably cheated on Jack before, especially when he was in the Marines, overseas. I've seen Ellen a few times. In fact, the last time I saw her, she was driving this car. She was a real knock-out, but she had that bar-look about her, you know what I mean? Hard to believe she was Laura's mom... or Jack's wife for that matter."

Carl scoffed, "She was a real winner. How much did Laura tell you about her mom?"

Jo blew warm air into her hands again, and said, "She told me her mom was cheating on her dad with his best friend, who also happened to be his boss at work."

Carl said, "Yeah, that was Don. He got killed in Chicago that first day. He was with Lynne and Jack, trying to get out of the city. I don't think we know the half of it. Jack's got to have lots of anger stored up, I know that. He really likes Lynne, but somehow, I think he still loves his wife.... even though she was a bitch. And that isn't from Jack. Laura told me about some of the stunts her mother pulled and how she made her life miserable. I had a couple run-ins with her at parent teacher conferences. She was a real piece of work and you're right; she was a knock-out. She could have been a model. Sometimes I think Jack believes she somehow survived that airplane crash and is alive and well someplace. He didn't know it, but she was about to leave him for Don. Laura said all her mom ever talked about was money, and apparently this Don guy had plenty of it. Laura is convinced her mom died in that crash and the fact that we are driving her car right now is the proof." Carl suddenly downshifted the car and came to a stop. "What is that up ahead, blocking the road?"

Jo said, "It looks like an old school bus that's been converted into a camper, and it's on fire. We're going to have to stop and back up. I don't want to go around it, we might drive into an ambush."

Carl said, "Wait a minute, look under the bus. Is that a little boy?"

Jo gasped, "That bus is about to completely go up. He's only a toddler, let's get him out of there!"

* * * * *

"Dad, it's getting dark, and I'm worried about them. They should have been back hours ago." Laura sat across from her dad at the kitchen table, alongside Lynne and Kay. They all looked at Jack, expecting an answer. "Dad, what are we going to do?"

"We're going to have to sit tight and wait. That little car is a reliable, I doubt if they had any problems with it. At any hint of a roadblock, they would turn around and maybe go miles out of their way to avoid it. They might have had to take detours several times, trying to avoid trouble going there and coming back. So, we're going to have to be patient. You girls are the prayer warriors, so say them. Have faith and let's finish our supper. I'm sure they'll be all right."

After dinner, Jack headed down into Charlie's basement and packed some logs into the woodstove before starting his nighttime watch. He closed the air-tight door and sat in a broken-down lawn chair across from it. Thinking he was alone in the darkness, he startled when he heard movement behind him.

"Kind of cozy down here in the dark. Mind if I pull up a chair and join you?"

"Sure, Kathy. I didn't think anyone was down here, grab a chair. It is nice here— comfortable. This could become my favorite spot this winter."

"Yes, it is. I might be joining you. She opened another lawn chair and sat next to him. I think it's going to be a bad one, it's too early to be this cold. Good Lord, what did people do in the 1700s? We're so used to turning on a weather report that instantly lets us know what's coming. We've really screwed ourselves; you know that? The more I think about it, the madder I get. Our government could have done something to protect us against this bullshit. Thousands of people are going to starve and freeze to death, just in our area alone. It's scary to think how many people would kill us to trade places right now. I keep asking myself how we're going to survive this?" They sat in silence for a few moments, their eyes slowly adjusting to the darkness. Barely able to see his face, Kathy leaned close to him, "Jack, do you ever get scared?"

She couldn't see him, as he slowly shook his head. "No. Maybe at first I was, but it wasn't for myself. I'm long past being scared. Lynne and I had this same discussion a while back. I prepare the best I can each day, and I'm willing to change in a second. I'll do whatever I have to do to keep us afloat. If I worry about anything, it's about Laura and Carl. I'd like her and Carl to have a future. The survivors of this thing are going to be a new breed, that's for sure."

Kathy sat back in her chair, facing the hot stove. "Yeah, that's how I feel. It's funny, I get scared, but not for myself. I'm worried about Laura, expecting a baby and having to deal with all this. Being pregnant without any doctors or hospitals—that's scary. I just thank God we have Lynne."

403

They sat in silence for a few seconds. Jack said, "You want a beer? I've got some handy in Charlie's old root cellar. I was about to start making my nighttime rounds, so I probably shouldn't, but what the hell, I'll get us a couple. You and I have never had any long conversations and long conversations always make me thirsty." Jack got up and made his way over to the far side of the basement. Finding a flashlight, he quickly returned with two bottles of beer. As he handed a cold bottle to Kathy, she said, "What are we going to do when we run out of suds?"

Popping the cap off his bottle, Jack laughed, "Carl's already got it covered, he's got some books on brewing. That kid is amazing." They each sat back and took a long drink of their beer.

Kathy laughed to herself. "You know, as bad as things are, we still have times like this, it's crazy. This is good right now, like you said, it's comfortable. It's cold outside, the wind is howling... the world's falling apart, and we're warm as toast down here having a cold brew."

Jack laughed, "That's the spirit. We have to stay positive and enjoy what moments we have."

Tossing her head back, she took a drink. "That's good, that's really good." She let out a little belch. "Jack, I want to ask you something. Do you pray? I mean specifically pray for things, when you wake up or before you go to sleep? You call me a prayer warrior and you're right, I am. I pray for all of us every day. I even have a list of names written down, some people I worked with and old friends who I hope are safe. Every night before I go to sleep, I think about them and pray for them all. I pray that Jim and his biker friends are safe in Wisconsin. I pray for Al and Lois, even though she hates me."

Taking a swig of beer, Jack sat silent for a moment. "I've always worried more than I pray. I find myself in a trap sometimes and I become my worst enemy. I worry too much, and worry can defeat you before you even get started. These past months, I've changed in a few ways and it's helped me. Instead of worrying so much, I try to do what Father Steve says, and turn it over to God. We face so much crap every day and most of it we're powerless over, so yeah, I pray about it. I pray every morning as I'm getting up, which I never used to do. I prayed for Carl and Jo today, but I turned it over to God and there is nothing else I can do. I know God heard my prayer the first time, and I figure he doesn't need me pestering him over and over about it. It's like sending him a cosmic email. I send it in the name of Jesus Christ, and I know he gets it and understands it. If I have to keep repeating the same prayers during the day, over and over, what does that say about my faith? So, to answer your question, of course I pray, but I also turn it over to the man after I do. I prayed earlier today that Ben and Father Steve stay safe. God has a plan for them, I guess I have to leave it at that. It's not that I'm not thinking of them during the day, of course I am. Even that girl, the one who Ben hates? I prayed for her this morning. I prayed that if he does find her, he forgives her. If I hadn't met Father Steve, I would never had done that. I keep it to myself, but I do pray for people, even people who have hurt me. As for you—you keep on praying your rosary, Kathy. All of us are different here, we all have our own ways. Me, Lynne, and even Ben, have watched you when you're sitting there praying your long prayers, and it helps us. I don't know if I can go as far as calling Ben an atheist, but he's pretty close to it, and you've made a positive difference on him. I don't understand Catholicism, what the heck, I'm Lutheran, and I never paid much attention to the nuts and bolts of that. But I'll tell you this: when we see you holding your rosary, so fervent and faithful, it shows us that there's still goodness in this world. When we see you sitting there and you have your eyes closed, we know you're praying, and it makes us feel better. God is working through you and that means your prayers are working. I know God hears all our prayers. So yeah, I pray, and I'm glad you do too." Jack kicked back his beer and finished it, saying, "I'll tell you one thing that concerns me now that Ben is gone. We're short one person for our nightly watch rotation. Glad your beer is finished, cause you're my relief." They both got up and started walking towards the stairs.

Upstairs, Kay and Lynne were having the same conversation. Kay said, "Listen to that wind, it's blowing so hard. I can't believe it's gotten so cold so quick. If it wasn't for old Charlie and his wood stove contraption, we'd be up the creek. I can feel the cold trying to get in here, it's seeping into every corner of the house. Thank God the kids are warm in that back bedroom. They're all sound asleep." Lynne bent forward and turned up the kerosene lamp that sat on the kitchen table. Kay nervously continued, "They have no idea of the danger we've been in."

Lynne said, "No they don't, do they? And thank God they don't. If this cold keeps up, entire families will freeze to death before winter even gets started. My God, look at us, all this modern crap around us and we're living like settlers. We may as well be out in the middle of nowhere." Lynne craned her neck, looking into the living room, "Where's Laura?"

"I think she's still sitting with the kids. She was reading them a bedtime story; she probably fell asleep." Kay exhaled impatiently, "I hate this waiting... God I pray they're all right. I still can't believe Ben went to that camp, looking for that girl. He's so stubborn and full of hate. Hate, it's such a terrible thing. You do it to yourself. Your own stubbornness blinds you, so you only see revenge." They sat there in silence for a few minutes. Kay said, "I'm scared, not for myself, but for the children. If anything happens to me, or to us—"

Lynne reached across the table, placing her hand on top of Kay's. "Kay, you're worrying yourself sick. Winter is just starting, but we'll make it. We have heat, food and fresh water. And thanks to you, we also have plenty of fire-power."

Kay nervously laughed. "I can't believe you actually said *fire-power*. It makes us sound like we're at some lonely outpost, surrounded by the enemy. That hardly makes me feel better. Carl compared us to the Alamo. The terrible thing is, the enemy is ordinary people, people just like us, who are desperate for their families to survive. Sure, there are evil people out there, but there are more good people who are just terrified. We were all so caught up in our computers, video games and the latest phones, and watching and listening to idiot Hollywood actors, who don't know their ass from a hole in the ground. That's how we got this way, Lynne. Thanks for letting me talk, I do feel better."

Lynne laughed, "Oh boy.... I can tell you've been around Jack for a while. *Ass from a hole in the ground?*"

"I'm sorry, Lynne, it's just that this whole thing makes me so sad. I'm going to miss Father Steve and his talks. I was so angry before he came here. Ben is angry, just like I was. Going into that camp and looking for that girl is crazy, but look who's with him...God sent Father Steve. That's how God works. I was always led to believe that God sent bad things to correct us and to test our faith. I was so wrong. He already knows every hair on our head and which way it will fall. He doesn't need to test anyone. He gives us the free will and *we* test ourselves; he uses the bad, but he wasn't the one who sent it. We know when we're wrong and he lets us decide our fate."

The two women stared at each other across the table, a sudden smile coming to both their faces. They both heard the unmistakable sound of a VW pulling into the driveway. Lynne picked up the kerosene lamp. Kay was already running for the door.

Jo came in first. She was carrying a little boy who was sound asleep. Carl was right behind her. They all sat down in Charlie's living room. The little boy was still sound asleep, now on Lynne's lap, as Carl and Jo explained why they were so late.

Carl said, "Sorry we're so late. If the radios were working right, I'd have called. Every main road was packed with people heading towards the camps. This cold weather is doing it. We didn't stop for anything and had to keep turning around to avoid being overrun by desperate people. We ran into other people with cars and trucks doing the same thing we were, driving around in circles, trying to avoid confrontations. Some had already been near the camps and warned us to turn around and go home."

Jo said, "We let Father Steve and Ben off about a mile and a half away from the place and God help them. The line to get in was at least a mile long. The entire road was packed solid. It was crazy, it was the same thing coming back home. We're late because we had to drive out of our way to avoid being trapped by a wall of people, every one of them wanting our car. That's how we found Andy. We saw an old grey school bus that had been converted into a camper stopped in the middle of an intersection. The whole back of it was on fire. We

406

decided to beat it out of there and turn around, not wanting to get caught up in whatever was going down. Then Carl spotted Andy. He was under the bus... we just couldn't leave him there. The whole thing was going up in flames above him. Carl pulled up next to it and I jumped out. I pulled him out of there, while Carl checked out the bus."

Carl said, "There was an older fellow inside, slumped over the steering wheel. His head looked like it had exploded. There was a bullet hole in the windshield. I couldn't get all the way in. The smoke and flames were too hot. There was a gray-haired lady lying on the floor in the aisle, her face was staring right up at me. God, I'm never going to forget her eyes. Her clothing up to her waist was on fire."

Upset by what he had seen, Carl stopped talking for a moment. "Sorry, the whole day was just crazy. Anyway, she was about to be cremated, so I got out of there. We got the little guy into the car and he started yelling for grandma. As we were pulling away, I think a propane tank inside the bus exploded and the whole thing went up in the air. We barely go out of there alive. Jeez, I could have been in there when it went."

Jo looked down at the little boy, still sound asleep on Lynne's lap. She said, "I asked him his name and he said, 'Andy'. He told us he was two years old, but I think he's closer to three. He kept asking for his grandma and grandpa nearly all the way here, until he fell asleep. His grandparents had to have been the two people murdered in the bus. God, our world is sick, how can people do things like this?"

Lynne bent down and kissed the sleeping boy on the forehead, "You're safe now, Andy. We'll take care of you."

Jack got up saying, "And we add one more to our little family... I better start making my rounds." As he reached for the front door knob, he shot a glance back to Carl and Jo, "Is our little VW still in one piece?"

Early the next morning Lynne was frying up some diced spam in brown sugar to mix with the scrambled eggs. Kathy opened some canned peaches, while Jo sliced some soda bread.

Jack said, "That coffee sure smells good. How's our latest little family member doing?"

Laura entered the kitchen and heard her dad's question. "He's just like the rest of us. He'll have some adjusting to do, but he's a good little boy, and a strong one too. With our love, Andy will be all right. He's playing with Wendel and Bobby. Kay is keeping a close eye on him."

Lynne said, "It's tragic about his grandparents. I wonder what happened to his mother and father? They could still be alive. Does he know his last name?"

Kay entered the kitchen, holding Andy, "It's Hamilton, he just told me!"

Andy said, "I want my Gramma."

407

Lynne turned away from the stove, glancing at Jack. The start of a tear was in the corner of her eye. She placed the frying pan she was holding down on the burner and went to Kay, taking Andy in her arms. "We love you, Andy, and we'll never let you go…"

DON'S

CHAPTER 4 0

Jack stood in the kitchen, apart from the others, and watched Lynne as she held the little boy. He suddenly felt a wave of loneliness clench onto him. He decided he couldn't put it off any longer, he'd have to go to Don's place today.

After breakfast, he pulled Carl aside. "Carl, I'm feeling the best I've felt in weeks. I think my side is finally healed up. I know you had a rough day yesterday, but I'd like to get out today. We could go to your aunt's house and pick up those hand tools, and maybe find one of those old phone books you're looking for. We might even find some parts in your uncle's workshop to fix the walkie talkies."

Carl sensed an urgency in Jack's tone, and Jack spotted the questioning look that Carl was giving him. In a low voice, Jack said, "Carl, I *have* to check out Don's condo. There's something that's bothering me. Things don't add up and I have to get to the bottom of it. Today is going to be another cold miserable day. I don't think we'll run into any trouble if we leave early enough. His place is only a 15-minute ride from your aunt's house." He moved close to Carl and cocked his head, "You think you could take me there and keep that part of our ride between ourselves? It won't take but a few minutes for what I have to do."

Carl nodded his head, "Sure, we can do that. I'll tell Laura we're leaving."

They pulled out of the subdivision about 20 minutes later. Passing the industrial park and the golf course, "Carl said, "Gosh, I hope we can find an old yellow page's phone book. Without the internet, we'll never locate a nearby source for seeds. I bet old Charlie could have told us where a farmer's co-op was."

Jack nodded his head in agreement. "Charlie and old timers like him know lots of things that six months ago would have been considered useless information by most folks." Jack sighed heavily, a dull ache still in his side. "Of the many things we're losing, loss of knowledge is going to be the worst. Knowledge about simple things that've been forgotten in our crazy computerized world. All those books that you and Laura salvaged from the library are like gold now. That's another stop we should make today. If we've got time, we should stop at the library. With our house starting to look like a day care, we'll need school books, kids' books and a good set of old-fashioned encyclopedias. We should grab that big dictionary they have on display in the public library's foyer, stand and all. Also, that big globe, if that stuff is still there."

Carl said, "I've been thinking the same thing. The kids will have to be schooled by us. Laura is over five months pregnant. We'll be adding another one to *our clan*. You're going to be a grandpa soon, imagine that, Grandpa Jack!" Carl looked at Jack, his face beaming.

Jack said, "Carl, better watch the road, we don't want to get stopped."

"Okay, we're almost at my aunt's. Want me to do a fast drive-by, like the last time?"

"Yeah, why not, let's play it safe. Speed up and drive past the place, like we're not interested. You know, it's weird driving down this road now. We haven't seen anyone out walking or any other cars. Did you notice the golf course, how high the weeds were on the fairway? Jeez, one summer with no one tending to the greens and it's already going back to prairie. Even the streets are different, all covered with leaves and broken tree branches."

Carl interrupted, "What's that by the side of the road, up ahead? It looks like a body. I'll speed up and drive by it, it could be a trap."

As they sped past the body, they didn't need to stop to see if someone was hurt. If it wasn't for the bloody and tattered clothing on it, it could have been mistaken for a deer carcass. Jack got the best look at it as they drove by, and he couldn't tell if it was male or female.

As they sped past, Jack said, "Whoa, something big has been gnawing on that one. It's mangled and almost cut in two, Jeez..."

They drove on in silence for about a quarter mile, seeing no other signs of life. Approaching the entrance to his aunt's street, Carl said, "Okay, my aunt's street is coming up. I'll do a drive by, let's take a look-see." Carl glanced at Jack, making a grim face, "We left those three bodies propped up on the front porch, not looking forward to seeing them again..."

Jack said, "Let's hope our warning worked and the house hasn't been cleaned out."

Carl sped the truck up as they approached the house, speeding past it, appearing uninterested. The street was short, and the three homes still looked vacant. Both of them craned their necks as they sped by, scanning the street, looking for any signs of life. They continued on another hundred yards before making a quick U-turn, heading back towards his aunt's house.

The three bodies they had left propped up on the front porch were gone! All that remained were some chewed bones and tattered clothing, scattered about the front yard. Carl stopped the truck and slowly got out, saying. "God, Jack, this is why I dreaded coming back here. Look at this mess, there's almost nothing left of those men. Coyotes must have got at them."

Jack got of the passenger side, carrying the modified AR-15 he had taken off one of the bodies months before. Both of them stayed near the truck for a

410

few moments. As Carl sadly stared at the men's scattered remains, Jack kept his eyes on the houses and, as always, searching. The sun was coming up and the day looked like it would stay cold and grey. Except for a busy woodpecker high in a nearby oak, everything around them was silent. Jack scanned the mostly leafless woods that surrounded the three homes on the street. He carefully eyed the tangle of buckthorn, where he had hidden watching the thieves loot the house months before. A layer of undisturbed brown oak leaves blanketed the entire street and the home's driveway, telling Jack no one had been there for some time.

Jack said, "The house next door has been broken into, but it must have been weeks ago. I think you're right about the coyotes. The front door is still nailed shut and so is the side door to the garage. Let's check the house out and see if our warning committee did any good."

Carl didn't move.

Jack said, "What's wrong, you see something?"

Carl was shaking his head, still looking mournfully down at what was left of the three men.

Carl said, "This shows me how far we've regressed. What we did here with those men's bodies and what I'm seeing now should be haunting us forever, but I don't think it will. A few minutes ago, we drove past a dead body on the road like it was a dead raccoon or something. It was a person and somebody loved that person. We couldn't tell if it was a guy or a girl. It could have been a friend of ours or a neighbor, and it doesn't even phase us anymore. God, Jack, what's happened to us?"

"I don't know, but we've had this conversation before, so let's re-hash it later, not here. Just so you know, it bothers me too— what we've done, but is there another way? We have a family back home who depends on us, and when we're confronted, we can't dick around or we'll end up being that dead body on the road, or bones scattered about like these. Now come on, don't let it start getting to you. Let's go inside and check out the place, then we'll check on the other two houses. If they're abandoned, we'll help ourselves to anything left inside. Let's get it done."

The two of them went to the back door and found the window next to it had been shattered, the pane of glass was completely missing. The short hallway leading to the kitchen was full of brown leaves and shards of broken glass, confirming to Jack it had been open for some time. The house had a cold and abandoned feeling to it and felt like an icebox. Any warmth and coziness the home had once held was long gone. Someone had been inside the house, scattering belongings and upsetting the furniture.

Carl's shoulders dropped, "Shit... look at what they've done. My aunt and uncle loved this house. It's good they're not alive to see this. This is damn

411

depressing. I've been coming here since I was a baby and it's completely trashed. It looks like animals have been living in here too, there's shit all over the place."

"Sorry, Carl, I guess our warning committee didn't work. Nothing scares people anymore, they're that desperate. You go through things in here, and I'll be outside keeping watch. I hope you find a phone book and some parts to fix the radios. Keep your pistol handy and yell if you need me."

Jack scouted around outside and took up a position alongside of the house. With most of the leaves off the trees, he had a clear view of the entire woods and both sides of the street. Dried oak leaves covered everything and each footstep he took sounded a loud crunch. The dry leaves would sound alarm of anyone approaching. While Carl was inside going through the house, Jack hunkered down into the fallen leaves alongside it. The only sound that could be heard was a squirrel running in circles around a huge oak tree. Jack crouched low and listened for any sound that was out of place. The sun was struggling to come out and the wind was picking up. Other than the squirrel, all he heard was a winter-like breeze blowing through the nearly leafless trees.

"I'm done." It was Carl, sticking his head around the back corner of the house. Convinced no one was prowling near them, Jack got up, but still took one last look around. He jumped in the truck, started it, and quickly backed it up from where it was hidden behind the house, stopping next to the back porch. He wasn't surprised by the large pile of books and hand tools Carl had assembled. Setting on top the pile of books was the grand prize, two dog-eared yellow page phone books. Carl pointed to them, saying, "Jackpot! I checked them out. There's a feed and grain store in West Chicago and another in Warrenville. The closest is in Warrenville. Also, there's a big pet store listed as selling livestock feed, we might find some chicken feed there. A farmer's co-op is listed, but it's way out in DeKalb. I think that's too far to risk driving."

They loaded up the truck with his aunt's and uncle's belongings and drove it next door to the neighbor's home. Parking the truck in the driveway, they sat there a few moments watching the house. The house was a newer brick ranch with an attached garage, and it looked vacant.

As he got out of his truck, Carl said, "I feel really sad. I had planned on Laura and I living in that house someday. By all rights, we should bury the remains of those men, but I can't. Everywhere we go, we find more bodies. Jo said she heard they stopped dumping them in the gravel pit almost two months ago. I don't know if it's true, but I can believe it."

"Shhhhh!" Jack slowly got out of the truck, his forefinger up to his lips. He pointed to the brown leaves that blanketed the ground. There was a clear path through the leaves, winding off to the open side entrance of the attached garage. He motioned Carl to stay back, as he silently crept up the cleared path. There was no warning. They charged out of the open garage, growling and baring their teeth, heading straight at Jack! He fired two rounds from the AR-15, ripping into

412

the massive head of the lead pit bull, nearly knocking it off. The second animal faltered, feigned to the side and went after Carl. Carl hurriedly fired two shots at it with his 38 revolver, missing both. Jack let loose three rounds into the side of the charging dog, sending it rolling into the leaves, its guts protruding out the other side of its body.

Jack's heart was racing as he walked up to the open side door of the garage. He was met by the stench of rotting flesh, as he entered into the darkened entrance. He heard something and immediately knew what it was. The large sixteen-foot garage door was closed tight, and he pushed it up. As it rolled upwards, he saw three small Pitbull pups huddled together, growling at him, and a fourth cowered in a corner. Jack stepped out of the garage and stood on the concrete apron in front of it. As Carl walked up, he handed Carl the AR-15. There was a spade hanging from a hook on the garage wall. Grabbing it, he plunged the flat blade into the head of each pup, killing them. Tossing the bloodied spade aside, he pointed to large chunks of rotten flesh scattered about on the garage floor, some with scraps of clothing still attached to it. Carl watched in disbelief as Jack nudged his boot toe into one of the bloody, fattened pups. "There's where those three bodies went, Carl. These pit bulls have been feasting on them, and maybe on that body lying in the street back there as well. This is going to become a common thing that we have to be on guard for. These pups would have grown up hunting us for their dinner. I can't imagine what's prowling around all those bodies in that gravel pit. Man—we're going to have to be extra careful. All right, let's finish our search. Hopefully it'll be worth our time and we don't run into any more of these things."

They searched the house, but it had been vacant before the EMP hit and was empty. Jack took his Army 45 out and gestured with it towards the final house. It was about 100 yards from where they were and looked vacant.

He said, "It doesn't look like anyone's been around there for a while either. You say you know those people?"

"Yeah, they're nice people. Bob and Susan and their two children, Ethan and Chrissy, both of them are in grade school. The grandfather lives with them. It used to be his house. He works at the cemetery."

"All right, you stay out here with the rifle and keep watch. Take a position behind that fallen tree over there, and I'll take a look inside. Remember what I taught you about firing it. Go easy, don't run yourself out of ammo with that bump stock... and Carl—don't be so nervous. You're going to need some more target practice. You should have hit that dog." Jack walked up the six concrete steps leading to the front door of the house. The door was wide open and the jamb was splintered. Someone had kicked it in. He could see into the living room and, like Carl's aunt's house, the place had been thoroughly ransacked weeks ago.

Warily, with gun drawn, he walked in. He went through the living room, past the kitchen, and then the stench of death hit him. A foul smell emitting from a back hallway gave lead as to what awaited in the master bedroom. Rotting human flesh is different from that of a wild animal, it smells worse. There were three adult bodies in the bedroom. Two were on the bed, each of them with their head face down into a pillow. Another body was on the floor lying on his back. That one had a bullet hole in his temple and a nickel plated snub-nosed 38 lying next to it. They had been dead for some time. The bodies on the beds were almost skeletal, with matted hair where a single bullet had been fired into back of their heads. A second bedroom had the bodies of the two children, also lying in bed. Like the adults, the head of a young girl was face down into a pillow. The boy must have lifted his head off the pillow and turned at the last moment, facing the shooter. A hole was in the center of his forehead; his vacant eye sockets stared at Jack. The remains of the family dog were at the boy's feet. For a split second, the horrible image passed through Jack's mind. The grandfather standing over his grandchildren, doing something he couldn't possibly do. His grandson looked up at him at the last second of his life, as he shot him in the head.

Jack felt his legs weaken and his stomach rise in his chest. He did an about-face, and stepped out of the small bedroom. Feeling like he was going to throw up, he gently closed the door behind him.

Slowly walking out of the house, his legs felt like they were weighted with lead. Thinking, *fuck it,* he grabbed a wooden rocking chair that was near the front door.

Carrying the rocker down the front steps, he met Carl at the bottom of them.

Jack said, "Kay said we could use another rocker, especially when Laura has the baby. This one's a nice one."

Carl nodded his head and started up the stairs, saying, "It sure is. Anything else in there worth taking with us?"

Jack placed the chair down, quickly grabbing hold of Carl's arm. "Don't go inside, Carl, it's bad in there. Suicide, you don't want to see it. It must have happened several weeks ago. The back half of the house is covered in dead flies—the place has been ransacked, but they left the bedrooms where the bodies were alone. Let's check out that big metal shed in the backyard and get the hell out of here."

Carl hesitated on the steps, "Jack... I know these people. The grandfather was a good friend of my aunt and uncle. We should at least bury them."

"No, Carl, I won't let you go in there. Come on, let's go see if there's something we can use in that shed."

Reluctantly and rigid, Carl walked with Jack to the large metal shed in the backyard. Jack saw him look back twice at the house. He stopped and turned to Carl, "Look, Carl, I know things are horrible. But there is *nothing*—we can do about it. There aren't enough hours in the day to bury all the dead we find, and we can't mourn everyone like they're family. They're gone, along with countless others. It's very sad, but it's not our fault. I keep telling you, you're going to have to cowboy-up and put all this shit out of your mind or, like I've tried to tell you before, you'll go crazy. Believe me...**you will go fucking crazy**.... And, I'll tell you something else, when we get back, don't rehash it over and over in your head. There's just too much shit and there's no room for it upstairs. We have to do what we've been doing, Carl. Just move on and forget about it." Jack looked back at the vacant house. "The best thing we could do would be to burn their house, with their bodies in it."

They faced each other silently for a few moments, that turned into a minute. Carl gazed past Jack into the woods and took a deep breath. "The air is crisp this morning. I love the smell of it. I don't think it's my imagination, but since everything stopped, it seems the air is cleaner, fresher." Carl looked up into the treetops, the fog of his breath hanging in the cold morning air. "We screwed up, Jack. We tried to ruin this planet, but it doesn't care, it's fixing itself. I realized that this morning, when we passed the golf course. Look around us, everything is going back to the wild. The greens on that golf course are gone, smothered in weeds. One summer and it's already going back to prairie. Look at these houses and their yards." Carl kicked at a small tree at his foot. "One summer without upkeep and this lawn is already choked with small trees, just like that farm field. The forest is steadily creeping back in, and in the grand scheme of things, it proves to me that the human race doesn't mean shit. This stuff will grow tall and surround these houses. All the subdivisions and towns will go back to prairie and forest, because most of the people, maybe all of them... will die this winter. A few years from now, there'll be natural wildfires, then all of these houses and every trace of us above the ground will be incinerated. That's how I see it, Jack. Maybe it's a good thing. Just like those dogs you just killed; everything is going back to the wild. And here I was worried about global warming." Carl started laughing, but his face wasn't smiling. "Al Gore really had me going for a while. Oh my God."

Neither of them said anything for a few moments. They stood there and watched a squirrel scramble up the side of an oak tree. Carl managed a smile. "That's one lucky squirrel, you know that? There's not many of them left in these woods." Still watching the squirrel, Carl said, "It's going to get worse, isn't it?"

"Carl, I know we look at things differently. You're a college guy and a teacher and, no matter how I try, I'll always be a Combat Marine." Jack gestured to the woods, making a sweeping motion with his arm. "You see a beautiful green forest and I see firewood. You see a wood carving and I see a gun stock. But try to see it my way. You have to be my main man because every so often... *I find myself drifting away*— Listen...it gets to me too. I left shit like this in Iraq and Afghanistan and figured it was over. Holy shit, nothing's fucking over! I need you.

415

I keep telling you and the girls that we haven't seen nothing yet. Believe me, it's going to get worse! We're not going to have to worry about wild dogs eating people. Come the dark days of winter—I give it another month or so, it'll be wild people—eating people like us. It's going to get that bad. We're going to have to supply up as much as we can and dig in this winter. Your wife and those little kids we're raising depend on us. They're our future, let's not let them down. We're not going to commit suicide like these people did. I keep telling you, we *will* make it. Now come on, let's both bully up and see what's in that big fucking shed back there."

A cold shudder went through Carl, his lips trembled, "Okay—I'm with you—all the way. I'll be better... I promise you."

The shed was unlocked and it was an untouched treasure trove full of goodies. Carl got the truck and drove it into the backyard, pulling up next to the large metal shed, as Jack was busy pulling things out.

Jack could see that Carl was doing his best to keep himself together and he was proud of him. He prayed he could keep himself together.

Carl inventoried their haul as they loaded it onto the truck. "Two 5-gallon cans of gas. Two 5-gallon cans of kerosene. One 2-gallon can of kerosene. We got several big bags of fertilizer, grass seed, bird seed and charcoal. Two chain saws and a bunch of hand tools and smaller items. We'll put all of this to good use."

Jack wheeled an ancient-looking boy's bike out of the back of the shed. "Look at this old bike. It must have belonged to the grandfather. I remember my Uncle Dave had one like it. He was always working on it. Everybody in the family called him "The Tinker," what an old grouch."

Carl eyed the old red bike with less excitement than Jack. "Looks like an old motorcycle, with those twin springs on the front of it. Is that a gas tank on it?"

"No, it's a horn tank. They made these bikes to look like motorcycles. That's why the kids loved them. Look at this rear carrier and these leather saddlebags, pretty cool, huh?" It's made in Chicago. It's a **Super Deluxe.** We're taking this bike with us. The grandfather must have had it as a kid and took good care of it. He wouldn't want it to rust away out here. I know I wouldn't. I'll fix this old boy up, maybe get rid of these clunky fenders though. It's funny, something like a dusty old bike actually cheers me a little. Let's get it loaded up. I have one more thing to take care of today, then I'll feel much better."

As they loaded the old bike into the truck, Carl said, "They sure made things good back then. I can't believe how heavy this thing is, and the amount of chrome on it, and it's not even rusty."

"Yep, made in the good old USA, back when people gave a shit, before fucking China came on the scene." They got into the truck and Carl drove it roughly through the yard, then back onto the smooth street.

Carl said, "Things are changing—never heard you use the f-word before."

Jack laughed. "I'll tell you something. When Laura was born, I cleaned up my act a little. I decided to stop using the f-word. I used to use it to describe everything. It was f-this and f-that. My dad constantly called my attention to it. He used to say that people who swear a lot have a weak mind. I guess my mind was pretty weak, but I finally managed to stop using that word after I got married. I still think it a lot, but seldom say it anymore. I just said it a minute ago, and you know what? It felt fuckin good!" Jack raised his face skyward, "Sorry, Dad."   He winked at Carl and saw he was smiling. "You're laughing—that's the first fuckin smile you've had this morning!" Again, looking skywards, Jack said, "Sorry, Dad, I do have a weak mind." Jack laughed, "I feel better, how about you?"

"Yeah, I feel fuckin better, Jack, lots better, thanks."

"All right, now that we're both in a better mood, lets head over to my old partner's condo. It's not far. Drive towards town and turn left on Kensington, and then hang a right on Riniker. His condo will be in the middle of the block. We gotta get back on the home page here. Sun is shining and there might be some crazies walking about, and we don't want to ruin our good moods."

"How's your fuckin side doing, Jack, still hurting?"

"Only when I fuckin laugh, Carl, Ha, Ha, Ha, Ha!"

Carl didn't know exactly why, but as bad as things were, it felt good to laugh and he did feel better. He said to himself, *I'll have to start using the F word more often...*

Carl started laughing to himself. Jack smiled and said, "What? Tell me what's so funny. I want to laugh too..."

Carl's smile quickly faded, "Look up ahead. Two guys just stepped onto the road. They got their thumbs out for a ride."

Jack eyed them for a second and said, "They're trouble. Hang a quick U and go back. We'll cut over a couple streets and go around them."

Carl hit the brakes and made a U-turn, as one of the two hitchhikers pulled out a small handgun and fired two shots at them.

Their bullets missed, and as they sped away, Carl yelled, "**Can't anyone be nice? Good God almighty!**"

Jack replied, "This AR-15 has them out gunned. It sounded like they were firing something small, like a 22. They definitely crawled out of the scum box. Want to take 'em out, before they kill someone?"

"No, we don't need any trouble. Let's just let them go."

Jack thinly smiled, "I figured you'd say that. I didn't want to go back either, tired of it. They'll pull that stunt again today, hopefully with the wrong guy, and there will be two more dead bodies on the road." Jack pointed ahead, "Okay, turn there. Go down to the end of the street and make a right, we'll be on Riniker Avenue." The streets were empty and they drove the rest of the way to Don's condo without incident. Jack pointed to a grey sided, two-story building, in the middle of the block. "His is the center unit. Don't slow down, let's do a quick drive by and check things out."

Carl drove past the house then around the block, viewing the building from every angle. He said, "Jeez, the whole block looks vacant, and every front door is wide open. I'll bet every place has been stripped clean, including your friend's. Where is everyone?"

"It's pretty cold out. It's nearly December, and none of these places have any heat. I bet three-quarters of these people went straight to the camps. You're right though, every place is wide open. They've all been broken into."

"You sure you want to stop? Your friend's place has probably been completely trashed."

"Yeah, I'm sure. I have to do this. Back into that driveway and wait for me. Keep the motor running and the rifle ready. Anything looks out of place, lay on the horn. I won't be long." Jack jumped out of the truck before Carl had come to a full stop. Carl did as Jack told him. He backed his truck into Don's concrete driveway and kept it running.

Jack had driven by Don's new condo, but had never been in it. He fished in his pocket and retrieved the brass key that he had found in the glove box of Ellen's car. There was no need to use it, as Don's front door was kicked in. The lockset was hanging loosely, almost out of the smashed door. He stuck the key into the dangling lock and turned the cylinder... *a perfect fit*!

He had his 45 drawn and hesitated at the door, eyeing the open interior. The place was exactly as he expected it to be, a mess. Thieves had broken in, looking for food, guns, bottled water, whatever. Every vacant home was fair game and Don's was no exception. Carl was right, it had been thoroughly trashed. Soundlessly, with gun drawn, he walked in, intending to check every room for unwanted guests. Instead he holstered the 45. There would be no one in any of these homes, it was like an icebox inside. He knew what he was looking for would be in the master bedroom, and he was right. As he entered the master bedroom walk-in closet, a familiar scent smacked him in the face. On the floor in a heap was a dark blue dress he recognized. As he bent over to pick it up, it hit him full force. It was as if Ellen was standing there in front of him. He grabbed two other dresses, one of them still half clinging to a wooden hanger. It was soft and filmy and smelling of her. The blue dress... he remembered when she had brought it home... *"Jack, how do you think I look in it? I just love it."* He felt his stomach turn. Thieves had pulled drawers out from a dresser and carelessly scattered their contents on the floor. He kicked at a small heap of clothing... her underwear and a sheer nightgown. More underwear and lingerie strewn across the floor... all *reeking* of *her*.

He felt himself becoming sick and left the bedroom. Walking into the dining room, there were crumpled copies of typewritten forms scattered about. Picking one of them up, the word DIVORCE stabbed into him! There were papers strewn everywhere on the floor, and he spotted one with Ellen's flamboyant cursive on it. The words, Jack's IRA and his father's coin collection, were underlined. *Fucking underlined!* There was a question mark after Laura's college account. He didn't have to pick it up to read it, he ground his boot heel into it, grinding it into the white carpet.

A small scrap of yellow paper, about six inches square and almost at his feet, looked familiar. It was torn off Ellen's kitchen notepad, and once again, he didn't have to pick it up to read it

On the bottom line of her shopping list was something he had written. *D –*

Batteries. He had added it to her list before handing it back to her. It was on that Sunday night, *the day before the power went off*. She was supposed to pick up the batteries at the grocery store. He kicked at the shopping list, the small piece of paper tearing in half. *You fucking bitch...you said you were going to Brenda's...* Deflated, he stood with his back to the dining room wall, looking down at the divorce papers laughing at him from the floor. *Aw man, I've been such a fool... Jack, you are a stupid, stupid fool... did you expect anything less? Am I that stupid? What if her stuff wasn't here...would I feel better?*

He hurried up the stairs, and for a few seconds stood outside Don's bedroom, the anger inside him wanting to burst from his chest. Everything went into the pile. The divorce papers, the dresses, the black lace undergarments, anything that reeked of her.

Don's belongings followed. His suits, his shirts, the contents of every drawer, and finally the drawers themselves. He struggled with Don's treasured antique mahogany desk, upending it as it fell into the pile. The heavy oak filing cabinets, filled with the contents of Don's life, tipped over as he pushed them into the bedroom. Don's past came tumbling out of them, splaying itself out in a mountain of jumbled paper. Family pictures, his birth certificate, his social security card. Everything that was Don went into the heap. Then the chairs, the tables, the dressers and their drawers, his golf clubs—all of it and everything that he and she had touched! The bed in the master bedroom was heaped high, touching the ceiling, extending into the skylight shaft above it. Only one last ingredient was needed.

Outside, Carl was patiently waiting in the truck, it's motor running, while he nervously eyed the empty street. *Come on, Jack, hurry it up, I'm on overtime out here...what are you doing? He talks about me losing it, jeez—what the....*

Carl was startled by Jack suddenly appearing at the driver's door.

"Carl, can I have one of those road flares you keep under the seat?"

Carl reached under the seat, and without a word, handed Jack a ten-minute red railroad flare. He watched Jack in his mirror, as he removed something out of the back of the pickup and went running back into the condo. He cursed to himself for giving him the flare, as he saw Jack disappear inside Don's front door with the two-gallon can of kerosene.

Once upstairs, Jack opened up several windows, letting a crisp breeze blow into the rooms. He had piled up just about everything he could haul into Don's bedroom, burying the entire bed. Unscrewing the cap on the plastic can, he quickly splashed the golden liquid on the pile. Tossing the empty can, he walked out of the room and stopped at the doorway, staring back into it. Everything that represented Don's life was only a moment away from being incinerated, burned out of existence forever. Standing outside the bedroom door, the pungent odor of kerosene filled his head. It was funny, he thought to himself, what would Father Steve say to him if he was here? *"Go home Jack. Let it go and forgive them. Don't put yourself in that hole..."* I forgive them Father, but first....

Jack smiled as the sizzling flare left his hand, settling into the huge pile. He knew he should get out of there, but he fought it, wanting to stay and watch everything burn.

Unlike with gas, the fire started slow and gracefully. It licked the sides of the jumbled furniture, gently climbing it, almost caressing it, and finally engulfing it. Suddenly it was roaring, its flames extending into the skylight shaft above, the room instantly filling with oily black smoke. He wanted to stay longer, it was like he was mesmerized, but it was going up fast, and the heat and smoke were becoming unbearable. He turned away, but he didn't run out. He slowly walked out, the intense heat at his back as he went down the stairs. As he stepped out onto Don's front porch, he realized he still had the brass door key in his jacket pocket. Flipping the key over his shoulder, the elation that he had just felt suddenly left. He paused on the porch for a moment, thinking about what he had just done.

Carl was still sitting in the truck. He turned his head towards Jack, staring at him for a few seconds. Jack knew what Carl must be thinking, and suddenly felt ashamed. He didn't want to face him, and walked back slowly, trying to think of something to say. Climbing into the front seat, he said, "I'm done. What do you say we go to the library and check out some books?"

Carl put the truck in gear, saying, "Everything all right, Jack?"

"Yeah, I guess so."

As they left Don's house, Carl checked the truck's rearview mirrors. Behind them he could see smoke billowing out from every window of the condo and flames shooting out from a hole in the roof. He looked sideways to Jack, then back into his mirrors, then back to Jack, thinking, *Holy shit, talk about me losing it....*

Jack sat peacefully next to him, holding the rifle, looking out his open window and humming something...

"Jack, are you sure you want to go to the library? How about we go some other time? We'll just go home."

420

"Why not? It's still early. It's only couple blocks away from here. We've still got room in the truck. Let's go back with a full load of books. It's going to be a long winter. They drove in silence for several minutes, the library almost in sight.

"Okay, here's the library—what the heck!" Carl stopped the truck. "Look at it. It's been burned! Holy shit, the roof is caved in. What happened?"

Carl eased the truck up in front of the building, a strong burnt odor immediately enveloping them.

Jack raised his eyebrows, but didn't seem surprised. "Looks like no books for us today. The place is a burned out shell. The hell with it, let's go home."

They drove in an awkward silence for a few minutes. Finally, Carl said, "At least we got the phone book and we know where we can find the seed we need. Picking up the seed will probably be our next road trip, you think?"

Jack sat silent for a few more seconds, "Yeah. I guess so. It might be awhile for me for me though, I pulled something in my side. My ribs are hurting again...shit."

"Jeez, Jack, what did you find when you were in your friend's place to make you burn it? The whole block is probably going up in smoke by now, you talk about me starting to lose it." Carl shook his head, "Jack, I don't understand you. You're always telling me to "buck up," but look at you, you just go off sometimes and scare everyone. It's like that stunt you pulled when Ken's house blew up, going after all those armed men with Jo. You could have gotten Jo killed, not to mention yourself."

"Yeah, I know. I don't understand it myself. Sometimes I just boil over. I did lots of thinking while I was laid up with these damned ribs hurting me, maybe too much thinking. There's something I didn't tell you. The day before that big lummox kicked the crap out of me, I found a key from Don's condo in Ellen's car. I was looking for some cigarettes and found it in the glovebox. I checked his briefcase and he had a key to my front door. You know how Ellen was, I'm sure Laura has filled you in on her. But you know, as a pain in the ass as she was, I still loved her. Don was like that too. Sometimes he could be such an asshole, but you know what? I loved them both and I overlooked things—lots of things. I knew Don since third grade and he always was a character. I had my suspicions that something was going on with Ellen, but never with Don, not in a million years. When I saw that key, I knew what it was for. I shouldn't have gone there. I don't know why I burned the place. I just snapped, I'm sorry. I'm weak, I guess. I'm sorry for getting down on you before. It's just sometimes I get really pissed off and go crazy." Jack turned his head out his window and spat. Rolling it up he said, "Well, the love affair is over now. It's not that I hate them, let's just say I love them from afar and   I'm ready to move on." Jack shifted in his seat. Placing his fingers against his sore ribs, he winced. "There were a lot of Ellen's things in Don's place, lots of personal stuff. I got pissed off and dragged all his shit into his bedroom, including a heavy antique desk. God, that thing weighed a ton. I think I pulled these ribs, or something, picking up that damn desk."

"Why didn't you ask me to help you?"

"Sure, Carl, let's see…. 'Hey Carl, give me a hand up here, will you? Help me move all Don's stuff into his bedroom, so I can burn his fucking place down.'"

Carl laughed, "Yeah, I see your point. But if I did go up there with you, I would have stopped you."

"Don't worry, I got it out of my system, but you're right and I was wrong. Thanks for calling me on it. Father Steve was right too, right about so many things… let's get home, Carl."

They drove on for about a block, and Carl said, "That big box…do you think Don and Ellen ended up in it?"

Jack slowly shook his head and didn't say anything for a few seconds. "No. I'd like to think that somehow they just lost their way."

They drove in silence for a few minutes and Jack said, "I'm going to slow down this winter. Damn, I wish we could have gotten some books out of that library. We really needed an old set of encyclopedias. Anyway, now that it's getting cold, I'll be moving into Charlie's with you guys."

"What about Lynne? Life is short, Jack."

Jack almost laughed, but his side was hurting him. "You been talking to Jo? She gave me that same pitch a while back. Tell me something, Carl, and be honest with me, does Laura approve? I mean *really* approve, or does she just think her old dad needs some company before he kicks the bucket?"

"Everyone likes Lynne, especially you. It's hard to miss it. She likes you too and you two go good together. I'll tell you what, this is the way I look at it. Ellen died six months ago, but from what Laura told me, she as good as left you years ago. A year ago, burning your friend's place would have gotten you put in jail. But given the way things have changed, well—you can't very well see a shrink. I guess you thought burning his place down was the next best thing, but it still wasn't right. It's a messed-up world now, and like you've said yourself, the rules are gone, but that doesn't mean that we have to act crazy too. That's what separates us from the idiots in that big box. While I'm thinking of it, I want to say something else. You once told me that Iraq and Afghanistan took something from you and changed you, changed you for the worse. I'll tell you something, if you hadn't changed and came back the way you are now, our family would have never made it this far. I believe in God, and like Father Steve said about God not sending us the bad things, but using them for an ultimate good. He didn't send you into that Middle East hell hole, but what you experienced and learned over there, has *saved* us. We'd all be dead if it wasn't for you, Jack. That's the good coming out of the bad." Carl pointed ahead, "I guess our little talk is about over, here's our subdivision."

They were barely in the house when Laura ran to them, kissing and hugging them both. Taking a step back, still facing them, she clasped her hands and joyfully asked, "Guess what?"

Jack said, "Jo shot a deer and tomorrow she's making venison sausage?"

"No, guess again!"

Carl said, "The power went back on?"

"Nope, better... Carl...**we're going to have twins**!"

"What?"

"Lynne heard two heartbeats. No wonder I'm so big... isn't it wonderful?"

Carl smiled at Jack, "Twins!"

That night Jack laid down on Charlie's old leather couch in the knotty pine den. The couch was worn and comfortable, and the warmth of the cozy room felt good. He had no intention of sleeping in the cold bedroom at his house again. It was pitch dark in the room and he felt himself sink into the comfortably worn couch. He closed his eyes, waiting for sleep to overtake him, saying softly to himself, "What a day, what a day..." He heard the oak floor boards squeak and opened his eyes.

"Are you talking to yourself again?"

Lynne was standing in the doorway with a small flashlight in her hand.

"Kids are all in bed. I was about to turn in myself, but I heard you in here. Can't go anywhere in this house quietly, with these squeaky old floors. It's funny how we all go to bed so early now... another benefit of having no power." Lynne hesitated a moment. "You want to talk about it?" She stepped into the room and sat down on the wide arm of the couch. "You and Carl were pretty quiet at supper. I've learned that the quieter you are, the rougher it was out there."

"Sure, I could use some company." Jack sat up and offered her the space next to him on the couch. "Figured I'd crash here tonight. The old homestead is freezing. I tried using the fireplace, but the only part of me that stays warm is the front of me, and that's if I'm facing the fire. I think that's where the term, 'freezing your ass off' came from."

Lynne sat down next to Jack and shut her flashlight off. "I hate using these things. It won't be long and we won't be able to find batteries for them. At least this house is nice and warm—the kids are all snug as a bug. And they're happy too. Isn't it wonderful about Laura? I am so happy for her. It's going to work out, Jack, don't worry, she'll do fine."

There was a pause, and neither of them spoke for a few seconds. The house was silent, the den was pitch black, and they were close, so very close.

Jack asked, "What about Lynne, is she happy?"

"I'm happy when I'm with you...."

Jack reached for her, wanting her, but intending only to take her hand in his. As he moved towards her, she moved towards him, and neither of them stopped until they were in each other's arms.

"What's wrong Jack?"

"Sorry, my ribs are hurting again. I think I overdid it today."

FEBRUARY

CHAPTER 4 1

Jack was in Charlie's basement with Carl, who was packing the wood stove before turning in for the night. Jack said, "I never thought we could burn up so much firewood so quickly. It looked like Charlie had so much stacked up. Who would have thought we'd be running low?"

Carl placed the last log into the firebox and closed the door. "It's been a bad winter, today was the first day in two weeks it was above freezing. With all those below zero days, we used up a lot. I think we'll make it through most of March, but that will pretty much be it. I wish we hadn't wasted so much of the good stuff in our campfires. I've been thinking, we should take the snowmobiles out tomorrow if it's warmer out. We could scout around those big homes surrounding the golf course."

"I don't know, all of them were looted to the bones last fall. It might be a waste of time."

"Yeah, but maybe not for firewood. You need a truck for firewood and very few people have one. Every one of those big homes have fireplaces and they have huge garages too. Be nice if we came across a couple piles of dry oak stashed in a garage. The clubhouse on the golf course has a big fireplace. They may have a full cord stored in one of those sheds. We should gather firewood every spare chance we get, then we'll have enough for next winter."

"That's a good point. I like your snowmobile idea too. We can avoid the roads and won't have to worry about getting stuck. If we find some wood, we'll head back with the truck to get it, when some of this snow melts. It'll do us both good to get out for a while, we've been cooped up in here too long. Besides, we're bound to come across some other things we need. We can hitch up that little trailer you made, so we can grab a few small things."

"Laura wants some more children's books. We should be able to find some. Maybe we can bag something to eat too. Let's tell Jo while she's still up. The snowmobiles are ready to go. We can leave before sun-up."

Jack thoughtfully rubbed his beard. "I'm not so sure about leaving the girls alone, but we haven't seen anyone snooping around in weeks. I guess it'll be all right. Heck, the last time we went out scouting was in the fall when we went to your aunt's house." Jack thought to himself, *and what a day that was...*

Reading Jack's expression, Carl started laughing. "I think that was the last time I heard you use the 'F' word."

"Yeah, Lynne keeps me on a short leash, but that's all right. Okay, Carl, it sounds like a plan. I'm going to turn in. I'll be ready before sun-up. Goodnight."

Next Morning

5 A M.

"Are you going to be warm enough in that snowmobile suit? Have you got your long-johns on? You sure those gloves are warm enough? What if you have to fire your gun, can you finger the trigger with those heavy gloves on?"

"Lynne, I'll be all right. It's in the 20s today, a regular heatwave. We're not going far and we'll have the radios with us. You girls stick in the house this morning. Don't go outside. We'll be back after noon sometime. Any problems, call us. We'll give you a call in about three hours to check on you. Love you..."

Lynne kissed him, saying, "Love you too, please be careful, Jack.... If you run across any romance novels, grab them for me. Don't forget, we need some new children's books too. You be careful and don't be swearing around Carl. Laura says he's picking up your bad habits."

Ten minutes later, Jack met Carl out front. Jack said, "I'm taking an AR-15 with me. Other than your side arm, what kind of firepower you bringing with us?"

I've got a sawed off 12-gauge pump. That leaves the girls with Ben's M16 and an AR-15."

"Sounds good, let's go." The pair started up their snowmobiles and cut across the virgin snow, heading towards the Melville Pines Country Club. They stopped on a ridge, overlooking what used to be a fairway off the 12th hole

Jack said, "Jeez, it's beautiful out this morning, the air is cold and crisp. It feels like we're far up north, way out in the country. This is more like being in North Dakota than outside Chicago. Look at it, where did all the people go?"

"Yeah, kind of scary, isn't it? No planes, no cars, no smoke coming from any chimneys and no noise, only us."

"Yep, just us, I hope. Still, we better keep alert. Let's check out those big houses over there. We'll start with the one on the far end of the pond."

Jack gunned his snowmobile across the frozen pond, followed by Carl. The first home they picked to check out was a gabled roof, two-story brick Georgian.

The snow on the ground around it was over a week old and undisturbed, assuring them the house was vacant.

Carl walked up onto the front porch and tried the door. "It's locked, I'm surprised it's not kicked in. Somebody must have been living here until recently."

They had made up some rules about entering vacant houses. One of them was to never enter into a locked home. Unless it had clearly been broken into by someone else first, locked homes were considered occupied.

Jack said, "The garage door might be unlatched from the electric opener, I'll give it a try. We owe it to ourselves to at least check out the garage." Jack bent down and gave the heavy 16-foot door a tug and it swiftly rolled up. The early daylight was dim, but it flooded the freezing garage, revealing a pristine 1960s Mustang convertible. The car had been backed into the garage. Jack was startled when he saw two people sitting in the front seat. A gray-haired man was behind the steering wheel. An attractive blond-haired woman was in the passenger seat, leaning on him. They looked as if they were asleep, but their skins bluish hue told Jack they weren't. "Damn! They about gave me a start! Looks like carbon monoxide poisoning." Jack opened the driver's door and leaned in. "The key is in the ignition, and I'll bet the gas tank is bone dry. God, there's a dog lying on the back seat, a big St. Bernard. There's hardly any smell. They're frozen stiff " Jack shook his head, "I'd be interested in this car, we know it runs but... the provenance that goes with it... I think I'll pass."

Carl stayed back, tired of finding dead bodies. "What do you think, suicide, or just trying to stay warm?"

"Suicide, definitely suicide. Nobody sits in their garage in a running car, with the overhead door closed. Nice looking couple too. Oh well, let's go inside and salvage what we can from this place." Entering through the garage, they passed through a laundry room and into a large kitchen. "Well, look at that. They had a nice stockpile of canned goods. Look at all this boxed up stuff. Looks like they were planning to take it somewhere."

Carl exhaled disgustedly, his breath fogging in the freezing room. "Yeah, look at it. —Cans of vegetables and bottles of water, soda, and beer. All of it frozen solid and busted wide open. Any canned food we find from now on is probably going to look like this." Carl held up a can of cut green beans. "Look at the seams on this can, they're bursting wide open. This cold weather is going to finish off whatever supplies that are left." He pointed to two large cardboard boxes. "There's a couple boxes of dry stuff we can take, the rest of this is pretty much garbage."

Jack picked up a frozen bottle of beer, it's top popped off, with frozen foam sticking out of it. "Hey Carl, look... beer sherbet!"

Tossing the frozen bottle into the sink, Jack said, "Let's look upstairs for some stuff. We can pile it in the front foyer and come back for it with the truck."

Within fifteen minutes, they had a sizable pile on the floor, next to the front door.

Carl said, "Look at this, it's the best thing here." He was holding an old lever action rifle. "Couldn't find any cartridges though."

"Close, but no cigar! I found a full case of shit paper. I think that trumps an old rifle with no ammo."

Carl frowned, "That sums it all up, when a pack of double ply toilet paper is worth as much or more than a gun." He gestured with his thumb to a fireplace in the dining room. "I checked and there's no firewood. The house has three fireplaces and they're all gas. Lotta good that did them, huh?" Having a fireplace that doesn't burn wood is like having a gun that only fires blanks, they're both worthless." They started to walk out through the garage, when Carl stopped and pointed ahead into it. "What about their bodies? Are we just going to leave them there? We could push the car out and burn it, cremate them."

Jack looked thoughtfully at the old convertible. "I suppose...but then again, maybe we should just torch the whole place. We come across so many dead people, I don't know what to do anymore. I really like that car though; I think it's a 67'. Let's go check out the house next door and then some of those big places across the street. Then we can discuss what we're going to do with them."

They stood outside and surveyed the expensive, snow-covered homes surrounding the golf course. Carl pointed to a large English Tudor set back in a wooded area, two football fields away. He said, "Get a load of that place over there, will you? Look at all those fancy brick chimneys, gosh, I count six of them."

Jack said, "Let's quickly go through the house next door and then check that big one out. With all those brick chimneys, they have to have wood burning fireplaces, maybe even a stove. We could use another stove."

Carl mounted his snowmobile, saying, "I don't see smoke coming out of any of them, so it's got to be vacant." Carl gave Jack a big smile. "There has to be a big load of firewood stacked around there someplace and it's got our name on it. Come on, let's go there first. I've got a good feeling about that place. I'll race you there!"

* * * * *

Laura said, "I hate it when they go out. I know they'll be calling in an hour or so, but I still don't like it."

Kathy put down the potato she was peeling and said, "They'll be fine. We can't stay inside holed up all winter. They have to go out and scrounge for

428

supplies, especially firewood. There's nobody roaming around since it got cold, everybody has bugged out to the boonies or gone to the camps. They'll be okay. We have the walkie talkies, call them now, if you want."

"No, I'm just restless, I guess. I'll wait until they call. I do wonder how Father Steve and Ben are doing? I wish there was some way we could contact them. I wonder if Ben found that girl?" I hope he didn't. We should have never let Ben go off to that camp."

Kathy said, "That girl couldn't have survived that river current. Let's just hope they've been eating okay and have been staying warm. Speaking of staying warm, how's the babies?"

Laura patted her large belly, "They're fine, very active this morning, that's for sure. It'll be nice having them born when the weather warms up. It'll be a beautiful way to start the spring. It's warming up out and winter will be over soon. It'll be nice to go outside and not be freezing."

Kathy quickly tossed the last peeled potato into the pot of water. "I just have to cut up some carrots and I'm done. But right now, I have a better idea. Let's take the kids outside and let them play in the snow for a while. It'll do us all some good to get out and get some fresh air. Jo is already out there and Lynne is downstairs with the kids, I'll go tell her."

"I don't know, Kath, my dad said for all of us to stay inside." Laura hesitated a couple seconds, thinking it over. "I guess it's all right though, just for a half hour or so. It'll do all of us some good to get out for a while."

Kay was sitting in Charlie's den, making a final inventory of mostly obsolete ammo and weapons. She overheard their conversation in the kitchen and yelled, "Great idea. I wish I could join you, but it's my turn to stay inside today."

Laura went into the den where Kay was sitting, "You don't have to sit around inside, Kay, we'll just be in the backyard. Come on—join us."

"Nope. Someone always has to stay inside. I'll be fine. I'm almost done going over all of Charlie's old guns. Jack is right, most of them are just wall hangers. I'm going to clean up this old 10-gauge double barrel." Kay pointed to an open box of long brass shotgun shells on Charlie's desk. Charlie bought those antique shells at a gun show. I was looking them over, thinking about trying them out, but Jack said not to. He said Charlie admitted that he'd been drinking when he re-loaded them and maybe put in too heavy of a load. I'd really love to shoot this old boy, but I don't want the barrels blowing up in my hands."

Laura eyed the box of shells, making a face. "What on earth would you shoot with those big things, an elephant?"

Kay picked up one of the large shells, handing it to Laura, "Believe it or not, it's loaded with birdshot. Guns like these were used for birds. I'd like to try it out on a big pumpkin, there'd be nothing left. You guys go out with the kids. Wendel needs to get out and play. He'll have fun, but I'll stay inside."

429

The four women left the house and played outside with the three boys. The snow was like powder. The boys chased one another, kicking an old soccer ball into the frozen drifts. Jo grabbed the ball and kicked it hard over the boy's heads, high into the crisp air, disappearing over the corner of the house.

Bobby ran ahead of the other two boys, rounding the corner of the house, chasing after the ball. Wendel and Andy were right behind Bobby, as he disappeared around the corner. Both of the children suddenly stopped and stood still, frozen in place. Neither of them moved, nor said a word.

Lynne sensed danger and so did Jo, but it was too late.

Kathy screamed, **"Boys, run!"**

"Gotcha, you little bastard!" A pig-faced Dirk Hayes stepped out from the corner of the house, scooping up Andy in his immense hands. Following him was his younger brother, Chuck, carrying a kicking Bobby, his gloved hand firmly clamped over the boy's mouth.

Holding Bobby up like a shield, Sherriff Hayes yelled, "Go ahead girls, you got guns, come on, use them! Shoot us! Break them out and we'll snap their little necks!" Hayes motioned to Jo, "Long time no see, bitch! Now you lay that bad-ass rifle of yours down in the snow, real gentle like...."

Andy screamed as Dirk tightened his grip, snarling at Jo, "You lay it down like he said, big girl, or I'll pop his little noggin like a zit!"

Lynne was clutching her chest, **"Oh my God, don't hurt them!"** Wendel ran behind Kathy, clinging to her legs. Jo defiantly glared at the Hayes brothers, as she carefully laid the M16 down.

"That's a good start lady. Now, all of you take off your coats.... **TAKE THEM OFF!** I want to see what's under them!" All of the girls quickly removed their coats, dropping them into the frozen snow.

"Well looky here... the skinny one is fat as a hog! Looks like somebody is about to have a baby... isn't that sweet? You're that jarhead's daughter, Laura, right? Ahh yeah, this is going to be fun. Look, Dirk! I told you, just as I suspected... All of them are packing— you fuckin bitches... Didn't I tell you, Dirk, every one of them would be armed to the teeth! All of them got cute little shoulder holsters with little bitty semi-auto's... all except her! He motioned at Jo, "Look at the cannon the bitch is carrying, Dirk. What the hell, a 44? And look at the big knife she's has. —Now all of you, with your left hand, remove your weapons and set them in the snow, real easy like. If you have anything hidden, you better get rid of it now.... One of them goes off, these kids are dead." The women gently laid their weapons on top the frozen snow and stood up, all of them standing silent. He motioned to Kathy, "Hey, blondie, I remember you.... grab that snot nosed kid behind you and let's all get in the house, cause I'm cold." Kathy bent down and picked Wendel up. He clung to her, shaking.

Suddenly the sheriff yelled in pain, "**Ouch! You little black bastard!** He bit me, Dirk, right through my fuckin glove! Jeez!" He held Bobby up by the scruff of

430

his neck like a captured animal, shaking and choking him. **"How do you like this, you little asshole, huh? How do you like it?"**

In a rage, Lynne madly charged at him. Like a sack of potatoes, the sheriff tossed Bobby headlong into her, knocking her down into the snow.

He sneered, "There you go, Buckwheat, go to grandma. Now we got things to do, so let's all of us go inside." He spit on Lynne, "Get up old lady and keep a hold of that brat. Get your big ass inside! Dirk, you go open that sliding glass door and get in the house first, in case one of these bitches has a gun handy in there. Come on girls, move your fat asses."

Bobby was behind Lynne, hanging onto her shoulder, growling at him. The sheriff spit a wad of tobacco on Lynne's chest, yelling, "I told you to get your ass up lady and take hold of that little animal before I shoot him!" As he herded them inside, he snarled, "We've been watching you people from that house behind you, standing upstairs, freezing our asses off since before dawn, but it was worth it. We saw that stupid jar head and his teacher buddy leave on them snowmobiles. They're going to have a real surprise when they get back." Jo was last in line and in front of him as he launched a painful kick into her backside. "Come on, tootsie, move that big ass of yours in there." Roughly slamming the door behind him, the sheriff stomped the snow off his boots, while removing a sawed-off shotgun from a holster beneath his coat. "Damn, my feet are cold, holy shit!"

Wendel started to fight Kathy, yelling for his mom. Dirk snarled, "Which one of you is his mom? You better shut the little bastard up, or I will!"

Kathy shot a frantic look at Lynne, who quickly said, "None of us. He's an orphan, he's always asking for his mother." Lynne thought, *they don't know about Kay... oh God, Kay?*

The sheriff pointed the short-barreled shotgun to a closed door saying, "Where's that door go to, is it a closet?"

Laura answered, "It's the pantry."

"Well you open it, missy. Shove these brats in it and close the fuckin door." She bent down to comfort the children, but was instantly screamed at. **"Hey!** I didn't tell you to start telling them bedtime stories, did I? **Get their little asses in there, now!"**

Laura guided the boys in the pantry and closed the door, standing in front of it.

"Good girl. Now, let's get down to brass tacks..."

Dirk grabbed Kathy, saying, "I want this one. Come here blondie!"

Kathy said nothing. Her lips trembled, looking over to Jo.

Chuck placed his shotgun behind Jo's ear and whispered, "Go on, help her. She's your girl, ain't she? You can do it..." He laughed, "Ha! Smart decision, bitch, because I'll blow your face off!"

431

The sheriff nodded his head, glancing about the kitchen. "We always wanted to see what the insides of old Charlie's house looked like. I bet there's a picture somewhere of his daughter. Remember her, Dirk?"

Dirk held Kathy roughly from behind, his bearded chin nuzzled tightly into her smooth neck. He sneered at his younger brother and smiled, showing his tobacco stained teeth. He lowly snarled in Kathy's ear, "I cut her heart out and cooked it. It tasted damn good—she was my first…"

Lynne's heart fell to her bowels, **"It's you!"**

The Sheriff howled, **"Yep, we've been having a field day for a long time around here!** It's always been fun and profitable, but now people got to eat… It's not just for the rich who want it."

He jerked his head to Dirk. "You got blondie, but I want this one, she's feisty!" He pointed his shotgun at Laura's stomach and said to Lynne, "You're padded nice old lady, you come here, or I'll blow this young mama to kingdom come."

Dirk started laughing, "He will too!"

Lynne obeyed, and slowly moved toward the sheriff, thinking, Oh *God, Kay, please, do something…kill them now*….

The Sheriff impatiently shook his little shotgun, "You gotta move a little faster girl, get that big fat ass of yours's over here!"

* * * * *

Kay had been silently sitting in Charlie's study, fingering one of the large antique shotguns shells the old man had reloaded. The old 10-gauge brass shell was heavy in her small hand. Like most of the remaining weapons and ammunition left in Charlie's study, it was little more than a conversation piece. The day before, she had finished re-assembling Charlie's prized Korean War era 1910 Browning Automatic Rifle. A magnificent weapon, it had been upgraded twice since it was manufactured before World War 1, and it was now in the living room. It looked oddly out of place, setting up on its tripod, and taking up the entire length of Dottie's oak coffee table. Cleaned up and ready to fire, Kay had three 20 round magazines filled with Charlie's 70-year-old 30-06 ammo. They had planned to try the old automatic rifle out that week. She hoped the vintage 1950 ammunition would still be good, as some of the brass cartridges had turned a dark green with age. If Charlie's large stockpile of ammo for it had gone bad, the magnificent old weapon would be useless to them. There were other guns they planned to test fire that week, but sadly, the old ten-gauge double barrel side by side that was on her lap would not be one of them. She didn't want to risk the barrels exploding from an antique shell that was possibly overloaded by someone

432

who had one too many beers. No longer manufactured, Charlie had reloaded two dozen of them for the old 10-gauge side-by-side. She had finished cleaning and inspecting all of Charlie's weapons the day before. The newer ones, mostly shotguns, were distributed throughout the house for defense, leaving a large hodgepodge of older, mostly obsolete and foreign weapons sitting in the racks. Charlie had weapons from every war the United States had fought in. Most of them would be considered as conversation pieces and hadn't been fired in years; many having no ammunition to fit them. Kay had been care-fully disassembling, cleaning, and inventorying all of them. There were several old lever action rifles, all from the 1800s, and even some original black powder muskets dating from before the Civil War.

The inventory of antique weapons was impressive, but the feasibility of actually using them for defense, especially with old and limited supplies of ammunition, was questionable. There would be no problem using them for hunting or target shooting, but to face an armed intruder with ammunition dating from before 1950? They didn't want to risk their lives on it. It was decided they would test fire every usable weapon they had ammo for and keep them loaded as a last-ditch defense. That morning she had laid some of the boxes of old ammunition across Charlie's large desk, trying to figure out what shells went with what gun and if they were still usable. She was about to take the heavy old shotgun off her lap when she heard yelling. As soon as the door slammed open, Kay's heart jumped! She heard a man screaming and he was in the next room, maybe 12 feet away from her. He had everyone his prisoner... everyone except her!

There were two usable weapons within her reach. Both with their ammunition directly in front of her. Charlie's old 10-gauge was still on her lap, with its newly reloaded shells directly in front of her. Dottie's old double barrel, 20-gauge ladies' model, was setting on top of the desk with a box of outdated paper shot-shells lying next to it. Both guns were old side-by-sides, most likely from the teens, and hadn't been fired in many years. Other than the 12-gauge pump in the gun cabinet, every other weapon was outdated and pretty much useless. An arsenal was at her fingertips, but only the modern 12-gauge pump was a sure thing. To get out of Charlie's squeaky old leather chair and reach the gun case, she would have to risk six feet of squeaky old oak flooring, and open the gun cabinet door. *Didn't its hinges squeak and the glass rattle too? How many seconds will that take, before I have the gun in my hand, ready to fire?* Kay cursed herself. She remembered she hadn't chambered a shell in the shotgun... *Stupid, stupid, stupid!* She'd have to rack a shell into it before she could fire it, giving them more time, *more warning...While they're holding a gun to my friend's heads... Oh God help me! How could I have not kept a shell chambered, when split-seconds count?*

433

Kay exhaled defeated, scared and disgusted with herself. The Browning Auto Rifle was only a few feet away in the living room, with three full 20 round magazines next to it, but it was heavy and unwieldy. To fire it in the house? She would probably kill everyone, including the children—*Who was she kidding? She'd never get to it.* The kitchen was quiet for a few seconds and she wondered if the sheriff had heard her. She clearly heard everything that was being said in the kitchen, as well as every movement they made. She was so close, too close... and if she moved, they would hear her. In seconds, a hundred scenarios ran through her brain.

The intruders think they have everyone accounted for, it's my only advantage. They have everyone, *except me!* Kay felt sick, it was as if her whole body was collapsing into Charlie's old leather chair. *My Shotmaster 9mm is still in my bedroom...in the nightstand! Stupid, stupid, stupid! How could I be so stupid to leave my sidearm upstairs?* She looked down at the heavy weapon, lying uncomfortably on her lap. She had fired many shotguns, including a 10 gauge, but only at her father's gun range and never against a person. It was so heavy...she'd have to fire it from her hip—she could miss... She knew the breech would silently open to load, but it would make a loud snap! —when closed. *They'd hear her!* Afraid to move a muscle, she was frozen in Charlie's squeaky leather chair. *I can't make any noise... I'm screwed... Oh God, I'm screwed and it's my own fault!*

Kay listened to the sheriff and his brother tell their sick plan and heard the children crying. She had made a terrible mistake. *I left my sidearm in the bedroom, oh my God, how could I be so stupid?* She looked down at the hardwood floor. The floor didn't have carpet and loudly squeaked with every footstep. Her brain screamed at her! *If you move an inch,* **they'll hear You!**

I should have had all these guns ready to fire! I'll make noise... waste precious seconds and they'll know someone else is in here! They'll kill the children! She silently hefted the weight of the old shotgun off her legs, remembering what her father had once said, "*People think they can't miss an intruder with a shotgun, but they're woefully wrong...*" Kay started to shake with fear. *Oh my God, these shells are loaded with birdshot, oh My God...*

She eyed the old double barrel 20 gauge lying on the desk. She remembered when she cleaned it, the breech opened and closed silently... but it was only a 20-gauge, and those old paper shotshells? When were they made, the fifties—forties, maybe the thirties? Would they still be good? She was already holding the powerful 10. Silently, she opened the breach of the 10 and slid the two long brass shells in. Knowing the 10 gauge's breach would close with a loud click, she left it open, waiting for the last moment to close it. She ran everything over in her mind, so much so that her head was spinning... Charlie thought he may have overloaded these shells...the barrels could blow up in my hands... I have to calm down, calm down. There are two armed men in the house, holding my

434

friends hostage in the next room…. I heard Laura tell the kids to get into in the pantry…. they're safe, but I only have two rounds, loaded with birdshot…. I'm close, it will hit them in one wad… I'll have to move fast— God help me…

* * * * *

Jack and Carl approached the massive house from the golf course, and Carl stopped his snowmobile at the end of a huge snow-covered pile. "Look at all that firewood, Jack, there's got to be more than two full cords. I knew this place would pan out!" Carl was puzzled. Jack didn't seem as excited as he was, and was staring off into the woods behind the house.

"What's up, Jack, trouble?"

"Maybe, maybe not, but I think I just realized where we are." Jack was pointing behind the house. "Look into that stand of pine trees back there. I think I can make out the remains of an old windmill. The blades are gone, but I think the metal stand is still there. See it? That looks like the metal framework of an old windmill stand, doesn't it? Let's go back there and check it out. If there's anything left of a multicolored brick silo behind it, I think I've seen it before. I think this could be what's left of the farm where Charlie's daughter was brutally murdered. Let's go take a look."

They drove across the hard, frozen snow, stopping their snowmobiles before the grove of tall pine trees. Both of them dismounted their snowmobiles and walked through some snow-covered brush, stepping into a tangle of low branches. Buried amongst the boughs of two tall Scotts pines was the rusted framework of an old windmill. A slanting mound of sheet metal was on the ground at its base. Leaning against the windmill's stand were the rusty remains of its blades. Directly behind it was the other thing Jack was looking for. Sticking up, covered in the frozen snow, was a large circular outline that could only be the remains of the old silo. Jack kicked into a mound of snow, uncovering pieces of shattered bricks with his boot heel. Beneath the debris, he dislodged two unbroken bricks. Bending down, he placed both of them face up, next to each other. When placed side by side, they completed the same brown checkerboard pattern he had seen in the photo. He had found the old brick silo.

Jack reeled towards the new house and faced it. In his mind, he pictured where the old farm house and barn had once stood. "Damn, this is where she was found. She was murdered here. I recognized it from an old photo I saw in the

435

newspaper. Where that new house is standing was a large dairy barn. I read the accounts of the murder and I've seen pictures of the farm buildings; they were all painted white. I tried to find remnants of it when I golfed here. Al and I had looked for it while golfing last summer, no wonder we didn't see anything. When you're on the course, this huge house blocks this patch of pines from view.

They stood there for a few moments. The sun had disappeared, and a chill ran through both of them. "Come on, Carl, let's go check out the house." They mounted their snowmobiles and drove around towards the front of the huge home.

Both of them saw the tire ruts carved into the virgin snow and instantly brought their machines to a halt. Jack slowly scanned the empty course, his eyes searching for any movement, the tiniest reflection. Shutting off their machines, they sat there for a minute, intently listening. The sky was dark and the wind was blowing powdered snow across the silent country club. Other than two hawks high above them, they were alone, and the only thing out of place was a set of fresh tire tracks in the hard snow.

Carl said, "Looks like they were made from a truck, something heavy, with extra wide wheels." The tracks ended in front of the house's massive six-car garage, and trailed off across the drive and out to the street. Both of them looked down the snow-covered street, where the tracks disappeared, winding into the woods. They dismounted, removing the keys from their machines. Carl bent down, checking out the tire ruts in the six-inch-deep snow. "These look pretty fresh, Jack, they're not drifted in at all. They could have been made this morning. Let's check out the house." They walked in the ruts that ended in front of a closed garage door.

"This isn't an ordinary truck, look how far apart these tire tracks are. The tires on it are huge, like one of those big high 4'x4's." He pointed to a large patch of melted snow. "It was parked here with its motor running for a while, long enough for its exhaust to melt that big hole into the snow." Both of them studied a maze of footprints where the truck had parked. Two people had gotten out of it, walked towards the house, and returned. Jack set his foot into one of the footprints on the driver's side, the huge print dwarfed his size twelve boot. "These belong to a big guy, bigger than me. The driver of this truck wore work boots, easily a size 18 or 20." Jack felt a slight tinge in his ribs. He only knew of one person for sure who had a four-wheel drive pickup still running, with wide off-road tires. That person also wore at least size 18 boots.

Carl saw the alarm on Jack's face and immediately came to the same conclusion. Pointing to the passenger's much smaller footprints, Carl sighed, "It's them, isn't it? Black clouds had permanently moved in, covering the whole sky like a bad omen, and a fine shower of ice crystals suddenly cut through the frigid air. Carl glanced around, nervously holding his rifle.

Jack motioned to where the boot prints ended at the closed garage door, saying, "Stand off to the side and be ready. Let's see if this door goes up." Jack lifted the door and it easily rolled up, yielding a huge vacant garage. Two sets of snow caked boot prints were visible. They trailed off across the dark grey concrete floor, towards a service door leading into the silent house.

About halfway across the garage, the snow faded out from the prints and another set could be seen leaving the house. Clearly imprinted on the floor was the faint trace of red heel marks coming from the house, growing stronger as they got close to the service door.

Carl said, "God, it looks like blood."

"Yeah, there's a pool of blood in this house somewhere, and the bigger guy must have stepped in it as he left."

"Aw shit. Here we go again. What are we going to do, Jack? How about we just leave?"

Jack grimaced, grinding his teeth together. Sharply exhaling, he said, "This place has a bad feeling about it, but I think we're alone." He pointed to the back of Carl's snowmobile. "Give me your shotgun, I'm going inside. You stay out here and stand watch. Keep an eye on the street. If I run into something, you'll know it. Anyone comes up that driveway, you take care of them, and no questions—got it? Just shoot them. I'll be right out. And, Carl, if we do get visitors, remember—don't go nuts firing that rifle, we don't want to run out of ammo."

"Okay, I got it. Please be careful in there."

Jack silently opened the door and entered into a dark hallway. Its white-tiled floor reflected up from the dim light behind him. More bloody boot prints greeted him, trailing through the hallway and ending at another closed door. The hallway was about 15 feet long, with two multi-door closets, their white painted doors flanking the entire lengths of both sides. One of the doors was slightly ajar. Fighting the urge to quickly turn around and fire the 12 gauge into the open closet door, he ignored it and followed the bloody boot prints *Damn...I got a bad feeling about this.* He hesitated... The door at the end of the hall wasn't fully closed. Like a grade "B" horror movie, its hinges squeaked, sounding alarm as he pushed it open. An expanse of gray daylight hit him from tall windows, revealing a massive kitchen. Facing him was the largest kitchen island he had ever seen, at least 20 feet long. His heart was beating fast and his finger ready to pull the trigger. He was sure he was alone in the house, but his senses were screaming at him. *Something is really bad here, Jack!* The iron taste of fresh blood hit him as soon as the door had swung open. He felt his heart jump and his stomach sink as he viewed the long kitchen island before him. The counter top that was once white Corian, was awash in thickened blood. Open entrails and smooth white bones, some with shreds of muscle still clinging to them, were heaped in a bloody mess on each end. Jack stood there frozen, the shotgun leveled and his heavy breath condensing in the kitchen's frigid air. Blood—there was a waterfall of it, mixed with the brown insides of intestines, clinging to the counter's edge. The bloody mess had cascaded down the sides of the white cabinet and pooled on the floor, creeping down the seams of the large, square white tiles. The bloody boot prints he had followed into the home led straight from it.

Stacked on a long counter top, next to an oversize farmhouse sink, was a pile of brick sized, wrapped packages, climbing at least two feet high. All of them were tightly wrapped in clean white butcher paper and neatly secured with caramel colored tape. Next to them was a large bloody cleaver and several razor-sharp knives. His eyes glided across to a battery-powered reciprocating saw, with its bloody white saw-toothed blade menacingly protruding from it, pointing directly at him. He moved towards the hill of packages, knowing what they must hold, but telling himself it couldn't be. No human being could do something like this. He stood over the securely wrapped packages, trying not to breathe in the evil that hovered over them. Each package had something in black marker neatly printed on it.

The pile nearest to him read, **PORK TENDERLOIN.** The packages next to it were labeled **STEW MEAT.**   Another group, the contents visible in their clear plastic bags, simply read: ground pork and soup bones. There had to be over 400 pounds of it.

Jack shuddered, his breath freezing in the stagnant air and his body yelling at his brain to make it run! Suddenly sick to his stomach, he stood there taking it all in. The kitchen was like a giant walk-in meat freezer; its counters laid out like a butcher shop. His brain screamed *Cannibalism! I have to get out of here and call the girls!*

Jack turned around too quickly, slipping on the blood-soaked floor. Catching his fall on the counter's edge, he nearly went headlong into three white plastic buckets. They were lined up in a row on the bloody floor, filled with severed hands, feet, and at least four human heads. Two Asian looking adults and two children. Three females and one male. The Chen family! Each skull had one or more holes from a small caliber gun, staring at him like extra eyes punched into their skulls. He turned away from them, losing his stomach when he looked into the bottom of the deep porcelain farmhouse sink. In it were three other severed heads that he recognized, staring up at him, their jaded white pupils vacant in the grey winter light. He recoiled from the sink and vomited onto the bloody floor.

His mind flashed back to the horror of seeing Christian Iraqi families who had been executed in their homes...but their kitchen didn't look like a slaughterhouse, and their body parts hadn't been packaged and then labeled—and he didn't know three of them. Jack wanted to run out of the kitchen, but he couldn't. The souls of his boots wouldn't let him. They were slipping and sticking, as he slowly mucked across the blood-sodden floor, leaving the way he had come in.

"Carl!"

"Yeah, we're clear! What did you find in there?"

"It's horrible, oh my God, don't come in here!" Jack stumbled into the garage, still slipping in his bloody boots, wiping vomit from his chin. "Get your radio out. We have to call the girls. We're going straight home! Oh my God, we should burn this place, but we don't have the time. Jack mounted his snowmobile, placing his hand on the handle of Father Steve's treasured baseball bat. He had carried it with him since Jo had given it to him. Firmly gripping the knob on the end of the bat he yelled, "We got to get home, **NOW!**"

* * * * *

Chuck Hayes was in his glory as he looked around the kitchen. "This is some great set-up you girls got here... Jeez, we might just have a change in plans. What do you think, Dirk? It's cozy in here, maybe we should make this place our new winter outpost?"

"Sounds like a plan to me, Chuck."

The sliding glass door opened and a tall lanky man stepped into the kitchen. He was carrying a large open cardboard box. The sheriff reached into it and withdrew a long, curve bladed knife.

He said to the tall man holding the box, "Hey Boner, gonna borrow one of your knives. I'll take this curved one. Man, this is like a razor, it'll do fine." He gestured with the knife towards the front of the house, "Tango better be out in front watching for them, or I'll use this knife on him."

Boner nodded his head, mumbling "Yeah Boss, he's out there. He's upstairs in the house across the street, Glen's old place."

"That's good, because we got a change in plans. You leave your saws and cleavers outside. We're not going to do them in here. I've decided we're going to stay in this place for a while." The sheriff looked at the girls, grinning. "I don't want to make a big fucking mess in here, if you know what I mean?"

He laid the curve bladed knife on the counter next to him, eyeing Jo. "There it is again, big girl, I just saw it... you just had a *dangerous thought*, didn't you? You wanna go for that knife, don't you? Stick it in me, huh?" Pointing his shotgun at Laura's stomach, he snarled, "Go for it, you got a chance, follow your dream, girl...**grab that knife!**"

Laura cried, "What are you going to do with us? Please, don't hurt the children."

Chuck smiled, "Well, Missy, I wouldn't worry about them, they won't go to waste."

439

Dirk started laughing, "No, no, no, we don't waste nothing! Tell them what we're going do, Chuck!"

The sheriff looked up at the ceiling, laughing, "Okay, that sounds good. We still got some time before the men come home. I get a kick out of this part anyway; it draws out the suspense. We've been having fun for a long, long, time, girls. Me and the boys here do all the dirty work, while the other two just sit on their ass ordering us around, but that's going to change. Lots of things are going to change." He shot a look to Dirk, and Dirk nodded his pig-faced head in agreement. "You see, we've been in a business. It started as a little side thing, but lately it's gotten big, really big. There's a lot of rich and elite people in this country who like to do some pretty sick things, but they're not like us. No, no, no, **they don't have the balls to do the legwork required!** They're too scared to kidnap a kid, let alone face an adult! So, we've been in the business of providing victims. Victims for people who don't have the stones to do the dirty work themselves. You see, they tell us what they got in mind and who they wish to do it to, and we make it happen for them. We're in the business of making nightmares come true!" He smiled at his brother.

Dirk stomped his huge boots and started laughing. "You think all the missing kids in this country just disappear? Some of them are consumed!" Dirk's meaty hands tightened around Kathy's throat. She started choking as he laughed and sneered, ***"The eaters!"***

Laura felt herself become sick. She placed her hands protectively on her stomach.

"Oh yeah, you don't know the half of it, girls! We got some real winners in this country; they even make me sick. Behind them locked doors, the screams are never heard. We don't even know who our clients are. We're not supposed too—they're just provided to us. They come and go. But I got eyes and some of them I recognize...famous people, if you know what I mean. It aint just us, this is a worldwide operation and it's hidden in plain sight. They fly in and we pick them up. We provide them their fun in a discreet place we got just west of here, and we bring them back to the airport afterwards. We provide them a video and a little souvenir. Usually it's a body part or two, or maybe a couple pints of their victim's blood. It's business, that's all it is. We had a good thing going, but those days are over with, the way it is and all. But now—people are starving... hell, I've heard that half the population of the Midwest is already dead, and I can believe it. Whole neighborhoods are fucking empty. So nowadays, it's like we're in the livestock business. There is nothing left to eat—anywhere. People are clawing under the snow, eating grass. You fat assed preppers thought you were so damn smart, hoarding away all your chow, but all you did was put yourself on the main menu. The camps need fresh meat, ladies, and we provide it to them by the truckload! *We get paid in* gold!"

None of the women said a word. Angered by their silence, Dirk loudly said, "We've been hitting cocky ass preppers left and right! Sooner or later, you let your guard down and we're there like a big dick. You got all the food and are fat and sassy, all holed up—but none of you are safe from us!"

The women stayed silent and Dirk got madder. "**Screw you bitches!** You should be sniveling, begging for your lives...**get on your knees and maybe we'll let you live**—you could be our slaves!"

Kathy was almost passed out. Dirk roughly shoved her to the floor and started unbuckling his filthy blue jeans. Chuck smiled widely at his brother, "What the hell big brother, don't blow a gasket. Let 'em play tough, enough talk, huh? Let's get this ball rolling. You girls are going to save us some work... remove your clothing, all of it...***now!*** Let's go, drop'em, gals! Then you're all going to tippy toe outside in the snow. By the time those two assholes pull up on them snowmobiles, it'll all be over for you gals. Then we're going to wait. My brother is going to get even for getting his head split open, right, Dirk?"

Dirk stood there, his belt unbuckled and hanging loose. "You're damn straight I am. Just like I took care of that old black preacher and those two kids. He hit me in the head with his stinking bat, so I cut theirs off! And now it's the jarhead's turn."

Lynne gasped, **"NO!"**

The sheriff smiled again, and moved in front of her, snarling through his yellow teeth, **"Finally! Some emotion! *I thought I'd never see it!*"** His grin turned evil, "That's right... those other two kids were your neighbors, weren't they?" Nodding his head, he paused a few seconds, "I forgot about that..." Grabbing Lynne by the collar of her blouse he screamed, **"Well look at you, you're wearing your little crooked silver cross."** He looked at the other women. "What the hell? You're all wearing them. You think that little cross has some kind of power? It's all in your mind girls, that cross doesn't save anything." Tightening his grip on Lynne, he started laughing, "Your friends are sausage, sweetie! Dirk shot 'em in the head, and sliced them up like buttered links, they're already wrapped and stacked! You'll be joining them this evening, then it's off to the government stew pots!" Horse, human or dog, they're not fussy. As long as it's fresh. . . chopped up or ground—they buy it all. The camps are starving. Don't you get it? There's *nothing* left to eat—anywhere! You so-called Christians will close your eyes and sell your soul for a meal!" Getting no reaction from them, he lowered his voice and in a friendly tone, said, "You girls don't believe me, do you? We were doing some business with the Chen family, in their big mansion over by the golf course. They were preppers too. You should see their set-up. They've got a big-ass bunker under their house. They were doing pretty good until we dropped in on them! On the way back from there, we ran into that black priest. We've been looking for his ass. That boy, Ben, and his pretty girlfriend were with him. They said they were coming back here, *that's* the reason *we* came here. That kid, Ben, he was really sick, he could barely walk. That preacher said he had to get him back here, *so you girls could take proper care of him*. We killed all three of them! That black priest begged us to take him, and let them two kids live." The sheriff's upper lip curled and he shook his head, "That stupid kid and his girlfriend were actually praying for us when Dirk put a bullet in their heads. Can you believe that, *praying... for us*? It doesn't get better than that. Will you girls pray for us, **pretty please**? **Will you pray for our blackened souls?**"

Lynne spat out, **"You're lying!** Ben was always healthy as an ox, and he wasn't religious, he never prayed. And he didn't have a girlfriend... you don't scare us with your bullshit story, you ugly prick! Someday, try washing your face, then shove a gun barrel in your mouth!"

Letting go of her blouse, he roughly grabbed Lynne by the neck and started laughing. ***"You are funny."*** Pulling her closer, his blackhead-studded nose an inch from hers, he snarled, "It doesn't matter what you think, bitch, but I ain't no liar! That priest must have had some kinda spell on them kids. He used that Christian mind control bullshit, cause the boy was praying for us, ***and so was she***! I've seen her before and she was a tough bitch like you...and   I   **LIKE THAT!"**

The sheriff paused for a second, breathing heavily, and glaring into Lynne's eyes. Then he continued his rant, "Before the shit hit, she was married to some long-haired sandal wearing puke, and lived on the next street over. So, **don't** bullshit me that she wasn't part of your little neighborhood prayer group." He roughly pulled Lynne closer, the tip of his tongue brushing wetly against her cheek. "Whoa— you got balls calling me ugly. You are *one—ugly—bitch* with that nasty scar on your face. This is the first time I've ever seen you up close. Holy crap! You looked good from far away, lady, but you are **far—far from good!**

But *you are interesting...* Now you girls get all them clothes off before I get really pissed!"

The sliding glass door opened, and the man called Boner entered the kitchen and stood next to the sheriff, stomping his snow-covered boots, "Ready any time you are, Boss. I got the saws and the grinder set up on that big picnic table. I'll use the kids' swing set to hook'em. It's *nice and sturdy*. It'll go quick." Boner eyed the women as they undressed, while the sheriff continued to hold Lynne close, licking his cracked lips.

* * * * *

Carl yelled, "I can't get them, they're not answering! The batteries must be low, the radio isn't working!"

"Screw the radio, let's go, we'll be there in minutes." As they pounded the snowmobiles across the golf course, Jack ran Charlie's words over and over in his head, **"You won't have to look for them, they'll find you!"**

* * * * *

Kay heard the sliding glass door open and someone stomping snow off their boots. The one they called Boner entered the kitchen from outside. He had to be standing to the right of the sheriff and was talking to him. She had only two shots with Charlie's old shotgun, and this would be her only chance at getting both of the men so close together. The sheriff sounded like he was standing directly in line with the hallway. She wanted to line up her shot, but if she dared take a look, he'd spot her instantly.

She could hear Dirk talking, and it sounded like he was around the corner by the kitchen table, across from the sheriff. She would just have to rush out and take her shot. She would be at about six feet, hitting the sheriff first. There would be no spread of the pellets, and there was a chance, even with the shotgun, that she'd miss. It sounded like he was holding Lynne close to him, maybe by her collar or her neck. That would mean his right side would be turned towards her. She couldn't risk wounding him, hitting him in his arm or shoulder....it had to be in his head or neck. While advancing, she would fire the right barrel into the sheriff first. The one called Boner would most likely shoot her or try to shield himself. She decided to fire the left barrel at the dead center of his body. Back or chest, it didn't matter. At that range she'd blow a hole clear through him. The big one, the one called Dirk, he was the wild card. He was out of sight, around the corner, maybe holding Kathy... She'd still be advancing, and have to turn and face him. She'd quickly turn the corner—club him, and beat him to death with the heavy gun... she'd shove the barrels up his ass if she got half the chance. He would probably be putting a bullet in her as she shot the one, they called Boner, but she'd go after that pig-faced bastard with her last breath.

A cold shudder went through her as a last image of little Wendel's sweet face faded. *Wendel I love you...* She whispered to herself, "Okay let's do it, Kay, time to kill these bastards." The heavy old shotgun felt good in her hands and the steel became a part of her. She quietly pushed herself up from the worn leather chair and eased up to the open door. Any sounds she made stepping into the hallway were masked by the sheriff's screaming and ranting at her friends.

443

She closed the breach and heard her dad's voice in her head...*Easy Kay, breathe easy, don't rush it, your shot is coming— you'll get it. Kill them.* It felt like Dad was right next to her, his strength pouring into her

* * * * *

Sheriff Hayes stood there, cock-fire sure of himself, but something changed. Over the years he had tortured and killed many people. They bargained, they cried and pleaded, finally to cower—and that was the men. In all of the murders he'd committed, there weren't many that he could recall who faced him, unnerved to the end. There was that husband and wife, the Connors. They held each other's hands while they prayed. And then that sonofabitch black preacher and his two young friends. He could sense these women he was about to kill were cut from the same cloth, and that bothered him... They were women... they should be trembling, pissing themselves and babbling, pleading for the lives of their children, their precious little babies. And in the end—it was always about their babies. But these women were different, it was like they didn't give a shit. They weren't afraid, and he thought again about taking the time to make them take off their clothes. He thought, *Maybe I should kill them now, inside the house. Something doesn't feel right.* As he pulled the scar-faced bitch closer to him, he had that split second of warning. It was amazing how much could run through a person's mind in half a second. This bitch was dangerous, he felt it; he could smell it. It was like putting your face too close to a pissed off cat and you knew what would be coming, but had run out of time. He was a split second from shoving her forehead into the sharp edge of the kitchen counter when he saw it. Her face showed fear, but her eyes didn't. Something was coming, but it was too late for him to do anything to stop it.

* * * * *

The man that Boner referred to as Tango had taken up a position across the street, in the second-floor master bedroom of Glen Sorensen's home. He had known Glen and was within three feet of him the night he was killed. He looked around Glen's bedroom, remembering the last time he had seen him, the look of shock on his face with those scissors sticking out of his neck. They had made it look like Barry's wife had stabbed the scissors in him while he was raping her. Glen had never even touched the woman. The whole thing was a set-up. They knew if the power went back on, they'd be arrested for the years of unsolved murders. But if it didn't go on and they killed that Dorfman and his friend, there would be no witnesses against them. Glen was sacrificed as a distraction to take the blame for killing the only two people that knew who was behind the decades' old murders. With that forensics cop and his friend dead, and the computers silenced forever, they had gotten away with it. Possibly the longest running string of abductions and murders in the country would never be solved. Now they would continue, only this time that crooked government agent was paying them. Paying them in gold...for fresh meat, that was supposedly pork.

The front bedroom of Glen's house had a large bay window, giving him a panoramic view of the entire street. Tango ripped down the curtains and opened the side double-hung windows. It was colder in Glen's house than it was outside, but he'd rather be cold than in the warm house across the street with the others. He sat down on the ice-cold oak floor and waited. Tango was tired of the killing. He was tired of all of it, and it was time to get out. *Damn, it's cold.* He thought of the farm he was raised on; it was cold there too. *Has it been 25 years since I left home?* He stared blankly at his rifle. It was an M16, and although he had been kicked out of the army early, he had learned the weapon well. He closed his eyes and waited. It would go down soon enough.

Unknown to Jack and the family, the sheriff and his cutthroat friends had been watching them that morning from before sun-up. Hidden in the upstairs of Barry's ice-cold and ransacked house, they were waiting for the right moment to attack. The Hayes brothers saw it as a stroke of luck when the two men left early that morning on their snowmobiles. Tango was pissed. He wanted to shoot both of the men as they mounted their snowmobiles, but the Hayes boys had other plans. The sheriff had told him they would wait for the men to return and then kill them. Meanwhile, he and Dirk, would take the defenseless women without firing a shot. The Marine and his friend would return on their snowmobiles, unaware that their women were already sliced like a lunchmeat buffet, and a bullet was waiting for them. Dirk had told him to kill the teacher and only wound the jar head. *Yeah, right...* No way would he do something as foolish as that, just so that stupid Dirk could get his revenge torturing him. He had seen the Marine in action, and that man had to be put down quickly and permanently. He wasn't to be played with. Taking off his leather gloves, Tango removed two hand warmers from his coat pocket. Tearing the small plastic packets open, he tightly clenched them in his ice-cold fists and waited for their warmth to sink in. He sat hunched down on the floor, looking out the window. His M16 rifle was across his lap, and he was hoping his wait wouldn't be much longer. Looking down the deserted snow-covered street, he thought about the Marine he was waiting in ambush for. While listening for the sound of the approaching snowmobiles, he cursed out loud to himself about the sheriff. "Damn him! He should have Boner set up, watching the back, instead of playing with his fuckin knives." He shook his head in disgust, running over in his mind what he would do if he was in charge. *The Hayes brothers are so sure these two assholes are just going to run their snowmobiles right down the middle of the street and waltz in the front door of their house...the same way they left. "Girls, we're home!" This Marine is a cagey bastard. What if he doesn't come in the front and I can't get my shot?* As he sat in the cold silence of Glen's empty house, Tango ran every option through his brain and none of them came out well. He thought again about his parent's farm...it was so long ago—*maybe I could go back?*

What the hell was that? He heard a blood curdling scream that couldn't have come from a woman. It was immediately followed by a gunshot! Tango cursed to himself, *saying out loud.* "That didn't sound good!" He swiveled his head, quickly looking towards the house across the street. He immediately heard another loud bang! —Followed by a blood curdling, guttural scream that definitely wasn't from a woman. There was another gunshot, this one louder, and more screams!

"Shit, something's gone wrong over there!" He tossed the hand warmer packets and grabbed his leather shooting gloves, quickly slipping them on. Standing up, he readied his rifle, preparing to fire across the street. **"Aw shit!"** He saw Dirk stagger around the corner of the house, holding in his gut. Even from the distance of Glen's house, he could see Dirk's bloody intestines, trailing out of his split belly. Thinking that the crazy Marine had returned the back way, he lowered his rifle, cursing to himself. "I knew it! I knew it! I tried to tell that idiot that those two assholes would sneak in the back way. Screw this, I'm getting out of here!"

* * * * *

The sheriff suddenly yanked Lynne's head close to his face. Her mind raced back to that morning in Chicago. Sitting in her stalled car, the young thug had roughly grabbed her throat, trying to pull her out of the car. It felt like it happened so long ago, but she could still taste his blood and feel his meaty hand in her mouth. It was happening again, and she knew what she would do. As the sheriff's wet tongue danced across her cheek, she felt her own tongue brush against the jagged edge of her chipped front tooth. With his fetid breath fowling her nostrils, she thought to herself, *pull me closer.... closer.*

She saw it in his eyes. *He knows what I'm going to do!* His grip tightened, but it was too late. Her mouth opened and, in an instant, her teeth were clamped through the sheriff's nose, her mouth immediately filling with his salty warm blood. Biting down as hard as she could, she felt her upper and lower teeth clash together, as they tore through the spongy flesh, crushing the cartilage underneath.

He screamed and violently shoved her back, jamming the butt of his sawed-off shotgun into her cheek, his nose parting with a gristly sucking sound from his face. She thrust her arms up. A sharp pain went through her wrist as she deflected the shotgun's barrels upwards. Pain shot through her face as he gun-butted her, smashing into her already scarred cheek. His eyes were wide with terror, blood was pouring out from the two gaping holes where his nose had been, and he continued to scream. It was the loudest scream any of the women had ever heard. His shotgun went off, blowing a cabinet door above Lynne to splinters, knocking it off its hinges. Her ears were ringing, the loud blast deafening her. Suddenly there was another loud **bang,** and the sheriff's face exploded! The right side of his jaw detached, ripped off his skull. Like a freshly cut pork chop, it *plopped* on the kitchen countertop, several yellowed teeth sticking up out of it.

The moment Lynne's jaws snapped over the sheriff's nose, Jo swiftly grabbed the curve bladed knife off the counter. Dirk stood there dazed, wasting a precious second, with a look of dumb astonishment across his face. His little brother was screaming and his nose was missing.

As the women undressed, Dirk had unbuckled his belt. The thick black leather ends dangled towards the floor, and the mountain of flesh that was his belly, hung over it. Jo went for it! With the razor-sharp blade facing upwards, she screamed as she underhanded the knife, thrusting it well below the pig faced man's hanging stomach. Ripping upwards and slicing through his pants' waistband, the thin bladed knife opened his bladder, and severed his intestines. The huge man's soft belly split like an overloaded sack, spewing its bloody contents over Jo's arm and splattering the white tiled floor.

Dirk screamed, flinging Jo to the floor like an old rag, where she landed on top of Kathy. Holding his dangling guts, he leapt past his brother, as a wild-eyed woman with an ancient shotgun blasted Boner in the chest. The blast blew a quarter-size hole clear through him, shattering the sliding glass door behind him. Pellet sized chunks of glass were still airborne, as Dirk pushed the mortally wounded Boner through the shattered door ahead of him. With his guts trailing

447

him, Dirk stumbled into the backyard, wildly shuffling through the snow. His intestine filled pants fell to his ankles, as he rounded the corner of the house. Hobbled and unable to run any further, he fell to the ground. Curling into fetal position, he screamed in agony.

Laura rushed at the sheriff, pushing him down, screaming, **"GET OUT!"** Kathy and Jo each took an arm, roughly yanking him off the bloody floor and flinging him out the back door, landing him face up on top of Boner. The sheriff was finished and looked a mess. The right side of his jaw was missing, still lying on the kitchen counter. The left side of his jaw hung loosely, swinging with each convulsive jerk, dangling off the side of his open neck. His nose was missing, somewhere on the floor where Lynne had spit it out. Blood steadily flowed from the gaping hole where his mouth had been; an artery was shredded, and soon he'd be dead.

With the blood from Hayes's amputated nose smeared across her face, Lynne yelled at the others, **"There's another one of them across the street, hiding in Glen's place. We have to kill him!"**

Jo and Kay ran to the front of the house, Jo hesitating at the living room. Everyone had thought that Charlie's old Browning Automatic Rifle seemed so out of place, set up on Dottie's living room coffee table. Ready and up on its tripod, there were three full 20 round magazines next to it. Jo grabbed a hold of the heavy weapon, yelling, **"I'm going to kill that bastard!"**

Kay turned around and faced Jo, "Let me get you the M16. You're not going to be able to carry that thing, it's too much for you!"

Placing one of the magazines into the Browning, Jo calmly looked at Kay, "Bullshit! I'm going to rip this guy a couple new assholes. Now, open the side door for me and get yourself the M16!" Jo anxiously looked at Lynne, whose face and blouse were covered in the sheriff's blood. She yelled, "You all right, Lynne?"

` "I'm fine, what do you want me to do?"

"You're going to take Kay's AR-15 around back and get to the west front corner of Ronnie's house. Fire two quick shots when you're there. I'll start raking the house with twenty rounds from the BAR, and you run like hell across the street. Get yourself in a position somewhere behind the house next to Glen's, where you can cover the back, if this prick runs out."

* * * * *

As Tango bolted out of Glen and Doris' bedroom, he quickly ran his odds through his head. *The Marine, his sidekick and them crazy broads—they got me out gunned. I'm out of here, I got to get to the truck!* Missing a step as he jumped into the stairway, he tumbled down the last six steps, yelling, **"SON OF A BITCH!"** His left foot twisted as he hit the slippery tiled floor, sending a searing pain up his leg. A bone had snapped in his ankle, and he knew right then and there he was finished. Painfully, he slowly braced himself to his feet. Using his rifle butt as a prop, he pushed himself up against the living room wall. Heavily breathing, he swore out loud, "Fuck me, aw shit—I broke my ankle, aw no, this is bad!"

He stood there a minute, the pain radiating up his leg, figuring out what he should do. *All right, calm down Tango, calm down… Maybe, they don't know I'm in here. Why would they?* Bracing himself with the rifle butt, he tried taking a step, but pain instantly bolted up his leg. *Okay… okay, I can wrap up my ankle, find something to use as a crutch and when it gets dark…get myself to the truck. I'll just stay here until it's dark. I'll make it out of here….*

It couldn't have been a minute later when bullets started ripping through the walls. He quickly let himself slide down the wall to the floor, trying to make himself part of it, as bullets rhythmically whizzed through the house. He silently screamed to himself, ***They know I'm in here!*** The shooting stopped. He knew what it was, someone was changing a twenty-round magazine. He thought of firing a burst from his M16 through the frame walls, but instead he screamed, **"Screw you. Come and get me!"** He hoped to hear a reply, but there was none, just the freezing silence of the empty house, and the crunching sounds of footsteps in the hard snow.

The house was dead silent and he could have heard a pin drop. Hearing muffled talking and the crunch of the frozen snow under running boots unnerved him. It seemed to be coming from all sides, caging him in. He knew the game. Someone had put down a line of heavy cover-fire, while the others crossed the street. *Shit, they got me boxed in!* As cold as it was, he was sweating, and a shiver ran through him as he watched his frozen breath hang in the frigid air. Tango looked up and about the room. It was dark and cold; the whole place was a mess. He said softly to himself, "Glen, you crazy bastard. You really trashed this place, didn't you?" The only undamaged thing in the whole downstairs was the fancy chandelier hanging over Doris' dining room table, and he was looking up at it. He wondered if it's dark lights would ever go back on.

Curling up on the floor, he closed his eyes, and placed the muzzle of the cold rifle barrel tightly under his chin. *God, I've messed my life up…. forgive me for what I've done.*

* * * * *

As the two snowmobiles cut through the frozen golf course, Jack signaled Carl to stop. Shutting his snowmobile off, Jack said, "These machines are too damn noisy. If these bastards are attacking the girls, or worse—they'll be waiting for us. They'll hear us and pick us off as we approach. My machine is louder than yours, so I'm going to hop on the back of yours with you." Jack pointed with his gloved hand to the north. "Head for the northern edge of the farm, they won't hear your machine from that far away. We'll park in the machinery shed and double-time it back home. If someone is there, we're going to hit them from the rear, and grease their ass good."

.

* * * * *

There was a single gunshot from the inside of Glen's house, followed by silence. Jo was on the side of Charlie's house, with the Browning on the hood of the old station wagon. She had just emptied 20 rounds of 70-year-old 30-06 into Glen's house, as Lynne ran across the street.

Kay was crouched down behind the car next to her. Making a gun gesture with her right hand and placing the forefinger to her temple, she said, "Suicide?"

Jo shook her head saying, "Maybe he killed himself, but maybe he wants us to think he did. Run back and get a can of gas and a couple of our grenades. Dead or alive, in a few minutes this asshole is going to be a crispy critter. I'll rake the shit outta the place with our friend here, while you cross the street like Lynne did. I'll put down some more cover-fire and blast all the windows out. You get alongside of the place and toss the gas can through that side window. Follow it with a grenade. Make sure that grenade goes inside that house and doesn't bounce back at you. Run like hell around the corner and hit the dirt. You've got about four seconds. He won't go anywhere because Lynne's got the rear. If he didn't kill himself, he'll wish he did!"

* * * * *

Suddenly aware she was half clothed, Laura covered herself with Lynne's sweater, and stood by the pantry door. The children were strangely silent and that frightened her more than if they were screaming.

"It's all right boys, the bad men are all gone. Are you all right in there?"

She heard Wendel say, "Andy opened the big bag of pretzels you were saving. Can me and Bobby have some?"

"You boys have whatever you want, you just stay in there until I say you can come out. **Do not open the door, do you understand?** You're going to hear some more loud bangs. It'll just be us—we're testing our guns." Feeling a slight kick in her belly, she placed her hand on her stomach, then stepped out into the cold through the shattered sliding door. Spotting Jo's heavy 44, she gently picked it out of the snow, shaking the icy crystals off of it as she held it up. Looking the ice-cold weapon over, she said, "This will do." She calmly walked over to the sheriff. His face and the snow around him were a mass of red, he had to be dead. *But was he?* He was partially lying on top of the other man and it was barely noticeable, but his mangled head was slowly jerking. It was rhythmically twitching back and forth, ever so slightly. The right side of his face was missing, but *he was still alive*! She heard a noise behind her. Startled, she turned and saw it was Kay, running to the shed. Laura slowly turned and faced the sheriff. Holding the gun with both hands, she pointed it at him, shooting him in the head. Next, she put one in the side of the tall man's skull, just to be sure. She was standing there barefoot, the icy snow crystals covered her toes, but she didn't feel the cold. Walking around the side of the house, she could see Jo setting up the Browning on top of the hood of the old station wagon. Jo gave her a "thumbs up." She waved back to Jo, noticing that she was wearing only her Dad's old military raincoat.

Looking down, their pig-faced tormentor lay a few feet before her. He was curled up in the crystal white snow, almost in a ball, and was whimpering like a baby, still trying to hold his ruptured guts in. His pants were down to his ankles and his huge ass was sticking up, facing her. Stepping safely around him, she kept the powerful handgun pointed at his face. "You're still alive, aren't you? Good. **I get to send you to hell!** Squeezing the trigger, the big gun jumped and his pig-like head exploded. She didn't need to, but she fired it again. There was no breeze and the smell of gunfire hung in the frigid air. It was done. She stood there holding the gun with both hands, still pointed at the mess that had once been his head.— The monster was dead.

Lowering the heavy handgun, she slowly walked back around the corner of the house. Kathy was standing at the back door, watching her.

"You all right, Laura? You—you better get your boots on...."

451

"Yeah, I'm coming inside."

"Good…. That's good. I've got to get back up front and cover Jo. They don't know if the guy across the street committed suicide or is playing possum. They know he's still in there because they heard him swearing, then a gunshot."

Holding the gun at her side, Laura stepped into the house. Facing Kathy, she calmly said, "I'll have the boys cover their eyes, so they don't see this mess." She spotted a knob of bloody flesh on the floor by the door and quickly kicked it out into the yard with her half-frozen toe, softly cursing, "You bastard." Turning back to Kathy, she said, "I'll get the boys downstairs, locked in the safe-room and play some cassettes. We'll sing some songs." Pointing the big 44 towards the ceiling, Laura added, "I'll be keeping this, and a shotgun, near my hand. Tell everyone to give me a yell… before they come in."

* * * * *

The staccato of rifle shots echoed across the open field from the subdivision. Jack and Carl had barely gotten off the snowmobile, when they heard what could only have been Charlie's old Browning. Someone was firing it on slow automatic.

Jack motioned to the snowmobile. "Let's get back on the snowmobile and get in a little closer. Whoever it is, they're not firing at us, it's out front. We can pull in behind Barry's house, and see what's going on before we go charging in. They zipped across the frozen farm field, bucking up and down on the snowmobile, trying to stay in the furrows that Father Steve and Carl had plowed. Exiting the field, they headed to Barry's backyard, and were both shocked at what they saw. There were two bodies, one on top of the other, lying just outside their shattered back door. Another one, a big man, was alongside of the house curled up in a ball. The gunfire momentarily stopped, then started again. Someone out front had just re-loaded and was laying down another barrage of fire from the BAR. They spotted Kay sprinting towards Glen's house, with what looked like one of the old metal gas cans from the shed.

Confused, Jack and Carl ran towards Charlie's house. They were barely over the back fence when there was a loud explosion.

Carl looked toward Jack, "What the hell is happening?"

They made it to the front corner of Charlie's house to see flames shooting out of the front downstairs' windows of Glen's house. Kay was in front of the house next door. When she spotted them, she waved them to stay back.

Carl pointed to Jo. "Look at her. What the hell is going on? Where is Laura?"

452

Jack didn't know what to think, as Jo was wearing only half laced combat boots and his old Marine issue raincoat. The BAR was on the hood of the old station wagon. Jo pointed to it, saying, "This old boy and its 70-year-old ammo works great! **We got them! We killed them all!**"

Jack heard his name being yelled; it was Lynne. She was across the street between the houses, waving at him from Glen's backyard. She was fully clothed, but the whole front of her white blouse had a dark stain running down the center of it. She was holding an M16 in one hand and waving at him with the other. She yelled, "Don't worry, I'm all right!" Hearing Kathy's voice behind them, they turned and faced her.

"Everyone is safe. Laura is downstairs with the children, she's fine! The evil bastards are dead!"

Carl said, "Thank God everyone's all right. It's a miracle no one was hurt."

Carl left to check on Laura and Jack walked back to Dirk's dead body. "Holy shit, just as we thought! The skinny one, with his head blown apart, is it the sheriff?"

Jo said, "Yeah. The tall guy underneath him was with them. They were the serial killers. All these years they got away with it until Barry's friend, that forensic cop, figured them out. When the computers went down, all the evidence was lost. He and Barry were the only ones who knew what they had done, so they killed them. Glen was part of their group too, but they killed him. You were right, they made it look like Glen killed Barry and his family, and the Dorfman's too. The sheriff bragged to us about it, he told us everything. But now they're finally dead. We killed them all!"

Lynne ran towards Jack, but hurriedly went past him, pushing him away when he tried to grab her. Her right eye was almost swollen shut, and her face and blouse were covered in blood. As she ran past, she yelled, "I'm covered in that bastard's blood. I have to clean up."

Kathy quickly said to him, "Don't worry, that's not her blood. The sheriff got his face too close to hers. She bit his nose clean off! Kay was hiding in the study. She jumped out and shot him in the face with Charlie's old shotgun. The sheriff's blood splattered everywhere. Lynne got the worst of it."

All Jack could say was, "*What?* She bit his nose off?"

"Yeah, she did!" Jo pointed to the man lying under the sheriff. "The tall one, they called him *Boner.* Kay blasted him point blank in the chest. He went backwards through the door. I slashed porky over there in his gut, with their own knife. He had unbuckled his pants. They were going to rape us, then butcher us. They're cannibals!" Jo's gazed turned to the huge meat grinder on the picnic table. "They've been killing people—then grinding them up and selling it to the camps. They're eating human flesh, like it's ground pork. I'd like to think they don't know what they're buying...." She hesitated, and looked down, her excitement gone. "They said they killed Father Steve... and Ben."

453

Jack swallowed hard, "It's true. We found a house on the other side of the golf course.... It was built on the site of the old farm where they killed Charlie's daughter. They tortured her there, all those years ago.... They butchered the current owner, his wife and two children. They also killed and butchered Father Steve, Ben and that black-haired girl, the one Ben was hunting, the girl who was behind the attack that killed Ken."

Kathy said, "Oh my God, how horrible! They cut them up?"

Jack slowly nodded his head, softly saying, "Yeah."

"So, it *was* her... and Ben had forgiven her—and they were coming back here? Oh my God, the sheriff was telling us the truth!"

Something exploded in Glen's house and everyone flinched, turning away from the burning home. The flames had spread upstairs, shooting out the windows and licking the roof. Jack pointed towards the burning home. "What happened over there?"

Kay said, "They had a sniper upstairs waiting for you and Carl to come back. He was going to kill Carl and wound you. They wanted you alive so they could torture you. We cornered him in there. We thought he killed himself, but we weren't sure. We didn't want to risk going in after him. Jo gave the place the once over with the BAR. I threw in a can of gas, followed by a grenade." Kay pointed back towards Barry's house. "They hid in the upstairs of Barry's place, maybe since last night, waiting for their chance to attack us. They were watching us this morning when you and Carl left."

Kathy was crying, "They caught us off guard. We were outside, playing with the children... after you told us not to go out."

Kay stepped up to Jack. Moving close to Jack, looking him in the eyes, she nervously wet her lips. Trembling, she rapidly said, "I let you down. I let everyone down. I nearly got us all killed, it's my fault."

Not understanding, Jack shook his head. "Slow down, Kay, what are you talking about? You killed Hayes and that other guy." Pointing to Glen's burning house, he added, "You risked your life throwing a grenade and can of gas into that house. That guy could have killed you. No one was harmed. **Kay— you girls won!**"

Kay started sobbing and her words came faster, "I stayed in the house as planned when the others went outside...but I forgot my weapon. I left it in my nightstand... that's why I used Charlie's old shotgun. I only had two shots. Two shots with an antique shotgun— filled with birdshot. A gun we decided was too dangerous to use. I messed up bad. I'm a target shooter, not a killer...or a fighter. I'm sorry."

Jack pulled her close to him and held her. "You didn't mess up, Kay, you didn't mess up at all. We're only human and we make mistakes. We can forgive others and we can forgive ourselves. Let's all go inside." As they stepped up on Charlie's front porch, Jack stopped and looked back to the burning house. "Man,

I can feel the heat from that fire all the way over here, and it feels good." Glancing at Jo, Jack quickly adverted his eyes. "Jo, how about closing that coat up. Jeez, aren't you cold?"

"No, not at all. I'm just getting warmed up."

As they walked through the front door, Jack said to Jo, "I've been kicking over an idea in my head since Ken's place was attacked." He shot a last look over to the burning home. "We're going to burn this whole neighborhood. Nobody will ever have the high ground around us again."

Kay said, "I'll go down and check on Laura and the kids, then help Lynne clean herself up. She's going to have another black eye."

Kay turned and went downstairs, leaving the other three crowded in the entryway of the kitchen. Hesitant to go all the way in, they stood there for a few seconds together, grimly looking at the mess before them. Kathy covered her face with her hands. "Oh my God, look at all the blood splattered on the walls."

All their eyes fell on it at once. There was a bloody chunk of jawbone, with at least half a dozen yellow teeth protruding from it, lying on the countertop. Quickly moving forward, Kathy grabbed a wet dishcloth off the sink, and tossed it over it. As if it would bite her, she gingerly picked it up with two fingertips and quickly shoved it into a white plastic bag. Tossing it out into the yard, she said, "UGH! That was part of the sheriff's jaw. The kids can't see any of this."

Kathy stood in front of the shattered door, vacantly looking at the two bodies lying in the yard. "What are we going to do with them?"

Jack stepped up next to her and stared down at the two dead men, fighting the sudden urge to piss on them. "Just more crap we have to clean up. Carl and I will load them into the truck and we'll dump them someplace like a load of shit. No burial for them. I don't want anyone to ever know where their bodies are. I'll throw a bunch of old tires on them and burn them to powder. They'll be erased from God's green earth." Jack paused, sticking his head out of the shattered glass door. He slowly surveyed the snow-covered backyard and the vacant houses behind them, muttering under his cold breath, "We're too damn vulnerable here, but not for long."

Before going into the basement to find Lynne, he picked Charlie's old shotgun off the floor. There was a thin split starting at the breach in the top of the right barrel. It got wider and was bulged out, right where someone would hold it, when firing it. Charlie was right, the old gun should have never been fired. Setting it against the wall, he went downstairs and found Lynne and Kay standing in the bathroom. A kerosene lantern on the vanity provided the only light.

Lynne's bloody clothes were heaped in a pile on the floor, next to her bare feet. Kay stood beside her, dabbing something antiseptic smelling on her swollen cheek.

"You're lucky, Lynne. Thank God the skin's not broken and you don't need stiches. You're going to have a real shiner though." Seeing Jack, Kay hesitated and capped the small bottle she held in her hand. Bending over, she picked up the bloody clothes, "I'll get rid of these and get some ice for your eye. I'll be back in a few minutes."

Jack stopped her. "Let me see your left hand."

She held both of them up. "I know, I'm lucky, they're all there. The right barrel split and almost blew out. I fired it from my hip. I was holding it further up. Charlie was right, he overloaded the shells. I took the risk. I'll let you two alone."

Lynne reached for a large bath towel and wrapped it tightly around her. "That was all *his* blood on me, it soaked completely through my clothes."

Jack said, "Thank God it was his blood. When I first saw you running across the street..."

"I know, I looked horrible. If my face didn't look bad enough already, look at it now."

"I know it hurts, but it's only a black eye. It'll go away. You'll look fine, Lynne."

Suddenly conscious of her wet, tangled hair, she tossed her head back, pulling it tight behind her. "Yeah right, my face will never look fine again." She started to cry. "I hope I got it all off me, Jack. Kay must have hit his carotid artery. It was like a fountain of blood shooting everywhere. I washed my mouth out with this." She held up a bottle of bourbon.

"I took a couple heavy belts of it too—I got some of that bastard's blood in my mouth when I bit him. I think I swallowed some... God knows what diseases he carried."

Jack placed his arms around her and she placed her head against his chest.

"Tell me it will get better, Jack. I don't know how much more of this I can take."

"It will, honey, we'll see good times again."

He gently pushed her at arm's length. "You bit off his nose?"

Lynne nodded her head. "Yeah, I did. He kept shoving his face in front of me. I flashed back to that gangbanger in Chicago, who wanted to kidnap me. I couldn't resist. I didn't think the whole thing would just tear off like that."

"Jeez, don't ever get pissed at me, okay?"

Lynne cupped her ear. "Jack, —I can't hear out of my right ear, it's just ringing. His shotgun went off, almost in my face. Am I going to be deaf?"

"Your hearing will come back, but the ringing, that might stay. I'm sorry."

They held each other tight for a few moments. Lynne said, "You better go check on Laura while I finish cleaning up. She's in the safe-room with the boys. Knock before you enter."

THE DAY AFTER

CHAPTER 4 2

"Good, I see you're finally awake." Jack laid down in the bed next to Lynne.

"Oh my gosh, Jack, what time is it?"

"Who knows? My clock stopped eight months ago. You've been out like a light. Figured you needed it, so I let you sleep in. How much of that bourbon did you have last night?"

"Plenty. I could still taste his blood in my mouth, so I downed a small glass of it before turning in. Gosh, my head hurts. I think I have a hangover. My wrist hurts too, from pushing his gun out of my face. My eye hurts and my ears are ringing. God, I feel a wreck."

"You're not a wreck, Lynne. You just take it easy. Your hearing will come back, your eye will get better, and we'll put all this bullshit behind us, with the rest of it. Carl and I found their truck. We even got an address as to where their place is. It's west of Geneva, in a little place called Pine Grove. I've been through there a couple times and there's not much there. Some small farms and old abandoned gravel pits, a perfect place to get away with murder. It's a rural address, probably an old farmstead. We burned their truck with them in it and they're toast. You girls did it, it's over for good."

Lynne suddenly sat up in bed. "**No, it's not!** I just remembered something that bastard said. The sheriff, he was screaming at us, bragging about the murders they had committed and gotten away with. He said something to his brother, I forgot about it until now. He said something like, 'We do all the dirty work, while the other two just sit on their ass, ordering us around.' Jack, there's two more of them and they're the leaders. Oh my God. We didn't kill them all, they're still out there!"

"Shit."

* * * * *

The next afternoon, they all gathered in the front yard. The temperature had sharply risen during the night, and a warm breeze blew through the frozen subdivision. The sun was shining and the snow was melting. For the first time in weeks, it was nice out. While the boys played in the melting snow, the family talked.

Jack said, "Jo, Kathy. Your thoughts?"

Jo said, "We get at least two dogs. We get them young and train them. At least one dog stays outside at all times."

Kathy said, "We can get some puppies at the flea market. We can barter chickens for them. They're slaughtering dogs for food, but we'll make guard dogs out of them. Somehow, we'll find the food to feed them."

Jack gave them a thumbs up, saying, "Good idea, ladies."

Carl said, "We can get more fencing at Walt's father's place. We'll fence these three, maybe four houses in. That will help keep intruders out and the dogs in. We have to do that because if the dogs roam, they'll be shot by someone for food. We still have to get more seeds for spring planting. We have what we've saved from the garden. It's a lot, but we need other stuff. Father Steve was right, we're no farmers and there is no way we are going to plant all that land, at least not this coming spring. But we can plant some of it, even if it's only an acre. We can comfortably survive on that and easily keep an eye on it. I'd like to get some sheep or goats too."

Kay said. "Everyone needs weapons training and more target practice."

Lynne said, "We need more medical supplies."

Laura patted her belly. "We're going to have to set up a nursery soon. We'll also need more books and toys for the children."

Jack agreed, "The children, yeah, we can't forget them. Man, we got our work cut out for us. There are some other issues we have to deal with that aren't pleasant. Lynne told me what our deceased sheriff said about there being two others in their group, the ones who run it. I've been thinking about those two bastards all morning. I think they're the ones that started it, way back when, so they have to be a lot older than any of them. That's why they weren't involved in the attack yesterday. The youngest they could be would be what, early 70's? Yesterday, Dirk was the only one who had any ID. We found it in his truck. He was 64, so in 1968, he'd have been almost 16. That puts him right in there, but still way too young to be behind something like this. I'm not going to worry about two old men who started these killings, because yesterday you girls wiped out

459

their strike force. My dad died when he was 74 and he was already in a wheelchair. That's what I'm picturing. Besides, I think we have the address of their house of horrors. Before we burned their bodies in Dirk's truck, we went through it. Carl found a folder crammed with paperwork. I've gone through it and one rural address west of Geneva keeps coming up, and it's not Dirk's. When everything clears up some, we may take a ride out to Pine Grove. If we see a couple dirty old men sitting in out front at that address, we'll know we have them and I'll shoot them on the spot. I'll kill anyone and everyone who's in that house, even if they're in wheelchairs. Then I'll burn it. Unfortunately, there are still others out there we have to defend against, but we'll be prepared for them. You guys got some good ideas and we'll act on them right away. Meanwhile, maybe, just maybe, times will get better."

Laura said, "Dad, are you really going to burn the whole neighborhood down?"

"No, not the whole neighborhood, honey, but these vacant houses near us, especially the two-story ones, yeah, they have to go. The houses on the next block that were wrecked by the tornado, have to go too. Most of our subdivision is uninhabitable anyway, so no one will care. Vacant houses, like Barry's, can and will be used to stage attacks against us. They're empty and too close to us, so we can't let them stand. We'll strip anything of value to us out of them and burn them. We have Ken's backhoe and it'll be easy to knock over anything left standing. It doesn't have to be done right away, but eventually what's left can be buried and leveled. We can plant crops where the houses were, as if they never existed."

"But Dad, what about our friends' houses? Jim and his biker friends, they might be back. And Uncle Al's?"

"I've thought about that, honey. We could board up Jim's place so no one can get inside it." Jack gave out a short laugh. "Uncle Al... good old Al. Funny you should mention him, I was thinking about him this morning. I would expect that as soon as winter is over, he'll be popping in. If anyone has survived this crap, it's him and Lois."

Jo gave a snort, "Lois.... ugh! Let's burn their place first."

"No, we'll let Al's place stand, but everything up to it, we'll level. We should take down your old place too, Jo, if that's all right with you?"

"Sure, the whole second floor is collapsing, we'll never rebuild it."

"Okay, are we all agreed?"

Everyone nodded their heads in agreement, and Kay said, "Where do we start?"

Jack replied, "Unfortunately, we have to retrieve what's left of our friends' bodies and the family that lived in that house, and bury them. There's—not much left of them. In my worst nightmare, I never dreamt we'd face something like this. From what little we know, Ben somehow forgave the girl who

460

masterminded the attack on his father's house. For him to forgive her is one thing, that's a miracle in itself. But to return here with her and Father Steve… there is more to Father Steve than we will ever know. Steve showing up here, showing us how to farm, saving my life, and teaching us how to forgive, was not a random happening. It's sad to say, but you know, I don't even remember the name of that black-haired girl. I only know we tried our best to kill her that day she escaped from us and jumped into the river. It's another miracle she survived that."

Carl said, "I think her first name was Candi, I never got her last. If this doesn't teach us the power of forgiveness, nothing will. We'll have to go back and get their remains… good God almighty, that's going to be tough. The ground is pretty much frozen solid, so I think it would be best to only dig one grave. We're going to have to use the backhoe to do it. Also, I hate to mention it—we can't forget about all that firewood. There're at least two full cords at that house. We badly need it, and that's another blessing, it can't be a coincidence."

Jack said, "Carl is right. I don't believe in coincidences anymore. I hate the thought of having to go back to that house to retrieve our friends remains. I'd like to never see it again. That house is on the property that's connected to this whole nightmare. We'll go get that firewood and anything else we can salvage, but the house has to be destroyed. We're fighting something evil here, pure demonic. I know everyone thinks that maybe I've gone a little overboard with wanting to burn things lately, but I'm torching that house. That house means something sacred to them, so it has to be destroyed, along with the remains of the old windmill. The rest of the month, we can strip anything we can use out of these homes around us and get the supplies to build our fence. We've been through a lot together these past months. I feel like we're all brothers and sisters because we've saved each other. I wouldn't be alive if it wasn't for you guys. We are surviving and we will continue to survive, because we're strong and we know who makes us strong. He loves us and I love all of you."

Chapter 4 3

"How are the twins doing?"

Lynne was beaming, smiling from ear to ear. "They're fine and so is Laura. Two little healthy girls. Can you believe it? They named them Dottie and Charli! My heavens, we're so blessed, Jack. We're so blessed!"

"Yes, we are. Grandma and Grandpa, that sure sounds good. Look, I have to go check out Ronnie's house, Carl says there's a leak in the roof. We got that place packed with supplies. I'm going to fix it before anything gets ruined. I'll see you a little later."

"Be careful, Jack. Don't fall off the roof."

He gave Lynne a kiss and left for Ronnie and Jake's house. It was a beautiful Spring day. The sun was out, the birds were chirping and he felt good. *I'm a grandpa.* It'd been almost a year since Ronnie had died. Like thousands of people who went to work that Monday, her husband never came home. Bobby was growing fast. He'd be big, like his dad. He wouldn't be called little Bobby as he got older, that was for sure. Other than using their house for storage, it was kept ready for Jake to return. But after almost a year, they had given up hope. For now, the house was vacant, but soon it would be fitted with a woodstove where the gas furnace stood. It was decided that Carl and Laura would move into the small home.

Jack opened the garage door and stared for a moment at Lynne's battered car. It hadn't been run in months and he wondered if it would start.

He was standing in front of Ronnie's garage, thinking about that Monday morning in Chicago when he had first seen Lynne. He laughed to himself, saying aloud, "You were driving this car like a mad lady, your hair flying in the wind...."

He clenched his teeth, his smile fading as he remembered his friend, Don. *Poor Donnie*, he thought. He leaned over the front of the car, placing both of his palms on the its dented hood. Donnie's ashen face, his blood bubbling from his mouth, *Jeez, why did it have to end that way?* The bad dreams had stopped, and that dark shade that used to descend from nowhere hadn't darkened Jack's days for months. Turning around, he sat on the edge of the car's hood. The good feeling, he had woken up with faded a little, but *it was okay.* It was okay to be sad for the loss of friends and family, he wouldn't be normal if he wasn't. But the nightmare and flashbacks to the Middle East and his anger at Ellen and Don were gone. *It never leaves…* He laughed to himself. The skills he learned in the Marine Corps would never fade, but the nightmares did. It was all so simple; he forgave others as they had forgiven him—but just as important, *he forgave himself.* No one had ever told him that. If there was anyone who didn't forgive him, that was their problem and not his. He could only pray that someday they would. *Father Steve was so right, "Anger and hate chains your soul to the bottom of a hole. Forgiveness is the key, and it unlocks those chains… all of them. All he had to say was, "Here I am Lord."*

Something shiny caught his eye, he turned and his heart jumped in his chest! Parked in the driveway of Al's house, was his black Olds convertible!

Like a toddler seeing a new toy, without even thinking, he started walking towards it. Wanting to run, he walked faster, suddenly feeling elated. He couldn't wait to tell them about Laura and the twins…**"AL, GUESS *WHAT? I'M A GRANDFATHER!"*** There would be so much to talk about, and Al would have the latest news on what was happening. He hadn't heard anything but the same rumors for months, but Al always knew the scoop on what was going on. As he rounded the corner into Al's open garage, doubt leapt into his mind. *What if something happened to the little guy? Maybe it's just Lois who is home, or maybe something happened to her?* He couldn't wait to see both of their faces So many people had died or never come home, Jack wanted to forget the past. They had their differences, but as he sprinted around Nancy, into Al's garage, he was ready to start his friendship anew… that's what forgiveness was all about.

"Come on in Jack, we've been waiting for you!"

The door to the kitchen was open and Lois and Al were waiting for him, standing behind the island counter.

"Lois, Al! Thank God you're alright!" Jack stepped forward to embrace them, but both of them held their hands up, stopping him.

Al said, "Good to see you, big guy, but you better stay back, can't take any chances. You know how it is."

Confused, Jack shook his head, "No, what's going on?"

Al shrugged his shoulders, "You kidding me?"

When Jack didn't reply, Lois said, "I don't think he knows."

Al said, "Half the population of the country is dead. Some kind of super-flu or something, it started in the camps and it spread everywhere. People were starving and dropping like flies. The shit is deadly. Now it's spread over the whole planet. You didn't know about it?"

"No, Al. We're all fine." Jack shook his head. "We haven't heard any news. We've been keeping to ourselves. Nobody's been sick."

"Have you heard that we've got a new government?"

"Al, we haven't heard anything lately, not even rumors."

" Well, get this big guy, the military runs the show now. A whole bunch of people were charged with treason, including that little rabble-rouser, Clanton. He was one of the ring leaders behind this whole EMP thing. They thought they could shit-can the constitution and the military and police would back them up. They figured wrong and got lined up against a wall. They hanged him. So much for the new world order—good riddance, I say. —I guess you didn't hear about the nuclear fallout either, huh?" Jack shook his head. "It's to the north and south of us, but this area's safe." Al looked at Lois, "I told you, honey, this place is like a secluded oasis back here."

Lois said, "Looks like you've been doing some urban renewal, either that or one hell of a fire roared through here."

Jack said, "Yeah. We've been under attack. Decided to eliminate nearby homes and cover."

"Good move, big guy, good move. Always better without pesky neighbors. I see your little farm idea paid off, huh? That's great. We knew you'd do it. Lois and I made it through the winter, but last week we got attacked. Two amigos tried to break into our place in the middle of the night. You'd be proud of me, big guy, I greased both of their asses, but good. Problem was, one of my bullets hit our propane tank, and our living quarters got charbroiled. We've been staying at an old farmstead, in a little town west of here called Pine Grove. I bet you never even heard of it. Nothing but empty corn fields and gravel pits. But hey, thanks for sparing our place here...we appreciate it. Nothing like home sweet home." Al seemed nervous and licked his lips. "You sure nobody is sick at your place? We don't want to catch no virus."

Suddenly feeling uneasy, Jack replied, "No, Al. Like I said, we're all fine."

"That's great news, Jack, you don't know how happy that makes us. Hey, I see you're back to wearing Little Red, your old 44. That's good, Jack, that big iron always looked good on you." Al shifted nervously, from one foot to the other. "How'd you know we were here, big guy? Oh, I know, I bet you saw Nancy parked out front, huh? Yeah, that old car's been a lifesaver for us."

Lois said, "You're starting to get a bad feeling—aren't you, Jack? Something doesn't feel right—I can see it in your eyes. Could it be something Al said? I think you better put your hands up and lock your fingers behind your head." Lois was suddenly pointing what looked like a Shotmaster 45 pistol at him. "Don't move a muscle, or I'll kill you."

Al yelled, "**Pumpkin!** I hope you're up there watching the street! Is anyone coming down here?"

From upstairs a female voice said, "No one, Dad."

Lois said, "What's the matter, Jack, at a loss for words? Look at him, Al, he looks like a little boy. Close your mouth, Jack. You look like you're at your first day of school."

Al said, "I told them two assholes to leave you alone. I pleaded with them, Jack, but they wouldn't listen, and now they're dead. You killed our whole fuckin crew, Jack. You and your band of angels down there, left me and poor Lois here— *defenseless*. Not to mention, you put us out of business."

Jack felt himself stiffen. A sick feeling shot through him. "You? You murdered all those children?"

Lois laughed, "**Bingo! He *finally* gets it!**"

"I always told you, Jack, you gotta know your neighbors. Didn't I, big guy, didn't I always say that?"

"Why? For what? What's wrong with you?"

"A fair question, Jack, I guess I owe you that much. But it's more of how and when, right, Lois? Let me regress—it was the winter of 1967-68, a particularly brutal record-breaking winter. It was Christmas Eve, and I had just bought my first new car, that's Nancy, that's sitting out front. Lois and I were dating. We were seniors in high school and she wanted to learn how to drive stick shift. Remember that, honey? Not a good time to learn to drive stick, it was snowing like hell, but she insisted."

Lois quickly snapped, "Give him an explanation, Al, but spare the details, we don't have much time, and Jack, please don't move."

"Well, that's an important detail, honey, I think. Anyway, in a nut-shell, Lois and I went out driving in Nancy. It was a blinding snowstorm. She was brand new and Lois was driving. She accidentally ran over a young girl that was walking down the middle of the street. It was Kirhman's big sister, you know, the Fire Chief. Honest, Jack, we didn't see her. It was an accident and we thought we killed her. We panicked; I don't know why... we were just two scared kids. So, we put her body in Nancy's trunk. We thought she was dead. We decided to dump her on a secluded road west of town... Like I said, we were scared. Problem was, she wasn't dead. I opened the trunk and she started screaming like hell. She was all busted up, so we tossed her out on the road. No one was around, so Lois put the car in reverse and backed over her again."

Lois's green eyes looked like they were on fire, "And again, Jack. I ran over her five, maybe six times. It was the greatest rush I ever experienced, and we got away with it."

Al said, "The next summer, after we graduated, we went on a road trip to California together. That was the summer of 1969, Jack. We were having so much fun we didn't want to leave. That's when we got into the witchcraft thing." Al chuckled to himself. "I'm a warlock, Jack, and Lois is a witch! We have, or should I say *had*, a coven.... Anyway, we met some very interesting and wealthy people out in California, and we told them what we did to that girl. You see, there's some people in Hollywood who are very into the occult. Some really sick weirdos out there. We were lucky, we met them at a party. They wanted to do something like that too, and would *pay* to do it. Anyway, we came back home

465

and later that fall, I became an apprentice butcher. Dirk was a kid who worked in the supermarket where I worked. He was crazy then too and he wanted to be a butcher like me. Him and Chuck killed their own mother for her money, could you believe that? They got away with it and everything just fell into place. Chuck, became a cop and everybody trusts a young cop, right? It was perfect, Jack, just perfect."

Lois said, "It was all my idea!"

"Yes, it was Dear, you always were the smart one. The Mills girl was our first contract and I remember it like it was yesterday. After that, the rest of them seem to blur together. But that first one. . . oh, it was a brutal one! A wealthy businessman from California flew into O'Hare and I picked him up at the airport. I remember it was raining that whole week. Friendly Officer Chuck offered her a ride home from school in his squad. She was at the wrong place at the right time and never made it home. Chuck took her over to the old farm, where the golf course is now. I had our client waiting there."

"I was there too!"

"Yeah, sorry, honey, how I could I forget? You helped Dirk dismember that girl." Al smiled, closing his eyes and reverently looked up to the ceiling. "Ahh yes, that big white barn, so peaceful there." His smile gone; Al's eyes gleamed at Jack. "Do you remember, Jack, last year when we were golfing and I helped you look for that old barn? I was saddened when they tore it down for those big houses, but at least part of the windmill is still standing. That place has special meaning to us, it's hallowed ground. You know, we recently commemorated our fiftieth anniversary there. We sacrificed some good friends of yours."

"You're sick, both of you. So, what are you going to do, eat me for your dinner? You're pedophiles and you're cannibals, sick and demented. You're both disgusting—filthy, scum!"

Lois laughed. "You sound just like your Ellen. We tried to recruit her into our little group. She didn't know about the killings, of course, but she knew about our coven and some of our animal sacrifices. She had a lot of nerve running us down, but you know, so do you, Jack. You shouldn't be so quick to throw stones... Remember our last cookout, the big one we had before we left? My *wonderful* pulled pork? Do you recall our young neighbors next door, the Connors? My oh my, they suddenly went missing! Oh, Jack, your mouth is hanging open again. You look so cute when you do that."

Al started laughing. "Yeah, Jack, you had what's called long pork! And, gas this,Jackster. . . we've served it to you and your little family before. In fact, the whole subdivision has eaten it, many times. Hey, don't look so sick, big guy, you've been a big help to me. Remember when you made that garbage run with your truck? You helped me dump all those big black plastic trash bags on the side of the road over by the sand pit, remember that?" Al smiled at Lois, laughing. "You should have seen that, Lois! He put the truck in reverse and floored it, then hit the brakes. Those big bags shot out of the back of that pickup like Billy Hell... man that was funny! But here's something you didn't know, Jack. I was mortified that those bags would bust open. You know what was in them? The better parts of the Connors, their heads, their feet, their hands, and all the bony soup parts, that we couldn't use. The rest went into Lois' pulled pork! *Nice and sweet tasting, wasn't it?*

Keeping her gun aimed at Jack, Lois yelled, "**Sheila!** Anyone else coming down here?"

"No, Mother, no one!

"**Then get down here, now!**" Enough of this reminiscing, Al.

Let's get on with it."

Al shrugged his shoulders, "You know, Jack, I did you a favor. I got rid of that pesky neighbor of yours, and Glen too. You should have seen the shock on Glen's face when Lois stuck those scissors in his neck." Al looked at Lois and started laughing. "Our plan, Jack, is simple. We shoot you. We let you bleed some, maybe you die, or you're almost dead, it doesn't matter. We load you into our merry little Oldsmobile and take you home." Al changed the expression on his face to one of concern, and said, "**Look!** Someone's shot our *poor* Jack! We tell them we found you on the street, mortally wounded! 'Why, who could have done such a thing?'" Al threw his arms in the air, shaking his head. "Your little family will open the front door, they'll run out, and crowd around poor Jackie boy." Al turned around and showed Jack an M16 rifle that had been hidden behind the counter. He proudly held it up high. "This weapon scares me, Jack. It's your favorite military issue, loaded and on full auto. I've never fired anything like this before, so I tried it out yesterday. It's awesome! It used to belong to a certain sheriff, **who your women killed!**" Al carefully placed the M16 on the counter in front of him. "It'll go down like this, big guy. Your little family comes out, gathers around you crying and everything, and I waste them with this! No words, no explanations, I just kill them all, then and there. All except the little black boy, because we *need* him. That's what it was all about. Since the day that black family moved in here, Lois and I wanted that little boy. You see, Bobby is special to us; he will *always* be special. We planned to take him. Problem was, that Monday after the power went out, old Charlie decided to check on the new black family. The old bastard actually cared. While he was knocking on Ronnie's front door, he interrupted Glen. That little Bobby is smart and he hid, so Glen had to leave without him. But we got him now! Don't worry, Jack, he's going to have a long, long life. He'll become a warlock...**just like me!** Lois and I will raise him... because he's special. *Lois read it in his stars!* Anyway, Jack, we've decided we're going to move into your little vegetable farm. It's like your Bible says, 'Man cannot live on meat alone,' or something like that. We're going to live there happily ever after, bringing up our. . . little . . . Bobby! Ain't that great?"

Jack stood in stunned silence as a familiar young woman joined them in the kitchen. "Mr. Hansen?" Sheila stared at Jack in disbelief, shooting an angry look at her mother. "He's the man who gave me the ride home from the store that day. This is Jack—the man you hate, the man you're going to kill?"

Lois smirked, "No, my dear, *you're* going to kill him. He'll be your first, but not your last." Lois kept the sarcastic grin on her face as she asked Jack, "Did she offer herself to you that day, the day you drove her home?" Lois cocked her head frowning at her daughter. She smiled at Jack, "Of course, she did."

Jack's mind flashed back to the day he gave Sheila a ride home in Lynne's car. *The woman with the long black-hair who was sitting on Sheila's' front porch, her back turned towards him.* "**That was *you* sitting on the porch!**"

"Of course, Jack. I'm her mother! I was afraid that you had recognized me." She turned to Sheila. "Shoot him."

"**No!** He was nice to me, Mother. He didn't even know me, yet he gave me a ride and then gave me all that extra money to *save me!* He wanted nothing in return— He's a good man, we can't do this!"

Al calmly said, "Do as your mother says, Shelia. Take your gun, point it at him and shoot him."

Lois screamed, "**SHOOT HIM, YOU LITTLE SLUT!**"

Shelia held a small stainless-steel revolver in her left hand, it's barrel wavering, slowly dropping down. Jack wanted to reach for his 44, but Lois still held her pistol aimed at his chest. Al appeared unarmed, but was wearing a short jacket with a slight telltale bulge under his left arm and the M16 was directly in front of him. Lois's finger was on the trigger of her weapon and he knew she would empty it into him. He would be dead before he could pull Little Red out of its holster.

Sheila screamed, "**I AM NOT LIKE YOU!** I'm a good person!" She fired her gun, but not at Jack. **BLAM! —BLAM!**

"**SHEILA, NO! WHAT HAVE YOU DONE?**" Al screamed again, "**NO!**"

Jack dove for cover behind the kitchen island as he yanked his 44 from its holster. The was another loud bang from Sheila's gun, and Jack saw Al flinch as he turned his back away from her. As if he could dodge the bullet, the little man covered his head with his hands. It caught him in the back of his neck, the 38-caliber bullet whipping him around, sending him spinning to the floor. Lois was out of sight behind the counter. Jack was on her in a second, his finger on the trigger, intending to finish her off. She was lying on her back, her heart instantly stopped by the two bullets that had cut through it. Jack spun around and faced Sheila, the barrel of her small silver handgun was pressed hard, under her chin.

"Sheila no. Please don't..."

The barrel lowered slightly. "Life's too hard, Mr. Jack."

BLAM!

For a moment Sheila stood there, river of blood gushing from her open mouth. Her eyes went vacant as she collapsed to the kitchen floor.

Jack quickly spun to Al, his 44 pointed at him, about to send the little man to hell. Al was lying face up, staring at the ceiling. A widening pool of blood was slowly seeping from the back of his neck.

"I can't move, Jack. I think I'm paralyzed; I can't feel a thing. Where's Sheila?"

"Sheila's dead, Al, she shot herself. Lois is dead too."

"Oh, God, not Sheila...no, oh please God... not my little Sheila."

Jack kept his gun pointed at Al. "So now you call on God? That beats it all, Al." Jack shook his head. "Father Steve was right, so right about everything."

"Go ahead and shoot me, Jack, it's okay. Do it—just do it."

"You're bleeding out, Al, you can die on your own." Jack holstered the 44, while bending over the little man. Grabbing the silver key chain that hung from Al's belt loop, he roughly ripped it from his pants. Gripping the front of his Al's jacket, he yanked it open and, as he suspected, Al was wearing a shoulder holster under his left arm. Jack removed a small 32 semi-auto. He patted Al's pant legs, saying, "Just in case you have another weapon, and suddenly regain your mobility." Removing the gun's magazine, Jack ejected a chambered round onto Al's chest, then tossed the pistol, sending it skidding across the tiled floor. "Al, does Nancy have a full tank of gas?" Al didn't answer him. Jack said, "I bet she does. Nobody drives anywhere these days unless they have a full tank. I'll bet you have a can of extra gas in her trunk too.... Yeah, you do, don't you, Al? Say goodbye to Nancy."

Al weakly asked, "Whatta you going to do to her, Jack? *Don't hurt her.* Jack ignored him and walked towards the garage, stopping to grab the M16 off the counter. Stepping through the kitchen door, he stopped. Al was softly mumbling something and Jack listened to the little man's dying words. "I never wanted this. All I ever wanted was a little restaurant. It was Lois, always Lois. Bless me Father for I have sinned...."

Glancing back at Sheila's body, Jack hesitated a second longer. Shouldering the rifle, he walked back to her. Bending down, he picked her up. She felt so light—he carried her out through the open garage. After gently laying Sheila and the rifle in the grass, he quickly walked over to Al's precious convertible. Fingering the key ring, he found the worn key that fit the trunk. His hands were shaking as he fit it into the trunk lock. It opened, and sure enough a spare 2-gallon can of gas was in it. In the corner of the trunk he found an emergency road kit, with two red road flares tucked inside. Removing a flare and the can of gas, he slammed the trunk lid and quickly walked back into the garage. His heart was racing as he opened the red plastic gas can. Like throwing a strike at a bowling alley, he stood at the open door to the kitchen and whipped the open can of gas into it. Quickly walking out of the garage, he opened the

469

convertible's door. Jamming himself into the driver's seat, he violently shoved the bucket seat all the way back. As soon as she started, the eight-track player came to life with Al's disco music, *"Gotta keep on rolling now...never gonna stop.... never gonna stop...."* Shoving the floor shift into first gear, he let Nancy's powerful Rocket V8 idle her into the garage. Leaving her running, he got out and walked outside. Turning and facing the back of Al's cherished black convertible, he didn't hesitate a second. Drawing Little Red from its holster, he emptied it into the lower trunk lid and back bumper, where he knew the gas tank sat behind. As a flood of gasoline splashed onto the floor, it was like the old car was bleeding to death. Nancy's dual exhaust sounded good and her stereo kept blaring, *Gotta keep on rolling now... gotta keep on rolling on never gonna stop, always gonna rock...never gonna stop....*

Jack heard his name and looked back towards his house. Everyone was standing out front and Carl was walking towards him. Lighting the road flare, Jack tossed it, spinning into the garage and under Al's convertible. There was a loud **Whoomph** and Nancy was in flames, still running, and her 8-track stereo loudly playing Al's favorite song. He waved Carl back and started walking home. He had gone about 30 feet, when there was another loud **Whoomph!** The gasoline fumes from the kitchen had worked their way down into the burning garage, and the whole first floor of Al's house was an inferno. As flames shattered the living room windows, he met up with Carl on the sidewalk.

"Jeez, Jack, we heard what sounded like your 44 going off and ran out to see what the shooting was about. I thought you weren't going to burn Uncle Al's house. Are you okay?"

"Yeah, just changed my mind, that's all."

470

5 YEARS LATER

"Jack are you awake? It's been a long day, but such a good one, and I'm really tired. It's nice we have enough gas to be able to use the pontoon boat. I enjoyed being out on it and so did the children. I don't know about you shooting those carp with that big shotgun though... If anyone would have told me six years ago that I would be happy again, I would have thought they were crazy. Yeah, it's been a long day, but a good day—goodnight dear, I love you... Jack are you awake? Jack?"

"Huh? —Did you say something?"

Fall 2119

"And that's how it was, sweetie, our family's story of survival. It took almost 50 years before we got out of darkness. In a matter of months, after the power went out, the wires started falling down. The years went by and they got all jumbled up. Buildings were destroyed and everything was a mess. The people who maintained the machines and built everything, were dead or scattered. Chicago was gone. All that was left was the ruins. We have to be thankful, because life *did* get better. Everybody in the family lived to an old age. We've now got plenty of food, nobody bothers us, and there's no more wars. So, write your story, it'll be a good one, that's for sure. There's about 50 years unaccounted for."

"There's no more wars, but we still got guns, Grandpa Bobby."

The old man started laughing. "Yeah, we sure do, don't we? Keeps those *nasty* politicians away. Come on, it's getting late, sweetie. It's almost supper. Let's get back home. Your mama's having my favorite—it's pulled pork night."